Tad Williams has held more jobs than any sane person should admit to – singing in a band, selling shoes, managing a financial institution, throwing newspapers and designing military manuals, to name just a few. He also hosted a syndicated radio show for ten years, worked in theatre and television production, taught, and worked in multimedia for a major computer firm. He is co-founder of an interactive television company, and is currently writing comic books and film and television scripts. Tad and his family live in London and the San Francisco Bay Area.

TO GREEN ANGEL TOWER: SIEGE

Memory, Sorrow and Thorn

Book Three

Tad Williams

orbit

An *Orbit* Book

First published in Great Britain by Legend Books 1993
Reprinted by Orbit 1998, 1999, 2000

A CIP catalogue record for this book
is available from the British Library.

ISBN 1 85723 787 0

Printed and bound in Great Britain by
Mackays of Chatham plc, Chatham, Kent

Orbit
A Division of
Little, Brown and Company (UK)
Brettenham House
Lancaster Place
London WC2E 7EN

This series is dedicated to my mother,
Barbara Jean Evans,
who taught me to search for other worlds,
and to share the things I find in them.

This final volume, *To Green Angel Tower,*
in itself a little world of heartbreak and joy,
I dedicate to Nancy Deming-Williams,
with much, much love.

The Nornfells

RIMMERSGARD

YIQANUC

The FROSTMARCH

The Wealdhelm

HERNYSTIR

ALDHEORTE

Hayholt (Asu'a)

ERKYNLAND

HIGH THRITHING

MEADOW THRITHING

Warinsten

PERDRUIN

LAKE THRITHING

NABBAN

Osten Ard

The WRAN

Author's Note

And death shall have no dominion.
Dead men naked they shall be one
With the man in the wind and the west moon;
When their bones are picked clean and the clean bones
*   gone*
They shall have stars at elbow and foot;
Though they go mad they shall be sane,
Though they sink through the sea they shall rise again;
Though lovers be lost love shall not;
And death shall have no dominion . . .

> ——DYLAN THOMAS
> (from *"And Death Shall Have No*
> *Dominion"*)

Tell all the truth but tell it slant,
Success in circuit lies,
Too bright for our infirm delight
The truth's superb surprise;

As lightning to the children eased
With explanation kind,
The truth must dazzle gradually
Or every man be blind.

> ——EMILY DICKINSON

Many people gave me a great deal of help with these books, ranging from suggestions and moral support to crucial logistical aid. Eva Cumming, Nancy Deming-Williams, Arthur Ross Evans, Andrew Harris, Paul

Hudspeth, Peter Stampfel, Doug Werner, Michael Whelan, the lovely folks at DAW Books, and all my friends on GEnie® make up only a small (but significant) sampling of those who helped me finish The Story That Ate My Life.

Particular thanks for assistance on this final volume of the Bloated Epic goes to Mary Frey, who put a bogglesome amount of energy and time into reading and—for lack of a better word—analyzing a monstrous manuscript. She gave me an incredible boost when I really needed it.

And, of course, the contributions of my editors, Sheila Gilbert and Betsy Wollheim, are incalculable. Caring a lot is their crime, and here at last is their well-deserved punishment.

To all of the above, and to all the other friends and supporters unmentioned but by no means unremembered, I give my most heartfelt thanks.

NOTE: There is a cast of characters, a glossary of terms, and a guide to pronunciation at the back of this book.

Synopsis of
The Dragonbone Chair

For eons the Hayholt belonged to the immortal Sithi, but they had fled the great castle before the onslaught of Mankind. Men have long ruled this greatest of strongholds, and the rest of Osten Ard as well. *Prester John*, High King of all the nations of men, is its most recent master; after an early life of triumph and glory, he has presided over decades of peace from his skeletal throne, the Dragonbone Chair.

Simon, an awkward fourteen year old, is one of the Hayholt's scullions. His parents are dead, his only real family the chambermaids and their stern mistress, *Rachel the Dragon*. When Simon can escape his kitchen-work he steals away to the cluttered chambers of *Doctor Morgenes*, the castle's eccentric scholar. When the old man invites Simon to be his apprentice, the youth is overjoyed—until he discovers that Morgenes prefers teaching reading and writing to magic.

Soon ancient King John will die, so *Elias*, the older of his two sons, prepares to take the throne. *Josua*, Elias' somber brother, nicknamed Lackhand because of a disfiguring wound, argues harshly with the king-to-be about *Pryrates*, the ill-reputed priest who is one of Elias' closest advisers. The brothers' feud is a cloud of foreboding over castle and country.

Elias' reign as king starts well, but a drought comes and plague strikes several of the nations of Osten Ard.

Soon outlaws roam the roads and people begin to vanish
from isolated villages. The order of things is breaking
down, and the king's subjects are losing confidence in his
rule, but nothing seems to bother the monarch or his
friends. As rumblings of discontent begin to be heard
throughout the kingdom, Elias' brother Josua disappears—to plot rebellion, some say.

Elias' misrule upsets many, including *Duke Isgrimnur*
of Rimmersgard and *Count Eolair,* an emissary from the
western country of Hernystir. Even King Elias' own
daughter *Miriamele* is uneasy, especially about the
scarlet-robed Pryrates, her father's trusted adviser.

Meanwhile Simon is muddling along as Morgenes'
helper. The two become fast friends despite Simon's
mooncalf nature and the doctor's refusal to teach him
anything resembling magic. During one of his meander-
ings through the secret byways of the labyrinthine
Hayholt, Simon discovers a secret passage and is almost
captured there by Pryrates. Eluding the priest, he enters a
hidden underground chamber and finds Josua, who is being held captive for use in some terrible ritual planned by
Pryrates. Simon fetches Doctor Morgenes and the two of
them free Josua and take him to the doctor's chambers,
where Josua is sent to freedom down a tunnel that leads
beneath the ancient castle. Then, as Morgenes is sending
off messenger birds to mysterious friends, bearing news
of what has happened, Pryrates and the king's guard come
to arrest the doctor and Simon. Morgenes is killed fighting Pryrates, but his sacrifice allows Simon to escape into
the tunnel.

Half-maddened, Simon makes his way through the
midnight corridors beneath the castle, which contain the
ruins of the old Sithi palace. He surfaces in the graveyard
beyond the town wall, then is lured by the light of a bonfire. He witnesses a weird scene: Pryrates and King Elias
engaged in a ritual with black-robed, white-faced creatures. The pale things give Elias a strange gray sword of
disturbing power, named *Sorrow.* Simon flees.

Life in the wilderness on the edge of the great forest
Aldheorte is miserable, and weeks later Simon is nearly

dead from hunger and exhaustion, but still far away from his destination, Josua's northern keep at Naglimund. Going to a forest cot to beg, he finds a strange being caught in a trap—one of the Sithi, a race thought to be mythical, or at least long-vanished. The cotsman returns, but before he can kill the helpless Sitha, Simon strikes him down. The Sitha, once freed, stops only long enough to fire a white arrow at Simon, then disappears. A new voice tells Simon to take the white arrow, that it is a Sithi gift.

The dwarfish newcomer is a troll named *Binabik,* who rides a great gray wolf. He tells Simon he was only passing by, but now he will accompany the boy to Naglimund. Simon and Binabik endure many adventures and strange events on the way to Naglimund: they come to realize that they have fallen afoul of a threat greater than merely a king and his counselor deprived of their prisoner. At last, when they find themselves pursued by unearthly white hounds who wear the brand of Stormspike, a mountain of evil reputation in the far north, they are forced to head for the shelter of *Geloë*'s forest house, taking with them a pair of travelers they have rescued from the hounds. Geloë, a blunt-spoken forest woman with a reputation as a witch, confers with them and agrees that somehow the ancient Norns, embittered relatives of the Sithi, have become embroiled in the fate of Prester John's kingdom.

Pursuers human and otherwise threaten them on their journey to Naglimund. After Binabik is shot with an arrow, Simon and one of the rescued travelers, a servant girl, must struggle on through the forest. They are attacked by a shaggy giant and saved only by the appearance of Josua's hunting party.

The prince brings them to Naglimund, where Binabik's wounds are cared for, and where it is confirmed that Simon has stumbled into a terrifying swirl of events. Elias is coming soon to besiege Josua's castle. Simon's serving-girl companion was Princess Miriamele traveling in disguise, fleeing her father, whom she fears has gone mad under Pryrates' influence. From all over the north and elsewhere, frightened people are flocking to Naglimund and Josua, their last protection against a mad king.

Then, as the prince and others discuss the coming battle, a strange old Rimmersman named *Jarnauga* appears in the council's meeting hall. He is a member of the *League of the Scroll,* a circle of scholars and initiates of which Morgenes and Binabik's master were both part, and he brings more grim news. Their enemy, he says, is not just Elias: the king is receiving aid from *Ineluki the Storm King,* who had once been a prince of the Sithi—but who has been dead for five centuries, and whose bodiless spirit now rules the Norns of Stormspike Mountain, pale relatives of the banished Sithi.

It was the terrible magic of the gray sword Sorrow that caused Ineluki's death—that, and mankind's attack on the Sithi. The League of the Scroll believes that Sorrow has been given to Elias as the first step in some incomprehensible plan of revenge, a plan that will bring the earth beneath the heel of the undead Storm King. The only hope comes from a prophetic poem that seems to suggest that "three swords" might help turn back Ineluki's powerful magic.

One of the swords is the Storm King's Sorrow, already in the hands of their enemy, King Elias. Another is the Rimmersgard blade *Minneyar,* which was also once at the Hayholt, but whose whereabouts are now unknown. The third is *Thorn,* black sword of King John's greatest knight, *Sir Camaris.* Jarnauga and others think they have traced it to a location in the frozen north. On this slim hope, Josua sends Binabik, Simon, and several soldiers off in search of Thorn, even as Naglimund prepares for siege.

Others are affected by the growing crisis. Princess Miriamele, frustrated by her uncle Josua's attempts to protect her, escapes Naglimund in disguise, accompanied by the mysterious monk *Cadrach.* She hopes to make her way to southern Nabban and plead with her relatives there to aid Josua. Old Duke Isgrimnur, at Josua's urging, disguises his own very recognizable features and follows after to rescue her. *Tiamak,* a swamp-dwelling

Wrannaman scholar, receives a strange message from his old mentor Morgenes that tells of bad times coming and hints that Tiamak has a part to play. *Maegwin,* daughter of the king of Hernystir, watches helplessly as her own family and country are drawn into a whirlpool of war by the treachery of High King Elias.

Simon and Binabik and their company are ambushed by *Ingen Jegger,* huntsman of Stormspike, and his servants. They are saved only by the reappearance of the Sitha *Jiriki,* whom Simon had saved from the cotsman's trap. When he learns of their quest, Jiriki decides to accompany them to Urmsheim Mountain, legendary abode of one of the great dragons, in search of Thorn.

By the time Simon and the others reach the mountain, King Elias has brought his besieging army to Josua's castle at Naglimund, and though the first attacks are repulsed, the defenders suffer great losses. At last Elias' forces seem to retreat and give up the siege, but before the stronghold's inhabitants can celebrate, a weird storm appears on the northern horizon, bearing down on Naglimund. The storm is the cloak under which Ineluki's own horrifying army of Norns and giants travels, and when the *Red Hand,* the Storm King's chief servants, throw down Naglimund's gates, a terrible slaughter begins. Josua and a few others manage to flee the ruin of the castle. Before escaping into the great forest, Prince Josua curses Elias for his conscienceless bargain with the Storm King and swears that he will take their father's crown back.

Simon and his companions climb Urmsheim, coming through great dangers to discover the Uduntree, a titanic frozen waterfall. There they find Thorn in a tomblike cave. Before they can take the sword and make their escape, Ingen Jegger appears once more and attacks with his troop of soldiers. The battle awakens *Igjarjuk,* the white dragon, who has been slumbering for years beneath the ice. Many on both sides are killed. Simon alone is left standing, trapped on the edge of a cliff; as the ice-worm bears down upon him, he lifts Thorn and swings it. The dragon's scalding black blood spurts over him as he is struck senseless.

Simon awakens in a cave on the troll mountain of Yiqanuc. Jiriki and *Haestan,* an Erkynlandish soldier, nurse him to health. Thorn has been rescued from Urmsheim, but Binabik is being held prisoner by his own people, along with *Sludig* the Rimmersman, under sentence of death. Simon himself has been scarred by the dragon's blood and a wide swath of his hair has turned white. Jiriki names him "Snowlock" and tells Simon that, for good or for evil, he has been irrevocably marked.

Synopsis of
Stone of Farewell

Simon, the Sitha *Jiriki*, and soldier *Haestan* are honored guests in the mountaintop city of the diminutive Qanuc trolls. But *Sludig*—whose Rimmersgard folk are the Qanuc's ancient enemies—and Simon's troll friend *Binabik* are not so well treated; Binabik's people hold them both captive, under sentence of death. An audience with the *Herder* and *Huntress,* rulers of the Qanuc, reveals that Binabik is being blamed not only for deserting his tribe, but for failing to fulfill his vow of marriage to *Sisqi,* youngest daughter of the reigning family. Simon begs Jiriki to intercede, but the Sitha has obligations to his own family, and will not in any case interfere with trollish justice. Shortly before the executions, Jiriki departs for his home.

Although Sisqi is bitter about Binabik's seeming fickleness, she cannot stand to see him killed. With Simon and Haestan, she arranges a rescue of the two prisoners, but as they seek a scroll from Binabik's master's cave which will give them the information necessary to find a place named the Stone of Farewell—which Simon has learned of in a vision—they are recaptured by the angry Qanuc leaders. But Binabik's master's death-testament confirms the troll's story of his absence, and its warnings finally convince the Herder and Huntress that there are indeed dangers to all the land which they have not understood. After some discussion, the prisoners are pardoned and Si-

mon and his companions are given permission to leave
Yiqanuc and take the powerful sword *Thorn* to exiled
Prince Josua. Sisqi and other trolls will accompany them
as far as the base of the mountains.

Meanwhile, Josua and a small band of followers have
escaped the destruction of Naglimund and are wandering
through the Aldheorte Forest, chased by the *Storm King's*
Norns. They must defend themselves against not only arrows and spears but dark magic, but at last they are met
by *Geloë,* the forest woman, and *Leleth,* the mute child
Simon had rescued from the terrible hounds of
Stormspike. The strange pair lead Josua's party through
the forest to a place that once belonged to the Sithi, where
the Norns dare not pursue them for fear of breaking the
ancient Pact between the sundered kin. Geloë then tells
them they should travel on to another place even more sacred to the Sithi, the same Stone of Farewell to which she
had directed Simon in the vision she sent him.

Miriamele, daughter of *High King Elias* and niece of
Josua, is traveling south in hope of finding allies for
Josua among her relatives in the courts of Nabban; she is
accompanied by the dissolute monk *Cadrach.* They are
captured by *Count Streáwe* of Perdruin, a cunning and
mercenary man, who tells Miriamele he is going to deliver her to an unnamed person to whom he owes a debt.
To Miriamele's joy, this mysterious personage turns out to
be a friend, the priest *Dinivan,* who is secretary to *Lector
Ranessin,* leader of Mother Church. Dinivan is secretly a
member of the League of the Scroll, and hopes that
Miriamele can convince the lector to denounce Elias and
his counselor, the renegade priest *Pryrates.* Mother
Church is under siege, not only from Elias, who demands
the church not interfere with him, but from the *Fire
Dancers,* religious fanatics who claim the Storm King
comes to them in dreams. Ranessin listens to what
Miriamele has to say and is very troubled.

Simon and his companions are attacked by snow-giants
on their way down from the high mountains, and the soldier Haestan and many trolls are killed. Later, as he
broods on the injustice of life and death, Simon inadver-

tently awakens the Sitha mirror Jiriki had given him as a summoning charm, and travels on the Dream Road to encounter first the Sitha matriarch *Amerasu,* then the terrible Norn Queen *Utuk'ku.* Amerasu is trying to understand the schemes of Utuk'ku and the Storm King, and is traveling the Dream Road in search of both wisdom and allies.

Josua and the remainder of his company at last emerge from the forest onto the grasslands of the High Thrithing, where they are almost immediately captured by the nomadic clan led by March-Thane *Fikolmij,* who is the father of Josua's lover *Vorzheva.* Fikolmij begrudges the loss of his daughter, and after beating the prince severely, arranges a duel in which he intends that Josua should be killed; Fikolmij's plan fails and Josua survives. Fikolmij is then forced to pay off a bet by giving the prince's company horses. Josua, strongly affected by the shame Vorzheva feels at seeing her people again, marries her in front of Fikolmij and the assembled clan. When Vorzheva's father gleefully announces that soldiers of King Elias are coming across the grasslands to capture them, the prince and his followers ride away east toward the Stone of Farewell.

In far off Hernystir, *Maegwin* is the last of her line. Her father the king and her brother have both been killed fighting Elias' pawn *Skali,* and she and her people have taken refuge in caves in the Grianspog Mountains. Maegwin has been troubled by strange dreams, and finds herself drawn down into the old mines and caverns beneath the Grianspog. *Count Eolair,* her father's most trusted liege-man, goes in search of her, and together he and Maegwin enter the great underground city of Mezutu'a. Maegwin is convinced that the Sithi live there, and that they will come to the rescue of the Hernystiri as they did in the old days, but the only inhabitants they discover in the crumbling city are the *dwarrows,* a strange, timid group of delvers distantly related to the immortals. The dwarrows, who are metalwrights as well as stonecrafters, reveal that the sword *Minneyar* that Josua's people seek is actually the blade known as *Bright-Nail,*

which was buried with *Prester John,* father of Josua and
Elias. This news means little to Maegwin, who is shattered to find that her dreams have brought her people no
real assistance. She is also at least as troubled by what
she considers her foolish love for Eolair, so she invents
an errand for him—taking news of Minneyar and maps of
the dwarrows' diggings, which include tunnels below
Elias' castle, the Hayholt, to Josua and his band of survivors. Eolair is puzzled and angry at being sent away, but
goes.

Simon and Binabik and Sludig leave Sisqi and the
other trolls at the base of the mountain and continue
across the icy vastness of the White Waste. Just at the
northern edge of the great forest, they find an old abbey
inhabited by children and their caretaker, an older girl
named *Skodi.* They stay the night, glad to be out of the
cold, but Skodi proves to be more than she seems: in the
darkness, she traps the three of them by witchcraft, then
begins a ceremony in which she intends to invoke the
Storm King and show him that she has captured the
sword Thorn. One of the undead *Red Hand* appears because of Skodi's spell, but a child disrupts the ritual and
brings up a monstrous swarm of *diggers.* Skodi and the
children are killed, but Simon and the others escape,
thanks largely to Binabik's fierce wolf *Qantaqa.* But Simon is almost mad from the mind-touch of the Red Hand,
and rides away from his companions, crashing into a tree
at last and striking himself senseless. He falls down a gulley, and Binabik and Sludig are unable to find him. At
last, full of remorse, they take the sword Thorn and continue on toward the Stone of Farewell without him.

Several people besides Miriamele and Cadrach have arrived at the lector's palace in Nabban. One of them is
Josua's ally *Duke Isgrimnur,* who is searching for
Miriamele. Another is Pryrates, who has come to bring
Lector Ranessin an ultimatum from the king. The lector
angrily denounces both Pryrates and Elias; the king's emissary walks out of the banquet, threatening revenge.

That night, Pryrates metamorphoses himself with a
spell he has been given by the Storm King's servitors, and

becomes a shadowy *thing*. He kills Dinivan and then brutally murders the lector. Afterward, he sets the halls aflame to cast suspicion on the Fire Dancers. Cadrach, who greatly fears Pryrates and has spent the night urging Miriamele to flee the lector's palace with him, finally knocks her senseless and drags her away. Isgrimnur finds the dying Dinivan, and is given a Scroll League token for the Wrannaman *Tiamak* and instructions to go to the inn named *Pelippa's Bowl* in Kwanitupul, a city on the edge of the marshes south of Nabban.

Tiamak, meanwhile, has received an earlier message from Dinivan and is on his way to Kwanitupul, although his journey almost ends when he is attacked by a crocodile. Wounded and feverish, he arrives at *Pelippa's Bowl* at last and gets an unsympathetic welcome from the new landlady.

Miriamele awakens to find that Cadrach has smuggled her into the hold of a ship. While the monk has lain in drunken sleep, the ship has set sail. They are quickly found by *Gan Itai,* a Niskie, whose job is to keep the ship safe from the menacing aquatic creatures called *kilpa.* Although Gan Itai takes a liking to the stowaways, she nevertheless turns them over to the ship's master, *Aspitis Preves,* a young Nabbanai nobleman.

Far to the north, Simon has awakened from a dream in which he again heard the Sitha-woman Amerasu, and in which he has discovered that Ineluki the Storm King is her son. Simon is now lost and alone in the trackless, snow-covered Aldheorte Forest. He tries to use Jiriki's mirror to summon help, but no one answers his plea. At last he sets out in what he hopes is the right direction, although he knows he has little chance of crossing the scores of leagues of winterbound woods alive. He ekes out a meager living on bugs and grass, but it seems only a question of whether he will first go completely mad or starve to death. He is finally saved by the appearance of Jiriki's sister *Aditu,* who has come in response to the mirror-summoning. She works a kind of traveling-magic that appears to turn winter into summer, and when it is finished, she and Simon enter the hidden Sithi stronghold of Jao é-Tinukai'i. It is a place of magical beauty and timelessness. When Jiriki welcomes him, Simon's joy is great; moments later, when he is taken to see *Likimeya* and *Shima'onari*, parents of Jiriki and Aditu, that joy turns to horror. The leaders of the Sithi say that since no mortal has ever been permitted in secret Jao é-Tinukai'i, Simon must stay there forever.

Josua and his company are pursued into the northern grasslands, but when they turn at last in desperate resistance, it is to find that these latest pursuers are not Elias' soldiers, but Thrithings-folk who have deserted Fikolmij's clan to throw in their lot with the prince. Together, and with Geloë leading the way, they at last reach Sesuad'ra, the Stone of Farewell, a great stone hill in the middle of a wide valley. Sesuad'ra was the place in which the Pact between the Sithi and Norns was made, and where the parting of the two kin took place. Josua's long-suffering company rejoices at finally possessing what will be, for a little while, a safe haven. They also hope they can now discover what property of the three Great Swords will allow them to defeat Elias and the Storm King, as promised in the ancient rhyme of *Nisses*.

Back at the Hayholt, Elias' madness seems to grow ever deeper, and *Earl Guthwulf*, once the king's favorite, begins to doubt the king's fitness to rule. When Elias forces him to touch the gray sword *Sorrow*, Guthwulf is almost consumed by the sword's strange inner power, and is never after the same. *Rachel the Dragon*, the Mistress of Chambermaids, is another Hayholt denizen dismayed by what she sees happening around her. She learns that the priest Pryrates was responsible for what she thinks was Simon's death, and decides something must be done. When Pryrates returns from Nabban, she stabs him. The priest has become so powerful that he is only slightly injured, but when he turns to blast Rachel with withering magics, Guthwulf interferes and is blinded. Rachel escapes in the confusion.

Miriamele and Cadrach, having told the ship's master Aspitis that she is the daughter of a minor nobleman, are treated with hospitality; Miriamele in particular comes in for much attention. Cadrach becomes increasingly morose, and when he tries to escape the ship, Aspitis has him put in irons. Miriamele, feeling trapped and helpless and alone, allows Aspitis to seduce her.

Meanwhile, Isgrimnur has laboriously made his way south to Kwanitupul. He finds Tiamak staying at the inn, but no sign of Miriamele. His disappointment is quickly overwhelmed by astonishment when he discovers that the old simpleton who works as the inn's doorkeeper is *Sir Camaris,* the greatest knight of Prester John's era, the man who once wielded Thorn. Camaris was thought to have died forty years earlier, but what truly happened remains a mystery, because the old knight is as witless as a very young child.

Still carrying the sword Thorn, Binabik and Sludig escape pursuing snow-giants by building a raft and floating across the great storm-filled lake that was once the valley around the Stone of Farewell.

In Jao é-Tinukai'i, Simon's imprisonment is more boring than frightening, but his fears for his embattled friends are great. The Sitha First Grandmother Amerasu calls for him, and Jiriki brings him to her strange house. She probes Simon's memories for anything that might help her to discern the Storm King's plans, then sends him away.

Several days later Simon is summoned to a gathering of all the Sithi. Amerasu announces she will tell them what she has learned of Ineluki, but first she berates her people for their unwillingness to fight and their unhealthy obsession with memory and, ultimately, with death. She brings out one of the Witnesses, an object which, like Jiriki's mirror, allows access to the Road of Dreams. Amerasu is about to show Simon and the assembled Sithi what the Storm King and Norn Queen are doing, but instead Utuk'ku herself appears in the Witness and denounces Amerasu as a lover of mortals and a meddler. One of the Red Hand is then manifested, and while Jiriki and the other Sithi battle the flaming spirit, *Ingen Jegger,* the Norn Queen's mortal huntsman, forces his way into

Jao é-Tinukai'i and murders Amerasu, silencing her before she can share her discoveries.

Ingen is killed and the Red Hand is driven away, but the damage has been done. With all the Sithi plunged into mourning, Jiriki's parents rescind their sentence and send Simon, with Aditu for a guide, out of Jao é-Tinukai'i. As he departs, he notices that the perpetual summer of the Sithi haven has become a little colder.

At the forest's edge Aditu puts him in a boat and gives him a parcel from Amerasu that is to be taken to Josua. Simon then makes his way across the rainwater lake to the Stone of Farewell, where he is met by his friends. For a little while, Simon and the rest will be safe from the growing storm.

Foreword

Guthwulf, Earl of Utanyeat, ran his fingers back and forth across the scarred wood of Prester John's Great Table, disturbed by the unnatural stillness. Other than the noisy breathing of King Elias' cupbearer and the clank of spoons against bowls, the great hall was quiet—far quieter than it should be while almost a dozen people ate their evening meal. The silence seemed doubly oppressive to blind Guthwulf, although it was not exactly surprising: in these days only a few still dined at the king's table, and those who spent time in Elias' presence seemed more and more anxious to get away again without tempting fate by anything so risky as supper-table conversation.

A few weeks before, a mercenary captain named Ulgart from the Meadow Thrithing had made the mistake of joking about the easy virtue of Nabbanai women. This was a common view among Thrithings-men, who could not understand women who painted their faces and wore dresses that displayed what the wagon-dwellers thought of as a shameless amount of bare flesh. Ulgart's coarse joke would generally have gone unremarked in the company of other men, and since there were few women still living in the Hayholt, only men sat around Elias' table. But the mercenary had forgotten—if he had ever known—that the High King's wife, killed by a Thrithings arrow, had been a Nabbanai noblewoman. By the time the after-supper custard arrived, Ulgart's head was already dangling from an Erkynguardsman's saddle horn, on its way to the

spikes atop the Nearulagh Gate for the delectation of the
resident ravens.

It was a long time since the Hayholt's tabletalk had
sparkled, Guthwulf reflected, but these days meals were
eaten in almost funereal silence, interrupted only by the
grunts of sweating servitors—each working hard to take
up the slack of several vanished fellows—and the occasional nervous compliments offered by the few nobles
and castle functionaries unable to escape the king's invitation.

Now Guthwulf heard a murmur of quiet speech and
recognized Sir Fluiren's voice, whispering something to
the king. The ancient knight had just returned from his
native Nabban, where he had been acting as Elias' emissary to Duke Benigaris; tonight he held the place of honor
at the High King's right hand. The old man had told
Guthwulf that his conference with the king earlier that
day had been quite ordinary, but still Elias had seemed
troubled all through the meal. Guthwulf could not judge
this by sight, but decades of time spent in his presence let
him put images to each straining inflection, each of the
High King's strange remarks. Also, Guthwulf's hearing,
smell, and touch, which seemed far more acute since he
had lost the use of his eyes, were sharper still in the presence of Elias' terrible sword Sorrow.

Ever since the king had forced Guthwulf to touch it,
the gray blade seemed to him almost a living thing, something that knew him, that waited quietly but with terrible
awareness, like a stalking animal that had caught his
scent. Its mere presence lifted his hackles and made all
his nerves and sinews feel tight-strung. Sometimes in the
middle of the night, when the Earl of Utanyeat lay
blackly awake, he thought he could feel the blade right
through the hundreds of cubits of stone that separated his
chambers from the king's, a gray heart whose beating he
alone could hear.

Elias pushed back his chair suddenly, the squeak of
wood on stone startling everyone into silence. Guthwulf
pictured spoons and goblets halted in midair, dripping.

"Damn you, old man," the king snarled, "do you serve me or that pup Benigaris?"

"I only tell you what the duke says, Highness," quavered Sir Fluiren. "But I think he means no disrespect. He is having troubles along his borders from the Thrithings-clans, and the Wran-folk have been balky. . . ."

"Should I care?!" Guthwulf could almost see Elias narrowing his eyes, so many times had he watched the changes that anger worked on the king's features. His pale face would be sallow and slightly moist. Lately, Guthwulf had heard the servants whispering that the king was becoming very thin.

"I helped Benigaris to his throne, Aedon curse him! And I gave him a lector who would not interfere!"

This said, Elias paused. Guthwulf, alone of all the company, heard a sharp intake of breath from Pyrates, who was seated across from the blind earl. As though sensing he might have gone too far, the king apologized with a shaky jest and returned to quieter conversation with Fluiren.

Guthwulf sat dumbstruck for a moment, then hurriedly lifted his spoon, eating to cover his sudden fright. What must he look like? Was everyone staring at him—could they all see his treacherous flush? The king's words about the lectorship and Pyrates' gasp of alarm echoed over and over in his mind. The others would no doubt assume that Elias referred to influencing the selection of the pliable Escritor Velligis to succeed Ranessin as lector—but Guthwulf knew better. Pyrates' discomfiture when it seemed the king might say too much confirmed what Guthwulf had already half-suspected: Pyrates had arranged Ranessin's death. And now Guthwulf felt sure that Elias knew it, too—perhaps had even ordered the killing. The king and his counselor had made bargains with demons and had murdered God's highest priest.

At that moment, sitting with a great company around the table, Guthwulf felt himself as alone as a man upon a windswept peak. He could not bear up under the burdens of deception and fear any longer. It was time to flee. Better to be a blind beggar in the worst cesspits of Nabban than stay a moment longer in this cursed and haunted keep.

Guthwulf pushed open the door of his chamber and paused in the frame to let the chill hallway air wash over him. It was midnight. Even had he not heard the procession of sorrowful notes ring from Green Angel Tower, he would have recognized the deeper touch of cold against his cheeks and eyes, the sharp edge that the night had when the sun was at its farthest retreat.

It was strange to use eyes to feel with, but now that Pryrates had blasted away his sight, they had proved to be the most sensitive part of him, registering every change in wind and weather with a subtlety of perception finer even than that of his fingertips. Still, useful as his blinded orbs were, there was something horrible about using them so. Several nights he had wakened sweating and breathless from dreams of himself as a shapeless crawling *thing* with fleshy stalks that pushed out from its face, sightless bulbs that wavered like snail's horns. In his dreams he could still see; the knowledge that it was himself that he looked at dragged him gasping up from sleep, time and again, back into the real darkness that was now his permanent home.

Guthwulf moved out into the castle hallway, surprised as always to find himself still in blackness as he stepped from one room to another. As he closed the door on the chamber, and thus on his brazier of smoldering coals, the chill grew worse. He heard the muffled chinking of the armored sentries on the walls beyond the open window, then listened to the wind rise and smother the rattle of their surcoats beneath its own moaning song. A dog yipped in the town below, and somewhere, past several turns of the hallway, a door softly opened and closed.

Guthwulf rocked back and forth uncertainly for a moment, then took a few more steps away from his door. If he were to leave, he must leave now—it was useless to stand maundering in the hallway. He should hurry and take advantage of the hour: with all the world blinded by night, he was almost on equal terms again. What other choice was left? He had no stomach for what his king had become. But he must go in secret. Although Elias now had little use for Guthwulf, a High King's Hand who could not ride to battle, still Guthwulf doubted that his once-friend would simply let him go. For a blind man to leave the castle where he was fed and housed, and also to flee his old comrade Elias, who had protected him from Pyrates' righteous anger, smacked too much of treachery—or at least it would to the man on the Dragonbone Chair.

Guthwulf had considered this for some time, had even rehearsed his route. He would make his way down into Erchester and spend the night at St. Sutrin's—the cathedral was all but deserted, and the monks there were charitable to any mendicants brave enough to spend nights inside the city walls. When morning came, he would mix with the straggle of outgoing folk on the Old Forest Road, traveling eastward into Hasu Vale. From there, who knew? Perhaps on toward the grasslands, where rumor whispered that Josua was building a rebel force. Perhaps to an abbey in Stanshire or elsewhere, some place that would be a refuge at least until Elias' unimaginable game finally threw down everything.

Now it was time to stop thinking. Night would hide him from curious eyes; daylight would find him sheltered in St. Sutrin's. It was time to go.

But even as he started down the hallway he felt a feather-light presence at his side—a breath, a sigh, the indefinable sense of *someone there*. He turned, hand flailing out. Had someone come to stop him after all?

"Who. . . ?"

There was no one. Or, if someone was indeed near, that one now stood silent, mocking his sightlessness. Guthwulf felt a curious, abrupt unsteadiness, as though the floor tilted beneath his feet. He took another step and suddenly felt the presence of the gray sword very strongly, its peculiar force all around. For a moment he thought the walls had fallen away. A harsh wind passed over and through him, then was gone.

What madness was this?

Blinded and unmanned. He almost wept. *Cursed.*

Guthwulf steeled himself and walked away from the security of his chamber door, but the curious sense of dislocation accompanied him as he made his way through the Hayholt's acres of corridors. Unusual objects passed beneath his questing fingers, delicate furnishings and smooth-polished but intricately figured balusters unlike anything he remembered from these halls. The door to the quarters once occupied by the castle chambermaids swung unbolted, yet though he knew the rooms to be empty—their mistress had smuggled all of her charges out of the castle before her attack on Pryrates—he heard dim voices whispering in the depths. Guthwulf shuddered, but kept walking. The earl already knew the shifting and untrustworthy nature of the Hayholt in these days: even before he lost his sight it had become a weirdly inconstant place.

Guthwulf continued to count his paces. He had practiced the journey several times in recent weeks: it was thirty-five steps to the turning of the corridor, two dozen more to the main landing, then out into the narrow, wind-chilled Vine Garden. Half a hundred paces more and he was back beneath a roof once again, making his way down the chaplain's walking hall.

The wall became warm beneath his fingers, then abruptly turned blazingly hot. The earl snatched his hand away, gasping in shock and pain. A thin cry wafted down the corridor.

"... *T'si e-isi'ha as-irigú...!*"

He reached a trembling hand out to the wall again and felt only stone, damp and night-cold. The wind fluttered his clothing—the wind, or a murmuring, insubstantial crowd. The feeling of the gray sword was very strong.

Guthwulf hurried through the castle corridors, trailing his fingers as lightly as he could over the frighteningly changeable walls. As far as he could tell, he was the only real living thing in these halls. The strange sounds and the touches light as smoke and moths' wings were only phantasms, he assured himself—they could not hinder him. They were the shadows of Pryrates' sorcerous meddling.

He would not let them obstruct his flight. He would not stay prisoned in this corrupted place.

The earl touched the rough wood of a door and found to his fierce joy that he had counted truly. He fought to restrain a cry of triumph and overwhelming relief. He had reached the small portal beside the Greater Southern Door. Beyond would be open air and the commons that served the Inner Bailey.

But when he pushed it open and stepped through, instead of the bitter night air the earl had expected, he felt a hot wind blowing and the heat of many fires upon his skin. Voices murmured, pained, fretful.

Mother of God! Has the Hayholt caught fire?

Guthwulf stepped back but could not find the doorway again. His fingers instead scrabbled at stone which grew hotter beneath his touch. The murmurs slowly rose into a drone of many agitated voices, soft and yet piercing as the hum of a beehive. Madness, he told himself, illusion. He must not give in. He staggered ahead, still counting his steps. Soon his feet were slipping in the mud of the commons, yet somehow at the same moment his heels clicked on smooth tiles. The invisible castle was in some terrible flux, burning and trembling one moment, cold and substantial the next, and all in total silence as its tenants slept on, unaware.

Dream and reality seemed almost completely interwoven, his personal blackness awash in whispering ghosts that confused his counting, but still Guthwulf struggled on with the grim resolve that had carried him through many dreadful campaigns as Elias' captain. He trudged on toward the Middle Bailey, stopping at last to rest for a moment near—according to his faltering calculations—the spot where the castle doctor's chambers had once stood. He smelled the sour tang of the charred timbers, reached out and felt them crumble into rotted powder beneath his touch, and distractedly remembered the conflagration that had killed Morgenes and several others. Suddenly, as though summoned up by his thoughts, crackling flames leaped all around him, surrounding him with fire. This could be no illusion—he could feel the deadly blaze! The heat enclosed him like a crushing fist, balking him no matter which way he turned. Guthwulf gave a choked cry of despair. He was trapped, trapped! He must burn to death!

"*Ruakha, ruakha Asu'a!*" Ghostly voices were crying from beyond the flames. The presence of the gray sword was inside him now, in everything. He thought he could hear its unearthly music, and fainter, the songs of its unnatural brothers. Three swords. Three unholy swords. They knew him now.

There was a rustle like the beating of many wings, then the Earl of Utanyeat suddenly felt an opening appear before him, an empty spot in the otherwise unbroken wall of flame—a doorway that breathed cool air. With nowhere else to turn, he threw his cloak over his head and stumbled down into a hall of quieter, colder shadows.

PART ONE

The
Waiting Stone

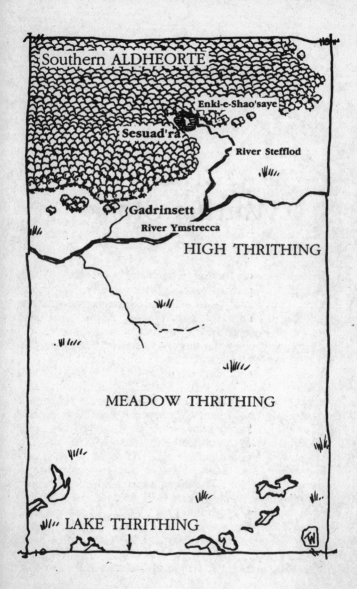

Southern ALDHEORTE

Enki-e-Shao'saye

Sesuad'ra

River Stefflod

Gadrinsett

River Ymstrecca

HIGH THRITHING

MEADOW THRITHING

LAKE THRITHING

1

Under Strange Skies

Simon squinted up at the stars swimming in the black night. He was finding it increasingly difficult to stay awake. His weary eyes turned to the brightest constellation, a rough circle of lights hovering what seemed a handsbreadth above the gaping, broken-eggshell edge of the dome.

There. That was the Spinning Wheel, wasn't it? It did seem oddly elliptical—as though the very sky in which the stars hung had been stretched into an unfamiliar shape—but if that wasn't the Spinning Wheel, what else could be so high in the sky in mid-autumn? The Hare? But the Hare had a little nubbly star close beside it—the Tail. And the Hare wasn't ever that big, was it?

A claw of wind reached down into the half-ruined building. Geloë called this hall "the Observatory"—one of her dry jokes, Simon had decided. Only the passing of long centuries had opened the white stone dome to the night skies, so Simon knew it couldn't really have been an observatory. Surely even the mysterious Sithi couldn't watch stars through a ceiling of solid rock.

The wind came again, sharper this time, bearing a flurry of snowflakes. Though it wracked him with shivers, Simon was thankful: the chill scraped some of his drowsiness away. It wouldn't do to fall asleep—not *this* night of all nights.

So, now I am a man, he thought. *Well, almost. Almost a man.*

Simon drew back the sleeve of his shirt and looked at

his arm. He tried to make the muscles stand up, then frowned at the less than satisfactory results. He ran his fingers through the hair on his forearm, feeling the places where cuts had become ridged scars: here, where a Hunë's blackened nails had left their mark; there, where he had slipped and dashed himself against a stone on Sikkihoq's slope. Was that what being grown meant? Having a lot of scars? He supposed it also meant learning from the wounds, as well—but what could he learn from the sort of things that had happened to him during the last year?

Don't let your friends get killed, he thought sourly. *That's one. Don't go out in the world and get chased by monsters and madmen. Don't make enemies.*

So much for the words of wisdom that people were always so eager to share with him. No decisions were ever as easy as they had seemed in Father Dreosan's sermons, where people always got to make a clean choice between Evil's Way and the Aedon's Way. In Simon's recent experience of the world, all the choices seemed between one unpleasant possibility and another, with only the faintest reference to good and evil.

The wind skirling through the Observatory dome grew more shrill. It put Simon's teeth on edge. Despite the beauty of the intricately sculpted pearlescent walls, this was still a place that did not seem to welcome him. The angles were strange, the proportions designed to please an alien sensibility. Like other products of its immortal architects, the Observatory belonged completely to the Sithi; it would never feel quite comfortable to mortals.

Unsettled, Simon got up and began to pace, the faint echo of his footsteps lost in the noise of the wind. One of the interesting things about this large circular hall, he decided, was that it had stone floors, something the Sithi no longer seemed to utilize. He flexed his toes inside his boots as a memory of Jao é-Tinukai'i's warm, grassy meadows tugged at him. He had walked barefoot there, and every day had been a summer day. Remembering, Simon curled his arms across his chest for warmth and comfort.

The Observatory's floor was made up of exquisitely cut and fitted tiles, but the cylindrical wall seemed to be one piece, perhaps the very stuff of the Stone of Farewell itself. Simon pondered. The other buildings here were also without visible joint or seam. If the Sithi had carved all the buildings on the surface directly from the hill's rocky bones, and had cut down into Sesuad'ra as well—the Stone seemed shot through with tunnels—how did they know when to stop? Hadn't they been afraid that if they made one hole too many the whole rock would collapse in on itself? That seemed almost as amazing as any other Sithi magic he had heard of or seen, and just as unavailable to mortals—knowing when to stop.

Simon yawned. Usires Aedon, but this night was long! He stared at the sky, at the wheeling, smoldering stars.

I want to climb up. I want to look at the moon.

Simon made his way across the smooth stone floor to one of the long staircases that spiraled gradually up around the circumference of the rooms, counting the steps as he went. He had already done this several times during the long night. When he got to the hundredth step, he sat down. The diamond gleam of a certain star, which had been midway along a shallow notch in the decayed dome when he made his last trip, now stood near the notch's edge. Soon it would disappear from sight behind the remaining shell of the dome.

Good. So at least some time had passed. The night was long and the stars were strange, but at least time's journey continued.

He clambered to his feet and continued up, walking the narrow stairway easily despite a certain light-headedness that he had no doubt would be cured by a long sleep. He climbed until he reached the highest landing, a pillar-propped collar of stone that at one time had circled the entire building. It had crumbled long ago, and most of it had fallen; now it extended only a few short ells beyond its joining with the staircase. The top of the high outer wall was just above Simon's head. A few careful paces took him along the landing to a spot where the breach in the dome dipped down to only a short distance above him. He reached up, feeling carefully for good finger-holds, then pulled himself upward. He swung one of his legs over the wall and let it dangle over nothingness.

The moon, wound in a wind-tattered veil of clouds, was nevertheless bright enough to make the pale ruins below gleam like ivory. Simon's perch was a good one. The Observatory was the only building within Sesuad'ra's outwall that stood even as high as the wall itself, which gave the settlement the appearance of one vast, low building. Unlike the other abandoned Sithi dwelling places he had seen, no towers had loomed here, no high spires. It was as though the spirit of Sesuad'ra's builders had been subdued, or as though they built for some utilitarian reason and not pure pride of craft. Not that the remains were unappealing: the white stone had a peculiar lambent glow all its own, and the buildings inside the curtain wall were laid out in a design of wild but somehow supremely logical geometry. Although it was built on a much smaller scale than what Simon had seen of Da'ai Chikiza and Enki-e-Shao'saye, the very modesty of its scope and uniformity of its design gave it a simple beauty different from those other, grander places.

All around the Observatory, as well as around the other major structures like the Leavetaking House and the House of Waters—names that Geloë had given them; Simon did not know if they were anything to do with their original purpose—snaked a system of paths and smaller buildings, or their remnants, whose interlocking loops and whorls were as cunningly designed yet naturalistic as the petals of a flower. Much of the area was overgrown by encroaching trees, but even the trees themselves revealed traces of some vestigial order, as the green space in the middle of a fairy-ring would show where the ancestral line of mushrooms had begun.

In the center of of what obviously had once been a settlement of rare and subtle beauty lay a strange tiled plateau. It was now largely covered with impertinent grass, but even by moonlight it still showed some trace of its original lushly intricate design. Geloë called this central place the Fire Garden. Simon, comfortably familiar only with the workings of human habitations, would have guessed it to be a marketplace.

Beyond the Fire Garden, on the other side of the Leavetaking House, stood a motionless wavefront of pale conical shapes—the tents of Josua's company, grown now to a sizable swell by the newcomers who had been trickling in for weeks. There was precious little room left, even on the broad tabletop summit of the Stone of Farewell; many of the most recent arrivals had made themselves homes in the warren of tunnels that ran beneath the hill's stony skin.

Simon sat staring at the flicker of the distant campfires until he began to feel lonely. The moon seemed very far away, her face cold and unconcerned.

He did not know how long he had been staring into empty blackness. For a moment he thought he had fallen asleep and was now dreaming, but surely this queer feeling of suspension was something real—real and frightening. He struggled, but his limbs were remote and nerveless. Nothing of Simon's body seemed to remain but his two eyes. His thoughts seemed to burn as brightly as the stars he had seen in the sky—when there had been a sky, and stars; when there had been something besides this unending blackness. Terror coursed through him.

Usires save me, has the Storm King come? Will it be black forever? God, please bring back the light!

And as if in answer to his prayer, lights began to kindle in the great dark. They were not stars, as they first seemed, but torches—tiny pinpoints of light that grew ever so slowly larger, as though approaching from a great distance away. The cloud of firefly glimmers became a stream, the stream became a line, looping and looping in slow spirals. It was a procession, scores of torches climbing uphill the way Simon himself had climbed up Sesuad'ra's curving path when he had first come here from Jao é-Tinukai'i.

Simon could now see the cloaked and hooded figures who made up the column, a silent host moving with ritual precision.

I'm on the Dream Road, he realized suddenly. *Amerasu said that I was closer to it than other folk.*

But what was he watching?

The line of torchbearers reached a level place and spread out in a sparkling fan, so that their lights were carried far out on either side of the hilltop. It *was* Sesuad'ra they had climbed, but a Sesuad'ra that even by torchlight was plainly different than the place Simon knew. The ruins that had surrounded him were ruins no longer. Every pillar and wall stood unbroken. Was this the past, the Stone of Farewell as it once had been, or was it some strange future version that would someday be rebuilt—perhaps when the Storm King had subjugated all Osten Ard?

The great company surged forward onto a flat place Simon recognized as the Fire Garden. There the cloaked figures set their torches down into niches between the tiles, or placed them atop stone pedestals, so that a garden of fire indeed bloomed there, a field of flickering, rippling light. Fanned by the wind, the flames danced; sparks seemed to outnumber the very stars.

Now Simon found himself suddenly pulled forward with the surging crowd and down toward the Leavetaking House. He plummeted through the glittering night, passing swiftly through the stone walls and into the bright-lit hall as though he were without substance. There was no sound but a continuous rushing in his ears. Seen closely, the images before him seemed to shift and blur along their edges, as though the world had been twisted ever so slightly out of its natural shape. Unsettled, he tried to close his eyes, but found that his dream-self could not shut out these visions: he could only watch, a helpless phantom.

Many figures stood at the great table. Globes of cold fire had been placed in alcoves on every wall, their blue, fire-orange, and yellow glows casting long shadows across the carved walls. More and deeper shadows were cast by the thing atop the table, a construct of concentric spheres like the great astrolabe Simon had often polished for Doctor Morgenes—but instead of brass and oak, this

was made entirely from lines of smoldering light, as
though someone had painted the fanciful shapes upon the
air in liquid fire. The moving figures that surrounded it
were hazy, but still Simon knew beyond doubt that they
were Sithi. No one could ever mistake those birdlike pos-
tures, that silken grace.

A Sitha-woman in a sky-blue robe leaned toward the
table and deftly scribed in trails of finger-flame her own
additions to the glowing thing. Her hair was blacker than
shadow, blacker even than the night sky above Sesuad'ra,
a great cloud of darkness about her head and shoulders.
For a moment Simon thought she might be a younger
Amerasu; but though there was much in this one that was
like his memories of First Grandmother, there was also
much that was not.

Beside her stood a white-bearded man in a billowing
crimson robe. Shapes that might have been pale antlers
sprouted from his brow, bringing Simon a pang of
unease—he had seen something like that in other, more
unpleasant dreams. The bearded man leaned forward and
spoke to her; she turned and added a new swirl of fire to
the design.

Although Simon could not see the dark woman's face
clearly, the one who stood across from her was all too
plain. That face was hidden behind a mask of silver, the
rest of her form beneath ice-white robes. As if in answer
to the black-haired woman, the Norn Queen raised her
arm and slashed a line of dull fire all the way across the
construct, then waved her hand once more to lay a net of
delicately smoking scarlet light over the outermost globe.
A man stood beside her, calmly watching her every move.
He was tall and seemed powerfully built, dressed all in
spiky armor of obsidian-black. He was not masked in silver or otherwise, but still Simon could see little of his
features.

What were they doing? Was this the Pact of Parting
that Simon had heard of—for certainly he was watching
both Sithi and Norn gathered together upon Sesuad'ra.

The blurred figures began to talk more animatedly.
Looping and crisscrossing lines of flame were thrown

into the air around the spheres where they hung in nothingness, bright as the afterimage of a hurtling fire-arrow. Their speech seemed to turn to harsh words: many of the shadowy observers, gesticulating with more anger than Simon had seen in the immortals he knew, stepped forward to the table and surrounded the principal foursome, but still he could hear nothing but a dull roaring like wind or rushing water. The flame globes at the center of the dispute flared up, undulating like a wind-licked bonfire.

Simon wished he could move forward somehow to get a better view. Was this the past he was watching? Had it seeped up from the haunted stone? Or was it only a dream, an imagining brought on by his long night and the songs he had heard in Jao é-Tinukai'i? Somehow, he felt sure that it was no illusion. It seemed so real, he felt almost as though he could reach out . . . he could reach out . . . and *touch*. . . .

The sound in his ears began to fade. The lights of torches and spheres dimmed.

Simon shivered back into awareness. He was sitting atop the crumbling stone of the Observatory, dangerously close to the edge. The Sithi were gone. There were no torches in the Fire Garden, and no living things visible atop Sesuad'ra except a pair of sentries sitting near the watchfire down beside the tent city. Bemused, Simon sat for a little while staring at the distant flames and tried to understand what he had seen. Did it mean something? Or was it just a meaningless remnant, a name scratched upon a wall by a traveler which remained long after that person was gone?

Simon trudged back down the stairway from the Observatory roof and returned to his blanket. Trying to understand his vision made his head hurt. It was becoming more difficult to think with every hour that passed.

After wrapping his cloak around himself more tightly—the robe he was wearing beneath was not very warm—he took a long swallow from his drinking skin. The water, from one of Sesuad'ra's springs, was sweet and cold against his teeth. He took another swig, savoring the aftertaste of grass and shade-flowers, and tapped his fingers on the stone tiles. Dreams or no dreams, he was supposed to be thinking about the things Deornoth had told him. Earlier in the night, he had repeated them over and over in his mind so many times that they had finally begun to seem like nonsense. Now, when he again tried to concentrate, he found that the litany Deornoth had so carefully taught him would not stay in his head, the words elusive as fish in a shallow pond. His mind roved instead, and he pondered all the strange happenings he had endured since running away from the Hayholt.

What a time it had been! What things he had seen! Simon was not sure that he would call it an adventure—that seemed a little too much like something that ended happily and safely. He doubted the ending would be pleasant, and enough people had died to make the word "safely" a cruel jest . . . but still, it was definitely an experience far beyond a scullion's wildest dreams. Simon Mooncalf had met creatures out of legends, had been in battles, and had even killed people. Of course, that had proved much less easy than he had once upon a time imagined it would be, when he had seen himself as a potential captain of the king's armies; in fact, it had proved to be very, very upsetting.

Simon had also been chased by demons, was the enemy of wizards, had become an intimate of noble folk—who didn't seem much better or worse than kitchen-and-pantry folk—and had lived as a reluctant guest in the city of the undying Sithi. Besides safety and warm beds, the only thing his adventure seemed to be lacking was beautiful maidens. He *had* met a princess—one he had liked even when she had seemed just an ordinary girl—but she was long gone, the Aedon only knew where. There had been precious little else in the way of feminine company since then, other than Aditu, Jiriki's sister, but *she* had been a little too far beyond Simon's awkward understanding. Like a leopard, she was: lovely but quite frightening. He yearned for someone a little more like himself—but better looking, of course. He rubbed his fuzzy beard, felt his prominent nose. A *lot* better looking. He was tired of being alone. He wanted someone to talk to—someone who would care, who would understand, in a way that not even his troll-friend Binabik ever could. Someone who would share things with him . . .

Someone who will understand about the dragon, was his sudden thought.

Simon felt a march of prickling flesh along his back, not caused by the wind this time. It was one thing to see a vision of ancient Sithi, no matter how vivid. Lots of people had visions—madmen by the score in Erchester's Battle Square shouted about them to one another, and Simon suspected that in Sesuad'ra such things might be even more common occurrences. But Simon had met a *dragon*, which was more than almost anyone could say. He had stood before Igjarjuk, the ice-worm, and hadn't backed down. He had swung his sword—well, *a* sword: it was more than presumptuous to call Thorn his—and the dragon had fallen. That was truly something wonderful. It was a thing no man but Prester John had ever done, and John had been the greatest of all men, the High King.

Of course, John killed his dragon, but I don't believe Igjarjuk died. The more I think about it, the more certain I am. I don't think its blood would have made me feel the way it did if the dragon was dead. And I don't think that I'm strong enough to kill it, even with a sword like Thorn.

But the strange thing was, although Simon had told everyone exactly what happened on Urmsheim and what he thought about it all, still some of the folk who now made the Stone of Farewell their home were calling him "Dragon Killer," smiling and waving when he passed. And although he had tried to shrug off the name, people seemed to take his reticence for modesty. He had even heard one of the new settlers from Gadrinsett telling her children the tale, a version that included a vivid description of the dragon's head struck loose from its body by the force of Simon's blow. Someday soon, what really happened wouldn't matter at all. The people who liked him—or liked the story, rather—would say he had single-handedly butchered the great snow dragon. Those who didn't care for him would say the whole thing was a lie.

The idea of those folk passing false stories of his life made Simon more than a little angry. It seemed to cheapen things, somehow. Not so much the imagined naysayers—they could never take away that moment of pure silence and stillness atop Urmsheim—but the others, the exaggerators and simplifiers. Those who told it as a story of unworrying bravery, of some imaginary Simon who sworded dragons simply because he could, or because dragons were evil, would be smearing dirty fingers across an unstained part of his soul. There was so much more to it than that, so much more that had been revealed to him in the beast's pale, emotionless eyes, in his own confused heroism and the burning instant of black blood . . . the blood that had shown him the world . . . the world. . . .

Simon straightened up. He had been nodding again. By God, sleep was a treacherous enemy. You couldn't face it and fight it; it waited until you were looking the other way, then stole up quietly. But he had given his word, and now that he would be a man, his word must be his solemn bond. So he *would* stay awake. This was a special night.

The armies of sleep had forced him to drastic measures by dawn's arrival, but they had not quite managed to defeat him. When candle-bearing Jeremias entered the Observatory, his entire frame tense with the gravity of his mission, it was to discover Simon sitting cross-legged in a puddle of fast-freezing water, wet red hair dangling in his eyes, the white streak that ran through it stark as an icicle. Simon's long face was alight with triumph.

"I poured the whole water skin over my head," he said with pride. His teeth were chattering so hard that Jeremias had to ask him to repeat himself. "Poured water over my head. To stay awake. What are you doing here?"

"It's time," the other said. "It's nearly dawn. Time for you to come away."

"Ah." Simon stood up unsteadily. "I stayed awake, Jeremias. Didn't sleep once."

Jeremias nodded. His smile was a cautious one. "That's

good, Simon. Come on. There's a fire at Strangyeard's place."

Simon, who felt weaker and colder than he had thought he would, draped his arm around the other youth's lean shoulder for support. Jeremias was so thin now that it was hard for Simon to remember him as he once had been: a suety chandler's apprentice, treble-chinned, always huffing and sweating. But for the haunted look that showed from time to time in his dark-shadowed eyes, Jeremias looked just like what he now was—a handsome young squire.

"A fire?" Simon's thoughts had at last caught up with his friend's words. He was quite giddy. "A good one? And is there food, too?"

"It's a very good fire." Jeremias was solemn. "One thing I learned ... down in the forges. How to make a proper fire." He shook his head slowly, lost in thought, then looked up and caught Simon's eye. A shadow flitted behind his gaze like a hare hunted in the grass, then his wary smile returned. "As for food—no, of course not. Not for a while yet, and you know it. But don't worry, pig, you will probably get a heel of bread or something this evening."

"Dog," Simon said, grinning, and purposefully leaned in such a way that Jeremias stumbled under the added weight. Only after much cursing and mutual insult did they avoid tumbling over onto the chilly stone flags. Together they staggered through the Observatory door and out into the pale gray-violet glow of dawn. Eastern light splashed all across the summit of the Stone of Farewell, but no birds sang.

Jeremias had been as good as his word. The blaze that burned in Father Strangyeard's tent-roofed chamber was gloriously hot—which was just as well, since Simon had stepped out of his robe and into a wooden tub. As he stared around at the white stone walls, at the carvings of tangled vines and minute flowers, the firelight rippled across the stonework so that the walls seemed to move beneath shallow pink and orange waters.

Father Strangyeard raised another pot of water and poured it over Simon's head and shoulders. Unlike his earlier self-inflicted bath, this water had at least been warmed; as it ran down his chilly flesh, Simon thought that it felt more like flowing blood than water.

". . . May this . . . may this water wash away sin and doubt." Strangyeard paused to fiddle with his eyepatch, his one squinting eye netted in wrinkles as he tried to remember the next passage of the prayer. Simon knew it was nerves, not forgetfulness: the priest had spent most of yesterday reading and rereading the short ceremony. "Let . . . let then the man so washed and made shriven fear not to stand before Me, so that I might look into the glass of his soul and see there reflected the fitness of his being, the righteousness of his oath . . . the righteousness of . . . of his oath . . ." The priest squinted again, despairingly. "Oh . . ."

Simon let the heat of the fire beat upon him. He felt quite boneless and stupid, but that was not such a bad way to feel. He had been sure he would be nervous, terrified even, but his sleepless night had burned away his fear.

Strangyeard, running his hand fitfully through his few remaining wisps of hair, at last summoned up the rest of the ceremony and hurried through to the ending, as though afraid the memory might slip away again. When he finished, the priest helped Jeremias to dry Simon off with soft cloths, then they gave him back his white robe, this time with a thick leather belt to wrap around his waist. Then, as Simon was stepping into his slippers, a small shape appeared in the doorway.

"Is he now ready?" Binabik asked. The troll spoke very quietly and gravely, as always full of respect for someone else's rituals. Simon stared at him and was filled with a sudden fierce love for the little man. Here was a friend, truly—one who had stood by him through all adversity.

"Yes, Binabik. I'm ready."

The troll led him out, Strangyeard and Jeremias following behind. The sky was more gray than blue, wild with fragmented clouds. The whole procession matched itself

to Simon's bemused, wandering pace as they made their
way in the morning light.

The path to Josua's tent was lined with spectators, perhaps ten score in all, mostly Hotvig's Thrithings-folk and
the new settlers from Gadrinsett. Simon recognized a few
faces, but knew that those most familiar to him were
waiting up ahead with Josua. Some of the children waved
to him. Their parents snatched at them and whispered
warningly, fearful of disrupting the solemn nature of the
event, but Simon grinned and waved back. The cold
morning air felt good on his face. A certain giddiness had
taken him over once more, so that he had to repress an
urge to laugh out loud. Who would ever have thought of
such a thing as this? He turned to Jeremias, but the
youth's face was closed, his eyes lowered in meditation
or shyness.

As they reached the open place before Josua's lodging,
Jeremias and Strangyeard dropped back, moving to stand
with the others in a rough semicircle. Sludig, his yellow
beard new-trimmed and braided, beamed at Simon like a
proud father. Dark-haired Deornoth stood beside him
dressed in knightly finery, with the harper Sangfugol, the
duke's son Isorn, and old Towser all close by—the jester,
wrapped in a heavy cloak, seemed to be muttering quiet
complaints to the young Rimmersman. Nearer the front of
the tent stood Duchess Gutrun and young Leleth. Beside
them stood Geloë. The forest woman's stance was that of
an old soldier forced to put up with a meaningless inspection, but as Simon caught her yellow eyes she nodded
once, as if acknowledging a job completed.

On the far side of the semicircle were Hotvig and his
fellow randwarders, their tall spears like a thicket of slim
trees. White morning light bled through the clotted
clouds, shining dully on their bracelets and spearheads.
Simon tried not to think about the others, like Haestan
and Morgenes, who should be present but were not.

Framed in the opening between these two groups was a
tent striped in gray, red, and white. Prince Josua stood before it, his sword Naidel sheathed at his side, a thin circlet
of silver upon his brow. Vorzheva was beside him, her

own dark cloud of hair unbound, lush upon her shoulders and moving at the wind's touch.

"Who comes before me?" Josua asked, his voice slow and measured. As if to belie his heavy tone, he showed Simon a hint of smile.

Binabik pronounced the words carefully. "One who would be made a knight, Prince—your servant and God's. He is Seoman, son of Eahlferend and Susanna."

"Who speaks for him and swears that this is true?"

"Binbiniqegabenik of Yiqanuc am I, and I am swearing that this is true." Binabik bowed. His courtly gesture sent a ripple of amusement through the crowd.

"And has he kept his vigil, and been shriven?"

"Yes!" Strangyeard piped up hurriedly. "He did—I mean, he has!"

Josua fought another smile. "Then let Seoman step forward."

At the touch of Binabik's small hand on his arm, Simon took a few steps toward the prince, then sank to one knee in the thick, rippling grass. A chill moved up his back.

Josua waited a moment before he spoke. "You have rendered brave service, Seoman. In a time of great danger, you have risked your life for my cause and returned with a mighty prize. Now, before the eyes of God and of your fellows, I stand prepared to lift you up and grant you title and honor above other men, but also to lay upon your shoulders burdens beyond those that other men must carry. Will you swear to accept them all?"

Simon took a breath so his voice would be steady, and also to make sure of the words Deornoth had so carefully taught him. "I will serve Usires Aedon and my master. I will lift up the fallen and defend God's innocents. I will not turn my eyes from duty. I will defend my prince's realm from enemies spiritual and corporeal. This I swear by my name and honor, with Elysia, Aedon's holy mother, as my witness."

Josua stepped closer, then reached down and laid his one good hand upon Simon's head. "Then I name you my man, Seoman, and lay on you the charges of knighthood." He looked up. "Squire!"

Jeremias stepped forward. "Here, Prince Josua." His voice shook a little.

"Bring his sword."

After a moment's confusion—the hilt had gotten tangled in Father Strangyeard's sleeve—Jeremias approached bearing the sword in its tooled leather scabbard. It was a well-polished but otherwise undistinguished Erkynlandish blade. Simon felt a moment of regret that the blade was not Thorn, then chastised himself as an overweening idiot. Could he never be satisfied? Besides, think of the embarrassment if Thorn did not submit to the ritual and proved heavy as a millstone. He would look a perfect fool then, wouldn't he? Josua's hand upon his head suddenly felt as weighty as the black sword itself. Simon looked down so that no one could see his spreading flush.

When Jeremias had carefully buckled the scabbard onto Simon's belt, Simon drew the sword, kissed its hilt, then made the sign of the Tree as he set it on the ground before Josua's feet.

"In your service, Lord."

The prince withdrew his hand, then pulled slender Naidel from its scabbard and touched Simon's shoulders, right, left, then right again.

"Before the eyes of God and of your fellows—rise, Sir Seoman."

Simon rose tottering to his feet. It was done. He was a knight. His mind seemed nearly as cloudy as the lowering sky. There was a long, hushed moment, then the cheering began.

Hours after the ceremony, Simon awoke gasping from a dream of smothering darkness to find himself half-strangled in a knot of blankets. Weak, wintery sunlight was beaming down on Josua's striped tent; bars of red light lay across Simon's arm like paint. It was daytime, he reassured himself. He had been sleeping, and it had only been a terrible dream. . . .

He sat up, grunting as he unwrapped himself from the tangle of bedclothes. The tent walls throbbed beneath the

wind. Had he cried out? He hoped not. It would be humil-
iating indeed to wake up screaming on the afternoon that
he had been knighted for bravery.

"Simon?" A small shadow appeared on the wall near
the door. "Are you awake?"

"Yes, Binabik." He reached over to retrieve his shirt as
the little man ducked in through the tent flap.

"Were you sleeping well? It is no thing of easiness to
stay awake all the night, and sometimes it is then making
it hard for sleeping after."

"I slept." Simon shrugged. "I had a strange dream."

The troll cocked an eyebrow. "Do you remember it?"

Simon thought for a moment. "Not really. It sort of
slipped away. Something about a king and old flowers,
about the smell of earth . . ." He shook his head. It was
gone.

"That, I am thinking, is just as well." Binabik bustled
around the prince's tent, looking for Simon's cloak. He
found it at last, then turned and tossed it to the new-made
knight, who was pulling on his breeches. "Your dreams
are often disturbing to you, but seldom of much help in
gaining more knowledge. Probably, then, it is best you are
not troubled with the memory of each one of them."

Simon felt vaguely slighted. "Knowledge? What do
you mean? Amerasu said that my dreams meant something. And so did you and Geloë!"

Binabik sighed. "I was meaning only that we are not
having much luck discovering their meaning. So, it seems
to me better that you are not troubled by them, at least for
this moment, when you should be enjoying your great
day!"

The troll's earnest face was enough to make Simon
thoroughly ashamed of his momentary ill humor. "You're
right, Binabik." He buckled on his sword belt. Its unfamiliar weight was one more unusual thing in a day of
wonders. "Today I won't think about . . . about anything
bad."

Binabik gave him a hearty hand-smack. "That is my
companion of many journeys that speaks! Let us go now.
Besides the kindness of his tent for your sleeping com-

fort, Josua has made sure that a fine meal awaits us all, and other pleasures, too."

Outside, the encampment of tents that stood in the shelter of Sesuad'ra's long northeastern wall had been hung with ribbons of many colors which snapped and streamed in the powerful wind. Seeing them, Simon could not help but think of his days in Jao é-Tinukai'i, memories he usually tried to hold at bay because of the complicated and unsettling feelings that came with them. All today's fine words couldn't change the truth, couldn't make the Storm King go away. Simon was tired of being fearful. The Stone of Farewell was a refuge only for a little while—how he longed for a home, for a safe place and freedom from terror! Amerasu the Ship-Born had seen his dreams. She had said he need carry no further burdens, hadn't she? But Amerasu, who had seen so many things, had also been blind to others. Perhaps she had been wrong about Simon's destiny as well.

With the last stragglers, Simon and his companions passed through the cracked doorway and into the torchlit warmth of the Leavetaking House. The vast room was full of people seated on spread cloaks and blankets. The tiled floors had been cleared of centuries of moss and grasses; small cookfires burned everywhere. There were few enough excuses for merriment in these hard days: the exiles of many places and nations gathered here seemed determinedly joyful. Simon was called upon to stop at several fires and share a congratulatory drink, so that it took some part of an hour before he at last made his way to the high table—a massive decorated stone slab that was part of the original Sithi hall—where the prince and the rest of his company waited.

"Welcome, Sir Seoman." Josua motioned Simon to the seat at his left. "Our settlers of New Gadrinsett have spared no effort to make this feast a grand one. There is rabbit and partridge; chicken, I think; and good silver trout from the Stefflod." He leaned over to speak more quietly. Despite the weeks of peace, Simon thought the prince's face seemed gaunt. "Eat up, lad. Fiercer weather is coming soon. We may need to live on our fat, like bears."

"New Gadrinsett?" Simon asked.

"We are but visitors on Sesuad'ra," said Geloë. "The prince rightly feels that it would be presumptuous to call our settlement by the name of their sacred place."

"And since Gadrinsett is the source of many of our residents, and the name is appropriate—'Gathering Place' in the old Erkynlandish tongue—I have named our tent city after it." He lifted his cup of beaten metal. "New Gadrinsett!" The company echoed his toast.

The sparse resources of valley and forest had indeed been put to good use; Simon ate with an enthusiasm that bordered on frenzy. He had gone unfed since the midday meal of the day before, and much of his nightlong vigil had been taken up with distracted thoughts of food. Eventually, sheer exhaustion had taken his appetite away, but now it had returned at full strength.

Jeremias stood behind him, refilling Simon's cup with watered wine each time he emptied it. Simon was not yet comfortable with the idea that his Hayholt companion should wait upon him, but Jeremias would have it no other way.

When the one-time chandler's boy had reached Sesuad'ra, drawn east by the rumor of Josua's growing army of the disaffected, Simon had been surprised—not only by the change in Jeremias' appearance, but by the very unlikeliness of meeting him again, especially in such a strange place. But if Simon had been surprised, Jeremias had been astounded to discover that Simon was alive, and even more amazed by the story of what had befallen his friend. He seemed to view Simon's survival as nothing less than a miracle, and had thrown himself into Simon's service as one entering religious orders. Faced with Jeremias' unswerving determination, Simon gave way with no little embarrassment. He was made uneasy by his new squire's selfless devotion; when, as sometimes happened, a hint of their old mocking friendship surfaced, Simon was much happier.

Although Jeremias made Simon tell and retell all the

things that had happened to him, the chandler's boy was unwilling to talk much about his own experiences. He would say only that he had been forced to work in the forges beneath the Hayholt, and that Inch, Morgenes' former assistant, had been a cruel master. Simon could sense much of the untold tale, and silently added to the slow-talking giant's tally of deserved retribution. After all, Simon was a knight now, and wasn't that something that knights did? Dispense justice...?

"You stare at nothing, Simon," said Lady Vorzheva, waking him from his thoughts. She was beginning to show the signs of the growing child within her, but still had a slightly wild look, like a horse or bird that would suffer human touch but would never be quite tame. He remembered the first time he had seen her across the courtyard at Naglimund, how he had wondered what could make such a lovely woman look so fiercely unhappy. She seemed more contented now, but a hard edge still remained.

"I'm sorry, Lady, I was thinking about ... about the past, I suppose." He flushed. What did one talk about at table with the prince's lady? "It is a strange world."

Vorzheva smiled, amused. "Yes, it is. Strange and terrible."

Josua rose and banged his cup on the stone tabletop until the crowded room at last fell silent. As the host of unwashed faces stared up at the prince's company, Simon had a sudden, startling revelation.

All those Gadrinsett folk, with their mouths hanging open as they watched Josua—they were him! They were like he had been! He had always been outside, looking in at the important folk. And now, wonderfully, unbelievably, *he* was one of the high company, a knight at the prince's long table, so that others stared at him enviously—but he was still the same Simon. What did it mean?

"We are gathered for many reasons," the prince said. "First, and most importantly, to give thanks to our God that we are alive and safe here upon this place of refuge, surrounded by water and protected from our enemies.

Also, we are here to celebrate the eve of Saint Granis' Day, which is a holy day to be observed by fasting and quiet prayer—but to be observed the night before with good food and wine!" He lifted his cup to cheers from the throng. When the noise had died down, he grinned and continued. "We also celebrate the knighthood of young Simon, now called Sir Seoman." Another chorus of cheers. Simon blushed and nodded. "You have all seen him knighted, seen him take his sword and swear his oath. But you have not seen—his banner!"

There was much whispering as Gutrun and Vorzheva bent over and hauled up a roll of cloth from beneath the table; it had been lying right at Simon's feet. Isorn stepped forward to help them, and together they lifted and unfurled it.

"The device of Sir Seoman of New Gadrinsett," the prince declared.

On a field of diagonal gray and red stripes—Josua's colors—lay the silhouette of a black sword. Twined about it like a vine was a sinuous white dragon, whose eyes, teeth, and scales had all been meticulously stitched with scarlet thread. The crowd hooted and cheered.

"Hooray for the dragon slayer!" a man cried; several echoed him. Simon ducked his head, face reddening again, then quickly drained his wine cup. Jeremias, smiling proudly, refilled it. Simon drank down that one, too. It was glorious, all of it, but still ... deep in his heart, he could not help feeling that some important point was being missed. Not just the dragon, although he hadn't slain it. Not Thorn, although it certainly wasn't Simon's sword, and might not even be of any use to Josua. Something was not quite right. . . .

S'Tree, he thought disgustedly, *don't you ever get tired of complaining, mooncalf?*

Josua was banging his cup again. "That is not all! Not all!" The prince seemed to be enjoying himself.

It must be nice for him to preside over cheerful events for once.

"There is more!" Josua cried. "One more present, Simon." He waved, and Deornoth stepped away from the table, heading for the back of the hall. The hum of conversation rose again. Simon drank a little more watered wine, then thanked Vorzheva and Gutrun for their work on his banner, praising the quality of the stitchery until both women were laughing. When a few people near the back of the crowd began to shout and clap their hands, Simon looked up to see Deornoth returning. The knight led a brown horse.

Simon stared. "Is it. . . ?" He leaped up, banging his knee on the table, and hurried limping across the crowded floor. "Homefinder!" he cried. He threw his arms around the mare's neck; she, less overwhelmed than he, nosed gently at his shoulder. "But I thought Binabik said she was lost!"

"She was," said Deornoth, smiling. "When Binabik and Sludig were trapped by the giants, they had to set the horses free. One of our scouting parties found her near the ruins of the Sithi city across the valley. Maybe she sensed something of the Sithi still there and felt safe, since you say she spent time among them."

Simon was chagrined to find himself weeping. He had been certain that the mare was simply one more addition to the list of friends and acquaintances lost in this terrible year. Deornoth waited until he wiped his eyes, then said: "I'll put her back with the other horses, Simon. I took her away from her feed. You can see her in the morning."

"Thank you, Deornoth. Thank you." Simon stumbled back to the high table.

As he settled in, accepting Binabik's congratulations, Sangfugol rose at the prince's request. "We celebrate Simon's knighthood, as Prince Josua has said." The harper bowed toward the high table. "But he was not alone on his journey, nor in his bravery and sacrifice. You also know that the prince has named Binabik of Yiqanuc and Sludig of Elvritshalla to be Protectors of the Realm of Erkynland. But even there, the tale is not all told. Of the six braves ones who set out, only three returned. I have made this song, hoping that in later days they will none of them be forgotten."

At a nod from Josua, he picked out a delicate succession of notes on the harp which one of the new settlers had crafted for him, then began to sing.

"In farthest north, where storm winds blow
And winter's teeth are fierce with rime,
Out of the deep eternal snows
Looms the mountain, cold Urmsheim.

At prince's call six men did ride
From out of threatened Erkynland,
Sludig, Grimmric, Binabik the troll,
Ethelbearn, Simon, and brave Haestan.

They sought Camaris' mighty sword
The black blade Thorn from old Nabban,
Splinter of fallen heaven-star
To save the prince's tortured land ..."

As Sangfugol played and sang, the whispering stopped, and a hush fell over the gathering. Even Josua watched, as though the song could make the triumph a real one. The torches wavered. Simon drank more wine.

It was quite late. Only a few musicians were still playing—Sangfugol had exchanged his harp for his lute, and Binabik had brought out his flute late in the proceedings—and the dancing had more or less degenerated into staggering and laughing. Simon himself had drunk a great deal of wine and danced with two girls from Gadrinsett, a pretty plump one and her thin friend. The girls had whispered back and forth between themselves almost the whole time, impressed by Simon, his youthful beard and grand honors. They had also giggled uncontrollably every time he tried to talk to them. At last, bewildered and more than a little irritated, he had bid them good night and kissed their hands, as knights were supposed to do, which had occasioned more flurries of nervous laughter. They were really little more than children, Simon decided.

Josua had seen Lady Vorzheva off to bed, then returned

to preside over the final hour of the feast. He sat now, talking quietly with Deornoth. Both men looked tired.

Jeremias was sleeping in a corner, determined not to go to bed while Simon was still up, despite the fact that his friend had the advantage of having slept until past noon. Still, Simon was beginning to think seriously about lurching off to bed when Binabik appeared in the doorway of Leavetaking House. Qantaqa stood beside him, sniffing the air of the great hall with a mixture of interest and distrust. Binabik left the wolf and came inside. He beckoned to Simon, then made his way over to Josua's chair.

". . . So they have made him a bed? Good." The prince turned as Simon approached. "Binabik brings news. Welcome news."

The troll nodded. "I do not know this man, but Isorn seemed to think that his coming was an important thing. Count Eolair, a Hernystirman," he explained to Simon, "has just been brought across the water by one of the fishermen, brought here to New Gadrinsett." He smiled at the name, which still seemed clumsily new-minted. "He is very tired now, but he is telling that he has important news for us, which he will give us in the morning if the prince is willing it."

"Of course." Josua stroked his chin thoughtfully. "Any news of Hernystir is valuable, although I doubt that much of Eolair's tale is happy."

"As it may be. However, Isorn was also saying," Binabik lowered his voice and leaned closer, "that Eolair claims to have learned something important about," his voice became quieter still, "the Great Swords."

"Ah!" muttered Deornoth, surprised.

Josua was silent for a moment. "So," he said at last. "Tomorrow, on Saint Granis' Day, perhaps we shall learn if our exile is one of hope or hopelessness." He rose and turned his cup over, giving it a spin with his fingers. "Bed, then. I will send for you all tomorrow, when Eolair has had a chance to rest."

The prince walked away across the stone tiles. The torches made his shadow jump along the walls.

"Bed, as the prince was saying," Binabik smiled.

Qantaqa pushed forward, thrusting her head beneath his hand. "This will be a day for long remembering, Simon, will it not?"

Simon could only nod.

2

Chains of Many Kinds

Princess Miriamele considered the ocean.

When she had been young, one of her nurses had told her that the sea was the mother of mountains, that all the land came from the sea and would return to it one day, even as lost Khandia was reputed to have vanished into the smothering depths. Certainly the ocean that had beaten at the cliffs beneath her childhood home at Meremund had seemed eager to reclaim the rocky verge.

Others had named the sea as mother of monsters, of kilpa and kraken, oruks and water-wights. The black depths, Miriamele knew, did indeed teem with strange things. More than once some great, formless hulk had washed up on Meremund's rocky beaches to lie rotting in the sun beneath the fearful, fascinated eyes of the local inhabitants until the tide rolled it away again into the mysterious deeps. There was no doubt that the sea birthed monsters.

And when Miriamele's own mother went away, never to return, and her father Elias sank into brooding anger over his wife's death, the ocean even became a kind of parent to her. Despite its moods, as varied as the hours of sunlight and moonlight, as capricious as the storms that roiled its surface, the ocean had provided a constancy to her childhood. The breakers had lulled her to sleep at night, and she had awakened every morning to the sound of gulls and the sight of tall sails in the harbor below her father's castle, rippling like great-petaled flowers as she stared down from her window.

The ocean had been many things to her, and had meant much. But until this moment, as she stood at the aft rail of the *Eadne Cloud* with the whitecaps of the Great Green stretching away on all sides, she had never realized that it could also be a prison, a holdfast more inescapable than anything built of stone and iron.

As Earl Aspitis' ship coursed southeast from Vinitta, bound toward the Bay of Firannos and its scatter of islands, Miriamele for the first time felt the ocean turn against her, holding her more surely than ever her father's court had bound her with ritual or her father's soldiers had hemmed her all around in sharp steel. She had escaped those wardens, had she not? But how was she to escape a hundred miles of empty sea? No, it was better to give in. Miriamele was tired of fighting, tired of being strong. Stone cliffs might stand proudly for ages, but they fell to the ocean at last. Instead of resisting, she would do better to float where the tides took her, like driftwood, shaped by the action of the currents but moving, always moving. Earl Aspitis wasn't a bad man. True, he did not treat her with quite the same solicitude as he had a fortnight ago, but still he spoke kindly—that is, when she did as he wished. So she would do as he wished. She would float like an abandoned spar, unresisting, until time and events dropped her onto land again. . . .

A hand touched the sleeve of her dress. She jumped, surprised, and turned to find Gan Itai standing beside her. The Niskie's intricately wrinkled face was impassive, but her gold-flecked eyes, though sun-shaded, seemed to glitter.

"I did not mean to startle you, girl." She moved up to the rail beside Miriamele and together they stared out over the restless water.

"When there's no land in sight," Miriamele said at last, "you might as well be sailing off the edge of the world. I mean, it seems as if there might not be any land anywhere."

The Niskie nodded. Her fine white hair fluttered around her face. "Sometimes, at night, when I am up on

the deck alone and singing, I feel as though I am crossing
the Ocean Indefinite and Eternal, the one my people
crossed to come to this land. They say that ocean was
black as tar, but the wave crests glowed like pearl."

As she spoke, Gan Itai extended her hand and clasped
Miriamele's palm. Startled and unsure of what to do, the
princess did not resist, but continued to stare out to sea.
A moment later the Niskie's long, leathery fingers pushed
something into her hand.

"The sea can be a lonely place." Gan Itai continued as
though unaware of what her own hand was doing. "Very
lonely. It is hard to find friends. It is hard to know who
can be trusted." The Niskie's hand dropped away, disappearing back into the wide sleeves of her robe. "I hope
you will discover folk you can trust ... Lady Marya."
The pause before Miriamele's false name was unmistakable.

"So do I," said the princess, flustered.

"Ah." Gan Itai nodded. A smile tilted her thin mouth.
"You look a little pale. Perhaps the wind is too much for
you. Perhaps you should go to your cabin." The Niskie
inclined her head briefly, then walked away, bare brown
feet carrying her artfully across the rocking deck.

Miriamele watched her go, then looked up to the tiller
where Earl Aspitis stood talking to the steersman. The
earl lifted his arm to free himself from his golden cloak,
which the wind had wrapped about him. He saw
Miriamele and smiled briefly, then returned to his conversation. Nothing about his smile was unusual, except perhaps its perfunctory quality, but Miriamele suddenly felt
chilled to the heart. She clutched the curl of parchment in
her fist more tightly, fearful that the wind might pull it
loose from her grasp and send it fluttering right up to
Aspitis. She had no idea what it was, but somehow she
knew beyond doubt that she did not want him to see it.

Miriamele forced herself to walk slowly across the
deck, using her empty hand to clutch the rail. She was not
nearly so steady as Gan Itai had been.

*   *   *

In the dim cabin, Miriamele carefully uncurled the parchment. She had to hold it up beside the candle flame to read the tiny, crabbed letters.

I have done many wrongs,

she read,

and I know you no longer trust me, but please believe that these words are honest. I have been many people, none of them satisfactory. Padreic was a fool, Cadrach a rogue. Perhaps I can become something better before I die.

She wondered where he had gotten the parchment and ink, and decided that the Niskie must have brought it to him. As she stared at the labored script, Miriamele thought of the monk's weak arms weighted by chains. She felt a stab of pity—what agony it must have been for him to write this! But why could he not leave her alone? Why could no one simply let her be?

If you are reading this, then Gan Itai has done as she promised. She is the only one on this ship you can trust ... except perhaps for me. I know that I have cheated and deserted you. I am a weak man, my lady, but in my warnings at least I have served you well, and still try to do so. You are not safe on board this ship. Earl Aspitis is even worse than I guessed him to be. He is not just a gilded creature of Duke Benigaris' court. He is a servant of Pryrates.

I have told you many lies, my lady, and there are also many truths that I have kept hidden. I cannot set all to right here. My fingers are tired already, my arms are sore. But I will tell you this: there is no one alive who knows the evil of the priest Pryrates better than I. There is no one alive who bears more responsibility for that evil, since I helped him become what he is.

It is a long and complicated tale. Enough to say that I, to my eternal and horrible shame, gave Pryrates the key to a door he should never have opened. Worse, I did so even after I knew him for the ravening beast he is. I gave in to him because I was weak and frightened. It is the worst thing I have ever done in a life of grievous errors.

Believe me in this, lady. To my sorrow, I know our enemy well. I hope you will also believe me when I say that Aspitis does not only the bidding of his lord Benigaris, but the work of the red priest as well. It was common knowledge in Vinitta.

You must escape. Perhaps Gan Itai can help you. Sadly, I do not think you will ever again go under such light guard as you did on Vinitta. My cowardly attempt at flight will assure that. I know not how or why, but I beg you to leave as soon as you can. Flee to the inn called Pelippa's Bowl, in Kwanitupul. I believe Dinivan has sent others there, and perhaps they can help you escape to your uncle Josua.

I must stop because I hurt. I will not ask you to forgive me. I have earned no forgiveness.

A smear of blood had stained the edge of the parchment. Miriamele stared at it, her eyes blurring with tears, until someone knocked sharply on the door and her heart erupted into frenzied pounding. She crumpled the note in her palm even as the door swung open.

"My sweet lady," said grinning Aspitis, "why do you hide yourself down here in the dark? Come, let us walk on the deck."

The parchment seemed to burn her, as though she clutched a smoldering coal.

"I . . . I do not feel well, my lord." She shook her head, trying to hide her shortness of breath. "I will walk another time."

"Marya," the earl chided, "I told you that it was your country openness that charmed me. What, are you becoming a moody court wench?" He reached her side in a long step. His hand trailed across her neck. "Come, it is no wonder you feel poorly, sitting in this dark room. You need air." He leaned forward and brushed his lips below her ear. "Or perhaps you prefer it here, in the dark. Perhaps you are merely lonely?" His fingers dragged delicately across her throat, soft as spiderwebs on her skin.

Miriamele stared at the candle. The flame danced before her, but all around it was sunken deep in shadow.

The stained glass windows of the Hayholt's throne room had been broken. Ragged curtains restrained the flurrying snow, but did not keep out the freezing air. Even Pryrates seemed to feel the cold: although he still went bareheaded, the king's counselor was wearing red robes lined with fur.

Alone of all the folk who came into the throne room, the king and his cupbearer did not seem to mind the chill air. Elias sat bare-armed and bare-footed on the Dragonbone Chair; but for the great scabbarded sword that hung from his belt, he was dressed as casually as if he lounged in his private chambers. The monk Hengfisk, the king's silent page, wore a threadbare habit and his customary lunatic grin, and appeared no less comfortable than his master in the frosty hall.

The High King slouched deep in the cage of dragon's bones, chin on chest, peering out from beneath his eyebrows at Pryrates. In contrast to the black malachite statues which stood on each side of the throne, Elias' skin seemed white as milk. Blue veins showed at his temples and along his wiry arms, bulging as though they might burst through the flesh.

Pryrates opened his mouth as if to say something, then closed it again. His sigh was that of an Aedonite martyr overwhelmed with the foolish wickedness of his persecutors.

"Damn you, priest," Elias snarled, "my mind is made up."

The king's advisor said nothing, but only nodded; the torchlight made his hairless skull gleam like a wet stone. Despite the wind that fluttered the curtains, the room seemed full of a curious stillness.

"Well?" The king's green eyes were dangerously bright.

The priest sighed again, more softly. His voice, when he spoke, was conciliatory. "I am your counselor, Elias. I only do what you would wish me to: that is, help you decide what is best."

"Then I think it best that Fengbald take soldiers and go east. I want Josua and his band of traitors driven out of their holes and crushed. I have delayed too long already with this business of Guthwulf and with Benigaris' fumblings in Nabban. If Fengbald leaves now, he and his troops will reach my brother's den in a month. You know what kind of winter it will be, alchemist—you of all people. If I wait any longer, the chance is lost." The king pulled at his face irritably.

"As to the weather, there is little doubt," Pryrates said equably. "I can only once again question the need to pursue your brother. He is no threat. Even with an army of thousands, he could not stop us before your glorious, complete, and permanent victory is assured. There is only a little while longer to wait."

The wind changed direction, making the banners that hung from the ceiling ripple like pondwater. Elias snapped his fingers and Hengfisk scuttled forward with the king's cup. Elias drank, coughed, then drank again until the goblet was empty. A bead of steaming black liquid clung to his chin.

"That is simple for you to say," the king snarled when he had finished swallowing. "Aedon's Blood, you have said it often enough. But I have waited long already. I am cursedly tired of waiting."

"But it will be worth the wait, Majesty. You know that."

The king's face grew momentarily pensive. "And my dreams have been getting more and more strange, Pryrates. More . . . real."

"That is understandable." Pryrates lifted his long fingers soothingly. "You bear a great burden—but all will soon be made right. You will author a reign of splendor unlike anything the world has seen, if you will only be patient. These matters have their own timing—like war, like love."

"Hah." Elias belched sourly, his irritation returning. "Damned little you know of love, you eunuch bastard." Pryrates flinched at this, and for a moment narrowed his coal-black eyes to slits, but the king was gazing down morosely at Sorrow and did not see. When he looked up again, the priest's face was as blandly patient as before. "So what is *your* payment for all this, alchemist? That I've never understood."

"Besides the pleasure of serving you, Majesty?"

Elias' laugh was sharp and short, like a dog's bark. "Yes, besides that."

Pryrates stared at him appraisingly for a moment. An odd smile twisted his thin lips. "Power, of course. The power to do what I want to do . . . need to do."

The king's eyes had swung to the window. A raven had alighted on the sill and now stood preening its oily black feathers. "And what do you want to do, Pryrates?"

"Learn." For a moment the priest's careful mask of statecraft seemed to slip; the face of a child showed through—a horrible, greedy child. "I want to know *everything*. For that I need power, which is a sort of permission. There are secrets so dark, so deep, that the only way to discover them is to tear open the universe and root about in the very guts of Death and Unbeing."

Elias lifted his hand and waved for his cup once more. He continued to watch the raven, which hopped forward on the sill and tilted its head to return the king's stare. "You talk strangely, priest. Death? Unbeing? Are they not the same?"

Pryrates grinned maliciously, although at what was not clear. "Oh, no, Majesty. Not remotely."

Elias suddenly whirled in his chair, craning his head around the yellowed, dagger-fanged skull of the dragon

Shurakai. "Curse you, Hengfisk, did you not see me call
for my cup!? My throat is burning!"

The pop-eyed monk hurried to the king's side. Elias
carefully took the cup from him and set it down, then hit
Hengfisk on the side of his head so swiftly and powerfully that the cupbearer was flung to the floor as if
lightning-struck. Elias then calmly drained the steaming
draught. Hengfisk lay boneless as a jellyfish for several
long moments then rose and retrieved the empty cup. His
idiot grin had not vanished; if anything, it had become
wider and more deranged, as though the king had done
him some great kindness. The monk bobbed his head and
backed into the shadows once more.

Elias paid him no attention. "So it is settled. Fengbald
will take the Erkynguard and a company of soldiers and
mercenaries and go east. He will bring me back my brother's smirking, lecturing head on a lance." He paused, then
said thoughtfully: "Do you suppose that the Norns would
go with Fengbald? They are fierce fighters, and cold
weather and darkness are nothing to them."

Pryrates raised an eyebrow. "I think it unlikely, my
king. They do not seem to like to travel by day; neither
do they seem to enjoy the company of mortals."

"Not much use as allies, are they?" Elias frowned and
stroked Sorrow's hilt.

"Oh, they are valuable enough, Majesty." Pryrates nodded his head, smiling. "They will render service when we
truly need them. Their master—your greatest ally—will
see to that."

The raven blinked its golden eye, then uttered a harsh
noise and took wing. The tattered curtain fluttered where
it passed out through the window and into the stinging
wind.

"Please, may I hold him?" Maegwin extended her
arms.

With a worried look on her dust-smeared face, the
young mother handed the baby to her. Maegwin could not

help wondering if the woman was frightened of her—the king's daughter, with her dark mourning clothes and strange ways.

"I'm just so afraid he'll be wicked, my lady," said the young woman. "He's been crying all day, till I nearly run mad. He's hungry, poor little thing, but I don't want him screaming 'round you, Lady. You've more important things to think about."

Maegwin felt the chill that had touched her heart thaw a little. "Never worry about that." She bounced the pink-faced baby, who did seem to be on the brink of another outburst. "Tell me his name, Caihwye."

The young woman looked up, startled. "You know me, Lady?"

Maegwin smiled sadly. "We are not so very many, any more. Far less than a thousand in these caverns all told. No, there are not so many people in Free Hernystir that I have trouble remembering them."

Caihwye nodded, wide-eyed. "It is terrible." She had probably been pretty before the war, but now she had lost teeth and was dreadfully thin. Maegwin was certain that she had been giving most of what food she had to her baby.

"The child's name?" Maegwin reminded her.

"Oh! Siadreth, my lady. It was his father's name." Caihwye shook her head sadly; Maegwin did not ask after the child's namesake. For most of the survivors, discussions about fathers, husbands, and sons were sadly predictable. Most of the stories ended with the battle at the Inniscrich.

"Princess Maegwin." Old Craobhan had been watching silently until now. "We must go. There are more people waiting for you."

She nodded. "You are right." Gently, she handed the child back to his mother. The small pink face wrinkled, preparing to shed tears. "He is very beautiful, Caihwye. May all the gods bless him, and Mircha herself give him good health. He will be a fine man."

Caihwye smiled and jiggled young Siadreth in her lap

until he forgot what he had been about to do. "Thank you,
Lady. I'm so glad you came back well."

Maegwin, who had been turning away, paused. "Came
back?"

The young woman looked startled, frightened she'd
said something wrong. "From under the ground, Lady."
She pointed downward with her free hand. "From down
in the deeper caverns. It is you the gods must favor, to
bring you back from such a dark place."

Maegwin stared for a moment, then forced a smile. "I
suppose. Yes, I am glad to be back, too." She stroked the
baby's head once more before turning to follow
Craobhan.

"I know that judging disputes is not so enjoyable a task
for a woman as dandling babies," Old Craobhan said over
his shoulder, "but this is something you must do anyway.
You are Lluth's daughter."

Maegwin grimaced, but would not be distracted. "How
did that woman know I had been in the caverns below?"

The old man shrugged. "You didn't work very hard to
keep it secret, and you can't expect people not to be interested in the doings of the king's family. Tongues will always wag."

Maegwin frowned. Craobhan was right, of course. She
had been heedless and headstrong about exploring the
lower caverns. If she wanted secrecy, she should have
started worrying about it sooner.

"What do they think about it?" she asked at last. "The
people, I mean."

"Think about your adventuring?" He chuckled sourly.
"I imagine there's as many stories as there are cookfires.
Some say you went looking for the gods. Some think you
were looking for a bolt hole out of this whole muddle."
He peered at her over his bony shoulder. His self-
satisfied, knowing look made her want to smack him. "By
the middle of winter they'll be saying you found a city of
gold, or fought a dragon or a two-headed giant. Forget
about it. Stories are like hares—only a fool tries to run after one and catch it."

Maegwin glowered at the back of his old bald head.

She didn't know which she liked less, having people tell lies about her or having people know the truth. She suddenly wished Eolair had returned.

Fickle cow, she sneered at herself.

But she did. She wished she could talk to him, tell him of all her ideas, even the mad ones. He would understand, wouldn't he? Or would it only confirm his belief in her wretchedness? It mattered little, anyway: Eolair had been gone for more than a month, and Maegwin did not even know if he still lived. She herself had sent him away. Now, she heartily wished that she had not.

Fearful but resolute, Maegwin had never softened the cold words she had spoken to Count Eolair down in the buried city of Mezutu'a. They had barely conversed during the few days that passed between their return from that place and his departure in search of Josua's rumored rebel camp.

Eolair had spent most of those days down in the ancient city, overseeing a pair of stronghearted Hernystiri clerks as they copied the dwarrows' stone maps onto more portable rolls of sheepshide. Maegwin had not accompanied him; despite the dwarrows' kindness, the thought of the empty, echoing city only filled her with sullen disappointment. She had been wrong. Not mad, as many thought her, but certainly wrong. She had thought the gods meant her to find the Sithi there, but now it seemed clear that the Sithi were lost and frightened and would be no help to her people. As for the dwarrows, the Sithi's once-servants, they were little more than shadows, incapable of helping even themselves.

At Eolair's parting, Maegwin had been so full of warring feelings that she could muster little more than a curt farewell. He had pressed into her hand a gift sent by the dwarrows—it was a glossy gray and white chunk of crystal on which Yis-fidri, the record-keeper, had carved her name in his own runic alphabet. It almost looked as though it might be part of the Shard itself, but it lacked that stone's restless inner light. Eolair had then turned and mounted his horse, struggling to hide his anger. She had

felt something tearing inside her as the Count of Nad
Mullach rode away down the slope and vanished into the
flurrying snow. Surely, she had prayed, the gods must
bear her up in this desperate time. The gods, though,
seemed slow to lend their aid these days.

Maegwin had thought at first that her dreams about an
underground city were signs of the gods' willingness to
help their stricken followers in Hernystir. Maegwin knew
now that somehow she had made a mistake. She had
thought to find the Sithi, the ancient and legendary allies,
to force her way in through the very gates of legend to
bring help to Hernystir—but that had been prideful foolishness. The gods invited, they were not invaded.

Maegwin had been mistaken in that small thing, but
still she knew that she was not altogether wrong. No matter what misdeeds her people had done, the gods would
not so easily desert them. Brynioch, Rhynn, Murhagh
One-Arm—they would save their children, she was sure
of it. Somehow, they would bring destruction to Skali and
Elias the High King, the bestial pair who had brought
such humiliation on a proud and free people. If they did
not, then the world was an empty jest. So Maegwin would
wait for a better, clearer sign, and while she waited, she
would go quitely about her duties . . . tending to her people and mourning her dead.

"What suits do I hear today?" she asked Old Craobhan.

"Some small ones, as well as a request for judgment
that should prove no joy," Craobhan replied. "That one
comes from House Earb and House Lacha, which were
neighboring holdings on the Circoille fringe." The old
man had been king's counselor since Maegwin's grandfather's day, and knew the fantastical ins and outs of
Hernystiri political life the way a master smith knew the
vagaries of heat and metal. "Both families shared a section of the woods as their vouchsafe," he explained,
"—the only time your father had to declare separate
rights to forest land and draw up a map of possession for
each, like the Aedonite kings do, just to keep Earb-men
and Lacha-men from slaughtering each other. They loathe

each other and the two houses have fought forever. They barely took time to go to war against Skali, and they may not have noticed that we lost." He coughed and spat.

"So what is wanted of me?"

Craobhan frowned. "What would you guess, Lady? They quarrel now over cavern space—" his voice rose in mockery, " '—this place is for me, this for thee. No, no, it's mine; no, mine.' " He snorted. "They squabble like piglets over the last teat, even as we all shelter together in danger and poor conditions."

"They sound a disgusting group." Maegwin had little temper for such petty nonsense.

"I couldn't have said fairer myself," the old man said.

Neither House Lacha nor House Earb benefited much from Maegwin's presence. Their dispute proved just as petty as Craobhan had predicted. A tunnel to the surface had been dug out and widened to useful size by men from both houses with the additional help of Hernystirmen from other, less important families who shared the common cavern. Now each of the feuding houses insisted that it alone was the tunnel's owner, and that the other house and all other cavern-dwellers should pay a tithe of goatsmilk for taking their flocks up and down the tunnel each day.

Maegwin was mightily disgusted by this and said so. She also proclaimed that if such rank nonsense as people "owning" tunnels ever came up again, she would have the remainder of Hernystir's fighting men gather up the malefactors, take them to the surface, and throw them from the highest cliffs that craggy Grianspog could provide.

Houses Lacha and Earb were not pleased by this judgment. They managed to put aside their differences long enough to demand that Maegwin be replaced as judge by her stepmother Inahwen—who was after all, they said, the late King Lluth's *wife*, and not merely his daughter. Maegwin laughed and called them conniving fools. The spectators who had gathered, along with the remaining families that shared the cavern with the feuding houses, cheered Maegwin's good sense and the humbling of the haughty Earb- and Lacha-folk.

The rest of the suits went quickly. Maegwin found herself enjoying the work, although some of the disputes were sad. It was something she did well—something that had little to do with being small or delicate or pretty. Surrounded by lovelier, more graceful women, she had always felt herself an embarrassment to her father, even at a rustic court like the Taig. Here, all that mattered was her good sense. In the past weeks, she had found—to her surprise—that her father's subjects valued her, that they were grateful for her willingness to listen and be fair. As she watched her people, tattered and smoke-smudged, she felt her heart tighten within her. The Hernystiri deserved better than this low estate. They would get it, somehow, if it was within Maegwin's power.

For a while, she managed to forgot almost entirely about her cruelty to the Count of Nad Mullach.

That evening, as she lay on the edge of sleep, Maegwin found herself abruptly falling forward into a darkness vaster and deeper than the ember-lit cavern where she made her bed. For a moment she thought some cataclysm had torn open the earth beneath her; a moment later, she was certain that she dreamed. But as she felt herself slowly spinning into emptiness, the sensation seemed far too immediate for a dream, and yet too strangely dislocated to be anything so real as an earth tremor. She had felt something like this before, those nights when she had dreamed of the beautiful city beneath the earth. . . .

Even as her confused thoughts fluttered in darkness like startled bats, a cloud of dim lights began to appear. They were fireflies, or sparks, or distant torches. They spiraled upward, like the smoke of a great bonfire, mounting toward some unimaginable height.

Climb, said a voice in her head. *Go to the High Place. The time is come.*

Swimming in nothingness, Maegwin struggled toward the distant peak where the flickering lights congregated.

Go to the High Place, the voice demanded. *The time is come.*

And suddenly she was in the midst of many gleaming lights, small and intense as distant stars. A hazy throng surrounded her, beautiful yet inhuman, dressed in all the colors of the rainbow. The creatures stared at each other with gleaming eyes. Their graceful forms were vague; although they were man-shaped, she somehow felt sure they were no more human than rain clouds or spotted deer.

The time is come, said the voice, now many voices. A smear of leaping, coruscating light glowed in the midst of them, as though one of the stars had fallen down from the vaulting sky. *Go to the High Place. . . .*

And then the fantastic vision was bleeding away, draining back into darkness.

Maegwin woke to discover herself sitting upright on her pallet. The fires were only glowing coals. There was nothing to be seen in the darkened cavern, and nothing to hear but the sound of other people breathing in sleep. She was clutching Yis-fidri's dwarrow-stone so tightly that her knuckles throbbed with pain. For a moment she thought a faint light gleamed in its depths, but when she looked again she decided she had fooled herself: it was only a translucent lump of rock. She shook her head slowly. The stone was of no importance, anyway, compared to what she had experienced.

The gods. The gods had spoken to her again, even more plainly this time. The high place, they had said. The time had come. That must mean that at last the lords of her people were ready to reach out and aid Hernystir. And they wanted Maegwin to do something. They must, or they would not have touched her, would not have sent her this clear sign.

The small matters of the day just passed were now swept from her mind. *The high place*, she told herself. She sat for a long time in the darkness, thinking.

After checking carefully to make sure that Earl Aspitis was still up on deck, Miriamele hurried down the narrow passageway and rapped on the low door. A murmuring voice inside fell silent at the sound of Miriamele's knock.

The reply came some moments later. "Yes? Who is there?"

"Lady Marya. May I come in?"

"Come."

Miriamele pushed against the swollen door. It gave grudgingly, opening on a tiny, austere room. Gan Itai sat on a pallet beneath the open window, which was little more than a narrow slit near the top of the wall. Something moved there; Miriamele saw a smooth expanse of white neck and a flash of yellow eye, then the seagull dropped away and vanished.

"The gulls are like children." Gan Itai showed her guest a wrinkled smile. "Argumentative, forgetful, but sweet-hearted."

Miriamele shook her head, confused. "I'm sorry to bother you."

"Bother? Child, what a foolish idea. It is daylight, I have no singing to do for now. Why would you be a bother?"

"I don't know, I just . . ." Miriamele paused, trying to collect her thoughts. She wasn't really certain why she had come. "I . . . I need someone to talk to, Gan Itai. I'm frightened."

The Niskie reached over to a three-legged stool which appeared to serve as a table. Her nimble brown fingers swept several sea-polished stones off the seat and into the pocket of her robe, then she pushed the stool over to Miriamele.

"Sit, child. Do not hurry yourself."

Miriamele arranged her skirt, wondering how much she dared to tell the Niskie. But if Gan Itai was carrying secret messages for Cadrach, how much could there be that she still did not know? She had certainly seemed to know that Marya was a false name. There was nothing to do but roll the dice.

"Do you know who I am?"

The sea-watcher smiled again. "You are Lady Marya, a noblewoman from Erkynland."

Miriamele was startled. "I am?"

The Niskie's laugh hissed like wind through dry grass. "Are you not? You have certainly told enough people that name. But if you mean to ask Gan Itai who you *truly* are, I will tell you, or at least I will start with this: Miriamele is your name, daughter of the High King."

Miriamele was curiously relieved. "So you *do* know."

"Your companion Cadrach confirmed it for me. I had suspicions. I met your father, once. You smell like him; sound like him, too."

"I do? You did?" Miriamele felt as though she had lost her balance. "What do you mean?"

"Your father met Benigaris here on this boat two years gone, when Benigaris was only the duke's son. Aspitis, *Eadne Cloud's* master, hosted the gathering. That strange wizard-creature was here, too—the one with no hair." Gan Itai made a smoothing gesture across her head.

"Pryrates." The name's evil taste lingered in her mouth.

"Yes, that is the one." Gan Itai sat up straighter, cocking her ear to some far-away sound. After a moment she turned her attention back to her guest. "I do not learn the names of all the folk who ride this boat. I do pay sharp attention to everyone who treads the gangplank, of course—that is part of the Navigator's Trust—but names are not usually important to sea-watchers. That time, though, Aspitis told me all their names, as my children used to sing to me their lessons about the tides and currents. He was very proud of his important guests."

Miriamele was momentarily distracted. "Your children?"

"By the Uncharted, yes, certainly!" Gan Itai nodded. "I am a great-grandmother twenty times over."

"I've never seen Niskie children."

The old woman looked at her dourly. "I know you are a southerner only by birth, child, but even in Meremund where you grew up there is a small Niskie town near the docks. Did you never go there?"

Miriamele shook her head. "I wasn't allowed."

Gan Itai pursed her lips. "That is unhappy. You should have gone to see it. We are fewer now than we once were, and who knows what will come on tomorrow's tide? My family is one of the largest, but there are fewer than ten score families all together from Abaingeat on the north coast all the way down to Naraxi and Harcha. So few for all the deep-water ships!" She shook her head sadly.

"But when my father and those others were here, what did they say? What did they do?"

"They talked, young one, but about what I cannot say. They talked the night away, but I was on deck, with the sea and my songs. Besides, it is not my place to spy on the ship's owner. Unless he wrongly endangers the ship, it is not my place to do anything at all except that which I was born for: to sing the kilpa down."

"But you brought me Cadrach's letter." Miriamele looked around to make sure the passageway door was closed. "That is not something Aspitis would want you to do."

For the first time, Gan Itai's golden eyes showed a trace of discontent. "That is true, but I was not harming the ship." A look of defiance crept onto the lined face. "We are Niskies, after all, not slaves. We are a free people."

She and Miriamele looked at each other for a moment. The princess was the first to look away. "I don't even care what they were talking about, anyway. I'm sick and tired of men and their wars and arguments. I just want to go away and be left alone—to climb into a hole somewhere and never come out."

The Niskie did not reply, only watched her.

"Still, I will never escape across fifty leagues of open water." The uselessness of it all pulled at her, making her feel heavy with despair. "Will we make land anytime soon?"

"We will stop at some of the islands in Firannos Bay. Spenit, perhaps Risa—I am not sure which ones Aspitis has chosen."

"Maybe I can escape somehow. But I'm sure I will be

heavily guarded." The leaden feeling seemed to grow stronger. Then an idea flickered. "Do you ever get off the ship, Gan Itai?"

The sea-watcher looked at her appraisingly. "Seldom. But there is a family of Tinukeda'ya—of Niskies—at Risa. The *Injar* clan. Once or twice I have visited them. Why do you ask?"

"Because if you can leave the ship, you could take a message for me. Give it to someone who might get it to my Uncle Josua."

Gan Itai frowned. "Certainly I will do it, but I am not sure that it will ever get to him. It would be a piece of long luck."

"What choice do I have?" Miriamele sighed. "Of course it's foolish. But maybe it would help, and what else can I do?" Tears abruptly welled in her eyes. She wiped them away angrily. "No one will be able to do anything, even if they want to. But I have to try."

Gan Itai stared in alarm. "Do not cry, child. It makes me feel cruel for having dragged you out of your hiding place in the hold."

Miriamele waved a tear-dampened hand. "Someone would have found us."

The Niskie leaned forward. "Perhaps your companion would have some idea of who to give your note to, or some special thing that could be written in it. He seems to me a wise man."

"Cadrach?"

"Yes. After all, he knew the true name of the Navigator's Children." Her voice was grave but proud, as though knowing her people's name was evidence of godlike wisdom.

"But how ..." Miriamele bit off the rest of her question. Of course Gan Itai knew how to get to Cadrach. She had already brought a note from him. But Miriamele was not quite sure that she wanted to see the monk. He had caused her so much pain, sparked so much anger.

"Come." Gan Itai rose from the pallet, climbing to her feet as easily as a young girl. "I will take you to him." She squinted out the narrow window. "They will not bring him food for almost another hour. That will leave plenty of time for a pleasant conversation." She grinned, then moved quickly across the small room. "Can you climb in that dress?"

The Niskie slid her fingers in behind a board on the bare wall and pulled. A panel, so closely fitted that it had been all but invisible, came free; Gan Itai set it down on the floor. A dark hole lined with pitch-smeared beams showed where the panel had been.

"Where does it lead?" Miriamele asked, surprised.

"Nowhere, particularly," Gan Itai said. She clambered through and stood up, so that only her thin brown legs and the hem of her robe showed in the opening. "It is merely a way to get quickly to the hold or the deck. A Niskie-hole, as it is called." Her muffled voice had a slight echo.

Miriamele leaned in behind her. A ladder stood against the far wall of the tiny cubicle. At the top of the confining walls, a narrow crawlspace extended in both directions. The princess shrugged and followed the Niskie up the ladder.

The passageway at the top was too low to be negotiated except on hands and knees, so Miriamele knotted the end of her skirt up out of her way, then crawled after Gan Itai. As the light of the Niskie's room disappeared behind them, the darkness pulled in closer, so that Miriamele could only follow her nose and the quiet sound of Gan Itai crawling. The beams creaked as the ship flexed. Miriamele felt as though she were creeping down the gullet of some great sea beast.

Some twenty cubits from the ladder, Gan Itai stopped. Miriamele bumped into her from behind.

"Careful, child." The Niskie's face was revealed in a growing wedge of light as she pried up another panel. When Gan Itai had peered through, she beckoned Miriamele forward. After the darkness of the crawlspace, the dim hold seemed a cheerful, sunlit place, though all that lit it was a propped hatchway at the far end.

"We must keep our voices low," the sea-watcher said. The hold was stacked nearly to the rafters with sacks and barrels, all tied down so they would not roll free in high seas. Against one wall, as though he, too, were restrained against capricious tides, was the huddled figure of the monk. A heavy length of chain was at his ankles; another depended from his wrists.

"Learned one!" called the Niskie. Cadrach's round head came up slowly, like a beaten dog's. He stared up into the shadowed rafters.

"Gan Itai?" His voice was hoarse and weary. "Is that you?"

Miriamele felt her heart plummet in her breast. Mercieful Aedon, look at him! Chained like a poor dumb brute!

"I have come to talk to you," the Niskie whispered. "Are the warders coming soon?"

Cadrach shook his head. His chains rattled quietly. "I think not. They never hurry to feed me. Did you give my note to . . . to the lady?"

"I did. She is here to talk to you."

The monk started as if frightened. "What? You brought her here?" He lifted his clanking shackles before his face. "No! No! Take her away!"

Gan Itai pulled Miriamele forward. "He is very unhappy. Speak to him."

Miriamele swallowed. "Cadrach?" she said at last. "Have they hurt you?"

The monk slid down the wall, becoming little more than a heap of shadows. "Go away, Lady. I cannot bear to see you, or to have you see me. Go away."

There was a long moment of silence. "Speak to him!" Gan Itai hissed.

"I am sorry they have done this to you." She felt tears coming. "Whatever has happened between us, I would never have wished to see you tormented this way."

"Ah, Lady, what a dreadful world this is." The monk's voice had a sobbing catch to it. "Will you not take my advice and flee? Please."

Miriamele shook her head in frustration, then realized he could not see her up in the shadow of the hatchway. "How, Cadrach? Aspitis will not let me out of his sight.

Gan Itai said she would take away a letter from me and try to get it to someone who will deliver it—but deliver it to whom? Who would help me? I do not know where Josua is. My mother's family in Nabban have turned traitor. What can I do?"

The dark shape that was Cadrach slowly stood up. "*Pelippa's Bowl*, Miriamele. As I told you in my letter. There may be someone there who can help." He did not sound very convinced.

"Who? Who could I send it to?"

"Send it to the inn. Draw a quill pen on it, a quill in a circle. That will get it to someone who can help, if anyone useful is there." He lifted a weighted arm. "Please go away, Princess. After all that has happened, I want only to be left alone. I do not wish to have you see my shame any longer."

Miriamele felt her tears overspill her eyes. It took a few moments before she could talk. "Do you want anything?"

"A jug of wine. No, a wineskin: it will be easier to hide. That's all I need. Something to make a darkness within me to match the darkness around me." His laughter was painful to hear. "And you safely escaped. That, too."

Miriamele turned her face away. She could not bear to look at the monk's huddled form any longer. "I'm so sorry," she said, then hurriedly pushed past Gan Itai and retreated a few cubits up the crawlspace. The conversation had made her feel ill.

The Niskie said some last words to Cadrach, then lowered the panel and plunged the tiny passageway into darkness once more. Her thin form pushed past, then she led Miriamele back to the ladder.

The princess was no sooner back into daylight when a fresh bout of sobbing came over her. Gan Itai watched uncomfortably for a while, but when Miriamele could not stop crying, the Niskie put a spidery arm around her.

"Stop, now, stop," she crooned. "You will be happy again."

Miriamele untied her skirt, then lifted the corner and

wiped her eyes and nose. "No I won't. Nor will Cadrach. Oh, God in Heaven, I am so lonely!" Another storm of weeping came over her.

Gan Itai held her until she stopped crying.

"It is cruel to bind any creature that way." The Niskie's voice was tight with something like anger. Miriamele, her head in Gan Itai's lap, was too drained to reply. "They bound Ruyan Vé, did you know? The father of our people, the great Navigator. When he would have taken the ships and set sail once more, they seized him in their anger and bound him in chains." The Niskie rocked back and forth. "And then they burned the ships."

Miriamele sniffled. She did not know who Gan Itai was talking about, nor did she care at this moment.

"They wanted us to be slaves, but we Tinukeda'ya are a free people." Gan Itai's voice became almost a chant, a sorrowful song. "They burned our ships—burned the great ships that we could never build again in this new land, and left us stranded here. They said it was to save us from Unbeing, but that was a lie. They only wanted us to share their exile—we, who did not need them! The Ocean Indefinite and Eternal could have been our home, but they took our ships away and bound mighty Ruyan. They wanted us to be their servants. It is wrong to put anyone in chains who has done you no harm. Wrong."

Gan Itai continued to hold Miriamele in her arms as she rocked back and forth and murmured of terrible injustices. The sun fell lower in the sky. The small room began to fill with shadow.

Miriamele lay in her darkened cabin and listened to the Niskie's faint song. Gan Itai had been very upset. Miriamele had not thought the sea-watcher held such strong feelings, but something about Cadrach's captivity and the princess' own tears had brought up a great outpouring of grief and anger.

Who were the Niskies, anyway? Cadrach called them Tinukeda'ya—Ocean Children, Gan Itai had said. Where did they come from? Some distant island, perhaps. Ships on a dark ocean, the Niskie had said, from somewhere far away. Was that the way of the world, that everyone longed to go back to some place or some time that was lost?

Her thoughts were interrupted by a knock at the door.

"Lady Marya? Are you awake?"

She did not answer. The door slowly swung open. Miriamele cursed herself inwardly: she should have bolted it.

"Lady Marya?" The earl's voice was soft. "Are you ill? I missed you at supper."

She stirred and rubbed her eyes, as if awakening from sleep. "Lord Aspitis? I'm sorry, I am not feeling well. We will talk tomorrow, if I feel better."

He came on cat-soft feet and sat down on the edge of her bed. His long fingers traced her cheek. "But this is terrible. What ails you? I shall have Gan Itai look to you. She is well-versed in healing; I would trust her past any leech or apothecary."

"Thank you, Aspitis. That would be kind. Now I should probably go back to sleep. I'm sorry to be such poor company."

The earl seemed in no hurry to leave. He stroked her hair. "You know, Lady, I am truly sorry for my rough words and ways of the other evening. I have come to care deeply for you, and I was upset at the idea that you might leave me so soon. After all, we share a deep lovers' bond, do we not?" His fingertips slid down to her neck, making the skin tighten and sending a chill through her.

"I fear I am not in good condition to talk about such things now, Lord. But I forgive you your words, which I know were hasty and not heartfelt." She turned her eyes to his face for a moment, trying to judge his thoughts. His eyes seemed guileless, but she remembered Cadrach's words, as well as Gan Itai's description of the gathering he had hosted, and the chill returned, bringing a tremor that she was hard-pressed to conceal.

"Good," he said. "Very good. I am glad you understand that. Hasty words. Exactly."

Miriamele decided to test that courtier's sincerity of

his. "But of course, Aspitis, you must understand my own unhappiness. My father, you see, does not know where I am. Perhaps already the convent will have sent word to him that I did not arrive. He will be sick with worry. He is old, Aspitis, and I fear for his health. You can see why I feel I must forsake your hospitality, whether I wish to or not."

"Of course," said the earl. Miriamele felt a flicker of hope. Could she have misread him after all? "It is cruel to let your father worry. We will send him word as soon as we next make landfall—on Spenit Island, I think. And we will give him the good news."

She smiled. "He will be very happy to hear I am well."

"Ah." Aspitis returned her smile. His long, fine jaw and clear eyes could have served as a sculptor's model for one of the great heroes of the past. "But there will be more good news than just that. We will tell him that his daughter is to marry one into of Nabban's Fifty Families!"

Miriamele's smile faltered. "What?"

"Why, we will tell him of our coming marriage!" Aspitis laughed with delight. "Yes, Lady, I have thought and thought, and although your family is not quite so elevated as mine—and Erkynlandish, as well—I have decided for love's sake to spit in the face of tradition. We will be married when we return to Nabban." He took her cold hand in his warm grip. "But you do not look as happy as I would have hoped, beautiful Marya."

Miriamele's mind was racing, but as in a dream of fearful pursuit, she could think of nothing but escape. "I . . . I am overwhelmed, Aspitis."

"Ah, well, I suppose that is understandable." He stood, then bent over to kiss her. His breath smelled of wine, his cheek of perfume. His mouth was hard against hers for a moment before he pulled away. "After all, it is rather sudden, I know. But it would be worse than ungentlemanly of me to desert you . . . after all we have shared. And I have come to love you, Marya. The flowers of the north are different than those of my southern home, but their scent is just as sweet, the blossoms just as beautiful."

He stopped in the doorway. "Rest and sleep well, Lady. We have much to talk about. Good night." The door fell shut behind him. Miriamele immediately leaped from her bed and drove home the bolt, then crawled back under her blanket, overcome by a fit of shivering.

3

East of the World

✦

"**I'm a knight** now, aren't I?" Simon ran his hand through the thick fur of Qantaqa's neck. The wolf eyed him impassively.

Binabik looked up from his sheaf of parchment and nodded. "By an oath to your god and your prince." The troll turned back to Morgenes' book once more. "That is seeming to me to fit the knightly particulars."

Simon stared across the tiled expanse of the Fire Garden, trying to think of how to put his thought into words. "But ... but I don't feel any different. I'm a knight—a man! So why do I feel like the same person?"

Caught up in something he was reading, Binabik took a moment to respond. "I am sorry, Simon," he said at last. "I am not being a good friend for listening. Please say what you were saying once more."

Simon bent and picked up a piece of loose stone, then flung it skittering across the tiles and into the surrounding undergrowth. Qantaqa bounded after it. "If I'm a knight and a grown man, why do I feel like the same stupid scullion?"

Binabik smiled. "It is not only you who has ever had such feelings, friend Simon. Because a new season has passed, or because a recognition has been given, still it is not changing a person very much on the inside. You were made Josua's knight because of bravery you showed on Urmsheim. If you were changing, it was not at the ceremony yesterday, but on the mountain that it was happening." He patted Simon's booted foot. "Did you not say that you had learned something there, and also from the spilling of the dragon's blood?"

"Yes." Simon squinted at Qantaqa's tail, which waved above the heather like a puff of smoke.

"People, both trolls and lowlanders, are growing in their own time," said the little man, "—not when someone says that it is so. Be content. You will always be extremely Simon-like, but still I have been seeing much change in the months we have been friends."

"Really?" Simon paused in mid-toss.

"Truth. You are becoming a man, Simon. Let it happen at the swiftness that it needs, and do not be worrying yourself." He rattled the papers. "Listen, I want to read something to you." He ran a stubby finger along the lines of Morgenes' spidery handwriting. "I am grateful beyond telling to Strangyeard, that he brought this book out of the ruin of Naglimund. It is our last tie to that great man, your teacher." His finger paused. "Ah. Here. Morgenes writes of King Prester John:

> "*. . . If he was touched by divinity, it was most evident in his comings and goings, in his finding the correct place to be at the most suitable time, and profiting thereby . . .*"

"I read that part," Simon said with mild interest.
"Then you will have noticed its significantness for our efforts," the troll replied.

> "*For John Presbyter knew that in both war and diplomacy—as also with love and commerce, two other not dissimilar occupations—the rewards usually do not fall to the strong or to even the just, but rather to the lucky. John also knew that he who moves swiftly and without undue caution makes his own luck.*"

Simon frowned at Binabik's pleased expression. "So?"
"Ah." The troll was imperturbable. "Listen further."

"Thus, in the war that brought Nabban under his imperial hand, John took his far-outnumbered troop through the Onestrine Pass and directly into the spear-points of Ardrivis' legions, when all knew that only a fool would do so. It was this very foolhardiness, this seeming madness, that gave John's smaller force a great advantage of surprise—and even, to the startled Nabbanai army, an aura of God-touched irresistibility."

Simon found the note of triumph in the little man's voice faintly disquieting. Binabik seemed to think that the point was somehow very clear. Simon frowned, thinking.

"Are you saying that we should be like King John? That we should try to catch Elias by surprise?" It was an astonishing idea. "That we should . . . attack him?"

Binabik nodded, his teeth bared in a yellow smile. "Clever Simon! Why not? We have only been reacting, not acting. Perhaps a change will be helpful."

"But what about the Storm King?" Shaken by the thought, he looked out at the beclouded horizon. Simon did not even like to say that name beneath the wide slate sky in this alien place. "And besides, Binabik, we are only a few hundred. King Elias has thousands of soldiers. Everybody knows it!"

The troll shrugged. "Who says we must be fighting army to army? In any case, our little company is growing every day, as more folk come across the meadows to . . . what was Josua's naming? Ah. New Gadrinsett."

Simon shook his head and flung another shard of wind-smoothed stone. "It seems stupid to me—no, not stupid. But too dangerous."

Binabik was not upset. He whistled for Qantaqa, who came trotting back across the stone flags. "Perhaps it is being just that, Simon. Let us walk for a little while."

✿

Prince Josua stared down at the sword, his face troubled. The good cheer he had shown at Simon's feast seemed entirely gone.

It was not that the prince was truly any happier of late, Sir Deornoth decided, but he had learned that his self-doubts made those around him uneasy. In times like these, people preferred a fearless prince to an honest one, so Josua labored to present a mask of calm optimism to his subjects. But Deornoth, who knew him well, had little doubt that Josua's responsibilities still weighed on him as heavily as they ever had.

He is like my mother, Deornoth realized. *A strange thing to think of a prince. But like her, he feels he must take the worries and fears of all onto himself, that no one else can bear the burden.*

And, as Deornoth had seen his mother do, Josua also seemed to be aging faster than those around him. Always slender, the prince had become very thin during the company's flight from Naglimund. He had regained a little of his girth, but there was a strange aura of fragility about him now that would not go away: Deornoth thought him a little unworldly, like a man just risen from a long illness. The gray streaks in his hair had increased drastically and his eyes, although still as sharp and knowing as ever, held a slightly feverish gleam.

He needs peace. He needs rest. I wish I could stand at the foot of his bed and protect him while he slept for a year. "God give him strength," he murmured.

Josua turned to look at him. "I'm sorry, my mind was wandering. What did you say?"

Deornoth shook his head, not wishing to lie, but not caring to share his thoughts either. They both turned their attention back to the sword.

Prince and liege-man stood before the long stone table in the building Geloë had named Leavetaking House. All traces of the previous night's feast had been cleared away, and now only one gleaming black object lay upon the smooth stone.

"To think that so many have died at the end of that blade," Deornoth said at last. He touched the cord-wrapped hilt; Thorn was as cold and lifeless as the rock on which it rested.

"And more recently," the prince murmured, "think of how many have died that we might have it."

"But surely, if it cost us so dearly, we should not just leave it lying here in an open hall where anyone may come." Deornoth shook his head. "This might be our greatest hope, Highness—our only hope! Should we not hide it away safe, or put it under guard?"

Josua almost smiled. "To what purpose, Deornoth? Any treasure can be stolen, any castle thrown down, any hiding place nosed out. Better it should lie where all can see and feel what hope is in it." He narrowed his eyes as he stared down at the blade. "Not that I feel much hope looking at it. I trust you will not think me any the less princely if I say it gives me a kind of chill." He slowly ran his hand down the length of the blade. "In any case, from what Binabik and young Simon have said, no one will take this sword where it does not wish to go. Besides, if it lies here in view of all, like Tethtain's ax in the heart of the fabled beech tree, perhaps someone will come forward to tell us how it may serve."

Deornoth was puzzled. "You mean one of the common people, Highness?"

The prince grunted. "There are all kinds of wisdom, Deornoth. If we had listened sooner to the common folk living on the Frostmarch when they told us that evil was abroad in the land, who knows what anguish we might have been spared? No, Deornoth, any word of wisdom about this sword is valuable to us now, any old song, any half-remembered story." Josua could not hide his look of discontent. "After all, we have no idea of what good it can do us—in fact, no idea that it will do good at all, but for an obscure and ancient rhyme. . . ."

A harsh voice sang out, interrupting him.

"When frost doth grow on Claves' bell
And shadows walk upon the road
When water blackens in the Well
Three Swords must come again."

The two men turned in surprise. Geloë stood at the doorway. She continued the rhyme as she walked toward them.

"When Bukken from the Earth do creep
And Hunën from the heights descend
When Nightmare throttles peaceful Sleep
Three Swords must come again.

"To turn the stride of treading Fate
To clear the fogging Mists of Time
If Early shall resist Too Late
Three Swords must come again.

"I could not help hearing you, Prince Josua—I have keen ears. Your words are very wise. But as to doubting whether the sword will help . . ." She grimaced. "Forgive an old forest woman for her bluntness, but if we do not believe in the potency of Nisses' prophecy, what else do we have?"

Josua tried to smile. "I was not disputing that it means something significant to us, Valada Geloë. I only wish I knew more clearly what kind of a weapon these swords will be."

"As do we all." The witch woman nodded to Deornoth, then flicked a glance at the black sword. "Still, we have one of the three Great Swords, and that is more than we had a season ago."

"True. Very true." Josua leaned back against the stone table. "And we are in a safe place, thanks to you. I have not grown blind to good fortune, Geloë."

"But you are worried." It was not a question. "It is becoming harder to feed our growing settlement, and harder to govern those who live here."

The prince nodded. "Many of whom are not even sure why they are here, except that they followed other settlers. After such a freezing summer, I do not know how we will survive the winter."

"The people will listen to you, Highness," said Deornoth. When the witch woman was present, Josua seemed more like a careful student than a prince. He had never learned to like it, and had only partially learned to hide his annoyance. "They will do what you say. We will survive the winter together."

"Of course, Deornoth." Josua laid his hand upon his friend's shoulder. "We have come through too much to be balked by the petty problems of today."

He looked as if he would say more, but at that moment they heard the sound of footsteps on the wide stairs outside. Young Simon and the troll appeared in the doorway, followed closely by Binabik's tame wolf. The great beast sniffed the air, then snuffled at the stone on all sides of the door as well before trotting off to lie down in a far corner of the hall. Deornoth watched her go with some relief. He had seen numerous proofs of her harmlessness, but he had been raised a child of the Erkynlandish countryside, where wolves were the demons of fireplace tales.

"Ah," Josua said cheerfully, "my newest knight, and with him the honored envoy from far Yiqanuc. Come, sit down." He pointed to a row of stools left from the previous evening's festivities. "We wait on only a few more, including Count Eolair." The prince turned to Geloë. "You saw to him, did you not? Is he well?"

"A few cuts and bruises. He is thin, too—he has ridden far with little food. But his health is good."

Deornoth thought she would not say much more if the Count of Nad Mullach had been drawn and quartered—but still would have him on his feet again soon. The witch woman did not show his prince proper respect, and had few traits that Deornoth considered womanly, but he had to admit that she was very good at the things she did.

"I am happy to hear it." Josua tucked his hand under his cloak. "It is cold here. Let us make a fire so we can speak without our teeth chattering."

As Josua and the others talked, Simon fetched pieces of wood from the pile in the corner and stacked them in the firepit, happy to have something to do. He was proud to be part of this high company, but not quite able to take his membership for granted.

"Stand them touching at the top, spread at the bottom," Geloë advised.

He did as she suggested, making a conical tent of fire-wood in the middle of the ashes. When he had finished, he looked around. The crude firepit seemed out of place on the finely-crafted stone floor, as though animals had taken up residence in one of the great houses of Simon's own kind. There seemed no Sithi-built equivalent of the pit anywhere in the long chamber. How had they kept the room heated? Simon remembered Aditu running barefoot on the snow and decided that they might not have bothered.

"Is Leavetaking House really the name of this place?" he asked Geloë as she came forward with her flint and steel. She ignored him for a moment as she squatted beside the firepit, putting a spark to the curls of bark that lay around the logs.

"It is as close a name as any. I would have called it 'Hall of Farewell,' but the troll corrected my Sithi grammar." She showed a tight smile. A thread of smoke floated up past her hands.

Simon thought she might have made a joke, but he wasn't quite sure. " 'Leavetaking' because this room was where the two families split up?"

"I believe it is the place where they parted, yes. Where the accord was struck. I imagine it has or had some other name for the Sithi, since it was in use long before the parting of those two tribes."

So he had been right: his vision had shown him the past of this place. Pondering, he stared along the pillared hall, at the columns of carved stone still clean and sharp-edged after countless years. Jiriki's people had once been mighty builders, but now their homes in the forest were as changeable and impermanent as the nests of birds. Perhaps the Sithi were wise not to put down deep roots. Still, Simon thought, a place that was always there, a home that did not change, seemed right now to be the finest treasure in the world.

"Why did the two families separate?"

Geloë shrugged. "There is never one reason for such a

great change, but I have heard that mortals had something
to do with it."

Simon remembered the last, terrible hour in the Yasirá.
"The Norn Queen—Utuk'ku. She was mad that the Sithi
hadn't . . . 'scourged the mortals from the land,' she said.
And she also said that Amerasu wouldn't leave the mortals be. Us mortals. Like me." It was hard to think of
Amerasu the Ship-Born without shame: her assassin had
claimed that he followed Simon to Jao é-Tinukai'i.

The witch woman stared at him for a moment. "I forget
sometimes how much you have seen, boy. I hope you do
not forget when your time comes."

"What time?"

"As to the parting of Sithi and Norn," she continued,
ignoring his question, "mortals came into it, but also it is
told that the two houses were uneasy allies even in the
land of their origin."

"The Garden?"

"As they call it. I do not know the stories well—such
tales have never been of much interest to me. I have always worked with the things that are before me, things
that can be touched and seen and spoken to. There was a
woman in it, a Sitha-woman, and a man of the Hikeda'ya
as well. She died. He died. Both families were bitter. It is
old business, boy. If you see your friend Jiriki again, ask
him. It is the history of his own family, after all."

Geloë stood and walked away, leaving Simon to warm
his hands before the flames.

*These old stories are like blood. They run through peo-
ple, even when they don't know it or think about it.* He
considered this idea for a moment. *But even if you don't
think about them, when the bad times come, the old stories come out on every side. And that's just like blood,
too.*

As Simon sat contemplating, Hotvig arrived with his
right-hand man Ozhbern. They were quickly followed by
Isorn and his mother, Duchess Gutrun.

"How is my wife, Duchess?" asked Josua.

"Not feeling well, your Highness," she replied, "or she

would have been here. But it is only to be expected. Children aren't just difficult *after* they arrive, you know."

"I know very little, good lady," Josua laughed. "Especially about this. I have never been a father before."

Soon Father Strangyeard appeared, accompanied by Count Eolair of Nad Mullach. The count had replaced his traveling garments with Thrithings clothes, breeches and shirt of thick brown wool. He wore a golden torque at his neck, and his black hair was pulled back in a long tail. Simon remembered seeing him long ago, at the Hayholt, and once again had to marvel at the strangeness of Fate, how it moved people about the world like markers in a vast game of *shent*.

"Welcome, Eolair, welcome," Josua said. "Thanks be to Aedon, it does my heart good to see you again."

"And mine, Highness." The count tossed the saddlebags he carried against the wall by the door, then touched a knee briefly to the ground. He rose to Josua's embrace. "Greetings from the Hernystiri nation in exile."

Josua quickly introduced Eolair to those he had not met. To Simon, the count said: "I have heard something of your adventures since I arrived." The smile on his thin face was warm. "I hope you will put aside some time to speak with me."

Flattered, Simon nodded. "Certainly, Count."

Josua led Eolair to the long table where Thorn waited, solemn and terrible as a dead king upon his bier.

"The famous blade of Camaris," said the Hernystirman. "I have heard of it so many times, it is strange to see it at last and realize it is a real thing, forged of metal like any other weapon."'

Josua shook his head. "Not quite like any other weapon."

"May I touch it?"

"Of course."

Eolair was barely able to lift the hilt from the stone table. The cords of his neck stood out in sharp relief as he strained at it. At last he gave up and rubbed his cramped fingers. "It is as weighty as a millstone."

"Sometimes." Josua patted his shoulder. "Other times

it is as light as goosedown. We do not know why, nor do we know what good it will do us, but it is all we have."

"Father Strangyeard told me of the rhyme," the count said. "I think I have more to tell you about the Great Swords." He looked around the room. "If this is the proper time."

"This is a war council," Josua said simply. "All these folk can be told anything, and we are anxious for any news about the swords. We also wish to hear of your people, of course. I understand that Lluth is dead. You have our great sympathy. He was a splendid man and a fine king."

Eolair nodded. "And Gwythinn, too, his son."

Sir Deornoth, seated on a stool nearby, groaned. "Oh, that is foul news! He set out from Naglimund shortly before the siege. What happened?"

"He was caught by Skali's Kaldskrykemen and butchered." Eolair stared down at the ground. "They dumped his body at the foot of the mountain, like offal, and rode away."

"A curse on them!" Deornoth snarled.

"I am ashamed to call them countrymen," said young Isorn.

His mother nodded her agreement. "When my husband returns, he will deal with Sharp-nose." She sounded as certain as if she spoke of sunset coming.

"Still, we are *all* countrymen, here," Josua said. "We are all one people. From this day forward, we go together against common enemies." He gestured to the stools that stood against the wall. "Come, everybody sit down. We must fetch and carry for ourselves: I thought that the smaller this group remained, the easier it would be to speak openly."

When all were arrayed, Eolair told of Hernystir's downfall, beginning with the slaughter at the Inniscrich and Lluth's mortal wounding. He had barely started when there was a commotion outside the hall. A moment later, the old jester Towser stumbled through the door with Sangfugol tugging at his shirt, trying to restrain him.

"So!" The old man fixed Josua with a reddened stare.

"You are no more loyal than your murdering brother!" He swayed as Sangfugol pulled at him desperately. Pink-cheeked and wild-haired—what little hair was left—Towser was clearly drunk.

"Come away, curse you!" the harper said. "I'm sorry, my prince, he just suddenly leaped up and ..."

"To think that after all my years of service," Towser spluttered, "that I should be ... should be ... *excluded*," he pronounced the word with proud care, unaware of the strand of spittle that hung from his chin, "should be shunned, barred from your councils, when I was the one closest to your father's heart. ..."

Josua stood up, regarding the jester sadly. "I cannot talk to you now, old man. Not when you are like this." He frowned, watching Sangfugol struggle with him.

"I will help, Prince Josua," Simon said. He could not bear to watch the old man shame himself a moment longer. Simon and the harper managed to get Towser turned around. As soon as his back was to the prince, the fight seemed to drain out of him; the jester allowed himself to be steered toward the door.

Outside, a bitter wind was blowing across the hilltop. Simon took off his cloak and draped it around Towser's shoulders. The jester sat down on the top step, a bundle of sharp bones and thin skin, and said: "I think I will be sick." Simon patted his shoulder and looked helplessly at Sangfugol, whose gaze was less than sympathetic.

"It is like taking care of a child," the harper growled. "No, children are better-behaved. Leleth, for example, who doesn't talk at all."

"*I* told them where to find that damnable black sword," Towser mumbled. "Told them where it was. Told them about the other, too, how 'Lias wouldn't hold it. 'Your father wants you to have it,' I told him, but he wouldn't listen. Dropped it like a snake. Now the black sword, too." A tear ran down his white-whiskered cheek. "He tosses me away like an orange rind."

"What is he talking about?" asked Simon.

Sangfugol curled his lip. "He told the prince some things about Thorn before you left to find it. I don't know what the rest's about." He leaned down and grasped Towser's arm. "Huh. Easy for him to complain—*he* doesn't have to play nursemaid to himself." He showed Simon a sour smile. "Ah, well, there are probably bad days in a knight's career, too, are there not? Like when people hit you with swords and so on?" He pulled the jester to his feet and waited for the old man to get his balance. "Neither Towser nor I are in a very good mood, Simon. Not your fault. Come see me later and we'll drink some wine."

Sangfugol turned and walked away across the waving grass, trying both to support Towser and simultaneously keep him as far as possible from the harper's clean clothes.

Prince Josua nodded his thanks when Simon reentered Leavetaking House; Simon felt odd being commended for such disheartening duty. Eolair was finishing his description of the fall of Hernysadharc and of his people's flight into the Grianspog Mountains. As he told of the remaining Hernystirfolk's retreat into the caves that riddled the mountain and how they had been led there by the king's daughter, Duchess Gutrun smiled.

"This Maegwin is a clever girl. You are lucky to have her, if the king's wife is as helpless as you say."

The count's smile was a pained one. "You are right, Lady. She is indeed her father's daughter. I used to think she would make a better ruler than Gwythinn, who was sometimes headstrong—but now I am not so sure."

He told of Maegwin's growing strangeness, of her visions and dreams, and of how those dreams had led Lluth's daughter and the count down into the mountain's heart to the ancient stone city of Mezutu'a.

As he told of the city and its unusual tenants, the dwarrows, the company listened in amazement. Only Geloë and Binabik did not seem astonished by Eolair's tale.

"Wonderful," Strangyeard whispered, staring up at Leavetaking House's arched ceiling as though he were even now deep in the bowels of Grianspog. "The Pattern Hall! What marvelous stories must be written there."

"You may read some of them later," Eolair said with some amusement. "I am glad that the spirit of scholarship has survived this evil winter." He turned back to the company. "But what is perhaps most important of all is what the dwarrows said about the Great Swords. They claim that they forged Minneyar."

"We are knowing some of Minneyar's story," said Binabik, "and the dwarrows—or *dvernings,* as the northmen call them—are in that story."

"But it is where Minneyar has gone that most concerns us," Josua added. "We have one sword. Elias has the other. The third . . ."

"Nearly everyone in this hall has seen the third," Eolair said, "and seen the place where it now lies as well—if the dwarrows are correct. For they say that Minneyar went into the Hayholt with Fingil, but that Prester John found it . . . and called it Bright-Nail. If they are right, Josua, it was buried with your father."

"Oh, my!" Strangyeard murmured. A moment of stunned silence followed his utterance.

"But I held it in my hand," Josua said at last, wonderingly. "I myself placed it on my father's breast. How could Bright-Nail be Minneyar? My father never said a word about it!"

"No, he did not." Gutrun was surprisingly brisk. "He would never even tell my husband. Told Isgrimnur it was an old, unimportant story." She shook her head. "Secrets."

Simon, who had been listening quietly, spoke up at last. "But didn't he bring Bright-Nail from Warinsten, where he was born?" He looked to Josua, suddenly fearful that he was being presumptuous. "Your father, I mean. That is the story I knew."

Josua frowned, considering. "That is the story that many told, but now that I think on it, my father was never one of them."

"Of course! Oh, of course!" Strangyeard sat up, slapping his long hands together. His eyepatch slid a little, so that its corner edged onto the bridge of his nose. "The passage that troubled Jarnauga so, that passage from Mor-

genes' book! It told how John went down to face the
dragon—but he carried a spear! A spear! Oh, goodness, how blind we were!" The priest giggled like a
young boy. "But when he came out, it was with Bright-
Nail! Oh, Jarnauga, if only you were here!"

The prince raised his hand. "There is much to think of
here, and many old tales that should be retold, but for the
moment there is a more important problem. If the
dwarrows are right, and somehow I feel that they are—
who could doubt such a mad tale, in this mad season?—we still must get the sword, call it Bright-Nail or
Minneyar. It lies in my father's grave on Swertclif, just
outside the walls of the Hayholt. My brother can stand on
his battlements and see the grave mounds. The Erkynguard parade on the cliff's edge at dawn and dusk."

The giddy moment was over. In the heavy silence that
followed, Simon felt the first stirrings of an idea. It was
vague and unformed, so he kept it to himself. It was also
rather frightening.

Eolair spoke up. "There is more, your Highness. I told
you of the Pattern Hall, and of the charts the dwarrows
keep there of all the delvings they have done." He rose
and walked to the saddlebags he had deposited near the
doorway. When he returned, he spilled them upon the
floor. Several rolls of oiled sheepskin tumbled out.
"These are the plans for the diggings beneath the
Hayholt, a task the dwarrows say they performed when
the castle was named Asu'a and belonged to the Sithi."

Strangyeard was the first down on his knees. He unfurled one of the sheepskins with the tender care of a
lover. "Ah!" he breathed. "Ah!" His rhapsodic smile
changed to a look of puzzlement. "I must confess," he
said finally, "that I am, ah, somewhat ... somewhat disappointed. I had not thought that the dwarrows' maps
would be ... dear me! ... would be so crude."

"Those are not the dwarrows' maps," said Eolair,
frowning. "Those are the painstaking work of two
Hernystiri scribes laboring in cramped near-darkness in a
frightening place, copying the stone charts of the

dwarrows onto something I could carry up to the surface."

"Oh!" The priest was mortified. "Oh! Forgive me, Count! I am so sorry. . . ."

"Never mind, Strangyeard." Josua turned to the Count of Nad Mullach. "This is an unlooked-for boon, Eolair. On the day when we can finally stand before the Hayholt's walls, we will praise your name to the heavens."

"You are welcome to them, Josua. It was Maegwin's idea, if truth be told. I am not sure what good they will do, but knowledge is never bad—as I'm sure your archivist will agree." He gestured to Strangyeard, who was rooting among the sheepskins like a shoat who had uncovered a clump of truffles. "But I must confess I came to you in hope of more than thanks. When I left Hernystir, it was with the idea that I would find your rebel army and we would together drive Skali of Kaldskryke from my land. As I see, though, you are scarcely in a position to send an army anywhere."

"No." Josua's expression was grim. "We are still very few. More trickle in every day, but it would be a long wait before we could send even a small company to the aid of Hernystir." He stood and walked a little way out across the room, rubbing the stump of his right wrist as though it pained him. "This whole struggle has been like fighting a war blindfolded: we have never known or understood the strength brought against us. Now that we begin to grasp the nature of our enemies, we are too few to do anything but hide here in the remotest regions of Osten Ard."

Deornoth leaned forward. "If we could strike back *somewhere,* my prince, people would rise on your behalf. Very few beyond the Thrithings even know that you still live."

"There is truth to that, Prince Josua," Isorn said. "I know there are many in Rimmersgard who hate Skali. Some helped to hide me when I escaped from Sharpnose's war camp."

"As far as that, Josua, your survival is only a dim rumor in Hernystir as well," said Eolair. "Just to carry that information back to my people in the Grianspog will make my journey here a great success."

Josua, who had been pacing, stopped. "You will take them more than that, Count Eolair. I swear to you, you will take them more hope than that." He passed his hand across his eyes, like one wakened too early. "By the Tree, what a day! Let us stop and take some bread. In any case, I would like to think about what I have heard." He smiled wearily. "Also, I should go and see my wife." He waved his arm. "Up, all, up. Except you, Strangyeard. I suppose you will stay behind?"

The archivist, surrounded by sheepskins, did not even hear him.

Immersed in dark and mazy thoughts, Pryrates did not for some time notice the sound.

When at last it cut through the fog of his preoccupation, he stopped abruptly, teetering on the edge of the step.

"Azha she'she t'chakó, urun she'she bhabekró . . ."

The sound that rose from the darkened stairwell was delicate but dire, a solemn melody that wove in and out of painful dissonance: it might have been the contemplative hymn of a spider winding its prey in sticky silk. Breathy and slow, it slid sourly between notes, but with a deftness that suggested the seeming tunelessness was intentional—was in fact based in an entirely different concept of melody.

"Mudhul samat'ai. Jabbak s'era memekeza sanayha-z'á Ninyek she'she, hamut 'tke agrazh'a s'era yé . . ."

A lesser man might have turned and fled back toward the upper reaches of the daylit castle rather than meet the singer of such an unsettling tune. Pryrates did not hesi-

tate, but set off downward once more, his boots echoing
on the stone steps. A second thread of melody joined the
first, just as alien, just as dreadfully patient; together they
droned like wind over a chimney hole.

Pryrates reached the landing and turned into the corridor. The two Norns who stood before the heavy oaken
door abruptly fell silent. As he approached, they gazed at
him with the incurious and faintly insulting expression of
cats disturbed while sunning.

They were big for Hikeda'ya, Pryrates realized: each
was tall as a very tall man, though they were thin as
starveling beggars. They held their silver-white lances
loosely, and their deathly pale faces were calm within the
dark hoods.

Pryrates stared at the Norns. The Norns stared at
Pryrates.

"Well? Are you going to gape or are you going to open
the door for me?"

One of the Norns slowly bowed his head. "Yes, Lord
Pryrates." There was not the slightest hint of deference in
his icy, accented speech. He turned around and pulled
open the great door, exposing a corridor red with torchlight and more stairs. Pryrates stepped between the two
guards and started downward; the door swung shut behind
him. Before he had gone ten steps, the eerie spider-
melody had begun once more.

Hammers rose and fell, clanging and clattering, pounding the cooling metal into shapes useful to the king who
sat in a darkened throne room far above his foundry. The
din was terrible, the stench—brimstone, white-hot iron,
earth scorched to dry salt, even the savory-sweet odor of
burned manflesh—even worse.

The deformity of the men who scurried back and forth
across the floor of the great forge chamber was severe, as
though the terrible, baking heat of this underground cavern had melted them like bad metal. Even their heavy,
padded clothing could not hide it. In truth, Pryrates knew,
it was only those hopelessly twisted in body or spirit or
both that still remained here, working in Elias' armory. A

few of the others had been lucky enough to escape early on, but most of the able-bodied had been worked to death by Inch, the hulking overseer. A few smallish groups had been selected by Pryrates himself to aid in certain of his experiments; what was left of them had eventually been returned here, to feed the same furnaces in death they had served in life.

The king's counselor squinted through the hanging smoke, watching the forge men as they struggled along beneath huge burdens or hopped back like scalded frogs when a tongue of flame came too close. One way or the other, Pryrates reflected, Inch had dealt with all those more lovely or clever than himself.

In fact, Pryrates thought, grinning at his own cruel levity, if that was the standard it was a miracle anyone at all remained to stoke the fires or tend the molten metals in the great crucibles.

There was a lull in the clangor of hammers, and in that moment of near-quiet, Pryrates heard a squeaking noise behind him. He turned, careful not to appear too hurried, in case someone was watching. Nothing could frighten the red priest: it was important that everyone know that. When he saw what made the sound, he grinned and spat onto the stone.

The vast water wheel covered most of the cavern wall behind him. The mighty wooden wheel, steel-shod and fixed on a hub cross-cut from a huge tree trunk, dipped water from a powerful stream that sluiced through the forge, then lifted it up and spilled it into an ingenious labyrinth of troughs. These directed the water to a number of different spots throughout the forge, to cool metal or to put out fires, or even—when the rare mood struck Inch—to be lapped at by the forge's parched and miserable laborers. The turning wheel also drove a series of black-scummed iron chains, the largest of which reached vertically up into the darkness to provide the motive force for certain devices dear to Pryrates' heart. But at this moment it was the digging and lifting of the wheel's paddles that engaged the alchemist's imagination. He wondered idly if such a mechanism, built mountain-large and spun by the straining sinews of several thousand whimpering slaves, could not dredge up the bottom of the sea and expose the secrets hidden for eons there in darkness.

As he contemplated what fascinating things the millenial ooze might disgorge, a wide, black-nailed hand dropped down upon his sleeve. Pryrates whirled and slapped it away.

"How dare you touch me?!" he hissed, dark eyes narrowing. He bared his teeth as though he might tear out the throat of the tall, stooping figure before him.

Inch stared back for a moment before replying. His round face was furred by a patchwork of beard and fire-scarred flesh. He seemed, as always, thick and implacable as stone. "You want to talk to me?"

"Never touch me again." Pryrates' voice was restrained now, but it still trembled with a deadly tension. "Never."

Inch frowned, his uneven brow wrinkling. The hole where one eye had been gaped unpleasantly. "What do you need from me?"

The alchemist paused and took a breath, forcing down the black rage that had climbed up into his skull. Pryrates was surprised at his own violent reaction. It was foolish to waste anger on the brutish foundrymaster. When Inch had served his purpose, he could be slaughtered like the dull beast he was. Until then, he was useful to the king's plans—and, more importantly, to Pryrate's own.

"The king wishes the curtain wall refortified. New joists, new cross-bracing—the heaviest timbers that we can bring from the Kynslagh."

Inch lowered his head, thinking. The effort was almost palpable. "How soon?" he said at last.

"By Candlemansa. A week later and you and all your groundlings will find yourselves above the Nearulagh Gate keeping company with ravens." Pryrates had to restrain a chuckle at the thought of Inch's misshapen head spiked above the gate. Even the crows would not fight over *that* morsel. "I will hear no excuses—that gives you a third of a year. And speaking of the Nearulagh Gate, there are a few other things you must do as well. A few very important things. Some improvements to the gate's defenses." He reached into his robe and produced a scroll. Inch unfurled it and held it up to better catch the fitful light of the forge fires. "That must also be finished by Candlemansa."

"Where is the king's seal?" Inch wore a surprisingly shrewd look on his puckered face.

Pryrates' hand flew up. A flicker of greasy yellow light played along his fingertips. After a moment the glow winked out; he let his hand drop back to his side, hidden in a voluminous scarlet sleeve. "If you ever question me again," the alchemist gritted, "I will blast you to flakes of ash."

The foundrymaster's face was solemn. "Then walls and gate will not be finished. No one makes them work as fast as Doctor Inch."

"Doctor Inch." Pryrates curled his thin lip. "Usires save me, I am tired of talking to you. Just do your job as King Elias wishes. You are luckier than you know, bumpkin. You will see the beginning of a great era, a golden age." *But only the beginning, and not much of that,* the priest promised himself. "I will be back in two days. You will tell me then how many men you need, and what other things."

As he strode away, he thought he heard Inch call something after him, but when Pryrates turned, the forgemaster was staring instead at the water wheel's thick spokes passing in a never-ending circle. The clatter of hammers was sharp, but still Pryrates could hear the ponderous, mournful creaking of the turning wheel.

Duke Isgrimnur leaned on the windowsill, stroking his new-sprouted beard and staring down at the greasy waterways of Kwanitupul. The storm had passed, the sprinkling of bizarrely unseasonal snow had melted, and the marshy air, though still oddly cool, had returned to its usual stickiness. Isgrimnur felt a strong urge to be moving, to do something.

Trapped, he thought. *Pinned down as surely as if by*

archers. It's like the damnable Battle of Clodu Lake all over again.

But of course there were no archers, no hostile forces of any kind. Kwanitupul, at least temporarily freed from the cold's grip and restored to its usual mercenary existence, paid no more attention to Isgrimnur than it did to any of the thousands of others who occupied its ramshackle body like so many busy fleas. No, it was circumstance that had trapped the former master of Elvritshalla, and circumstance was right now a more implacable enemy than any human foes, no matter how many and how well-armed.

Isgrimnur stood up with a sigh and turned to look at Camaris, who sat propped against the far wall, tying and untying a length of rope. The old man, once the greatest knight in Osten Ard, looked up and smiled his soft, idiot-child's smile. For all his white-haired age, his teeth were still good. He was strong, too, with a grip most young tavern brawlers would envy.

But weeks of constant effort on Isgrimnur's part had not altered that maddening smile. Whether Camaris was bewitched, wounded in the head, or simply deranged with age, it all came to the same end: the duke had not been able to summon forth even a flicker of recollection. The old man did not recognize Isgrimnur, did not remember his past or even his own true name. If the duke had not once known Camaris so well he might even have begun to doubt his own senses and memory, but Isgrimnur had seen John's paramount knight at every season, in every light, in good times and evil times. The old man might no longer know himself, but Isgrimnur was not mistaken.

Still, what should be done with him? Whether he was hopelessly mad or not, he should be helped. The most obvious task was to get the old man to those who would remember and revere him. Even if the world Camaris had helped build was now crumbling, even if King Elias had laid waste to the dream of Camaris' friend and liege-lord John, still the old man deserved to spend his last years in some better place than this backwater pesthole. Also, if anyone yet survived of Prince Josua's folk, they should know that Camaris lived. The old man could be a powerful emblem of hope and of better days—and Isgrimnur, a shrewd statesman for all his bluff disavowals, knew the value of a symbol.

But even if Josua or some of his captains had somehow survived and regrouped somewhere to the north of here, as Kwanitupul market rumor suggested, how could Isgrimnur and Camaris reach them through a Nabban full of enemies? How could he leave this inn in any case? Father Dinivan, with his dying breath, had told Isgrimnur to bring Miriamele here. The duke had not found her before being forced to flee the Sancellan Aedonitis, but Miriamele might already know of this place—perhaps Dinivan himself had mentioned it to her! She might come here, alone and friendless, and find Isgrimnur already gone. Could the duke risk that? He owed it to Josua—whether the prince was living or dead—to do his best to help her.

Isgrimnur had hoped that Tiamak—who in some unspecified way was an intimate of Dinivan's—might know something about Miriamele's whereabouts, but that hope had been immediately dashed. After much prodding, the little brown man had admitted that Dinivan had sent him here as well, but without explanation. Tiamak had been very preoccupied with the news of the deaths of Dinivan and Morgenes and afterward had offered nothing helpful to Isgrimnur at all. In fact, the duke thought him somewhat sullen. Although the marsh man's leg was obviously painful—a cockindrill had bitten him, he said—still Isgrimnur thought that Tiamak could do more to help solve the various riddles that plagued them both, Dinivan's purpose uppermost among them. But instead he seemed content just to sulk around the room—a room paid for by Isgrimnur!—or to spend long hours writing or limping along the wooden walkways of Kwanitupul, as he was doubtless doing now.

Isgrimnur was about to say something to silent Camaris when there was a knock at the door. It creaked open to reveal the landlady, Charystra.

"I've brought the food you asked for." Her tone im-

plied that she had made some great personal sacrifice instead of merely taking Isgrimnur's money for grossly
overpriced bed and board. "Some nice bread and soup.
Very nice. With beans." She set the tureen on the low table and clanked down three bowls beside it. "I don't understand why you can't come down to eat with everyone
else." Everyone else was two Wrannaman feather merchants and an itinerant gem cutter from Naraxi who was
looking for work.

"Because I pay not to," Isgrimnur growled.

"Where's the marsh man?" She ladled out the
unsteaming soup.

"I don't know, and I don't think it's business of yours,
either." He glowered. "I saw you go off with your friend
this morning."

"To the market," she sniffed. "I can't take my boat, because *he*—" hands full, she waggled her head in the direction of Camaris, "—never fixed it."

"Nor will I let him, for the sake of his dignity—and
I'm paying you for that, too." Isgrimnur's sour temper
was rising. Charystra always tested the boundaries of the
duke's chivalry. "You are very quick with your tongue,
woman. I wonder what you tell your friends at the market
about me and your other strange guests."

She darted an apprehensive look in his direction.
"Nothing, I'm sure."

"That had better be true. I gave you money to keep silent about . . . about my friend here." He looked at
Camaris, who was happily spooning oily soup into his
mouth. "But in case you think to take my money and still
spread tales, remember: if I find you have talked about
me or my business . . . *I will make you wish you hadn't.*"
He let his deep voice rumble the words like thunder.

Charystra took a step back in alarm. "I'm sure I
haven't said nothing! And you've no cause to be threatening me, sir! No cause! It's not right!" She started toward
the door, waving the ladle as if to fend off blows. "I said
I wouldn't say anything and I won't. Anyone will tell
you—Charystra keeps her word!" She quickly made the

sign of the Tree, then slipped out into the hall, leaving a spatter of soup spots on the plank flooring.

"Hah," Isgrimnur snorted. He stared at the grayish fluid still rippling in the bowl. Pay for her silence, indeed. That was like paying the sun not to shine. He had been throwing money around as though it were Wran water—soon it would run out. Then what would he do? It made him angry just to think about it. "Hah!" he said again. "Damn me."

Camaris wiped his chin and smiled, staring at nothing.

Simon leaned around the standing stone and peered downward. The pale sun was nearly straight overhead; it knifed down through the undergrowth, revealing a flicker of reflection on the hillside.

"Here it is," he called back, then leaned against the wind-smoothed pillar to wait. The white stone had not yet shed its morning chill, and was even colder than the surrounding air. After a moment, Simon began to feel his bones turning to ice. He stepped away and turned to survey the line of the hill's edge. The standing stones circled Sesuad'ra's summit like the spikes of a king's crown. Several of the ancient pillars had fallen down, so the crown had a somewhat bedraggled look, but most stood tall and straight, still doing their duty after a span of unguessable centuries.

They look just like the Anger Stones on Thisterborg, he realized.

Could that be a Sithi place, too? There were certainly enough strange stories told about it.

Where were those two? "Are you coming?" he called.

When he received no answer, he clambered around the stone and made his way a short distance down the hillside, careful to keep a solid grip on the sturdy heather despite the resultant prickling: the ground was muddy and potentially treacherous. Below, the valley was full of gray water that barely rippled, so that the new lake around the hill seemed solid as a stone floor. Simon could not help

thinking of the days when he had climbed to the
bellchamber of Green Angel Tower and felt himself sitting cloud-high above the world. Here on Sesuad'ra, it
was as though the entire hill of stone had just now been
born, thrusting up from the primordial muck. It was easy
to pretend there was nothing beyond this place, that this
was how it must have felt when God stood atop Mount
Den Haloi and made the world, as told in the Book of the
Aedon.

Jiriki had told Simon about the coming of the
Gardenborn to Osten Ard. In those days, the Sitha had
said, most of the world had been covered in ocean, just as
the west still was. Jiriki's folk had sailed out of the rising
sun, across unimaginable distances, to land on the verdant
coastline of a world innocent of humanity, a vast island in
a great surrounding sea. Some later cataclysm, Jiriki had
implied, had then changed the face of the world: the land
had risen and the seas had drained away to east and south,
leaving new mountains and meadows behind them. Thus,
the Gardenborn could never return to their lost home.

Simon thought about this as he squinted out toward the
east. There was little to see from atop Sesuad'ra but
murky steppes, lifeless plains of endless gray and dull
green, stretching to where vision failed. From what Simon had heard, the eastern steppes had been inhospitable
territory even before this dread winter: they grew increasingly barren and shelterless the farther east of Aldheorte
Forest one went. Beyond a certain point, travelers
claimed, even the Hyrkas and Thrithings-folk did not
journey. The sun never truly shone there and the land was
sunken in perpetual twilight. The few hardy souls who
had crossed that murky expanse in search of other lands
had never returned.

He realized he had been staring a long time, yet he was
still alone. He was just about to call again when Jeremias
appeared, picking his way carefully through the brambles
and waist-high grass toward the edge of the hill. Leleth,
barely visible in the swaying undergrowth, held the young
squire's hand. She seemed to have taken a liking to Jeremias, although it was shown only by her constant proxim-

ity. She still did not speak, and her expression remained perpetually solemn and abstracted, but when she could not be with Geloë, she was nearly always with Jeremias. Simon guessed that she might have sensed in the young squire something like her own pain, some shared affliction of the heart.

"Does it go down into the ground," Jeremias called, "or over the edge?"

"Both," said Simon, pointing.

They had been following the path of this spring from the point where it appeared in the building Geloë had named the House of Waters. Issuing mysteriously from the rocks, it did not drain away after pooling at the base of the spring—where it provided fresh drinking water for New Gadrinsett, and thus had become one of the centers of gossip and commerce for the infant settlement—but rather gurgled out of the little pond in a narrow streamlet, passing out of the House of Waters, which was at one of the highest points on Sesuad'ra, then running across the summit as a tiny rivulet, appearing and disappearing as the features of the ground changed. Simon had never seen or heard of a spring that behaved in such a way—who had ever heard of a spring on a hilltop, anyway?—and he was bound and determined to discover its path, and perhaps its origin, before the storms returned and made the hunt impossible.

Jeremias joined Simon a little way down the hillside. They both stood over the swift-flowing rivulet.

"Do you think it goes all the way down," Jeremias gestured to the vast gray moat around the base of the Stone of Farewell, "or does it go back into the hill?"

Simon shrugged. Water that sprang from the heart of a Sithi sacred mountain might indeed pass back into the rock once more, like some incomprehensible wheel of creation and destruction—like the future approaching to absorb the present, then quickly falling away again to become the past. He was about to suggest further exploration, but Leleth was making her way down the hill. Simon worried for her, although she herself seemed to pay little attention to the hazardous trail. She could easily slip, and the slope was steep and dangerous.

Jeremias took a couple of steps up and reached for her, catching her under her thin arms and lifting her down to stand beside them. As he did so, her loose dress rode up, and for a brief moment Simon saw her scars, long inflamed weals that covered her thighs. They must be far worse on her stomach, he reflected.

He had been thinking all morning about what he had heard in Leavetaking House about the Great Swords and other things. These matters had seemed abstract, as though Simon, his friends and allies, Elias, even the dreadful Storm King himself, were no more than pieces on a shent board, tiny things that could be considered in a hundred different configurations. Now, suddenly, he was reminded of the true horrors of the recent past. Leleth, an innocent child, had been terrorized and savaged by the hounds of Stormspike; thousands more just as innocent had been made homeless, been orphaned, tormented, killed. Anger suddenly made Simon sway on his feet, as if the very force of his fury might knock him stumbling. If there was any justice, someone would pay for what had happened—for Morgenes, Haestan, Leleth, for Jeremias with his now-thin face and unspoken sorrows, for Simon himself, homeless and sad.

Usires have mercy on me, I would kill them all if I could. Elias and Pryrates and their white-faced Norns—if only I could, I would kill them with my own hands.

"I saw her at the castle," said Jeremias. Simon looked up, startled. He had clenched his fists so tightly that his knuckles hurt.

"What?"

"Leleth." Jeremias nodded at the child, who was smearing her dirty face as she stared out across the flooded valley. "When she was Princess Miriamele's handmaiden. I remember thinking, 'what a pretty little girl.' She was all dressed in white, carrying flowers. I thought she looked very clean." He laughed quietly. "Look at her now."

Simon found he did not want to talk about sorrowful

things. "And look at you," he said. "You're one to be talking about clean."

Jeremias would not be distracted. "Did you really know her, Simon? The princess, I mean."

"Yes." Simon didn't want to tell Jeremias that story again. He had been bitterly disappointed to find Miriamele was not with Josua, and horrified that no one knew where she was. He had dreamed of telling her his adventures, of the way her bright eyes would go wide as he told her of the dragon. "Yes," he repeated, "I knew her."

"And was she beautiful, like a princess should be?" Jeremias asked, suddenly intent.

"I suppose so." Simon was reluctant to talk about her. "Yes, she was—I mean, she is."

Jeremias was about to ask something else, but was interrupted. "Ho!" a voice cried from above. "There you are!"

A strange, two-headed silhouette was looking down at them from beside the standing stone. One of the heads had pointed ears.

"We're trying to find out where the spring comes from and where it goes, Binabik," Simon called.

The wolf tilted her head and barked.

"Qantaqa thinks you should stop your water-following for now, Simon," Binabik laughed. "Besides, Josua has asked all to be returning to the Leavetaking Hall. There is much to talk about."

"We're coming."

Simon and Jeremias each took one of Leleth's small cold hands and clambered back up toward the hillcrest. The sun stared down on them all like a milky eye.

All who had been gathered in the morning had returned to Leavetaking House. They talked quietly, perhaps over-awed by the size and strange dimensions of the hall, so much more unsettling when it was not filled with a dis-tracting crowd as it had been the night before. The sickly afternoon light leaked in through the windows, but with so little strength that it seemed to come from no direction at all, smearing all the room equally; the meticulous wall-carvings gleamed as though by their own faint inner light, reminding Simon of the shimmering moss in the tunnels beneath the Hayholt. He had been lost there in choking, strangling blackness. He had been in a place beyond despair. Surely to survive that meant something. Surely he had been spared for a reason!

Please, Lord Aedon, he prayed, *don't bring me so far just to let me die!*

But he had already cursed God for letting Haestan perish. It was doubtless too late for making amends.

Simon opened his eyes to find that Josua had arrived. The prince had been with Vorzheva, and assured them all that she was feeling better.

Accompanying Josua were two who had not been at the morning council, Sludig—who had been scouting the perimeter of the valley—and a heavyset young Falshireman named Freosel, who had been chosen by the settlers as constable of New Gadrinsett. Despite his relative youth, Freosel had the wary, heavy-lidded look of a veteran street fighter. He was liberally scarred and two of his fingers were missing.

After Strangyeard had spoken a short blessing, and the new constable had been cautioned to hold secret the things he would hear, Prince Josua stood.

"We have many things to decide," he said, "but before we begin, let me talk to you of good luck and of more hopeful days.

"When it seemed that there was nothing left but despair and defeat, God favored us. We are now in a safe place, when a season ago we were scattered over the world, the castaways of war. We undertook a quest for one of the three Great Swords, which may be our hope of victory, and that quest has succeeded. More people flock to our banner every day, so that if we only can wait long enough, we will soon have an army that will give even my brother the High King pause.

"Our needs are still great, of course. Out of those people driven from their homes throughout Erkynland, we can indeed mount an army, but to overcome the High

King we will need many more. It is also certain that we are already hard-pressed to feed and shelter those who are here. And it is even possible that no army, however large and well-provided, will be great enough to defeat Elias' ally the Storm King." Josua paused. "Thus, as I see it, the important questions we must answer this day are three: What does my brother plan to do? How can we assemble a force that will prevent it? And how can we retrieve the other two swords, Bright-Nail and Sorrow, that we may have a hope of defeating the Norns and their dark master and mistress?"

Geloë lifted her hand. "Your pardon, Josua, but I think there is one more question: How much time do we have to do any of these things?"

"You are right, Valada Geloë. If we are able to protect this place for another year, we might gather a great enough force to begin disputing Elias on his own ground, or at least his outermost holdings—but like you, I doubt we will be left unmolested so long."

Others raised their voices, asking about what further strength could be expected from the east and north of Erkynland, territories that chafed beneath King Elias' heavy hand, and where other allies might be found. After a while, Josua again called the room to silence.

"Before we can solve any of these riddles," he declared, "it is my thought that we must solve the first and most important one—namely, what does my brother want?"

"Power!" said Isorn. "The power to cast men's lives around as if they were dice."

"He had that already," Josua replied. "But I have thought long, and can think of no other answer. Certainly the world has seen other kings who were not content with what they had. Perhaps the answer to this most crucial question may remain hidden from us until the very end. If we knew the shape of Elias' bargain with the Storm King, perhaps then we would understand my brother's secret intent."

"Prince Josua," Binabik spoke up, "I myself have been puzzling about a different thing. Whatever your brother is wishing to do, the Storm King's power and dark magics will be helping him. But what is the Storm King wanting in return?"

The great stone hall went silent for a moment, then the voices of those assembled rose once more, arguing, until Josua had to stamp his boot on the floor to silence them.

"You ask a dreadful question, Binabik," said the prince. "What indeed could that dark one want?"

Simon thought about the shadows beneath the Hayholt where he had stumbled in a terrible, ghost-ridden dream. "Maybe he wants his castle back," he said.

Simon had spoken softly, and others in the room who had not heard him continued to talk quietly among themselves, but Josua and Binabik both turned to stare at him.

"Merciful Aedon," said Josua. "Could it be?"

Binabik thought for a long moment, then shook his head slowly. "There is being something wrong in that thought—although it is clever thinking, Simon. Tell me, Geloë, what is it that I am half-remembering?"

The witch woman nodded. "Ineluki cannot ever come back to that castle. When Asu'a fell, its ruins were so priest-blessed and so tightly wound in spells that he could not return before the end of time. No, I do not think he *can* have it back, much as he no doubt burns to reclaim it . . . but he may wish to rule through Elias what he cannot rule himself. For all their power, the Norns are few— but as the shadow behind the Dragonbone Chair, the Storm King could reign over all the lands of Osten Ard."

Josua's face was grave. "And to think that my brother has so little care for either his people or his throne that he would sell them for some trifling prize to the enemy of mankind." He turned to the others assembled there, anger poorly hidden on his thin features. "We will take this as truth for now, that the Storm King wishes to rule mankind through my brother. Ineluki, I am told, is a creature sustained mostly by hatred, so I do not need to tell you what sort of reign his would be. Simon has told us that the Sitha-woman Amerasu foresaw what the Storm King desired for men, and she called it 'terrible.' We must do all that we can—even up to tithing our lives, if necessary—to halt them both. Now the other questions must be addressed. How do we fight them?"

In the hours that followed many plans were proposed. Freosel cautiously suggested that they merely wait in this place of refuge as disaffection with Elias grew throughout Osten Ard. Hotvig, who for a plainsman seemed to be taking well to stone-dweller intrigue, put forward a bold scheme to send men who, with Eolair's maps, would sneak into the Hayholt and kill both Elias and Pryrates. Father Strangyeard seemed distressed at the idea of sending the precious maps off with a band of brutish murderers. As the merits of these and other proposals were introduced and debated, tempers grew hot. When at one point Isorn and Hotvig, who normally were cheerful comrades, had nearly come to blows, Josua at last ended the discussion.

"Remember that we are friends and allies here," he said. "We all share a common desire to return our lands to freedom." The prince looked around the room, calming his excited advisers with a stern gaze, as a Hyrka trainer was said to quiet horses without touching them. "I have heard all, and I am grateful for your help, but now I must decide." He placed his hand on the stone table, near Thorn's silver-wrapped hilt. "I agree that we must wait yet a while before we will be ready to strike at Elias," he nodded in Freosel's direction, "—but we may not stand still, either. Also, our allies in Hernystir are trapped. They could be a valuable irritant on Elias' western flank if they were free to move once more. If the westerners were to gather together some of their scattered countrymen, they could be even more than that. Thus, I have decided to combine two purposes and see if they cannot serve each other."

Josua beckoned forward the lord of Nad Mullach. "Count Eolair, I will send you back to your people with more than thanks, as I promised. With you will go Isorn, son of Duke Isgrimnur." Gutrun could not restrain a muffled cry of sadness at this, but when her son turned to comfort her, she smiled bravely and patted his shoulder.

Josua bowed his head toward her, acknowledging her sorrow. "You will understand when you hear my plan, Duchess, that I do not do this without reason. Isorn, take with you a half-dozen or so men. Perhaps some of Hotvig's randwarders will consent to accompany you: they are brave fighters and tireless horsemen. On your journey to Hernystir, you will gather as many of your wandering countrymen as you can. I know that most of them do not love Skali Sharpnose, and many I hear are now unhomed on the Frostmarch. Then, on your own judgment, you can put those you find to service—either helping to break Skali's siege of Eolair's folk, or if that is not possible, returning with you here to help us in our fight against my brother." Josua looked fondly at Isorn, who was listening with eyes downcast in concentration, as though he wished to learn each word by heart. "You are the duke's son. They respect you, and they will believe you when you tell them that this is the first step in regaining their own lands."

The prince turned back to the assembly. "While Isorn and the others undertake this mission, we here will work to further our other causes. And there is indeed much to do. The north has been so thoroughly savaged by winter, by Skali, by Elias and his ally the Storm King, that I fear that however successful Isorn is, the lands north of Erkynland will not prove sufficient to provide all the forces we need. Nabban and the south are firmly in the grip of Elias' friends, especially Benigaris, but I must have the south myself. Only then will we truly have the number of fighting men to confront Elias. So, we will work, and talk, and think. There must be some way of cutting Benigaris off from Elias' help, but at the moment I cannot see it."

Simon had been listening impatiently, but had held his tongue. Now, when it seemed as though Josua had finished with what he had to say, Simon could not stay quiet any longer. While the others had been shouting, he had been thinking with growing excitement about the things he had discussed with Binabik that morning.

"But Prince Josua," he cried, "what about the swords?"

The prince nodded. "Those, too, we will have to think about. Do not worry, Simon: I have not forgotten them."

Simon took a breath, determined to plunge on. "The best thing to do would be to surprise Elias. Send Binabik and Sludig and me to get Bright-Nail. It's outside the walls of the Hayholt. With just the three of us, we could go to your father's grave and find it, then be away before the king even knew we'd been there. He'd never suspect that we'd do such a thing." Simon had a momentary vision of how it would be: he and his companions bearing Bright-Nail back to Sesuad'ra in glory, Simon's new dragon banner flapping above them.

Josua smiled but shook his head. "No one doubts your bravery, Sir Seoman, but we cannot risk it."

"We found Thorn when no one thought we could."

"But the Erkynguard did not march past Thorn's resting place every day."

"The dragon did!"

"Enough." Josua raised his hand. "No, Simon, it is not yet time. When we can attack Elias from west or south and thus distract his eye away from Swertclif and the grave mounds, then it will be time. You have earned great honor, and you will no doubt earn more, but you are now a knight of the realm, with all the responsibilities that go with your title. I regretted sending you away in search of Thorn and despaired of ever seeing you again. Now that you have succeeded beyond all hope, I would have you here for a while—Binabik and Sludig, too ... whom you neglected to consult before volunteering them for this deadly mission." He smiled to soften the blow. "Peace, lad, peace."

Simon was filled with the same stifling, trapped feeling that had beset him in Jao é-Tinukai'i. Didn't they understand that to wait too long to strike could mean they would lose their chance? That evil would go unpunished? "Can I go with Isorn?" he pleaded. "I want to help, Prince Josua."

"Learn to be a knight, Simon, and enjoy these days of relative freedom. There will be enough danger later on." The prince stood. Simon could not help seeing the weariness in his expression. "That is enough. Eolair, Isorn, and whoever Isorn chooses should make ready to leave in two days' time. Let us now go. A meal has been prepared—not as lavish as the meal celebrating Simon's knighthood, but something that will do us all good, nevertheless." With a wave of his hand, he ended the gathering.

Binabik approached Simon, wanting to talk, but Simon was angry and at first would not answer. It was back to this, was it? *Wait, Simon, wait. Let others make the decisions. You'll be told what to do soon enough.*

"It was a good idea," he muttered.

"It will still be a good idea later," said Binabik, "when we are then distracting Elias, as Josua was telling."

Simon glared at him, but something in the troll's round face made his anger seem foolish. "I just want to be useful."

"You are far more than that, friend Simon. But everything is having its season. *'Iq ta randayhet suk biqahuc,'* as we say in my homeland: 'Winter is not being the time for naked swimming.' "

Simon thought about this for a moment. "That's supid," he said at last.

"So," Binabik responded testily. "You may be saying what you please—but do not then come weeping to *my* fire when you have chosen the wrong season for swimming."

They walked silently across the grassy hill, haunted by the cold sun.

4

The Silent Child

Although the air was warm and still, the dark clouds seemed unnaturally thick. The ship had been almost motionless all day, sails slack against the masts.

"I wonder when the storm is coming," Miriamele said aloud.

A young sailor standing nearby looked up in surprise. "Lady? You say to me?"

"I said that I wondered when the storm was coming." She gestured at the clot of overhanging clouds.

"Yes, Lady." He seemed uneasy talking with her. His command of Westerling speech was not great: she guessed that he was from one of the smaller southern islands, on some of which the residents didn't even speak Nabbanai. "Storm coming."

"I know it's coming. I was wondering *when*."

"Ah." He nodded his head, then looked around furtively, as though the valuable knowledge he was about to impart might draw thieves. "Storm come *very soon*." He showed her a wide, gummy smile. His gaze traveled up from her shoes to her face and his grin widened. "Very pretty."

Her momentary pleasure in having a conversation, however limited, was dashed. She recognized the look in this sailor's eyes, the insulting stare. However free he was in his inspection, he would never dare to touch her, but that was only because he considered her a toy that rightfully belonged to the ship's master, Aspitis. Her flash of indignation was mixed with a sudden uncertainty. Was he

right? Despite all the doubts she now harbored about the
earl—who, if Gan Itai spoke rightly, had met with
Pryrates, and if Cadrach spoke rightly, was even in the
red priest's employ—she at least had believed that his announced plan to marry her was genuine. But now she
wondered if it might only be a ruse, something to keep
her pliant and grateful until he could discard her in
Nabban and go looking for new flesh. He no doubt
thought she would be too ashamed to tell anyone what
had happened.

Miriamele was not sure which upset her more at this
point, the possibility of being forced to marry Aspitis or
the conflicting possibility that he could lie to her with the
same airy condescension he might show to a pretty tavern
whore.

She stared coldly at the sailor until at last, puzzled, he
turned and made his way back toward the bow of the
ship. Miriamele watched him go, silently willing him to
trip and bash his smug face on the deck, but her wish was
not granted. She turned her eyes back to the sooty gray
clouds and the dull, metallic ocean.

A trio of small objects were bobbing in the water off
the stern, a good stone's throw from the ship. As
Miriamele watched, one of the objects moved closer, then
opened its red hole of a mouth and hooted. The kilpa's
gurgling voice carried well across the calm waters;
Miriamele jumped in surprise. At her motion, all three
heads swung to face her, wet black eyes staring, mouths
gaping loutishly. Miriamele took a step back from the rail
and made the sign of the Tree, then turned to escape the
empty eyes and almost knocked over Thures, the young
page who served Earl Aspitis.

"Lady Marya," he said, and tried to bow, but he was
too close to her. He banged his head against her elbow
and gave out a little squeak of pain. When she reached
out to soothe him, he pulled away, embarrassed. "'S
Lordship wants you."

"Where, Thures?"

"Cabin." He composed himself. "In his cabin, Lady."

"Thank you."

The boy stepped back as if to lead her, but Miriamele's eyes had again been caught by a movement in the water below. One of the kilpa had drifted away from the other two and now swam slowly up next to the ship. With its empty eyes fixed on hers, the sea-thing lifted a slick gray hand from the water and ran its long fingers along the hull as if casually searching for climbing holds. Miriamele watched with fascinated horror, unable to move. After a moment, the unpleasantly manlike creature dropped away again, vanishing smoothly into the sea to reappear a few moments later a stone's throw back from the ship. It floated there, mouth glistening, the gills on its neck bulging and shrinking. Miriamele stared, frozen as if in a nightmare. Finally she tore her eyes away and forced herself back from the rail. Young Thures was looking at her curiously.

"Lady?"

"I'm coming." She followed him, turning to look back only once. The three heads bobbed in the ship's wake like fishermen's floats.

Thures left her in the narrow passageway outside Aspitis' cabin, then vanished back up the ladder, presumably to perform other errands. Miriamele took advantage of the moment of solitude to compose herself. She could not shake off the memory of the kilpa's viscous eyes, its calm and deliberate approach toward the ship. The way it had stared—almost insolently, as though daring her to try to stop it. She shuddered.

Her thoughts were interrupted by a series of quiet clinking noises from the earl's cabin. The door was not completely closed, so she stepped forward and peered through the crack.

Aspitis sat at his tiny writing table. A book of some kind was open before him, its parchment pages reflecting creamy lamplight. The earl swept two more piles of silver coins off the table and into a sack, then dropped the clinking bag into an open chest at his feet, which seemed nearly full with other such sacks. Aspitis then made a notation of some kind in the book.

A board creaked—whether from her weight upon it or from the movement of the ship Miriamele did not know—but she moved back hurriedly before Aspitis could look up and see her in the narrow slit of open doorway. A moment later, she stepped forward and knocked firmly.

"Aspitis?" She heard him close the book with a muffled thump, then another sound she guessed was the chest being dragged across the floor.

"Yes, my lady. Come in."

She pushed on the door and walked through, then closed it gently behind her but did not let the latch fall. "You asked for me?"

"Sit down, pretty Marya." Aspitis gestured to the bed, but Miriamele pretended she had not noticed and instead perched on a stool beside the far wall. One of Aspitis' hounds rolled aside to make room for her feet, thumped its heavy tail, then fell asleep again. The earl was wearing his osprey crest robe, the one she had admired so much at their first shared supper. Now she looked at the gold-stitched talons, perfect machines for catching and clutching, and was filled with remorse for her own foolishness.

Why did I ever let myself become entrapped in these stupid lies! She would never have told him so, but Cadrach had been right. If she had said she was only a commoner, Aspitis might have left her alone; even if he had forcibly bedded her, at least he would not be planning to wed her as well.

"I saw three kilpa swimming beside the ship." She stared at him defiantly, as if he might deny that it was true. "One swam up alongside and looked like it was going to climb aboard."

The earl shook his head, but he was smiling. "They will do no such thing, Lady, do not fear. Not on *Eadne Cloud*."

"It touched the ship!" She raised her hand, shaped into a groping claw. "Like this. It was looking for handholds."

Aspitis' smile faded. He looked grim. "I will go on deck when we have finished talking. I will put a few arrows into them, the fishy devils. They do not touch my ship."

"But what do the kilpa want?" She could not get the gray things out of her mind. Also, she was in no hurry to talk with Aspitis about whatever he was thinking. She was positive now that no good could come to her out of any of the earl's plans.

"I do not know what they want, Lady." He wagged his head impatiently. "Or rather, I do know—food. But there are many easier ways for the kilpa to catch their meals than to come onto a ship full of armed men." He stared at her. "There. I should not have said it. Now you are frightened."

"They eat . . . people?"

Aspitis shook his head, this time with greater vehemence. "They eat fish, and sometimes birds that do not take off swiftly from floating on the water." He absorbed her skeptical look. "Yes, other things, too, when they can find them. They have sometimes swarmed small fishing boats, but nobody knows why for certain. Anyway, it does not matter. I told you, they will not harm *Eadne Cloud*. There is no better sea-watcher than Gan Itai."

Miriamele sat silently for a moment. "I'm sure you're right," she said at last.

"Good." He stood up, ducking beneath a beam of the low cabin roof. "I am glad Thures found you—although you could not go very far on a ship at sea, could you?" His smile seemed a little harsh. "We have many things to discuss."

"My lord." She felt a strange sense of lassitude sweep over her. Perhaps if she did not resist, did not protest, especially if she did not care, then things would just go on in this unsatisfactory but impermanent way. She had promised herself that she would drift, drift. . . .

"We are becalmed," said Aspitis, "but I think that there will be winds coming soon, far ahead of the storm. With a little luck, we could be on the island of Spenit tomorrow night. Think of that, Marya! We will be married there, in the church sacred to Saint Lavennin."

It would be so easy not to resist, but just to float, like *Eadne Cloud* herself, borne slowly along on the wind's unambitious breath. Surely there would be some chance to escape when they made landfall at Spenit? Surely?

"My lord," she heard herself saying, "I . . . there are . . . problems."

"Yes?" The earl cocked his golden head. Miriamele thought he looked like someone's trained hound, miming civilization while he sniffed for prey. "Problems?"

She gathered the material of her dress in her damp hand, then took a deep breath. "I cannot marry you."

Unexpectedly, Aspitis laughed. "Oh, how foolish! Of course you can! Do you worry about my family? They will come to love you, even as I have. My brother married a Perdruinese woman, and now she is my mother's favorite daughter. Do not fear!"

"It's not that." She clutched her dress more tightly. "It's . . . it's just that . . . there is someone else."

The earl frowned. "What do you mean?"

"I am already promised to someone else. Back home. And I love him."

"But I asked you! You said to me there was no one. And you gave yourself to me."

He was angry, but so far he had kept his temper. Miriamele felt her fear ease somewhat. "I had an argument with him and refused to marry him; that is why my father sent me to the convent. But I have realized that I was wrong. I was unfair to him . . . and I was unfair to you." She detested herself for saying this. It seemed only a very slight chance that she was truly being unfair to Aspitis; he had certainly not been over-chivalrous with her. Still, this was the time to be generous. "But of the two of you, I loved him first."

Aspitis took a step toward her, his mouth twisting. There was a strange, trembling tension to his voice. "But you gave yourself to me."

She lowered her eyes, anxious not to cause offense. "I was wrong. I hope you will forgive me. I hope that he will forgive me, although I do not deserve it."

The earl abruptly turned his back on her. His words were still tight, barely controlled. "And that is that, you think? You will just say, 'Farewell, Earl Aspitis!' That is what you think?"

"I can only rely on your gentleman's honor, my lord." The little room seemed even smaller. She thought she could feel the very air tighten, as if the threatening storm was reaching down for her. "I can only pray for your kindness and pity."

Aspitis' shoulders began to shake. A low, moaning noise welled up from him. Miriamele shrunk back against the wall in horror, half-certain he would turn into a ravening wolf before her eyes, as in some old nurse's tale.

The earl of Eadne and Drina whirled. His teeth were indeed bared in a lupine grimace, but he was laughing.

She was stunned. *Why is he...?*

"Oh, my lady!" He was barely able to control his mirth. "You are a clever one!"

"I don't understand," she said frostily. "Do you think this is funny?"

Aspitis clapped his hands together. The sudden thunder crack of noise made Miriamele jump. "You are so clever." He shook his head. "But you are not quite as clever as you think ... Princess."

"Wh—what?"

He smiled. It was no longer even remotely charming. "You think quickly and you invent pretty little lies very well—but I was at your grandfather's funeral, and your father's coronation as well. You are Miriamele. I knew that from the first night you joined me at my table."

"You ... you ..." Her mind was full of words, but none of them made sense. "What...?"

"I suspected something when you were brought to me." He reached out a hand and slid it along Miriamele's face into her hair, his strong fingers clasping her behind the ear. She sat unmoving, holding her breath. "See," he said, "your hair is short, but the part closest to your head is quite golden ... like mine." He chuckled. "Now, a young noblewoman on her way to a convent *might* cut her hair before she got there—but dye it, too, when it was already such a handsome color? You can be sure I looked at your face very closely at supper that night. After that, there was not much difficulty. I had seen you before, if not closely. It was common knowledge that Elias' daughter was at Naglimund, and missing after the castle fell." He snapped his fingers, grinning. "So. Now you *are* mine, and we *will* be married on Spenit, since you might find some way to escape in Nabban, where you still have family." He chortled again, pleased. "Now they will be my family, too."

It was difficult to speak. "You really want to marry me?"

"Not because of your beauty, my lady, though you are a pretty one. And not because I shared your bed. If I had to marry all the women I have dallied with, I would need to give my army of wives their own castle, like the Nascadu desert kings." He sat down on the bedcover, leaning back until he could rest his head against the cabin wall. "No, you will be my wife. Then, when your father's conquests are over and he grows tired at last of Benigaris, as I did long ago—did you know, after he killed his father he drank wine and cried all night long! Like a child!— when your father grows tired of Benigaris, who better to rule Nabban than the one who found his daughter, fell in love with her, and brought her back home?" His smile was a knife-glint. "Me."

She stared at him, her skin turning cold; she almost felt she could spit venom like a serpent. "And if I tell him that you kidnapped and dishonored me?"

He shook his head, amused. "You are not so good a schemer as I thought, Miriamele. Many witnessed you board my boat with a false name, and saw me pay court to you, although I had been told you were a minor baron's daughter. Once it is known that you have been— dishonored, you said?—do you think your father would offend a legitimate and high-born husband? A husband who is already his ally, and who has done your father many,"—he reached over and patted his hand against something Miriamele could not see—"important services?"

His bright eyes burned into hers, mocking and immensely pleased. He was right. There was nothing she could do to prevent him. He owned her. *Owned her.*

"I am going." She rose unsteadily.

"Do not cast yourself in the ocean, pretty Miriamele. My men will be watching to make sure you play no such tricks. You are far too valuable alive."

She pushed at the door, but it would not open. She was hollow, empty and hurting as if all the air had been forced out of her.

"Pull it," Aspitis suggested.

Miriamele staggered out into the corridor. The shadowed hall seemed to lurch crazily.

"I will come to your cabin later, my beloved," the earl called. "Prepare for me."

She was barely off the ladder and onto the deck before she sank to her knees. She wanted to fall into blackness and disappear.

Tiamak was angry.

He had gone through a great deal for the sake of his drylander associates—the League of the Scroll, as they called themselves, although Tiamak sometimes thought that a group of a half-dozen or so was a bit small to be called a league. Still, Doctor Morgenes had been a member and Tiamak revered the doctor, so he had always done his best when someone in the league wanted information that only the little Wrannaman could provide. The drylanders didn't often need marsh-wisdom, Tiamak had noticed, but when they did—when, for instance, one of them needed a sample of twistgrass or Yellow Tinker, herbs not to be found in any drylander marketplace—they would scratch off a note to Tiamak quickly enough. Occasionally, as when he had arduously prepared a bestiary of marsh animals for Dinivan, complete with his own painstaking illustrations, or had studied and reported to old Jarnauga which rivers reached the Wran, and what happened when their fresh water met the salt of the Bay of Firannos, he would receive a long letter of gratitude from the recipient—in fact, Jarnauga's letter had so burdened its carrier that the pigeon's journey had taken twice the usual time. In these grateful letters, League members would occasionally hint that someday soon Tiamak might be officially counted in their number.

Little appreciated by his own villagefolk, Tiamak was terribly hungry for such recognition. He remembered his time in Perdruin, the hostility and suspicion he had felt from the other young scholars, who had been astonished to find a marsh lad in their midst. If not for Morgenes' kindness, he would have fled back to the swamps. Still, beneath Tiamak's diffident exterior, there was more than a trace of pride. Had he not, after all, been the first Wrannaman ever to leave the swamplands and study with the Aedonite brothers? Even his fellow villagers knew there was no other marsh-dweller like him. Thus, when he received encouraging words from Scrollbearers, he had sensed that his time was coming. Some day he would be a member of the League of the Scroll, the very highest of scholarly circles, and travel every three years to the home of one of the other members for a gathering—a gathering of equals. He would see the world and be a famously learned man ... or so he had often imagined.

When the hulking Rimmersman Isgrimnur came to *Pelippa's Bowl* and gave him the coveted Scrollbearer's pendant—the golden scroll and feather pen—Tiamak's heart had soared. All his sacrifices had been worth the reward! But a moment later Duke Isgrimnur had explained that the pendant came from Dinivan's dying hand, and when stunned Tiamak had asked about Morgenes, Isgrimnur gave him the shattering news that the doctor was dead, too, that he had died almost half a year ago.

A fortnight later, Isgrimnur still did not understand Tiamak's desperation. He seemed to think that although it was sad that the two men had died, Tiamak's brooding melancholy was extreme. But the Rimmersman had brought no new strategy, no useful advice; he was not, he admitted, even a member of the League! Isgrimnur did not seem to comprehend that this left Tiamak—who had waited many painful weeks for word of what Morgenes planned—terribly adrift, spinning like a flatboat in an eddy. Tiamak had sacrificed his duty to his people for a drylander errand—or so it sometimes seemed when he was angry enough to forget that it had been the crocodile attack that had forced him to give up his embassy to Nabban. In any case, he had clearly failed the people of Village Grove.

Tiamak did have to admit that at least Isgrimnur was paying for his room and board at a time when the Wrannaman's own credit had run out. That was something, anyway—but then again, it was only fair: the drylanders had made money from the sweat of the marshfolk for untold years. Tiamak himself had been threatened, chased, and abused in the markets of Ansis Pelippé.

Morgenes had rescued him then, but now Morgenes was dead. Tiamak's own people would never forgive him for failing them. And Isgrimnur was obsessed with old Ceallio the doorkeeper, who he claimed was the great knight Camaris; Isgrimnur no longer seemed to care whether the little marsh man was alive or dead. Taken all together, it was clear to Tiamak that he was now as useless as a crab with no legs.

He looked up, startled. He had wandered far away from *Pelippa's Bowl* into a section of Kwanitupul that he did not recognize. The water here was even grayer and greasier than usual, dotted with the corpses of fish and seabirds. The derelict buildings that overlooked the canals seemed almost to bend beneath the weight of centuries of grime and salt.

A dizzying sense of bleakness and loss swept over him. *He Who Always Steps on Sand, let me come safely back to my home again. Let my birds be alive. Let me . . .*

"*Marsh man!*" The braying voice interrupted his prayer. "*He's coming!*"

Startled, Tiamak looked around. Three young drylanders dressed in white Fire Dancer robes stood on the far side of the narrow canal. One of them pushed back his hood to display a partially shorn head, uncut tufts of hair still sticking up like weeds. His eyes, even from a distance, seemed wrong.

"He's coming!" this one shouted again, his voice cheerful, as though Tiamak were an old friend.

Tiamak knew who and what these men were; he wanted no part of their madness. He turned and limped back along the uneven walkway. The buildings he passed were boarded up, empty of life.

"Storm King's coming! He'll fix that leg!" On the far side of the canal, the three Fire Dancers had turned as well. They paced along directly across from Tiamak, matching him step for hobbling step, shouting as they walked. "Haven't you heard yet? Sick and the lame will be scourged! Fire burn 'em, ice bury 'em!"

Tiamak saw a gap in the long wall to his right. He turned into it, hoping it was not a dead end. The jeers of the Fire Dancers followed him.

"Where do you go, little brown man? When he comes, the Storm King will find you if you hide in the deepest hole or on the highest mountain! Come back and talk with us or we will come and get you!"

The doorway led into a large open court that might once have been a ship-building yard, but now contained only a few castoffs of its vanished owners, a litter of weather-twisted gray spars, splintered tool handles, and pieces of shattered crockery. The planks of the courtyard floor were so warped that when he looked down he could see long stripes of the muddy canal flowing beneath him.

Tiamak made his way carefully across the dubious flooring to a door on the far side of the yard, then out onto another walkway. The cries of the Fire Dancers grew fainter, but seemed nevertheless to become more fiercely angry as he quickly strode away.

For a Wrannaman, Tiamak was quite familiar with cities, but even the residents found it easy to get lost in Kwanitupul. Few of the buildings remained in use for long, or even remained standing; the small, select group of establishments that had existed as long as a century or two had also changed location a dozen times—the sea air and the murky water chewed away at paint and pilings alike. Nothing was permanent in Kwanitupul.

After walking for a while Tiamak began to recognize a few familiar landmarks—the rickety spire of crumbling Saint Rhiappa's, the bright but decaying paint of the Market Hall dome. As his nervousness about being lost and threatened receded, he began to ponder his dilemma once more. He was trapped in an unfriendly city. If he wished to make a living, he must sell his services as a scribe and translator. This would mean living near the marketplace, since evening business, especially the small transactions on which Tiamak made his livelihood, would never wait until daylight. If he did not work, he was dependent on the continuing charity of Duke Isgrimnur. Tiamak had no urge to suffer the hospitality of the dreadful Charystra a moment longer, and in an attempt to solve this very problem he had suggested to Isgrimnur that they all move closer to the market so Tiamak could earn money while the duke nursed the idiot doorkeeper. The Rimmersman, however, had been adamant. He was certain there was a good reason Dinivan had wanted them to wait at *Pelippa's Bowl*—although what that reason might be, he could not say. So, although Isgrimnur did not like the innkeeper any more than Tiamak did, he was not ready to leave.

Tiamak was also worried about whether he was actually a member of the League of the Scroll. He had apparently been chosen to join, but the members he knew personally were dead and he had heard nothing from any of the others for months. What was he supposed to do?

Last, but certainly not the least of his problems, he was having bad dreams. Or rather, he corrected himself, not *bad* dreams so much as odd ones. For the last several weeks, his sleep had been haunted by an apparition: no matter what he dreamed, whether it was of being chased by a crocodile with an eye in every one of its thousand teeth, or of eating a splendid meal of crab and bottomfish with his resurrected family in Village Grove, a ghostly child was present—a little dark-haired drylander girl who watched everything in utter silence. The child never interfered, whether the dream was frightening or enjoyable, and in fact seemed somehow even less real than the dreams themselves. Were it not for the constancy of her presence from dream to dream, he would have forgotten her entirely. Lately she seemed to be getting fainter each time she appeared, as though her image was receding into the murk of the dreamworld, her message still unvoiced. . . .

Tiamak looked up and saw the barge-loading dock. He remembered beyond doubt that he had passed it on his way out. Good. He was back on familiar territory.

So here was another mystery—who or what was this silent child? He tried to remember what Morgenes had told him of dreams and the Dream Road and what such an apparition might signify, but he could remember nothing useful. Perhaps she was a messenger from the land of the dead, a spirit sent by his late mother, wordlessly chastising him for his failure. . . .

"The little marsh man!"

Tiamak whirled to see the three Fire Dancers standing on the walkway a few paces behind him. This time, no canal separated them from him.

The leader stepped forward. His white robe was less than pristine, smeared with dirty handprints and splotches of tar, but his eyes were even more frightening than they had been at a distance, bright and burning as if with some inner light. His stare seemed almost to jump out of his face.

"You don't walk very fast, brown man." He grinned, showing crooked teeth. "Somebody bend your leg, yes? Bend it bad?"

Tiamak backed up a few steps. The three young men waited until he stopped, then slouched forward, casually regaining their proximity. It was clear that they were not going to let him walk away. Tiamak lowered his hand onto the hilt of his knife. The bright eyes widened, as though the slender marsh man proposed a newer and more interesting game.

"I have done nothing to you," Tiamak said.

The leader laughed soundlessly, skinning his lips back

and showing his red tongue like a dog. "*He* is coming, you know. You cannot run from Him."

"Does your Storm King send you to devil innocent strollers?" Tiamak tried to put strength in his voice. "I cannot believe that such a being would stoop so low." He gently eased the knife loose in its sheath.

The leader made a humorous face as he looked to his fellows. "Ah, he talks good for a little brown man, doesn't he?" He turned his gleaming eyes back on Tiamak. "The master wants to see who is fit, who is strong. It will go hard on the weak when He comes."

Tiamak began to walk backward, hoping either to reach a place where there might be others to help him—not very likely in this backwater section of Kwanitupul—or at least to find a spot where his back would be protected by a wall and where these three would not have such freedom of movement on either side of him. He prayed to They Who Watch and Shape that he would not stumble. He would have liked to be able to feel behind him with his hand, but knew he might need that arm to ward off the first blow and give himself a chance to draw his knife.

The three Fire Dancers followed him, each face as innocent of consideration as a crocodile's. In fact, Tiamak thought, trying to make himself brave, he had fought a crocodile and survived. These beasts were little different, except that the crocodile would at least have eaten him. The youths would kill him for pure pleasure, or for some warped idea of what their Storm King wanted. Even as he walked backward, locked in a strange death-dance with his persecutors, even as he desperately sought some place to make a stand, Tiamka could not help wondering how the name of a little-known demon legend from the North should these days be upon the lips of street bullies in Kwanitupul. Things had changed indeed since he had last left the swamps.

"Careful, little man." The leader looked past Tiamak. "You will fall in and drown."

Startled, Tiamak glanced backward over his shoulder, expecting to see the unfenced canal just behind him. When he realized instead that he was at the mouth of a

short alleyway, and that he had been tricked, he turned
back quickly to his pursuers, just in time to avoid the
hurtling downstroke of an iron-tipped cudgel which
crashed against the wooden wall beside him. Splinters
flew.

Tiamak pulled his knife free of the sheath and slashed
at the cudgel-wielding hand, missing but tearing the
sleeve of a white robe. Two Fire Dancers, one of them
waving a tattered sleeve in mockery, moved to either side
of him as the leader took up his own position directly in
front. Tiamak backed into the alley, waving his knife in
an attempt to keep all three at bay. The leader laughed as
he pulled his own cudgel out from beneath his robe. His
eyes were full of a terrifying, guiltless glee.

The youth on the left suddenly made a quiet sound and
disappeared back around the mouth of the alleyway onto
the walkway they had just deserted. Tiamak guessed that
he was serving as lookout while his friends finished with
their victim. An instant later the vanished youth's cudgel
reappeared without its owner, hurtling into the alleyway
and striking the Fire Dancer on Tiamak's right hand,
flinging him against the wall of the alleyway. His head
left a red smear down the planking as he crumpled into a
white-robed heap. As the shaven-headed leader stood,
staring in astonishment, a tall shape stepped into the alley
behind him, grasped him firmly around the neck and then
whipped him through the air and into the walkway railing, which shattered into flinders as though struck by a
catapult stone. The limp body sagged free of the remnants
of the walkway and tumbled into the canal; then, within
a long, silent moment, it sank out of sight in the oily water.

Tiamak discovered he was trembling uncontrollably
with excitement and terror. He looked up into the kind,
slightly confused face of Ceallio, the doorkeeper.

Camaris. The duke said he is Camaris, was Tiamak's
dazed thought. *A knight. Sworn to, sworn to . . . to save
the innocent.*

The old man laid his hand on Tiamak's shoulder and
led him back out of the alleyway.

*   *   *

That night the Wrannaman dreamed of white-shrouded figures with eyes that were flaming wheels. They came at him across the water like sails flapping. He was splashing in one of the sidestreams of the Wran, desperate to escape, but something held his leg. The more he struggled, the harder it became to keep afloat.

The little dark-haired girl watched him from the bank, solemn and silent. She seemed so faint this time that he could hardly see her, as though she were made of mist. Eventually, before the dream ended and he woke up gasping, she faded entirely.

Diawen the scryer had made her cave in the mountain's depths into something very much like the small house she had once inhabited on the outskirts of Hernysadharc, close by the Circoille fringe. The small cavern was closed off from its neighbors by woolen shawls hung across the doorway. When Maegwin gently tugged one of the curtaining shawls aside, a wave of sweetish smoke billowed out.

The dream of flickering lights had been so vivid and so obviously important that Maegwin had found it difficult to go about her business all morning. Although her people's needs were many, and she had done her best to satisfy them, she had moved all day in a kind of fog, far away in her heart and mind even as she touched the trembling hands of an old person or took one of the children in her arms.

Diawen had been a priestess of Mircha many years ago, but had broken her vows—no one knew why, or at least no one could say for certain, though speculation was constant—then left the Order to live by herself. She had a reputation as a madwoman, but was also known for true-telling, for dream-reading and healing. Many a troubled citizen of Hernysadharc, after leaving a bowl of fruit and a coin for Brynioch or Rhynn, waited until after dark and then went to Diawen for more immediate assistance.

Maegwin remembered seeing her once in the market near the Taig, her long, pale brown hair fluttering like a pennant. Maegwin's nurse had quickly pulled her away, as though even looking at Diawen might be dangerous.

So, faced with a powerful but confusing dream, and having made a grave mistake in her last interpretation, Maegwin had this time decided to seek help. If anyone would understand the things that were happening to her, she felt sure, it was Diawen.

For all the smoky haze that hung thick as Inniscrich fog, the inside of the scryer's cave was surprisingly neat. She had carefully arranged the few possessions saved from her home in Hernysadharc, a collection of shiny things that might have aroused the envy of a nesting magpie. Dozens of gleaming bead necklaces hung on the cave's rough walls and caught the light of the fire like dew-spotted spiderwebs. Small mounds of shiny baubles—mostly beads of metal and polished stone—were arranged on the flat rock that was Diawen's table. In various niches around the chamber stood the equally shiny tools of the scryer's craft, mirrors ranging in size from a serving tray to a thumbnail, made of polished metal or costly glass, some round, some square, some elliptical as a cat's eye. Maegwin was fascinated to see so many in one place. A child of a rustic court, where a lady's hand mirror was, after her reputation, perhaps her most cherished possession, she had never seen anything like it.

Diawen had been beautiful once, or so everyone always said. It was hard to tell now. The scryer's upturned brown eyes and wide mouth were set in a gaunt, weathered face. Her hair, still exceptionally long and full, had turned a very ordinary iron gray. Maegwin thought she looked like nothing more than a thin woman growing old fast.

Diawen smiled mockingly. "Ah, little Maegwin. Come for a love dram, have you? If it's the count you're after, you'll have to heat his blood first or the charm won't take. He's a careful one, he is."

Maegwin's initial surprise was quickly overtaken by shock and rage. How could this woman know of her feel-

ings for Eolair? Did everyone know? Was she the object
of laughter at every cookfire? For a moment, her deep
sense of responsibility for her father's subjects evaporated. Why should she fight to save such a pack of snig-
gering ingrates?

"Why do you say that?" she snapped. "What makes
you think I love anyone?"

Diawen laughed, untouched by Maegwin's anger. "I am
the one who knows. That is what I do, king's daughter."

For a long moment, her eyes smarting from the clinging smoke and her pride stinging from Diawen's bold as-
sessment, Maegwin wanted only to turn and leave. At
last, her sensible side took charge. There might be loose
talk about Lluth's daughter, certainly—as Old Craobhan
had pointed out, there always was. And Diawen was just
the type to prowl about listening for valuable castoffs—
useful little facts that, when polished up and then cunningly disclosed, would make her prophesying seem more
uncanny. But if Diawen was the type to rely on such
trickery, would she be any use to Maegwin's current
need?

As if sensing her thoughts, Diawen gestured for her to
take a seat on a smooth lump of stone covered with a
shawl and said: "I have heard talk, it's true. No magical
arts were needed to reveal your feelings for Count
Eolair—just seeing you together once taught me all I
needed to know. But there is more to Diawen than keen
ears and sharp eyes." She poked at the fire and set sparks
to hopping, unleashing another billow of yellowish
smoke, then turned a calculating look upon Maegwin.
"What do you want, then?"

When Maegwin told her that she wished the scryer's
help interpreting a dream, Diawen became quite business-
like. She refused Maegwin's offers of food or clothing.
"No, king's daughter," she said with a hard smile, "I will
help you now and you will owe me a favor. That will suit
me better. Agreed?"

After being assured that the favor was not to be repaid
with her firstborn son, or with her shadow, or soul, or
voice, or any other such thing, she consented.

"Do not fret," Diawen chuckled. "This is no fireplace tale. No, someday I will simply want help ... and you will give it. You are a child of Hern's House and I am only a poor scryer, yes? That is my reason."

Maegwin told Diawen the substance of the dream, and of the other strange things she had dreamed in the months before, as well as what had happened when she let the visions lead her down into the earth with Eolair.

The smoke in the little chamber was so thick that when she finished telling of Mezutu'a and its denizens, she had to step out past the hanging for a while to breathe. Her head had begun to feel very strange, as if it were floating free of her body, but a few moments out in the main cavern restored her to clear-mindedness.

"That story is almost payment enough, king's daughter," the scryer said when Maegwin returned. "I had heard the rumors, but did not know whether to believe them. The dwarrow-folk alive in the earth below us!" She made a strange hooking gesture with her fingers. "Of course, I have always thought there was something more to the Grianspog tunnels than just the dead past."

Maegwin frowned. "But what about my dream? About the 'high place'—about how the time has come."

Diawen nodded. The scryer crawled to the wall on her hands and knees. She ran her fingers over several of the mirrors, then at last selected one and brought it back to the fireside. It was small, set in a wooden frame gone nearly black from untold years of handling.

"My grandmother used to call this a 'wormglass,'" Diawen said, holding it out for Maegwin's inspection. It looked like a very ordinary mirror, the carving worn down until it was almost completely smooth.

"A wormglass? Why?"

The scryer shrugged her bony shoulders. "Perhaps in the days of Drochnathair and the other great worms, it was used to watch for their approach. Or perhaps it was made from the claws or the teeth of a worm." She grinned, as though to show that she herself, despite her livelihood, did not hold with such superstition. "Most likely the frame was once carved to look like a dragon. Still, it is a good tool." .

She held the mirror above the flames, moving it in slow circles for a long while. When at last she turned it upright once more, a thin film of soot covered its surface. Diawen held it up before Maegwin's face; the reflection was obscured, as though by fog. "Think of your dream, then blow."

Maegwin tried to fix in her mind the strange procession, the beautiful but alien figures. A tiny cloud of soot puffed from the mirror's face.

Diawen turned the glass around and studied it, biting her lower lip as she concentrated. With the firelight directly below her, her face seemed even thinner, almost skeletal. "It is strange," the scryer said finally. "I can see patterns, but they are all unfamiliar to me. It is as though someone is speaking loudly in a house nearby, but in a tongue I have never heard before." Her eyes narrowed. "Something is wrong, here, king's daughter. Are you sure this was your own dream and not one that someone told to you?" When Maegwin angrily reaffirmed her ownership, Diawen frowned. "I can tell you little, and nothing from the mirror."

"What does that mean?"

"The mirror is as good as silent. It is speaking, but I do not understand. So, then, I will release you from your promise to me, but I will also tell you something—give you my own advice." Her voice implied that this would be just as good as whatever the mirror might have told them. "If the gods truly mean for this to be made clear to you, do what they say." She briskly wiped the mirror clean with a white cloth and set it back into its niche in the cavern wall.

"What is that?"

Diawen pointed up, as though at the ceiling of the cave. "Go to the high place."

Maegwin felt her boots sliding on snow-slicked rock and flung out a gloved hand to catch a prong of stone beside the steep path. She bent her knees and edged her feet

under her body until she had regained her balance, then
stood straight once more, looking back down the white
hillside at the dangerous distance she had already
climbed. A slip here could easily topple her off the narrow path; after that, nothing would stop her tumble down
the slope but the tree trunks that would dash out her
brains long before she reached the bottom.

She stood panting, and found to her mild surprise that
she was not very frightened. Such a fall would certainly
end in death one way or another—either immediately, or
by leaving her crippled on a snowy mountain in the
Grianspog—but Maegwin was giving her life back into
the hands of the gods: what difference could it make if
they decided to take her now rather than later? Besides, it
was glorious to be out beneath the sky again, no matter
how cold and grim it might be.

She shuffled a little farther toward the outside edge of
the trail and turned her gaze upward. Almost half the
height of the hill still loomed between Maegwin and her
destination—Bradach Tor, which jutted from the pinnacle
like the prow of a stone ship, its underside blackly naked
of the snow that blanketed the slopes. If she went hard at
it, she should reach the summit before the weak morning
sun, which now shone full in her face, had climbed far
past noon.

Maegwin shouldered her pack and turned her attention
back to the path, noting with satisfaction that the fluttering snow had already erased most of the marks of her recent passage. At the base of the hill where she had begun,
the tracks had no doubt been completely obliterated. If
any of Skali's Rimmersmen came sniffing around this
part of the Grianspog, there would be no sign she had
been here. The gods were doing their share. That was a
good sign.

The steep path forced her to make most of the ascent
leaning forward, grasping at the handholds that presented
themselves. She felt a small, sour pride at the strength of
her body, at the way her muscles stretched and knotted,
pulling her up the slope just as swiftly as most men could
climb. Maegwin's height and strength had always been

more of a curse to her than a blessing. She knew how un-
womanly most thought her, and had spent most of her life
pretending not to care. But still, it was somehow very satisfying to feel her capable limbs work for her. Sadly, it
was her body itself that was the greatest impediment to
her given task. Maegwin felt sure she would be able to let
it go if she had to, although it would not be easy, but it
had been even harder to turn against Eolair, to pretend a
contempt for him that was the opposite of her feelings.
Still, she had done it, however sick it made her feel.
Sometimes doing the gods' bidding required a hardened
heart.

The climb did not get easier. The snowy path that she
followed was really little more than an animal track. In
many places it vanished altogether, forcing her to make
her way awkwardly over outcroppings of stone, trusting
tangles of leafless heather or the branches of wind-twisted
trees to hold her weight until she could haul herself up to
another area of relative safety.

She made several stops to catch her breath, or to
squeeze her sodden gloves dry and rub the feeling back
into her fingers. The clouded sun was well into the western sky by the time she clambered up the last rise and
found herself atop Bradach Tor. She scraped away snow,
then slumped down in a heap on the black, wind-polished
rock.

The forested skirts of the Grianspog spread below her.
Beyond the mountain's base, hidden from her eyes by
swirling snow, stood Hernysadharc, the ancestral home of
Maegwin's family. There, Skali the usurper strode the
oaken halls of the Taig and his reavers swaggered through
Hernysadharc's white-clad streets. Something had to be
done; apparently it was something only the daughter of
the king could do.

She did not rest long. The heat generated by her exertion was being rapidly sucked away by the wind, and she
was growing chilled. She emptied her pack, pouring all
the possessions she thought she would need in this world
onto the black stone. She wrapped herself in the heavy

blanket, trying not to dwell childishly on how the onset of
night might deepen the already unpleasant cold. Her
leather sack of flints and her striking stone she put to one
side: she would have to clamber back off the tor to find
some firewood.

Maegwin had brought no food, not only to show trust
in the gods, but also because she was tired of acceding to
her body's demands. The flesh she inhabited could not
live without meals, without love—in truth, it was the low
clay of which she was made that had confused her with
its constant need for food and warmth and the good will
of others. Now it was time to let such earthy things fall
away so that the gods could see her essence.

There were two articles nestled in the bottommost folds
of her sack. The first was a gift from her father, a carved
wooden nightingale, emblem of the goddess Mircha. One
day, when a younger Maegwin had cried inconsolably
over some childhood disappointment, King Lluth had
stood and plucked the graceful bird from the rafters of the
Taig where it hung among the myriad of other god-
carvings, then put it into her small hands. It was all that
she had left to remind her of how things had been, of
what had been lost. After pressing it for a moment against
her cold cheeks, she set it on a rounded outcropping of
stone where it rocked in the brisk wind.

The last treasure in the bag was the stone that Eolair
had given her, the dwarrow's gift. Maegwin frowned,
rolling the strange object between her palms. She had pretended that the reason she packed it was because she had
been holding it when she had the god-sent dream, but really she knew better. The count had given it to her, then
he had ridden away.

Tired and stupefied from her climb, Maegwin stared at
the stone and her name-rune until her head hurt. It was a
perfectly useless thing—her name given a sort of false
immortality, as much of a cheat as the great stone city beneath the ground. All things of the heavy earth were suspect, she now understood.

At the gods' own clear urging, she had come to this
high place. This time, Maegwin had decided, she would

let the gods do what they wished, not struggle to antici-
pate them. If they wanted to bring her to stand before
them, then she would plead for salvation of her folk and
the destruction of Skali and the High King, the bestial
pair who had brought such humiliation on a blameless
people; if the gods did not wish to help her, she would
die. But no matter the ultimate result, she would sit here
atop the tor until the gods made their wishes known.

"Brynioch Sky-lord!" she shouted into the wind.
"Mircha cloaked in rain! Murhagh Armless, and bold
Rhynn! I have heard your call! I await your judgment!"

Her words were swallowed up in gray and swirling
white.

Waiting, Miriamele fought against sleep, but Aspitis
hovered on the edge of wakefulness for a long time,
mumbling and shifting on the bed beside her. She found
it very hard to keep her own thoughts fixed. When the
knock came on her cabin door, she was floating in a sort
of a half-slumber, and did not at first realize what the
noise was.

The knock came again, a little louder. Startled,
Miriamele rolled over. *"Who is it?"* she hissed. It must be
Gan Itai, she decided—but what would the earl think
about the Niskie visiting Miriamele in her room? A second thought followed swiftly: she did not want Gan Itai to
see Aspitis here in her bed. Miriamele had no illusions
about what the Niskie knew, but even in her wretchedness
she wished to preserve some tiny fragments of self-
respect.

"Is the master there?" The voice, to both her shame and
relief, was male—one of the sailors.

Aspitis sat up in bed beside her. His lean body was unpleasantly warm against her skin. "What is it?" he asked,
yawning.

"Pardon, my lord. You're needed by the helmsman.
That is, he begs your pardon, and asks for you. He thinks
he sees storm signs. Odd ones."

The earl sagged onto his back once more. "By the Blessed Mother! What is the hour, man?"

"The Lobster's just gone over the horizon, Lord Aspitis. Mid-watch, four hours till dawn. Very sorry, my lord."

Aspitis swore again, then reached down to the cabin floor for his boots. Although he must have known that Miriamele was awake, he did not say a word to her. Miriamele saw the sailor's bearded face etched in lamplight when the door opened, then listened as the two sets of footsteps passed down the corridor to the deck ladder.

She lay in the darkness for dragging minutes, listening to her own heartbeat, which was louder than the still-becalmed ocean. It was plain that all the sailors knew where Aspitis was—they *expected* to find the earl in his doxy's bed! Shame choked her. For a moment she thought of poor Cadrach down in the shadowed hold. He was bound by iron chains, but were her own fetters any more comfortable for being invisible?

Miriamele could not imagine how she could ever again walk across the deck under the eyes of those grinning sailors—could not imagine it any more than she could imagine standing naked before them. It was one thing to be suspected, another to be part of the casual knowledge shared by the entire ship: when he was needed in the night watches, Aspitis could be found in her bed. This latest degradation seemed to creep over her like a heavy, numbing chill. How could she ever leave the cabin again? And even if she did, what did she have to look forward to in any case but a forced marriage to the golden-haired monstrosity? She would rather be dead.

In the dark, Miriamele made a small noise. Slowly, as if approaching a dangerous animal, she considered this last idea for a moment—it was stunning in its power, even as an unvoiced thought. She had promised herself that she could outlast anything, that she could float with any tide and lie happily beneath the sun on whatever beach received her—but was it true? Could she even marry Aspitis, who had made her his whore, who had aided in murdering her uncle and was a willing catspaw

of Pryrates? How could a girl—no, a woman now, she reflected ruefully—how could a woman with the blood of
Prester John in her veins allow such a thing to happen to
her?

But if the life that stretched before her was so unbear-
able that death seemed preferable, then she need be afraid
no longer. She could do anything.

Miriamele slipped from the bed. After dressing quickly,
she edged out into the narrow passageway.

Miriamele climbed the ladder as quietly as she could,
lifting her head above the hatchway just far enough to
make sure that Aspitis was still talking to the helmsman.
They seemed to be having a very animated discussion,
waving their lamps so that the flaming wicks left streaks
across the black sky. Miriamele dropped down to the passageway as quickly as she could. A kind of cold cleverness had come over her along with her new resolution,
and she moved quietly and surely along the corridor to
Aspitis' doorway. When she had slipped through the door
and closed it behind her, she took the hood off her lamp.

A quick examination of Aspitis' room turned up nothing useful. The earl's sword lay across his bed like some
heathen wedding token, a slim, beautifully wrought blade
with a hilt in the shape of a spread-winged seahawk. It
was the earl's favorite possession—except perhaps for
her, Miriamele thought grimly—but it was not what she
sought. She began to investigate a little more thoroughly,
checking the folds of all his clothing, rummaging through
the caskets in which he kept his jewelry and gaming-dice.
Although she knew that time was growing ever shorter,
she forced herself to refold each garment and lay it back
where it had been. It would do her cause no good to alert
Aspitis.

When she had finished, Miriamele stared around the
cabin in frustration, unwilling to believe that she could
simply fail. Abruptly, she remembered the chest into
which she had seen Aspitis pushing bags of money.
Where had that gone? She dropped down onto her knees
and pushed aside the bed's hanging coverlet. The chest
was there, draped by Aspitis' second-best cloak. Certain

that any moment the Earl of Eadne and Drina would walk
through the door, Miriamele forced herself under the bed
and dragged it out into the light, wincing at the loud
scraping as its metal corners cut into the plank floor.

The chest was, as she had seen, full of bags of money.
The coins were mostly silver, but each sack contained
more than a few gold Imperators as well. It was a small
fortune, but Miriamele knew that Aspitis and his family
were the possessors of a very large fortune beside which
this was a mere handful. She carefully lifted out a few of
the sacks, trying to keep them from jingling, noting with
some interest that her hands, which should have been
shaking, were as steady as stone. Hidden beneath the top
row of sacks was a leather-bound ledger. It contained lists
in Aspitis' surprisingly fastidious handwriting of places
the *Eadne Cloud* had stopped—Vinitta and Grenamman,
as well as other names that Miriamele decided must have
been ports visited on other voyages; beside each entry
was a line of cryptic markings. Miriamele could make no
sense of it, and after a moment's impatient study she put
it aside. Beneath the ledger, rolled into a bundle, was a
hooded robe of coarse white cloth—but this was not what
she was looking for either. The trunk contained no further
secrets, so she repacked it as well as she could, then
pushed it back beneath the bed.

Time was running short. Miriamele sat on the floor, full
of a dreadful, cold hatred. Perhaps it would be easiest just
to slip up on deck and throw herself into the ocean. It was
hours until dawn; no one would know where she had
gone until it was too late to stop her. But she thought of
the kilpa, patiently waiting, and could not imagine joining
them in the black seas.

As she stood, she saw it at last. It had been hanging on
a hook behind the door all along. She took it down and
slipped it into her belt beneath her cloak, then stepped
into the doorway. When she was certain that no one was
coming, she hooded her lamp and made her way back to
her own cabin.

Miriamele was crawling under her blanket when she
suddenly understood the significance of the white robe. In

her oddly detached state, this realization was only one more tally added to the earl's overloaded account, but it helped to stiffen her resolve. She lay unmoving, breathing quietly, waiting for Aspitis' return, her mind set on her course so firmly that she would not allow any thoughts to distract her—not memories of her childhood and her friends, not regrets about the places she would never see. Her ears brought her every creak of the ship's timbers and every slap of the waves on the hull, but as the trudging hours passed, his booted footsteps never sounded in the passageway. Her door did not creak open. Aspitis did not come.

At last, as dawn was glimmering in the sky above-decks, she fell into a heavy, muddy sleep with the earl's dagger still clutched in her fist.

She felt the hands that shook her, and heard the quiet voice, but her mind did not want to return to the waking world.

"Girl, wake up!"

At last, groaning, Miriamele rolled over and opened her eyes. Gan Itai peered down at her, a look of concern furrowing her already wrinkled brow. Morning light from the hatch in the passageway outside spilled in through the open door. The achingly painful memories of the day before, absent for the first few moments, rolled back over her.

"Go away," she told the Niskie. She tried to push her head back under the blanket, but Gan Itai's strong hands clutched her and pulled her upright.

"What is this I hear on deck? The sailors are saying that Earl Aspitis is to be married on Spenit—married to you! Is that true?"

Miriamele covered her eyes with her hands, trying to keep out the light. "Has the wind come up?"

Gan Itai's voice was puzzled. "No, we are still becalmed. Why do you ask such a strange question?"

"Because if we can't get there, he can't marry me," Miriamele whispered.

The Niskie shook her head. "By the Uncharted, then it is true! Oh, girl, this is not what you want, is it?"

Miriamele opened her eyes. "I would rather be dead."

Gan Itai made a little humming noise of dismay. She helped Miriamele to get her feet out of bed and onto the floor, then brought over the small mirror that Aspitis had given to Miriamele when he had still been pretending kindness.

"Do you not wish to brush your hair straight?" the Niskie asked. "It looks rumpled and windblown, and that is not how you like it, I think."

"I don't care," she said, but the look on Gan Itai's face touched her: the sea-watcher could think of no other way to help. She reached out her hand for the mirror. The hilt of Aspitis' dagger, which had been covered in the folds of blanket, caught in her sleeve and clattered onto the floor. Both Miriamele and the old Niskie stared at it for a moment. Suddenly, chillingly, Miriamele saw her one door of escape closing. She leaped from the bed to grab it, but Gan Itai had bent first. The Niskie held it up to the light, a look of surprise in her gold-flecked eyes.

"Give it to me," said Miriamele.

Gan Itai gazed at the silver osprey carved so that it seemed to be alighting on the dagger's pommel. "This is the earl's knife."

"He left it here," she lied. "Give it to me."

The Niskie turned to her, solemn-faced. "He did not leave it here. He only wears this with his best clothes, and I saw how he was dressed when he came on deck in the night. In any case, he was wearing his other dagger on his belt."

"He gave it to me as a present, a gift. . . ." Abruptly, she burst into tears, great convulsive sobs that shook her whole body. Gan Itai jumped up in alarm and pushed the cabin door shut.

"I hate him!" Miriamele moaned, rocking from side to side. Gan Itai curled a thin dry arm around her shoulders. "I hate him!"

"What are you doing with his knife?" When she received no answer, she asked again. "Tell me, girl."

"I'm going to kill him." Miriamele found strength in saying it; for a moment, her tears subsided. "I'm going to stab that whoremongering beast, and then I won't care what happens."

"No, no, this is madness," the Niskie said, frowning.

"He knows who I am, Gan Itai." Miriamele gulped air. It was hard to speak. "He knows I am the princess, and he says he will marry me . . . so he can be master of Nabban when my father has conquered all the world." The idea seemed unreal, yet what could prevent it from happening? "Aspitis helped kill my uncle Leobardis, too. And he is giving money to the Fire Dancers."

"What do you mean?" Gan Itai's eyes were intent. "The Fire Dancers, they are madmen."

"Maybe, but he has a chest filled with sacks of silver and gold, and there is a book that lists payments made. He also has a Fire Dancer's robe rolled up and hidden away. Aspitis would never wear such a coarse weave." It had been so clear, suddenly, so laughably obvious: Aspitis would die before wearing something so common . . . unless there was a reason. And to think she had once been impressed by his beautiful clothes! "I am certain he goes among them. Cadrach said that he does Pryrates' bidding."

Gan Itai lifted her arm from Miriamele's shoulder and sat back against the wall. In the silence, the sound of men moving about on deck drifted down through the cabin ceiling. "The Fire Dancers burned down part of Niskietown in Nabban," the old woman said slowly. "They wedged doors shut, with children and old ones inside. They have burned and slaughtered in other places where my people live, too. And the Duke of Nabban and other men do nothing. Nothing." She ran her hand through her hair. "The Fire Dancers always claim some reason, but in truth there never is a reason, just love of other folks' suffering. Now you say that my ship's master is bringing them gold."

"It doesn't matter. He'll be dead before landfall."

Gan Itai shook her head in what looked like astonishment. "Our old masters put Ruyan the Navigator into

chains. Our new masters burn our children, and ravage
and kill their own young as well." She put a cool hand on
Miriamele's arm and left it there for a long time. Her up-
turned eyes narrowed in thought. "Hide the knife," she
said at last. "Do not use it until I speak to you again."

"But . . ." Miriamele began. Gan Itai squeezed hard.

"No," the Niskie said harshly. "Wait! You must wait!"
She stood and walked out of the room. When the door
shut behind her, Miriamele was left alone, tears drying on
her cheeks.

5

Wasteland of Dreams

❦

The sky was filled with swirling streamers of gray. A thicker knot of clouds loomed like an upraised fist on the distant northern horizon, angry purple and black.

The weather had gone bitterly cold again. Simon was very grateful for his thick new wool shirt. It had been a present from a thin New Gadrinsett girl, one of the two young women who had attached themselves to him at his knighthood feast. When the girl and her mother had come to bestow the gift, Simon had been properly polite and thankful as he imagined a knight should be. He just hoped they didn't think he was going to marry the girl or something. He had met her half a dozen times now, but she had still said scarcely anything to him, although she giggled a lot. It was nice to be admired, Simon had decided, but he couldn't help wishing that someone was doing the admiring besides this silly girl and her equally silly friend. Still, the shirt was well-made and warm.

"Come, Sir Knight," Sludig said, "are you going to use that stick, or are we going to give up for the day? I'm as tired and frozen as you are."

Simon looked up. "Sorry. Just thinking. It *is* cold, isn't it?"

"It is seeming our short taste of summer has come to its ending," Binabik called from his seat on a fallen pillar. They were in the middle of the Fire Garden, with no shelter from the brisk, icy wind.

"Summer!?" Sludig snorted. "Because it stopped

snowing for a fortnight? There is still ice in my beard every morning."

"It has been, in any case, an improvement of weather over what we were suffering before," said Binabik serenely. He tossed another pebble at Qantaqa, who was curled in a furry loop on the ground a few steps away. She peered at him sideways, but then, apparently deciding that an occasional pebble was not worth the trouble of getting up and biting her master, closed her yellow eyes once more. Jeremias, who sat beside the troll, watched the wolf apprehensively.

Simon picked up his wooden practice sword once more and moved forward across the tiles. Although Sludig was still unwilling to use real blades, he had helped Simon lash bits of stone to the wooden ones so that they were more truly weighted. Simon hefted his carefully, trying to find the balance. "Come on, then," he said.

The Rimmersman waded forward against the surging wind, heavy tunic flapping, and brought his sword around in a surprisingly quick two-handed swipe. Simon stepped to one side, deflecting Sludig's blow upward, then returned his own counterstroke. Sludig blocked him; the echo of wood smacking wood floated across the tiles.

They practiced on for most of an hour as the shrouded sun passed overhead. Simon was finally beginning to feel comfortable with a sword in his hand: his weapon often felt as though it were part of his arm, as Sludig was always saying it should. It was mostly a question of balance, he now realized—not just swinging a heavy object, but moving with it, letting his legs and back supply the force and letting his own momentum carry him through into the next defensive position, rather than flailing at his opponent and then leaping away again.

As they sparred, he thought of shent, the intricate game of the Sithi, with its feints and puzzling strikes, and wondered if the same things might work in swordplay. He allowed his next few strokes to carry him farther and farther off-balance, until Sludig could not help but notice; then, when the Rimmersman swept in on the heels of one of Simon's flailing misses with the aim of catching him leaning too far and smacking him along the ribs, Simon let his swing carry him all the way forward into a tumbling roll. The Rimmersman's wooden sword hissed over him. Simon then righted himself and whacked Sludig neatly on the side of his knee. The northerner dropped his blade and hopped up and down, cursing.

"*Ummu Bok!* Very good, Simon!" Binabik shouted. "A surprising movement." Beside him, Jeremias was grinning.

"That hurt." Sludig rubbed his leg. "But it was a clever thought. Let us stop before our fingers are too numb to hold the hilts."

Simon was very pleased with himself. "Would that work in a real battle, Sludig?"

"Perhaps. Perhaps not if you are wearing armor. Then you might go down like a turtle and not be able to get up in time. Be very sure before you ever leave your feet, or you will be more dead than you are clever. Still, it was well done." He straightened up. "The blood is freezing in my veins. Let us go down to the forges and warm up."

Freosel, New Gadrinsett's young constable, had put several of the settlers to work building a smithy in one of the airier caves. They had taken to the task briskly and efficiently, and were now melting down what little scrap metal could be found on Sesuad'ra, hoping to forge new weapons and repair the old ones.

"The forges, for warming," Binabik agreed. He clicked his tongue at Qantaqa, who rose and stretched.

As they walked, shy Jeremias dropped behind until he trailed them by several paces. The wind blew cuttingly across the Fire Gardens, and the sweat on the back of Simon's neck was icy. He found his buoyant mood settling somewhat. "Binabik," he asked suddenly, "why couldn't we go to Hernystir with Count Eolair and Isorn?" That pair had departed the previous day in the gray of early morning, accompanied by a small honor guard made up mostly of Thrithings horsemen.

"I am thinking that the reasons Josua gave you were true ones," Binabik replied. "It is not good for the same people always to be having the risks—or gaining the glories." He made a wry face. "There will be enough for all to do in coming days."

"But we brought him Thorn. Why shouldn't we try to at least get Minneyar as well—or Bright-Nail, rather?"

"Just because you are a knight, boy, does not mean you will have your way all the time," Sludig snarled. "Count your good fortunes and be content. Content and quiet."

Taken by surprise, Simon turned to the Rimmersman. "You sound angry."

Sludig looked away. "Not me. I am only a soldier."

"And not a knight." Simon thought he understood. "But you know why that is, Sludig. Josua is not king. He can only knight his own Erkynlanders. You are Duke Isgrimnur's man. I'm sure he will honor you when he returns."

"*If* he returns." There was bitterness in Sludig's voice. "I am tired of talking about this."

Simon thought carefully before speaking. "We all know what part you played, Sludig. Josua told everyone—but Binabik and I were there and we will *never* forget." He touched the Rimmersman's arm. "Please don't be angry with me. Even if I am a knight, I am still the same mooncalf you've been teaching how to swing a sword. I am still your friend."

Sludig peered at him for a moment from beneath bushy yellow brows. "Enough," he said. "You are a mooncalf indeed, and I need something to drink."

"And a warm fire." Simon tried not to smile.

Binabik, who had listened to the exchange in silence, nodded solemnly.

Geloë was waiting for them at the edge of the Fire Garden. She was bundled up against the cold, a scarf wrapped about her face so that only her round yellow eyes showed. She raised a chill-reddened hand as they approached.

"Binabik. I wish you and Simon to join me just before sundown, at the Observatory." She gestured to the ruined shell several hundred paces to the west. "I need your assistance."

"Help from a magical troll and a dragon-slaying knight." Sludig's smile was not entirely convincing.

Geloë turned her raptor's stare on him. "It is no honor. Besides, Rimmersman, even if you could, I don't think you would wish to walk the Road of Dreams. Not now."

"The Dream Road?" Simon was startled. "Why?"

The witch woman waved toward the ugly boil of clouds in the northern sky. "Another storm is coming. Besides wind and snow, it will also bring closer the mind and hand of our enemy. The dream-path grows ever riskier and soon may be impossible." She tucked her hands back beneath her cloak. "We must use the time we have." Geloë turned and walked away toward the ocean of rippling tents. "Sundown!" she called.

"Ah," said Binabik after a moment's silence. "Still, there is time for the wine and the hand-warming we were discussing. Let us go to the forges with haste." He started away. Qantaqa bounded after him.

Jeremias said something that could not be heard over the rising voice of the wind. Simon stopped to let him catch up.

"What?"

The squire bobbed his head. "I said that Leleth wasn't with her. When Geloë goes out to walk, Leleth always walks with her. I hope she's well."

Simon shrugged. "Let's go and get warm."

They hurried after the retreating forms of Binabik and Sludig. Far ahead, Qantaqa was a gray shadow in the waving grass.

Simon and Binabik stepped through the doorway into the lamplit Observatory. Beyond the sundered roof, twilight made the sky seem a bowl of blue glass. Geloë was absent, but the Observatory was not empty: Leleth sat on a length of crumbled pillar, her thin legs drawn up beneath her. She did not even turn her head at their entrance. The child was usually withdrawn, but there was something about the quality of her stillness that alarmed Simon. He approached and spoke her name softly, but although her eyes were open, fixed on the sky overhead, she had the slack muscles and slow breath of one who slept.

"Do you think she's sick?" Simon asked. "Maybe that's why Geloë asked us to come." Despite worry over Leleth, he felt a glimmering of relief: thoughts of traveling the Dream Road made him anxious. Even though he had reached the safety of Sesuad'ra, his dreams had continued to be vivid and unsettling.

The troll felt the child's warm hand, then let it drop back into her lap. "Little there is that we could do for her that Geloë could not be doing better. We will wait with patientness." He turned and looked around the wide, circular hall. "I am thinking this was a very beautiful place once. My people have long been carving into the living mountain, but we are having not a tenth of the skill the Sithi had."

The reference to Jiriki's people as though they were a vanished race bothered Simon, but he was not yet ready to give up the subject of Leleth's well-being. "Are you sure we shouldn't get something for her? Perhaps a cloak? It's so cold."

"Leleth will be well," said Geloë from the doorway. Simon jumped guiltily, as if he had been plotting treason. "She is only traveling a little way on the Dream Road without us. She is happiest there, I think."

She strode forward into the room. Father Strangyeard appeared behind her. "Hello, Simon, Binabik," the priest said. His face was as happy and excited as a child's at Aedontide. "I'm going to go with you. Dreaming, I mean. On the Dream Road. I have read of it, of course—it has long fascinated me—but I never imagined . . ." He waggled his fingers as if to demonstrate the delightful unlikeliness of it all.

"It is not a day of berry-picking, Strangyeard," Geloë said crossly. "But since you are a Scrollbearer now, it is good that you learn some of the few Arts left to us."

"Of course it is not—I mean, of course it *is* good to learn. But berry-picking, no—I mean . . . oh." Defeated, Strangyeard fell silent.

"Now I am knowing why Strangyeard joins us,"

Binabik said. "And I may be good for helping, too. But why Simon, Valada Geloë? And why here?"

The witch woman passed her hand briefly through Leleth's hair, eliciting no response from the child, then sat down on the pillar beside her. "As to the first, it is because I have a special need, and Simon perhaps can help. But let me explain all, so no mistakes will be made." She waited until the others had seated themselves around her. "I told you that another great storm is coming. The Road of Dreams will be difficult to walk, if not impossible. There are other things coming, too." She held up her hand to forestall Simon's question. "I cannot say more. Not until I speak to Josua. My birds have brought news to me—but even they will go to their hiding places when the storm comes. Then we atop this rock will be blind."

As she spoke, she deftly built a small pile of sticks on the stone floor, then lit it with a twig she had set aflame from one of the lamps. She reached into her cloak pocket and produced a small sack. "So," she continued, "while we can, we will make a last try to gather those who may be useful to us, or who need the shelter we can give. I have brought you here because it is the best spot. The Sithi themselves chose it when they spoke with each other over great distance, using, as the old lore says, 'Stones and Scales, Pools and Pryes'—what they called their Witnesses." She poured a handful of herbs from the sack, weighing them on her palm. "That is why I named this place the 'Observatory.' As clerics in the observatories of the old Imperium once watched the stars from theirs, so the Sithi once came to this place to look over their empire of Osten Ard. This is a powerful spot for seeing."

Simon knew more than a little about the Witnesses—he had summoned Aditu with Jiriki's mirror, and had seen Amerasu's disastrous use of the Mist Lamp. He suddenly remembered his dream from the night of his vigil—the torchlit procession, the Sithi and their strange ceremony. Could the nature of this place have something to do with his clear, strong vision of the past?

"Binabik," Geloë said, "you may have heard of

Tiamak, a Wrannaman befriended by Morgenes. He sent messages sometimes to your master Ookekuq, I think." The troll nodded. "Dinivan of Nabban also knew Tiamak. He told me that he had instigated some well-meaning plan, and had drawn the Wrannaman into it." Geloë frowned. "I never found out what it was. Now that Dinivan is dead, I fear the marsh man is lost and without friends. Leleth and I have tried to reach him, but have not quite managed. The Dream Road is very treacherous these days."

She reached across the pillar and lifted a small jar of water from the rubble-strewn floor. "So I hope your added strength will help us find Tiamak. We will tell him to come to us if he needs protection. Also, I have promised Josua that I will try to reach Miriamele once more. That has been even stranger—there is some veil over her, some shadow that prevents me from finding her. You were close to her, Simon. Perhaps that bond will help us finally to break through."

Miriamele. Her name sent a rush of powerful feelings through Simon—hope, affection, bitterness. He had been angry and disappointed to discover that she was not at Sesuad'ra. In the back of his mind he had been somehow certain that if he won through to the Stone of Farewell she would be there to welcome him; her absence seemed like desertion. He had been frightened, too, when he discovered that she had vanished with only the thief Cadrach for company.

"I will help any way I can," he said.

"Good." Geloë stood, rubbing her hands on her breeches. "Here, Strangyeard, I will show you how to mix the mockfoil and nightshade. Does your religion forbid this?"

The priest shrugged helplessly. "I don't know. It might ... that is, these are strange days."

"Indeed." The witch woman grinned. "Come, then, I will show you. Consider it a history lesson, if you wish."

Simon and Binabik sat quietly while Geloë demonstrated the proportions for the fascinated archivist.

"This is the last of these plants until we leave this

rock," she said when they had finished. "Another encouragement to succeed this time. Here." She dabbed a little on Simon's palms, forehead, and lips, then did the same for Strangyeard and Binabik before setting down the pot. Simon felt the paste grow chill against his skin.

"But what about you and Leleth?" Simon asked.

"I can get by without it. Leleth has never needed it. Now, sit and clasp hands. Remember, the Road of Dreams is strange these days. Do not be frightened, but keep your wits about you."

They put one of the lamps on the floor and sat in a circle beside the crumbling pillar. Simon clutched Binabik's small hand on one side and Leleth's equally small hand on the other. A smile spread slowly across the little girl's face, the blind smile of someone who dreams of happy surprises.

The icy sensation spread up Simon's arms and all through him, filling his head with a kind of fog. Although twilight should still have been clinging overhead, the room swiftly grew dark. Soon Simon could see nothing but the wavering orange tongues of the fire, then even that light passed into blackness . . . and Simon fell through.

Beyond the black all was a universal, misty gray—a sea of nothingness with no top or bottom. Out of that formless void a shape slowly began to coalesce, a small, swift-moving figure that darted like a sparrow. It took only a moment before he recognized Leleth—but this was a dream-Leleth, a Leleth who whirled and spun, her dark hair flying in an unfelt wind. Although he could hear nothing, he saw her mouth curl in delighted laughter as she beckoned him forward; even her eyes seemed alive in a way he had never seen. This was the little girl he had never met—the child who, in some inexplicable way, had not survived the mauling jaws of the Stormspike Pack. Here she was alive again, freed from the terrors of the waking world and from her own scarred body. His heart soared to watch her unfettered dance.

Leleth swept along before him, beckoning, silently pleading with him to hurry, to follow her, to follow! Simon tried, but in this gray dream place it was he who was lamed and lagging. Leleth's small form quickly quickly became indistinct, then vanished into the undending grayness. His dream-self felt a kind of warmth disappear with her. Suddenly, he was alone again and drifting.

What might have been a long time passed. Simon floated without purchase until something tugged at him with gentle, invisible fingers. He felt himself pulled forward, gradually at first, then with growing speed; he was still unbodied, but nevertheless caught up by some incomprehensible current. A new shape began to form out of the emptiness before him—a dark tower of unstable shadow, a black vortex shot through with red sparks, like a whirlpool of smoke and fire. Simon felt himself drawn toward it even more swiftly and was suddenly fearful. Death lay in that whirling dark—death or something worse. Panic welled up in him, stronger than he had imagined it could be. He forced himself to remember that this was a dream, not a place. He did not have to dream this dream if he did not want it. A part of him remembered that at this very moment, in some other place, he was holding the hands of friends. . . .

As he thought of them, they were there with him, invisible but present. He gained a little strength and was able to halt his slide inward toward the boiling, sparking blackness. Then, bit by bit, he pulled himself away, his dream-self somehow swimming against the current. As he put distance between himself and the black roil, the whirlpool abruptly fell in upon itself and he was free and sailing into some new place. The grayness was placid here, and there was a different quality to the light, as though the sun burned behind thick clouds.

Leleth was there before him. She smiled at his arrival, at the pleasure of having him with her in this place— although Simon knew now beyond a doubt that he could never share all she experienced.

The formlessness of the dream began to change; Simon felt as though he hovered above something much like the waking world. A shadowed city lay below him, a vast tract of structures formed from a haphazard collection of unlikely things—wagon wheels, children's toys, statues of unfamiliar animals, even toppled siege-towers from some long-ago war. The haphazard streets between the madly unlikely buildings were full of scurrying lights. As he stared down, Simon felt himself drawn toward one particular building, a towering structure made entirely of books and yellowing scrolls, which seemed ready at any moment to collapse into a rubbish heap of old parchment. Leleth, who had been moving around him in circles, swift as a bumblebee, now whirled down toward a gleaming window in the book-tower.

Upon a bed lay a figure. Its shape was unclear, as something seen through deep water. Leleth spread her thin arms above the bed and the dark shape tossed in uneasy sleep.

"Tiamak," said Leleth—but it was Geloë's voice, and it contained traces of his other companions' voices as well. *"Tiamak! Wake to us!"*

The shape on the bed moved more fitfully, then slowly sat up. The figure seemed to ripple, and the sense of being underwater was strengthened. Simon thought he heard it speak, but the voice at first was wordless.

". . . . . ??"

"It is Geloë, Tiamak—Geloë of the Aldeheorte Forest. I want you to come and join me and others at Sesuad'ra. You will be safe there."

The figure rippled again. *". . . .dreaming? . . ."*

"Yes—but it is a true dream. Come to the Stone of Farewell. It is hard to speak to you. Here is how you can find it." Leleth stretched her arms over the shadowy figure once more, and this time a blurry image of the Stone began to form.

". . . Dinivan . . . wanted . . ."

"I know. All is changed now. If you need refuge, come to Sesuad'ra." Leleth lowered her hands and the wavering picture was gone. The form on the bed also began to fade.

". . . ! . . ." It was trying to tell some urgent thing, but it was rapidly vanishing into mist, even as the tower in which it lay and the surrounding city were vanishing, too.

"*. . . from the North . . . grim . . . found the old night . . .*"
There was a lag, then a last heroic effort. "*. . . Nisses'
book . . .*"

The dream-shadow vanished and all was murky gray
once more.

As the intangible mist surrounded him once more, Simon's thoughts turned to Miriamele. Surely, since they
had somehow reached Tiamak, Geloë would now turn her
attention to the missing princess. And indeed, even as
Miriamele's image came to his mind—he saw her as she
had been in Geloë's house, dressed in boy's clothing, hair
blackened and close-shorn—that very picture began to
form in the nothingness before him. Miriamele shimmered for a moment—he thought her hair might have
turned gold, its natural hue—then it dissolved into something else. A tree? A tower? Simon felt a sense of cold
foreboding. He had seen a tower in many dreams, and it
never seemed to signify anything good. But no, this was
more than one tall shape. Trees? A forest?

Even as he strained to make the image clearer, the
shadowy vision began to coalesce, until he at last could
see that it was a ship, as blurry and imprecise as had been
the dream-Tiamak in his parchment tower. The tall masts
were hung with lank sails and fluttering ropes, all made
from cobwebs, gray and dusty and tattered. The ship
rocked as though in a great wind. The black waters beneath were studded with glowing whitecaps, and the sky
overhead was just as black. Some force pushed at Simon,
holding him away from the vessel despite his desperation
to approach. He fought hard against it. Miriamele might
be there!

Exerting his will to the utmost, Simon tried to force
himself nearer to the ghostly ship, but a great dark curtain
swept before him, a storm of rain and mist so thick as to
be almost solid. He stopped, lost and helpless. Leleth was
suddenly beside him, her smile gone, her small face set in
a grimace of effort.

Miriamele! Simon cried. His voice pealed out—not
from his own, but from Leleth's mouth. *Miriamele!* he
shouted again. Leleth forced herself a little nearer to the

phantom, as though carrying his words as close as she could before they spilled from her mouth. *Miriamele, come to the Stone of Farewell!*

The boat had now vanished entirely and the storm was spreading to cover all the black sea. At its heart, Simon thought he saw jumping arcs of red light like those that had pierced the great whirlpool. What did this mean? Was Miriamele somehow endangered? Were her dreams invaded? He forced himself to a final effort, pushing hard against the swirling dream-storm, but to no avail. The ship was gone. The storm itself had completely surrounded him. It growled and hummed through his very being like the tolling of huge brazen bells, shaking him so powerfully that he thought he could feel himself breaking apart. Now Leleth was gone, too. The spark-shot blackness held him like an inky fist, and he suddenly thought that he would die here, in this place that was no place.

A patch of light appeared in the distance, small and gray as a tarnished silver coin. He moved toward it as the blackness battered him and the red sparks sizzled through him like tiny lances of fire. He tried to feel his friends' hands but could not. The gray seemed to be no closer. He was tiring, as would a swimmer far out at sea.

Binabik, help me! he thought, but his friends were lost beyond the unending blackness. *Help me!* Even the tiny spot of gray was fading. *Miriamele,* he thought, *I wanted to see you again. . . .*

He reached for the spot of light one last time and felt a touch, as of a fingertip pressing his, although he had no hands to touch or be touched. A little strength came, and he slipped closer to the gray . . . closer, with black all around . . . closer. . . .

Deornoth thought that in different circumstances, he would have laughed. To see Josua sitting, listening with such rapt and respectful attention to this unusual pair of counselors—a hawk-faced woman with mannish hair and man's clothing, and a waist-high troll—was to see the upside-down world personified.

"So what do you hope that this Tiamak will bring, Valada Geloë?" the prince asked. He moved the lamp closer. "If he is another wise one like Morgenes and yourself, I am sure we will welcome him."

The witch woman shook her head. "He is not a wielder of the Art, Josua, and he is certainly not a planner of wars. In truth, he is a shy little man from the swamp who knows much about herbs that grow in the Wran. No, I have tried to call him here only because he was close to the League, and because I fear for him. Dinivan had some plan to use him, but Dinivan is dead. Tiamak should not be abandoned. Before the storm arrives, we must save all we can."

Josua nodded his head, but without much enthusiasm. Beside him, Vorzheva looked no happier. Deornoth thought that the prince's wife might resent any more responsibilities being piled on her husband's shoulders, even one very small responsibility from the marsh country.

"Thank you for that, Geloë," he said. "And thank you for trying again to reach my niece Miriamele. I grow increasingly worried for her."

"It is strange," the witch woman replied. "There is something odd there, something I cannot make sense of. It is almost as though Miriamele has erected some barrier to us, but she has no such talents. I am puzzled." She straightened, as if dismissing a useless thought. "But there is more to tell you."

Binabik had been shifting from foot to foot. Before Geloë could continue, he touched her arm. "Forgive me, but I should be looking to Simon, to make sure the unpleasantness of the Dream Road has left him and that he is resting well."

Geloë almost smiled. "You and I can speak later."

"Go, Binabik," urged Josua. "I will go to him later myself. He is a brave boy, although perhaps a bit overeager."

The troll bowed low and trotted out through the tent's door flap.

"I wish my other news was good, Prince Josua," Geloë said, "but the birds have brought me worrisome tidings. There is a large force of armored men coming toward us from the west."

"What?" Josua sat up, startled. Beside him, Vorzheva draped her hands protectively across her belly. "I don't understand. Who has sent you this message?"

The witch woman shook her head. "I do not mean birds like Jarnauga's, who carry little scraps of parchment. I mean the birds of the sky. I can speak with them . . . somewhat. Enough to understand the sense of things. There is a small army on the march from the Hayholt. They have ridden through the valley towns of Hasu Vale and are now following the southern border of the great forest toward the grasslands."

Deornoth stared at her. When he spoke, his voice sounded weak and querulous, even to his own ears. "You talk with *birds?*"

Geloë turned a sharp glance on him. "Your life may have been saved by it. How do you think I knew to come to you on the banks of the Stefflod, when you would have fought Hotvig's men in the dark? And how do you think I found you in the first place in all the vastness of Aldheorte?"

Josua had laid his hand on Vorzheva's shoulder as if to soothe her, although she looked quite calm. When he spoke, his voice was unusually harsh. "Why have you not told us of this before, Geloë? What other information could we have had?"

The forest woman seemed to suppress a sharp reply. "I have shared everything vital. There has been precious little to share during this yearlong winter. Most of the birds are dead, or hiding from the cold—certainly not flying. Also, do not misunderstand: I cannot talk to them as you and I are speaking now. Their thoughts are not people's thoughts, and words do not always fit them, nor can I always understand. Weather they understand, and fear, but those signs have been clear enough for us to read ourselves. Beyond that, it is only something as plain as a large body of men on foot and horseback that can even catch their attention. Unless some man is hunting them, they think very little about us."

Deornoth realized he was staring and looked away. He thought she did more than just talk with birds—he remembered the winged thing that had struck at him in the copse above the Stefflod—but he knew it was foolish to bring it up. It was more than foolish, he decided suddenly, it was rude. Geloë had been a loyal ally and helpful friend. Why did he begrudge her the secrets on which her life was plainly founded?

"I think Valada Geloë is correct, sire," he said quietly. "She has proven time and again that she is a valuable ally. What is important now is the news she brings."

Josua stared at him for a moment, then nodded once in assent. "Very well, Geloë, have your winged friends any idea how many men are coming, and how fast?"

She thought for a moment. "I would say the number is somewhere in the hundreds, Josua, although that is a guess. Birds do not count as we do, either. As for when they will be here, they seem to be traveling without hurry, but still, I should not be surprised to see them inside a month."

"Aedon's Blood," Josua swore. "It is Guthwulf and the Erkynguard, that would be my wager. So little time. I had hoped we might have until the coming spring to prepare." He looked up. "Are you sure they come here?"

"No," said Geloë simply. "But where else?"

For Deornoth, the fear this announcement brought was almost overwhelmed by a surprising sense of relief. It was not what they had wanted, not so soon, but the situation was by no means hopeless. Despite their own scant numbers, as long as they held this eminently defensible rock entirely surrounded by water, there was at least a small chance they could fight off a besieging force. And it would be the first chance to strike back at Elias since the destruction of Naglimund. Deornoth felt the knife-edge of violence pressing against him. It would not be entirely bad to simplify the world, since there seemed to be

TO GREEN ANGEL TOWER 171

no other choice. What was it that Einskaldir used to say? *"Fight and live, fight and die, God waits for all."* Yes, that was it. Simple.

"So," Josua said finally. "Caught between a bitter new storm and my brother's army." He shook his head. "We must defend ourselves, that is all. So soon after we have found this place of refuge, we must fight and die again." He stood up, then turned and bent to kiss his wife.

"Where are you going?" Vorzheva raised a hand to touch his cheek, but did not meet his eyes. "Why do you leave?"

Josua sighed. "I should go and speak to the lad Simon. Then I will walk for a while and think."

He strode out into the night and the swift wind.

In the dream, Simon was seated upon a massive throne made of smooth white stone. His throne room was not a room at all, but a great sward of stiff green grass. The sky overhead was as unnaturally blue and depthless as a painted bowl. A vast circle of courtiers stood before him; like the sky, their smiles seemed fixed and false.

"The king brings rebirth!" someone cried. The nearest of the courtiers stepped up to the throne. It was a dark-eyed woman dressed in gray with long straight hair; there was something terribly familiar about her face. She set before him a doll woven of leaves and reeds, then stepped away again and, despite the absence of hiding places on all sides, disappeared. The next person moved into place. *"Rebirth!"* someone shouted; *"Save us!"* cried another. Simon tried to tell them that he had no such power, but the desperate faces continued to circle past, continuous and indistinguishable as the spokes of a turning wheel. The pile of offerings grew larger. There were other dolls, and sheaves of summer-yellow wheat, as well as bunches of flowers whose brightly colored petals seemed as artificial as the paint-blue sky. Baskets of fruit and cheeses were placed before him, even farm animals, goats and calves whose bleating rose above the importuning voices.

"I can't help you!" Simon cried. *"There's nothing to be done!"*

The endless parade of faces continued. The cries and moans began to swell, an ocean of pleading that made his ears ache. At last he looked back down and saw that a child had been placed on the spreading mass of offerings, as though atop a funeral bier. The infant's face was somber, the eyes wide.

Even as Simon reached out to the child, his eye was caught by the doll that had been the first gift. It was rotting before his eyes, blackening and sagging until it became little more than a smear upon the obscenely bright grass. The other offerings were changing, too, decaying at a horrible rate—the fruits first bruising and dimpling, then seeming almost to froth as a blanket of mold swept over them. The flowers dried to ashy flakes, the wheat diminished to gray dust. As Simon watched in horror, even the tethered animals sagged, bloated, then were skeletonized in heartbeats by a pulsing mass of squirming white grubs.

Simon tried to clamber down off his throne, but the unlikely seat had begun buckling and sliding beneath him, pitching as though in an earth tremor. He tumbled to his knees in the muck. Where was the baby? Where? It would be consumed like the rest, crumbled into putrefaction unless he rescued it! He dove forward, shoveling through the rotting, stinking humus that had been the pile of offerings, but there was no sign of the child—unless that was a wink of gold, down there in the heap. . . . Simon scraped down into the dark mass until it was all around him, clogging his nose and filling his eyes like graveyard earth. Was that gold, there, beaming through the shadows? He must go deeper. Hadn't the child worn a golden bracelet? Or had it been a ring, a golden band. . . ? Deeper. It was so hard to breathe. . . .

He awoke in the dark. After a moment of panic, he fought free of his cloak and rolled toward the doorway, then fumbled open the flap so he could see the few stars not smothered by clouds. His heart slowed its pounding.

He was in the tent he and Binabik shared. Geloë and Strangyeard and the troll had helped him stumble here from the Observatory. Once they had laid him down on his pallet, he had fallen into sleep and dreamed a strange dream. But there had been another dream as well, hadn't there—the journey on the Dream Road, a shadow house and then a haunted ship? It was hard now to remember which had been which, and where the separation was. His head felt heavy and cobwebbed.

Simon pushed his head out and breathed the cold air, drinking it in as though it were wine. Gradually his thoughts became clearer. They had all gone to the Observatory to walk the Dream Road, but they had not found Miriamele. That was the important thing, far more important than some nightmare about dolls and babies and golden rings. They had tried to reach Miriamele, but something had prevented it, as Geloë had warned might happen. Simon had refused to give up. Pushing on when the others did not, he had almost lost himself in something bad—something very bad indeed.

I almost reached her! Almost! I know I could do it if I tried again!

But they had used the last of Geloë's herbs, and in any case, the time when the Dream Road could be walked had almost ended. He would never have another chance . . . *unless* . . .

The idea—a frightening, clever idea—had just begun to make its presence felt when he was startled from his thoughts.

"I am surprised to find you awake." The lamp Josua held limned his thin face in yellow light. "Binabik said he had left you sleeping."

"I just woke up, your Highness." Simon tried to stand, but tangled himself in the tent flap and nearly fell down again.

"You should not be up. The troll said you had a difficult time. I do not quite understand all that you four were doing, but I know enough to think you should be abed."

"I'm well." If the prince thought him sickly, he would never let him go anywhere. Simon did not want to be left out of any further expeditions. "Truly. It was only a sort of bad dream. I'm well."

"Hmm." Josua stared at him skeptically. "If you say it is so. Come, then—walk with me for a little while. Perhaps afterward you will be able to go back to sleep."

"Walk. . . ?" Inwardly, Simon cursed himself. Just at a time when he truly wanted to be alone, his stupid pride had tricked him again. Still, it was a chance to talk to Josua.

"Yes, just a short way across the hilltop. Get something to wrap yourself in. Binabik will never forgive me if you catch some ague under my care."

Simon ducked back into the tent and found his cloak.

They walked for a while in silence. The light of Josua's lamp reflected eerily from the broken stones of Sesuad'ra.

"I want to be a help to you, Prince Josua," he said at last. "I want to get your father's sword back."

Josua did not reply.

"If you let Binabik go with me, we will never be noticed. We are too small to attract the king's attention. We brought you Thorn, we can bring you Bright-Nail as well."

"There is an army coming," said the prince. "It seems my brother has learned of our escape and seeks to remedy his earlier laxness."

As Josua related Geloë's news, Simon felt a surprising sense of satisfaction growing within him. So he would not be denied his chance to do something after all! A moment later he remembered the women and children and old folk who now made New Gadrinsett their home and was ashamed at his pleasure. "What can we do?" he asked.

"We wait." Josua stopped before the shadowy bulk of the House of Waters. A dark rivulet ran down the crumbling stone sluice at their feet. "All other roads are closed to us, now. We wait, and we prepare. When Guthwulf or whoever leads this troop arrives—it could even be my brother himself—we will fight to defend our new home. If we lose . . . well, then all is finished." The hilltop wind lifted their cloaks and tugged at their clothing. "If somehow God grants that we win, we will try to move forward and make some use of our victory."

The prince sat down on a fallen block of masonry, then gestured for Simon to sit beside him. He set the lamp down; their shadows were cast giant-sized on the walls of the House of Waters. "We must live our lives day to day, now. We must not think too far ahead or we will lose what little we have."

Simon stared at the dancing flame. "What about the Storm King?"

Josua drew his cloak tighter. "I do not know—it is too vast a matter. We must stick to the things we can understand." He lifted his hand toward the slumbering tent city. "There are innocents to be protected. You are a knight now, Simon. That is your sworn task."

"I know, Prince Josua."

The older man was silent for a while. "And I have my own child to think of, as well." His grim smile was a small movement in the lampglow. "I hope it is a girl."

"You do?"

"Once, when I was a younger man, I hoped my first-born would be a son." Josua lifted his face to the stars. "I dreamed of a son who would love learning and justice, but have none of my failings." He shook his head. "But now, I hope our child is a girl. If we lost and he survived, a son of mine would be hunted forever. Elias could not let him live. And if we were to win somehow . . ." He trailed off.

"Yes?"

"If we were to win, and I took my father's throne, one day I would have to send my son off to do something I could not do—something dangerous and glorious. That is the way of kings and their sons. And I would never sleep again, waiting to hear that he had been killed." He sighed. "That is what I hate about ruling and royalty, Simon. It is living, breathing people with whom a prince plays the games of statecraft. I sent you and Binabik and the others into danger—you, who were little more than a child. No, I know you are now a young man—who knighted you, after all?—but that does not ease my remorse. With

Aedon's mercy, you survived my attention—but other companions of yours did not."

Simon hesitated a moment before speaking. "But being a woman does not save anyone from being caught by war, Prince Josua. Think of Miriamele. Think of your wife, Lady Vorzheva."

Josua nodded slowly. "I fear you are right. And now there will be more fighting, more war—and more helpless ones will die." After a moment's thought he looked up, startled. "Elysia, Mother of God, this is wonderful medicine for someone suffering from nightmares!" He grinned shamefacedly. "Binabik will kick me for this—taking his ward out and talking to him of death and misery." He put his arm around Simon's shoulder for a brief instant, then rose to his feet. "I will take you back to your tent. The wind is getting fierce."

As the prince bent to retrieve the lamp, Simon watched his spare features and felt a painful kind of love for Josua, a love mixed with pity, and wondered if all knights felt this way about their lords. Would Simon's own father Eahlferend have been stern but kind like Josua if he had lived? Would he and Simon have talked together about such things?

Most important of all, Simon thought as they pushed through the waving grass, would Eahlferend have been proud of his son?

They saw Qantaqa's gleaming eyes before they could make out Binabik, a small dark figure standing beside the tent door.

"Ah, good," the troll said. "I was, I must confess, full of worrying when I found you gone, Simon."

"It is my fault, Binabik. We were talking." Josua turned to Simon. "I leave you in able hands. Sleep well, young knight." He smiled and took his leave.

"Now," said Binabik sternly, "it is back to your bed that you should go." He directed Simon through the door, then followed him inside. Simon suppressed a groan as he lay down. Was this to be a night when everyone in New Gadrinsett would wish to talk with him?

His groan became actual as Qantaqa, following them into the tent, stepped on his stomach.

"Qantaqa! *Hinik aia!*" Binabik swatted at the wolf. She growled and backed out of the door flap. "Now, time for sleeping."

"You're not my mother," Simon muttered. How could he ever do anything about his idea with Binabik hanging about? "Are you going to sleep now, too?"

"I cannot." Binabik took an extra cloak and threw that over Simon as well. "I am on watch with Sludig this night. I will return to the tent with quietness when it is finished." He crouched at Simon's side. "Are you wishing to talk for a while? Was Josua telling you about the armed men who are coming here?"

"He told me." Simon feigned a yawn. "I'll talk to you about it tomorrow. I *am* sleepy, now that you mention it."

"You have had a day of great difficulty. The Dream Road was treacherous, as Geloë was warning."

Simon's desire to get on with his plans was blunted for a moment by curiosity. "What *was* that, Binabik—that thing on the Dream Road. Like a storm, with sparks in it? Did you see it, too?"

"Geloë is not knowing, and neither am I. Some disturbance, she called it. A storm is a good word, because I am thinking it was something like bad weather on the Road of Dreams. But what was causing it is something for guessing about, only. And even the guessing is not good for nighttime and the dark." He stood up. "Sleep well, friend Simon."

"Good night, Binabik." He listened as the troll made his way outside and whistled for Qantaqa, then he lay quietly for a long time after, counting ten score heartbeats before he slid out from beneath the sheltering cloaks and went searching for Jiriki's mirror.

He found it in the saddlebags Binabik had saved from Homefinder. The White Arrow was there, too, as was a heavy drawstring sack that momentarily puzzled him. He hefted it, then struggled with the knotted cord that held it shut. Memory came back to him suddenly: Aditu had given it to him at their parting, saying it was something

sent from Amerasu to Josua. Curious, Simon wondered
for a moment if he should take it with him and open it in
a more private place, but he felt time pressing. Binabik
might come back sooner than expected; it would be better
to be berated for being absent than to be stopped before
he had a chance to try out his idea. He reluctantly pushed
the sack back into the saddlebag. Later, he promised himself. Then he would give it to the prince, as he had promised.

Stopping only to root out the small pouch containing
his flints, he slipped out of the tent and into the cold
night.

Scant moonlight leaked through the clouds, but it was
enough for him to find his way across the hilltop. A few
shadowy figures were moving through the tent city on
one sort of errand or another, but none challenged him,
and soon he had passed out of New Gadrinsett and into
the central ruins of Sesuad'ra.

The Observatory was deserted. Simon crept through the
deep-shadowed interior until he found the remains of
the fire Geloë had made. The ashes were still warm. He
added a few pieces of kindling that lay beside the embers,
then sprinkled it with a handful of sawdust from his
pouch. He struck at the blunt edge of his iron with his
flint until he finally managed to catch a spark. It died before he could breathe it into full life, so he laboriously repeated the procedure, cursing quietly. At last he managed
to start a small fire burning.

The carved rim of Jiriki's mirror seemed warm to his
touch, but the reflecting surface, when he held it near his
cheek, was as cold as a sheet of ice. He breathed on it as
he had breathed on the hard-won spark, then held it up
before his face.

His scar had lost some of its angry flame; it was now
a red and white line curving down his cheek from his eye
to his jaw. It gave him, he thought, a certain soldierly
look—the appearance of one who had fought for what
was right and honorable. The snow-white streak running
through his hair also seemed to add a touch of maturity.
His beard, which he could not resist fluffing with his fin-

gers while he stared, made him look, if not like a knight, at least like a young man rather than a boy. He wondered what Miriamele would think if she could see him now.

Maybe I'll find out soon.

He tilted the mirror a little, so that the firelight illumined only half his face, leaving the remainder in red-tinged shadow. He thought carefully about what Geloë had said about the Observatory, how it had once been a place where the Sithi saw and spoke to each other over great distances. He tried to pull its antiquity and silence around him like a cape. He had found Miriamele once before in the mirror, without trying: why not now, in this potent place?

As he stared at his own halved reflection, the quality of the firelight seemed to change. The flicker became a gentle wavering, then slowed to a methodical pulse of scarlet light. The face in the mirror dissolved into smoky gray, and as he felt himself falling forward into it, he had time for a brief, triumphant thought.

And nobody wanted to teach me magic!

The frame of the mirror had vanished and the grayness was all around him. After his journeyings earlier in the day, he was undaunted: this was old and familiar territory. But even as he told himself this, another thought suddenly came to him. He had always had a guide before, and other travelers with him. This time there would be no Leleth to share his troubles, and no Geloë or Binabik to help him if he should go too far. A thin frost of fear descended, but Simon fought it back. He had used the mirror to call Jiriki once, had he not? There had been no one to help him then. Still, a small part of him guessed that calling for help might be a little less difficult than exploring the Road of Dreams by himself.

But Geloë had said that time was running short, that soon the Dream Road would be impassable. This might be his last chance to reach Miriamele, his last chance to save her and guide her back. If Binabik and the others found out, it would certainly be his last chance. He must go forward. Besides, Miriamele would be so astonished, so pleased and surprised. . . .

The gray void seemed thicker this time. If he swam, it was in gelid, muddy waters. How did one find his way here, without landmarks or signs? Simon formed the image of Miriamele in his mind, the same that he had held at sunset, dream-traveling with the others. This time, though, the picture would not hold together. Surely that was not what Miriamele's eyes looked like? And her hair, even when she had dyed it for disguise, was never that shade of sorrel brown? He fought with the recalcitrant vision, but the features of the lost princess would not come right. He was even having trouble remembering what they *should* look like. Simon felt as though he tried to build a stained glass window with colored water: the shapes ran and merged together, heedless of his efforts.

Even as he struggled, the grayness around him began to change. The difference was not immediately obvious, but if Simon had been in his body—which he suddenly wished he were—the hair on the back of his neck would have risen and goosebumps would have carbuncled his skin. Something shared the void with him, something much vaster than he was. He felt the outward wash of its power, but unlike the dream-storm that had caught at him before, this thing was no mindless force: it exuded intelligence and evil patience. He felt its remorseless scrutiny as a swimmer in the open sea might sense a great-finned thing pass beneath him in the black depths.

Simon's solitude suddenly seemed a kind of dreadful nakedness. He struggled, desperate to make contact with something that might pull him away from this shelterless void. He felt himself dwindling with fear, guttering like a candleflame—he did not know how to get away! How could he leave this place? He tried to startle himself out of the dream, to come awake, but as in childhood nightmares, there was no breaking the spell. He had entered this dream without sleeping, so how could he wake from it?

The blurry image that was not Miriamele remained. He tried to force himself toward it, to pull away from whatever great, slow thing was stalking him.

Help me! he screamed silently, and felt a glimmer of

recognition somewhere on the horizon of his thoughts. He reached for it, grasping at it like a castaway at a spar. This new presence became a little stronger, but even as it grew in strength, the thing that shared the void with him extended a fraction more of its own power, just enough to keep him from escaping. He sensed a malicious alien humor that delighted in his hopeless struggle, but he also sensed that the thing was tiring of the diversion and would soon end the game. A kind of deadening force reached out and surrounded him, a coldness of the soul that froze his efforts even as he reached out one more time toward the faint presence. He touched her then, across a dreadful span of dream, and clung.

Miriamele? he thought, praying that it was so, terrified to let loose of the tenuous contact. Whoever she was, she seemed finally to realize that he was there, but the thing that had him did not falter now. A black shadow moved over and through him, smothering light and thought. . . .

Seoman!? Another presence was with him suddenly— not the hesitant feminine one, not the dark, deadly other. *Come to me, Seoman!* it called. *Come!*

A warmth touched him. The chill grasp of the other squeezed more tightly for a moment, then let go—not overpowered, he sensed from its retreating thought, but bored and unwilling to trouble with such small matters, as a cat might lose interest in a mouse that had run under a stone. The gray came back, still featureless and directionless, then began to swirl like breeze-twisted clouds. A face formed before him—thin-boned, with eyes like liquid gold.

"*Jiriki!*"

"*Seoman,*" the other said. His face was worried. "*Are you in danger? Do you need help?*"

"*I am safe now, I think.*" Indeed, the lurking presence seemed gone completely. "*What was that horrible thing?*"

"*I do not know for sure what had you, but if it was not of Nakkiga, there is more evil in the world than even we suspected.*" Despite the strange disconnectedness of dream-vision, Simon could see the Sitha studying him carefully. *"Do you mean to say you did not call me for a reason?"*

"I didn't mean to call you at all." Simon replied, a little shamed now that the worst was over. *"I was trying to find Miriamele—the king's daughter. I told you about her."*

"By yourself, on the Road of Dreams?" With the anger, there was a kind of chilly amusement. *"Idiot manchild! If I had not been resting, and thus near to the place you are—near in thought, I mean—then only the Grove knows what would have become of you."* After a moment, the feeling of his presence warmed. *"Still, I am glad you are well."*

"I'm happy to see you, too." And he was. Simon had not realized how much he missed Jiriki's calm voice. *"We are at the Stone of Farewell—Sesuad'ra. Elias is sending troops. Can you help us?"*

The Sitha's angular face turned grim. *"I cannot come to you any time soon, Seoman. You must keep yourself safe. My father Shima'onari is dying."*

"I'm ... I'm sorry."

"He slew the hound Niku'a, greatest beast ever whelped in the kennels of Nakkiga, but he took his death-wound in the doing of it. It is another knot in the overlong skein—another blood-debt to Utuk'ku and ..." he hesitated, *"the other. Still, the Houses are gathering. When my father at last is taken to the Grove, the Zida'ya will ride to war again."* After his earlier flash of anger the Sitha had returned to his customary implacability, but Simon thought he could detect an underlying feeling of tension, of excitment.

Simon's hopes rose. *"Will you join with Josua? Will you fight with us?"*

Jiriki frowned. *"I cannot say, Seoman—and I would not make false promises. If I have my way, we will, and one last time the Zida'ya and Sudhoda'ya will fight together. But there are many who will speak when I speak, and many will have their own ideas. We have danced the year's end many hundreds of times since all the Houses were together for a war-council. Look!"*

Jiriki's face shimmered and faded, and for a moment Simon could see a cloudy scene, a vast circle of silver-leaved trees that stretched tall as towers. Gathered at their feet was a great host of Sithi, hundreds of immortals clad in armor of wildly different forms and colors, armor that glinted and shimmered in the columns of sunlight that spilled down through the treetops.

"*Look. The members of all the Houses are joined at Jao é-Tinukai'i. Cheka'iso Amber-Locks is here, as is Zinjadu, Lore-Mistress of lost Kementari, and Yizashi Grayspear. Even Kuroyi the tall horseman has come, who has not joined with the House of Year-Dancing since Shi'iki and Senditu's day. The exiles have returned, and we will fight as one people, as we have not done since Asu'a fell. In this, anyway, Amerasu's death and my father's sacrifice will not be in vain.*"

The vision of the armored host faded, then Jiriki faced Simon once more. "*But I have only a little power to guide this gathering of forces,*" he said, "*and we Zida'ya have many obligations. I cannot promise we will come, Seoman, but I will do my best to uphold my own duties to you. If your need is great, call me. You know I will do what I can.*"

"I know, Jiriki." There seemed many other things that he should tell him, but Simon's mind was in a whirl. "I hope we see each other soon."

At last, Jiriki smiled. "*As I said once before, manchild, a very unmagical wisdom tells me we shall meet again. Be brave.*"

"I will."

The Sitha's face grew serious. "*Now go, please. As you have found, the Witnesses and the Dream Road are no longer reliable—in fact, they are dangerous. I also doubt that words spoken here are safe from listening ears. That the Houses are gathering is no secret, but what the Zida'ya will do is. Avoid these realms, Seoman.*"

"But I need to find Miriamele," Simon said stubbornly.

"*You will only find trouble, I fear. Leave it alone. Besides, perhaps she is hiding from things that might not find her unless, without meaning to, you lead them to her.*"

Simon thought guiltily of Amerasu, but realized Jiriki had not intended to remind him of that, but only to caution him. "*If you say so,*" he acceded. So it had all been for nothing.

"*Good.*" The Sitha narrowed his eyes, and Simon felt his presence begin to fade. A sudden thought came.

"*But I don't know how to get back!*"

"*I will help you. Farewell for now, my Hikka Staja.*"

Jiriki's features blurred and evaporated, leaving only shimmering gray. As even that emptiness began to fade, Simon felt again a faint touch, the feminine presence to which he had reached out in his moment of fear. Had she been with them all along? Was she a spy, as Jiriki had warned about? Or was it indeed Miriamele, separated from him somehow, but nonetheless feeling that he was near? Who was it?

As he came back to himself, shivering in the cold beneath the Observatory's broken dome, he wondered if he would ever know.

6

The Sea-Grave

Miriamele had paced back and forth across the small cabin so many times that she could almost feel the plank flooring wearing away beneath her slippered feet.

She had nerved herself to an exquisite pitch, ready to slit the earl's throat as he lay sleeping. But now, at Gan Itai's direction, she had hidden the pilfered dagger and was waiting—but she did not know for what. She was trembling, and no longer just with anger and frustration: the gnawing fear, which she had been able to suppress with the thought that all would be over quickly, had returned. How long could it be until Aspitis noticed the theft of his knife? And would he have even a moment's doubt before he fixed the blame in the obvious place? This time, he would come to her wary and prepared; then, instead of the bindings of shame and society, she would go to her impending wedding in chains as real as Cadrach's.

As she paced, she prayed to blessed Elysia and Usires for help, but in the offhand way that one spoke to an ancient relative who had long ago gone deaf and numb-witted. She had little doubt that whatever happened to her on this drifting ship was of scant interest to a God who could allow her to reach this sorry state in the first place.

She had been proved wrong twice. After a childhood surrounded by flatterers and lackeys, she had been certain the only way to make a life worth living was to listen only to her own counsel and then push forward against any impediment, letting no one stay her from whatever

seemed important—but it was just that course which had
brought her to this horrible position. She had fled her uncle's castle, certain that she alone could help change the
course of events, but the faithless tides of time and history had not waited for her, and the very things she hoped
to prevent had occurred anyway—Naglimund fallen,
Josua defeated—leaving her without purpose. So it had
seemed wisest to cease fighting, to put an end to a lifetime's worth of stubborn resistance and simply let events
push her along. But that plan had proven as foolish as the
first, for her listlessness had brought her to Aspitis' bed,
and soon would make her his queen. For a while this realization had toppled Miriamele back into heedlessness—
she would kill him, and then likely be killed by Aspitis'
men; there would be no mucking about in the middle
ground, no complicated responsibilities. But Gan Itai had
stopped her, and now she drifted and circled just as the
Eadne Cloud idled on the windless waters.

This was an hour of decision, the sort Miriamele had
learned about from her tutors—as when Pelippa, the pam-
pered wife of a nobleman, had to decide whether to declare her belief in the condemned Usires. The pictures in
her childhood prayer book were still fresh in her memory.
As a young princess, she had been chiefly fascinated by
the silver paint on Pelippa's dress. Miriamele had given
little thought to Pelippa herself, to the actual people
caught up in the legends, written of in stories, painted on
walls. Only recently had it occurred to her to wonder how
it felt to be one of those folk. Had the warring kings im-
mortalized in the Sancellan's tapestries walked back and
forth in their ancient halls as they agonized over decisions, thinking little of what people would say in centuries unborn, but rather sorting the small facts of the
moment, trying to see a pattern that might guide them to
a wise choosing?

As the ship gently rocked and the sun rose into the sky,
Miriamele paced and thought. Surely there must be some
way to be bold without being stupid, to be resilient without becoming malleable and yielding as candle wax.
Along some course midway between these two extremes,

might there be a way she could survive? And if there was, could she then fashion from it a life worth living?

In the lamplit cabin, hidden from the sun, Miriamele pondered. She had not slept much the night before and she doubted she would sleep in the night that was coming ... if she lived to see it.

When the knock came upon her door, it was a quiet one. She thought herself ready to face even Aspitis, but her fingers trembled as they reached for the door handle.

It was Gan Itai, but for a moment Miriamele thought that some other Niskie had come aboard, so changed did the sea-watcher look. Her golden-brown skin seemed almost gray. Her face was loose and haggard and her sunken, red-rimmed eyes seemed to gaze out at Miriamele across a vast distance. The Niskie had wrapped her cloak closely about her, as though even in the swollen, humid air that presaged a storm, she feared catching a chill.

"Mercy of Aedon!" Miriamele hustled her inside and pushed the door closed. "Are you ill, Gan Itai? What has happened?" Aspitis had discovered the theft and was on his way, of course—that could be the only reason for the Niskie to look so dreadful. Miriamele faced this resolution with a kind of cold relief. "Do you need something? Water to drink?"

Gan Itai raised her weathered hand. "I need nothing. I have been ... thinking."

"Thinking? What do you mean?"

The Niskie shook her head. "Do not interrupt, girl. I have things to say to you. I made my own decision." She sat down on Miriamele's bed, moving as though two score years had been added to her age. "First, do you know where the landing boat is?"

Miriamele nodded. "Near midship on the starboard side, hanging from the windlass ropes." There was at least some advantage to having lived among waterfaring folk most of her young life.

"Good. Go to it this afternoon, when you are sure you are unobserved. Hide these there." The Niskie lifted her

cloak and dumped several bundles out onto the bed. Four
were water skins, tight-filled; two more were packages
wrapped in sacking. "Bread, cheese, and water," Gan Itai
explained. "And some bone fishhooks, so you may perhaps have some flesh to eke out your provisions. There
are a few other small things that may also prove useful."

"What does this mean?" Miriamele stared at the old
woman. Gan Itai still looked as though she carried some
dreadful burden, but her eyes had lost some of the
clouded look. They glinted now.

"It means you are escaping. I cannot sit and watch such
wickedness forced on you. I would not be one of the Navigator's true children if I did."

"But it cannot happen!" Miriamele fought against the
rush of witless hope. "Even if I could get off the ship,
Aspitis would hunt me down within a few hours. The
wind will come up long before I reach land. Do you think
I can vanish in a dozen leagues of empty sea, or outrow
the *Eadne Cloud?*"

"Outrow her? No." There was a strange pride in Gan
Itai's expression. "Of course not. She is fleet as a dolphin. But as to how . . . leave that to me, child. That is
the rest of *my* duty. You, however, must do one other
thing."

Miriamele swallowed her arguments. Heedless, stubborn pushing had done her little good in the past.
"What?"

"In the hold, in one of the barrels near the starboard
wall, tools and other metal goods are packed in oil. There
is writing on the cask, so do not fear you will not find it.
Go to the hold after sunset, take a chisel and a mallet
from the barrel, and strike off Cadrach's chains. Then he
must hide the fact that the chains are broken, in case
someone comes."

"Break his chains? But everyone on the ship will hear
me." Weariness descended on her. Already it seemed
clear that the Niskie's plan could never succeed.

"Unless my nose betrays me, the storm will be here
soon. A ship at sea in heavy wind makes many noises."

Gan Itai lifted her hand to still further questions. "Just do those tasks, then leave the hold and go to your cabin or anywhere, but *do not let anybody bolt you in.*" She waggled her long fingers for emphasis. "Even if you must feign sickness or madness, do not let anyone put a bolt between you and freedom." The golden eyes stared into her own until Miriamele felt her doubts wither away.

"Yes," she said. "I will."

"Then, at midnight, when the moon is just *there,*" the Niskie pointed at a spot on the ceiling, as if the sky were spread directly over them, "get your learned friend and help him to the landing boat. I will make sure you get a chance to put it overboard." She looked up, caught by a sudden thought. "By the Uncharted, girl, make sure that the oars are in the boat! Look for them when you hide the food and water."

Miriamele nodded. So the matter was resolved. She would do her best to live, but if she failed, she would not struggle against the inevitable. Even as her husband, Aspitis Preves could not keep her alive against her will. "And what will you do, Gan Itai?" she asked.

"What I have to."

"But it was not a dream!" Tiamak was growing angry. What did it take to convince this great brute of a Rimmersman? "It was Geloë, the wise woman of Aldheorte Forest. She talked to me through a child who has been in all my dreams of late. I have read of this. It is a trick of the Art, something adepts can do."

"Calm yourself, man. I didn't say you imagined it." Isgrimnur turned from the old man, who was waiting patiently for the next question the duke might ask him. Although unable to answer, he-who-had-been-Camaris seemed to get a quiet, childlike satisfaction from the attention, and would sit smiling back at Isgrimnur for hours. "I have heard of this Geloë. I *believe* you, man. And when we can leave, your Stone of Farewell is as good a destination as any—I have heard that Josua's camp is somewhere near where you say the place is. But I cannot let a dream of any kind, no matter how urgent it seems, take me away just yet."

"But why?" Tiamak was not even sure himself why it seemed so important that they leave. All he knew was that he was tired of feeling worthless. "What can we do here?"

"I am waiting for Miriamele, Prince Josua's niece," said the Rimmersman. "Dinivan sent me to this godforsaken inn. Perhaps he sent her as well. Since it is my sworn duty to find her, and I have lost the trail, I must stay for a time here where the track ends."

"If he sent her, then why is she not here now?" Tiamak knew he was making trouble, but could not help himself.

"Perhaps she's been delayed. It is a long journey on foot." Isgrimnur's mask of calm slipped a little. "Now be quiet, damn you! I have told you all I can. If you wish to go, then go! I won't stop you."

Tiamak closed his mouth with a snap, then turned and limped unhappily to his bundle of belongings. He began to sort through them in halfhearted preparation for departure.

Should he leave? It was a long journey, and would certainly be better made with companions, however shortsighted and uncaring of his feelings they might be. Or maybe it would be better just to slink back to his house in the banyan tree, deep in the marsh outside Village Grove. But his people would demand to know what had become of his forsaken errand to Nabban on their behalf, and what would he tell them?

He Who Always Steps on Sand, Tiamak prayed, *save me from this terrible indecision!*

His restless fingers touched heavy parchment. He drew out the page of Nisses' lost book and cradled it briefly in his hands. This small triumph, anyway, no one could take from him. It was he and no one else who had found it. But, sadness of sadnesses, Morgenes and Dinivan were no longer alive to marvel at it!

"... Bringe from Nuanni's Rocke Garden,"

he read silently,

> *"... The Man who tho' Blinded canne See*
> *Discover the Blayde that delivers The Rose*
> *At the foote of the Rimmer's greate Tree*
> *Find the Call whose lowde Claime*
> *Speakes the Call-bearer's name*
> *In a Shippe on the Shallowest Sea—*
> *—When Blayde, Call, and Man*
> *Come to Prince's right Hande*
> *Then the Prisoned shall once more go Free ..."*

He remembered the dilapidated shrine to Nuanni he had
found in his wanderings a few days earlier. The wheezing,
half-blind old priest had been able to tell him little of import, although he was quite happy to talk after Tiamak
dropped a pair of cintis-pieces into the offering bowl.
Nuanni was, apparently, a sea god of ancient Nabban whose
glory days had passed even before the upstart Usires appeared. Old Nuanni's followers were few indeed these days,
the priest had assured him: were it not for the tiny pockets
of worship still clinging to life in the superstitious islands,
no one living would remember Nuanni's name, although the
god had once bestrode the Great Green, first in the hearts of
all seafarers. As it was, the old priest guessed that his was
the last shrine still on the mainland.

Tiamak had been pleased to hear the now-familiar
name from his parchment at last given substance, but had
thought little more of it than that. Now he let his mind
run on the first line of the puzzling rhyme and wondered
if "Nuanni's rock garden" might not refer to the scattered
islands of Firannos Bay themselves...?

"What do you have there, little man? A map, hey?"
From the sound of his voice, Isgrimnur was trying to be
friendly, perhaps in an effort to offset his earlier
gruffness—but Tiamak was having none of it.

"Nothing. It is not your business." He quickly rolled

the parchment and pushed it back into his clump of belongings.

"No need to bite my head off," the duke growled. "Come, man, talk to me. Are you truly leaving?"

"I do not know." Tiamak did not want to turn and look at him. The Rimmersman was so large and imposing that he made the Wrannaman feel terribly small. "I might. But it would be a long way for one to go alone."

"How would you go, anyway?" Isgrimnur's interest sounded genuine.

Tiamak considered. "If I did not go with you two, there would be no need to be inconspicuous. So I would go the straightest way possible, overland across Nabban and the Thrithings. It would be a long walk, but I am not afraid of exertion." He frowned, thinking of his injured leg. It might never heal, and certainly was not now capable of carrying him a long distance. "Or perhaps I would buy a donkey," he added.

"You certainly speak fine Westerling for a Wran-man," Isgrimnur smiled. "You use words I don't know myself."

"I told you," Tiamak replied stiffly. "I studied with the Aedonite brothers in Perdruin. And Morgenes himself taught me much."

"Of course." Isgrimnur nodded. "But, hmm, if you did have to travel—inconspicuously, I think you said? If you did have to travel without being noticed, what then? Some secret marsh-man tunnels, or something like?"

Tiamak looked up. Isgrimnur was watching him carefully. Tiamak quickly lowered his gaze, trying to hide a smile of his own. The Rimmersman was trying to trick him, as though Tiamak were a child! It was funny, actually. "I imagine I would fly."

"Fly!?" Tiamak could almost hear the look of incredulity twist the duke's features. "Are you mad?"

"Oh, no," said Tiamak earnestly, "it is a trick known to all Wran-dwellers. Why do you think that we are only observed in places like Kwanitupul, where we choose to be seen? Surely you know that great blundering drylanders come into the Wran and never see a living soul. It is because when we have to, we can fly. Just like birds." He darted a sideways glance. Isgrimnur's baffled face was everything he could hope. "Besides, if we could not fly ... how would we reach the treetop nests where we lay our eggs?"

"S'Red Blood! Aedon on the Tree!" Isgrimnur swore explosively. "Damn you, marsh man! Mock me, will you?!"

Tiamak cringed in expectation of having some heavy object thrown at him, but a moment later looked up to see the duke grinning and shaking his head. "I suppose I asked for that. You Wrannamen have a sense of humor, it seems."

"Perhaps some drylanders do also."

"Still, the problem remains." Isgrimnur glowered. "Life seems nothing but difficult choices these days. By the Ransomer's Name, I have made mine and must live with it: if Miriamele does not appear by the twenty-first day of Octander—Soul's Day, that is—then I, too, will say 'enough' and head north. There is my choice. Now you must make yours: stay or go." He turned back to the old man, who had observed their entire conversation with benign incomprehension. "I hope you stay, little man," the duke added quietly.

Tiamak stared for a moment, then stood and walked to the window. Below, the murky canal gleamed like green metal in the afternoon sun. He pulled himself up onto the sill and dangled his wounded leg out the window.

"Inihe Red-Flower had dark hair,"

he crooned, watching a flatboat bob past,

"Dark hair, dark eyes. Slender as a vine she was,
And she sang to the gray doves.
Ah-ye, ah-ye, she sang to them all the night long.

"Shoaneg Swift-Rowing heard her,
Heard her, loved her. Strong as a banyan he was,
But he had no children.
Ah-ye, ah-ye, he had no one to carry his name.

"*Shoaneg called out to Red-Flower,*
Wooed her, won her. Swift as dragonflies their love
     was,
And she came back to his home.
Ah-ye, ah-ye, her feather hung over his door.

"*Inihe, she bore a boy-child,*
Nursed him, loved him. Sweet as cool wind he was,
And he bore Swift-Rowing's name.
Ah-ye, ah-ye, water was safe to him as sand.

"*The child grew up to wander,*
Rowing, running. Footloose as a rabbit he was,
Traveled far from his home.
Ah-ye, ah-ye, he was stranger to the hearth.

"*One day his boat came empty,*
Spinning, drifting. Empty as a nutshell it was,
Red-Flower's child was gone.
Ah-ye, ah-ye, he had blown away like thistledown.

"*Shoaneg said forget him,*
Heartless, thoughtless. Like a foolish nestling he was,
Who flies from his home.
Ah-ye, ah-ye, his father cursed his name.

"*Inihe could not believe it,*
Missed him, mourned him. Sad as drifting leaves she
     was,
Her tears soaked the floor-reeds.
Ah-ye, ah-ye, she cried for her missing son.

"*Red-Flower burned to find him,*
Hoping, praying. Like a hunting owl she was,
Who would search for her son.
Ah-ye, ah-ye, she would find her lost child.

"*Shoaneg said he forbade her,*
Shouted, ordered. Angry as a beehive he was,

If she went, he had no wife.
Ah-ye, ah-ye, he would blow her feather from his door . . ."

Tiamak broke off. A barge, crewed by shouting Wrannaman, was being poled awkwardly into a narrow side-canal. It scraped hard against the wharf pilings which jutted at the front of the inn like rotten teeth. The surface of the water boiled with waves. Tiamak turned to look at Isgrimnur, but the duke had left the room. Only the old man remained, his eyes fixed on nothing, his face vacant but for a small, secretive smile.

It was long since Tiamak's mother had sung that song to him. The tale of Inihe Red-Flower's terrible choice had been her favorite. Thinking of her brought a tightness to Tiamak's throat. He had betrayed the trust she would have wanted him to keep—the debt he owed to his own people. Now what should he do? Wait here with these drylanders? Go to Geloë and the other Scrollbearers who had asked him to come? Or return in shame to his own Village Grove? Wherever he went, he knew that his mother's spirit would watch him, mourning because her son had turned his back on his people.

He frowned as if tasting something bitter. Isgrimnur was right about one thing, anyway. These days, these bleak days, life seemed nothing but difficult choices.

"Pull her back!" the voice said. "Quickly!"

Maegwin woke to find herself staring straight down into white nothingness. The transition was so strange that for a moment she thought she still dreamed. She leaned forward, trying to move through this emptiness as she had moved through the gray dream-void, but something restrained her. She gasped as she felt the fierce, biting cold. She was leaning out over an abyss of swirling snow. Rough hands were clutching at her shoulders.

"Hold her!"

She flung herself backward, scrabbling for safety,

struggling against those who held her. When she could feel stone solidly beneath her on all sides, she let out a deep rush of close-held breath and went limp. The flurrying snowflakes were quickly filling the indentations left by her knees along the outer edge of the precipice. Nearby, the ashes of her small campfire had all but disappeared under a mantle of white.

"Lady Maegwin—we are here to help you!"

She looked around, dazed. Two men still held her tightly; a third stood a few paces behind her. All were heavily cloaked, and wore scarves wrapped around their faces. One wore the tattered crest of the Croich clan.

"Why have you brought me back?" Her voice seemed slow and clumsy. "I was with the gods."

"You were about to fall, Lady," the man at her right shoulder said. She could feel from the hand that gripped her that he was shivering. "We have been searching for you three days."

Three days! Maegwin shook her head and looked at the sky. From the indistinct gleam of the sun, it was only a little after dawn. Had she really been with the gods all that time? It had seemed scarcely an instant. If only these men had not come....

No, she told herself. *That is selfish. I had to come back—and I would have been of no use if I had tumbled down the mountain and died.*

After all, she now had a duty to survive. She had more than duty.

Maegwin unwrapped her chilled fingers from the dwarrow-stone, letting it tumble to the ground. She felt her heart swell inside her. She had been right! She had climbed Bradach Tor as the dream had bidden her. Now, here in the high place she had dreamed again, dreams just as compelling as the ones that had brought her here.

Maegwin had felt the messenger of the gods reaching out for her, a messenger in the form of a tall, red-haired youth. Although his features had been misted by the dream, she guessed that he was very beautiful. Perhaps he was a fallen hero of old Hernystir, Airgad Oakheart or

Prince Sinnach, taken to live in the sky with Brynioch and the rest!

During the first vision back in the cavern she had merely sensed him looking for her, but when she tried to reach out to him the dream had dissolved, leaving her chill and lonely atop her rock. Then, when she had fallen back into sleep, she had felt the messenger searching for her once more. She had felt that his need was urgent, so she had strained herself to the utmost, trying to burn as bright as a lamp so that he could find her, stretching herself out through the substance of the dream so she could reach him. Then, when she had touched him at last, he had instantly carried her to the threshold of the land where the gods lived.

And surely that had been one of the gods she had seen there! Again, the dream-vision had been fogged—perhaps living mortals could not witness the gods in their true forms—but the face that had appeared before her was nothing born of man or woman. If nothing else, the burning, inhumanly golden eyes would have proved that. Perhaps she had seen cloud-bearing Brynioch himself! The messenger, whose spirit had remained with her, seemed to tell the god something about a high place—which could only be the spot where Maegwin's sleeping body lay while her soul flitted in dream—then the messenger and the god spoke of a king's daughter and a dead father. It had all been very confusing, the voices seeming to come to her garbled and echoing, as if through a very long tunnel or across a mighty chasm—but who else could they have been speaking of but Maegwin herself and her own father Lluth, who had died protecting his people?

Not all the words spoken reached her, but the sense of them was clear: the gods were readying themselves for battle. Surely that could only mean they were going to intervene at last. For a moment she had even been vouchsafed a glimpse into the very halls of Heaven. A mighty host of them had waited there, fiery-eyed and streaming-haired, clad in armor as colorful as the wings of butterflies, their spears and swords shimmering like lightning in a summer's sky. Maegwin had seen the gods themselves in their power and glory. It was true, it must be! How could there be any doubt now? The gods meant to take the field and to wreak revenge on Hernystir's enemies.

She swayed back and forth and the two men steadied her. She felt that if she leaped from Bradach Tor at this moment she would not fall, but would fly like a starling, arrow-swift down the mountain to tell her people the wonderful news. She laughed at herself and her foolish ideas, then laughed again with joy that she should be chosen by the gods of field, water, and sky to bear their message of coming redemption.

"My lady?" The man's worry was clear in his tone. "Are you ill?"

She ignored him, afire with ideas. Even if she could not truly fly, she must hurry down the mountain to the cave where the Hernystiri nation labored in its exile. It was time to go!

"I have never been better," she said. "Lead me to my people."

As her escorts helped her back along the tor, Maegwin's stomach rumbled. Her hunger, she realized, was returning swiftly. Three days she had slept and dreamed and stared into the snowy distance from this high place, and in that time she had eaten almost nothing. Full of the words of heaven, she was now also hollow as an empty barrel. How would she ever fill herself up? She laughed uproariously and paused, smacking the snow from her clothing in powdery bursts of white. It was bitterly cold, but she was warmed. She was far from her home, but she had her leaping thoughts for company. She wished she could share this sense of triumph with Eolair, but even the thought of him did not sadden her, as it always had before. He was doing what he should do, and if the gods had planted the seed of his going in her mind, there must be some reason for it. How could she doubt, when all else that had seemed promised had been given— all but the last and greatest gift, which she knew was coming soon?

"I have spoken with the gods," she told the three worried men. "They are with us at this terrible time—they will come to us."

The man nearest her looked quickly at his companions, then did his best to smile as he said: "Praise to all their names."

Maegwin gathered her sparse possessions into her sack so hastily that she chipped the wooden wing of Mircha's bird. She sent one of the men back to get the dwarrow-stone, which she had dropped in the snow at the cliff's edge. Before the sun had moved a handsbreadth above the horizon, she was making her way down the Grianspog's snowy slope.

She was hungry and very tired, and she had also finally begun to feel the cold. Even with the help of her rescuers, the journey down was even more difficult than the climb up. Still, Maegwin felt joy pulsing quietly within her like a child waiting to be born—a joy that, like a child, would grow and become ever more splendid. Now she could tell her people that help was coming! What could be more welcome after this bleak twelvemonth?

But what else should be done, she suddenly wondered. What should the Hernystiri people do to prepare for the return of the gods?

Maegwin turned her thoughts to this as the party made its careful way down and the morning slipped away across the face of the Grianspog. She decided at last that before anything else, she must speak to Diawen again. The scryer had been right about Bradach Tor and had understood instantly the importance of the other dreams. Diawen would help Maegwin decide what to do next.

Old Craobhan met the search party, full of angry words and poorly-hidden worry, but his fury at her heedlessness rolled off Maegwin like rain from oiled leather. She smiled and thanked him for sending men to bring her safely down, but would not be hindered; she ignored him as he first demanded, then asked, then at last begged her to rest and be tended. Finally, unable to convince her to accompany them, unwilling to use force in a cavern full of curious onlookers, Craobhan and his men gave up.

Diawen was standing before her cave as though she had expected Maegwin to come at just that time. The scryer took her arm and guided her into the smoky chamber.

"I can see by your face." Diawen peered solemnly into Maegwin's eyes. "Praise Mircha, you have had another dream."

"I climbed up to Bradach Tor, just as you suggested." She wanted to shout her excitment. "And the gods spoke to me!"

She related all that she had experienced, trying not to exaggerate or glorify—surely the bare reality was marvelous enough! When she had finished, Diawen gazed back at her in silence, eyes bright with what looked like tears.

"Ah, praise be," said the scryer. "You have been given a Witnessing, as in the old tales."

Maegwin grinned happily. Diawen understood, just as Maegwin had known she would. "It's wonderful," she agreed. "We will be saved." She paused as the thought she had been holding made itself felt. "But what should we do?"

"The gods' will," Diawen replied without hesitation.

"But what is that?"

Diawen searched among her collection of mirrors, at last selecting one made of polished bronze with a handle in the shape of a coiling serpent. "Quiet now. I did not walk in dreams with you, but I have my own ways." She held the mirror above the smoldering fire, then blew away the accumulated soot. For a long time she stared into it, her dark brown eyes seemingly fixed on something beyond the mirror. Her lips moved soundlessly. At last, she put the mirror down.

When Diawen spoke, her voice was remote. "The gods help those who are bold. Bagba gave cattle to Hern's folk because they had lost their horses fighting on behalf of the gods. Mathan taught the art of weaving to the women who hid her from her husband Murhagh's rage. The gods help those who are bold." She blinked and pushed a lock of gray hair from her eyes. Her voice resumed its ordinary tone. "We must go to meet the gods. We must show them that Hern's children are worthy of their help."

"What does that mean?"

Diawen shook her head. "I am not sure."

"Should we take up arms ourselves? Go forth and challenge Skali?" Maegwin frowned. "How can I ask the people to do that, few and weak as we are?"

"Doing the will of the gods is never easy," Diawen sighed. "I know. When I was young, Mircha came to me in a dream, but I could not do what she asked. I was afraid." The scryer's face, lost in memory, was full of fierce regret. "Thus I failed in my moment and left her priesthood. I have never felt her touch since, not in all the lonely years. . . ." She broke off. When she turned her gaze to Maegwin once more, she was brisk as a wool merchant. "The will of the gods can be frightening, king's daughter, but to refuse it is to refuse their help as well. I can tell you no more."

"To take arms against Skali and his reavers . . ." Maegwin let the thought flow through her like water. There was a certain mad beauty in the idea, a beauty that might indeed please the heavens. To lift the sword of Hernystir once more against the invaders, even for one brief moment. Surely the gods themselves would shout to see such a proud hour! And surely at that moment the sky could not help but open up, and all of Rhynn's lightnings leap forth to burn Skali Sharp-nose and his army into dust. . . .

"I must think, Diawen. But when I speak to my father's people, will you stand with me?"

The scryer nodded, smiling like a prideful parent. "I will stand with you, king's daughter. We will tell the people how the gods spoke."

A shower of warm rain was falling, the first outrider of the approaching storm. The thick bank of clouds along the horizon was mottled gray and black, touched at the

edges by the orange glare of the late afternoon sun it had
almost swallowed. Miriamele narrowed her eyes against
the spattering drops and looked carefully all around. Most
of the sailors were busy preparing for the storm, and none
seemed to be paying any attention to her at all. Aspitis
was in his cabin, where she prayed he would be too engrossed in his charts to notice the theft of his fanciest
dagger.

She slid the first of the water skins out from beneath
her belted cape, then loosened a knot that held the heavy
cloth cover in place over the open landing boat. After one
more quick survey of the surroundings, she let the water
skin slide down into the boat to nestle beside the oars,
then quickly sent down the other. As she stood on tiptoe
to push the parcels of bread and cheese in, somebody
shouted in Nabbanai.

"*Hoy! Stop that!*"

Miriamele froze like a cornered rabbit, heart pounding.
She let the food bundles slide out of her fingers and down
into the boat, then slowly turned.

"*Fool! You've put it wrongside-round!*" the sailor
screamed from his perch in the rigging. Twenty cubits up,
he was staring indignantly at another sailor working
above him on the mast. The object of his criticism gave
him the goat-sign and cheerfully continued doing whatever it was that had proved so offensive. The first sailor
shouted for a while longer, then laughed and spat through
the wind before resuming his own labors.

Miriamele closed her eyes as she waited for her knees
to stop shaking. She took a deep breath, filling her nose
with the scents of tar, wet planks, and the sodden wool of
her own cloak, as well as the bristly, secretive odor of the
approaching storm, then opened her eyes again. The rain
had grown stronger and was now running off her hood, a
tiny cascade falling just beyond the tip of her nose. Time
to get below-decks. It would be sunset soon and she did
not want to defeat Gan Itai's plan through simple care-
lessness, however faint the hope of success. Also, while it
was not inexplicable that Miriamele should be on deck in
this rapidly worsening rain, if she encountered Aspitis it

might stick in his mind as a curious thing. Miriamele did not know exactly what the Niskie was arranging, but she knew it would not be helped by putting the earl on guard.

She made her way down the hatchway stairs without attracting attention, then padded silently along the corridor until she reached the Niskie's sparsely furnished room. The door had been left unbolted and Miriamele quickly slipped inside. Gan Itai was gone—out preparing the master-stroke of her plan, Miriamele felt sure, however hopeless even the Niskie thought it to be. Gan Itai had certainly seemed weary and heartsick when she had seen her this morning.

After Miriamele had tied up her skirt, she pulled free the loose section of wall paneling, then agonized for a long moment over whether to bolt the outer door of the room. Unless she could replace the panel perfectly from the inside of the hidden passageway, anyone entering the room would instantly know someone had gone through, and might be interested enough to investigate. But if she threw the bolt, Gan Itai might return and be unable to get in.

After a little consideration, she decided to leave the door alone and take her chances with accidental discovery. She took a stub of candle from her cloak and held it to the flame of Gan Itai's lamp, then climbed through and pulled the panel closed behind her. She held the candle-end in her teeth as she climbed the ladder, saying a silent prayer of thanks that her hair was wet and still cropped short. She hastily dismissed an image of what might happen if someone's hair caught fire in a narrow place like this.

When she reached the hatchway, she dripped some wax on the passageway floor to hold the candle, then lifted the trapdoor and peered through the crack. The hold was dark—a good sign. She doubted that any of the sailors would be walking around among the precariously stacked barrels without light.

"Cadrach!" she called softly. "It's me! Miriamele!"

There was no reply, and for an instant she was sure that she had come too late, that the monk had died here in the

darkness. She swallowed down the clutch in her throat,
retrieved her candle, then climbed carefully down the ladder fixed to the sill of the hatchway. It ended short of the
ground, and when she dropped the remaining distance she
struck sooner than she expected to. The candle popped
from her hand and rolled across the wooden flooring. She
scrambled after it, burning herself with a panicky grab,
but it did not go out.

Miriamele took a deep breath. "Cadrach?"

Still unanswered, she snaked her way through the leaning piles of ship's stores. The monk was slumped on the
floor beside the wall, head sunken on his breast. She
grabbed his shoulder and shook, making his head wobble.

"Wake up, Cadrach." He moaned but did not awaken.
She shook harder.

"Ah, gods," he slurred, "that *smearech fleann* . . . that
cursed book . . ." He flailed as if caught in a terrible
nightmare. "Close it! Close it! I wish I had never opened
it. . . ." His words fell away into unintelligible mumbling.

"Curse you, wake up!" she hissed.

His eyes opened at last. "My . . . my lady?" His confusion was pitiable. Some of his substance had withered
away during his captivity: his skin hung loosely on the
bones of his face and his eyes peered blearily out of deep
sockets. He looked like an old man. Miriamele took his
hand, wondering a little that she should do so without
hesitation. Wasn't this the same tosspot traitor she had
pushed into the Bay of Emettin and hoped to watch
drown? But she knew he was not. The man before her
was a miserable creature who had been chained and
beaten—and not for any real crime, but only for running
away, for trying to save his own life. Now she wished she
had run with him. Miriamele pitied the monk, and remembered that he had not been entirely bad. In some
ways, he had even been a friend.

Miriamele suddenly felt ashamed of her callousness.
She had been so certain about things, so sure about what
was right and what was wrong that she had been ready to
let him drown. It was hard to look at Cadrach now, his
eyes wounded and frightened, his head bobbing above the

stained robe. She squeezed his cold hand and said: "Don't fear—I will return in a moment." She took her candle and went off to search the ranked barrels for Gan Itai's promised tools.

She squinted at faded markings as footsteps echoed back and forth overhead. The ship rolled abruptly, creaking in the grasp of the storm's first winds. At last she found a barrel helpfully marked *"Otillenaes."* When she had also located a pry-bar that hung near the ladder, she unlidded the cask. A treasure trove of tools were packed inside, all neatly wrapped in leather and floating in oil like exotic supper birds. She bit her lip and forced herself to work calmly and carefully, unwrapping the oozing parcels one at a time until she found a chisel and a heavy mallet. After wiping them off on the inside of her cloak, she took them back to Cadrach.

"What are you doing, Lady? Do you plan to favor me with a blow from that pig-slaughterer? It would be a true favor."

She frowned, fixing the candle to the floor with hot wax. "Don't be a fool. I'm going to cut your chains. Gan Itai is helping us to escape."

The monk stared at her for a moment, his pouchy gray eyes surprisingly intent. "You must know that I cannot walk, Miriamele."

"If I have to, I will carry you. But we will not go until tonight. That will give you a chance to rub some life back into your legs. Perhaps you can even stand up and try pacing a bit, if you are quiet about it." She pulled at the chain that hung from his ankles. "I suppose I must cut this on each side or you will rattle when you walk, like a tinker." Cadrach's smile, she guessed, was mostly for her sake.

The long chain between his leg irons ran through one of the tying-bolts in the floor of the hold. Miriamele pulled one side taut, then set the chisel's sharp blade against the nearest link to the shackle. "Can you hold it for me?" she asked. "Then I can use both hands on the hammer."

The monk nodded and clutched the spike of iron.

Miriamele hefted the mallet a few times to get the feel of it, then raised it above her head.

"You look like Deanagha of the Brown Eyes," he whispered.

Miriamele was trying to listen to the creaking rhythm of the boat's movement, hoping to find a noisy moment in which to strike. "Like who?"

"Deanagha of the Brown Eyes." He smiled. "Rhynn's youngest daughter. When his enemies surrounded him and he lay sick, she pounded on his bronze cauldron with her spoon until the other gods came to rescue him." He stared at her. "Brave she was."

The boat rolled and the timbers gave out a long, shuddering groan.

"My eyes are green," Miriamele said, then brought the mallet down as hard as she could. The clank seemed loud as thunder. Certain that Aspitis and his men must now be racing toward the hold, she looked down. The chisel had bitten deep, but the chain was still uncut.

"Curse it," she breathed and paused to listen for a long, anxious moment. There seemed no unusual sounds from the deck above, so she lifted the mallet, then had a thought. She took off her cloak and folded it over, then folded it once more. She slid this cushion beneath the chain. "Hold this," she ordered, and struck again.

It took several cuts, but the cloak helped soften the noise, though it also made striking a hard blow more difficult. At last the iron link parted. Miriamele then pounded laboriously through the other side as well, and even managed to sever one side of Cadrach's wrist chains before she had to stop. Her arms felt as though they were afire; she could no longer lift the heavy mallet above her shoulder. Cadrach tried, but was too weak. After he had struck at it several times without making an appreciable dent, he handed her back the hammer.

"This will be sufficient," he said. "One side is enough to free me, and I can wrap the chain about my arm so it will make no noise. The legs were what mattered, and they are free." He wiggled his feet carefully to demonstrate. "Do you think you could find some dark cloth in this hold?"

Miriamele looked at him curiously, but got up and began a weary search. At last she returned. Aspitis' knife, which had been tied to her leg with a scarf, was in her hand. "There's nothing around. If you really need it, we'll take it off the hem of my cloak." She kneeled and held the blade over the dark fabric. "Shall I?"

Cadrach nodded. "I will use it to tie the chains together. That way they will hold unless someone pulls them hard." He exerted the effort to grin. "In this light, my guards will never notice that one of the links is made of soft Erkynlandish wool."

When they had done this, and when all the tools had been wrapped and replaced, Miriamele picked up her candle and stood. "I will be back for you at midnight, or just before."

"How is Gan Itai planning to work this little trick?" There was a flavor of his old ironic tone.

"She has not told me. Probably she thinks it's best I know little, so I will worry less." Miriamele shook her head. "There she has failed."

"It is not likely that we will get off the boat, nor that we will get far even if we do." The painful effort of the last hour showed in Cadrach's every halting movement.

"Not likely at all," she agreed. "But Aspitis knows that I am the High King's daughter and he is forcing me to marry him, so I do not care what is likely or unlikely." She turned to go.

"No, Lady, I imagine you do not. Until tonight, then."

Miriamele paused. Somewhere in the hour just passed, as the chains were falling away, an unspoken understanding had arisen between the two of them . . . a sort of forgiveness.

"Tonight," she said. She took the candle and made her way back up the ladder, leaving the monk sitting in darkness once more.

The hours of evening seemed to inch past. Miriamele

lay in her cabin listening to the mounting storm, wondering where she would be this time tomorrow.

The winds grew stronger. The *Eadne Cloud* heaved and rolled. When the earl's page came and rapped at the door to say that his master bid her come to a late supper, she claimed illness from the restless seas and declined the invitation. A while later, Aspitis himself arrived.

"I am sorry to hear you are sick, Miriamele." He lounged in the doorway, loose-jointed as any predator. "Perhaps you would like to sleep in my cabin tonight, so you will not be alone with your misery?"

She wanted to laugh at such hideous irony, but resisted. "I am sick, Lord. When you marry me, I will do what you say. Leave me this last night to myself."

He seemed inclined to argue, but shrugged instead. "As you wish. I have had a long evening, preparing for the storm. And, as you say, we still have our entire lives before us." He smiled, a line thin as a knife-slash. "So, good night." He stepped forward and kissed her cold cheek, then stepped to the small table and pinched the wick of her lamp, snuffing the flame. "This will be a rough night. You do not want to start a fire."

He walked out, pulling the door closed behind him. As soon as his steps had receded down the passageway, she leaped from her bed to make sure he had not somehow locked her in. The door swung open freely, revealing the dark corridor. Even with the upper hatchway closed, the wail of the wind was loud, full of wild power. She closed the door and went back to her bed.

Propped upright, swaying to the ship's powerful movements, Miriamele drifted in and out of a light, restless sleep, surfacing with a start from time to time, the rags of dream still clinging, then hastening to the passageway and up the ladder to sneak a look at the sky. Once she had to wait so long for the moon to reappear in the stormclouded heavens that, still not completely awake, she feared that it had vanished altogether, chased away somehow by her father and Pryrates. When it appeared at last, a winking eye behind the murk, and she saw that it was still far from the place of which the Niskie had spoken, Miriamele glided back to her bed.

It even seemed that once, as she lay half-awake, Gan Itai opened the door and peered in at her. But if it was truly her, the Niskie said nothing; a moment later, the doorway was empty. Soon after, in a lull between gusts of wind, Miriamele heard the sea-watcher's song keening across the night.

When she could wait no longer, Miriamele rose. She pulled out the bag she had hidden underneath the bed and removed her monk's clothing, which she had put away in favor of the lovely dresses Aspitis had provided. After donning the breeches and shirt and belting the loose robe close about her waist, she donned her old boots, then threw a few select articles into the bag. Aspitis' knife, which she had worn that afternoon, she now thrust under her belt. Better to have it available than to worry about discovery. If she met someone between here and Gan Itai's cabin, she would have to try and hide the blade under the robe's wide sleeve.

A quick inspection proved the corridor empty. Miriamele tucked her sack under her arm and moved as silently as she could down the passageway, aided in her stealth by the rain that was beating down on the deck above her head like a drum struck by a thousand hands. The Niskie's song, rising above the storm noises, had a weird, unsettled quality, far less pleasant to the ear than usual. Perhaps it was the Niskie's obvious unhappiness coming out in her song, Miriamele thought. She shook her head, disturbed.

Even a brief glance out through the hatchway left her drenched. The torrential rains were being swept almost sideways by the wind, and the few lamps still burning in their hoods of translucent horn banged and capered against the masts. The *Eadne Cloud*'s crewmen, wound in flapping cloaks, hurried about the decks like panicked apes. It was a scene of wild confusion, but even so, Miriamele felt her heart grow heavy. Every seaman aboard seemed to be on deck and hard at work, eyes alert for a tearing sail or a flapping rope. It would be impossi-

ble for her and Cadrach to sneak from one side of the
boat to the other unobserved, let alone lower the heavy
landing boat and escape over the side. Whatever Gan Itai
had planned, the storm would surely bring the scheme to
ruin.

The moon, though almost completely obscured, looked
to be near the place that the Niskie had indicated. As
Miriamele squinted into the rain, a pair of cursing sailors
approached the hatchway dragging a heavy coil of rope.
She quickly lowered the door and scrambled back down
the ladder, then hurried along the passage to Gan Itai's
room and the Niskie-hole that led to Cadrach.

The monk was awake and waiting. He seemed a little
improved, but his movements were still weak and slow.
As Miriamele wrapped the length of chain around his arm
and secured it with the strips from her cloak, she worried
about how she would manage to get him across the deck
to the landing boat unobserved.

When she had finished, Cadrach lifted his arm and
wagged it bravely. "It is almost no weight at all, Lady."

She stared at the heavy links, frowning. He was lying,
of course. She could see the strain in his face and his posture. For a moment she considered reopening the barrel
and having another try with hammer and chisel, but she
feared to take the time. Also, with the ship pitching so
strongly, there was a great chance she might somehow
wound herself or Cadrach by accident. She doubted their
escape would succeed, but it was her only hope. Now that
the time had come, she was determined to do her best.

"We must go soon. Here." She pulled a slim flask out
of her sack and handed it to Cadrach. "Just a few swallows."

He took it with a wondering look. After the first gulp,
a smile spread over his face. He took several more long
drinks.

"Wine." He licked his lips. "Good red Perdruin! By
Usires and Bagba and ... and everyone else! Bless you,
Lady!" He took a breath and sighed. "Now I can die
happy."

"Don't die. Not yet. Let me have that."

Cadrach looked at her, then reluctantly handed over the flask. Miriamele upended it and drank the last few swallows, feeling the warmth trickle down her throat and nestle into her stomach. She hid the empty vessel behind one of the barrels.

"Now we will go." She picked up her candle and led him to the ladder.

When Cadrach at last made his way up the ladder and into the passageway of the Niskie-hole, he stopped to catch his breath. As he wheezed, Miriamele considered the next step. Overhead, the ship hummed and vibrated beneath the downpour.

"There are three ways we can get out," she said aloud. Cadrach, steadying himself against the rocking of the ship, did not seem to be listening. "The hatchway out of the hold—but that opens directly in front of the aft deck, where there is always a steersman. In this weather someone will certainly be there and be wide awake. So that's out." She turned to look at the monk. In the small circle of candlelight, he was staring down at the passageway boards beneath him. "We have two choices. Up through the hatchway in the main passage, right past Aspitis and all his sailors, or down this passage to the far end, which probably opens onto the foredeck."

Cadrach looked up. "Probably?"

"Gan Itai never told me and I forgot to ask. But this is a Niskie-hole; she said she uses it to get across the ship quickly. Since she always sings from the foredeck, that must be the place it leads to."

The monk nodded wearily. "Ah."

"So I think we should go there. Perhaps Gan Itai is waiting for us. She didn't say how we should get to the landing boat or when she would meet us."

"I will follow you, Lady."

As they crawled along the narrow passageway, a huge concussive thump made the very air in their ears seem to burst. Cadrach let out a muffled cry of terror.

"Gods, what is it?" he gasped.

"Thunder," said Miriamele. "The storm is here."

"Usires Aedon in His mercy, save me from boats and the sea," Cadrach groaned. "They are all cursed. Cursed."

"From one boat to another, and even closer to the sea." Miriamele began inching along again. "That's where we're going—if we're lucky." She heard Cadrach come scrambling after her.

Thunder tolled two more times before they reached the end of the passage, each peal louder than the last. When at last they crouched beneath the hatchway, Miriamele turned and laid her hand on the monk's arm.

"I'm going to snuff the candle. Now be quiet."

She inched the heavy door up until the opening was as wide as her hand. Rain flew and splashed. They were just below the forecastle—the steps mounted up only a few paces from the hatch—and some twenty cubits from the portside railing. A glare of lightning momentarily illuminated the whole deck. Miriamele saw the silhouetted shapes of crewmen all around, caught in mid-gesticulation as though painted on a mural. The sky was pressing down on the ship, a roil of angry black clouds that smothered the stars. She dropped down and let the hatchway close as another smack of thunder rattled the night.

"There are people all around," she said when the echoes had faded. "But none of them are too close. If we get to the rail and wear our hoods up, they may not notice we are not of the crew. Then we can make our way aft to the boat."

Without the candle she could not see the monk, but she could hear him breathing in the narrow space beside her. She had a sudden thought.

"I did not hear Gan Itai. She was not singing."

There was a moment's silence before Cadrach spoke. "I am afraid, Miriamele," he said hoarsely. "If we are to go, let us go soon, before I lose what little nerve I have left."

"I'm afraid, too," she said, "but I need to think for a bit." She reached out and found his chilly hand, then held it while she pondered. They sat that way for some while before she spoke again. "If Gan Itai is not on the foredeck, then I don't know where she is. Maybe waiting for us at the landing boat, maybe not. When we get there, we'll have to undo the tie-ropes that hold it to the ship—all but one. I'll go look for her, and when I come back we'll drop the boat down and jump into the water. If I don't come back, you must do it yourself. It will only be one knot, though. It won't take much strength."

"Jump . . . into the water?" he stammered. "In this terrible storm? And with those demon-creatures, those *kilpa,* swimming there?"

"Of course, jump," she whispered, trying to hold down her annoyance. "If we let the boat go while we're in it, we'll probably break our backs. Don't worry, I'll go first and give you an oar to hang onto."

"You shame me, Lady," the monk said, but did not let go of her hand. "It should be me protecting you. But you know I hate the sea."

She squeezed his fingers. "I know. Come on, then. Remember, if someone calls to you, pretend you can't hear them properly and keep walking. And keep your hand on the railing, for the deck is sure to be slippery. You don't want to go overboard before we get the landing boat into the water."

Cadrach's laugh was giddy with fright. "You are right about that, Lady. God save us all."

Another sound abruptly rose over the roar of the storm, a little quieter than the thunder but somehow just as powerful. Miriamele felt it surge through her and had to brace herself against the wall for a moment as her knees became weak. She could not think what it might be. There was something terrible about it, something that went to her heart like a spike of ice, but there was no time left to hesitate. A moment later, when she had mastered herself once more, she pushed up the hatchway door and they clambered out into the driving rain.

The strange sound was all around, piercingly sweet yet as frightfully compelling as the pull of a riptide. For a moment it seemed to soar up beyond the range of mortal ears, so that only a ghost of its fullness remained and her skull was full of echoes that piped like bats; then, a moment later, it descended just as swiftly, swooping down so rumblingly deep that it might be singing the slow and stony language of the ocean's floor. Miriamele felt as though she stood inside a humming wasp's nest big as a cathedral: the sound quivered right down to her innards. A part of her burned with the need to fling her body into sympathetic motion, to dance and scream and run in circles; another part of her wanted only to lie down and beat her head against the desk until the sound stopped.

"God save us, what is that horrible noise?" Cadrach wailed. He lost his balance and tumbled to his knees.

Clenching her teeth, Miriamele put her head down and forced herself to inch away from the forecastle steps toward the rail. Her very bones seemed to rattle. She grabbed at the monk's sleeve and pulled him with her, dragging him like a sledge across the slippery planks. "It's Gan Itai," she gasped, fighting against the stunning power of the Niskie's song. "We're too close."

The velvety darkness, lit only by the yellow-streaming lanterns, suddenly went stark blue and white. The rail before her, Cadrach's hand in hers, the empty blackness of the sea beyond both—all were seared on her eyes in an explosive instant. A heartbeat later the lightning flared again, and Miriamele saw, imprisoned in the flash, a smooth round head poking up above the portside rail. As the lightning faded and thunder double-cracked, another half-dozen loose-jointed shapes came swarming onto the ship, slick and gleaming in the dim lantern light. Realization struck, hard as a physical blow; Miriamele turned, stumbling and sliding, then plunged toward the starboard side of the ship, dragging Cadrach after her.

"What is happening?" he shouted.

"It's Gan Itai!" Ahead of her sailors ran back and forth like ants from a scattered nest, but it was no longer the *Eadne Cloud*'s crew she feared. "It is the Niskie!" Her mouth filled with rainwater and she spat. "She is singing the kilpa *up!*"

"Aedon save us!" Cadrach shrieked. "Aedon save us!"

Lightning glared again, revealing a host of gray, froglike bodies slithering over the starboard rail. As the kilpa flopped down onto the deck, they swung their gape-

mouthed faces from side to side, staring like pilgrims who
had finally reached a great shrine. One of them threw out
a thin arm and caught a reeling crewman, then seemed to
fold around him, dragging the screaming man down into
darkness as the thunder bayed. Sickened, Miriamele
turned and hurried along the length of the ship toward the
spot where the landing boat hung. Water tugged at her
feet and ankles. As in a nightmare, she felt that she could
not run, that she was going slower and slower. The gray
things continued to spill over the side, like ghouls from a
childhood tale swarming out of an unhallowed grave. Behind her Cadrach was shouting incoherently. The Niskie's
maddening song hung over all, making the very night
pulse like a mighty heart.

The kilpa seemed to be everywhere, moving with a terrible, lurching suddenness. Even through the noise of the
storm and Gan Itai's singing, the deck echoed with de-
spairing cries from the beleaguered crewmen. Aspitis and
two of his officers were backed against one of the masts,
holding off a half-dozen of the sea beasts; their swords
were little more than thin glints of light, darting, flashing.
One of the kilpa tottered backward, clutching at an arm
that was no longer attached to its body. The creature let
the limb fall to the deck, then hunched over it, gills puffing. Black blood fountained from the stump.

"Oh, merciful Aedon!" Ahead, Miriamele could finally
see the dark shadow that was the boat. Even as she
dragged Cadrach toward it, one of the lamps burst against
the crosstree overhead, raining burning oil down onto the
watery deck. Gouts of steam leaped up all around and a
smoldering spark caught on Miriamele's sleeve. As she
hastily beat out the flame, the night erupted into orange
light. She looked up into a blinding torrent of raindrops.
A sail had caught fire, despite the storm, and the mast
was rapidly becoming a torch.

"The knots, Cadrach!" she shouted. Nearby, someone's
choking scream was buried in the rumble of thunder. She
grabbed at the rain-slicked rope and struggled, feeling
one of her fingernails tear as she tried to loose the swollen rope. At last it slipped free and she turned to the one

beside it. The landing boat swung with the roll of the ship, bumping her away from her task, but she hung on. Nearby, Cadrach, pale as a corpse, struggled with another of the four ropes that held the windlass over the deck of the *Eadne Cloud*.

She felt a wave of cold even before the thing touched her. She whirled, slipping and falling back against the hull of the landing boat, but the kilpa took a step closer and caught her trailing sleeve in its web-fingered hand. Its eyes were black pools that glowed with the flames of the burning sail. The mouth opened and then shut, opened and shut. Miriamele screamed as it dragged her nearer.

There was a sudden rush of movement from out of the shadows behind her. The kilpa fell back but retained its grip on her arm, dragging her down after it so that her outflung hand smacked the slippery resilience of its belly. She gasped and tried to rip herself loose, but the webbed hand gripped her too tightly. Its stench enwrapped her, brine and mud and rotting fish.

"*Run*, Lady!" Cadrach's face appeared behind the creature's shoulder. He had pulled his chain taut around its throat, but even as he tightened the strangling hold, Miriamele saw the gills on the kilpa's neck pulsing in the half-light, translucent wings of delicate gray flesh, pink at the edges. She realized with a numbing sense of defeat that the beast did not need its throat to breathe: Cadrach had the chain too high. Even as he strained, the kilpa was drawing her in toward the other reaching arm, toward its slack mouth and gelid eyes.

Gan Itai's song ended abruptly, although its echo seemed to linger for long moments. The only sounds that rose above the wind now were screams of fear and the dull hoots of the swarming sea-demons.

Miriamele had been fumbling at her belt, but at last her hand closed around Aspitis' hawk-knife. Her heart skipped as the hilt caught in a fold of her sodden robe, but with a tug it came free. She shook it hard to knock loose the sheath, then slashed at the gray arm that held her. The knife bit, freeing a line of inky blood, but failed to loosen the creature's grip.

"Ah, God help us!" Cadrach screeched.

The kilpa rounded its mouth but made no sound, only pulled her closer until she could see the rain beading on its shiny skin and the soft, pale wetness behind its lips. With a cry of disgusted rage, Miriamele threw herself forward, plunging the knife into the thing's gummy midsection. Now it did make a sound, a soft, surprised whistle. Blood bubbled out over Miriamele's hand and she felt the creature's grasp weaken. She stabbed again, then again. The kilpa spasmed and kicked for what seemed an eternity, but at last fell limp. She rolled away. Then, shuddering, she plunged her hands down into cleansing water. Cadrach's chain was still wrapped about the thing's neck, making a grisly tableau for the next flash of lightning. The monk's eyes were wide, his face stark white.

"Let it go," Miriamele gasped. "It's dead." Thunder echoed her.

Cadrach kicked the thing, then crawled on his hands and knees toward the landing boat, struggling for breath. Within moments he had recovered enough to fumble open his two knots, then he helped Miriamele, whose hands were shaking uncontrollably, to finish hers. With one of the oars they swung the scaffolding out from the side of the ship, guiding it until it was perpendicular to the deck and only one tie held the boat suspended from the windlass over the dark, surging water.

Miriamele turned to look back across the ship. The mast was burning like an Yrmansol tree, a pillar of flame whipped by the winds. There were pockets of struggling men and kilpa scattered across the deck, but there also seemed to be a relatively clear line between the landing boat and the forecastle.

"Stay here," she said, pulling her hood down to obscure her face. "I must find Gan Itai."

Cadrach's look of astonishment quickly turned to rage. "Are you mad? *Goirach cilagh!* You will find your death!"

Miriamele did not bother to argue. "Stay here. Use the oar to protect yourself. If I don't come back soon, drop the boat and follow it. I will swim to you if I can." She turned and trotted back across the deck with the knife clutched in her fist.

Pretty *Eadne Cloud* had become a hell-ship—something that might have been crafted by the devil's boatwrights to torment sinners on the deepest seas of damnation. Water covered much of the deck, and the fire from the central mast had spread to some of the other sails. Burning rags rode the winds like demons. The few bloodied sailors who still remained topside had the crushed, brutalized look of prisoners punished far past what any crime could warrant. Many kilpa had been slaughtered, too—a pile of their corpses lay near the mast where Aspitis and his officers had fought, although at least one human leg protruded from the heap—and quite a few more of the sea creatures seemed to have seized a meal and leaped back overboard, but others still hopped and slid after survivors.

Miriamele waded to the foredeck without being set upon, although she had to pass much closer than she wished to several groups of feeding kilpa. A part of her was amazed to find that she could look on such things without being overcome by terror. Her heart, it seemed, had hardened: a year before, any one of these atrocities would have had her weeping and searching for a place to hide. Now she felt that if she had to, she could walk through fire.

She reached the stairs and made her way swiftly up to the forecastle. The Niskie had not stopped singing altogether: a thin drone of melody still hung over the foredeck, a thin shadow of the power that had outstormed even the wind. The sea watcher sat cross-legged on the deck, bent forward so that her face nearly touched the planks.

"Gan Itai," Miriamele said. "The boat is ready! Come!"

At first the Niskie did not respond. Then, when she sat up, Miriamele gasped. She had never seen such wretchedness on the face of a living creature.

"Ah, no!" the Niskie croaked. "By the Uncharted, go away! *Go!*" She waved her hand feebly. "I have done this for your freedom. Do not make the crime pointless by failing your escape!"

"But aren't you going to come?!"

The Niskie moaned. Her face seemed to have aged a hundred years. Her eyes were sunken deep into her head, their luster burned away. "I cannot leave. I am the ship's only hope to survive. It will not change my guilt, but it will ease my ruined heart. May Ruyan forgive me—it is an evil world that has brought me to this!" She threw back her head and gave out a groan of misery that brought Miriamele to tears. "Go!" the Niskie wailed. "Go! I beg you!"

Miriamele tried again to plead with her, but Gan Itai lowered her face to the deck once more. After a long silence, she at last resumed her weak, mournful song. The rain eased for a moment as the wind changed direction. Miriamele saw that only a few figures still moved on the firelit deck below. She stared at the huddled Niskie, then made the sign of the Tree and went down the stairs. She would think later. Later she would wonder why. Later.

It was a wounded sailor, not a kilpa, who grabbed at Miriamele on her return. When she slashed at his hand the crewman let go and collapsed back onto the sloshing deck. A few steps farther along she waded past the body of Thures, the earl's young page. There were no signs of violence upon him. The boy's dead face was peaceful beneath the shallow water, his hair undulating like seaweed.

Cadrach was so happy to see her he did not utter a single word of reproach or ask any questions about her solitary return. Miriamele stared at where the last windlass-rope was tied, then reached out with the dagger and sawed through it, leaning back as the cut end whipped free. The winding-drum spun and the landing boat plummeted down. A fountain of white spray sprang up as it hit the waves.

Cadrach handed her the oar he had been clutching. "Here, Miriamele. You're tired. It will help you float."

"Me?" she said, surprised almost into a smile.

A third voice interrupted them. "*There* you are, my darling."

She whirled to see a ghastly figure limping toward them. Aspitis had been slashed bloody in a dozen places, and a long cut that snaked down his cheek had closed one eye and flecked his golden locks with gore, but he still held his long sword. He was still as beautiful and terrifying as a stalking leopard.

"You were going to leave me?" he asked mockingly. "Not stay and help clean up after our . . ." he grinned, a dreadful sight, and gestured toward him, ". . . our *wedding guests?*" He took another step forward, waving the sword slowly from side to side. It glinted in the light of burning sails like a whisker of red-hot iron. It was strangely fascinating to watch it pass back and forth . . . back and forth. . . .

Miriamele shook her head and stood up straighter. "Go to hell."

Aspitis' smile dropped away. He leveled the tip of the sword toward her eye. Cadrach, who stood behind her, cursed helplessly. "Should I kill you," the earl mused, "or will you still be useful?" His eyes were as inhuman as a kilpa's.

"Go ahead and kill me. I would die before I let you have me again." She stared at him. "You are paying the Fire Dancers, aren't you? For Pryrates?"

Aspitis shook his head. "Some only. Those who are not . . . firm believers. But they are *all* useful." He frowned. "I do not wish to talk of such unimportant things. You are mine. I must decide . . ."

"I have something that *is* yours," she said, and raised the dagger before her. Aspitis smiled oddly, but lifted his sword-blade to fend off a sudden throw. Instead, Miriamele tossed the knife into the water at his feet. His dreaming eye caught its glitter and followed it down. As his head dipped, ever so slightly, Miriamele thrust the oar handle into his gut. He gasped for breath and took a staggering step backward, his sword jabbing blindly like the sting of an injured bee. Miriamele brought the oar up again with both hands, then swung it with all the might of her arms and back, sweeping it around in a great arc that ended with a crunch of bone. Aspitis shrieked and fell to the deck holding his face. Blood spurted from between his fingers.

"Hah!" Cadrach shouted with exultant relief. "Look at you, you devil! Now, you will have to find something else to bait your woman-trap with!"

Miriamele fell to her knees, then pushed the oar across the slippery deck to Cadrach. "Go," she panted. "Take this and jump."

The monk stood in confusion for a moment, as if he could not remember where he was, then staggered to the side of the ship. He closed his eyes and muttered some words, then plunged overboard. Miriamele rose and took a last look at the earl, who was bubbling red froth out onto the deck, then scrambled over the railing and pushed herself out into emptiness. For a moment she was falling, flying through the dark. When the water closed on her like a cold fist, she wondered if she would ever come back up, or if instead she would just continue downward into the ultimate depths, into blackness and quiet. . . .

She did come up. When she had reached the boat and helped Cadrach to clamber aboard, they fitted the oars and began to row away from the wounded ship. The storm still hovered overhead, but it was diminishing. *Eadne Cloud* grew smaller behind them until it was only a point of burning light on the black horizon, a tiny flame like a dying star.

7

Storm King's Anvil

At the nothernmost edge of the world the mountain stood, an upthrusting fang of icy stone that shadowed the entire landscape, towering high above even the other peaks. For long weeks the smokes and steams and vapors had crept from vents in the mountain's side. Now they wreathed Stormspike's crown, spinning in the awesome winds that circled the mountain, gathering and darkening as though they sucked the very substance of ultimate night from between the stars.

The storm grew and spread. The few scattered folk who still lived within sight of the terrible mountain huddled in their longhouses as the beams creaked and the wind howled. What seemed an unceasing blizzard of snow piled above their walls and onto their roofs, until all that remained were white mounds like so many grave barrows, marked as dwellings of the living only by the thin pennants of smoke that fluttered above the chimney-holes.

The vast expanse of open land known as the Frostmarch was also engulfed by driving snows. Only a few years before, the vast plain had been dotted with small hamlets, thriving towns and settlements fed by the traffic of the Wealdhelm and Frostmarch roads. After half a dozen seasons of continuous snow, with crops long dead and virtually all the animals fled or eaten, the land had become a desolate waste. Those who huddled in the foot-hills along its border or in the sheltering forests knew it as the home only of wolves and wandering ghosts, and

had come to call the Frostmarch by a new name—the
Storm King's Anvil. Now an even greater storm, a dreadful hammer of frost and cold, was pounding on that anvil
once more.

The storm's long hand reached out even beyond
Erkynland to the south, sending gusts of freezing wind
across the open grasslands, turning the Thrithings bone-
white for the first time in memory. And snow returned to
Perdruin and Nabban—the second time in a season, but
only the third time in five centuries, so that those who
had once scoffed at the Fire Dancers and their dire warnings now felt a squeeze of fear on their hearts, a fear
much more chilling than the powdery snow sifting down
onto the domes of the two Sancellans.

Like a tide moving toward some unimaginable high
water mark, the storm spread farther than ever before,
bringing frost to southern lands that had never felt its
touch and draping a great cold shroud over all of Osten
Ard. It was a storm that numbed hearts and crushed spirits.

"That way!" the leading rider shouted, pointing to the
left. "*Á prenteiz,* men—up and after!" He spurred forward
so swiftly that his clouded breath was left hanging in the
air behind him. Snow spouted from beneath his horse's
hooves.

He bore down on the empty space between two tumbledown, snow-covered dwellings, his mount slashing
through the drifts as effortlessly as through fog. A dark
shape bolted out into the open from behind one of the
buildings and dashed away, bounding erratically across
the flat. The leading pursuer vaulted a low, snow-buried
fence, landed, and followed close after. The horse's
pounding strides obliterated the smaller prints of its fleeing quarry, but there was no need now for tracking: the
end was in sight. Half a dozen other riders came hurtling
from between the houses and spread out like an opening
fan, surrounding the quarry like a riverman's fishing net.

A moment to draw the net closed—the riders reining in as a narrowing circle—then the hunt was over. One of the men who had ridden the wing leaned down until his lance touched the captive's heaving side. The leader dismounted and took a step forward.

"Well run," said Duke Fengbald, grinning. "That was excellent sport."

The boy stared up at him, eyes wide with terror.

"Shall I finish him, Lord?" asked the rider with the lance. He gave the boy a hard poke. The child squealed and flinched away from the sharp lance-head.

Fengbald peeled off his gauntlet, then turned and flung it into the rider's face. Its metal beadwork left a cross-hatching on the man's cheek that welled with blood. "Dog!" Fengbald scowled. "What am I—a demon? You will be whipped for that." The rider shied away, pulling his horse a few steps back from the circle. Fengbald glared after him. "I do not murder innocent children." He turned his eyes down to the cowering boy. "We had a game, that is all. Children love games. This one has played with us as well as he could." The duke retrieved his gauntlet and put it back on, then smiled. "And a merry chase you led us, boy. What is your name?"

The child grimaced, baring his teeth like a treed cat, but made no sound.

"Ah, too bad," Fengbald said with a philosophical air. "If he will not talk, he will not talk. Put him with the rest—one of these shack-women will feed him. They say a bitch will always nurse a stranger's pups."

One of Fengbald's men-at-arms dismounted and grabbed the boy, who put up no resistance as he was draped across the front of the soldier's saddle.

"I think he is the last," said Fengbald. "The last of our sport, too. A shame—but still, better than if we let them run ahead of us and spoil our surprise." He grinned broadly, pleased with his own wit. "Come. I want a warm cup of wine to take off the chill. This was a hard, cold ride."

He vaulted up into the saddle, then swung his mount

around and led his company back into the snow-
smothered remnants of Gadrinsett.

Duke Fengbald's red tent sat in the middle of the
snowy meadow like a ruby in a puddle of milk. The silver
falcon, the duke's family emblem, stretched its wings
from corner to corner above the door-flap; in the stiff
winds that blew down the river valley, the great bird
trembled as though longing to take flight. The tents of the
duke's army were clustered all around, but set at a respectful distance.

Inside, Fengbald reclined on a pile of figured cushions,
his cup of mulled wine—several times refilled since he
had returned—held loosely, his dark hair unbound and
trailing down across his shoulders. At Elias' coronation
Fengbald had been lean as a young hound. Now the master of Falshire, Utanyeat, and the Westfold had grown a
little soft in the waist and jowls. A fair-haired woman
kneeled on the floor near his feet. A thin page, pale and
anxious-looking, waited at his lord's right hand.

On the far side of the brazier that warmed the tent was
a tall man, squint-eyed and bearded, dressed in the leather
and rough wool of the Thrithings-dweller. Refusing to sit
as city-folk did, he stood spread-legged, arms crossed.
When he shifted, his necklace of finger-bones made a
clinking music.

"What else is there to know?" he demanded. "Why
more talking?"

Fengbald stared at him, eyes slowly blinking. He was a
little befuddled by drink, which for once seemed to curb
his belligerence. "I must like you, Lezhdraka," he said at
last, "because otherwise I would have become sick of
your questions long ago."

The mercenary chieftain stared back, unimpressed.
"We know where they are. What more do we ask?"

The duke took another drink, then wiped his mouth
with the sleeve of his silken shirt and gestured to his
page. "More, Isaak." He returned his attention to
Lezhdraka. "I learned some things from old Guthwulf, for
all his failings. I have been given the keys to a great king-

dom. They are in my hand, and I will not throw them away by acting too fast."

"Keys to a kingdom?" said the Thrithings-man scornfully. "What stone-dweller nonsense is that?"

Fengbald seemed pleased by the mercenary's incomprehension. "How do you plains-folk ever hope to drive me and the other city-dwellers into the sea, as you are always babbling about? You have no craft, Lezhdraka, no craft at all. Just go and fetch the old man. You like the night air—do your people not sleep, eat, piss, and sport beneath the stars?" The duke chuckled.

The High King's Hand, having turned to watch his page fill his cup, did not witness the Thrithings-man's venomous look as he left the tent. But for the wind strumming the fabric, the tent fell quiet.

"So, my sweet," Fengbald said at last, prodding the silent woman with his slippered foot, "how does it feel to know that you belong to the man who will one day hold all the land in his grasp?" When she did not reply, he pushed her again, more roughly. "Speak, woman."

She looked up slowly. Her pretty face was empty, drained of life as a corpse's. "It is good, my lord," she murmured at last, the Westerling words thickly accented by a Hernystiri burr. She let her head sink back down, her hair falling like a curtain before her features. The duke looked around impatiently.

"And you, Isaak? What do you think?"

"It is well, master," the page said hurriedly. "If you say it will happen, it will happen."

Fengbald smiled. "Of course it will. How can I fail?" He paused for a moment, frowning at the boy's expression, then shrugged. There were worse things than being feared.

"Only a fool," he resumed, quickly warming to the topic once more, "only a fool, I say, could not see that King Elias is a dying man." He waved his hand expansively, slopping a little wine over the rim of his cup. "Whether he has caught some wasting illness, or whether the priest Pyrates is slowly poisoning him, I do not care. The red priest is an idiot if he thinks he can rule the kingdom—he is the most hated man in Osten Ard. No, when Elias dies, only someone of noble blood will be able to rule. And who will that be? Guthwulf has gone blind and run away." He laughed shortly. "Benigaris of Nabban? He cannot even rule his own mother. And Skali the Rimmersman is no more noble or civilized than that animal Lezhdraka. So when I have killed Josua—if he even truly lives—and put down this petty rebellion, who else will be fit to rule?" Excited by his own words, he drained the remainder of his cup in a single draught. "Who else? And who would oppose me? The king's daughter, that fickle slut?" He paused and eyed the page intently, so that the young boy lowered his gaze. "No, perhaps if Miriamele came begging to me on her knees, I *might* make her my queen—but I would keep her closely watched. And she would be punished for spurning me." He smirked and leaned forward, placing his hand on the pale neck of the woman who knelt before him. "But never fear, little Feurgha, I would not cast you aside for her. I will keep you, too." As she shrunk away he tightened his hand, holding her, enjoying the tension of her resistance.

The tent flap bulged and flapped inward. Lezhdraka entered, snowflakes shimmering in his hair and beard. He held the arm of an old man whose bald head was red with too much sun and whose white ruff of beard was stained and discolored by the juices of citril root. Lezhdraka roughly shoved the man forward. The captive took a few stumbling steps, then fell stiffly to his knees at Fengbald's feet and did not look up. His neck and shoulders, exposed by the open collar of his thin shirt, were covered with yellowing bruises.

When the nervous page had filled the duke's cup once more, Fengbald cleared his throat. "You look somewhat familiar. Do I know you?" The old man wagged his head from side to side. "So. You may look up. You claim to be the Lord Mayor of Gadrinsett?"

The old man nodded slowly. "I am," he croaked.

"You *were*. Not that there would be much glory in being mayor of this pesthole in any case. Tell me what you know about Josua."

"I . . . I don't understand, Lord."

Fengbald leaned forward and gave him a brief but solid push. The Lord Mayor toppled over to lie on his side; he did not seem to have the strength to sit up again. "Don't play the fool with me, old man. What have you heard?"

Still curled on his side, the Lord Mayor coughed. "Nothing that you have not learned, Duke Fengbald," he quavered, "nothing. Riders came from the evil-omened valley up the Stefflod. They said that Josua Lackhand had escaped from his brother, that he and a band of warriors and magicians had driven out the demons and made a stronghold on the witch-mountain in the middle of the valley. That all who came to join him there would be fed, and have places to live, and that they would be protected from bandits and from . . . and from . . ." his voice dropped, ". . . from the High King's soldiers."

"And you think it is a pity you did not listen to these treasonous rumors, eh?" Fengbald asked. "You think that perhaps Prince Josua might have saved you from the king's vengeance?"

"But we did no wrong, my lord!" the old man moaned. "We did no wrong!"

Fengbald looked at him with perfect coldness. "You harbored traitors, since everyone who joins Josua is a traitor. Now, how many are with him on this witch-mountain?"

The mayor shook his head vehemently. "I do not know, lord. In time, some few hundred of our folk went. The first riders who came said there were five or six score there already, I think."

"Counting women and children?"

"Yes, lord."

Fengbald snapped his fingers. "Isaak, go find a guards-man and bid him come to me."

"Yes, sire." The youth hurried out, happy with any er-rand that took him out of his master's reach for a few moments.

"A few more questions." The duke settled back against the cushions. "Why did your people believe it was Josua?

Why should they leave a safe haven to go to a place of bad reputation?"

The old man shrugged helplessly. "One of the women who lived here claimed she had met Josua—that she had sent him to the rock herself. A gossipy creature, but well-known. She swore that she had fed him at her fire and had marked him instantly as the prince. Many were convinced by her. Others went because ... because they heard you were coming, Duke Fengbald. People from Erkynland and the western Thrithings came here, fleeing ... moving east ahead of your lordship's progress." He cringed as if expecting a blow. "Forgive me, lord." A tear ran down his wrinkled cheek.

The tent flap rustled. Isaak the page entered, followed by a helmeted Erkynguardsman. "You wanted me, lord?" the soldier said.

"Yes." Fengbald gestured toward the old man. "Take this one back to the pens. Treat him roughly, but do not hurt him. I will wish to speak to him again later." The duke turned. "You and I have things to talk about, Lezhdraka." The guardsman dragged the mayor to his feet. Fengbald watched the process with contempt. "Lord Mayor, is it?" he snorted. "There is not a drop of lordly blood in you, peasant."

The old man's rheumy eyes opened wide, staring at Fengbald. For a moment, it seemed he might do something entirely mad; instead, he shook his head like someone waking from a dream. "My brother was a nobleman," he said hoarsely, then a fresh outpouring of tears spilled down his cheeks. The soldier grabbed his elbow and hastened him out of the tent.

Lezhdraka stared insolently at Fengbald. " 'Do not hurt him?' I thought you were harder than that, city-man."

A slow, drunken smile spread across Fengbald's face. "What I said was, 'treat him roughly but do not hurt him.' I don't want the rest of his folk to know he will spill his guts any time I ask. And he may prove useful to me somehow, either as a spy in the pens or as a spy among Josua's folk. Those traitors take in all who flee my terrible wrath, do they not?"

The Thrithings-man squinted. "Do you think my horse-men and your armored city-dwellers cannot smash your king's enemies?"

Fengbald waved an admonitory finger. "Never throw a weapon away. You never know when you may need it. That's another lesson that sightless fool Guthwulf taught me." He laughed, then waved his cup. His page scurried after the wine ewer.

Outside, darkness had fallen. The duke's tent glowed crimson, smoldering like an ember half-buried in fireplace ashes.

A rat, Rachel thought bitterly. *Now I'm no better than a rat in the walls.*

She peered out at the darkened kitchen and suppressed a bitter curse. It was just as well that Judith had long since quit the Hayholt. If the huge, galleon-stately Mistress of the Kitchens were to see the condition of her beloved domain, it would probably kill her dead. Rachel the Dragon's own work-callused hands itched as she felt herself torn between a desire to repair the damage and an equally strong urge to throttle whoever had let the castle fall into this dreadful state.

The Hayholt's great kitchen might have become a den of wild dogs. The pantry doors were off their hinges and the few remaining sacks of foodstuffs lay ripped and scattered about the chamber. It was the waste as much as the filth that set a fire of anger burning in Rachel's heart. Flour lay all across the floors, ground into the cracks between flagstones, crisscrossed with the prints of heedless, booted feet. The great ovens were black with grease, the baking paddles charred from inexpert use. Staring out at the wreckage from her hiding hole behind a hanging curtain, Rachel felt tears coursing down her face.

God should strike those who did this dead. This is wickedness with no purpose—devil's work.

And the kitchen, for all the damage done, was one of the places least affected by the evil changes that had overtaken the Hayholt. Rachel had seen much in her forays out of hiding, all of it disheartening. The fires were no longer set in most of the great chambers and the dark hallways were almost misty with cold. The shadows seemed to have lengthened, as though a strange twilight had settled over the castle: even on the days when the sun broke through the clouds, the Hayholt's passages and gardens were steeped in shade. But the night itself had become almost too frightening to bear. When the dim sun set, Rachel found herself hiding-places in the abandoned places of the castle and did not stir until dawn. The unearthly sounds that floated through the darkness were enough to make her pull her shawl over her head, and sometimes as evening came along there were shifting, unsolid shapes that hovered just at the edge of vision. Then, when the bells rang midnight, dark-robed demons silently walked the halls.

Clearly some dreadful magic was at work all around. The ancient castle seemed almost to breathe, imbued with a chilling vitality that it had never had before, for all its illustrious history. Rachel could feel a crouching presence, patient but alert as a predatory beast, that seemed to inhabit the very stones. No, this ruined kitchen was only the smallest, mildest sample of the evil Elias had brought down on her beloved home.

She waited, listening, until she was certain no one was about, then pushed her way out past the curtain. The closet behind this hanging had a false back hung with shelves of vinegar and mustard jars; the shelves hid a passageway into one of the network of corridors that ran behind, above, and beneath the Hayholt's walls. Rachel, who for many weeks now had made her home in these between-places, still marveled at the web of secret ways that had surrounded her all her life, unseen and unrecognized as a riot of mole tunnels beneath a formal garden.

Now I know where that rascal Simon used to disappear to. By the Blessed Mother, no wonder I sometimes thought the boy'd been swallowed up by the earth when there was work to be done.

She made her way out to the center of the kitchen,

moving as quietly as her stiff old bones would allow so
she would not obscure the sounds of anyone approaching.
There were few people left in the great keep these days—
Rachel did not think of the king's white-faced demons as
people—but there were still some mercenaries from the
Thrithings and elsewhere billeted in the castle's scores of
empty rooms. It was such barbarians as those, Rachel felt
sure, who had reduced Judith's kitchen to its hideous condition. Surely abominations like those devil-Norns did not
even eat earthly food. Drank blood most likely, if the
Book of the Aedon was any guide—and it had been Rachel's only guide since she was old enough to understand
what the priests said.

There was nothing remotely fresh to be found anywhere. More than once Rachel opened a jar to discover
the contents rotted, covered with blue or white mold, but
after much patient searching she was able to find two
small containers of salted beef and a jug of vegetables
pickled in brine that had rolled beneath a table and somehow been missed. She also discovered three loaves of
bread, hard and stale, wrapped in a napkin in one of the
pantries. Although the sample piece she pulled from a
loaf was painfully hard to chew—Rachel had few teeth
left, and felt sure that such fare as this would finish off
the survivors—it was edible, and when dipped in the beef
brine would make a nice change indeed. Still, this raid
had turned up scant results. How much longer would she
be able to keep herself alive on what she could thieve
from the Hayholt's untended larders? Thinking of the
days ahead, she shivered. It was horribly cold, even in the
rock fastness of the castle's internal passageways. How
long could she go on?

She wrapped the fruits of her scavenging in her shawl
and dragged the heavy bundle across the floor toward the
closet and its hidden door, doing her best to obscure the
tracks she made in the flour. When she reached the closet,
where the flour—so eerily like the snow outside—had not
yet drifted, she unwrapped her take for a moment and
used the shawl to brush away all the nearest marks, so

that no one might wonder at tracks that disappeared into an abandoned closet and failed to come out again.

As she was rebundling her salvage, she heard voices in the hallway outside. A moment later, the great kitchen doors began to swing inward. Her heart suddenly beating as swiftly as a bird's, Rachel leaned forward and caught at the curtain with fumbling fingers, then pulled the hanging across the closet entrance just as the outer door thumped back against the wall and booted footsteps sounded on the flagstones.

"Damn him and his grinning face, where is he?!"

Rachel's eyes widened as she recognized the king's voice.

"I know I heard someone in here!" Elias shouted. There was a crash as something was swept off one of the knife-scarred tables, then the rhythmic clatter of someone pacing back and forth across the great length of the kitchen floor. "I hear everything in this castle, every footstep, every murmur, until my head pounds with it! He must have been here! Who else could it be?"

"I told you, Majesty, I do not know."

The Mistress of Chambermaids' heart skipped and seemed to stumble between beats. That was Pryrates. She thought of him as he had stood before her—her knife standing from his back, no more effective than a twig— and felt herself sagging toward the floor. She reached out a hand to steady herself and brushed against a copper trivet hanging on the wall, setting it swinging. Rachel grasped it, holding its heavy weight out from the wall so that it would make no noise.

Like a rat! Her thoughts were wild and fragmented. *Like a rat. Trapped in the walls. Cats outside.*

"Aedon burn and blast him, he is not to leave my side!" Elias' hoarse voice, teetering on the edge of some strange despair, seemed almost to reflect Rachel's own panic. "Hengfisk!" he shouted. "Damn your soul, where are you!?" The sound of the king's furious pacing resumed. "When I find him, I will slit his throat."

"*I* will prepare your cup for you, Majesty. I will do it for you now. Come."

"It's not just that. What is he doing? Where could he be? He has no right to go off wandering!"

"He will be back soon, I'm sure," the priest said. He sounded impatient. "His needs are few, and easily satisfied. Come now, Elias, we should go back to your chamber."

"He's hiding!" Rachel could hear the king's steps suddenly grow louder. He stopped, and she heard a squeak of hinges as he yanked at one of the broken doors. "He is hiding in the shadows somewhere!"

The footsteps approached. Rachel held her breath, trying to be as still as stone. She heard the king come nearer, muttering angrily as he yanked at doors and kicked piles of fallen hangings out of his way. Her head whirled. Darkness seemed to descend before her eyes, a darkness threaded with fluttering sparks of light.

"Majesty!" Pryrates voice was sharp. The king stopped thrashing and quiet descended on the kitchen. "This is accomplishing nothing. Come. Let me prepare your cup. You are overtired."

Elias groaned softly, a terrible sound like a beast in final pain. At last, he said: "When will it all end, Pryrates?"

"Soon, Majesty." The priest's voice resumed its soothing tone. "There are certain rituals to be performed on Harrow's Eve. Then, after the year turns, the star will come and that will show that the final days are at hand. Soon after, your waiting will be over."

"Sometimes I cannot bear the pain, Pryrates. Sometimes I wonder if anything is worth this pain."

"Surely the greatest gift of all is worth any price, Elias." Pryrates' footfalls moved closer. "Just as the pain is beyond what others must bear, so are you brave beyond other men. Your reward will be equally splendid."

The two men moved away from her hiding spot. Rachel let out her breath in a near-silent hiss.

"I am burning up."

"I know, my king." The doors thumped shut behind them.

Rachel the Dragon sank to a crouch on the closet floor. Her hand shook as she traced the sign of the Tree.

Guthwulf could feel stone at his back and stone beneath his feet, and yet at the same moment he felt that he stood before a great abyss. He folded to his knees and reached cautiously before him, patting at the ground, certain that any moment he would feel his hand waving in empty space. But nothing was before him but more of the endless stone of the passageway floor.

"God help me, I am cursed!" he shouted. His voice rattled and echoed from a distant ceiling, obliterating for a moment the whispering chorus that had surrounded him for a length of time he could not guess. "Cursed!" He fell forward, cradling his face on his outstretched arms in an unconscious attitude of prayer, and wept.

He knew only that he must be somewhere beneath the castle. Since the moment he had stepped through the unseen doorway, fleeing from flames that burned so hot that he was certain they would char him to cinders, he had been as lost as a damned soul. He had wandered through these mazy depths so long that he could no longer remember the feeling of wind and sunshine on his face, no longer recall the taste of food other than cold worms and beetles. And always the ... *others* ... had accompanied him, the quiet murmurs just below the level of intelligibility, the ghostly things that seemed to move beside him but mocked his blindness by slipping away before he could touch them. Countless days he had stumbled unseeing through this netherworld of mournful whispers and shifting forms, until life was only that which made him sensible to torment. He had become little more than a cord tight-stretched between terror and hunger. He was cursed. There could be no other explanation.

Guthwulf rolled over onto his side and slowly sat up. If Heaven was punishing him for the wickedness of his life, how long would it go on? He had always scoffed at the priests and their talk of eternity, but now he knew that even an hour could stretch to a terrible, infinite length. What could he do to end this dreadful sentence?

"I have sinned!" he screamed, his voice a hoarse croak. "I have lied and killed, even when I knew it was wrong! *Sinned!*" The echoes flew and dissipated. "Sinned," he whispered.

Guthwulf crawled forward another cubit, praying that the pit he had sensed was truly there before him, a hole into which he would tumble and perhaps find the release of death—if he were not already dead. Anything was preferable to this unending emptiness. Were it not as grave a sin as the murder of another, he would have long since smashed his head against the stone that surrounded him until life fled, but he feared that he would only find himself awakened to an even more dreadful sentence after the added crime of self-slaughter. He groped ahead in desperation, but his crawling fingers found nothing but more stone, the unending, winding passageway floor.

Surely this was but another element of his punishment, the shifting reality of his prison. Just as a moment earlier he had known beyond doubt that a great chasm lay before him—a chasm that his fingers now proved did not exist—he had at other times encountered great columns that rose to the ceiling, and had run his hands over their intricate carvings, trying to read in their crafted textures some message of hope, only to find a moment later that he stood in the midst of a great and empty chamber as vacant of columns as it was of other human company.

What of the others, he suddenly wondered? What of Elias and the devil Pryrates? Surely if divine justice had been meted out, they had not escaped—not with crimes on their souls vaster and more evil by far than Guthwulf's poor tally. What had happened to them, and to all the other uncountable sinners who had lived and died on the spinning earth? Was each condemned to his or her own solitary damnation? Did others as afflicted as Guthwulf wander just on the other side of the stone walls, wondering if they, too, were the last creatures in the universe?

He clambered to his feet and stumbled toward the wall, pounding on it with the flat of his hand. "Here I am!" he cried. "I am!" He let his fingers drag down the cool, faintly damp surface as he slumped to the floor again.

In all the years when he had been alive—for he could not help but feel that his life was now over, even if he still seemed to inhabit a body that hurt and hungered— Guthwulf had never realized the simple wonder of companionship. He had enjoyed his associations with others—the rough company of men, the satisfying compliance of women—but he had always been able to do without them. Friends had died or left. Some Guthwulf had been forced to turn his back on when they opposed him, some one or two he had been forced to remove, despite previous comradeship. Even the king had turned on him at last, but Guthwulf had been strong. To need was to be weak. To be weak was not to be a man.

Now Guthwulf thought of the most precious thing he had. It was not his honor, for he knew he had given that up when he did not raise a hand to help Elias combat his growing madness; it was not his pride, for he had lost that with his sight, when he became a staggering invalid who had to wait for a servant to bring him a chamber pot. Even his courage was no longer his to give or receive, for it had fled when Elias made him touch the gray sword and he had felt the blade's horrible, cold song run through him like poison. No, the only thing left to him was the most ephemeral of all, the tiny spark that still lived and still hoped, buried though it was beneath such a weight of despair. Perhaps that was a soul, that thing the priests prattled about, and perhaps it wasn't—he no longer cared. But he did know that he would give even that last, crucial spark away if he could only have companionship once more, if there could be some end to this hideous loneliness.

The empty darkness suddenly filled with a great wind, a wind that blew through him but did not rustle a hair on his head. Guthwulf groaned weakly: he had felt this before. The void that surrounded him filled with chittering voices that brushed by him moaning and sighing words that he could not understand, but that he felt were full of loss and dread. He stretched out a hand, knowing as he

did so that there was nothing to grasp . . . but his hand
touched something.

With a gasp of shock, Guthwulf snatched the hand
back. A moment later, as the rush of wailing shades dwindled down the endless corridor, something touched him
again, this time bumping against his outstretched leg. He
squeezed his eyelids shut, as though whatever was there
might horrify even the eyes of a blind man. There was another insistent push at his leg. He slowly reached out once
more and felt . . . fur.

The cat—for surely that was what it was: he could feel
its back arching beneath his hand, the sinuous tail sliding
between his fingers—thumped his knee with its small,
hard head. He let his fingers rest on it, not daring to move
for fear of frightening it away. Guthwulf held his breath,
half-certain that this would prove to be like other things
of this inconstant netherworld, that a moment's time
would find it vanished into air. But the cat seemed
pleased with its own substantiality; it put two paws up on
his thin leg, delicately sinking its claws into his skin as it
moved beneath his careful touch.

For a moment, as he scratched and patted, and as the
unseen animal wriggled with pleasure, he remembered
that he had eaten nothing but crawling things since he had
come to this place of damnation. The warm flesh moved
beneath his hand, a starving man's banquet of meat and
hot, salty blood separated from him only by a thin layer
of fur.

It would be so easy, he thought, his fingers gently circling the cat's neck. *Easy. Easy.* Then, as his fingers tightened just a little bit, the cat began to purr. The vibrations
moved up through its throat and into his fingers, a throb
of contentment and trust as piercingly beautiful as any
music of angelic choirs. For the second time in an hour,
Guthwulf burst into tears.

When the one-time Earl of Utanyeat awoke, he had no
idea how long he had been asleep, but for the first time in
many days he felt as though he had truly rested. His moment of peace ended quickly when he realized that the

TO GREEN ANGEL TOWER 239

warm body that had nestled in his lap was gone. He was alone once more.

Just as the emptiness swept back down upon him, there was a soft pressure against his leg, then a small cold nose pressed against his hand.

"Back," he whispered. "You came back." He reached down to touch the cat's head, but instead found he was pressing something smaller, something warm and slickly wet. The cat purred as he felt the thing that it had pushed against his hip: it was a rat, recently killed.

Guthwulf sat up, saying a silent prayer of thanks, and pulled the offering apart with trembling fingers. He returned an equal portion to the founder of the feast.

Deep beneath the dark bulk of Stormspike Mountain, the eyes of Utuk'ku Seyt-Hamakha suddenly opened. She lay motionless in the onyx crypt that was her bed, staring up into the perfect blackness of her stone chamber. She had wandered far along her web, into places in the dream-world that only the eldest of the immortals could go—and in the shadows of the most distant improbabilities, she had seen something she had not expected. A sharp sliver of unease pierced her ancient heart. Somewhere at the outermost edges of her designs, a strand had snapped. What that meant, she could not know, but an uncertainty had been added, a flaw in the pattern she had woven so long and so faultlessly.

The Norn Queen sat up, her long-fingered hand clawing for her silver mask. She placed it on her face, so that once more she appeared as serenely emotionless as the moon, then she sent out a cold and fleeting thought. A door opened in the blackness and dark shapes entered, bringing with them a little light, for they, too, wore masks, theirs of faintly glowing pale stone. They helped their mistress to rise from her vault and brought her royal robes of ice-white and silver, which they wrapped about her with the ritual care of burial priests swaddling the dead. When she was dressed, they scuttled away, leaving

Utuk'ku alone once more. She sat for a while in her lightless chamber; if she breathed, she made no sound doing
so. Only the almost imperceptible creaking of the mountain's roots sullied the pure silence.

After some time, the Norn Queen rose and made her
way out through the twisting corridors that her servants
had carved from the mountain's flesh in the deeps of the
past. She came at last to the Chamber of the Breathing
Harp and took her seat upon the great throne of black
rock. The Harp hovered in the mists that rose from the
vast well, its shifting dimensions glinting in the lights that
shone from the deeps below. The Lightless Ones were
chanting somewhere in the depths of Stormspike, their
hollow voices tracing the shapes of songs that had been
old and already forbidden back in the Lost Garden,
Venyha Do'Sae. Utuk'ku sat and stared at the Harp, letting her mind trace its complexities as the steams of the
pit met the chamber's icy air and turned to frost upon her
eyelashes.

Ineluki was not there. He had gone, as he sometimes
did, into that place that was no place, where he alone
could go—a place as far beyond the dreamworld as
dreams were beyond waking, as far beyond death as death
was beyond living. For this time, the Norn Queen would
have to keep her own counsel.

Although her shining silver face was as impassive as
ever, Utuk'ku nevertheless felt a shadow of impatience as
she stared into the untenanted Well. Time was growing
short now. A lifetime for one of the scurrying mortals was
a scant season for the eldest, so the short span that
stretched between now and the hour of her triumph could
seem scarcely more than a few heartbeats if she chose to
perceive it so. But she did not choose that. Every moment
was precious. Every instant brought victory closer—but
for that victory to come to pass, there could be no mistakes.

The Queen of the Norns was troubled.

8

Nights of Fire

Simon's blood seemed almost to boil in his veins. He looked around him, at the white-blanketed hills, at the dark trees bending in the fierce, chilling winds, and wondered how he could feel so full of fire. It was excitement—the thrill of responsibility . . . and of danger. Simon felt very much alive.

He leaned his cheek against Homefinder's neck and patted her firm shoulder. Her wind-cooled skin was damp with sweat.

"She is tired," Hotvig said, cinching the strap on his own mount's saddle. "She is not meant for such fast traveling."

"She's fine," Simon shot back. "She's stronger than you think."

"The Thrithings-folk know horses if they know anything," Sludig said over his shoulder. He turned away from the tree trunk, lacing his breeches. "Do not be so proud, Simon."

Simon stared at the Rimmersman for a moment before speaking. "It is not pride. I rode this horse a long way. I will keep her."

Hotvig raised his hand placatingly. "I did not mean to make you angry. It is just that you are thought of well by Prince Josua. You are his knight. You could have one of our fleet clan-horses for the asking."

Simon turned his stare on the braid-bearded grasslander, then tried to smile. "I know you meant it well, Hotvig, and one of your horses would be a gift indeed. But this is different. I called this horse Homefinder, and that is where she will go with me. Home."

"And where is that home, young thane?" asked one of the other Thrithings-men.

"The Hayholt," Simon said firmly.

Hotvig laughed. "The place where Josua's brother rules? You and your horse must be mighty travelers indeed, to ride into such fierce weather."

"That's as may be." Simon turned to look at the others, squinting against the oblique afternoon light streaming past the trees. "If you're all ready, it's time to go. If we wait longer, the storm may die. We'll be under the light of an almost full moon tonight. I'd rather have the snow and the sentries all hunkered down over a fire."

Sludig started to say something, then thought better of it. The Thrithings-men nodded in agreement and swung easily into their saddles.

"Lead on, thane." Hotvig's laugh was short but not unfriendly. The little company eased down out of the copse and back into the bitter clutches of the wind.

Simon was almost as grateful for the simple chance to *do* something as he was of this evidence of Josua's trust. The days of increasingly bad weather, coupled with the important duties granted to his companions but not to him, had left Simon restless and ill-tempered. Binabik, Geloë, and Strangyeard were in deep discussion over the swords and the Storm King; Deornoth oversaw the arming and preparing of New Gadrinsett's ragtag army; even Sangfugol, thankless as he found the task, had Towser to watch. Before Prince Josua had called him to his tent, Simon had begun to feel as he had in days he had hoped long past—like a drummer boy hurrying along after the Imperator's soldiers.

"Just a little spying work," Josua had called this task, but to Simon it was almost as splendid as the moment he had been knighted. He was to take some of Hotvig's grasslanders and ride out for a look at the approaching force.

"Don't do *anything,*" the prince had said emphatically.

"Just look. Count tents—and horses if you see them. Look for banners and crests if there's enough light. But don't be seen, and if you are, ride away. Quickly."

Simon had promised. A knight leading men to war: that was what he had become. Impatient to be off on this glorious quest, he had squirmed—unobtrusively, he hoped—as he waited for Josua to finish with his instructions.

Sludig, surprisingly, had asked to come along. The Rimmersman was still smarting over Simon's high honors, but Simon suspected that, like Simon himself, Sludig was feeling a little left out, and would even prefer being Simon's subordinate for a short time to the frustration of waiting atop Sesuad'ra. Sludig was a warrior, not a general: the Rimmersman was interested only when the fighting became real, blade on blade.

Hotvig had also offered his services. Simon guessed that Prince Josua, who had come to both like and trust the Thrithings-man, might have asked Hotvig to go along and keep an eye on his youngest knight. Surprisingly, this possibility did not bother Simon. He had begun to understand a little of the burden of power, and knew that Josua was trying to do his best for all concerned. So, Simon had decided, let Hotvig be Josua's eye: he would give the grasslander something good to report.

The storm was worsening. All the Stefflod river valley was covered with snow, the river itself only a dark streak running through a field of white. Simon pulled his cloak tight and wrapped his woolen scarf more tightly around his face.

The Thrithings-men, for all their confident bantering, were more than a little frightened by the changes the storm winds had brought to their familiar grasslands. Simon saw their eyes widen as they looked around, the uneasy way they spurred their horses through the deeper drifts, the small reflexive signs to ward evil that they made with crossed fingers. Only Sludig, child of the frozen north, seemed unaffected by the bleak weather.

"This is truly a black winter," said Hotvig. "If I had

not already believed Josua when he said there was an evil spirit at work, I would believe him now."

"A black winter, yes—and summer only just ended." Sludig flicked snow from his eyes. "The lands north of the Frostmarch have not seen a spring for more than a year. We fight against more than men."

Simon frowned. He did not know how superstitious the clan men were, but he did not want to stir up any fears that might interfere with their task. "It *is* a magical storm," he said loudly enough to be heard over the cloak-snapping wind, "but it's still only a storm. The snows can't hurt you—but they might freeze off your tail."

One of the Thrithings-men turned to him with a grin. "If tails freeze, then you will suffer most, young thane, riding that bony horse." The other men chortled. Simon, pleased at the way he had changed the conversation, laughed with them.

Afternoon swiftly melted into evening as they rode, a journey almost silent but for the soft chuffing of the horses' hooves and the eternal moaning of the wind. The sun, which had been overmatched by clouds all day, at last gave up and dropped down below the low hills. A violet, shadowless light enveloped the valley. Soon it was almost too dark for the little company to see where they rode; the moon, enmeshed in clouds, was all but invisible. There was no sign of stars.

"Should we stop and make camp?" Hotvig shouted above the wind.

Simon considered for a moment. "I don't think so," he said at last. "We are not too far away—maybe another hour's riding at most. I think we could risk a torch."

"Should we also blow some trumpets?" Sludig asked loudly. "Or perhaps we could find some criers to run ahead and announce that we are coming to spy out Fengbald's position."

Simon scowled but did not rise to the bait. "We still have the hills between us and Fengbald's camp at Gadrinsett. If the people who fled his army are right about where he is, we can easily put our light out before we are within sight of his sentries." He raised his voice for emphasis. "Do you think it would be better to wait until morning light, when Fengbald's men are rested and there is sun to make us even easier to spot?"

Sludig waved his hand, conceding.

Hotvig produced a torch—a good, thick branch, wrapped in strips of cloth and soaked in pitch—and struck a spark with his flints. He shielded the flame from the winds until it was burning well, then raised the brand and rode a few paces ahead of the others, mounting the slope of the riverbank as he headed for the greater shelter of the hillside. "Follow, then," he called.

The procession resumed, moving a little more slowly now. They passed across the uneven terrain of the hills, letting the horses feel their way. Hotvig's torch became a jogging ball of flame, the only thing throughout the storm-darkened valley that could hold a wandering eye: Simon almost felt he tracked a will-of-the-wisp across the misty barrens. The world had become a long black tunnel, an endless corridor spiraling down into the earth's light-less heart.

"Anybody know a song?" Simon asked at last. His voice sounded frail lifted against the mournful wind.

"A song?" Sludig wrinkled his brow in surprise.

"Why not? We are still far off from anyone. In any case, you are an arm's length away and I can scarcely hear you over this damnable wind. So, a song, yes!"

Hotvig and his Thrithings-men did not volunteer to sing, but they seemed to have no objection. Sludig made a face, as if the very idea was foolish beyond belief.

"Up to me, then?" Simon smiled. "Up to me. Too bad that Shem Horsegroom isn't here. He knows more songs and stories than anyone." He wondered briefly what had happened to Shem. Was he still living happily in the Hayholt's great stables? "I'll sing you one of his. A song about Jack Mundwode."

"Who?" asked one of the Thrithings-men.

"Jack Mundwode. A famous bandit. He lived in Aldheorte Forest."

"If he lived at all," scoffed Sludig.

"If he lived at all," Simon agreed. "So I'll sing one of

the songs about Mundwode." He wrapped his reins around his hand once more, then leaned back in the saddle, trying to remember the first verse.

  "Bold Jack Mundwode,"

he began at last, timing the song to the thudding rhythm of Homefinder's pace;

  "Said: 'I'll go to Erchester,
  I've heard that there's a maiden sweet
  Who is a-living there.'

  " 'Hruse her name is:
  Hair of softly flowing gold,
  Shoulders pale as winter snows,
  Hruse young and fair.'

  "Jack's bandits warned him,
  Said: 'The town's no place for you.
  Their lord has sworn to take your head,
  He's a-waiting there.'

  "Jack only laughed then.
  Lord Constable he knew of old
  Many times had Jack escaped him
  By a slender hair.

  "Jack put on rich dress,
  Shining silks and promise-chain
  Told Osgal: 'You're the servant
  Who'll stand behind my chair.

  " 'Duke of Flowers I'll be,'
  Said Jack, '—a wealthy nobleman.
  A man of grace and gifts and gold
  Come to the county's fair.' "

Simon sang just loudly enough to let his voice carry above the wind. It was a long tune, with many verses.

They followed Hotvig's torch through the hills as Simon continued the story of how Jack Mundwode entered into Erchester in disguise and charmed Hruse's father, a baron who thought he had found a wealthy suitor for his daughter. Although Simon had to pause from time to time to catch his breath, or to remember words—Shem had taught him the song a very long time ago—his voice grew more sure as the ride progressed. He sang about how Jack the trickster paid court to the beautiful Hruse—sincerely, since he had fallen in love at his first sight of her—and sat beside the unknowing Lord Constable at the baron's supper. Jack even convinced the greedy baron to take a magical rose bush as Hruse's dowry, a bush whose delicate blossoms each contained a shining gold Imperator, and which, the supposed Duke of Flowers assured Hruse's father and the constable, would bear fresh coins every season as long as its roots were in the ground.

It was only as Simon neared the end of the song—he had begun the verse that told how a drunken remark by the bandit Osgal spoiled Jack's disguise and led to his capture by the constable's men—that Hotvig reined up his horse and waved his arm for silence.

"I think that we are very close." The Thrithings-man pointed. The hillside sloped downward ahead, and even through the swirling snows it was clear that open land lay before them.

Sludig rode up beside Simon. The Rimmersman's frosty breath hung in the air around his head. "Finish the song on the way back, lad. It is a good tale."

Simon nodded.

Hotvig rolled over his saddle and down onto the ground, then snuffed his torch in a drift of snow. He patted it dry on his saddle blanket before slipping it under his belt and turning to Simon with an expectant look.

"Let's go, then," Simon said. "But carefully, since we have no light."

They spurred their horses forward. Before they had gone halfway down the long hill, Simon saw distant lights, a sparse collection of gleaming dots.

"There!" he pointed, and immediately worried he had

spoken too loudly. His heart was hammering. "Is that Fengbald's camp?"

"It is what is left of Gadrinsett," said Sludig. "Fengbald's camp will be near it."

In the valley before them, where the invisible Stefflod met the equally unseeable Ymstrecca, only a scatter of fires burned. But on the far side, camped near what Simon felt sure was the Ymstrecca's northern bank, a greater concentration of lights lay spread across the darkened meadows, a myriad of fiery points arranged in rough circles.

"You're right." Simon stared. "That will be the Erkynguard there. Fengbald is probably in the middle of those rings of tents. Wouldn't it be nice to put an arrow through *his* blanket."

Hotvig rode a little nearer. "He is there, yes. And I would like to kill him myself, just to pay him for the things he said about the Stallion Clan when we last met. But we have other things to do tonight."

Stung, Simon took a breath. "Of course," he said at last. "Josua needs to know the strength of armies." He paused to think. "Would it be useful to count the fires? Then we should know how many troops he has brought."

Sludig frowned. "Unless we know how many men share each fire, it will mean little."

Simon nodded, musing. "Yes. So we count the fires now, then ride closer and find out if each tent has one, or every dozen."

"Not too close," Sludig warned. "I like a fight as much as any God-fearing man, but I like odds that are a little better."

"You are very wise," Simon smiled. "You should take Binabik on as your apprentice."

Sludig snorted.

After counting the tiny points of flame, they rode down the hill.

"We are lucky," Hotvig said quietly. "I think the stone-dweller sentries will be standing close to their campfires tonight, staying out of the wind."

Simon shivered, bending a little closer to Homefinder's neck. "Not all stone-dwellers are that smart."

As they came down onto the snowy meadows, Simon again felt his heart racing. Despite his fear, there was something heady and exciting about being so close to the enemy, about moving silently through the darkness scarcely more than an arrow flight from armed men. He felt very alive, as though the wind blew right through his cloak and shirt, making his skin tingle. At the same time, he was half-convinced that Fengbald's troops had already spotted his little company—that even at this moment the entire Erkynguard was crouching with bows drawn, eyes glittering in the deep darkness between the shadowy tents.

They made a slow circuit around the outside of Fengbald's camp, trying to move from the shelter of one clump of trees to another, but trees were in unpleasantly short supply on the edge of the grasslands. It was only when they came close to the riverside and the western-most end of the encampment that they felt themselves safe for a while from staring eyes.

"If there are less than a thousand men at arms here," Sludig declared, "then I'm a Hyrka."

"There are Thrithings-men in that camp," Hotvig said. "Men-of-no-clan from the Lake Thrithing, if I know anything."

"How can you tell?" Simon asked. At this distance the tents showed no markings or distinctive features—many of them were little more than cloth shelters staked to the ground and then roped to bushes or standing stones—and none of the inhabitants of the camp's perimeter were out in such fierce weather.

"Listen." Hotvig cupped his hand behind his ear. His scarred face was solemn.

Simon held his breath and listened. The windsong covered everything, drowning even the sound of the men riding beside him. "Listen to what?"

"Listen with more care," said Hotvig. "It is the harnesses." Beside him, one of his clansmen nodded his head solemnly.

Simon strained to hear what the grasslander did. He

thought he could make out a faint clinking. "That?" he asked.

Hotvig smiled, showing the gap in his teeth. He knew it was an impressive feat. "Those horses are wearing Lakeland harnesses—I am sure of it."

"You can tell what kind of harnesses they wear by the sound?" Simon was astonished. Did these meadow-men have ears like rabbits?

"Our bridles are different as the feathers of birds," one of the other Thrithings-men said. "Lakeland and Meadow and High Thrithings harness are all different to our ears as your voice is from the northerner's, young thane."

"How else could we know our own horses at night, from a distance?" Hotvig frowned. "By the Four-Footed, how do you stone-dwellers stop your neighbors stealing from you?"

Simon shook his head. "So we know where Fengbald's mercenaries are from. But can you tell how many of the men down there are Thrithings-folk?"

"By their shelters, I guess that more than half these troops are from the unclanned," Hotvig replied.

Simon's expression turned grim. "And good fighters, I'd wager."

Hotvig nodded. There was more than a trace of pride in the set of his jaw. "All the grasslanders can fight. But the ones without clans are the most . . ." he searched for a word, ". . . the most fierce."

"And the Erkynguard are no sweeter." Sludig's voice was sour, but his eyes held a faintly predatory spark. "It will be a strong and bloody battle when iron and iron meet."

"Time to go back." Simon looked out to the stripe of dark emptiness that was the Ymstrecca. "We've been lucky so far."

The little company crossed back over the exposed spaces. Simon again felt their vulnerability, the closeness of a thousand enemies, and thanked the heavens that the stormy weather had enabled them to come close to the camp without having to leave their horses behind. The idea of having to flee on foot if they were discovered by mounted sentries—and flee through wind and snow at that—was a disheartening one.

They reached the shelter of a copse of wind-stripped elders that stood forlornly on the slope of the lowest-lying foothills. As Simon turned to stare back at the sprinkling of lights that marked the edge of Fengbald's placid camp, the anger that had been hidden by his excitement suddenly began to well inside him—a cold fury at the thought of all those soldiers lying securely in their tents, like caterpillars that had gorged on the leaves of a beautiful garden and now lay safely wrapped in their cocoons. These were the despoilers, the Erkynguardsmen who had come to arrest Morgenes, who had tried to throw down Josua's castle at Naglimund. Under Fengbald, they had crushed the whole town of Falshire as thoughtlessly as a child might kick over an anthill. Most importantly to Simon, they had driven him from his home, and now they would try to drive him from Sesuad'ra as well.

"Which of you has a bow?" he said abruptly.

One of the Thrithings-men looked up in surprise. "I do."

"Give it to me. Yes, and an arrow, too." Simon took the bow and hooked it over his saddle horn, still staring out at the dark shapes of the clustered tents. "Now give me that torch, Hotvig."

The Thrithings-man stared at him for a moment, then pulled the unlit brand from his belt and handed it to him. "What will you do?" he asked quietly. His expression betrayed nothing but calm interest.

Simon did not reply. Instead, with his concentration on other matters freeing him for a moment from self-consciousness, he swung down from the saddle with surprising ease. He unpeeled the pitchy rag from the end of the torch and wrapped it instead around the head of the arrow, tying it tightly with the length of leather thong that had bound his Qanuc sheath against his thigh. Kneeling, sheltered from the wind by Homefinder's bulk, he produced his flints and iron bar.

"Come, Simon." Sludig sounded midway between

worry and anger. "We have done what we came for. What are you up to?"

Simon ignored him, striking at the iron until a spark nestled in the sticky folds of the rag wound around the arrow's tip. He blew on it until the flame caught, then pocketed his flints and swung back up into the saddle. "Wait for me," he said, and spurred Homefinder out of the stand of trees and down the slope. Sludig started after him, but Hotvig reached out a hand and caught the harness of the Rimmersman's mount, pulling him up short. They fell into an animated, but whispered, argument.

Simon had found little chance to practice with a bow, and none at all to shoot one from horseback since the terrible, swift battle outside of Haethstad when Ethelbearn had been killed. Still, it was not accuracy or skill that was important now so much as his desire to do *something*, to send a small message to Fengbald and his confident troops. He nocked the arrow while still holding the reins, clinging with his knees to the saddle as Homefinder jounced across the uneven snow. The flame blew back along the arrow's shaft until he could feel it hot on his knuckles. At last, as he swept down onto the valley floor, he pulled up. He used his legs to turn Homefinder slowly in a wide circle, then pulled the bowstring back to his ear. His lips moved, but Simon himself did not know what he was saying, so all-absorbing was the ball of flame quivering at the end of the shaft. He took a breath, then let the arrow go.

It flew out, bright and swift as a shooting star, and arched across the night sky like a finger dipped in blood being drawn across black cloth. Simon felt his heart leap as he watched its erratic flight, watched the wind that nearly extinguished the flame carry it first to this side, then that, then drop it at last in among the crowded shadows of the camp. A few moments later a bright blossom of light arose as one of the tents caught fire. Simon watched for a moment, his heart beating as swiftly as a bird's, then turned and spurred Homefinder back up the hill.

He did not say anything about the arrow when he

caught up with the rest of his companions. Even Sludig did not question him. Instead, the little company fell in around Simon and together they rode swiftly through the darkened hills with the wind blowing chill against their faces.

"I wish you would go and lie down," Josua said.

Vorzheva looked up. She was sitting on a mat beside the brazier with the cloak she was repairing spread out on her lap. The young New Gadrinsett girl who was helping her also looked up, then quickly lowered her eyes to the mending once more.

"Lie down?" Vorzheva said, cocking her head quizzically. "Why?"

Josua resumed his pacing. "It . . . it would be better."

Vorzheva ran a hand through her black hair as she watched him cross from one wall of the tent to the other then start back again, a journey of little more than ten cubits. The prince was tall enough that he could only stand upright at the very center of the tent, which gave his pacing progress an odd, hunchbacked look.

"I do not want to lie down, Josua," she said at last, still watching him. "What is wrong with you?"

He stopped and flexed his fingers. "It would be better for the baby . . . and for you . . . if you did lie down."

Vorzheva stared at him for a moment, then laughed. "Josua, you are being foolish—the child will not come until the end of winter."

"I worry for you, Lady," he said plaintively. "The bitter weather, the hard life we live here."

His wife laughed again, but this time there was a slight edge in her voice. "The women of the Stallion Clan, we give birth standing up on the grasslands, then we go back to work. We are not city women. What is wrong with you, Josua?"

The prince's thin face flushed violently. "Why must you always disagree with me?" he demanded. "Am I not your husband? I fear for your health and I do not like to see you working so strenuously, late into the night."

"I am no child," Vorzheva snapped, "I only am carrying one. Why do you walk here and back, here and back? Stand and talk to me!"

"I try to talk with you, but you quarrel with me!"

"Because you tell me what things I should do, like you tell a child. I am not a fool, even though I do not speak like your castle ladies!"

"Aedon curse it, I never said you were a fool!" he shouted. The moment the words were out of his mouth, he stopped his agitated walking. After staring at the ground for a moment, he raised his eyes to Vorzheva's young helper. The girl was huddled in mortification, doing her best to vanish into the shadows. "You," he said. "Would you leave us for a while? My wife and I would like to be alone."

"She is helping me!" Vorzheva said angrily.

Josua fixed the girl with his hard gray eyes. *"Go."*

The young woman leaped to her feet and fled out through the tent flap, leaving her mending in a heap on the floormats. The prince stared after her for a moment, then turned his attention back to Vorzheva. He seemed about to say something, then stopped and swiveled around to the tent flap.

"Blessed Elysia," he murmured. It was hard to tell whether it was a prayer or a curse. He walked toward the doorway and out of the tent.

"Where do you go?" Vorzheva called after him.

Josua squinted into the darkness. At last he saw a lighter shape against one of the tents not far away. He walked toward it, clenching and unclenching his fist.

"Wait." He reached out to touch the young woman's shoulder. Her eyes widened. She had backed herself against the tent; now she raised her hands before her as if to ward off a blow. "Forgive me," he said. "That was an ungentle thing for me to do. You have been kind to my lady and she likes you. Please forgive me."

"For—forgive *you,* Lord?" she sniffled. "Me? I am no one."

Josua winced. "God values each soul at the same measure. Now please, go to Father Strangyeard's tent over there. There, you can see the light of his fire. It will be warm, and I'm sure he will give you something to eat and drink. I will come to fetch you when I have finished talking to my wife." A sad, tired smile crept onto his lean face. "Sometimes a man and woman must have some time alone, even when they are the prince and his lady."

She sniffled again, then tried to curtsy, but was pressed back so firmly against the fabric of the tent that she could not bend. "Yes, Prince Josua."

"Go on, then." Josua watched her hurry across the snowy ground toward the circle of Strangyeard's fire. He saw the archivist and someone else stand to greet her, then he turned and walked back to the tent.

Vorzheva stared at him as he entered, curiosity clearly mixed with anger on her face. He told her what he had done.

"You are the strangest man I have ever known." She took a deep, shaky breath, then looked down, squinting at her needlework.

"If the strong can bully the weak without shame, then how are we different from the beasts of forest and field?"

"Different?" She still avoided his eyes. "How is it different? Your brother chases us with soldiers. People die, women die, children die, all for grazing land and names and flags. We *are* beasts, Josua. Have you not seen that?" She looked up at him again, more kindly this time, as a mother at a child who has not learned life's harsh lessons. She shook her head and returned to her task.

The prince moved to the pallet, then sat down among the piles of cushions and blankets. "Come sit with me." He patted the bed beside him.

"It is warmer here, close to the fire." Vorzheva seemed engrossed in her stitchery.

"It would be just as warm if we sat together here."

Vorzheva sighed, then put down her sewing, stood, and walked to the bed. She fell down beside him and leaned back upon the cushions. Together they stared up at the roof of the tent, which sagged beneath its burden of snow.

"I am sorry," Josua said. "I did not mean to be harsh. But I worry. I fear for your health, and for the child's health."

"Why is it that men think they are brave and women are weak? Women see more blood and pain than men ever do, unless men are fighting—and that is foolish blood." Vorzheva grimaced. "Women tend the hurts that cannot be helped."

Josua did not reply. Instead, he slid his arm around her shoulder and let his fingers move in the dark curls of her hair.

"You have no need to fear for me," she said. "Clan women are not weak. I will not cry. I will make our child and it will be strong and fit."

Josua maintained his silence for a while, then took a deep breath. "I blame myself. I did not give you a chance to understand what you were doing."

She turned suddenly to look at him, her face twisting in fear. She reached up and plucked his hand from her hair, then held it tightly. "What are you saying?" she demanded. "Tell me."

He hesitated, looking for words. "It is a different thing being a prince's wife than it is being a prince's woman."

She swiftly moved a little way across the bed so she could turn and face him. "What are you saying? That you would bring some other woman to take my place? I will kill you and her, Josua! I swear on my clan!"

He laughed softly, although at that moment she looked quite capable of carrying out her threat. "No, that is not what I mean. Not at all." He looked at her and his smile faded. "Please, my lady, never think anything like that." He reached out and clasped her hand again. "I meant only that as prince's wife, you are not like other women—and our child is not like other children."

"So?" The fear still lingered. She was not yet appeased.

"I cannot let anything happen to you, or to our child. If I am lost, the life you bear within you might be the only remaining link to the world as it was."

"What does that mean?"

"It means that our child must live. If we fail—if

Fengbald defeats us, or even if we survive this battle, but I die—then one day our child must avenge us." He rubbed his face. "No, that is not what I mean. This is more important than vengeance. Our child could be the last light against an age of darkness. We do not know if Miriamele will come back to us, or if she even lives. If she is lost, then a prince's son—or a prince's daughter, for that matter—a grandchild of Prester John, would raise the only banner that could bring together a resistance to Elias and his ungodly ally."

Vorzheva was relieved. "I told you, we Thrithings-women bear strong children. You need have no worry—our child will live to make you proud. And we will win here, Josua. You are stronger than you know." She moved closer to him. "There is too much worry in you."

He sighed. "I pray that you are right. Usires and His mercy, is there anything worse than being a ruler? How I wish I could simply walk away."

"You would not do that. My husband is no coward." She lifted herself to look at him closely, as if he might be an impostor, then settled back once more.

"No, you are right. It is my lot—my test, perhaps . . . my own Tree. And each nail is sharp and cold indeed. But even the condemned man is allowed to dream of freedom."

"Do not talk of this any more," she said into his shoulder. "You will bring bad luck."

"I can stop speaking, my love, but I cannot so easily silence my thoughts."

She pushed her head against him like a young bird trying to force its way out of an egg. "Be quiet now."

The worst of the storm had passed, moving southeast. The moon, although curtained and invisible, still shed enough light to give a faint shine to the snow, as though all the river valley between Gadrinsett and Sesuad'ra were sprinkled with powdered diamonds.

Simon watched the snow fountain up from the hooves

of Sludig's horse and wondered if he would live to look back on this year. What might he be, if by some odd chance he managed to survive? A knight, of course, which was already something so grand he had only imagined it in his most childish daydreams—but what did a knight do? Fought for his liege in war, of course, but Simon did not want to think about wars. If there were peace someday, and if he lived to see it—two possibilities that seemed sadly remote—what sort of life would he have?

What did knights do? Ruled over their fiefdoms, if they had land. That was more or less like being a farmer, wasn't it? It certainly didn't seem grand, but suddenly the idea of coming home from a wet day spent walking through the fields seemed very appealing. He would pull off his cloak and boots and wiggle into his slippers, then warm himself in front of a great roaring fire. Someone would bring him wine, and mull it with a hot poker . . . but who? A woman? A wife? He tried to conjure a suitable face out of the darkness, but could not. Even Miriamele, if she lost her legacy and consented to marry a commoner, and if she would choose Simon in any case—if the rivers ran uphill and fish flew, in other words—Miriamele would not be, he sensed, the kind of woman who would wait quietly at home for her husband to return from the fields. To imagine her thus was almost to think of a beautiful bird with its wings tied.

But if he did not marry and have a household, what then? The thought of tournaments, that staple of the knight's spring and summer entertainment which had occupied his excited thoughts for several years, nearly sickened him now. That healthy men would hurt each other for no reason, lose eyes and limbs and even their lives for a game when the world was already such a dreadful and dangerous place, made Simon furious. "Mock-war" some called it, as though any mere sport, no matter how hazardous, could approach the horror of the things Simon had seen. War was like a great wind or an earth tremor, something dreadful that should not be trifled with. To imitate it seemed almost blasphemous. Practicing at tilting and swordwork was something you did to stay alive if

war caught you. When this all ended—*if* it ended—Simon
wanted to get as far away from war, mock or otherwise,
as he could.

But one did not always go looking for war, for pain and
terror; certainly death did not need to be sought out. So
shouldn't a knight always be ready to do his duty defending himself and others? That was what Sir Deornoth said,
and Deornoth did not strike Simon as the kind who fought
needlessly or happily. And what was it that Doctor Morgenes had said once about the great Camaris? That he
blew his famous battle horn Cellian not to summon help
or make himself glorious, but to let his enemies know he
was coming so they could safely escape. Morgenes had
written time after time in his book that Camaris took no
pleasure in battle, that his mighty skills were only a burden, since they drew attackers to him and forced him to
kill when he did not want to. *There* was a paradox. No
matter how adept you were, someone would always wish
to test you. So was it better to prepare for war or to avoid
it?

A clump of snow fell from a branch overhead and, as
if it had life, avoided his heavy scarf and slid easily down
the back of his neck. Simon gave a muffled squeak of dismay, then quickly looked around, hoping none of the others had heard him make such an unmanly noise. No one
was looking at him; the attention of all his companions
seemed fixed on the silver-gray hills and spiky, shadowy
trees.

So which was better? To flee war, or to try to make
yourself so strong that no one could hurt you? Morgenes
had told him that such problems were the stuff of king-
ship, the sort of questions that kept goodhearted mon-
archs awake at night when all their subjects were
sleeping. When Simon had complained about such a
vague response, the doctor had smiled sadly.

"That answer is certainly unsatisfactory, Simon," the
old man had said. *"So are all possible answers to such
questions. If there were correct answers, the world would
be as orderly as a cathedral—flat stone on flat stone,
pure angle mating with pure angle—and everything as*

solid and unmoving as the walls of Saint Sutrin's." He
had cocked his beer jug in a sort of salute. *"But would
there be love in such a world, Simon? Beauty or charm,
with no ill-favor to compare them to? What kind of place
would a world without surprises be?"* The old man had
taken a long drink, wiped his mouth, then changed the
subject. Simon had not thought any more of what the doctor had said again—until this moment.

"Sludig." Simon's voice was startlingly loud as it broke
the long silence.

"What?" Sludig turned in his saddle to look back.

"Would you rather live in a world without surprises? I
mean without good ones and bad ones both?"

The Rimmersman glared at him for a moment. "Don't
talk foolishness," he grunted, then turned back, using his
knees to urge his horse around a boulder standing stark
against the white drifts.

Simon shrugged. Hotvig, who had also looked back,
stared intently for a moment, then swiveled around once
more.

The thought would not quite go away, however. As
Homefinder plodded along beneath him, Simon remembered a bit of a recent dream—a field of grass whose
color was so even that it might have been painted, a sky
as cold and unchanging as a piece of pottery, the whole
landscape eternal and dead as stone.

I'll take surprises, I think, Simon decided. *Even with
the bad ones included.*

They heard the music first, a thin, piping melody that
wove in and out through the noise of the wind. As they
came down the hillside into the bowl-shaped valley
around Sesuad'ra, they saw a small fire burning at the
edge of the great black tarn that surrounded the hill. A little round shape rose from beside the fire, draped in
shadow, silhouetted by flame as it lowered a bone flute.

"We heard you playing," Simon said. "Aren't you worried that someone else might hear you, too? Someone unfriendly?"

"I have protection of sufficiency." Binabik smiled just

a little. "So, you are returned." He sounded studiedly calm, as if worrying was absolutely the last thing he might have been doing. "Are you all well?"

"Yes, Binabik, we're well. All Fengbald's sentries were staying close to their fires."

"As I have myself been doing," the troll said. "The flatboats are over there, where I am pointing. Would you like to rest and warm yourselves, or should we be going up the hill now?"

"We should probably get the news to Josua as soon as possible," Simon decided. "Fengbald has something near a thousand men, and Hotvig says that almost half of them are Thrithings mercenaries." He was distracted by a shape moving along the shadowy shore. When it passed before a high snow drift, he saw that it was Qantaqa slipping along the water's edge like a driblet of quicksilver. The wolf turned to look toward him, her eyes reflecting the firelight, and Simon nodded. Yes, Binabik was indeed protected: no one would sneak up on Qantaqa's master without first dealing with her.

"That is not truly good news, but I am thinking it could be less good," Binabik said as he gathered together the pieces of his walking-stick. "The High King could have thrown all his forces upon us, as he was doing at Naglimund." He sighed. "Still, a thousand soldiers is not a comforting thought." The troll pushed the assembled stick through his belt and took Homefinder's reins. "Josua is gone to sleep for the night, but I think you are sensible when you say you will go straight up. Better we all go to the safeness of the Stone. Even if the king's armies are still distant, this is a wild place, and I am thinking that the storm may bring strange things out into the night."

Simon shivered. "Then let's get ourselves out of the night and into a warm tent."

They followed Binabik's short steps down to the edge of the lake. It seemed to have an odd sheen.

"Why does the water look so strange?" Simon asked.

Binabik grimaced. "That is my news, it gives me sorrow to say. I fear that this last storm has brought us more evil luck than we had guessed. Our moat, as you castle-dwellers would call it, is becoming frozen."

Sludig, who was standing close by, cursed richly. "But the lake is our best guard against the king's troops!"

The little man shrugged. "It is not all frozen yet—otherwise there would be terrible difficulties to get our boats back across. Perhaps we will be having a thaw, and then it will be a shield to us again." The look on his face, shared by Sludig, suggested that it was not very likely.

Two large flatboats waited at the lake's edge. "Men and wolves are to go in this one," Binabik said, gesturing. "The other will take the horses and one man for watching them. Although, Simon, I am thinking your horse has been with Qantaqa enough to bear the trip in our boat."

"It's me you should worry about, troll," growled Sludig. "I like boats less than I like wolves—and I don't like wolves much more than the horses do."

Binabik waved a small, dismissive hand. "You are making jokes, Sludig. Qantaqa has risked her life at your side many times, and that you are knowing."

"So now I have to risk my own again on another of your damned boats," the Rimmersman complained. He seemed to be suppressing a smile. Simon was surprised again by the strange fellowship that seemed to have grown between Binabik and the northerner. "Very well, then," Sludig said, "I will go. But if you trip over that great beast and fall in, I am the last person who will jump in after you."

"Trolls," Binabik said with great dignity, "do not 'fall in.' "

The little man plucked a burning brand from the flames, extinguished the campfire with a few handfuls of snow, then clambered onto the nearest flatboat. "Your torches have too much brightness," he said. "Put them out. Let us be enjoying this night, when some stars can at last be seen." He lit the horn-shielded lamp hanging at the front of the barge, then stepped gingerly from one rocking deck to the other and fired the wick on the other boat as well. The lamplight, lunar and serene, spread out across the water as Binabik dropped his torch overboard. It disappeared with a hiss and a belch of steam. Simon and the others doused their own brands and followed the troll aboard.

One of Hotvig's clansmen was deputed to ferry the horses in the second barge, but the mare Homefinder, as Binabik had predicted, seemed unruffled by Qantaqa's presence and so was deemed fit to ride with the rest of the company. She stood in the stern of the leading boat and gazed back at the other horses like a duchess eyeing a gang of drunkards carousing beneath her balcony. Qantaqa curled up at Binabik's feet, tongue lolling, and watched Sludig and Hotvig as they poled the first barge out onto the lake. Mist rose up all around; in a moment the land behind them had vanished and the two boats were floating through a netherworld of fog and black water.

In most places the ice was little more than a thin skin across the water, brittle as sugar candy. As the front of the boat pushed through, the ice crackled and rang, a delicate but unnerving sound that made the back of Simon's neck prickle. Overhead, the passage of this wave of the storm had left the sky almost clear; as Binabik had said, a few stars could indeed be seen blinking in the murk.

"Look," the troll said softly. "While men prepare for fighting, Sedda still goes about her business. She has not caught her husband Kikkasut yet, but she does not stop her trying."

Simon stood beside him and stared up into the deep well of the sky. But for the soft tinkling of the water's frozen crust parting before them, and an occasional muffled thump when they struck a larger piece of floating ice, the valley was supernaturally silent.

"What's that?" Sludig said abruptly. "There."

Simon leaned to follow his gaze. The Rimmersman's fur-cloaked arm pointed out across the water to the dark edge of the Aldheorte, which stood like a castle outwall above the north shore of the lake.

"I can't see anything," Simon whispered.

"It's gone now," Sludig said fiercely, as though Simon

had spoken from disbelief instead of inability. "There were lights in the forest. I saw them."

Binabik stepped closer to the edge of the boat, peering out into the darkness. "That is near where the city Enki-e-Shao'saye stands, or what is remaining of it."

Hotvig now moved forward as well. The barge rocked gently. Simon thought it good that Homefinder still stood placidly in the stern, otherwise the shallow flatboat might have overbalanced. "In the ghost city?" The Thrithings-man's scarred features were suddenly childlike in their apprehension. "You see lights there?"

"I did," Sludig said. "I swear by the Blood of Aedon I did. But they are gone now."

"Hmm." Binabik looked troubled. "It could be that somehow our own lamps were shining back from some mirroring surface there in the old city."

"No." Sludig was firm. "One was bigger than any lamp of ours. But they went dark so quickly!"

"Witch lights," said Hotvig grimly.

"It is also possible," Binabik offered, "that you only saw them for a moment through trees or broken buildings, then after that we passed from where we could be seeing them." He thought for a moment, then turned to Simon. "Josua has set tonight's task for you, Simon. Should we back water for a way to see if we can be finding these forest lights again?"

Simon tried to think calmly of what was best, but he truly did not want to know what was on the far side of the black water. Not tonight.

"No." He tried to make his voice measured and steady. "No, we will not go and look. Not when we have news that Josua needs. What if it is a scouting party for Fengbald? The less they see of us, the better." Stated that way, it sounded rather reasonable. He felt a moment of relief, but that was quickly followed by shame that he should try to falsely impress these men, who had risked their lives under his command. "And also," he said "I am tired and worried—no, frightened is what I am. This has been a hard night. Let's go and tell Josua what we've seen, including the lights in the forest. The prince should decide." As he finished, he was suddenly aware of a vast presence at his shoulder. He turned quickly, unnerved, to be confronted with the great bulk of Sesuad'ra looming up from the water beside him; it had appeared so unexpectedly through the fog that it might have just that moment pushed up from beneath the lake's obsidian surface like a breaching whalefish. He stood and stared up at it, openmouthed.

Binabik stroked Qantaqa's broad head. "I am thinking Simon speaks with good sense. Prince Josua should be deciding what to do about this mystery."

"They were there," Sludig said angrily, but shook his head as though not as sure now as he had been.

The flatboats sailed on. The forested shore vanished once more into the cloaking mist, like a dream receding before the light and noises of morning.

Deornoth watched Simon as the youth made his report, and found that he liked what he was seeing. The young man was flushed with the excitement of his new responsibilities, and the gray morning light was reflected in eyes that were perhaps a little too bright for the gravity of the things discussed—namely, Fengbald's army and its overwhelming superiority in numbers, equipment, and experience—but Deornoth noted with pleasure that the youth did not rush through his explanations, did not jump toward unwarranted conclusions, and thought carefully before answering each of Prince Josua's questions. This new-minted knight had seen and heard much in his short life, it seemed, and had paid attention. As Simon related their adventure and Sludig and Hotvig nodded agreement with the young man's conclusions, Deornoth found himself nodding, too. Though Simon's beard still had the chick-feathered look of youth, Deornoth's experienced eye saw beneath it the makings of a fine man. He guessed that the lad might someday be one such as other men might follow to their benefit.

Josua was holding his council before his tent, where a

blazing fire kept the morning chill at bay and served as a centerpiece to their deliberations. As the prince questioned and probed, Freosel, New Gadrinsett's stocky constable, cleared his throat to gain Josua's attention.

"Yes, Freosel?"

"Strikes me, sire, that all things your knight here says he saw, well, they be like what the Lord Mayor told us."

Simon turned to the Falshireman. "Lord Mayor? Who's that?"

"Helfgrim, who was once mayor of Gadrinsett," Josua explained. "He came to us just after you and the others rode out. He escaped from Fengbald's camp and made his way here. He is sickly and I have ordered him to bed, otherwise he would be with us this moment. He had a long, cold journey on foot, and Fengbald's men had treated him badly."

"As I said, your Highness," Freosel resumed, polite but determined, "what Sir Seoman here says bears out all Helfgrim's talk. So when Helfgrim says he knows how Fengbald will attack, and where, and when . . ." the young man shrugged, "well, seems we should pay heed. Would be a boon to us, and we have small enough to work with."

"Your point is well taken, Freosel. You said the mayor is a trustworthy man, and you, as another Falshireman, know him best." Josua looked around the circle. "What think you all? Geloë?"

The witch woman looked up quickly, surprised. She had been staring into the shifting orange depths of the fire. "I do not pretend to be a war strategist, Josua."

"That I know, but you are a keen judge of people. How much weight can we place on the old Lord Mayor's words? We have few enough forces—we cannot spare anything on a bad gamble."

Geloë thought for a moment. "I have only spoken with him briefly, Josua, but I will say this: there is a darkness in his eyes I do not like—a shadow. I suggest you take great care."

"A shadow?" Josua looked at her intently. "Could it be

a mark of his suffering, or are you saying you read treachery in him?"

The forest woman shook her head. "No, I would not go so far as to say anything about treachery. It could be pain, certainly. Or he could be addled by harsh treatment, and the thing I see is a mind hiding from itself, hiding behind imaginings of knowing what the great ones are thinking and doing. But go carefully, Josua."

Deornoth sat up straighter. "Geloë is wise, sire," he said quickly, "—but we shouldn't make the error of a caution so great we fail to use what could save us."

Even as he spoke, Deornoth wondered whether he was so concerned that the witch woman might talk his master into passivity that he was ignoring the possible truth of what she said. Still, it was important in these final days to keep Josua resolved. If the prince was bold and decisive, it would overcome many small mistakes—that, in Deornoth's experience, was the way of war. If Josua wavered and hesitated too long, over this matter or any others, it might steal away what little fighting spirit remained to New Gadrinsett's army of survivors.

"I say we pay close attention to what Helfgrim the mayor has to offer," he asserted.

Hotvig spoke up in Deornoth's support, and Freosel was clearly already in agreement. The others held their peace, although Deornoth could not help noticing that Binabik the troll had an uneasy look on his round face as he poked at the fire with a length of stick. The little man put too much stock in Geloë and her magical trappings, Deornoth thought. This was different, though. This was war.

"I think I will have a talk with the Lord Mayor tonight," Josua said at last. "Providing he is strong enough, that is. As you say, Deornoth, we cannot afford to be too proud to accept help. We are needy, and God, it is said, provides what His children need if they trust Him. But I will not forget your words, Geloë. That would also be throwing away valuable gifts."

"Your pardon, Prince Josua," Freosel said. "If you be done with this, there are other things I need speak on."

"Of course."

"We have more problems than just readying to fight," the Falshireman said. "You know food is dreadful scarce. We fished the rivers until they be nearly empty—but now ice has come, we cannot even do that. Every day hunters go farther and come back with less. This woman," he nodded toward Geloë, "helped us find plants and fruits we did not know were good to eat, but that only helps stretch stores gone mighty thin." He stopped and swallowed, anxious about speaking so forwardly, but determined to say what was needed. "Even do we win here and beat off siege . . ." at the word, Deornoth felt an almost imperceptible shudder travel around the circle, ". . . we'll not be able to stay. Not enough food to last us through winter, that is the length of it."

The baldness of his statement dropped the makeshift council into silence.

"What you say is not truly a surprise," Josua said at last. "Believe me, I know the hunger our people are feeling. I hope the settlers of New Gadrinsett are aware that you and I and these others are not eating any better than they are."

Freosel nodded. "They know, your Highness, and that's stopped any worse trouble than grumbling and complaining. But if people starve, they won't care that you be starving, too. They'll go. Some be gone already."

"Goodness!" said Strangyeard. "But where can they go? Oh, the poor creatures!"

"Don't matter." Freosel shook his head. "Back to tag along the edges of Fengbald's army begging for scraps, or back across plains toward Erkynland. Only a few be gone. So far."

"If we win," Josua said, "we will move on. That was my plan, and this only proves to me that I was right. If the wind swings in our favor, we would be fools not to move while it blows at our backs." He shook his head. "Always more troubles. Fear and pain, death and hunger—how much my brother has to answer for!"

"It's not just him, Prince Josua," Simon said, his face tight with anger. "The king didn't make this storm."

"No, Simon, you are correct. We cannot afford to forget my brother's allies." Josua seemed to think of something, for he turned toward the young knight. "And now I am reminded. You spoke of seeing lights on the northeast shore last night."

Simon nodded. "Sludig saw them—but we are certain they were there," he hastened to add, then darted a look over at the Rimmersman, who was listening attentively. "I thought it best we tell you before doing anything."

"This is another puzzle. It could be some feint of Fengbald's, I suppose—some attempt to outflank us. But it makes little sense."

"Especially with his main army still so far away," Deornoth said. It did not seem like Fengbald's method, anyway, he thought. The duke of Falshire had never been the subtle sort.

"It seems to me, Simon, that it could be your friends the Sithi coming to join us. That would be a happy chance." Josua cocked an eyebrow. "I believe you had some conversation recently with your Prince Jiriki?"

Deornoth was amused to see the young man's cheeks turn bright scarlet. "I . . . I did, your Highness," Simon mumbled. "I shouldn't have done it."

"That is not to the point," Josua said dryly. "Your crimes, such as they were, are not for this gathering. Rather, I wish to know if you think it might be them."

"The fairy-folk?" blurted out Freosel. "This lad talks to the fairy-folk?"

Simon ducked his head in embarrassment. "Jiriki seemed to say that it would be a long time before he could join us, if he even could. Also—and I cannot prove this, Highness, it is just a feeling—I think he would let me know somehow if he were coming to bring us help. Jiriki knows how impatient we mortals are." He smiled sadly. "He knows how much it would lift our spirits if we knew they were coming."

"Merciful Aedon and His mother." Freosel was still stunned. "Fairies!"

Josua nodded thoughtfully. "So. Well, if the folks who make those lights are not friends, they are most likely enemies—although, now that I think on it, perhaps you saw the campfires of some of the folk Freosel spoke of, those who have fled Sesuad'ra." He frowned. "I will think on this, too. Perhaps we will send a scouting party tomorrow. I do not wish to remain ignorant of whoever might be sharing our little corner of Osten Ard." He stood, brushing ashes from his breeches, and tucked the stump of his right wrist into his cloak. "That will be all. I release you to find what slim provender you can to break your fast."

The prince turned and walked into his tent. Deornoth watched him go, then turned to look out at the edge of the great hill, where the standing stones loomed against a gray mist, as though Sesuad'ra floated in a sea of nothingness. He frowned at the thought and moved closer to the fire.

In the dream, Doctor Morgenes stood before Simon, dressed as though for a long journey, wearing a traveling cloak with a tasseled hood and scorchmarks blackening its hem, as though its owner had ridden through flames. Little of the old man's face could be seen in the darkened depths of the hood—a glint from his spectacles, the white flash of his beard; other than that, the doctor's face was only hint and shadow. Behind Morgenes lay no familiar vista, but only a swirling patch of pearlescent nothingness like the eye of a blizzard.

"It is not enough merely to fight back, Simon," the doctor's voice said, *". . . even if you are only fighting to stay alive. There must be more."*

"More?" As delighted as he was to see this dream-Morgenes, Simon somehow knew he had only moments to grasp what the old man said to him. Precious time was slipping away. *"What does that mean, 'more'?"*

"It means you must fight for *something. Otherwise you are no more than a straw man in a wheatfield—you can scare the crows away, you can even kill them, but you will*

never win them over. You cannot stone all the crows in the world. . . ."

"Kill crows? What do you mean?"

"Hate is not enough, Simon . . . it is never enough." The old man seemed about to say more, but the white emptiness behind him was abruptly slashed by a great stripe of vertical shadow which seemed to grow out of the very nothingness. Although without substance, still the shadow seemed oppressively heavy—a thick column of darkness that could have been a tower, or a tree, or the upright rim of an oncoming wheel; it bisected the void behind the doctor's hooded figure as neatly as a heraldic blazon.

"Morgenes!" Simon cried, but in this dream his voice was suddenly weak, almost stifled by the weight of the long shadow. *"Doctor! Don't leave!"*

"I had to leave a long time ago," the old man cried, his voice faint, too. *"You've done the work without me. And remember—the false messenger!"* The doctor's voice suddenly slid upward in pitch until it became a piping shriek. *"False!"* he cried. *"Faaaallllsssse!"*

His hooded shape began to crumple and shrink, the cloak flapping madly. At last, the old man was gone; where he had stood, a tiny silver bird beat its wings. It suddenly darted up into the emptiness, circling first sunwise, then widdershins, until it was only a speck. An instant later it was gone.

"Doctor!" Simon squinted after it. He reached up, but something was restraining his arms, a heavy weight that clung to him and pushed him down, as though the milky void had become thick as a sodden blanket. He struggled against it. *"No! Come back! I need to know more. . . ."*

"It is me, Simon!" Binabik hissed. "More quiet, please!" The troll shifted his weight once more until he was almost sitting on the young man's chest. "Stop now! If you keep up these struggling-about movements, you will hit my nose again."

"What. . . ?" Simon gradually stopped thrashing. "Binabik?"

"From bruised nose to wounded toes," the troll sniffed. "Have you finished with your flinging of arms and legs?"

"Did I wake you up?" Simon asked.

Binabik slid down and crouched beside the pallet. "No. *I* was coming to wake *you*—that is the truth of it. But what was this dream that caused you so much worry and fearfulness?"

Simon shook his head. "It's not important. I don't remember it very well, anyway."

He actually remembered every word, but he wished to think about it a while longer before he discussed the subject with Binabik. Morgenes had seemed more vivid in this dream than he had in others—more *real*. In a way, it had almost been like having a last meeting with his beloved doctor. Simon had grown covetous of the few things he could call his own: he did not yet wish to share this small thing with anybody. "Why did you wake me?" He yawned to cover the change of subject. "I don't have to stand guard tonight."

"That is true." Binabik's surprising smile was a brief pale blur in the light of the dying embers. "But I am wishing you to get up, put on your boots and other clothes for traveling out of doors, and then be coming with me."

"What?" Simon sat up, listening for the sound of alarum or attack, but heard nothing louder than the ever-present wind. He slumped back down into his bed and rolled over, turning his back to the troll. "I don't want to go anywhere. I'm tired. Let me go back to sleep."

"This is a thing that you will be finding is worth your trouble."

"What is it?" he grumbled into his upper arm.

"A secret, but a secret of great excitingness."

"Bring it to me in the morning. I'll be very excited then."

"Simon!" Binabik was a little less jovial. "Do not be so lazy. This is being very important! Do you have no trust in me?"

Groaning as though the entire weight of the earth had been tipped onto his shoulders, Simon rolled over again and levered himself into a sitting position. "Is it really important?"

Binabik nodded.

"And you won't tell me what it is?"

Binabik shook his head. "But you will soon be discovering. That is my promise."

Simon stared at the troll, who seemed inhumanly cheerful for this dark hour of the night. "Whatever it is, it's certainly put you in a good mood," he growled.

"Come." Binabik stood up, excited as a child at the Aedontide feasting. "I have Homefinder with her saddle upon her back already. Qantaqa is also waiting with immense wolfly patience. Come!"

Simon allowed himself to be coerced into boots and a thick wool shirt. Dragging his bed-warm cloak about him, he stumbled out of the tent after Binabik, then nearly turned and stumbled right back in again. "S'Bloody Tree!" he swore. "It's cold!"

Binabik pursed his lips at the oath, but said nothing. Now that Simon had been made a knight, the troll seemed to have decided that he was a grown man and could curse if he wished to. Instead, the little man lifted a hand to gesture toward Homefinder, who stood pawing at the snowy ground a few paces away, bathed in the light of a torch thrust handle-first into the snow. Simon approached her, stopping to stroke her nose and whisper a few muzzy words in her warm ear, then dragged himself clumsily into the saddle. The troll gave a low whistle and Qantaqa appeared silently out of the darkness. Binabik sank his fingers in her thick gray fur and clambered onto her broad back, then leaned over to pick up the torch before urging the wolf forward.

They made their way out of the close-quartered tent city and across the broad summit of Sesuad'ra, across the Fire Garden where the wind whirled little eddies of snow across the half-buried tiles, then past Leavetaking House, where a pair of sentries stood. Not far beyond the armed men was a standing stone which marked the edge of the wide road that wound down from the summit. The sentries, bundled up against the cold so that only the gleam of their eyes could be seen below their helms, raised their spears in salute. Simon waved, puzzled.

"They don't seem very curious about where we're going."

"We have permission." Binabik smiled mysteriously.

The skies overhead were almost clear. As they made their way down the hill along the crumbling stones of the old Sithi road, Simon looked up to see that the stars had returned. It was a cheering sight, although he was bemused to find that none of them seemed quite familiar. The moon, appearing for a moment from behind a spit of clouds, showed him that it was earlier than he had at first thought—perhaps only a few hours after sunset. Still, it was late enough that almost the whole of New Gadrinsett was abed. Where on earth could Binabik be leading him?

Several times as they made their spiraling circuit of the Stone, Simon thought he saw lights sparkling in the distant forest, tiny points dimmer even than the stars high overhead. But when he pointed them out, the troll merely nodded as though such a sight was no more than he had expected.

By the time they reached the place where the old road widened out once more, pale Sedda had vanished behind a curtain of mist on the horizon. They came down onto the sloping shoulder of land at the hill's base. The waters of the great lake lapped against the stone. A few drowned treetops still protruded above the surface like the heads of giants sleeping beneath the black waters.

Without a word, Binabik dismounted and led Qantaqa to one of the flatboats moored near the end of the road. Simon, lulled into an unquestioning dreaminess, slid down from the saddle and led his horse aboard. Once Binabik had lit the lamp in the bow, they lifted their poles and pushed out onto the freezing water.

"Not many more trips can we make this way," Binabik said quietly. "Luckily, that will not matter soon."

"Why won't it matter?" Simon asked, but the troll only waved his small hand.

Soon the slope of the submerged valley began to fall away beneath the boat, until at last their poles reached down and touched nothing. They took up the paddles that were lying in the barge's shallow bottom. It was hard work—the ice seemed to grab and cling to hull and paddle-blade alike, as though urging the boat to stop and become part of the greater solidification. Simon did not notice for a while that Binabik had steered them toward the northeast shore, where Enki-e-Shao'saye had once stood and where the strange glimmerings had appeared.

"We're going to the lights!" he said. His voice seemed to sigh and quickly fade, vanishing into the enormity of the darkened valley.

"Yes."

"Why? Are the Sithi there?"

"Not the Sithi, no." Binabik was staring out across the wind-rippled water, his posture that of one who could barely contain himself. "I am thinking that you spoke truly: Jiriki would not keep his coming a secret."

"Then who is there?"

"You will see."

The troll's whole attention was now fixed on the far shore, which grew ever closer. Simon saw the great breakfront of trees looming up, shadowy and impenetrable, and suddenly remembered how the writing-priests back at the Hayholt would lift their heads almost as one movement when some errand brought him into their sanctuary—a vast crowd of ancient men tugged up from their parchmenty dreams by his blundering entrance.

Soon the bottom of the boat scraped, then ran aground. Simon and Binabik stepped out and pulled it up onto a more secure spot while Qantaqa loped in wide, splashing circles around them. When Homefinder had been coaxed out onto the shore, Binabik relit his torch and they rode into the forest.

The trees of the Aldheorte grew close together here, as though huddling for warmth. The torch revealed an incredible profusion of leaves in an uncountable variety of shapes and sizes, as well as what seemed to be every variety of creeper, lichen, and moss, all grown together into a disordered riot of vegetation. Binabik led them onto a narrow deer track. Simon's boots were wet and his feet were cold and getting colder. He wondered again what they were doing in this place at such an hour.

He heard the noise long before he could see anything but the choke of trees, a whining, discordant skirling of flutes that wound in and out around a deep, almost inaudible drumbeat. Simon turned to Binabik, but the troll was listening and nodding and did not see Simon's inquiring glance. Soon they could see light, something warmer and less steady than moonlight, flickering through the thick trees. The odd music grew louder, and Simon felt his heart began to beat more swiftly. Surely Binabik knew what he was doing, he chided himself. After all the dreadful times they had survived together, Simon could trust his friend. But Binabik seemed so strangely distracted! The little man's head was cocked to one side in an attitude that mirrored Qantaqa's, as though he heard things in the weird melody and incessant drums that Simon could not even guess at.

Simon was full of nervous anticipation. He realized that he had been smelling something vaguely familiar for a long while. Even after he could no longer ignore it, he was at first certain that it was nothing more than the scent of his own clothing, but soon the pungency, the *aliveness* of it could no longer be denied.

Wet wool.

"Binabik!" he cried—then, recognizing the truth, he began to laugh.

They came down into a wide clearing. The crumbled ruins of the old Sithi city lay all around, but now the dead stone was painted with leaping flames: life had returned, if not the life its builders had intended. All along the upper part of the dell, crowding and quietly clamoring, bumped a great herd of snow-white rams. The bottom of the dell, where the fires burned merrily, was equally filled with trolls. Some were dancing or singing. Others were playing on trollish instruments, producing the skittering, piping music. Most simply watched and laughed.

"*Sisqinanamook!*" Binabik shouted. His face was stretched in an impossibly delighted smile. "*Henimaatuq! Ea kup!*"

A score of faces, two score, three score or more, all turned to stare up at the spot where he and Simon stood. In an instant a great crowd was pushing up past the disgruntled, sour-bleating rams. One small figure outstripped the rest and within moments had reached Binabik's widespread arms.

Simon was surrounded by chattering trolls. They shouted and chuckled as they tugged at his garments and patted him; the good will on their faces was unmistakable. He felt himself suddenly in the midst of old friends and found that he was beaming back at them, his eyes overbrimming. The strong scent of oil and fat that he remembered so well from Yiqanuc rose to his nostrils, but at this moment it was a very pleasant scent indeed. He turned, dazed, and looked for Binabik.

"How did you know?" he cried.

His friend stood a little way distant, an arm wrapped around Sisqi. She was smiling almost as widely as he, and the color had come out in her cheeks. "My clever Sisqinanamook was sending me one of Ookequk's birds!" Binabik said. "My people have been at camp here for two days, building boats!"

"Building boats?" Simon felt himself gently jostled from side to side by the ocean of little people that hemmed him close.

"To come across our lake for joining Josua," Binabik laughed. "One hundred brave trolls is Sisqi bringing to help us! Now you will truly see why the Rimmersmen still frighten their children with whispered stories of Huhinka Valley!" He turned and embraced her again.

Sisqi ducked her head into the side of his neck for a moment, then turned and faced Simon. "I read Ookekuq book," she said, her Westerling awkward but understandable. "I speak more now, your talk." Her nod was almost a bow. "Greetings, Simon."

"Greetings, Sisqi," he said. "It is good to see you again."

"This is why I was wanting you to come, Simon." Binabik waved his hand around the clearing. "Tomorrow will be enough time for talking of war. Tonight, friends are being together again. We will sing and dance!"

Simon grinned at the joy evident in Binabik's face, a happiness that was mirrored in the dark eyes of his betrothed. Simon's own weariness had melted away. "I'd like that," he said, and meant it.

9

Pages in an Old Book

Clawlike hands grasped at her. Empty eyes stared. They were all around her, gray and shiny as frogs, and she could not even scream.

Miriamele awakened with her throat so tightly constricted that it ached. There were no clutching hands, no eyes, only a sheet of cloth above her and the sound of slapping waves. She lay on her back for long moments, fighting for breath, then sat up.

No hands, no eyes, she promised herself. The kilpa, apparently sated by their feast on the *Eadne Cloud,* had scarcely troubled the landing boat.

Miriamele slid out from beneath the makeshift awning she and the monk had constructed from the boat's oiled broadcloth cover, then squinted, trying to find some trace of the sun so she could gauge the time of day. The ocean that surrounded her had a dull, leaden look, as though the vast sheet of water surrounding the boat had been hammered out by a legion of blacksmiths. The gray-green expanse stretched in every direction, featureless but for the wave-crests glimmering in the diffuse light.

Cadrach was sitting before her on one of the front benches, the oar handles held beneath his arms while he stared down at his hands. The bits of cloak he had wrapped around his palms for protection were in tatters, shredded by the repetitive slide of the oar handles.

"Your poor hands." Miriamele was surprised by her own rasping voice. Cadrach, more startled than she, flinched.

"My lady." He peered at her. "Is all well?"

"No," she said, but tried to smile. "I hurt. I hurt all over. But look at your hands, they are terrible."

He stared ruefully at his ragged skin. "I have rowed a little too much, I fear. I am still not strong."

Miriamele frowned. "You are mad, Cadrach! You have been in chains for days—what are you doing pulling at oars? You will kill yourself!"

The monk shook his head. "I did not work at it long, my lady. These wounds on my hands are a tribute to the weakness of my flesh, not the diligence of my labors."

"And I have nothing to put on them," Miriamele fretted, then looked up suddenly. "What time of the day is it?"

It took the monk a moment to answer the unexpected question. "Why, early evening, Princess. Just after sunset."

"And you let me sleep all day! How could you?"

"You needed to sleep, Lady. You had bad dreams, but I'm sure that you are still much better for ..." Cadrach trailed off, then lifted his curled fingers in a gesture of insufficiency. "In any case, it was best."

Miriamele hissed her exasperation. "I will find something for those hands. Perhaps in one of Gan Itai's packages." She kept her mouth firm, despite the quiver she felt at the corners when she spoke the Niskie's name. "Stay there, and do not move those oars an inch if you value your life."

"Yes, my lady."

Moving gingerly for the comfort of her painful muscles, Miriamele at last turned up the small oilcloth packet of useful articles that Gan Itai had bundled with the water skins and food. It contained the promised fishhooks, as well as a length of strong and curiously dull-colored cord of a type Miriamele had not seen before; there was also a small knife and a sack that contained a collection of tiny jars, none of them bigger than a man's thumb. Miriamele unstoppered them one by one, sniffing each cautiously.

"This one's salt, I think," she said, "—but what would

someone at sea need with salt, when they could get their
own by drying water?" She looked to Cadrach, but he
only shook his round head. "This one has some yellowish
powder in it." She closed her eyes to take another sniff.
"It smells fragrant, but not like something to eat. Hmm."
She opened three more, discovering crushed petals in one,
sweet oil in the second, and a pale unguent in the third
which made her eyes water when she leaned close.

"I know that scent," said Cadrach. "Mockfoil. Good
for poultices and such—the staple of a rustic healer's
apothecary."

"Then that's what I was looking for." Miriamele cut
some strips from the nightshirt she still wore underneath
her masculine clothing, then rubbed the unguent into
some of the strips and bound them firmly around
Cadrach's blistered hands. After she had finished, she
wrapped a few bits of dry cloth around the outside to
keep the others clean.

"There. That will help some, anyway."

"You are too kind, Lady." Although his tone was light,
Miriamele saw an unexpected glimmer in his eye, as
though a tear had blossomed. Embarassed and a little
unsure, she did not look too closely.

The sky, which had long since bled out its brighter colors, was now rapidly going purple-blue. The wind quickened, and Miriamele and Cadrach both drew their cloaks
closer about their necks. Miriamele leaned back against
the railing of the boat for a long, silent moment, feeling
the long craft roll from side to side on the cradling waters.

"So what do we do now? Where are we? Where are we
going?"

Cadrach was still prodding at the dressings on his
hands. "Well, as to where we are at this moment, Lady, I
would say we were somewhere between Spenit and Risa
Islands, in the middle of the Bay of Firannos. We're most
likely about three leagues off shore—a few days' rowing,
even if we pull oars the day long. . . ."

"There's a good thought." Miriamele crawled forward
to the bench Cadrach had occupied and lowered the oars

into the water. "Might as well keep moving while we're
talking. Are we facing the right direction?" She laughed
sourly. "But how could you say when we probably don't
know where we're going?"

"In truth, we should do well as we are headed, Princess. I'll look again when the stars come out, but the sun
was all I needed to know that we are pointing northeast,
and that is as fine as we need to be for now. But are you
sure you should tire yourself? Perhaps I can manage a little more. . . ."

"Oh, Cadrach, you with your bleeding hands!? Nonsense." She dipped the oarblades into the water and
pulled, slipping backward on the seat when one of them
popped free of the water. "No, don't show me," she said
quickly. "I learned how when I was little—it's only that
I haven't done it for a long time." She scowled in concentration, searching for the half-remembered stroke. "We
used to practice on some of the Gleniwent's small backwaters. My father used to take me."

The memory of Elias on a rowing bench before her,
laughing as one of the oars floated away across green-
scummed water, blew through her. In that snatch of recollection, her father seemed scarcely older than she now
was herself—perhaps, she suddenly realized with a kind
of startled wonder, he had been in some ways still a boy,
for all his manly age. There was no question that the imposing weight of his mighty, fabled, and beloved father
had pressed down upon him hard, forcing him to wilder
and wilder feats of valor. She remembered her mother
fighting back fearful tears at some report of Elias' battlefield madness, tears that the tale-bringers never understood. It was strange to think about her father this way.
Perhaps for all his bravery he had been unsure and
afraid—terrified that he would stay a child forever, a son
with an undying sire.

Unsettled, Miriamele tried to sweep the curiously
clinging memory from her mind and concentrate instead
on finding the ancient rhythm of oars in water.

"Good, my lady, you do very well." Cadrach settled
back, his bandaged hands and round face pale as mush-

room flesh in the swiftly darkening evening. "So, we know where we are—add or subtract a few million buckets of seawater. As to where we are going ... well, what say you, Princess? *You* are the one who rescued *me,* after all."

She suddenly felt the oars heavy as stone in her hands. A fog of purposelessness rolled over her. "I don't know," she whispered. "I have nowhere to go."

Cadrach nodded his head as though he had expected her answer. "Then let me cut you a bit of bread and a cintis-worth of cheese, Lady, and I will tell you what I am thinking."

Miriamele did not want to stop rowing, so the monk kindly consented to feed her bites between strokes. His comical look while dodging the backswing of the oars made her laugh; a dry crust stuck in her throat. Cadrach thumped her back, then gave her a swig of water.

"That is enough, Lady. You must stop for a moment and finish your meal. Then, if you wish, you may start again. It would fly in the face of God's mercy to escape the kil ... the many dangers we have, then to die of a foolish strangulation." He watched her critically as she ate. "You are thin, too. A girl your age should be putting meat on her bones. What did you eat on that cursed ship?"

"What Gan Itai brought me. The last week, I could not bear to sit at the same table with ... that man." She fought back another wave of despair and instead waved her heel of bread indignantly. "But look at you! You are a skeleton—a fine one to talk!" She forced the lump of cheese he had given her back into his hand. "Eat that."

"I wish I had a jug." Cadrach washed the morsel down with a small swallow of water. "By Aedon's Golden Hair, a few dribbles of red Perdruin would do wonders."

"But you don't have any," Miriamele replied, irritated. "There is no wine for ... for a very long way. So do something else instead. Tell me where you think we should go, if you really do have an idea." She licked her fingers, stretched until her bruised muscles twinged, then reached for the oars. "And tell me anything else you want as well. Distract me." She slowly resumed her rhythmic pulling.

For a while, the chop-swish of the blades diving and surfacing was the only sound except for the endless murmuration of the sea.

"There is a place," said Cadrach. "It is an inn—a hostel, I suppose—in Kwanitupul."

"The marsh-city?" Miriamele asked, suspicious. "Why would we want to go there—and if we did, what difference would it make which inn we chose? Is the wine so good?"

The monk put on a look of injured dignity. "My lady, you wrong me." His expression became more serious. "No, I suggest it because it may be a place of refuge in these dangerous times—and because it is where Dinivan was going to send you."

"Dinivan!" The name was a shock. Miriamele realized that she had not thought about the priest in many days, despite his kindness, despite his terrible death at Pyrates' hands. "Why on earth would you know what Dinivan wanted to do? And why should it matter now anyway?"

"How I know what Dinivan wanted is easy enough to explain. I listened at keyholes—and other places. I heard him discuss you with the lector and tell of his plans for you . . . although he did not inform the lector of all the reasons why."

"You did such a thing!?" Miriamele's outrage was quickly dampened by the memories of doing just such a thing herself. "Oh, never mind. I am beyond surprise. But you must change your ways, Cadrach. Such skulking—it goes with the drinking and lying."

"I do not think you know much about wine, my lady," he said with a wry smile, "so I may not consider you much of a teacher in that study. As for my other flaws— well, 'necessity beckons, self-interest comes following,' as they say in Abaingeat. And those flaws may prove the saving of us both, at least from our current situation."

"So why did Dinivan plan to send me to this inn?" she asked. "Why not let me stay at the Sancellan Aedonitis, where I would be safe?"

"As safe as Dinivan and the lector were, my lady?" Despite the harshness, there was real pain in his voice. "You know what happened there—although, the gods be thanked, you were spared seeing it with your poor young eyes. In any case, Dinivan and I had a falling out, but he was a good man and no fool. Too many people in and out of that place, too many folk with too many different needs and wants and problems to solve . . . and most of all, too many wagging tongues. I swear, they call Aedon's monument Mother Church, but at the Sancellan she is the most babble-breathed old gossip in the history of the world."

"So he planned to send me to some inn in the marshes?"

"I think so, yes—he spoke in a general way even to the lector, with no naming of names. But I am convinced I have it right because it is a place we all knew. Doctor Morgenes helped its owner to buy it. It is a place closely entangled with the secrets Dinivan and Morgenes and I shared."

Miriamele brought the oars to an awkward stop, leaning on the poles as she stared at Cadrach. He gazed back calmly, as though he had said nothing unusual. "My lady?" he asked at last.

"Doctor Morgenes . . . of the Hayholt?"

"Of course." He lowered his chin until it seemed to rest on his collarbone. "A great man. A kind, kind man. I loved him, Princess Miriamele. He was like a father to so many of us."

Mist was beginning to hover above the surface of the water, pale as cotton wool. Miriamele took a deep breath and shivered. "I don't understand. How did you know him? Who is 'us'?"

The monk let his gaze pass from her face out onto the shrouded sea. "It is a long story, Princess—a very long one. Have you ever heard of something called the League of the Scroll?"

"Yes! At Naglimund. The old man Jarnauga was part of it."

"Jarnauga." Cadrach sighed. "Another good man, although the gods know, we have had our differences. I hid from him while I was at Josua's stronghold. How was he?"

"I liked him," Miriamele said slowly. "He was one of those people who really listen—but I only talked with him a few times. I wonder what happened to him when Naglimund fell." She looked sharply at Cadrach. "What does all that have to do with you?"

"As I said, it is a long tale."

Miriamele laughed; it quickly turned into another shiver. "We don't have much else to do. Tell me."

"Let me first find something else to keep you warm." Cadrach crawled back into the shelter and brought out her monk's cloak. He draped it around Miriamele's shoulders and pulled the hood over her short hair. "Now you look like the convent-bound noblewoman you once claimed to be."

"Just talk to me—then I won't notice the cold."

"You are still weak, though. I wish you would put the oars down and let me take a turn, or at least lie down under the awning, out of the wind."

"Don't treat me like a little girl, Cadrach." Although she frowned, she was strangely touched. Was this the same man she had tried to drown—the same man who had tried to sell her into slavery? "You're not going to touch the oars tonight. When I get too tired, we'll drop the anchor. Until then, I'll row slowly. Now talk."

The monk waved his hands in a gesture of surrender. "Very well." He fluffed his own cloak around him, then settled down with his back against a bench and his knees drawn up before him so that he looked up at her from the darkness of the boat's bottom. The sky had gone almost completely black, and there was just enough moonlight to show his face. "I am afraid that I don't know where exactly to begin."

"At the beginning, of course." Miriamele raised the oars from the water and slid them back in again. A few drops of spray spattered her face.

"Ah. Yes." He thought for a moment. "Well, if I go back to the true beginnings of my story, then perhaps the later parts will be easier to understand—and that way I can also postpone the most shameful tales for a little while longer. It is not a happy story, Miriamele, and it winds through a great deal of shadow ... shadow that has now fallen over many people besides a drunken Hernystiri monk.

"I was born in Crannhyr, you know—when I say I am Cadrach ec-Crannhyr, only the last part is true. I was born Padreic. I have had other names, too, few of them pleasant, but Padreic I was born, and Cadrach I now am, I suppose.

"I stretch no truth when I say that Crannhyr is one of the strangest cities in all of Osten Ard. It is walled like a great fortress, but it has never been attacked, nor is there anything particularly worth stealing in it. The people of Crannhyr are secretive in a way that even other Hernystiri do not understand. A Crannhyr-man, it is said, would sooner buy everyone at the inn a drink than let even his closest friend into his home—and no one yet has seen a Crannhyr-man buy anyone's drink but his own. Crannhyr folk are close; that is the best word, I think. They talk in few words—how unlike the rest of the Hernystiri, in whose blood runs poetry!—and they make no show of wealth or luck at all, for fear that the gods will become jealous and take it back. Even the streets are close as conspirators, the buildings leaning so near together in some spots that you have to blow out all your breath before you go in and cannot suck in more air until you come out at the far end.

"Crannhyr was one of the first cities built by men in Osten Ard, and that age breathes in everything, so that people talk quietly from birth, as though they are afraid that if they speak too loud the old walls will tumble down and expose all their secrets to the light of day. Some people say that the Sithi had a hand in the making of the place, but although we Hernystirmen are never foolish enough to disbelieve in the Sithi—unlike some of our neighbors—I for one do not think the Peaceful Ones had anything to do with Crannhyr. I have seen Sithi ruins, and they are nothing like the cramped and self-protective walls of the city in which I spent my childhood. No, men built it—frightened men, if my eye tells me anything."

"But it sounds a terrible place," Miriamele said. "All that whispering!"

"Yes, I did not like it much myself." Cadrach smiled, a tiny gleam in the shadow. "I spent most of my childhood wanting to get away. My mother died when I was young, you see, and my father was a hard, cold man, fitly made for that hard, cold city. He never spoke a word more to me or my brothers and sisters than was necessary, and did not embellish even those words with kindness. He was a coppersmith, and I suppose that hammering at a hot forge all day to put food into our mouths showed that he recognized his obligations, so he felt bound to do no more. Most Crannhyri are like that—dour, and scornful of those who are not. I could not wait to make my own way in the world.

"Strangely, though—and it is often the way—for one so bedeviled by secrets and quietude, I developed a surprising love for old books and ancient learning. Seen through the eyes of the ancients—scholars like Plesinnen Myrmenis and Cuimnhe's Frethis—even Crannhyr was wonderful and mystical, its secretive ways hiding not just old unpleasantness, but strange wisdoms that freer, less arcane places could not boast. In the Tethtain Library— founded in our city centuries ago by the great Holly King himself—I found the only kindred souls in that entire walled prison, people who, like myself, lived for the lights of earlier days, and who enjoyed running down a bit of lost lore the way some men revel in chasing down a buck deer and putting an arrow in its heart.

"And that is where I met Morgenes. In those days— and this is almost two score years ago, my young princess—he was still inclined to travel. If there is a man who has seen more than Morgenes, who has been to more places, I have never heard of him. The doctor spent many hours among the scrolls of the Tethtain Library and knew the archives better than even the old priests who watched over them. He saw my interest in matters of history and forgotten lore and took me in hand, guiding me toward useful paths that I would otherwise never have found. When some years had passed, and he saw that my devotion to learning was not a thing to be sloughed off with childhood, he told me of the League of the Scroll, which was formed long ago by Saint Eahlstan Fiskerne, the Hayholt's Fisher King. Eahlstan inherited Fingil's castle and his sword Minneyar, but he wanted nothing to do with the Rimmersman's heritage of destruction—especially the destruction of learning. Eahlstan wanted instead to conserve knowledge that might otherwise vanish into shadow—and to use that knowledge when it seemed necessary."

"Use it for what?"

"We often argued about that, Princess. It was never 'for Good' or 'for Righteousness'—the Scrollbearers realized that once such a broad ideal is in place, one must meddle in *everything*. I suppose the clearest explanation is that the League acts to protect its own learning, to prevent a dark age that would bury again the secrets it has so laboriously unearthed. But at other times the League has acted only to protect itself rather than its products.

"However, I knew little of such difficult questions then. For me, the League sounded like a dream of heaven—a happy brotherhood of extraordinary scholars searching out the secrets of Creation together. I was deliriously eager to join. Thus, when our shared love of scholarship had ripened into a friendship—although on my part it was more like a love for a kind father—Morgenes took me to meet Trestolt, who was Jarnauga's father, and old Ookekuq, a wise man of the troll people who live in the far north. Morgenes put me forward as fit for the League, and those two took me in without hesitation, as wholeheartedly and trustfully as if they had known me all their lives—but that was because of Morgenes, you see. With the exception of Trestolt, whose wife had died a few years before, none of the other Scrollbearers was married. This has often been the case throughout the League's centuries of existence. Its members are generally the kind of folk—and it is true of the women who have carried the Scroll as well—who are more in love with knowledge than with mankind. Not that they do not care for other people, you must understand, but they love them better when they can keep them at a distance; in practice, people are a distraction. So for the Scrollbearers, the League itself became a kind of family. Thus, it was no surprise that any candidate put forward by the doctor should be warmly greeted. Morgenes—although he resisted any move to grant him power—was in a way a father to all the League's members, despite the fact that some of them seemed older than he did. But who will ever know when or where Morgenes was born?"

Down in the darkness of the hull, Cadrach laughed. Miriamele slowly dipped the oars into the water, listening dreamily to his words as the boat rose and fell.

"Later," he continued, "I met the other Scrollbearer, Xorastra of Perdruin. She had been a nun, although by the time I met her she had left her order. The inn at Kwanitupul that I spoke of earlier belongs to her, by the way. She was a fiercely clever woman, denied by her sex the life she would otherwise have led: she should have been a king's minister, that one. Xorastra also accepted me, then introduced me to a pair of her own candidates, for she and Morgenes had long had it in their minds to bring the numbers of the League back up to seven, which had traditionally been its full measure.

"Both of them were younger than I was. Dinivan was a mere youth at the time, studying with the Usirean brothers. Sharp-eyed Xorastra had seen the spark in him, and thought that if he were brought into contact with Morgenes and the others, that spark might become a great and warming fire by which the church she still loved could greatly benefit. The other that she put forward was a clever young priest, just ordained, who came from a poor island family, but who had made his way into a small sort of prominence by the swiftness of his mind. Morgenes, after much talk with Xorastra and their two northern colleagues, accepted these two new additions. When we all met the next year in Tungoldyr at the longhouse of Trestolt, the numbers of the League of the Scroll were seven once more."

Cadrach's words had become heavy and slow, and when at last he paused, Miriamele thought he might be falling asleep. But instead, when he spoke again there was a terrible hollowness to his voice. "Better they had kept us all out. Better that the League itself had fallen back into the dust of history."

When he did not speak more, Miriamele straightened up. "What do you mean, Cadrach? What could you have done that was so bad?"

He groaned. "Not me, Princess—my sins came later. No, it was in the moment we brought that young priest into our midst . . . for that was Pryrates."

Miriamele sucked in a deep breath, and for a moment, despite her warming feelings for Cadrach, felt the web of some terrible conspiracy gathering around her. Were all her enemies in alliance? Was the monk playing some deeper game, so that now she was in his hands utterly, adrift on an empty sea? Then she remembered the letter that Gan Itai had brought her.

"But you told me that," she said, relieved. "You wrote to me and said something about Pryrates—that you had made him what he was."

"If I said that," Cadrach replied sadly, "then I was ex- aggerating in my grief. The seeds of great evil must have been in him already, otherwise it could never have flow- ered so swiftly and so forcefully . . . or such is my guess. My own part came much later, and my shame is that al- though I already knew him for a black-souled and heart- less creature, I helped him anyway."

"But why? And helped him how?"

"Ah, Princess, I feel the drunken honesty of the Hernystiri on me tonight without even tasting a swallow of wine—but still there are things I would rather not tell. The story of my downfall is mine alone. Most of my friends who were near me in those years are dead now. Let me say only this: for many reasons, both because of the things that I studied, many of which I wish I had left alone, and because of my own pain and the many drunken nights I spent trying to kill it, the joy that for a time I found in life soon faded away. When I was a child, I believed in the gods of my people. When I was older, I came to doubt them, and believed instead in the single god of the Aedonites—single, though He is dreadfully mixed up with Usires His son and Elysia the blessed mother. Later, in the first blossoming of my scholarship, I came to disbelieve in all gods, old and new. But a certain dread gripped my heart when I became a man, and now I believe in the gods once more ... Ah, how I believe! ... for I know myself to be cursed." The monk quietly wiped his eyes and nose on his sleeve. He was sunken now in a shadow even the moonlight could not pierce.

"Cursed? What do you mean? Cursed how?"

"I do not know, or I would have found some hedge-wizard to grind me up a powder-charm a long time ago. No, I am joking, my lady, and a bleak joke it is. There are curses in the world no spell can dismiss—just as, I presume, there is good luck that no evil eye or envious rival can overthrow, but which can only be lost by its possessor. I only know that long ago the world became a heavy burden on me, one that my shoulders have proved too weak to bear. I became a drunkard in earnest—no local clown who drinks too many pots and sings the neighbors awake on his way home, but a chill-spirited, heart-lonely seeker of oblivion. My books were my only solace, but even they seemed to me full of the breath of tombs: they spoke only of dead lives, dead thoughts, and worst of all, dead and juiceless hopes, a million of them stillborn for every one that had a brief butterfly moment under the sun.

"So I drank, and I railed at the stars, and I drank. My drunkenness sent me down into the pit of despond, and my books, especially the volume with which I was then most deeply involved, only made my dread worse. So oblivion seemed even more desirable. Soon I was not wanted in the places where once I had been everyone's friend, which made me even more bitter. When the keepers of the Tethtain Library told me I would no longer be welcomed there, I fell down as into a deep hole, a season-long riot of black drunkenness from which I awoke to find myself by the side of a road outside Abaingeat, naked and without a cintis-piece. Clothed only in brambles and leaves like the lowest beast, I made my way by night to the house of a nobleman I knew, a good man and a lover of learning who had been, from time to time, my willing patron. He let me in, fed me, then gave me a bed for the night. When the sun rose, he gave me a monk's gown that had belonged to his brother and wished me good luck and Godspeed away from his house.

"There was disgust in his eyes that morning, Lady, a kind of loathing that I pray you never see in the eyes of another person. He knew of my habits, you see, and my tale of abduction and robbery did not fool him. I knew, as I stood in his doorway, that I had passed beyond the walls that surrounded my fellow men, that I was now as one unclean from plague. You see, all my drinking and wretched acts had only done this: it had made my curse as plain for others to see as it had been to me long before."

Cadrach's voice, which had grown more deathly during this recitation, now trailed off in a hoarse whisper. Miriamele listened to him breathing for a long while. She could think of nothing to say.

"But what had you actually done?" she tried at last. "You speak of being cursed, but you hadn't done anything wrong—besides drinking too much wine, that is."

Cadrach's laugh was unpleasantly cracked. "Oh, the wine was only to dull the pain. That is the thing with these stains, my lady. Though others, especially innocents like yourself, cannot always see them, the stain is there nevertheless, and others sense it, as the beasts of the field sense one of their number who is sick or mad. You tried to drown me yourself, didn't you?"

"But that was different!" Miriamele said indignantly. "That was for something you did!"

"Never fear," the monk murmured. "I have done enough wrong since that night by the road in Abaingeat to justify any punishment."

Miriamele pulled the oars in. "Is it shallow enough to drop the anchor?" she asked, trying to keep her voice calm. "My arms are tired."

"I will find out."

While the monk rooted the anchor out of the hold and made sure that its cord was tied firmly to the boat, Miriamele tried to think of something she could do to help him. The more she made him talk, the deeper the wounds seemed to be. His earlier good cheer, she sensed, was nothing but a thin skin that had grown over these raw places. Was it better to make him speak, when it was obviously painful, or simply to let it go? She wished that Geloë were here, or little Binabik with his shrewd and careful touch.

When the anchor had splashed over the side and the rope had fizzed down into the depths behind it, the two of them sat quietly for a while. At last, Cadrach spoke, his voice a little lighter than it had been.

"The cord only played out twenty ells or so before it struck bottom, so we may be closer to shore than I had thought. Still, you should try to sleep again, Miriamele. The day will be long tomorrow. If we are to reach shore, we will have to take turns at those oars so we can keep moving all day."

"Might there not be a ship around somewhere that might see us and pick us up?"

"I don't know if that would be the luckiest thing for us. Do not forget that Nabban now belongs utterly to your father and Pryrates. I think we will be happiest if we can make our way quietly to shore and disappear into the poorer parts of Nabban, then find our way to Xorastra's inn."

"You never explained about Pryrates," she said boldly, inwardly praying that it was not a mistake. "What happened between the two of you?"

Cadrach sighed. "Would you really force me to tell you such black things, Lady? It was only weakness and fear that led me to mention them in my letter, when I was frightened you would mistake the Earl of Eadne for something better than he was."

"I would not force you to do anything that would hurt you more, Cadrach. But I would like to know. These are

the secrets that are behind our troubles, remember? It is
not the time to hold them back, however bad they are."

The monk nodded slowly. "Spoken like a king's
daughter—but spoken well. Ah, gods of earth and sky, if
I had known that one day I would have to tell such stories
and say 'that is my life,' I think I would have pushed my
head into my father's kiln."

Miriamele made no reply but pulled her cloak tight.
Some of the mist had blown away, and the sea stretched
away beneath them like a great black tabletop. The stars
overhead seemed too small and chill to give off light;
they hung unsparkling, like flecks of milky stone.

"I did not leave the fellowship of ordinary men completely empty-handed," Cadrach began. "There were certain things I had obtained—many of them legitimately, in
my early days of scholarship. One was a great treasure
which no one knew that I had. My possessions—those I
had not sold to buy wine—remained in the care of an old
friend. When it was decided I was no longer fit for the
company of those I had known, I took them back from
him . . . against his protestations, for he knew I was not a
reliable keeper. Thus, when times became particularly
bad, I could usually find a dealer in rare manuscripts or
church-forbidden books and—usually at prices so low as
to approach robbery—get some money in exchange for
one of my prized books. But, as I said, one thing that I
had found was worth a thousandfold more than all the
rest. The story of its getting is a night's tale in itself, but
it was for long the one thing with which I would not part,
however desperate my circumstances. For you see, I had
found a copy of *Du Svardenvyrd*, the fabled book of mad
Nisses, the only copy that I have ever heard to exist in
modern days. Whether it was the original I do not know,
for the binding had long since disappeared, but the . . .
person from whom I obtained it swore that it was genuine; indeed, if it was a forgery, it was a work of brilliance
in itself. But copy or no, it contained the actual words of
Nisses—of that there was no doubt. No one could read
the dreadful things that I did, then look at the world
around him, and disbelieve."

"I have heard of it," said Mirimele. "Who *was* Nisses?"

Cadrach laughed shortly. "A question for the ages. He was a man who came out of the north beyond Elvritshalla, from the land of the Black Rimmersmen who live below Stormspike, and presented himself to Fingil, King of Rimmersgard. He was no court conjuror, but it is said that he gave Fingil the power that enabled him to conquer half of Osten Ard. That power may have been wisdom, for Nisses knew the facts of things that no one else had even dreamed existed. After Asu'a was conquered and Fingil died at last, Nisses served Fingil's son Hjeldin. It was during those years that he wrote his book—a book that contained part of the dreadful knowledge he had brought with him when he appeared in a murderous snowstorm outside Fingil's gates. He and Hjeldin both died in Asu'a—the young king by throwing himself out the window of the tower that bears his name. Nisses was found dead in the room from which Hjeldin had leapt, with no mark upon him. There was a smile on his face; the book was clutched in his hands."

Miriamele shuddered. "That book. They spoke of it at Naglimund. Jarnauga said that it supposedly tells of the Storm King's coming and other things."

"Ah, Jarnauga," Cadrach said sadly. "How he would have loved to see it! But I never showed it to him, nor to any of the Scrollbearers."

"But why? If you had it, even a copy, why didn't you show it to Morgenes and the others? I thought that was just the sort of thing that your League was for."

"Perhaps. But by the time I had finished reading it, I was no longer a Scrollbearer. I knew it in my heart. From the moment I turned the last page I gave up the love of learning for the love of oblivion—the two cannot live together. Even before I found Nisses' book, I had gone far down the wrong paths, learning things that no man should learn who wishes to sleep well at night. And I was jealous of my fellow Scrollbearers, Miriamele, jealous of their simple happiness with their studies, angry with their calm assurance that all that could be examined could be understood. They were so certain that if they could look closely enough at the nature of the world they could divine all its purposes ... but *I* had something they did not, a book the mere reading of which would not only prove to them things I had already suggested, but would crumble the pillars of their understanding. I was full of rage, Miriamele, but I was also full of despair." He paused, the pain clear in his voice. "The world is different once Nisses has explained it. It is as though the pages of his book were dipped in some slow poison that kills the spirit. I touched them all."

"It sounds horrible." Miriamele remembered the image she had seen in one of Dinivan's books, a horned giant with red eyes. She had seen that image since, in many troubling dreams. Could it be better not to know some things, to be blind to certain pictures and ideas?

"Horrible indeed, but only because it reflected the true terror that lurked beneath the waking world, the shadows which are the obverse image of sunlight. Still, even such a powerful thing as Nisses' book eventually became nothing more to me than another instrument of forgetting: when I had read it so many times that it made me sick even to stare at it, I began to sell its pages off, one by one."

"Elysia, Mother of Mercy! Who would buy such a thing?"

Cadrach chortled harshly. "Even those who were sure it was a deft forgery stumbled over themselves in their haste to take a single page from my hands. A banned book has a powerful fascination, young one, but a truly evil book— and there are not many—draws the curious as honey lures flies." His laughter grew for a moment, then was choked off in what sounded like a sob. "Sweet Usires, I wish that I had burned it!"

"But what about Pryrates?" she prodded. "Did you sell pages to him?"

"Never!" Cadrach almost shouted. "Even then, I knew he was a demon. He was forced out of the League long before my own downfall, and every one of us knew what a danger he was!" He recovered his composure. "No, I suspect that he merely frequented the same peddlers of antiquities that I did—it is a rather small community, you know—and that some scraps made their way into his hands. He is tremendously learned in dark matters, Princess, particularly the most dangerous areas of the Art. It was not difficult, I'm sure, for him to discover who had possessed the powerful thing from which those pages came. Neither was it hard for him to find me, despite the fact that I had sunk myself as deeply into shadows as I could, bending all my own learning into making myself unimportant to the point of invisibility. But, as I said, he found me. He sent some of your father's own guardsmen after me. You see, he had already become a counselor to princes—or in your sire's case, kings-to-be."

Miriamele thought of the day she had first met Pryrates. The red priest had come to her father's apartments in Meremund, bringing Elias information about events in Nabban. Young Miriamele had been having a difficult time speaking to her father, struggling to think of something she could tell him that might make him smile even for a moment, as he often had in the days when she was the light of his eye. Matters of state providing a useful excuse for avoiding another uncomfortable conversation with his daughter, Elias had sent her away. Curious, she had caught Pryrates' gaze on her way out the door.

Even as a young girl, Miriamele had become used to the variety of different looks she inspired among her father's courtiers—irritation from those who considered her an impediment to their affairs, pity from those who recognized her loneliness and confusion, honest calculation from those who wondered who she might marry someday, or whether she would grow into an attractive woman, or whether she would be a pliable queen after her father's death. But never until that moment had she been examined with anything like Pryrates' inhuman regard, a stare cold as a plunge in ice water. There seemed not the slightest bit of human feeling in his black eyes: she had known somehow that had she been flayed meat on a butcher's table his expression would have been no different. At the same time, he had seemed to see right into her and through her, as though her every thought were being made to walk naked before him, squirming beneath his inspection. Aghast, she had turned from his terrible gaze and fled down the corridor, inexplicably weeping. Behind, she heard the dry buzz of the alchemist's voice as he began to speak. She realized she meant no more to this new intimate of her father's than would a fly—that he would ignore her with never another thought, or crush her without a qualm if it suited his purposes. To a girl raised in the nurturing certainty of her own importance, an importance that had even outlasted her father's love, it was a horrifying realization.

Her father, for all his faults, had never been a monster of that sort. Why, then, had he brought Pryrates into his inner circle, so that eventually the devil-priest became his closest and most trusted advisor? It was a deeply troubling question, and one for which she had never discovered an answer.

Now, in the gently pitching boat, she struggled to keep her voice steady. "Tell me what happened, Cadrach."

The monk plainly did not want to start. Miriamele could hear his fingers scratching quietly against the wooden seat, as though he searched for something in the darkness. "They found me in the stable of an inn in south Erchester," he said slowly, "sleeping in the muck. The guardsmen dragged me out, then threw me in the back of a wagon and we rode toward the Hayholt. It was during the worst year of that terrible drought, and in the late afternoon light everything was gold and brown, even the trees stiff and dull as dried mud. I remember staring, my head ringing like a church bell—I had been sleeping off a long bout of drinking, of course—and wondering if the same dryness that made my eyes and nose and mouth feel as though they were packed with dust had somehow leached away all the colors of the world as well.

"The soldiers, I'm sure, thought I was nothing but another criminal, and one not fated for a long life beyond that afternoon. They talked as though I were already dead, complaining about the onerous duty of having to carry out and bury a corpse as fetid and unwashed as mine. A guardsman even said he would demand an extra hour's pay for the unpleasant labor. One of his companions smirked and said: 'From Pryrates?'. The braggart fell silent. Some of the other soldiers laughed at his discomfort, but their voices were forced, as though the mere thought of demanding anything from the red priest was enough to spoil the day. This was the first time I had any inkling of where I was going, and I knew it to be a great deal worse than simply being hung as a thief or a traitor—both of which I was. I tried to throw myself out of the cart, but was quickly pulled back in again. 'Ho,' one of them said, 'he knows the name!'

" 'Please,' I begged, 'do not take me to that man. If there is Aedonite mercy in you, do anything else with me you like, but do not give me to the priest.' The soldier who had last spoken stared at me, and I think there might have been some pity in his hard eyes, but he said: 'And bring his anger down on us? Leave our children fatherless? No. Bear up, and face it like a man.'

"I wept all the way to the Nearulagh Gate.

"The cart stopped at the iron-banded front door of Hjeldin's Tower and I was dragged inside, too weak with despair to resist—not that my wasted body would have served me for much against four armed Erkynguards. I was half-carried through the anteroom, then up what seemed like a million steps. At the top, two great oaken doors swung open. I was shoved through like a sack of meal and fell to my knees on the hard flags of a cluttered chamber.

"The first thing I thought, Princess, was that I had tumbled somehow into a lake of blood. The entire room was scarlet, every niche and cranny; my very hands held before my face had changed their color as well. I looked up in horror to the tall windows. Every one was fitted from top to bottom with panes of bright red glass; the setting sun streamed through them, dazzling the eye, as though each window were a great ruby. The red light stripped everything inside the room of color, just as evening does. There seemed no shades but black and red. There were tables and tall, leaning shelves, none of which touched the chamber's single curving outer wall, but instead were clustered toward the middle of the room. Every surface was draped in books and scrolls and . . . and other things, many of which I could not bear to look at for long. The priest has a terrible curiosity. There is nothing he will not do to discover the truth about something—or such truths as are important to him. Many of the subjects of his inquiries, mostly animals, were locked in cages stacked haphazardly among the books; most of them were still alive, although it would have been better for them if they had not been. Considering the chaos in the center of the room, the wall was curiously uncluttered, naked except for certain painted symbols.

" 'Ah,' a voice said. 'Greetings, fellow Scrollbearer.' It was Pryrates, of course, seated on a narrow, high-backed chair at the center of this strange nest. 'I trust your journey was a comfortable one?'

" 'Let us not bandy words,' I said. With despair had come a certain resignation. 'You are a Scrollbearer no longer, Pryrates, nor am I. What do you want?'

"He grinned. He was in no mood to speed what was, for him, an enjoyable diversion. 'Once a member of the League, always a member, I should think,' he chuckled. 'For are we not both still intimately concerned with old things, old writings . . . old books?'

"When he said this last, my heart stumbled in my chest. At first I had thought he wanted only to torment me, to take revenge for his ousting from the League— although others were more responsible for that than I was; I had already begun my slide into darkness when he was forced out. Now I realized he wanted something quite different. He plainly desired some book he thought I had—and I had little doubt as to which book that might be.

"I dueled with him for part of an hour, using words as a swordsman does his blade, and for a while held my own—the last thing a drunkard loses, you see, is his cunning: it outlasts his soul by a long season—but we both knew that I would give in at the end. I was tired, you see, very tired and sick. As we spoke, two men came into the

room. These were not more Erkynguardsmen, but rather
somber-robed, shaven-headed men who had the dark-
haired, dark-skinned look of southern islanders. They neither of them spoke—perhaps they were mutes—but
nevertheless, their purpose was clear: they would hold me
so that Pryrates might have his hands and attention unim-
peded as he moved on to more strenuous means of nego-
tiation. When the two grabbed my arms and dragged me
close to the priest's chair, I gave up. It was not the pain
I feared, Miriamele, or even the other soul-horrors that he
could have inflicted. I swear that to you, although why it
should matter I don't know. Rather, I simply no longer
cared. Let him have what he would of me, I thought. Let
him do what he pleased with it. It was not, I told myself,
as though this sin-blackened world might receive unde-
served punishment . . . for I had dwelt in the depths so
long that I saw nothing left that was good but nothingness
itself.

   " 'You have been making free with pages from a certain old volume, Padreic,' he said. 'Or do I remember that
you call yourself something different now? No matter. I
need that book. If you tell me where you keep it hidden,
you will walk free into the evening air.' He gestured to
the world beyond the scarlet windows. 'If not . . .' He
pointed at certain objects that were lying on the table
close by his hand, objects already filthy with hair and
blood.

   " 'I do not have it anymore,' I told him. That was the
truth. I had sold the remaining few pages a fortnight
earlier: I had been sleeping off the last of the proceeds in
that noisome stable.

   "He said: 'I do not believe you, little man,' then his
servants did something to me until I screamed. When I
still could not tell him where it was, he began to take a
more active hand himself, stopping only when I could
shriek no longer and my voice was a cracked whisper.
'Hmm,' he said, scratching his chin as though aping Doctor Morgenes, who would often muse that way over a delicate translation. 'Perhaps I must believe you after all. I
find it hard to think that offal such as you would stay si-

lent on purely moral grounds. Tell me who you sold it to—all the pieces.'

"Damning myself silently for the murder of these various merchants—for Pryrates, I knew, would have them killed and their wares confiscated without a moment's hesitation—I told him all the names I could remember. When I hesitated, I was helped along by ... by ... his servants. ..."

Cadrach suddenly broke into deep, chesty sobs. Miriamele heard him trying to repress them, then he broke off in a fit of coughing. She leaned forward and caught his cold hand, squeezing hard to let him know that she was there. After a while, his breathing became more regular.

"I am sorry, Princess," he rasped. "I do not like to think of it."

There were tears in Miriamele's eyes as well. "It's my fault. I should never have made you talk about it. Let's stop, and you can sleep."

"No." She could feel him shaking. "No, I have begun it. I will not sleep well in any case. Perhaps it will help me if I finish the tale." He reached out and patted her head. "I thought he had gotten everything from me he could wish, but I was wrong. 'What if these gentlemen no longer have the pieces I need, Padreic?' he asked. Ah, gods, there is nothing fouler than that priest's smile! 'I think you should tell me what you remember—there is still some wit left in that wine-soaked head, is there not? Come, recite for me, little acolyte.'

"And tell him I did, every bit and every line that I could recall, the order as tumbled as you would expect from a creature as wretched as I was. He seemed most interested in Nisses' cryptic words on death, especially something termed 'speaking through the veil,' which I gathered to be the rituals that allow one to reach what Nisses had called 'songs of the upper air'—that is, the thoughts of those who are somehow beyond mortality, both the dead and the never-living. I disgorged it all, aching to please, with Pryrates sitting there nodding, nodding, his shiny head gleaming in the strange light.

"Somehow, in the middle of this terrible experience, I noticed something strange. It took a while, as you can imagine, but since I had begun to talk freely about my memories of Nisses' book I had been left unharmed—one of the unspeaking servitors even gave me a cup of water so that I could speak more clearly. While I rattled on, answering Pryrates' every question as eagerly as a child at its first holy mansa, I noticed something disturbing about the way the light was moving across the room. At first, in my weary, pained state, I was convinced that somehow Pryrates had managed to make the sun roll backward in its tracks, for the light that should have been passing from east to west across the bloody windows was slipping the other way instead. I mused on this—at such times, it is good to have something to think about other than what is happening to you—and realized at last that the laws of heaven had not been countermanded after all. Rather, it was the tower itself, or at least the topmost section where we were, that was spinning slowly sunward, a little faster than the passage of the sun itself—so slowly that, when combined with the sameness of the tower's uppermost story, I would guess that none have ever marked it from the outside.

"So that was why nothing was allowed to lean against the stones of these chamber walls, I thought! Even in the extremity of my pain and terror, I marveled at the huge gears and wheels that must be moving silently behind the mortar or below my feet. Such things were once a joy of mine—I spent many hours of my youth studying the mechanical laws of the spinning globe and the heavens. And, the gods help me, it gave me something to think about beside what had been done to me, and what I, in turn, was doing to my fellow men.

"Looking around the circular room as I continued my prattling, I saw for the first time the subtle marks incised in the red window glass, and how those marks, thrown forward as faint lines of darker red, crossed over the strange symbols marked all around on the tower's interior wall. I could think of no other explanation but that Pryrates had turned the top of Hjeldin's Tower into some kind of vast water clock, a time-keeping device of fantastic size and intricacy. I have pondered and pondered, but to this day I still can think of nothing else that fits the facts as well. The black arts in which Pryrates has become involved, I suppose, have made hourglass and sundial unhelpfully imprecise."

Miriamele let him pause for a long time. "So what happened, Cadrach?"

Cadrach still hesitated. When he resumed, he spoke a little more swiftly, as though this part was even more troubling than what had preceded it. "After I had finished telling Pryrates all I knew, he sat thinking for the time it took the last sliver of the sun to drop out one of the windows and appear at the edge of the next. Then he stood, waved a hand, and one of his servants stepped up behind me. Something struck me on the head and I knew no more. I woke up lying in a thicket in the Kynslagh, my torn clothes stained with the fluids of my own body. I believe they thought me dead. Certainly Pryrates did not believe me worth any more effort, not even the effort to kill me properly." Cadrach stopped to take a deep breath.

"You would think that I would have been deliriously happy to be alive, to have survived when I did not expect to, but all I could do was crawl deeper into the underbrush and wait for death. But those were warm, dry days; I did not die. When I was enough recovered, I made my way down into Erchester. There I stole some clothing and some food. I even bathed in the Kynslagh, so that I could go to into the places where wine was sold." The monk groaned. "But I could not leave the town, although I burned to. The sight of Hjeldin's Tower looming up above the Hayholt's outwall terrified me, but still I could not flee: I felt as though Pryrates had pulled out a part of my soul to keep me tethered, as though he could call me back any time he wished and I would go. This despite the fact that he clearly did not care if I was alive or dead. I remained in the town, thieving, drinking, trying without success to forget the terrible, treacherous thing I had done. I have not forgotten it, of course—I will *never* forget it—although I eventually grew strong enough to wrench myself free of the tower's shadow and flee Erchester." He looked for a moment as though he might say something more, but shuddered and fell silent.

Miriamele again clutched the monk's hand, which had been scraping fretfully at the wooden bench. Somewhere to the south a seagull raised its lonely cry. "But you can't blame yourself, Cadrach. That is foolish. Anyone would have done what you did."

"No, Princess," he murmured sadly. "Some would not have. Some would have died before telling such dreadful secrets. And more importantly, others would not have given up a treasure in the first place—especially a dangerous treasure like Nisses' book—for the price of a few jugs of wine. I had a sacred trust. That is what the League of the Scroll is meant for, Miriamele—to preserve knowledge, and also to preserve Osten Ard from those like Pryrates who would use the old knowledge for power over others. I failed on both those counts. And the League was also meant to watch for the return of Ineluki, the Storm King. There I failed most miserably of all, for it seems clear to me that I gave Pryrates the means of finding that terrible spirit and interesting it in humankind once more—and all this evil I accomplished simply so I could guzzle wine, so I could make my already dim brain a little darker."

"But why did Pryrates want to know all that? Why was he so interested in death?"

"I don't know." Cadrach was weary. "His is a mind that has gone rotten like a piece of old fruit—who knows what strange prodigies will hatch from such a thing?"

Angry, Miriamele squeezed his hand. "That is no answer."

Cadrach sat up a little straighter. "I'm sorry, my lady, but I have no answers. The only thing I can say is that from the questions Pryrates asked me, I do not think that he was seeking to contact the Storm King—not at first. No, he had some other interest in, as he called it, 'speaking through the veil.' And I think that when he began to explore in those lightless regions, he was noticed. Most living mortals who are discovered there are destroyed or made mad, but my guess is that Pryrates was recognized as a possible tool for a vengeful Ineluki. From what you and others have told me, he has been a very useful tool indeed."

Miriamele, chilled by the night breeze, crouched lower. Something in what Cadrach had just said tugged at her mind, asking to be examined. "I want to think," she said.

"If I have disgusted you, my lady, it is only reasonable." He seemed very distant. "I have grown unutterably disgusted with myself."

"Don't be an idiot." Impulsively, she lifted his cold hand and pressed it against her cheek. Startled, he left it there for a moment before pulling it back again. "You have made mistakes, Cadrach. So have I, so have many others." She yawned. "Now we need to sleep, so we can get up in the morning and start rowing again." She crawled past him toward the boat's makeshift cabin.

"My lady?" the monk said, surprise evident in his voice, but she did not say anything more.

Some time later, as Miriamele was drifting toward sleep, she heard him crawl in beneath the oilcloth shelter. He curled up near her feet, but his breathing stayed quiet, as though he, too, were thinking. Soon, the gentle smack of the waves and the rocking of the anchored boat pulled her down into dreams.

10

Riders of the Dawn

Despite the chill morning mists that covered
Sesuad'ra like a gray cloak, New Gadrinsett was in almost a festival mood. The troop of trolls, led back across
the slowly freezing lake by Binabik and Simon, were a
new and pleasant wonder in a year whose other oddities
had been almost entirely bad. As Simon and his small
friends made their way up the last winding stretch of the
old Sithi road, a rush of chattering children who had
legged out ahead of their parents and older siblings began
to gather around them. The mountain rams, hardened by
the din of Qanuc villages, did not break stride. Some of
the smaller children were lifted up by rough brown hands
and dropped into the saddle to ride with troll herders and
huntresses. One little boy, not expecting such a sudden
and intimate introduction to the newcomers, broke into
loud crying. Grinning worriedly through his sparse beard,
the troll-man who had picked him up held the struggling
lad gently but firmly in place lest he fall and be hurt
among the horn-bumping rams. The boy's wailing outstripped even the shouting of the other children and the
unrestrained banging and tootling of Qanuc marching music.

Binabik had told Josua of his folk's arrival before taking Simon down to the forest; in turn, the prince had done
his best to see that a suitable welcome was prepared. The
rams were taken to warm cavern stables where they
cropped hay contentedly beside New Gadrinsett's horses,
then Sisqi and the rest of her troll contingent marched to

the wind-burnished hulk of Leavetaking House, still surrounded by a flock of gaping settlers. Sesuad'ra's meager stores were combined with the traveling food of the trolls and a modest meal was shared. There were now enough citizens in New Gadrinsett that the addition of five score of even such diminutive men and women filled the cavernous Sithi hall to its limits, but the closeness made it a warmer place. There was little food, but the company was exotically exciting.

Sangfugol stood, dressed in his best—if perhaps a little threadbare—doublet and hose, and presented a few favorite old songs. The trolls applauded by smacking their boots with the palms of their hands, a custom that much amused the citizens of New Gadrinsett. A man and woman of the Qanuc, urged on by their fellows, next presented an acrobatic dance that employed two of their hooked sheep-herder's spears and involved much leaping and tumbling. Most of the people of New Gadrinsett, even those who had entered the hall suspicious of these small strangers, found themselves warming to the newcomers. Only among those few settlers originally from Rimmersgard did there seem to be any lingering ill-feeling: the longtime enmity of trolls and Rimmersmen would not be banished by a single banquet and a little dancing and singing.

Simon sat and watched proudly. He did not drink, since the blood was still thudding uncomfortably in his head from the previous night's *kangkang,* but he felt as pleasurably giddy as if he had just downed a skinful. All Sesuad'ra's defenders were grateful for the arrival of new allies—any allies. The trolls were small, but Simon remembered from Sikkihoq what brave fighters they were. There was still little chance that Josua's folk would be able to hold off Fengbald, but at least the odds were better than they had been the day before. Best of all, however, Sisqi had solemnly asked Simon to fight alongside the trolls. From what he could gather, they had never asked another *Utku,* which made it an honor indeed. The Qanuc thought very highly of his bravery, she told him, and the loyalty he had shown to Binabik.

Simon could not help gloating a little, although he had decided to keep it to himself for the time being. Still, he could not keep from grinning cheerfully down the long table at anyone whose eye he caught.

When Jeremias appeared, Simon forced him to sit down beside him. In the company of the prince and the other "high folk," as Jeremias called them, the onetime chandler's boy was still generally more comfortable waiting on Simon as his body-servant—something that Simon did not find comfortable at all.

"It's not right," Jeremias grunted, staring down at the cup that Simon had placed in front of him. "I'm your squire, Simon. I shouldn't be sitting at the prince's table. I should be filling *your* cup."

"Nonsense." Simon waved his hand airily. "That's not the way things work here. Besides, if you had gotten out of the castle when I did, it would have been you that had the adventures, and me who wound up in the cellar with Inch. . . ."

"Don't say that!" Jeremias gasped, eyes full of sudden fright. "You don't know. . . !" He struggled to control himself. "No, Simon, don't even say it—you'll bring bad luck, make it come true!" His expression changed, the fear gradually giving way to a look of wistfulness. "Besides, you're wrong. Such things wouldn't have happened to me, Simon—the dragon, the fairy-folk, any of that. If you can't see that you're special, then . . ." He took a deep breath, ". . . then you're just being stupid."

This kind of talk made Simon even more uncomfortable. "Special or stupid, make up your mind," he growled.

Jeremias stared at him as if sensing his thought. He seemed to consider pursuing the subject, but after some moments his face twisted into a mocking smile instead. "Hmm. 'Specially stupid' would be about right, now that you mention it."

Relieved to find himself back on safer footing, Simon dipped his fingers in his wine cup and flicked droplets onto Jeremias' pale face, making his friend splutter. "And you, sirrah, are no better. I have anointed thee, and now I dub thee 'Sir Stupidly Special.' " He gravely flicked a few more drops. Jeremias snarled and swiped at the cup, spilling the dregs onto Simon's shirt, then they began to arm-wrestle, laughing and swatting back and forth with their free hands like sportive bear cubs.

"Specially Stupid!"

"Stupidly Special!"

The contest, although still good-natured, soon became a little more heated; those guests seated closest to the combatants moved back to give them room. Prince Josua, despite certain reservations, found it hard to maintain his look of detached propriety. Lady Vorzheva laughed out-right.

The trolls, whose state occasions took place in the awe-some vastness of Chidsik ub Lingit and never included anything as trivial as two friends wrestling and rubbing wine in each other's hair, watched the proceedings with grave interest. Several wondered aloud if any particular augury or prophesy was determined by the result of this contest, others whether it would be insulting to their hosts' religious beliefs if they made a few quiet wagers on who might be the winner. Regarding this last, a quiet consensus developed that what was not noticed could not offend; the odds changed several times as one or the other of the combatants seemed on the brink of crushing defeat.

As long moments passed and neither warrior showed any sign of surrender, the interest of the trolls grew. For such a thing to go on so long at a celebratory banquet in the cavern of these lowlanders' Herder and Huntress— well, clearly, the more cosmopolitan of the Qanuc folk explained, it must be more than a mere contest. Rather, they told their fellows, it was obviously a very compli-cated sort of dance that solicited luck and strength from the gods for the upcoming battle. No, others said, it was likely nothing more intricate than a combat for the right to mate. Rams did it, so why not lowlanders?

When Simon and Jeremias realized that almost every-one in the room was watching them, the arm-wrestling match suddenly came to a halt. The two embarrassed con-testants, red-faced and sweating, straightened their chairs and addressed themselves to their food, not daring to look

up at any of the other guests. The trolls whispered sadly.
What a shame it was that neither Sisqi nor Binabik had
been present to translate their many questions about the
odd ritual. A chance for a greater appreciation of *Utku*
customs had been lost, at least for the time being.

Outside Leavetaking Hall, Binabik and his betrothed
stood ankle-deep in the snow that blanketed the crumbling tiles of the Fire Garden. The cold bothered them not
at all—late spring in Yiqanuc could be far worse, and
they had not been alone together in a long time.

The hooded pair stood close, face to face, warming
each other's cheeks with their breath. Binabik reached up
a gentle hand and brushed a melting particle of sleet from
Sisqi's cheek.

"*You are even more beautiful,*" he said. "*I had thought
that my loneliness was playing tricks on me, but you are
more lovely even than I remembered.*"

Sisqi laughed and pulled him close. "*Flattery, Singing
Man, flattery. Have you been practicing on these huge
lowland women? Be careful, one of them might take offense and smash you flat.*"

Binabik made a mock-frown. "*I see no one else but
you, Sisqinanamook, nor have I since the first time your
eyes opened before mine.*"

She wrapped her arms about his chest and squeezed as
tightly as she could. When she let him go, she turned and
began walking once more. Binabik fell into step beside
her.

"*Your news was welcome,*" he said. "*I have worried for
our people since the day I left Blue Mud Lake.*"

Sisqi shrugged. "*We will get on. Sedda's children always do. Still, it was like taking a stone from the foot of
an angry ram to convince my parents to let me bring even
this small mustering of our folk.*"

"*The Herder and Huntress may be reconciled to the
truth of what Ookequk wrote,*" said Binabik, "*but just because an unpleasant thing is known to be true does not
make it more palatable. Still, Josua and the others are
truly grateful—every arm, every eye, will help. The

Herder and Huntress have done a good thing, however unwillingly." He paused. "*And you have done a good thing also. I thank you for your kindness to Simon.*"

Sisqi looked at him, puzzled. "*What do you mean?*"

"*Asking him to join the Qanuc troop. That meant much to him.*"

She smiled. "*It was no favor, beloved. It is a deserved honor, and our choice—and not just mine, Binabik, but that of the folk who came with me.*"

Binabik stared at her, surprised. "*But they do not know him!*"

"*Some do. A few of those who survived our march down Sikkihoq are among this hundred. You saw Snenneq, surely? And those who were at Sikkihoq brought back stories to the rest. Your young friend has made a strong impression on our folk, beloved.*"

"*Young Simon.*" Binabik thought about this for a moment. "*It is strange to think it, but I know you speak the truth.*"

"*He has grown much, your friend, even since we parted at the lake. Surely you have seen that?*"

"*I know you do not mean in size—he has always been large, even for one of his folk.*"

Sisqi laughed and squeezed him again. "*No, of course not. I mean that since he came down from our mountains, he looks like one who has taken the Walk of Manhood.*"

"*The lowlanders do not do as we do, my love—but I think that the whole of the last year has been, in a way, his manhood-walk. And I do not think it is over yet.*" Binabik shook his head, then folded her hand in his. "*But still, I have done Simon a disservice by guessing you had given this as a kindness. He is young and he is changing quickly. I am so close to him, perhaps I do not see the changes as clearly as you do.*"

"*You see more clearly than any of us, Binbiniqegabenik. That is why I love you—and that is also why no harm must come to you. I gave my parents no rest until I could be at your side with a troop of your own folk.*"

"*Ah, Sisqi,*" he said wistfully, "*a thousand, thousand of the stoutest trolls could not keep us safe in these terrible times—but better than a million spears is having you close to me again."*

"Flattery again," she laughed. *"But so wonderfully spoken."*

Arm in arm, they walked through the snow.

Provisions were scarce, but wood was not: inside Leavetaking House, the fire had been banked high with logs so that the smoke blackened the ceiling. Normally, Simon would have been upset by such a smirching of the Sithi's sacred place, but tonight he saw it as no more than what was needed—a brave and happy gesture in a time scant of hope. He looked toward the circle of people that had formed around the blaze once supper was finished.

Most of the settlers had wandered back to their tents and sleeping caves, tired after a long day and an unexpected celebration. Some of the trolls had also gone off, a few to look in on the rams—for what, they had asked themselves, did lowlanders *truly* know about sheep?—and others to bed down in the caverns the prince's folk had prepared for them. Binabik and Sisqi were now sitting at the high table with the prince, talking quietly, their faces far more serious than those of the rest of the revelers, who were passing a few precious wineskins around the fire-circle. Simon debated for a moment, then headed toward the group gathered near the fire.

Lady Vorzheva had left the prince's table and was moving toward the door—Duchess Gutrun was walking beside her, delicately holding the Thrithings-woman's elbow like a mother ready to restrain an impulsive child—but when Vorzheva saw Simon, she paused. "There you are," she said, and beckoned. The child growing in her was beginning to show, a bulge at her middle.

"My lady. Duchess." He wondered if he should bow to them, then remembered that they had both seen him thumping Jeremias earlier. He blushed and bent hastily to hide his face.

Vorzheva sounded as though she was smiling. "Prince

Josua says that these trolls are your sworn allies,
Simon—or should I call you Sir Seoman?"

It was getting worse and worse. His cheeks felt woefully hot. "Please, my lady, just Simon." He sneaked a
look, then slowly straightened.

Duchess Gutrun chuckled. "Heaven help you, lad, don't
get so worried. Let him go and join the others, Vorzheva—
he's a young man and wants to stay up late, drinking and
bragging."

Vorzheva looked at her sharply for a moment, then her
expression softened. "I wanted only to tell him ..." She
turned to Simon. "I wanted only to tell you that I wish I
knew more about you. I had thought *our* lives since going
from Naglimund were strange, but when Josua tells me
things you have seen ..." She laughed again, a little
sadly, and spread her long fingers on her stomach. "But it
is good of you to bring help to us. I have never seen anything like these trolls!"

"You have known ... *mmmmhh* ... Binabik for a long
time," Gutrun said, yawning behind her hand.

"Yes, but seeing one small person is different than seeing many, so many." Vorzheva turned to Simon as if for
help. "Do you understand?"

"I do, Lady Vorzheva." He grinned, remembering.
"The first time I saw the city where Binabik's people
live—hundreds of caves in the mountainside, and swinging rope bridges, and more trolls than you can imagine,
young and old—yes, it was far different than knowing
only Binabik."

"Just so." Vorzheva nodded. "Well, again I thank you.
Perhaps one day you will come to tell me more of your
travels. I am sick now some days, and Josua worries so
much for me when I go out and walk around—" she
smiled again, but there was a touch of bitterness in it,
"—so it is good to have company."

"Of course, Lady. I would be honored."

Gutrun tugged at Vorzheva's sleeve. "Come along now,
Vorzheva. Let the young man go and talk to his friends."

"Yes. Well, good night to you, Simon."

"Ladies." He bowed again as they left, a little more

gracefully this time. Apparently it was something that improved with practice.

Sangfugol glanced up as Simon reached the fire. The harper looked tired. Old Towser was seated beside him, carrying on one half of a rambling argument—an argument that Sangfugol seemed to have abandoned a while earlier.

"There you are," said the harper. "Sit down. Have some wine." He offered a skin.

Simon took a swallow just to be friendly. "I liked that song you did tonight—the one about the bear."

"The Osgal tune? It is a good one. I remembered you saying that they have bears up in the trollish country, so I thought they would like it."

Simon did not have the heart to reveal that only one of their hundred new guests spoke even a single word of Westerling—that the harper could have sung about swamp fowl for all they would have noticed. However, although the subject matter had been a complete mystery, the Qanuc *had* enjoyed the song's energetic choruses and Sangfugol's goggling facial expressions. "They certainly clapped for it," Simon said. "I thought the roof would come down."

"Smacked on their boots—did you see?" Thinking back on such a triumph, Sangfugol visibly lifted himself straighter. He might be the only harper ever to be applauded by troll feet—such a thing was not said even of the legendary Eoin-ec-Cluias.

"Boots?" Towser leaned forward and clutched at Sangfugol's knee. "And who taught 'em to wear boots at all, that's what I'd like to know. Mountain savages don't wear boots."

Simon started to reply, but Sangfugol shook his head, irritated. "You're talking nonsense again, Towser. You don't know the first thing about trolls."

Abashed, the jester looked around, the lump in his throat bobbing. "I just thought it strange that . . ." He looked at Simon. "And you know them, son? These little people?"

"I do. Binabik is my friend—you've seen him here often, haven't you?"

"So I have, so I have." Towser nodded, but his watery eyes were vague; Simon was not sure that he truly did remember.

"Well, after we left Naglimund and went to the dragon-mountain," Simon said carefully, "—the mountain that *you* helped us find, Towser, with your memories about the sword Thorn—after we were on the mountain, we went to the place where Binabik's people live and met their king and queen. And now they have sent these folks to be our allies."

"Ah, very kind. That's very kind." Towser squinted suspiciously across the fire at the nearest group of trolls, half a dozen men who were laughing and throwing dice in the damp sawdust. The aged jester looked up, brightening. "And they're here because of what I said!"

Simon hesitated, then said: "In a way, yes. That's true."

"Hah!" Towser grinned, exposing the stumps of his few remaining teeth. He looked truly happy. "I told Joshua and all those others about the sword, didn't I? About both swords." He looked at the trolls again. "What are they doing?"

"Throwing dice."

"Since I brought 'em here, I should show 'em how a real game is played. I should teach 'em Bull's Horn." Towser rose and stumbled a few paces to where the trolls were gambling, then flopped himself down cross-legged in their midst and began to try to explain the playing of Bull's Horn. The trolls chortled at his obvious drunkenness, but also seemed to be enjoying his visit. Soon the jester and the newcomers were engaged in a hilarious dumb show as Towser, already befuddled by drink and the excitement of the evening, tried to explain the more delicate nuances of the dice game to a group of tiny mountain men who could not understand his words.

Laughing, Simon turned back to Sangfugol. "That will probably keep him occupied for a few hours, at least."

Sangfugol made a sour face. "I wish I'd thought of that

myself. I would have sent him over to pester them a long
time ago."

"You don't have to be Towser's keeper. I'm sure that if
you told Josua how much you dislike the task, he'd ask
someone else to do it."

The harper shook his head. "It's not that simple."

"Tell me." From close up, Simon could see dark grit in
the shallow creases around Sangfugol's eyes, a smudge
on his forehead beneath his curly brown hair. The harper
seemed to have lost more than a little of his fastidious-
ness, but Simon was not sure that this was a good thing:
an unkempt Sanfugol seemed a blow against nature, like
a slovenly Rachel or a clumsy Jiriki.

"Towser was a good man, Simon." The harper's words
came out slowly, grudgingly. "No, that is not fair. He *is*
a good man still, I suppose, but these days he is mostly
old and foolish—and drunk whenever he can be. He is not
wicked, he is just tiresome. But when I first began my
craft, he took the time to help me although he owed me
nothing. It was all from kindness. He taught me songs and
tunings I did not know, helped me learn to use my voice
properly so that it would not fail me in time of need."
Sangfugol shrugged. "How can I turn away from him just
because he wearies me?"

The voices of the trolls nearby had risen, but what
seemed for a moment the beginning of an argument was
instead the swelling of a song, a guttural and jerky chant;
the melody was strange as could be, but the humor so evident even in an unfamiliar tongue that Towser, in the
midst of the singers, giggled and clapped his hands.

"Look at him," Sangfugol said with a touch of bemusement. "He is like a child—and so may we all be, someday. How can I hate him, any more than I would hate an
infant that did not know what it did?"

"But he seems to drive you mad!"

The harper snorted. "And do children not sometimes
drive parents mad? But someday, the parents become as
children themselves and are revenged on their sons and
daughters, for then it is the old parents who cry and spit
and burn themselves at the cookfire, and it is their chil-

dren who must suffer." There was little mirth in his laugh. "I thought myself well away from my own mother when I went off to make my fortune. Now, see what I have inherited for my unfaithfulness." He gestured at Towser, who, with head thrown back, was singing along with the trolls, baying wordlessly and tunelessly as a dog beneath a harvest moon.

The smile that this sight engendered faded quickly from Simon's face. At least Sangfugol and others had a choice about staying or not staying with parents. It was different for orphans.

"Then there is the other side." Sangfugol turned to look at Josua, who was still in deep conversation with the Qanuc. "There are those who, even when their parents die, still cannot get free of them." The gaze he leveled at his prince was full of love and, surprisingly, anger. "Sometimes he seems to be almost afraid to move, for fear he might have to step across the shadow of old King John's memory."

Simon stared at Josua's long, troubled face. "He worries so much."

"Yes, even when there is no use in it." As Sangfugol spoke, Towser came swaggering back. The *kangkang* of his Qanuc dicing partners seemed to have lifted the old man to a newer and more alert stage of drunkenness.

"We are about to be attacked by Fengbald and a thousand troops, Sangfugol," Simon growled. "That is certainly some reason for Josua to worry. Sometimes worry is called 'planning,' you know."

The harper waved his hand in apology. "I know, and I do not criticize him as a war-leader. If anyone can think of a way of winning this fight, it will be our prince. But I swear, Simon, I sometimes think that if he ever looked down at his feet and noticed the ants and fleas he must kill with every pace, he would never walk again. You cannot be a leader—let alone a king—when every hurt done to one of your people galls as though it happened to you. Josua suffers too much, I think, ever to be happy on a throne."

Towser had been listening, his eyes bright and intent. "He is his father's child, that's certain."

Sangfugol looked up, annoyed. "You are talking nonsense again, old fellow. Prester John was the very opposite, as everybody knows—as *you* should know better than anybody!"

"Ah," Towser said solemnly, his face unexpectedly serious. "Ah. Yes." After a moment's silence, when it seemed he might say more, the jester turned abruptly and walked away again.

Simon shrugged off the old man's strange remark. "How can a good king not hurt when his people are in pain, Sangfugol?" he asked. "Shouldn't he care?"

"Certainly he should. Aedon's Blood, yes!—otherwise he'd be no better than Josua's mad brother. But when you cut your finger, do you lay down and not move until it is healed again? Or do you staunch the blood and get on with what you have to do?"

Simon considered this. "You mean that Josua is like the farmer in that old story—the one who bought the finest, fattest pig at the fair, then couldn't bear to slaughter it, so he and his family starved but the pig lived."

The harper laughed. "I suppose, yes. Although I am not saying that Josua should let his people be butchered like swine—just that sometimes bad things happen, no matter how hard a kind prince tries to prevent it."

They sat staring into the fire as Simon thought about what his friend had said. When Sangfugol at last decided that Towser would be safe in the company of the Qanuc— the old jester was laboriously teaching them ballads of dubious propriety—the harper wandered off to sleep. Simon sat and listened to the concert for a while until his head began to hurt, then went to have a few words with Binabik.

His troll friend was still talking with Josua, although Sisqi was now practically asleep, her head propped on Binabik's shoulder, her long-lashed eyes half-closed. She smiled muzzily as Simon approached, but said nothing. The two lovers and Josua had been joined by the burly constable Freosel and a thin old man Simon did not rec-

ognize. After a moment he realized that this must be
Helfgrim, the onetime Lord Mayor of Gadrinsett who had
fled from Fengbald's camp.

As he watched Helfgrim, Simon remembered Geloë's
doubts about him. He certainly looked anxious and unsettled as he spoke to the prince, as though at any moment
he might say the wrong thing and bring some terrible
punishment down on himself. Simon could not help wondering how far they should trust this twitchy old man, but
a moment later he chided himself for such callousness.
Who knew what torments poor old Helfgrim had suffered
that made him look the way he did? Hadn't Simon himself wandered like a wild animal in the woods after his
escape from the Hayholt? Who could have seen him then
and still thought him reliable?

"Ah, friend Simon." Binabik looked up. "I am glad to
see you. I am doing a thing for which your help will be
needed tomorrow."

Simon nodded to show his availability.

"In truth," Binabik said, "it is being two things. One is
that I must teach you some Qanuc, so that you can be
talking to my folk in battle."

"Of course." Simon was pleased that Binabik remembered. It made it more real, to hear it spoken in the serious presence of Josua. "If I have the prince's leave to
fight with the Qanuc, of course." He looked at Josua.

The prince said: "Binabik's folk will help us most if
they can understand what we need from them. Their own
safety will also be best served that way. You have my
leave, Simon."

"Thank you, Highness. What else, Binabik?"

"We must also be collecting all the boats that belong to
the folk of New Gadrinsett." Binabik grinned. "There
must be two score of them all counted together."

"Boats? But the lake around Sesuad'ra is frozen. What
good will they do us?"

"Not the boats themselves will be doing good," said the
troll. "But parts of them will."

"Binabik has a plan for the defense of this place,"
Josua elaborated. He looked doubtful.

"It is not just being a plan." Binabik was smiling again. "Not just an idea that has landed on me like a stone. It is a certain Qanuc way that I will show to you *Utku*—and that is a great luckiness for you." He chuckled with self-satisfaction.

"What is it?"

"I will tell you tomorrow as we are at our boat-hunting task."

"One other thing, Simon," Josua said. "I know I have spoken of it before, but I feel it is worth asking again. Do you think there is any chance that your friends the Sithi will come? This is their sacred place, is it not? Will they not defend it?"

"I do not know, Josua. As I said, Jiriki seemed to think that his people would need a great deal of convincing."

"A pity." Josua drew his fingers through his short-cropped hair. "In truth, I fear we are just too few, even with the arrival of these brave trolls. The aid of the Fair Ones would be a great boon. Ha! Life is strange, is it not? My father prided himself that he had driven the last of the Sithi into hiding; now his son prays for them to come and help defend the remnants of his father's kingdom."

Simon shook his head sadly. There was nothing to say. The old Lord Mayor, who had listened silently to this exchange, now looked up at Simon, examining him closely. Simon tried to see some hint of the old man's thoughts in his watery eyes, but could make out nothing.

"Wake me up when it's time to go, Binabik," Simon said at last. "Good night, all. Good night, Prince Josua." He turned and walked toward the doorway. The singing of the trolls and lowlanders around the fire had quieted, the tunes grown slow and melancholy. The fire, dwindling, set red light shimmering along the shadowy walls.

The late morning sky was almost empty of clouds. The air was bitterly cold; Simon's breath clouded before his face. He and Binabik had been practicing a few important words in the Qanuc speech since first light, and Simon, showing greater than usual patience, was making good progress.

"Say 'now.' " Binabik cocked an eyebrow.

"*Ummu.*"

Qantaqa, trotting beside them, lifted her head and huffed, then found her voice for a short bark. Binabik laughed.

"She is not understanding why you are now speaking to her," he explained. "These are words she hears only from me."

"But I thought you said that your people had a whole different language that you spoke to your animals." Simon banged his gloved hand together to keep his fingers from turning into icicles.

Binabik gave him a look of reproach. "I am not talking to Qantaqa as we trolls are speaking to our rams, or to birds or fish. She is my friend. I speak to her as I would to any friend."

"Oh." Simon eyed the wolf. "How do you say 'I'm sorry,' Binabik?"

"*Chem ea dok.*"

He turned and patted the wolf's wide back. "*Chem ea dok,* Qantaqa." She grinned hugely up at him, panting steam.

After they had walked a little farther, Simon said: "Where are we going?"

"As I was telling the night before: we are going to go and collect the boats. Or rather, we are to be sending the boat-owners to the forge, where Sludig and others will be breaking the boats up. But we will give each person one of these—" he displayed a wad of parchment scraps with Josua's rune printed large on each, "—so that they know they are having the prince's word that they will be repaid."

Simon was puzzled. "I still don't understand what you're going to do. Those people need their boats to catch fish, to feed themselves and their families."

Binabik shook his head. "Not when even the rivers are now so thick with ice. And if we do not win here, it will matter little what plans the folk of New Gadrinsett are having."

"So are you going to tell me what *your* plan is?"

"Soon, Simon, soon. When we are finished with this morning's work, I will take you to the forge and you will then be seeing."

They strode along toward the settlement.

"Fengbald will probably attack soon."

"I am certain," said Binabik. "This cold must wear down the spirits of his men, even if they are having payment from the king's gold."

"But they'll be too few to lay siege, don't you think? Sesuad'ra is quite large, even for a thousand men."

"I am agreeing with your thought, Simon." Binabik considered. "Josua and Freosel and others were speaking of this last night. They are thinking that Fengbald will not try to besiege the hill. In any case, I am doubting that he knows how sad is our preparedness or scant our supplies."

"So what will he do, then?" Simon tried to think like Fengbald. "I guess that he'll simply try to overwhelm us. From what I've heard about him, he's not the patient type."

The troll looked up at him appraisingly, a twinkle in his dark eyes. "I think that you have thought well, Simon. That is seeming most likely to me, also. If you could lead a force of spying men to Fengbald's camp, it is only sense that he has sent spies here as well—Sludig and Hotvig think they have seen evidence of this, tracks of horses and such. So, he will know that there is a broad road that leads up the hill, and while it is something we can be defending, it is not like a castle wall where stones can be thrown down from above. I am guessing that he will try to overwhelm the resistance with his more strong and fearsome soldiers and drive all the way to the hilltop."

Simon pondered this. "We have more men than he may know, now that your folk are here. Maybe we can hold him longer than he thinks."

"Without doubt," Binabik said briskly. "But ultimately we will fail. They will be finding other ways up the slope—also unlike a castle, the hill can be climbed by men of determination, even in this cold and slippery weather."

"Then what can we do—nothing?"

"We can be using our brains as well as our hearts, friend Simon." Binabik smiled—a gentle, yellow smile. "That is why we are now hunting for boats—or rather, for the nails that are holding boats together."

"Nails?" Simon was even more puzzled.

"You will see. Now quick, give me the word that is meaning 'attack'!"

Simon thought. *"Nihuk."*

Binabik reached over and gave him a little shove on the hip. *"Nihut.* With the sound of 't,' not 'k.' "

"Nihut!" Simon said loudly.

Qantaqa growled and looked around, searching for an enemy.

Simon dreamed that he stood in the great throne room of the Hayholt, watching Josua and Binabik and a host of others search for the three swords. Although they were hunting in every corner, lifting each tapestry in turn and even looking beneath the malachite skirts of the statues of the Hayholt's former kings, only Simon seemed able to see that black Thorn, gray Sorrow, and a third silvery blade that must be King John's Bright-Nail were propped in plain sight on the great throne of yellowing ivory, the Dragonbone Chair.

Although Simon had never seen this third sword from any nearer than a hundred feet when he had lived at the Hayholt, it was remarkably clear to his dream-vision, the golden hilt worked in the curve of a holy Tree, the edge so polished that it sparkled even in the dim chamber. The blades leaned against each other, hilts in the air, like some unusual three-legged stool; the great, grinning skull of the dragon Shurakai stretched over them, as though at any moment it would gobble them down, sucking them out of sight forever. How could Josua and the others not see

them? It was so obvious! Simon tried to tell his friends
what they were missing, but could find no voice. He tried
to point, to make some sound that would draw their attention, but he had somehow lost his body. He was a ghost,
and his beloved friends and allies were making a terrible,
terrible mistake. . . .

"Damn you, Simon, get up!" Sludig was shaking him
roughly. "Hotvig and his men say Fengbald is marching.
He will be here before the sun is above the tree line."

Simon struggled to a sitting position. "What?" he gurgled. "What?"

"Fengbald is coming." The Rimmersman had retreated
to the doorway. "Get up!"

"Where is Binabik?" His heart was beating swiftly
even as he fought toward full wakefulness. What was he
supposed to do?

"He is already with Prince Josua and the others. Come
now." Sludig shook his head, then grinned with fierce exhilaration. "Finally—someone to fight!" He ducked
through the tent flap and was gone.

Simon scrambled out from beneath his cloak and fumbled on his boots, snagging a thumbnail in his chill-
fingered hurry. He swore quietly as he threw on his outer
shirt, then found his Qanuc knife and strapped on the
sheath. The sword Josua had given him was wrapped in
its polishing cloth beneath his pallet; when he unwrapped
it, the steel was icy against his hand. He shuddered.
Fengbald was coming. It was the day they had talked of
for so many weeks. People would die, perhaps some of
them before the gray sun even reached noon. Perhaps Simon himself would be one of them.

"Bad thoughts," he mumbled as he buckled his sword
belt. "Bad luck." He made the sign of the Tree to ward
off his own ill-speaking. He had to hurry. He was needed.

As he foraged in the corner of the tent for his gloves he
came upon the strangely-shaped bundle that Aditu had
given him. He had forgotten it since the night he had stolen out to the Observatory. What was it? He had a sudden
and sickening recollection that Amerasu had wanted it
given to Josua.

Merciful Aedon, what have I done?

Was it something that might have saved them? Had he, in his foolishness, in his mooncalf forgetfulness, neglected a weapon that might help keep his friends alive? Or was it something with which to summon the aid of the Sithi? Would it now be too late?

Heart thudding at the magnitude of his mistake, he snatched up the bag—noticing even in his fearful haste the odd, slithering softness of its weave—then dashed out into the icy dawn light.

A huge crowd was gathering in the Leavetaking House, caught up in a frenzy of activity that seemed ready at any moment to spill over into panicked flailing. At the center of it all Simon found Josua and a small group that included Deornoth, Geloë, Binabik, and Freosel. The prince, any trace of indecision vanished, was calling out orders, reviewing plans and arrangements, and exhorting some of the more anxious of New Gadrinsett's defenders. The brightness of Josua's eye made Simon feel like a traitor.

"Your Highness." He took a step forward, then dropped to a knee before the prince, who looked down in mild surprise.

"Up, Simon," Deornoth said impatiently. "There is work to do."

"I'm afraid I've made a terrible mistake, Prince Josua."

The prince paused, visibly willing himself to calm attention. "What do you mean, son?"

Son. The word struck Simon very hard. He wished that Josua could truly have been his father—there was certainly something in the man that he loved. "I think I have done a foolish thing," he said. "Very foolish."

"Speak with care," said Binabik. "Tell just the facts that have importance."

Prince Josua's alarmed expression eased as he listened to Simon's worried explanation. "Give it to me, then," he said when Simon had finished. "There is no point in tormenting yourself until we know what it is. I feared from the look on your face that you had done something to leave us open to attack. As it is, your bundle is most likely only some token."

"A fairy gift?" Freosel asked doubtfully. "Be those not perilous?"

Josua squatted and took the bag from Simon. It was difficult for him to untie the knotted drawstring with only one hand, but no one dared offer him aid. When the prince had at last worked it open, he upended the bag. Something wrapped in an embroidered black cloth rolled out into his lap.

"It is a horn," he said as he pulled away the covering and held it up. It was made of a single piece of ivory or unyellowed bone, chased all over with fine carvings. The lip and mouthpiece were sheathed in a silvery metal, and the horn itself hung on a black baldric as sumptuously worked as the wrapping. There was something unusual in the shape of it, some compelling but not quite recognizable essence. Although age and much use were suggested by its every line, still at the same time it shone as though newly made. It was potent, Simon saw: though it was not like Thorn, which sometimes almost seemed to breathe, the horn had something in it which drew the eye.

"It is a beautiful thing," Josua murmured. He tilted it from side to side, squinting at the carvings. "I can read none of these, although some look like writing-runes."

"Prince Josua?" Binabik held out his hands. Josua passed the horn to him. "They are all Sithi runes—not a surprising thing on a present from Amerasu."

"But the winding-cloth and the baldric are of mortal weave," Geloë said abruptly. "That is a strange thing."

"Can you read any of the writing?" Josua asked.

Binabik shook his head. "Not now. It might be so with some studying."

"Perhaps you can read this." Deornoth leaned forward and plucked a scrap of shimmery parchment out of the bell of the horn. He opened it, whistled in surprise, then handed it to Josua.

"It is written in our Westerling letters!" said the prince. " *'May this be given to its rightful owner when all seems lost.'* Then there is a strange sign—like an 'A.' "

"Amerasu's mark." Geloë's deep voice was sorrowful. "Her mark."

"But what can it mean?" Josua asked. "What is it, and who could be its rightful owner? It is clearly something of worth."

"Beggin' pardon, Prince Josua," Freosel said nervously, "but p'raps would be best not to meddle with such things—p'raps there be curse on it or somewhat like that. The gifts of the Peaceful Ones, they say, can cut both ways."

"But if it is meant to summon aid," said Josua, "then it seems a shame not to use it. If we are vanquished today, all will not just *seem* lost, it will *be* lost."

He hesitated for a moment, then lifted the horn to his lips and blew. Astonishingly, there was no sound at all. Josua stared into the bell of the horn in search of some obstruction, then puffed his cheeks again and blew until he was bent almost double, but still the horn was silent. He straightened with a shaky laugh. "Well, I do not seem to be the thing's rightful owner. Someone else try—anyone, it matters not."

Deornoth at last accepted it from him and lifted it, but had no more luck than Josua. Freosel waved it away. Simon took it, and although he puffed until black flecks whirled before his eyes, the horn remained mute.

"What is it for?" Simon panted.

Josua shrugged. "Who can say? But I do not think you have done any harm, Simon. If it is meant to serve some purpose, that purpose has not yet been revealed to us." He wrapped the horn again, then placed it back into the sack and put it down beside his feet. "We have other things to occupy us now. If we survive this day, then we will look at it again—perhaps Binabik or Geloë will be able to puzzle out its carvings. Now, bring me the tally of men, Deornoth, and let us make final dispositions."

Binabik pulled away from the group and came and took Simon's arm. "There are still a few things you should have," he said, "then you should go to be with your Qanuc troop."

Simon followed his small friend across the milling confusion of the Leavetaking House. "I hope your schemes work, Binabik."

The troll made a hand sign. "As I am hoping, too. But we will do what is our best to do. That is all the gods, or your God, or our ancestors can be expecting."

Against the far corner of the western wall a line of men stood before a dwindling pile of wooden shields, some of which still bore river-moss stains from their previous existence as boat timbers. Sangfugol, wearing a sort of battle-dress of ragged gray, was overseeing the distribution.

The harper looked up. "There you are. It's in the corner. Ho, stop that, you!" he snarled at a bearded older man who was pawing through the pile. "Take the one that's on top."

Binabik went to the place Sangfugol had indicated and drew something out from beneath a pile of sacking. It was another wooden shield, but this one had been painted with the arms Vorzheva and Gutrun had created for Simon's banner, the black sword and white dragon intertwined over Josua's gray and red.

"It is not done with the hand of art," the troll said. "But it was done with the hand of friendship."

Simon bent and embraced him, then took the shield and thumped it with the heel of his hand. "It's perfect."

Binabik frowned. "I am only wishing that you were having more time for practicing with its use, Simon. It is not easy to be riding and using a shield and fighting, too." His look grew more worried as he gripped Simon's fingers in his own small fist. "Do not be foolish, Simon. You are yourself of great importance, and my people are being very important as well . . . but the finest of *all* things that I am knowing will be with you, also." He turned his round face away. "She is a huntress of our folk and brave as a thunderstorm, but—*Qinkipa!*—how I wish Sisqi were not in this fighting today."

"Aren't you going to be with us?" Simon asked, surprised.

"I will be with the prince, acting as messenger since Qantaqa and I can be moving with swiftness and quiet where a bigger man on a horse might be observed." The troll laughed softly. "Still, I will be carrying a spear for the first time since my manhood-walk. It will be a strangeness to have that in my hand." His smile vanished. " 'No' is the answer to your questioning, Simon—I will not be with you, at least not closely by. So please, my good friend, keep an eye out for Sisqinanamook. If you are keeping her from harm, you keep away a blow to my own heart that might be the killing of me." He squeezed Simon's hand again. "Come. There are things we must still be doing. It is not enough to have clever schemes," he tapped his forehead and smiled mockingly, "if they are not completed with properness."

They met at last in the Fire Garden, all of Sesuad'ra's defenders, those who would fight and those who would stay behind, gathered together on the great commons-yard of tiles. Although the sun was well into the sky, the day was dark and very cold; many had brought torches. Simon felt a pang at seeing the flames fluttering in this open place, as they had in his vision of the past. A thousand Sithi had once waited here, just as his friends and allies now waited, for something that would change their lives forever.

Josua stood on a section of broken wall so that he could look out over the hushed crowd. Simon, standing close beside him, saw the prince's look of disappointment. The defenders were so few, his face said clearly, and so poorly prepared.

"People of New Gadrinsett and our kind allies of Yiqanuc," Josua called, "there is little need to speak about what we are doing. Duke Fengbald, who slaughtered the women and children of his own fiefdom in Falshire, is coming. We must fight him. There is little more to it than that. He is the tool of a great evil, and that evil must be stopped here or there will be none left to resist it. A victory here will not by any means overthrow our enemies, but if we lose it will mean that those enemies have won a great and total victory. Go and do your best, both those who will fight and those who will remain behind with their own tasks to do. Surely God is watching and will see your bravery."

The murmurs that had risen when Josua spoke of evil turned into cheers as he finished. The prince then reached down to help Father Strangyeard climb into place to say the benediction.

The archivist fretfully smoothed his few strands of hair. "I am certain I will muddle it," he whispered.

"You know it perfectly," said Deornoth. Simon thought he meant it kindly, but the knight could not keep impatience from his voice.

"I fear I am not meant to be a war-priest."

"Nor should you be," Josua said harshly. "Nor should any priest, if God were doing all that he ought to."

"Prince Josua!" Startled, Father Strangyeard sucked in air and coughed. "Beware of blasphemy!"

The prince was grim. "After these last two years of torment across the land, God must have learned to be a little . . . flexible. I am sure He will understand my words."

Strangyeard could only shake his head.

When the priest had finished his blessing, much of which was inaudible to the large crowd, Freosel mounted the wall with the ease of one used to climbing. The heavyset man had taken on an increasing burden of the defense, and seemed to be thriving under the responsibility.

"Come on, then," he said loudly, his rough voice reaching out to every one of the several hundred gathered in that cold, windy place. "You heard what Prince Josua said. What more need you know? Defending our home's what we be doing. Even a badger'll do that without thinking a moment. Will you let Fengbald and them come and take your home, kill your families? Will you?"

The assembled folk called back a ragged but heartfelt denial.

"Right. So, let's go to it."

Simon was caught up for a moment by Freosel's words. Sesuad'ra *was* his home, at least for now. If he had any hope of finding something more permanent, he would have to survive this day—and they would also have to beat back Fengbald's army. He turned to Snenneq and the other trolls who were waiting quietly a little apart from the rest of the defenders.

"*Nenit, henimaatuya,*" Simon said, waving them toward the stables where the rams—and Simon's horse—were waiting patiently. "Come on, friends."

Despite the chill of the day, Simon found himself sweating heavily beneath his helmet and chain mail. As he and the trolls turned off from the main road and started downslope through the clinging brush, he realized that he was, in a way, all alone—that no one would be near who could truly understand him. What if he showed himself a coward in front of the trolls, or something happened to Sisqi? What if he let Binabik down?

He pushed the thoughts away. There were things to do that would require his concentration. There could be no mooncalf foolishness, as with the forgotten gift from Amerasu.

As they neared the base of the hill and the hidden places near the foot of the road, Simon's company dismounted and led their beasts into place. The hill slope was covered here with ice-blasted bracken that snatched at feet and tore cloaks, so it took them a good part of an hour before they had finally selected their spots and the crackling and rustling had ceased. When all the troop was settled in, Simon climbed up out of the shallow gulley so that he could see the barricade of felled trees that Sludig and others had built at the skirt of the hill, blocking entrance to the wide, stone-paved road. It was to be his responsibility to relay the prince's commands.

Out beyond the expanse of ice that had once been Sesuad'ra's floodwater moat, the near shore was covered with a dark, seething mass. It took Simon a few startled moments to realize that this was Fengbald's army, settled in along the edge of the frozen water. It was more than an army, for the duke appeared to have brought a large section of the squatter town of Gadrinsett with him: tents and cookfires and makeshift forges spread lumpily into the distance, filling the small valley with smokes and steams.

Simon knew it was an army of only a thousand or so, but to one who had not seen the army ten times larger that had besieged Naglimund, it seemed as vast as the legendary Muster of Anitulles that had covered the hills of Nabban like a blanket of spears. Chill sweat began to bead on his forehead once more. They were so near! Two hundred ells or more separated Fengbald's forces from Simon's hidden perch, yet he could clearly see individual faces among the armored men. They were people, living people, and they were coming to kill him. Simon's companions would in turn try to kill as many of these soldiers as possible. There would be many new widows and orphans at the end of this day.

An unexpected trill of melody behind him made Simon jump. He whirled to see one of the trolls rocking slowly from side to side, his head lifted in quiet song. The troll, alerted by Simon's sudden movement, looked up at him questioningly. Simon tried to smile and waved for the little man to continue. After a moment the troll's plaintive voice rose once more into the freezing air, lonely as a bird in a leafless tree.

I don't want to die, thought Simon. *And God, please, I want to see Miriamele again—I truly, truly do.*

A vision of her came to him suddenly, a memory of their last desperate moment near the Stile, when the giant had come crashing down on them just as Simon had finally sparked his torch alight. Her eyes, Miriamele's eyes . . . they had been frightened but resolute. She was brave, he remembered helplessly, brave and lovely. Why had he never told her how much he admired her—even if she *was* a princess?

There was a movement downslope near the barricade of tumbled trunks. Josua, his crippled right arm marking him even at a distance, was climbing onto the makeshift wall. A cloaked and hooded trio mounted to stand beside him.

Josua cupped his hand before his mouth. *"Where is Fengbald?"* he shouted. His voice echoed out across the frozen lake and reverberated in the hollows of the close-looming hills. *"Fengbald!"*

After some moments a small group of figures detached themselves from the horde along the shore and came a short way out onto the ice. In their midst, mounted on a tall charger, rode one who was armored in silver and cloaked in bright scarlet. A silver bird flared its wings upon his helmet, which he removed and tucked beneath his arm. His long hair was black, and fluttered in the stiff wind.

"So you are there after all, Josua," the rider shouted. "I was wondering."

"You are trespassing on free lands, Fengbald. We do not acknowledge my brother Elias here, for his crimes have stolen away his right to rule my father's kingdom. If you leave now, you may go away freely and tell him so."

Laughing, Fengbald threw back his head in what seemed quite genuine amusement. "Very good, Josua, very good!" he bellowed. "No, it is you who must consider *my* offer. If you will surrender yourself to the king's justice, I promise that all but the guiltiest few of your traitorous mob will be allowed back to take their place as honorable subjects. Surrender, Josua, and they will be spared."

Simon wondered what effect this promise would have on the frightened and unhopeful army of New Gadrinsett. Fengbald was doubtless wondering the same.

"You lie, murderer!" someone shouted from near Josua, but the prince lifted his hand in a calming gesture.

"Did you not make that same promise to the wool merchants of Falshire," Josua called, "before you burned their wives and children in their beds?"

Fengbald was too distant for his expression to be discernible, but from the way he straightened in the saddle, pushing against his stirrups until he was almost standing, Simon could guess at the anger surging through him. "You are in no position to speak so insolently, Josua," the duke shouted. "You are a prince of nothing but trees and a few tattered, hungry sheepherders. Will you surrender and save much bloodshed?"

Now one of the other figures standing beside Josua stepped forward. "Hear me!" It was Geloë; she pulled back her hood as she spoke. "Know that I am Valada Geloë, protectress of the forest." She waved her cloaked arm toward the shadowy face of the Aldheorte, which loomed on the hillcrest like a vast and silent witness. "You may not know me, lord from the cities, but your Thrithings allies have heard of me. Ask your mercenary friend Lezhdraka if he recognizes my name."

Fengbald did not reply, but appeared to be in conversation with someone standing near him.

"If you would attack us, think of this," Geloë called. "This place, Sesuad'ra, is one of the Sithi's most sacred spots. I do not think they would like it spoiled by your coming. If you try to force your way in, you may find that they make a more terrible enemy than you can guess."

Simon was sure, or at least thought he was sure, that the witch woman's speech was an idle threat, but he found himself wishing again that Jiriki had come. Was this what a condemned man felt as he sat looking through the window slit at his gallows a-building? Simon felt a dull certainty that he and Josua and the rest could not win. Fengbald's army seemed a great infection upon the snowy plain beyond the lake, a plague that would destroy them all.

"I see," Fengbald shouted suddenly, "that you have not only gone mad yourself, Josua, but that you have surrounded yourself with other mad folk as well. So be it! Tell the old woman to hurry and call out to her forest spirits—perhaps the trees will come and rescue you. I have lost patience!" Fengbald waved his hand and a flurry of arrows spat out from the men along the shoreline. They all fell short of the barricade and skittered along the ice. Josua and the others clambered down into the undergrowth surrounding the pile of logs, disappearing once more from Simon's view.

At another cry from Fengbald, something that looked like a huge barge moved slowly out onto the ice. This war-engine was pulled by stout dray horses who were themselves covered in padded armor, and as it scraped along the ice it made a continual shrieking noise. From the dreadful sound, it might have been a market cart full of damned souls. The bed of the sledge was piled high with bulging sacks.

Simon could not help shaking his head, impressed despite his sudden fear. Someone in Fengbald's camp had been planning well.

As the great sledge moved out across the ice, the meager swarm of arrows coming back from the defenders—they had few to begin with, and Josua had warned them repeatedly against waste—bounced ineffectually from its steel-shod sides, or stuck harmlessly in the armor of the horses that drew it until they began to resemble some fabulous species of long-legged porcupines. Where the sledge passed, its crosswise runners scraped the ice raw. From holes in the mountain of sacks, a wide shower of sand dribbled down the sledge's sloping bed and spattered across the frozen surface of the lake. Fengbald's soldiers, following the sledge in a wide column, found much firmer footing than Josua and the defenders had ever suspected they might.

"Aedon curse them!" Simon felt his heart sink within his breast. Fengbald's army, a pulsing column like a stream of ants, moved forward across the moat.

One of the trolls, eyes wide, said something Simon could only partially understand.

"*Shummuk.*" For the first time Simon felt real fear coiling inside him like a serpent, crushing hope. He must keep to the plan, although all now seemed doubtful. "Wait. We will wait."

Far from Sesuad'ra, and yet somehow strangely near, there was a movement in the heart of the ancient forest Aldheorte. In a deep grove that was touched only lightly by the snows that had blanketed the woods for many months, a horseman rode out from between two standing stones and turned his impatient mount around and around at the center of the clearing.

"Come out!" he cried. The tongue he spoke was the oldest in Osten Ard. His armor was blue and yellow and silver-gray, polished until it gleamed. "Come through the Gate of Winds!"

Other riders and their mounts began to make their way out between the tall stones until the dell was foggy with the clouds of their breath.

The first rider reined up his horse before the assembled throng. He lifted a sword before him, lifted it as though it might pierce the clouds. His hair, bound only by a band of blue cloth, had once been lavender. Now it was as white as the snow clinging to the tree branches.

"Follow me, and follow Indreju, sword of my grandfather," Jiriki cried. "We go to the aid of friends. For the first time in five centuries, the Zida'ya will ride."

The others lifted their weapons, shaking them at the sky. A strange song began to build, deep as the booming of marsh bitterns, wild as a wolf cry, until all were singing and the glade shook with the force of it.

"Away, Houses of the Dawn!" Jiriki's thin face was fierce, his eyes alight, burning like coals. "Away, come away! And let our enemies tremble! The Zida'ya ride again!"

Jiriki and the rest—his mother Likimeya on her tall black horse, Yizashi of the gray spear, bold Cheka'iso Amber-Locks, even Jiriki's green-clad uncle Khendraja'aro with his longbow—all spurred their horses out of the clearing with a great shout and a singing. So great was the tumult of their going that the trees seemed to bend away before them and the wind, as if abashed, was momentarily silent in their wake.

11

The Road Back

Miriamele slouched lower inside her cloak, trying to vanish. It seemed that every person who passed by slowed to look at her, the slender Wrannamen with their calm brown eyes and rigorously expressionless faces as well as the Perdruinese traders in their slightly shabby finery. All seemed to be pondering the appearance of this crop-haired girl in a stained monk's habit, and it was making her very anxious. Why was Cadrach taking so long? Surely she should have known better by now than to let him go into an inn by himself.

When the monk appeared at last he wore an air of self-satisfaction, as though he had completed some immensely difficult task.

"It is down by Peat Barge Quay, as I should have remembered. A none-too-savory district."

"You have been drinking wine." Her tone was harsher than she wanted it to be, but she was cold and fretful.

"And how could I expect a publican to give me good directions if I bought nothing?" Cadrach was not to be so easily thrown off stride. He seemed to have rebounded from the despair that had filled him on the boat, although Miriamele could see where it was imperfectly hidden, where the deadly bleakness peered past the ragged edges of the jollity he had drawn over himself like a cloak.

"But we have no money!" she complained. "That's why we have to walk all over this cursed town, trying to find a place you said you knew!"

"Hush, my lady. I made a small wager on a coin-flip

and won—and just as well, too, since I'd no coin to
match the bet. But all's well now. In any case, it is traveling on foot through this city of canals that has confused
me, but with the innkeeper's instructions, we will have no
more problems."

No more problems. Miriamele had to laugh at that, if
bitterly. They had been living like beggars for three
weeks—parched on the boat for several days, then slog-
ging through the coast towns of southeastern Nabban begging meals where they could and taking rides on farm
wagons when they were lucky enough to get them. The
largest portion of the time had been spent walking, walking, walking, until Miriamele felt that if she were to
somehow remove her legs from her body they would continue pacing along without her. This kind of life was not
unfamiliar to Cadrach, and he seemed to have returned to
it complacently, but Miriamele was growing more than
tired of it. She could never live in her father's court
again, but suddenly the stifling surroundings of Uncle
Josua's castle at Naglimund seemed a great deal more appealing than they had a few months before.

She turned to say something else sharp to Cadrach—
she could smell the wine on his breath at an arm's
distance—and caught him by surprise, unguarded. He had
let his buoyant expression slip; the hollowness in his once
round cheeks and the shadows beneath his haunted eyes
chastened Miriamele into a kind of irritated love.

"Well . . . come on, then." She took his arm. "But if
you don't find this place soon, I'm going to push you into
the canal."

Since they did not have the price of a boatman's fare,
it took the better part of the morning for Cadrach and
Miriamele to make their way through the daunting maze
of Kwanitupul's wooden walkways to Peat Bog Quay. Every turn seemed to bring them to another dead end, another passage that ended in an abandoned boatyard or a
locked door with rusty hinges or a rickety fence beyond
which was only yet another of the ubiquitous waterways.
Thwarted, they would retrace their steps, try another turn-

ing, and the maddening process would begin again. At
last, with the noon sun whitening the cloudy sky, they
stumbled around the corner of a long and very deterio-
rated warehouse and found themselves staring at a salt-
rotted wooden sign that proclaimed the inn before which
it hung as *Pelippa's Bowl.* It was indeed, as Cadrach had
warned, in a rather unsavory district.

While Cadrach searched for the door—the front of the
building was an almost uniform wall of gray, weathered
wood—Miriamele wandered out onto the inn's front deck
and stared down at a wreath of yellow and white flowers
floating on the choppy canal near the wharf ladder.

"That's a Soul's Day wreath," she said.

Cadrach, who had found the door, nodded.

"Which means it was more than four months ago that
I left Naglimund," she said slowly. The monk nodded
again, then pulled the door open and beckoned.
Miriamele felt a wild sorrow course through her. "And it
was all for nothing! Because I was a headstrong fool!"

"Things would have gone no better, and perhaps worse,
if you had stayed with your uncle," Cadrach pointed out.
"At least you are alive, my lady. Now, let us go and see
if *Soria* Xorastra will remember an old, if fallen, friend."

They entered the inn through the dooryard, past the
corroding hulks of a pair of fishing boats, and quickly received two unpleasant surprises. The first was that the inn
itself was ill-kept and smelled distinctly of fish. The second was that Xorastra had been dead for three years, and
her jut-jawed niece Charystra quickly proved to be quite
a different sort of innkeeper than her predecessor.

She stared at their threadbare and travel-stained clothing. "I don't like the look of you. Let me see your
money."

"Come, now," Cadrach said as soothingly as he could.
"Your aunt was a good friend of mine. If you let us have
a bed for the night, we will have money to pay you by the
morning—I am well known in this town."

"My aunt was mad and worthless," Charystra said, not
without some satisfaction, "—and her stinking charities
left me with nothing but this tumbledown barn." She

waved her hand at the low-ceilinged common room, which seemed more like a burrow belonging to some disheartened animal. "The day I let a monk and his doxy stay without paying is the day they take me back to Perdruin in a wooden box."

Miriamele could not help looking forward to such a day, but she knew better than to let the innkeeper know it. "Things are not as they appear," she said. "This man is my tutor. I am a nobleman's child—Baron Seoman of Erkynland is my father. I was kidnapped, and my tutor here found me and saved me. My father will be very kind to anyone who helps with my return." Beside her, Cadrach straightened up, pleased to be the hero of even a mythical rescue.

Charystra squinted. "I've heard more than a few wild stories lately." She chewed at her lip. "One of them turned out to be true, but that doesn't mean yours will." Her expression turned sour. "I've got to make a living, whether your father is a baron or the High King at the Hayholt. Go out and get the money, if you say it's so easy. Let your friends help you."

Cadrach began once more to wheedle and flatter, now taking up the strands of story Miriamele had begun and weaving them into a richer tapestry, one in which Charystra would retire with bags of gold, a gift from the grateful father. Hearing the wild way in which the story grew beneath Cadrach's manipulation, Miriamele almost began to feel sorry for the woman, whose practicality was obviously being strained by her greed, but just before Miriamele was about to ask him to give it up, she saw a large man coming slowly down the stairway into the commons room. Despite his clothes—he wore a cowled cloak much like Cadrach's, belted with a rope—and a beard that was scarcely a finger's breadth thick, he was so instantly familiar that for a moment Miriamele could not believe what she was seeing. As he came down into the light of the tallow lamps, the man also stopped, wide-eyed.

"Miriamele?" he said at last. His voice was thick and hesitant. "Princess?"

"Isgrimnur!" she shrieked. "Duke Isgrimnur!" Her

heart seemed to expand within her breast until she thought she might choke. She ran across the cluttered room, dodging past the crooked-legged benches, then flung herself against his broad belly, weeping.

"Oh, you poor thing," he said, squeezing her, crying himself. "Oh, my poor Miriamele." He lifted her away for a moment, staring with reddened eyes. "Are you hurt? Are you well?" He caught sight of Cadrach and his eyes narrowed. "And there's the rogue who stole you!"

Cadrach, who like Charystra had been staring open-mouthed, flinched. Isgrimnur cast a large shadow.

"No, no," Miriamele laughed through her tears. "Cadrach is my friend. He helped me. I ran away—don't blame him." She hugged him again, burying her face in his reassuring bulk. "Oh, Isgrimnur, I have been so unhappy. How is Uncle Josua? And Vorzheva, and Simon, and Binabik the troll?"

The duke shook his head. "I know little more than you do, I would guess." He sighed, his breath trembling out. "This is a miracle. God has heard my prayers at last. Blessed, blessed. Come, sit down." Isgrimnur turned to Charystra and waved his hand impatiently. "Well? Don't just stand there, woman! Bring us some ale, and some food, too!"

Charystra, more than a little stunned, went lurching away.

"Wait!" Isgrimnur shouted. She turned to face him. "If you tell anyone about this," he roared, "I'll pull your roof down with my own hands."

The innkeeper, beyond surprise or fear, nodded slackly and headed for the sanctuary of her kitchen.

Tiamak hurried along, although his lame leg allowed him scarcely more speed than what would have been a normal walking pace. His heart was thumping against his ribs, but he forced himself to keep the worry from his face.

He Who Always Steps on Sand, he murmured to himself, *let no one notice me! I am almost there!*

Those who shared the narrow walkways with him

seemed determined to hinder his progress. One burly
drylander carrying a basket full of sandfish thumped into
him and almost knocked him down, then turned to shout
insulting names as Tiamak limped on. The little man
ached to say something—Kwanitupul was a Wrannaman
town, after all, no matter how many drylander traders
built expensive stilt houses on the edge of Chamul Lagoon, or had their massive trading barges poled through
the canals by sweating crews of Tiamak's folk—but he
dared not. There was no time to waste in quarrels, however justified.

He hurried through *Pelippa's Bowl*'s common room,
sparing barely a glance for the proprietress, despite
Charystra's strange expression. The innkeeper, clutching
a board laid with bread and cheese and olives, was swaying at the foot of the stairs as though deciding whether to
go up or not was an overwhelming strain.

Tiamak angled past her and hobbled up the narrow
staircase, then onto the landing and the first warped, ill-
hung door in the passageway. He pushed it open, his chest
already filling with air to spill out his news, then stopped,
surprised by the odd tableau before him.

Isgrimnur was sitting on the floor. In the corner stood
a short, husky man, dressed as was the duke in the cos-
tume of a pilgrim Aedonite monk, his squarish face curiously closed. Old Camaris sat on the bed, his long legs
crossed sailor-style. Beside him sat a young woman with
yellow hair close-cropped. She, too, wore a monk's robe,
and her pretty, sharp-featured face was set in an expression of bemusement almost as complete as Charystra's.

Tiamak closed his jaw with a snap, then opened it once
more. "What?" he said.

"Ah!" Isgrimnur seemed immensely cheerful, almost
giddy. "And this is Tiamak, a noble Wrannaman, a friend
of Dinivan and Morgenes. The princess is here, Tiamak.
Miriamele has come."

Miriamele did not even look up, but continued to stare
at the old man. "This is . . . Camaris?"

"I know, I know," Isgrimnur laughed. "I couldn't credit
it myself, God strike me—but it is him! Alive, after all

this time!" The duke's face suddenly became serious. "But his wits are gone, Miriamele. He is like a child."

Tiamak shook his head. "I ... I am glad, Isgrimnur. Glad that your friends are here." He shook his head again. "I have news, too."

"Not now." Isgrimnur was beaming. "Later, little man. Tonight we celebrate." He lifted his voice. "Charystra! Where are you, woman!?"

The inn's proprietress had just begun to push the door open when Tiamak turned and shut it in her face. He heard a surprised grunt and the thud of a heavy bread loaf bounding down the stairway. "No," Tiamak said. "This cannot wait, Isgrimnur."

The duke frowned at him, thick brows beetling. "Well?"

"There are men searching for this inn. Nabbanai soldiers."

Isgrimnur's impatience suddenly dropped away. He turned his full attention to the little Wrannaman. "How do you know?"

"I saw them down by Market Hall. They were asking questions of the boatmen there, treating them very roughly. The leader of the soldiers seemed desperate to find this inn."

"And did they find out?" Isgrimnur rose to his feet and walked across the room, taking up his sword Kvalnir from where it stood bundled in the corner.

Tiamak shrugged. "I knew I would not be able to go much faster than the soldiers, even though I am sure I know the city better than they do. Still, I wanted to delay them, so I stepped forward and told the soldiers that *I* would talk to the boatmen since they were all Wrannamen like me." For the first time since beginning his recitation, Tiamak turned to look at the young woman. Her face had gone quite pale, but the dazed expression had vanished. She was listening carefully. "In our swamp-language I told the boatmen that these were bad men, that they should talk only to me, and only in our tongue. I told them that when the soldiers left, they should leave, too, and not come back to the Market Hall until later. After I

had talked with them for a few moments longer, pretending to receive directions from them—in truth they
were merely telling me that these drylanders acted like
madmen!—I told the leader of the soldiers where he and
his men could find *Pelippa's Bowl.* Don't scowl so, Duke
Isgrimnur! I told them that it was on the other side of
town from here, of course! But it was so strange: when I
told that man, he shivered all over, as though knowing
where this place was made him itch."

"What ... what did the leader look like?" There was
strain in Miriamele's voice.

"He was very odd." Tiamak hesitated. He did not know
how to address a drylander princess, even one dressed
like a man. "He was the only one not dressed as a soldier.
Tall and strong-looking, wearing rich drylander's clothes,
but his face was purple with bruises, his eyes red as a
boar's, full of blood. He looked as though his head had
been crushed in a crocodile's jaws. He was missing teeth,
as well."

Miriamele groaned and slid down from the pallet onto
the floor. "Oh, Elysia, save me! It is Aspitis!" Her ragged
voice was now entirely given over to desperation.
"Cadrach, how could he know where we were going?!
Have you betrayed me again?"

The monk winced, but his words held no anger. "No,
my lady. Obviously he got back to shore, and I would
guess that he then somehow exchanged messages with his
true master." Cadrach turned toward Isgrimnur. "Pryrates
knows this place well, my lord Duke, and Aspitis is his
creature."

"Aspitis?" Isgrimnur, strapping his sword belt around
his broad middle, shook his head in bafflement. "I do not
know him, but I gather that he is no friend."

"No." Cadrach looked to Miriamele where she sat on
the floor, head in hands. "He is no friend."

Isgrimnur made a noise deep in his throat. Tiamak
turned to him with a startled look, for the duke sounded
like nothing less than an angry bear, but Isgrimnur was
only thinking, twisting his fingers in his short beard. "Enemies are at our heels," he said at last. "Even were we sit-

ting with the Camaris of forty years ago—ah, Lord love him, Miriamele, he was the mightiest man of all—still I would not like the odds. So, then, we must leave . . . and leave quickly."

"Where can we go?" asked Cadrach.

"North to Josua." Isgrimnur turned to Tiamak. "What did you say that time, little man? That if you were traveling with Camaris and me as fugitives, you would find another way?"

Tiamak felt his throat tighten. "Yes. But it will not be easy." He felt a chill, as though the cold breath of She Who Waits to Take All Back whispered against his neck. He suddenly did not like the idea of taking these drylander friends into the mazy Wran.

Miriamele arose. "Josua is alive?"

"So rumor says, Princess." Isgrimnur shook his head. "Northeast of the Thrithings, it is claimed. But it may be false hope."

"No!" Miriamele's face, still tearstained, wore a strange look of surety. "I believe it."

Cadrach, still leaning in the corner like a neglected house-god, shrugged. "There is nothing wrong with belief, if it is all we can cling to. But what is this other way?" He turned his brooding eyes on the marsh man.

"Through the Wran." Tiamak cleared his throat. "It will be nearly impossible for them to follow us, I think. We can make our way north to the outermost part of the Lake Thrithing."

"Where we will be trapped on foot in the middle of a hundred leagues of open ground," said Cadrach grimly.

"Damn it, man," Isgrimnur snarled, "what else can we do? Try to make our way through Kwanitupul, past this Aspitis fellow, then across all of hostile Nabban? Look at us! Can you imagine a more unlikely and memorable company? A girl, two monks—one bearded—a childish old giant and a Wrannaman? What choice do we have?"

The Hernystirman seemed prepared to argue, but after a moment's hesitation he shrugged once more, drawing back into himself like a tortoise retreating inside its shell. "I suppose there is no choice," he said quietly.

"What should we do?" Miriamele's fear had receded a
little. Though still shaken, she seemed bright-eyed and
determined. Tiamak could not help admiring her spirit.

Isgrimnur rubbed his large paws together. "Yes. We
must leave, certainly by the time an hour has passed,
sooner if we can, so there is no more time to waste.
Tiamak, go and watch from the front of the inn. Someone
else may give these soldiers better directions than you
did, and if they catch us unaware, we are lost. You will be
the least likely to be noticed." He looked around, thinking. "I will put Camaris to work patching the less man-
gled of those boats in the dooryard. Cadrach, you will
help him. Remember, he is simple-witted, but he has been
working here for years—he knows what to do and he understands many words, though he does not speak. I will
finish gathering up the rest of our things, then I will come
help you finish the boat and carry it down to the water."

"What about me, Isgrimnur?" Miriamele was actually
bouncing from one foot to the other in her need for something to do.

"Take that shrew of an innkeeper and go down to the
kitchens and provision us. Get things that will keep, since
we don't know how long we must go without . . ." He
paused, snagged by a sudden thought. "Water! Fresh water! Sweet Usires, we are going to the swamps. Get all
you can, and I will come help you carry the jugs or whatever you find to put it in. There is a rain barrel in the yard
behind the inn—full, I think. Hah! I knew this foul
weather would be good for something!" He tugged at his
fingers, thinking frantically. "No, Princess, don't go yet.
Tell Charystra she will be paid for everything we take,
but don't dare say a word of where we are going! She
would peddle our immortal souls for a bent cintis-piece
each. I wish I were the same, but I will pay her for what
we take, though it will empty my purse." The duke took
a deep breath. "There! Now go to. And wherever you are,
all of you, listen for Tiamak's call and run to the dooryard
if you hear it."

He turned and pulled open the door. Charystra was sitting on the top step in a scattering of foodstuffs, her face

a mask of confusion. Isgrimnur looked at her for a moment, then stepped over to Miriamele and bent to her ear; Tiamak was close enough to hear his whisper.

"Don't let her stray from you," the duke murmured. "We may have to take her with us, at least far enough away to protect the secret of which way we've gone. If she kicks up rough, just shout and I'll be there in a moment." He took Miriamele's elbow and guided her toward Charystra's seat on the steps.

"Greetings again, goodwife," the princess said to her. "My name is Marya. We met downstairs. Come now, let us go to the kitchen and get some food for my friends and me—we have been traveling and we are very hungry." She leaned down and helped Charystra to her feet, then bent again to retrieve the bread and cheese that had fallen. "See?" she said cheerfully, taking the dumbfounded woman by the arm. "We will be sure to waste nothing, and we will pay for all."

They disappeared down the stairs.

Miriamele found herself working in a sort of haze. She was concentrating so intently on the task at hand that she lost all track of the reasons for what she was doing until she heard Tiamak's excited cry and his rabbitlike thumping on the roof overhead. Her heart speeding, she snatched up a last handful of wizened onions—Charystra went to few pains to keep her larder well-stocked—and bolted for the dooryard, hurrying the protesting innkeeper along before her.

"Here, what do you think you're at?" Charystra complained. "There's no cause to be treating me this way, whoever you are!"

"Hush! All will be well." She wished she believed it.

As she reached the common room door, she heard Isgrimnur's heavy footsteps on the stairs. He quickly moved up behind, allowing the balking Charystra no room for escape, and together they pushed through into the dooryard. Camaris and Cadrach were working so intently that they did not look up at the entrance of their comrades. The old knight held a pitch-smeared brush, the monk a strip of heavy sailcloth which he was hacking at with a knife.

A moment later Tiamak came slithering down from the rafters. "I saw soldiers, not far distant," he said breathlessly. "They are a thousand paces away, maybe fewer, and they are coming here!"

"Are they the same ones?" Isgrimnur asked. "Damn me, of course they are! We must go. Is the boat patched?"

"I would guess that it will keep the water out for a while," Cadrach said calmly. "If we bring these things with us," he indicated the pitch and sailcloth, "we can do a better and more thorough job when we stop."

"If we get a chance to stop at all," the duke growled. "Very well. Miriamele?"

"I have stripped the larders. Not that it took much work."

Charystra, who had regained a little of her haughtiness, drew herself up. "And what are my guests and I going to eat?" she demanded. "The finest table in Kwanitupul, I'm known for."

Isgrimnur's snort fluttered his whiskers. "It's not your table that's the problem, it's the muck you put on top of it. You'll be paid, woman—but first you're going to take a little voyage."

"What?" Charystra shrieked. "I'm a God-loving Aedonite woman! What are you going to do with me?"

The duke grimaced and looked at the others. "I do not like this, but we cannot leave her here. We will put her off somewhere safe—with her money." He turned to Cadrach. "Take some of that rope and tie her up, will you? And try not to hurt her."

The last few preparations were finished to the accompaniment of Charystra's outraged protests. Tiamak, who seemed quite worried that Isgrimnur might have forgotten some precious items of their baggage, ran upstairs to make certain nothing had been left behind. When he returned, he joined the others in their efforts to move the large boat out through the broad side-door of the yard.

"Any decent boatyard would have a windlass," Isgrimnur complained. Sweat was pouring down his face.

Miriamele worried that one of the two older men might hurt themselves, but Camaris, for all his years, seemed utterly untroubled by carrying his share of the weight, and Isgrimnur was still a powerful man. Rather, it was Cadrach, wrung out by their misadventures, and slender Tiamak who had the most trouble. Miriamele wanted to help, but did not dare leave bound Charystra alone for a moment for fear she would raise an alarm or fall into the water and drown.

As they staggered down the ramp to the rear dock, Miriamele was certain she could hear the tramping bootsteps of Aspitis and his minions. The progress of the boat seemed horrifically slow, a blind eight-legged beetle that snagged itself on every narrow turning.

"Hurry!" she said. Her charge Charystra, understanding nothing but her own plight, moaned.

At last they reached the water. As they eased the boat over the edge of the floating dock, Cadrach reached down between the benches and lifted out the heavy maul from the pile of tools they had brought for patching the hull, then went back up the ramp toward the inn.

"What are you doing?" Miriamele shouted. "They'll be here at any moment!"

"I know." Cadrach broke into an uneven trot, the huge hammer cradled against his chest.

Isgrimnur glowered. "Is the man mad?"

"I don't know." Miriamele urged Charystra toward the boat, which was scraping gently against the side of the dock. When the innkeeper resisted, old Camaris stood up and lifted her down as easily a father might his small daughter, then placed her on the bench beside him. The woman huddled there, a tear snaking down her cheek; Miriamele could not help but feel sorry for her.

A moment later Cadrach reappeared, pelting down the gangway. He clambered into the boat with the help of the others, then pushed it away from the dock. The nose swung out toward the middle of the canal.

Miriamele helped the monk squeeze onto the bench. "What were you doing?"

Cadrach took a moment to catch his breath, then carefully laid the maul back down atop the bundle of sail-cloth. "There was another boat. I wanted to make sure that it would take them a lot longer to patch it than we took on this. You can't chase anyone through Kwanitupul without a boat."

"Good man," said Isgrimnur. "Although I'm sure they will get a boat soon enough."

Tiamak pointed. "Look!" A dozen blue-cloaked, hel-meted men were passing along the wooden walkway to-ward *Pelippa's Bowl.*

"First they will knock," Cadrach said quietly. "Then they will push down the door. Then they will see what we've done and start searching for a boat."

"So we'd better take advantage of our head start. Row!" Suiting action to word, Isgrimnur bent to his sweep. Camaris also bent, and as their two oar-blades bit at the green water the little boat leaped forward.

In the stern, Miriamele peered back at the diminishing inn. In the antlike movement of people near the entrance-way, she thought she could discern a momentary flash of golden hair. Stricken, she dropped her eyes to the choppy canal and prayed to God's mother and several saints that she would never have to see Aspitis again.

"It is only a little farther." The wall-eyed Rimmersman looked at the palisade of gnarled pine trees as fondly as at a familiar street. "There you can rest and eat."

"Thank you, Dypnir," Isorn said. "That will be good." He might have said more, but Eolair had caught at his bri-dle and slowed his horse. Dypnir, who had not seemed to notice, let his own mount carry him a little ahead until he was only a shadow in the forest dusk.

"Are you sure you can trust this man, Isorn?" the Count of Nad Mullach asked. "If you are not, let us de-mand some further proof of him now, before we ride into an ambush."

Isorn's wide brow furrowed. "He is of Skoggey. Those folk are loyal to my father."

"He *says* that he is from Skoggey. And they *were* loyal to your father." Eolair shook his head, amazed that the son of a duke could have so little craft. Still, he could not help admiring Isorn's kind and open heart.

Anyone that can keep himself so, in the midst of all this horror, is someone to be treasured, the count thought, but he felt a responsibility for, among other things, his own skin that would not let him be silent, even if it risked offending Duke Isgrimnur's son.

Isorn smiled at Eolair's worry. "He knows the folk he should know. In any case, this is a rather tricksy way to go about ambushing a half-dozen men. Don't you think that if this fellow was Skali's we would simply have been fallen upon by a hundred Kaldskrykemen?"

Eolair frowned. "Not if this fellow is only a scout, and looking to earn his spurs with a clever capture. Enough, then. But I will keep my sword loose in the sheath."

The young Rimmersman laughed. "As will I, Count Eolair. You forget, I spent much of my childhood with Einskaldir, Aedon rest him—the most mistrusting man who ever drew breath."

The Hernystirman found himself laughing a little, too. Einskaldir's impatience and quick temper had always seemed more in keeping with the old pagan Rimmersgard whose gods were as volatile as the weather, hard as the Vestivegg Mountains.

Eolair and Isorn and the four Thrithings-men sent by Hotvig had been traveling together for several weeks now. Hotvig's men were friendly enough, but the journey through the civilized lands of eastern Erkynland—civilized with houses and fields that bore the marks of cultivation, though at the moment it seemed largely unpopulated—had filled them with a certain unease. More and more, as the trek wore on and the grasslanders found themselves farther each day from the plains of their birth, they became moody and sullen, speaking almost entirely to each other in the guttural Thrithings tongue, sitting up at night around the fire singing the songs of their homeland. As a result, Isorn and Eolair had been thrown back almost entirely on each other's company.

To the count's relief, he had found there was a great deal more to the duke's yellow-haired bear of a son than was at first apparent. He was brave, there was little doubt of that, but it seemed unlike the courageousness of many brave men Eolair had known, who felt that to be otherwise was to fail somehow in the sight of others. Young Isorn simply seemed to know little fear, and to do the things he did only because they were right and necessary. Not that he was completely nerveless. His shuddersome story about his captivity among the Black Rimmersmen, of the torture he and his fellows had suffered and of the haunting presence of pale-skinned immortal visitors, still affected him so strongly that he found it difficult to tell. Yet Eolair, with his sharp intriguer's eye, thought that anyone else who had suffered such an experience would have taken it even more to heart. To Isorn it was a terrible time that was now over, and that was that.

So, as the little company had passed along the hillsides above eerily empty Hasu Vale and through the fringes of the Aldheorte, wide-skirting the menace of snowbound Erchester and the Hayholt—and also, Eolair could not help recalling, of tall Thisterborg—the Count of Nad Mullach had found himself growing more and more fond of this young Rimmersman, whose love for his father and mother was so firm and uncomplicated, whose love of his people was almost as strong and was virtually inseparable from his feelings for his family. Still, Eolair, tired and bruised by events, sick already of the horrors of war before this most recent one had begun, could not help wondering if he himself had *ever* been as young as Isorn.

"Almost there." Dypnir's voice brought Eolair's mind back to the dim forest track.

"I only hope they have something to drink," Isorn said, grinning, "and enough of it to share."

As Eolair opened his mouth to reply, a new voice cracked through the evening.

"Hold! Stand where you are!" It was Westerling, spoken with the thickness of Rimmersgard. Isorn and Eolair reined up. Behind them, the four Thrithings-men brought

their horses to an effortless halt. Eolair could hear them whispering among themselves.

"It's me," their guide called, leaning his bearded head to the side so the hidden watcher could mark him. "Dypnir. I bring allies."

"Dypnir?" There was a note of doubt in the question. It was followed by a flurry of Rimmerspakk. Isorn seemed to be listening carefully.

"What do they say?" Eolair whispered. "I cannot follow when they speak so fast."

"About what you would expect. Dypnir has been gone several days, and they ask him why. He explains about his horse."

Eolair and his companions had found Dypnir beside a forest trail in the western Aldheorte, hiding near the corpse of his mount, whose leg had been broken in a hole and whose throat Dypnir himself had slit a few moments before. After sharing out the burdens of one of the packhorses, they had given that mount to the Rimmersman in exchange for his aid in finding men who could help them—they had not been too specific about the type of help they needed, except that it seemed understood by all parties that it would not be to the benefit of Skali Sharpnose.

"Very well." The hidden sentry returned to Westerling speech. "You will follow Dypnir. But you will go slow, and with your hands where we can see them. We have bows, so if you think to play foolish games with us in a dark forest, you will be sorry."

Isorn sat straighter. "We understand. But play no games with us, either." He added something in Rimmerspakk. After a moment of silence, some sign was given and Dypnir started forward, Eolair's party behind him.

They plodded on for a little while into the deepening evening.

At first all that the Count of Nad Mullach could see were tiny sparks like red stars. As they rode forward and the lights wavered and danced, he realized that he was seeing the flames of a fire through close-knit, needled branches. The company turned abruptly and rode through a hedge of trees, ducking at Dypnir's whispered insistence, and the warm light of the blaze rose up all around them.

The camp was what was called a woodsman's hall, a clearing in a copse of trees that had been walled against the wind by bundles of pine and fir branches tied between the trunks. In the center of the open space, ranged about the firepit, sat perhaps three or four dozen men, their eyes glinting with reflected light as they silently observed the strangers. Many of them wore the dirty and tattered remnants of battle costumes; all bore the look of men who had long slept out-of-doors.

Rhynn's Cauldron, it is a camp of outlaws. We will be robbed and killed. Eolair felt a brief clutch of dismay at the thought that his quest should end so pointlessly, and of disgust that they should have ridden so trustingly to their deaths.

Some of the men nearest the entrance to the copse drew their weapons. The Thrithings-men shifted on their horses, hands snaking down to their own hilts. Before anyone's untoward movement could touch off a fatal confrontation, Dypnir flapped his hands in the air and slid down from his borrowed steed. The husky Rimmersman, far less graceful on land than on horseback, stumped to the center of the clearing.

"Here," he said. "These men are friends."

"No one is a friend who comes to eat out of our pot," one of the grimmest-looking growled. "And who is to say they are not Skali's spies?"

Isorn, who had been watching as quietly as Eolair, suddenly leaned forward in the saddle. "Ule?" he said wonderingly. "Are you not Ule, the son of Frekke Grayhair?"

The man stared at him, eyes narrowed. He was perhaps Eolair's age. So much dirt was on his lined, weathered face that he seemed to be wearing a mask. A hand-ax with a pitted blade was thrust through his belt. "I am Ule Frekkeson. How do you know my name?" He was stiff, tensed as if to spring.

Isorn dismounted and took a step toward him. "I am Isorn, son of Duke Isgrimnur of Elvritshalla. Your father

was one of my own father's most loyal companions. Do
you not remember me, Ule?"

A dry rustle of movement around the clearing and a
few whispered comments were all this revelation engendered. If Isorn expected the man before him to leap up
and joyfully embrace him, he was disappointed. "You
have grown since I last saw you, manling," said Frekke's
son, "but I see your father's face in yours." Ule stared at
him. Something was moving behind the man's quiet anger. "Your father is duke no longer, and all of his men are
outlaws. Why do you come to plague us?"

"We come to ask your help. There are many beside
yourself unhomed, and they have begun to gather together
to take back what was stolen from them. I bring you tidings from my father, the rightful duke—and from Josua of
Erkynland, who is his ally against Skali Sharp-nose."

The murmur of surprise grew louder. Ule paid no attention. "This is a sad trick, boy. Your father is dead at
Naglimund, your Prince Josua with him. Do not come to
us with goblin stories because you think it would be nice
to rule over a pack of house-carls again. We are free men
now." Some of his companions growled their agreement.

"Free men?" Isorn's voice suddenly grew tight with
fury. "Look at you! Look at this!" He gestured around the
clearing. Watching, Eolair marveled to see this sudden
passion in the young man. "Free to skulk in the woods
like dogs who have been whipped from the hall, do you
mean? Where are your homes, your wives, your children?
My father is alive. . . !" He paused, steadying his voice.
Eolair wondered if the thought had entered Isorn's head
that Isgrimnur's safety was not quite so sure as he made
it sound. "My father will have his lands back," he said.
"Those who help him will have their own steadings back
as well—and more beside, because when we are finished
Skali and his Kaldskrykemen will leave behind many un-
husbanded women, many an untended field. Any true
men that we find to follow us will be well rewarded."

A harsh laugh rose up from the watching men, but it
was one of enjoyment at the boast, not mockery. Eolair,

sensibilities honed by years of courtly sparring, could feel
the spirit of the moment beginning to turn their way.

Ule suddenly rose, his bearlike body wide in his ragged
furs. The noise of the onlookers dwindled away. "Tell me
then, Isorn Isgrimnurson," he demanded. "Tell me what
happened to my father, who served your father all his life.
Does he wait for me at the end of your road, like the man-
hungry widows and the wide, masterless fields you speak
of? Will he be waiting to embrace his son?" He was shaking with rage.

Clear-eyed Isorn did not flinch. He took a slow breath.
"He was at Naglimund, Ule. The castle fell before the
siege of King Elias. Only a few escaped, and your father
was not one of them. If he died, though, he died bravely." He paused, lost for a moment in memory. "He was
always very kind to me."

"The damned old man loved you like his own grandchild," Ule said bitterly, then took a lurching step forward. In the moment of stunned silence Eolair fumbled
for his sword, cursing his own slowness. Ule grabbed
Isorn in a rib-cracking embrace, dragging the duke's son
forward and lifting the taller man off the ground.

"God curse Skali!" Tears made pale tracks on Ule's
dirty face. "The murderer, the devil-cursed murderer! It is
bloodfeud forever." He let Isorn go and wiped his face
with his sleeve. "Sharp-nose must die. Then my father
will laugh in heaven."

Isorn stared at him for a moment, then tears came to
his eyes. "My father loved Frekke, Ule. I loved him, too."

"Blood on the Tree, is there nothing to drink in this
wretched place!?" Dypnir shouted. All around, the tattered men came pressing forward to welcome Isorn home.

"What I am going to say to you will sound most
strangely," Maegwin began. More nervous than she had
thought she would be, she took a moment to smooth the
folds of her old black dress. "But I am the daughter of
King Lluth, and I love Hernystir more than I love my own

life. I would sooner tear out my own heart than lie to you."

Her people, gathered together in the largest of the caverns beneath the Grianspog, the great high-ceilinged catacomb where justice was dispensed and food was shared out, listened attentively. What Maegwin said might indeed prove strange, but they were going to hear her out. What could be so odd as to be unbelievable in a world as mad as the one in which they found themselves?

Maegwin looked back to Diawen, who stood just behind her. The scryer, eyes radiant with some personal happiness, smiled her approval. "Tell them!" Diawen whispered.

"You know that the gods have spoken to me in dreams," Maegwin said loudly. "They put a song of the elder days into my head and taught me to bring you here into the rocky caverns where we would be safe. Then Cuamh Earthdog, the god of the depths, led me to a secret place that had not been seen since before Tethtain's time—a place where the gods had a gift in store for us. You!" She pointed at one of the scribes who had descended to Mezutu'a with Eolair to copy the dwarrow's maps. "Stand and tell the people what you saw."

The old man rose unsteadily, leaning for support on one of his young pupils. "It was indeed a city of the gods," he quavered, "deep in the earth—bigger than all Hernysadharc, set in a cavern wide as the bay at Crannhyr." He threw his thin arms apart in a helpless attempt to indicate the stone city's vastness. "There were creatures in that place like none I have seen, whispering in the shadows." He raised his hand as several of the onlookers made signs against evil. "But they did us no harm, and even led us to their secret places, where we did what the princess asked us to do."

Maegwin gestured for the scribe to sit down. "The gods showed me the city, and there we found things that will help turn the tide of battle against Skali and his master, Elias of Erkynland. Eolair has taken those gifts to our allies—you all saw him go."

Heads nodded throughout the crowd. Among people as

isolated as these earth-dwellers had become, the departure of the Count of Nad Mullach on a mysterious errand had been the subject of several weeks' worth of gossip.

"So twice the gods have spoken to me. Twice they have been correct."

But even as she spoke, Maegwin felt a twinge of worry. Was that really true? Hadn't she cursed herself for misinterpreting—even at times blamed the gods themselves for sending her cruel, false signs? She paused, suddenly beset by doubt, but Diawen reached forward and touched her shoulder, as if the scryer had heard her troubled thoughts. Maegwin found the courage to go on.

"Now the gods have spoken to me—a third time, and with the mightiest words of all. I saw Brynioch himself!" For surely, she thought, it must have been him. The strange face and golden stare burned in her memory like the afterimage of sun against the blackness of closed eyelids. "And Brynioch told me that the gods would send help to Hernystir!"

A few of the audience, caught up in Maegwin's own fervor, raised their voices in a cheer. Others, unsure but hopeful, exchanged glances with their neighbors.

"Craobhan," Maegwin called. "Stand and tell our people how I was found."

The old counselor got up with obvious reluctance. The look on his face told all: he was a statesman, a practical man who did not hold with such high-flown things as prophecies and the gods speaking to princesses. The folk gathered in the cavern knew that. For this reason, he was Maegwin's master stroke.

Craobhan looked around the chamber. "We found Princess Maegwin on Bradach Tor," he intoned. His voice could still carry powerfully despite his years; he had used it to great effect in the service of Maegwin's father and grandfather. "I did not see, but the men who brought her down are known to me, and . . . and trustworthy. She had been three days on the mountain, but had taken no hurt from the cold. When they found her she was . . ." he looked helplessly at Maegwin, but saw nothing in her

stern face that would allow him to escape this moment,
". . . she was in the grip of some deep, deep dream."

The gathering buzzed. Bradach Tor was a place of
strange repute, and it was stranger still that it should be
climbed by a woman during frozen winter.

"Was it just a dream?" Diawen said sharply from behind Maegwin. Craobhan looked at her angrily, then
shrugged.

"The men said it was like no dream they had ever
seen," he said. "Her eyes were open, and she spoke as
though to someone who stood before her . . . but nothing
was there but empty air."

"Who was she speaking to?" Diawen asked.

Old Craobhan shrugged again. "She . . . was speaking
as though she addressed the gods—and she listened be-
times, as though they were speaking to her in turn."

"Thank you, Craobhan," Maegwin said gently. "You
are a loyal and honest man. It is no wonder my father valued you so highly." The old counselor sat down. He did
not look happy. "I know that the gods have spoken to
me," she continued. "I was given a sight of the place
where the gods dwell, of the gods themselves in their in-
vincible beauty, caparisoned for war."

"For war?" someone shouted. "Against who, my lady?
Who do the gods fight?"

"Not who," Maegwin said, raising an admonitory finger. "But *for whom*. The gods will fight for *us*." She
leaned forward, quelling the rising murmur of the crowd.
"They will destroy our enemies—but only if we give our
hearts to them wholly."

"They have our hearts, lady, they do!" a woman cried.

Someone else shouted: "Why have they not helped us
before now? We have always honored them."

Maegwin waited until the clamor died down. "We have
always honored them, it is true, but in the manner that
one honors an old relative, out of grudging habit. We
have never shown them honor worthy of their power,
their beauty, worthy of the gifts they have given our people!" Her voice rose. She could feel again the nearness of
the gods; the sensation rose inside her like a spring of

clear water. It was such an odd, heady feeling that she
burst out laughing, which brought amazement to the faces
of the people around her. "No!" she shouted. "We have
performed the rites, polished the carvings, lit the sacred
fires, but very few of us have ever asked what more the
gods might wish as proof that we are worth their aid."

Craobhan cleared his throat. "And what do they want,
Maegwin, do you think?" He addressed her in a way that
seemed untowardly familiar, but she only laughed again.

"They want us to show our trust! To show our devotion, our willingness to put our lives in their hands—as
our lives have been all along. The gods will help us, this
I have seen for myself—but only if we show that we are
worthy! Why did Bagba give cattle to men? Because men
had lost their horses fighting in the wars of the gods, in
the time of the gods' truest need."

Even as she spoke, it all suddenly became clear to
Maegwin. How right Diawen had been! The dwarrows,
the frightened Sitha-woman who had spoken through the
Shard, the frighteningly endless winter—it was all so
clear now!

"For you see," she cried, "the gods themselves are at
war! Why do you think that snow has fallen, that winter
has come and never left although more than a dozen
moons have changed? Why do ancient terrors walk the
Frostmarch—things not seen since Hern's day? Because
the gods are at war even as we are at war. As the soldier-
ing games of children ape the combats of warriors, so is
our small conflict beside the great war that rages in the
heavens." She took a breath and felt the god-feeling bubbling inside her, filling her with joyful strength. She was
sure now that she had seen the truth. It was bright as sunlight to a new-wakened sleeper. "But just as the learning
of childhood is what shapes the wars of grown folk, so
does our strife here on the green earth affect the wars of
heaven. So if we wish the help of the gods, we must help
them in turn. We must be bold, and we must trust in their
beneficence. We must work the greatest magic against
darkness that we have."

"Magic?" a voice cried, an old man's distrustful rasp. "Is that what the scryer woman's taught you?"

Maegwin heard Diawen's hiss of indrawn breath, but she was feeling too bold for anger. "Nonsense!" she shouted. "I do not mean the fumblings of conjurors. I mean the sort of magic that speaks as loudly in heaven as it does upon the earth. The magic of our love for Hernystir and the gods. Do you wish to see our enemies vanquished? Do you wish to walk your green land again?"

"Tell us what we must do!" a woman near the front shouted.

"I will." Maegwin felt a great sense of peace and strength. The cavern had grown silent, and several hundred faces peered intently up at her. Just before her, old Craobhan's deep-lined, skeptical brow was creased with anger and worry. Maegwin loved him at that moment, for she saw in his defeated look the vindication of her suffering and the proof of the power of her dreams. "I will tell you all," she said again, louder, and her voice echoed and echoed again through the great cavern, so strong, so full of triumphant certainty that few could doubt that they were indeed hearing the chosen messenger of the gods.

Miramele and her companions lingered only a few moments to put Charystra ashore on an isolated dock in the furthest outskirts of Kwanitupul. The innkeeper's violated feelings were only partially soothed by the bag of coins Isgrimnur tossed onto the weathered boards at her feet.

"God will punish you for treating an Aedonite woman this way!" she cried as they rowed away. She was still standing on the edge of the rickety dock, waving a fist and shouting incomprehensibly, as their slow-sliding boat nosed down a canal lined by twisted trees and she was lost from view.

Cadrach winced. "If what we have experienced lately has been God's way of showing His favor, I think I would be willing to try a little of His punishment, just for a change."

"No blasphemy," Isgrimnur growled, leaning hard on his oar. "We are still alive, against all reason, and still free. That is indeed a gift."

The monk shrugged, unimpressed, but said no more.

They floated out into an open lagoon, so shallow that stalks of marsh-grass poked from the surface and wavered in the wind. Miriamele watched Kwanitupul slipping away behind them. In the late afternoon light, the low gray city seemed a collection of drifting flotsam that had snagged on a sandbar, vast but purposeless. She felt a terrible longing for some place to call home, for even the most mindless and stifling routines of everyday life. At the moment there was not a single scrap of charm left in the idea of adventuring.

"There is still no one behind us," Isgrimnur said with some satisfaction. "Once we reach the swamps, we will be safe."

Tiamak, sitting in the bow of the boat, gave a curious, strangled laugh. "Do not say such a thing." He pointed to the right. "There, head for that small canal, just between those two large baobab trees. No, do not talk like that. You might attract attention."

"What attention?" asked the duke, irritated.

"They Who Breathe Darkness. They like to take men's brave words and bring them back to them in fear."

"Heathen spirits," Isgrimnur muttered.

The little man laughed again, a sad and helpless giggle. He slapped his hand against his bony thigh so that the smack rang echoing across the sluggish water, then he sobered abruptly. "I am so ashamed. You people must think me a fool. I studied with the finest scholars in Perdruin—I am as civilized as any drylander! But now we are going back to my home . . . and I am frightened. Suddenly the old gods of my childhood seem more real than ever."

Next to Miriamele, Cadrach was nodding in a coldly satisfied way.

* * *

The trees and their raiment of clinging vines grew thicker as the afternoon wore on, and the canals down which Tiamak directed them grew progressively smaller and less well-defined, full of thick weeds. By the time the sun was scudding toward the leafy horizon, Camaris and Cadrach—Isgrimnur was taking a well-deserved rest—could hardly drag their oars through the mossy water.

"Soon we will have to use the oars as poles only." Tiamak squinted at the murky waterway. "I hope that this boat is small enough to go where we must take it. There is no doubt we will soon have to find something with a more shallow draft, but it would be good to be farther in, so that there will be less chance our pursuers will discover what we have done."

"I don't have a cintis-piece left." Isgrimnur fanned away the cloud of tiny insects that hovered around his head. "What will we use to trade for another boat?"

"This one," Tiamak said. "We will not get anything so sturdy in return, but whoever trades with us will know that they can sell this in Kwanitupul for enough to buy two or three flatboats, and also a barrel of palm wine."

"Speaking of boats," Cadrach said, resting against his sweep for a moment, "I can feel more water around my toes than I like. Should we not stop soon and patch this one, especially if we are condemned to keep it for a few more days? I would not care to look for a camping place on this mucky ground in the dark."

"The monk is right," Tiamak told Isgrimnur. "It is time to stop."

As they glided slowly along, with the Wrannaman standing in the bow inspecting the tangled coastline for a suitable mooring place, Miriamele occasionally caught a glimpse through the close-leaning trees of small, ramshackle huts. "Are those your people's houses?" she asked Tiamak.

He shook his head, a slight smile curving his lips. "No, lady, they are not. Those of my folk who must live in Kwanitupul for their livelihood live *in* Kwanitupul. This is not the true Wran, and to live in this place would be worse for them than simply enduring the two seasons a year they spend in the city, then returning to their villages after their money is earned. No, those who live here are drylanders mostly, Perdruinese and Nabbanai who have left the cities. They are strange folk who are not much like their brethren, for many of them have lived long on the edge of the marshes. In Kwanitupul they are called 'shoalers' or 'edge-hoppers,' and are thought to be odd and unreliable." He smiled again, bashfully, as if embarrassed by his long explanation, then returned to his search for a campsite.

Miriamele saw a wisp of smoke trailing upward from one of the hidden houses, and wondered what it would be like to live in such an isolated place, to hear no human voice from the start of the day until the end. She looked up at the overarching trees and their strange shapes, the roots twisted like serpents where they ran down to the water, the branches gnarled and grasping. The narrow watercourse, now shadowed from the dying sun, seemed lined by lonely shapes that reached out as if to clutch at the small boat and hold it fast, to pinion it until the waters would rise and the mud and roots and vines would swallow it. She shivered. Somewhere in the shaded hollows, a bird screeched like a frightened child.

12

Raven's Dance

At *first* the battle did not seem real to Simon. From his
position on the lower slopes of Sesuad'ra, the great expanse of frozen lake lay before him like a marble floor,
and beyond it the snow-stippled downs stretched to the
snow-blanketed, wooded hills across the valley. Everything was so small—so far away! Simon could almost
trick himself into believing that he had returned to the
Hayholt and was peering down from Green Angel Tower
on the busily harmless movements of castle folk.

From Simon's vantage point, the initial sally of
Sesuad'ra's defenders—meant to keep Duke Fengbald's
troops out on the ice and away from the log barricade that
protected the entrance to the Sithi road—seemed a capering display of intricate puppetry. Men waved swords and
axes, then fell to the ice pierced by invisible arrows,
dropping as suddenly as if some titanic master had loosed
their strings. It all seemed so distant! But even as he marveled at the miniature combat, Simon knew that what he
was watching was in deadly earnest, and that he would be
seeing it closer soon enough.

The rams and their riders were both growing restive.
Those of Simon's Qanuc troop whose hiding places did
not allow them a view of the frozen lake were calling
whispered questions to those who could see. The steamy
breath of the entire company hung close overhead. All
around, the branches of the trees shimmered with droplets
of melting snow.

Simon, as impatient as his trollish companions, leaned

into Homefinder's neck. He inhaled her reassuring smell and felt the warmth of her skin. He wanted so to do the right thing, to help Josua and his other friends; at the same time, he was mortally afraid of what might happen down there on the glassy surface of the frozen lake. But for now, he could only wait. Both death and glory would have to be put off, at least for Simon and these small warriors.

He watched carefully, trying to make sense of the chaos before him. The line of Fengbald's soldiers, which was holding tightly to the sandy path laid for them by their battle-sledges, rippled as the wave of defenders struck them. But although they wavered, Fengbald's force held, then struck back at their attackers, hitting and then dispersing the initial clump into several smaller groupings. The leading company of Fengbald's soldiers then swarmed around their attackers, so that the firm line of the Duke's forces quickly became a number of actively moving points, each small skirmish largely self-contained. Simon could not help thinking of wasps clustering around a scatter of scraps.

The muffled sounds of combat were rising. The faint clanking as swords and axes struck armor, the dim bellows of rage and terror, all added to the sense of remoteness, as though the battle were being fought beneath the frozen lake instead of atop it.

Even to Simon's untrained eye, it quickly became obvious that the defenders' opening sally had failed. The survivors were breaking away from Fengbald's line, which was still swelling as more and more of his army made its way out onto the lake. Those of Josua's soldiers who could pull free were skidding and crawling back over the naked ice to the dubious safety of the barricade and the wooded hillside.

Homefinder snorted beneath Simon's stroking hand and wagged her head restively. Simon gritted his teeth. They had no choice, he knew. The prince wished them to wait until they were called, even if it looked as if all might be lost before their time came.

Waiting. Simon let out an angry sigh. Waiting was so hard. . . .

Father Strangyeard was hopping about in an agony of worry.

"Oh!" he said, almost slipping on the muddy earth. "Poor Deornoth!"

Sangfugol reached out a hand and snagged the archivist's sleeve, saving the priest from a long tumble down the hillside.

Josua was standing upslope, peering down at the battle site. His red Thrithings-horse, Vinyafod, stood nearby, reins tied loosely around a low branch. "There!" Josua could not keep the exultation from his voice. "I see his crest—he is still on his feet!" The prince leaned forward, teetering precariously. Below, Sangfugol made a reflexive gesture to go toward him, as though the harper might have to catch his master as he had rescued the priest. "Now he has broken free!" Josua cried, relief in his voice. "Brave Deornoth! He is rallying the men and they are falling back, but slowly. Ah, God's Peace, I love him dearly!"

"Praise Aedon's name." Strangyeard made the sign of the Tree. "May they all come back safely." He was flushed with exertion and excitement, his eyepatch a black spot atop the mottled pink.

Sangfugol made a bitter noise. "Half of them are lying bloody on the ice, already. What is important is that some of Fengbald's men are doing the same." He clambered atop a stone and squinted down at the milling shapes. "I think I see Fengbald, Josua!" he called.

"Aye," the prince said. "But has he taken the feint?"

"Fengbald is an idiot," Sangfugol replied. "He will take it like a trout takes a shadfly."

Josua looked away from the battle for a moment, turning to the harper with a look of cool, if somewhat distracted, amusement. "Oh, he will, will he? I wish I had your confidence, Sangfugol."

The harper flushed. "I beg your pardon, Highness. I only meant that Fengbald is not the tactician that you are."

The prince returned his attention to the lake below. "Don't waste time with flattery, harper—at this moment, I fear I'm too busy to appreciate it. And don't make the mistake of underestimating an enemy, either." He stared, shading his eyes against the glare of the shrouded sun, which was climbing behind the clouds. "Damnation! He *hasn't* taken it, not entirely! There, see, he has only brought part of his troop forward. The rest are still huddled at the edge of the lake."

Embarrassed, Sangfugol said nothing. Strangyeard was hopping up and down again. "Where is Deornoth? Oh, curse this old eye!"

"Still falling back." Josua leaped down from his perch, then made his way down the hill to where they stood. "Binabik has not yet returned from Hotvig and I cannot wait any longer. Where is Simon's boy?"

Jeremias, who had been crouching beside a toppled log, trying to stay out of the way, now leaped to his feet. "Here, Your Highness."

"Good. Go now, first to Freosel, then down the hill to Hotvig and his riders. Tell them to make ready—that we will strike now after all. They will hear my signal shortly."

Jeremias bowed quickly, his face pale but composed, then turned and dashed up the trail.

Josua was frowning. Down on the ice, Fengbald's army of Erkynguardsmen and mercenaries indeed seemed to be moving forward only hesitantly, despite their success in the first engagement. "Welladay," said the prince, "Fengbald has grown more cautious with his advancing years and greater burdens. Damn his eyes! Still, we have no choice but to pull the trapdoor shut on whatever of his force we can catch." His laugh was sour. "We will leave tomorrow for the Devil."

"Prince Josua!" gasped Strangyeard, so shocked that he ceased hopping. He sketched another hasty Tree in the air before him.

The hot breath of men and horses hung over the lake as a mist. It was hard to see clearly for more than a few ells in any direction, and even those men Deornoth could see were dim and insubstantial, so that the clamor of combat seemed to come from some ghost battle.

Deornoth caught the guardsman's downward stroke on his hilt. The impact nearly shivered his blade loose from his grip, but he managed to retain it in his tingling fingers long enough to bring it up for a counterswipe. His stroke missed, but slashed the guardsman's mount on an unprotected leg. The dappled horse shrieked and bounced back a few steps, then lost its footing and tumbled to the ragged ice with a crash and a spurt of powdery snow. Deornoth reined in Vildalix; they danced away from the fallen charger, who was thrashing wildly. Its rider was trapped beneath, but unlike the horse, he was making no noise.

Breath whistling in the confines of his helmet, Deornoth raised his sword and hammered it against his shield as loud as he could. His hornsman, one of the young and untrained soldiers from New Gadrinsett, had gone down in the first crush, and now there was no one to blow the retreat.

"Hark to me!" Deornoth shouted, redoubling the clatter. "Fall back, all men, fall back!"

As he looked around, his mouth filled with something salty and he spat. A gobbet of red flew out through the helmet's vertical slot and onto the ice. The wetness on his face was blood, probably the wound he had gotten when another of the guardsmen had dented his headgear. He could not feel it—he never did feel such small hurts while the fight was raging—but he offered a quick prayer to Mother Elysia that the blood would not run into his eyes and blind him at an important moment.

Some of his men had heard and were collapsing back around his position. They were not true fighting men yet, God knew, but so far they had shown themselves bravely against a formidable line of Erkynguards. They were not

meant to break Fengbald's leading force, but only to slow
them, and perhaps to lure them incautiously toward the
barricade and the first of Josua's surprises: New
Gadrinsett's few dependable archers and their small hoard
of arrows. Bowmen alone would not change the course of
this battle—the mounted knights on both sides were too
well-armored—but they would wreak some havoc, and
force Fengbald's men to think twice before launching an
unbridled assault against the base of Sesuad'ra. So far,
very few arrows had flown from either side, although a
few of Deornoth's makeshift troops had gone down in the
first moments of their assault with shafts quivering in
their throats or even punched through chain mail into a
chest or stomach. Now the fog caused by the rising sun
would make it even more difficult for Fengbald's men to
make use of their bows.

Thank God it is Fengbald we are fighting, Deornoth
thought. He was almost immediately forced to duck, surprised by the flailing blade of a mounted guardsman who
appeared without warning out of the murk. The horse
clattered by, receding into insubstantiality once more.
Deornoth took a few quick, deep breaths.

*Mounted knights and kerns we can deal with, at least
for a while. Only Fengbald would be so foolhardy as to
besiege a fortified hill without a company or two of
longbowmen! They could have cut us all down in the first
moments.*

Of course, for all his arrogance, Fengbald had not
proved quite as foolish as Josua and the others had hoped.
They had prayed that he would send at least a major force
of the Thrithings-men in first, trusting to their superior
horsemanship on the treacherous ice. The grasslanders
were fearsome fighters, but they loved the heroisim of individual combat. The prince had felt sure that a few net-
tling attacks from Deornoth's troop would lure the
mercenaries out of formation, where they would be more
easily dealt with, and which would also throw Fengbald's
advance into confusion. But they had all reckoned without the sledges—and whose clever plan was *that,*
Deornoth could not help wondering—and the improved

footing brought by the blanket of sand had allowed the
duke to send in his disciplined Erkynguard.

There was a sound as of a swelling drum roll. Deornoth
looked up to see that the guardsman who had missed on
his first pass had finally turned his horse around—the
footing was so dreadful and necessitated such careful
movement by both sides that the entire battle had the look
of some strange underwater dance—and was now bearing
down on him out of the fog again, slowly this time, urging his horse forward at no more than a cautious walk.
Deornoth gave Vildalix a polite heel, bringing the bay
around to face the attacker, then lifted his sword. The
Erkynguardsman raised his in turn, but still continued his
approach at little more than a man's hiking pace.

It was strange to see the green livery of the Erkynguard
draping an enemy. It was stranger still to have so much
time to deliberate on the oddness of it while waiting for
that enemy to make his measured way across the ice. The
guardsman ducked a wild sword-swing from one of
Deornoth's comrades, a blow that flashed out of the mist
like a serpent's darting tongue—Josua's men were all
around, fighting desperately now to pull close enough together for an orderly retreat—and came on, undaunted.
Deornoth could not help wondering for a brief moment if
the face beneath this bold soldier's helm was one he
would recognize, someone he had drunk with, diced
with. . . .

Vildalix, who despite his bravery seemed sometimes as
sensitive as flayed skin, took Deornoth's minute pull on
the reins and lurched heavily to one side just as the attacker reached them, so that the guardsman's first stroke
scraped harmlessly across Deornoth's shield. Vildalix
then danced in place for a moment, trying to avoid stepping on the crumpled form of the rider who had earlier
gone down beneath his own mount, and thus Deornoth's
own return blow missed widely. The attacking guardsman
pulled up, his horse's legs spreading slightly as it skidded
in an attempt to make a sudden stop. Seeing his opening,
Deornoth dragged Vildalix around and went after him.
The Thrithings-horse, who had been trained on ice as

Josua's men prepared, was able to turn fairly easily, so that Deornoth caught up with the Erkynguard before he had completed his own awkward revolution.

Deornoth's first blow caromed off the guardsman's lifted shield, raising a brief plume of sparks, but he let the sword's own momentum carry it around for a second blow, rotating his wrists and leaning almost sideways in the saddle so he would not be forced to break his grip. He caught the green-liveried guardsman a powerful backhand blow to the head just as the man lowered his shield once more; the side of the Erkynguardsman's helmet crumpled inward at a hideous angle. Blood already sluicing down his neck and onto his byrnie, the guardsman toppled out of his saddle, tangling for a moment in his stirrups, then clanged to the ice where he lay twitching feebly. Deornoth turned away, pushing any regrets from his mind with the ease of long experience. This bleeding hulk might once have been someone he knew, but now any Erkynguardsman was only an enemy, no more.

"Hark, men, hark!" Deornoth shouted, standing upright in his stirrups so that he could better view their position through the mist. "Follow me on the retreat! Careful as you go!" It was hard to tell, but he thought he saw something more than half the force he had taken out now ringing him round. He raised his sword high, then spurred Vildalix in the direction of the great log barricades. An arrow whipped past his head, then another, but the aim was poor, or else the archers were confused by the mist. Deornoth's men lifted a thin cheer as they rode.

"Where is Binabik?" Josua fumed. "He was to be my messenger, but he has not come back from Hotvig." The prince made a face. "God grant me patience, listen to me! Perhaps something has happened to him." He turned to young Jeremias, who stood by, panting. "And Hotvig said Binabik left his side some time ago?"

"Yes, Highness. He said the sun has lifted a hand since the troll left, whatever that means."

"Damnable luck." Josua began pacing, but his eyes never left the battle below. "Well, there is nothing for it. I do not trust the call to carry so far, lad, so go to Simon and tell him that if hears nothing by the time he has counted five hundreds or so after Hotvig's men have ridden out, then he and the trolls are to rush in. Do you have that?"

"If he doesn't hear the horn, wait to a count of five hundreds after Hotvig appears, then rush in, yes." Jeremias considered before adding: "Your Highness."

"Fine. Go, then—run. We are at the time when moments matter." Josua waved him off, then turned to Sangfugol. "And you are ready, too?"

"Yes, sire," the harper said. "I have been trained by the best. I should have little difficulty wringing a few honking sounds out of something so simple as a horn."

Josua chuckled grimly. "There is something reassuring about your insolence, Sangfugol. But remember, master musician, you must do more than honk: you must play a victory call."

Simon was looking over the small company, mostly to keep himself busy, when he suddenly realized that Sisqi was not among the gathered trolls. He quickly went among the Qanuc, checking every face but finding no sign of Binabik's betrothed. She was their leader—where could she have gone? After a moment's thought, Simon realized that he had not seen her since the muster before Leavetaking House.

Oh, Aedon's mercy, no, he thought desperately. *What will Binabik say? I've lost his beloved before the battle even begins!*

He turned to the nearest of the trolls. "Sisqi?" he asked, trying to show by shrugs and gestures that he wished to know her whereabouts. Two troll women looked at him uncomprehendingly. Damn, that was what Binabik called her. What was her full name? "Sis—Sisqimook?" he tried. "Sisqinamok?"

One of the women nodded urgently, pleased to have understood. *"Sisqinanamook."*

"Where is she?" Simon could not think of the troll words. "Sisqinanamook? Where?" He pointed around to all sides and then shrugged again, trying to convey his question. His small companions seemed to grasp his meaning: after a long round of murmuring Qanuc-speech, those nearest indicated to him with perfectly understandable gestures that they did not know where Sisqinanamook had gone.

Simon was cursing roundly when Jeremias arrived.

"Hullo, Simon, isn't this glorious?" his squire asked. Jeremias seemed quite excited. "It's just like what we used to dream of back in the Hayholt."

Simon made a pained face. "Except we were hitting each other with barrel staves, and those men down there will use sharp steel instead. Do you know where Sisqi is—you know, the one Binabik is going to marry? She was supposed to be here with the other trolls."

"No, I don't, but Binabik's missing, too. Stop, though, Simon—I have to give you Josua's message first." Jeremias proceeded to relay the prince's instructions, then dutifully ran through them a second time, just in case.

"Tell him that I'm ready . . . that *we're* ready. We'll do what we're supposed to. But Jeremias, I have to find Sisqi. She's their leader!"

"No, you don't." His squire was complacent. "You've become a trollish war chieftain now, Simon, that's all. I have to run back to Josua. With Binabik gone, I'm his chief messenger. It happens that way in battles." He said it lightly, but with more than a touch of pride.

"But what if they won't follow me?" Simon stared at Jeremias for a moment. "You seem very cheerful," he growled. "Jeremias, people are being killed here. We may be next."

"I know." He became serious. "But at least it's our choice, Simon. At least it's an honorable death." A strange look flitted over his face, twisting his features as though he might suddenly burst into tears. "For a long time, when I was . . . under the castle . . . a quick, clean death seemed like it would be a wonderful thing." Jeremias turned away, hunching his shoulders. "But I suppose I must stay alive now. Leleth needs me as a friend—and you need someone to tell you what to do." He sighed and then straightened up, gave Simon an oddly flat smile and a half-wave, then trotted back into the shrouding greenery, disappearing in the direction from which he had come. "Good luck, Simon—Sir Seoman, I mean."

Simon started to call after him, but Jeremias was already gone.

Binabik's return was abrupt and somewhat startling. Josua heard a soft rustling noise and looked up to find himself staring into the yellow eyes and sharp-toothed maw of Qantaqa, panting on a rise just above him. The troll, seated atop her back, pushed some branches away from his round face and leaned forward. "Prince Josua," he said calmly, as though they were meeting at some court function.

"Binabik!" Josua took a backward step. "Where have you been?"

"I ask your pardoning, Josua." The troll slid off Qantaqa and made his way down to the level place where the prince stood. "I saw some of Fengbald's men who were exploring where they should not be going. I followed them." He gave Josua a significant look. "They were looking for a place with better climbing. Fengbald is not being so foolish as we were thinking—it is clear he is knowing he may not dislodge us with this first attack."

"How many were there?"

"Not a great number. Six . . . five."

"You couldn't tell? How closely did you watch them?"

Binabik's gentle smile did not reach his eyes. "There were six at first." He patted his walking-stick, and the hollow tube and darts contained therein. "Then one was falling down the hill again."

Josua nodded. "And the rest?"

"After they had been led away from the places they

should not be, I left Sisqi behind for distracting them while I went quickly up the hill. Some of the women of New Gadrinsett came down to help us."

"The women? Binabik, you are not to place women and children in danger."

The little man shook his head. "You know that they will be fighting just as bravely for saving their home as any men—we have never known any other thing among the Qanuc. But be of quieter heart. All they did was come for helping Sisqi and myself in the rolling of some large stones." He flattened his hand in a gesture of completion. "Those men will be no danger to us any more, and their searching will bring no reward for Fengbald."

Josua sighed in frustration. "I trust that at least you did not drag my wife along to help roll your stones?"

Binabik laughed. "She was eager to go, Prince Josua, that I will say. You have a wife of some fierceness—she would make a good Qanuc bride! But Gutrun was not allowing her a step out of camp." The troll looked around. "What is happening below? I could not easily be watching as I made my way back."

"Fengbald, as you said, was better prepared than we expected. They have built some kind of sleds or carts that roughen the ice so that the soldiers can move more easily. Deornoth's attack was pushed back, but Fengbald's Erkynguard did not chase him; they are still massing on the lake. I am about to—but enough. You will see what I am about to do."

"And do you need me to go to Hotvig?" Binabik asked.

"No. Jeremias has taken on your tasks while you were introducing Fengbald's spies to the ladies of New Gadrinsett." Josua smiled briefly. "Thank you, Binabik. I knew that if you were not hurt or trapped, you would be doing something important—but try to let me know next time."

"Apologies, Josua. I was fearing to wait too long."

The prince turned and beckoned to Sangfugol, who came quickly to his side. Father Strangyeard and Towser were both standing solemnly, watching the battle, although Towser seemed to be listing slightly, as if even the deadly combat below was not enough excitement to keep him from his midday nap much longer.

"Blow for Freosel," Josua said. "Three short bursts, three long."

Sangfugol lifted the horn to his lips, puffed out his thin chest, and blew. The call echoed down the wooded hillside, and for a moment the flurry of battle on the ice seemed to slow. The harper gasped in another great draught of air, then blew again. When the echoes died, he gave the call a third time.

"Now," Josua said firmly, "we shall see how ready Fengbald is for a real fight. Do you mark him down there, Binabik?"

"I think I am seeing him, yes. In the red flapping cape?"

"Yes. Watch and see what he does."

Even as Josua spoke, there was a sudden convulsion in the front line of Fengbald's army. The clot of soldiers nearest the wooden barricades abruptly stopped and swirled back in disorder.

"Hurrah!" Strangyeard shouted and leaped; then, seeming to remember his priestly gravity, he donned his look of worried concern once more.

"Aedon's Blood, see how they jump!" Josua said with fierce glee. "But even this will not stop them for long. How I wish we had more arrows!"

"Freosel will be making good use of those we are having," Binabik said. " 'A well-aimed spear is worth three,' as we say in Yiqanuc."

"But we must use the confusion Freosel's bowmen have given us." Josua paced distractedly as he watched. When a little time had passed, and he evidently could bear the waiting no longer, he cried: "Sangfugol— Hotvig's call, now!"

The trumpet blared again, two long, two short, two long.

The flight of arrows from Sesuad'ra's defenders caught Fengbald's men by surprise: they spilled back in confusion, leaving several score of their fellows lying skewered on the ice, some trying to crawl back across the slippery surface, trailing smears of blood like the tracks of snails. In the chaos, Deornoth and his remaining force were able to make their escape.

Deornoth himself went back three times to help carry the last of the wounded past the great wall of logs. When he was sure there was no more he could do, he slumped to the trampled mud in the shadow of the high barricade and pulled off his helmet. The sounds of struggle still raged close by.

"Sir Deornoth," someone said, "you are bleeding."

He waved the man away, disliking to be fussed over, but took the piece of cloth that was offered to him. Deornoth used the rag and a handful of snow to wipe the blood from his face and hair, then probed at his head wound with chilled fingers. It was only a shallow cut. He was glad he had sent the man off to aid those in greater need. A strip of the now bloodied cloth made an adequate bandage, and the pressure as he knotted it helped to soothe the ache in his head.

When he had finished looking over his other injuries—all quite minor, none as bloody as the nick in his scalp—he pulled his sword out of its scabbard. It was a plain blade, the hilt leather-wrapped, the pommel a crude hawk's head worn almost featureless by long handling. He wiped it down with an unbloodied corner of the cloth, frowning in displeasure at the new notches it had gained, however honorably. When he had finished, he held it up to catch the faint sunlight and squinted to make sure he had not left any blood to gnaw at the honed edge.

This is no famous blade, he thought. *It has no name, but it has still served well for many years. Like me, I suppose.* He laughed quietly to himself; a few of the other soldiers resting nearby looked at him. *No one will remember me, I think, no matter how long the names of Josua and Elias are spoken. But I am content with that. I do what the Lord Usires would have me do—was He any less humble?*

Still, there were times when Deornoth wished that the people of Hewenshire could see him now, see the way he fought loyally for a great prince, and how that prince depended on him. Was that too prideful for a good Aedonite? Perhaps. . . .

Another horn call shrilled from the hillside above, disrupting his thoughts. Deornoth scrambled to his feet, anxious to see what was afoot, and began to climb the barricade. A moment later, he dropped down and went back for his helmet.

Pointless to take an arrow between the eyes if I can avoid it, he decided.

He and several other men carefully lifted themselves so they could nose over the topmost logs and peer out through the crude observation slots that Sludig and his helpers had cut with their hand-axes. As they squeezed into place, they heard a great shout: a company of riders was breaking from the trees a short distance to the east, heading out onto the ice and directly toward Fengbald's rallying forces. There was something different about this company, but in the confusion of mists and flailing men and horses it took a moment to see what it was.

"Ride, Hotvig!" Deornoth shouted. The men beside him picked up the cry, cheering hoarsely. As the Thrithings-men pounded across the frozen lake, it quickly became apparent that they were moving far more easily and skillfully than Fengbald's men. They might almost have been riding on firm ground, so sure was their horsemanship.

"Clever Binabik," Deornoth breathed to himself. "You may save us yet!"

"Look at them ride!" one of the other men called, a bearded old fellow who had last joined a battle when Deornoth was a swaddled baby. "Those troll-tricks work, sure enough."

"But we are still far outnumbered," cautioned Deornoth. "Ride, Hotvig! Ride!"

In a matter of moments, the Thrithings-men were sweeping down on Fengbald's guardsmen, the horses' hooves making an oddly clangorous thunder on the ice.

They struck the first lines of men like a club, smashing a path through them without difficulty. The noise, the clashing of weapon and shield, the shrieking of men and horses, seemed to double in a moment. Hotvig himself, his beard festooned with scarlet war-ribbons, was plying his long spear as swiftly as an expert river-fisher; every time he darted it forward it seemed to find a target, bringing forth flaring sprays of blood as red as the silken knots in his whiskers. He and his grasslanders sang as they fought, a shouting chant with little tune but a horrible sort of rhythm which they used to punctuate each thrust and slash. They wheeled around Fengbald's men with amazing ease, as though the battle-hardened Erkynguardsmen were swimming in mud. The leading edges of the duke's forces wavered and fell back. The Thrithings-men's fierce song grew louder.

"God's Eyes!" Fengbald screamed, waving his long sword in purposeless fury, "hold your lines, damn you!" He turned to Lezhdraka. The mercenary captain was staring with slitted, feral eyes at Hotvig and his riders. "They have some damnable Sithi magic," the duke raged. "Look, they move across the ice as though they were on a tourney field."

"No magic," Lezhdraka growled. "Look at their horses' hooves. They wear some special shoe—see, the spikes are flashing! Somehow your Josua has shod his horses with metal nails, I think."

"*Damn* him!" Fengbald stood high in his stirrups and looked around. His pale, handsome face was beaded with sweat. "Well, it is a brave trick, but it is not enough. We are still far too many for him, unless he has an army three times that size hidden up there—which he has not. Bring up your men, Lezhdraka. We will shame my Erkynguard into giving a better account of themselves." He rode a little way toward his leading forces and raised his voice in a shriek. "Traitors! Hold your lines or you will go to the king's gibbet!"

Lezhdraka grunted in disgust at Fengbald's frenzy, then turned to his first company of Thrithings mercenaries, who had been sitting stolidly in their saddles, caring little for what happened until their own turn should come to ply their trade. They all wore boiled leather cuirasses and metal-rimmed leather helmets, the armor of the grasslands. At Lezhdraka's gesture, the large company of scarred and silent men straightened. A light seemed to kindle in their eyes.

"You carrion dogs," Lezhdraka shouted in his own tongue, *"listen! These stone-dwellers and their High Thrithing pets think that because they have ice-shoes on their horses, they will scare us off. Let us go and bare their bones!"* He spurred his horse forward, taking care to stay on the path provided by one of the battle sledges. With a single grim shout, his mercenaries fell in behind him.

"Kill them all," Fengbald shouted, riding in circles beside their column and waving his sword. "Kill them all, but especially, *do not let Josua leave the field alive.* Your master, King Elias, demands his death!"

The mercenary captain stared at the duke with poorly-hidden contempt, but Fengbald was already spurring his horse forward, screeching at his faltering Erkynguard. *"I care little for these stone-dweller quarrels,"* Lezhdraka shouted to his men in the Thrithings-tongue, *"but I know something that idiot does not: a live prince will get us better pay than Fengbald would ever give us—so I want the one-handed prince alive. But if Hotvig or any other whelp of the High Thrithing walks living from this field, I will make you scum eat your own guts."*

He waved again and the column surged forward. The mercenaries grinned in their beards and patted their weapons. The smell of blood was in the air—a very familiar smell.

Deornoth and his men were struggling back into their battle array when Josua appeared, leading Vinyafod. Father Strangyeard and the harper Sangfugol straggled after him, muddy and disarrayed.

"Binabik's ice-shoes have worked—or at least they have helped us catch Fengbald off-guard," Josua called.

"We have been watching, Highness." Deornoth gave the inside of his helmet another thump with his sword-hilt, but the dent was too deep for such simple repairs. He cursed and pulled it on anyway. There was nowhere near enough armor to go around; New Gadrinsett had strained to supply even what small weaponry and gear they had, and if Hotvig's Thrithings-men had not brought their own leather chestplates and headware, less than a quarter of the defenders would have been armored. There were certainly no replacements available, Deornoth knew, except those which could be gleaned from the newly dead. He decided he would stick with his original helm, dented or not.

"I am glad to see you ready," said Josua. "We must press whatever advantage we have, before Fengbald's numbers overwhelm us."

"I only wish we had more of the troll's boot-irons to pass around." As he spoke, Deornoth strapped on his own set, numbed hands fumbling awkwardly. He fingered the metal spikes that now jutted from his soles. "But we have used every piece of metal we could spare."

"Small price if it saves us, meaningless if it does not," Josua said. "I hope you gave preference to the men who must fight on foot."

"I did," Deornoth replied, "although we had enough for nearly all the horses, anyway, even after outfitting Hotvig's grasslanders."

"Good," Josua said. "If you have a moment, help me fit these on Vinyafod." The prince smiled an uncharacteristically straightforward smile. "I had the good sense to put them aside yesterday."

"But my lord!" Deornoth looked up, startled. "What do you want them for?"

"You do not think that I will watch the whole battle from this hillside, do you?" Josua's smile vanished. He seemed honestly surprised. "It is for my sake that these brave men are fighting and dying down on the lake. How could I not stand with them?"

"But that is precisely the reason." Deornoth turned to Sangfugol and Strangyeard, but those two merely looked away shamefacedly. Deornoth guessed that they had already argued this point with the prince and lost. "If something happens to you, Josua, any victory will be a hollow one."

Josua fixed Deornoth with his clear gray eyes. "Ah, but that is not true, old friend. You forget: Vorzheva now bears our child. You will protect her and our baby, just as you promised you would. If we win today and I am not here to enjoy it, I know that you will carefully and skillfully lead the people on from here. People will flock to our banner—people who will not even know or care if I am alive, but will come to us because we are fighting my brother, the king. And Isorn will soon return, I am sure, with men of Hernystir and Rimmersgard. And if his father Isgrimnur finds Miriamele—well, what more legitimate name could you have to fight behind than King John's granddaughter?" He watched Deornoth's face for a moment. "But, here, Deornoth, do not put on such a serious face. If God means me to overthrow my brother, not all the knights and bowmen of Aedon's earth can slay me. If He does not—well, there is no place to hide from one's fate." He bent and lifted one of Vinyafod's feet. The horse shifted anxiously but held its position. "Besides, man, this is a moment when the world is delicately balanced. Men who see their prince beside them know that they are not being asked to sacrifice themselves for someone who does not value that sacrifice." He fitted the leather sack with the stiffened bottom and protruding spikes over Vinyafod's hoof, then wrapped the long ties back and forth around the horse's ankle. "It is no use arguing," he said without looking up.

Deornoth sighed. He was desperately unhappy, but a part of him had known his prince might do this—indeed, would have been surprised if he had not. "As you wish, Highness."

"No, Deornoth." Josua tested the knot. "As I must."

Simon cheered as Hotvig's riders smashed into
Fengbald's line. Binabik's clever stratagem appeared to
be working: the Thrithings-men, although still riding
more slowly than normal, were far swifter than their op-
ponents, and the difference in maneuverability was startling. Fengbald's leading troops were falling back, forced
to regroup several hundred cubits back from the barricade.

"Hit them!" Simon shouted. "Brave Hotvig!" The trolls
cheered, too, strange bellowing whoops. Their time was
fast approaching. Simon was counting silently, although
he had already lost track once or twice and had to guess.
So far, the battle was unfolding just the way Josua and the
others had said.

He looked at his strange companions, at their round
faces and small bodies, and felt an overwhelming affection and loyalty sweep through him. They were his responsibility, in a way. They had come far to fight in
someone else's cause—even if it might ultimately prove
to be everyone's cause—and he wanted them all to reach
their homes safely once more. They would be fighting
bigger, stronger men, but trolls were accustomed to fighting in these wintry conditions. They, too, wore boot-irons,
but of a far more elaborate type than those Binabik had
taught the forge men to make. Binabik had told Simon
that among his people these boot-spikes were precious
now, since the trolls had lost the trade routes and the trading partners which had once made it possible to bring
iron into Yiqanuc; in this present era, each pair of boot-
spikes was handed down from parent to child, and they
were carefully oiled and regularly repaired. To lose a pair
was a terrible thing, for there was now almost no way to
replace them.

Their saddled rams, of course, had no need for such tri-
fles as iron shoes: their soft, leathery hooves would cling
to the ice like the feet of wall-walking flies. A flat lake
was little challenge when compared to the treacherous
frozen trackways of high Mintahoq.

"I come," someone said behind him. Simon turned to find Sisqi looking up at him expectantly. The troll woman's face was flushed and pearled with sweat, and the fur jacket she wore beneath her leather jerkin was tattered and muddy, as if she had crawled through the undergrowth.

"Where were you?" he said. He could see no trace of a wound on her, and was grateful for that.

"With Binabik. Help Binabik fight." She lifted her hands to mime some complicated activity, then shrugged and gave up.

"Is Binabik well?" Simon asked.

She thought for a moment, then nodded. "Not hurt."

Simon took a deep breath, relieved. "Good." Before he could say more, there was a flurry of movement down below. Another group of shapes suddenly scrambled forth from near the log barricade, hurrying to join the battle. A moment later Simon heard the faint, mournful cry of a horn. It blew a long note, then four short, then two long blasts that echoed thinly along the hillside. His heart leaped and he felt suddenly cold and yet tingling, as though he had fallen into icy water. He had forgotten his count, but it did not matter. That was the call—it was time!

Despite his nervous excitement, he was careful not to scrape Homefinder's side with his irons as he scrambled into the saddle. Most of the Qanuc words Binabik had so carefully taught him were blasted from his head.

"Now!" he shouted. "Now, Sisqi! Josua wants us!" He drew his sword and waved it in the air, catching it for a moment in a low-hanging tree branch. What was the word for "attack"? *Ni*-something. He turned and caught Sisqi's eye. She stared back, her small face solemn. She knew. The troll woman waved her arm and called out to her troops.

Everybody knows what happens now, he realized. *They don't need me to tell them anything.*

Sisqi nodded, giving him permission.

"Nihut!" Simon shouted, then spurred down the muddy trail.

* * *

Homefinder's hooves skidded as they struck the frozen lake, but Simon—who had ridden her unshod on the same surface a few days before—was relieved when she quickly caught her balance. The noise of conflict was loud before them, and now his trollish comrades were shouting too, bellowing strange war-cries in which he could discern the names of one or two of the mountains of Yiqanuc. The din of battle swiftly rose until it crowded all other thoughts from his mind. Then, before it seemed that he even had time to think, they were in the thick of it.

Hotvig's initial attack had split Fengbald's line and scattered it away from the safety of the sledge-scraped track. Deornoth's soldiers—all but a few on foot—had then surged out from behind the barricade and flung themselves on those Erkynguard who had been cut off from their own rearguard by Hotvig's action. The fighting near the barricade was particularly fierce, and Simon was startled to see Prince Josua in the thick of it, standing tall in red Vinyafod's saddle, his gray cloak billowing, his shouted words drowned in the confusion. Meanwhile, though, Fengbald had brought up his Thrithings mercenaries, who, instead of helping to stiffen the line behind the retreating Erkynguardsmen, were swarming around the broken column in their haste to engage Hotvig's horsemen.

Simon's troop struck the mercenaries from the blind side; those closest to the oncoming Qanuc had only a moment to look around in amazement before being skewered by the short spears of the trolls. A few of the Thrithingsmen seemed to regard the onrushing Qanuc with a shock that seemed closer to superstitious terror than mere surprise. The trolls howled their Qanuc war-cries as they charged, and whirled stones on oiled cords over their head, which made a dreadful buzzing sound like a swarm of maddened bees. The rams moved swiftly between the slower horses, so that several of the mercenaries' mounts reared and threw their masters; the trolls also used their darting spears to poke at the horses' undefended bellies.

More than one Thrithings-man was killed beneath his own toppled steed.

The din of battle, which at first had seemed to Simon a great roaring, quickly changed as the conflict drew him in, and became instead a kind of silence, a terrible humming quiet in which snarling faces and the steaming, white-toothed and red-throated mouths of horses loomed up from the mist. Everything seemed to move with a horrible sluggishness, but Simon felt that he was moving even more slowly. He swung his sword around, but although it was mere steel, it seemed at that moment as heavy as black Thorn.

A hand-ax struck one of the troll-men beside Simon. The small body was flung from the saddled ram and seemed to tumble slowly as a falling leaf until it disappeared beneath Homefinder's hooves. Through the droning emptiness, Simon thought he heard a faint, high-pitched shriek, like the cry of a distant bird.

Killed, he thought distractedly as Homefinder stumbled and again found her footing. *He was killed.* A moment later he had to fling his own blade up before him to ward off a swordstroke from one of the mounted mercenaries. It seemed to take forever for the two swords to meet; when they did, with a thin *clink,* he felt the shock down his arm and into his chest. Something brushed by him from the other side. When he looked down, he saw that his makeshift corselet had been torn and blood was rilling up in a wound along his arm; he could feel only a line of icy numbness from wrist to elbow. Gaping, he lifted his sword to strike back, but there was no one within reach. He pulled Homefinder around and squinted through the mist rising off the ice, then spurred her toward a knot of tangled shapes where he could see some of the trolls at bay.

After that the battle rose around him like a smothering hand and nothing made very much sense. In the midst of the nightmare, he was struck in the chest by someone's shield and tumbled from his saddle. As he scrambled to find purchase, he quickly realized that even shod with Binabik's magic spikes, he was still a man struggling for footing on a glassy sheet of ice. By luck, the reins had stayed tangled around his hand so that Homefinder did not bolt, but this same luck almost killed him.

One of the mounted Thrithings-men came out of the murk and pressed Simon backward, trapping him against Homefinder's flank. The gaunt swordsman had a face so covered with ritual scars that the skin showing beneath his helm looked like tree bark. Simon was in a terrible position, his shield arm still snagged in the reins so that he could barely get half of his shield between himself and his attacker. The grinning mercenary wounded him twice, a shallow gouge along his sword arm parallel to his first blooding of the day and a stab in the fat part of his thigh below his mail shirt. He would almost certainly have killed Simon in a few more moments, but someone else came up suddenly out of the fog—another Thrithings-man, Simon noted with dazed surprise—and accidentally collided with Simon's adversary, knocking the man's horse toward Simon and pushing the mercenary part of the way out of his saddle. Simon's half-desperate thrust, more in self-defense than anything else, slid up the man's leg and into his groin; he fell to the ground, blood fountaining from his wound, then screamed and writhed until his convulsions shook his helmet from his head. The man's thin, staring-eyed face, contorted with pain, brought back to Simon a Hayholt memory of a rat that had fallen into a rain barrel. It had been horrible to see it paddling desperately, teeth bared, eyes bulging. Simon had tried to save it, but in its terror the rodent had snapped at his hand, so he had run away, unable to bear watching it drown. Now an older Simon stared at the shrieking mercenary for a moment, then stepped on his chest to stop him rolling and pushed his sword blade into the man's throat, holding it there until all movement had stopped.

He felt curiously light-headed. Several long moments passed during which he tore loose the corpse's baggy sleeve and cinched it tightly around the wound in his own leg. It was only when he had finished and put his foot into Homefinder's stirrup that he realized what he had just done. His stomach heaved, but he had not made the mistake of eating that morning. After a brief pause he was able to drag himself up into the saddle.

Simon had thought he would be a sort of second-in-command of the trolls, Josua's hand among the prince's Qanuc allies, but he quickly discovered that it was hard enough work just to stay alive.

Sisqi and her diminutive troops were scattered all over the misty battlefield. At one point he had managed to find the area where they were most concentrated, and for a while he and the trolls had stood together—he saw Sisqi then, still alive, her slim spear as swift as a wasp sting, her round face set in a mask so fierce she looked like a tiny snow-demon—but at last the ebb and flow of combat had broken them apart again. The trolls did not do their best fighting in an orderly line, and Simon quickly saw that they were more useful when they moved quickly and unobtrusively among Fengbald's bigger horsemen. The rams seemed sure-footed as cats, and although Simon could see many small shapes of Qanuc dead and wounded scattered here and there among the other bodies, they seemed to be giving as good as they were getting, and perhaps better.

Simon himself had survived several more combats, and had killed another Thrithings-man, this time in a more or less fair fight.

It was only as he and this other were hacking at each other that Simon abruptly realized that to these enemies he was no child. He was taller than this particular mercenary, and in his helmet and mail-shirt, he doubtless seemed a large and fearsome fighter. Abruptly heartened, he had renewed his attack, driving the Thrithings-man backward. Then, as the man stopped and his horse came breast to breast with Homefinder, Simon remembered his lessons from Sludig. He feinted a clumsy swing and the mercenary seized the bait, leaning too far forward with his return stroke. Simon let the man's sword carry him well off-balance, then slammed his shield against the man's leather helm and followed with a sword thrust that slid between the two halves of the man's chest armor and into his unprotected side. The mercenary stayed in his saddle as Simon pulled Homefinder back, tugging loose his sword, but before Simon turned away his opponent had already fallen awkwardly to the bloody ice.

Panting, Simon had looked around him and wondered who was winning.

Whatever beliefs about the nobility of war that Simon still retained died during that long day on the frozen lake. In the midst of such terrible carnage, with fallen friends and enemies alike scattered about, maimed and bloodied, some even made faceless by terrible wounds; with the crying and pleading of dying men ringing in his ears, their dignity ripped away from them; with the air rank with the stenches of fear-sweat, blood, and excrement, it was impossible to see warfare as anything other than what Morgenes had once termed it: a kind of hell on earth that impatient mankind had arranged so it would not have to wait for the afterlife. To Simon, the grotesque unfairness of it was almost the worst of all. For every armored knight dragged down, half a dozen foot-soldiers were slaughtered. Even animals suffered torments that should not have been visited on murderers and traitors. Simon saw screaming horses, hamstrung by a chance blow, left to roll on the ice in agony. Although many of the horses belonged to Fengbald's troops, no one had asked them if they wanted to go to war; they had been forced to it, just as had Simon and the rest of the folk of New Gadrinsett. Even the king's Erkynguard might have wished to be elsewhere, rather than here on this killing ground where duty brought them and loyalty prisoned them. Only the mercenaries were here by choice. To Simon, the minds of men who would come to this of their own will were suddenly as incomprehensible as the thoughts of spiders or lizards—less so, even, for the small creatures of the earth almost always fled from danger. These were madmen, Simon realized, and that was the direst problem of the world: that madmen should be strong and unafraid, so that they could force their will on the weak and peace-loving. If God allowed such madness to be, Simon could not help thinking, then He was an old god who had lost His grip.

The sun was vanished high above, hiding behind clouds: it was impossible to tell how long the battle had raged when Josua's horn blew again. This time it was a summons note that sliced through the misty air. Simon, who did not think he had ever been wearier in his life, turned to the few trolls nearby and shouted: "*Sosa!* Come!"

A few moments later he nearly ran down Sisqi, who stood over her slaughtered ram, her face still strangely emotionless. Simon leaned toward her and extended his hand. She grasped it in her cold dry fingers and pulled herself up to his stirrup. He helped her into the saddle.

"Where is Binabik?" she asked him, shouting above the din.

"I don't know. Josua is calling us. We go to Josua now."

The horn blew again. The men of New Gadrinsett were falling back rapidly, as though they could not have fought a moment longer—which might not have been far from the truth—but they were retreating so swiftly that they seemed almost to evaporate around Simon, like the deposited foam of a sea-wave vanishing into the beach. Their departure left a knot of half a dozen trolls and a couple of Deornoth's foot-soldiers encircled by a ring of mounted Erkynguardsmen some fifty ells out on the ice. Without help, Simon knew, the defenders would be smothered. He looked around at the small company and grimaced. Too few to do any good, certainly. And those trolls had heard the retreat just as Simon and the others had—was it his duty to rescue everyone? He was tired and bleeding and frightened, and sanctuary was only a few moments away—he had survived, and that was almost a miracle!—but he knew he could not leave those brave folk behind.

"We go there?" he said to Sisqi, pointing to the clump of beleaguered defenders.

She looked and nodded wearily, then screamed something to the few surrounding Qanuc as Simon pulled Homefinder around and moved toward the Erkynguards at a slithering trot. The trolls fell in behind. There were no howls this time, no singing: the little company rode in the silence of utter exhaustion.

And then there was another nightmare of hacking and slashing. The top of Simon's shield was smashed by a sword blow, splinters of painted wood flying through the air. Several of his own blows struck against solid objects, but the chaos prevented him knowing what he had hit. The encircled trolls and men, seeing that help had come, redoubled their effort and managed to cut their way out, although at least one more of the Qanuc fell. His blood-spattered ram, when it had shaken its dead master's boot loose from the stirrup, leaped away from the corpse and ran off across the lake as though pursued by demons, zigzagging wildly until it vanished into the darkening mist. The weary Erkynguards, who after the initial moments seemed no more willing to prolong the struggle than Simon and his company, fought fiercely but gave ground, trying to herd Simon and the rest back toward the strength of Fengbald's forces. Simon finally saw an opening and shouted to Sisqi. With a last convulsion of soldiers and horses and trolls and rams, Simon's company broke away from the Erkynguards and fled toward Sesuad'ra and the waiting barricades.

Josua's horn was blowing again as Simon and the trolls—less than two score gathered together, he noted with dismay—reached the great wall of logs at the base of the hill-trail. Many of Sesuad'ra's other defenders were around them, and even those who were unwounded looked as beaten down and gray as dying men. A few of Hotvig's Thrithings-folk, however, were singing hoarsely, and Simon saw one of them had what looked like a pair of bloody heads dangling from his saddle-horn, bouncing to the horse's strides.

An immense feeling of relief struck Simon as he saw Prince Josua himself standing before the barricade, waving Naidel in the air like a banner and shouting to the returning combatants. The prince was grim, but his words were meant to be heartening.

"Come on," he cried. "We have given them a taste of their own blood! We have showed them some teeth! Back now, back—they will come no more this day!"

Again, even through the chill that had settled on his heart like a frost, Simon felt a deep and loving loyalty toward Josua—but he also knew that the prince had little left to offer except brave words. Sesuad'ra's defenders had nearly held their own against better trained and better equipped forces, but they could hardly match Fengbald body for body—the duke had almost three times as many men—and now any element of surprise, such as Binabik's boot-irons, had been played to its utmost. From here on, the war would be one of attrition, and Simon knew that he would be on the losing side.

On the ice behind them the ravens were already feeding on the fallen. The birds hopped and pecked and argued raucously among themselves. Half-hidden by the mist, they might have been tiny black demons come to gloat at the destruction.

Sesuad'ra's defenders limped up the hillside, leading their panting mounts. Although he felt curiously numb, Simon was still pleased to see that more of the Qanuc had survived than just those he and Sisqi had led off the ice. These other survivors rushed forward to greet their kin with cries of happiness, although there were sounds of keening sorrow, too, as the trolls counted their losses.

For Simon, an even greater joy came when he saw Binabik standing with Josua. Sisqi saw him, too. She leaped down from Simon's saddle and rushed to her betrothed. The two of them embraced at Josua's side, heedless of the prince or anyone else.

Simon watched them for a moment before staggering on. He knew he should look for his other friends, but at the moment he felt so battered and wrung out that it was as much as he could do just to put one foot before the other. Someone walking beside him passed him a cup of wine. When he had drunk it off and handed the cup back, he took a few limping steps up the hill to where the

campfires had been lit. Now that the day's fighting had
ended, some of the women of New Gadrinsett had come
down to bring food and to help care for the wounded.
One of them, a young girl with stringy hair, handed Simon a bowl of something that faintly steamed. He tried to
thank her, but could not summon the strength to speak.

Although the sun was just now touching the western
horizon and the day was still quite light, Simon had no
sooner finished his thin soup than he found himself lying
on the muddy ground, still wearing all of his armor but
for his helm, his head cushioned on his cloak. Homefinder stood nearby, cropping at the few thin stalks of
grass that had survived the general trampling. A moment
later Simon felt himself sliding down toward sleep. The
world seemed to tilt back and forth around him, as though
he lay on the deck of some huge, slow-rolling ship.
Blackness was coming on fast—not the black of night,
but a deep and smothering dark that welled up from inside him. If he dreamed, he knew, for once it would not
be of towers or giant wheels. He would see screaming
horses, and a rat drowning in a rain barrel.

Isaak, the young page, leaned close to the brazier, trying to absorb some warmth. He was chilled right through.
Outside, the wind strummed on the ropes and poked at the
rippling walls of Duke Fengbald's vast tent as though
seeking to uproot it and carry it away into the night. Isaak
wished he had never been forced to leave the Hayholt.

"Boy!" Fengbald cried. There was an edge of violence
in his voice, barely contained. "Where is my wine?"

"Just mulling, Lord," Isaak said. He took the iron out
of the pitcher and hurried to replenish the duke's goblet.

Fengbald ignored him as he poured, turning his attention to Lezhdraka, who stood by scowling, still dressed in
his bloodied leather armor. By contrast, the duke was
bathed—Isaak had been forced to heat innumerable pots
of water on the one small bed of coals—and wore a robe
of scarlet silk. He had put on a pair of doeskin slippers,

and his long, black hair hung on his shoulders in wet ringlets. "I will listen to no more of this nonsense," he told the mercenary captain.

"Nonsense?" Lezhdraka snarled. "You say that to me! I saw the magic folk with my own eyes, stone-dweller!"

Fengbald's eyes narrowed. "You had better learn to speak more respectfully, plainsman."

Lezhdraka clenched his fists, but kept his arms at his side. "Still, I saw them—you did, too."

The duke made a noise of disgust. "I saw a troop of dwarfs—freaks, such as can be seen tumbling and capering before most of the thrones of Osten Ard. Those were not the Sithi, whatever Josua and this scrub-woman Geloë might claim."

"Dwarfs or fairy-folk I cannot prove, but that other is no ordinary woman," Lezhdraka said darkly. "Her name is well-known in the grasslands—well-known and well-feared. Men who go into her forest do not return."

"Ridiculous." Fengbald drained his cup. "I do not quickly mock the dark powers ..." he trailed off, as though some uncomfortable memory was clamoring for attention, ". . . I do not mock, but neither will I *be* mocked. And I will not be frightened by conjuring tricks, however they may affect superstitious savages."

The Thrithings-man stared at him for a moment, his face suddenly gone serenely cold. "Your master, from what you have said before, has dabbled much in what you call 'superstition.' "

Fengbald's return glance was equally chilly. "I call no man master. Elias is the king, that is all." The moment of imperiousness quickly dissolved. "Isaak!" he called petulantly. "More wine, damn you." As the page scurried to serve him, Fengbald shook his head. "Enough quibbling. We have a problem, Lezhdraka. I want to solve it."

The mercenary chief folded his arms. "My men do not like the idea of Josua having magical allies," he growled, "—but do not fear. They are not womanish. They will fight anyway. Our legends have long told us that fairy-blood spills just as man-blood does. We proved that today."

Fengbald made an impatient gesture. "But we cannot afford to beat them this way. They are stronger than I thought. How can I return to Elias with most of his Erkynguard dead at the hands of a few cornered peasants?" He tapped his finger on the rim of his goblet. "No, there are other ways, ways that will assure that I return to Erkynland in triumph."

Lezhdraka snorted. "There are no other ways. What, some secret track, some hidden road as you talked of before? Your spies did not come back, I notice. No, the only way now is the way we have started. We will beat them down until none are left."

Fengbald was no longer paying attention. His gaze had shifted to the door flap of the tent and a soldier who stood there, unsure of whether to come in. "Ah," the duke said. "Yes?"

The soldier dropped to one knee. "The captain of the guard has sent me, Lord . . ."

"Good." Fengbald settled back in his chair. "And you have brought with you a certain person, yes?"

"Yes, Lord."

"Bring him in, then wait outside until I summon you again."

The soldier went, trying to hide a look of dismay at having to stand outside the tent in the jagged wind. Fengbald threw a mocking glance toward Lezhdraka. "One of my spies *has* come back, it appears."

A moment later the tent flap opened again. An old man stumbled in, his ragged clothes speckled with snowflakes.

Fengbald grinned hugely. "Ah, you have returned to us! Helfgrim, is it not?" The duke turned to Lezhdraka, his good humor returning as he played out his little show. "You remember the Lord Mayor of Gadrinsett, don't you, Lezhdraka? He left us for a while to go a-visiting, but now he has returned." The duke's voice became harsh. "Did you get away unseen?"

Helfgrim nodded miserably. "Things are confused. No one has seen me since the battle started. There are others missing, too, and bodies still lost on the ice and in the forest along the hill's base."

"Good." Fengbald snapped his fingers, pleased. "And of course you have done what I asked?"

The old man lowered his head. "There is nothing, Lord."

Fengbald stared at him for a moment. Color rose in the duke's face and he began to stand, then sat down again, clenching his fists. "So. You seem to have forgotten what I told you."

"What is all this?" Lezhdraka asked, irritated.

The duke ignored him. "Isaak," he called, "fetch the guard."

When the shivering soldier had come in, Fengbald summoned him to his side, then whispered a few words in his ear. The soldier went out through the flap once more.

"We will try again," Fengbald said, turning his attention back to the Lord Mayor. "What did you find out?"

Helfgrim could not seem to meet his eyes. The old man's weak-chinned, reddish face worked as though with some barely hidden grief. "Nothing of use, my lord," he said at last.

Fengbald had evidently gained control of his anger, for he only smiled tightly. A few moments later, the tent flap bulged once more. The guard came in, accompanied this time by two more guardsmen. They were escorting a pair of women, both of middle years, with threads of gray in their dark hair, both of them grimy and dressed in threadbare cloaks. The ashen, fearful expressions of the women changed to startlement as they saw the old man who cringed before Fengbald.

"Father!" one of them cried.

"Oh, merciful Usires," the other said, and made the sign of the Tree.

Fengbald surveyed the scene coolly. "You seemed to have forgotten who holds the whip hand, Helfgrim. Now, let me try again. If you lie to me, I will have to cause your daughters pain, much as it troubles my Aedonite conscience. Still, it will be your conscience that will suffer most, for it will be your fault." He smirked. "Speak."

The old man looked at his daughters, at the terror on their faces. "God forgive me," he said. "God forgive for a traitor!"

"Don't you do it, Father," one of the women cried. The other daughter was sobbing helplessly, her face buried in the sleeve of her cape.

"I cannot do other." Helfgrim turned to the duke. "Yes," he said quaveringly. "There is another way onto the hill, one that only a few of the folk there know. It is another old Sithi track. Josua has put a guard onto it, but only a token force, since the bottom of it is hidden by overgrowth. He showed it to me when we were planning his defense."

"A token force, eh?" Fengbald grinned and looked triumphantly at Lezhdraka. "And this track, it is wide enough for how many?"

Helfgrim's voice was so low as to be almost inaudible. "A dozen could march abreast, once the first few cubits of brambles are cleared away."

The mercenary captain, who had listened quietly for a long time, now stepped forward. He was angry, and his scars showed white against his dark face. "You are too trusting," he snarled at Fengbald. "How do you know this is no trap? How do you know that Josua will not be waiting for us with his whole army?"

Fengbald was unmoved. "You grasslanders are too simple-minded, Lezhdraka—did I not tell you that before? Josua's army will be busy trying to fight off our frontal assault tomorrow—far too busy to spare any more soldiers than his token force—when we go to make our surprise visit on Helfgrim's other road. *We* will take a sizable company. And just to make sure that there is no treachery, we will take the Lord Mayor with us."

At this, the two women burst into tears. "Please, do not take him into battle," one said desperately. "He is but an old man!"

"That is true." Fengbald appeared to consider the point. "And hence he might not be afraid to die, if there *is* some kind of trap—if Josua's force is more than token. So we will take you, too."

Helfgrim leaped up. "No! You cannot risk their lives! They are innocent!"

"And they will be safe as doves in a dovecote," Fengbald grinned, "as long as your story has been true. But if you have tried to betray me, they will die. Quickly, but painfully."

The old man begged him again, but the duke slouched back in his chair, unmoved. At last the Lord Mayor went to his daughters. "It will be well." He patted them awkwardly, inhibited by the presence of cruel strangers. "We will be together. No harm will come." He turned to Fengbald, anger showing beneath his trembling features; for a moment his voice almost lost its quaver. "There is no trap, damn you—you will see—but there are a few dozen men, as I said. I have betrayed the prince for you. You must show honor toward my children, and keep them out of danger if there is fighting. Please."

Fengbald waved his hand expansively. "Never fear. I promise on my honor as a nobleman that when we hold this dreadful hill and Josua is dead, you and your daughters will go free. And you will tell those you meet that Duke Fengbald keeps his bargains." He rose and gestured to the guards. "Now take them all three away—and keep them separate from the rest of their folk."

After the prisoners had been removed, Fengbald turned to Lezhdraka. "Why so silent, man? Can you not admit you were wrong—that I have solved our problem?"

The Thrithings-man seemed to want to argue, but instead reluctantly nodded his head. "These stone-dwellers are soft. No Thrithings-man would betray his people for the sake of two daughters."

Fengbald laughed. "We stone-dwellers, as you call us, treat our women differently than you louts do." He walked to the brazier and warmed his long hands over the coals. "And tomorrow, Lezhdraka, I shall show you how *this* stone-dweller treats his enemies—especially those who have defied him as Prince Josua has." He narrowed his lips. "That cursed fairy-hill will run red with blood."

He stared into the gleaming embers, a smile curling the corners of his mouth. The wind wailed outside and rubbed against the tent cloth like an animal.

13

The Nest Builders

Tiamak stared at the still water. His mind was only half on his task, so when the fish appeared, a dark shadow flitting between the water lilies, the Wrannaman's strike was far too late. Tiamak stared down at the handful of dripping vegetation in disgust and dropped the clump of weeds back into the muddied water. Any fish in the vicinity would be long gone now.

They Who Watch and Shape, he thought miserably, *why have you done this to me?*

He moved closer to the edge of the waterway and sloshed as delicately as he could down to the next backwater, then set himself in place to begin his wait once more.

Ever since he had been a small boy, it seemed, he had gotten less than he wanted. As the youngest of six children, he had always felt that his brothers and sisters ate better than he did, that when the bowl came at last to Tiamak, there was little left. He had not grown up as large as any of his three brothers or his father Tugumak, nor had he ever been able to catch fish as well as his swift sister Twiyah, or find as many useful roots and berries as his clever sister Rimihe. When at last he had found something he could do better than anyone else—namely, master the drylander skills of reading and writing, and even learn to speak the drylander tongues—this also proved too small a gift. This scurrying after the knowledge of drylanders made scant sense to his family, or to the other residents of Village Grove. When he went away to

Perdruin to study in a drylander school, were they proud? Of course not. Despite the fact that no other Wrannaman in memory had done it—or perhaps because of that—his family could not understand his ambitions. And the drylanders themselves, all but a very few, were openly scornful of his gifts. The indifferent teachers and mocking students had let young Tiamak know in no uncertain terms that no matter how many scrolls and books and learned discussions he devoured, he would never be anything better than a savage, a performing animal who had mastered a clever trick.

So it had been for all of his life until this fatal year, his only meager comforts found in his studies and the occasional correspondence of the Scrollbearers. Now, as if They Who Watch and Shape sought to pay all back in a single season, everything that came to him was *too much*—far, far too much.

This is how the gods mock us, he thought bitterly. *They take our fondest wish, then grant it in such a way that we beg to be released from it. And to think that I had stopped believing in them!*

They Who Watch and Shape had set the trap neatly enough, of that there was no doubt. First they had forced him to choose between his kin and his friends, then they had sent the crocodile that forced him to fail his kin. Now his friends needed to be conducted through the vast marshlands, in fact depended on him for their very lives, but the only safe route would take him back through Village Grove, back to the people he had forsaken. Tiamak only wished that he himself could have learned to build such a faultless snare—he would have eaten crabs for supper every night!

He stood hip-deep in the greenish water and pondered. What could he do? If he returned to his village, his shame would be known to all. It might even be possible that they would not let him go again, holding him as a traitor against the clan. But if he tried to avoid the wrath of the villagers, he would have to go leagues out of the way to find a suitable boat. The only other villages close to this end of the Wran, High Branch Houses, Yellow Trees, or

Flower-in-the-Rock, were all farther to the south. To go to
one would mean leaving the main arterial waterways and
crossing some of the most dangerous stretches of the entire marsh. Still, there was no choice: they had to stop in
Village Grove or one of the farther settlements, for without a flatboat Tiamak and his companions would never
reach the Lake Thrithing. As it was, their present craft
was leaking badly. They had already been forced to make
several dangerous trips across the unpredictable mud,
carrying the boat around places in the waterway that were
too shallow.

Tiamak sighed. What was it that Isgrimnur himself had
said? Life seemed nothing but difficult choices these
days—and he was right.

There was a flirt of shadow between his knees. Tiamak
swiftly darted a hand down and felt his fingers close
around something small and slippery. He lifted it high,
holding tightly. It was a fish, a pinch-eye, although not a
very large one. Still, it was better than no fish at all. He
turned and pulled up the cloth sack that floated beside
him, anchored to a thick root. He dropped the wriggling
thing in, tightened the drawstring, then lowered the sack
back into the water. A good omen, perhaps. Tiamak
closed his eyes to make a short prayer of thanks, hoping
that the gods, like children, could be confirmed in good
behavior by praise. When he had finished, he gave his attention back to the green water once more.

Miriamele was doing her best to keep the fire going,
but it was difficult. Since entering the marshes they had
found nothing that resembled dry wood, and the small
blazes they had been able to light burned fitfully at best.

She looked up as Tiamak returned. His thin brown face
was closed, and he only nodded as he put down a leaf-
wrapped bundle, then continued to where Isgrimnur and
the others were working on the boat. The Wrannaman
seemed very shy: he had said only a few words to
Miriamele in the two days since they had left Kwanitupul.

She wondered briefly if he might be embarrassed by his lilting Wrannaman accent. Miriamele dismissed the thought: Tiamak spoke the Westerling tongue better than most people who had grown up with it, and Isgrimnur's thick consonants and Cadrach's musical Hernystiri vowels were far more noticeable than the slight up and down quality of the marsh man's speech.

Miriamele unbundled the fish Tiamak had brought and gutted them, wiping her knife clean on the leaves before sheathing it again. She had never cooked in her life before fleeing the Hayholt, but traveling with Cadrach she had been forced to learn, if only to avoid starving on those frequent nights when he was too drunk to be of any help. She wondered if there was some marsh plant that might add flavor—perhaps she could wrap the fish in the leaves and steam them. She wandered over to ask the Wrannaman for advice.

Tiamak stood watching as Isgrimnur, Cadrach, and Camaris tried for the fourth or fifth time to seal the leaks that kept the bottom of their small boat almost constantly full of water. The marsh man held himself a little apart, as though to stand shoulder to shoulder with these drylanders might be presumptuous, but Miriamele suddenly found herself wondering if she might have it backward: maybe Wrannamen did not feel that those who lived outside the marsh were worth very much. Could Tiamak's stolidity be pride rather than shyness? She had heard that some savages, like the Thrithings-men, actually looked down on those who lived in cities. Could that be true with Tiamak, too? She realized now that she knew little about people outside the courts of Nabban and Erkynland, although she had always thought herself a shrewd judge of humanity. However, it was a much larger and more complicated world on the other side of the castle walls than she had ever suspected.

She reached out a hand toward the Wrannaman's shoulder, then pulled it back again. "Tiamak?" she said.

He jumped, startled. "Yes, Lady Miriamele?"

"I would like to ask you some questions about plants—for the cook-pot, that is."

He lowered his eyes and nodded. Miriamele could not believe that this was a man too proud to speak. The two of them walked back to the fire. After she had asked him a few questions and had shown that she was genuinely interested, he began to talk more freely. Miriamele was astonished. Although his reserve did not completely vanish, the Wrannaman turned out to be so full of plant lore, and so pleased to share some of it, that she quickly found herself overwhelmed with information. He found for her half a dozen flowers and roots and leaves that could be safely used to add savor to food, plucking them as he walked her around the campsite and down to the water's edge, and he listed a dozen more that they would encounter as they traveled through the Wran. Caught up, he began to point out other bits of greenery that were useful as medicine or ink or countless other things.

"How do you know so much?"

Tiamak stopped as if he had been struck. "I am sorry, Lady Miriamele," he said quietly. "You did not wish to hear all this."

Miriamele laughed. "I think it's wonderful. But where did you learn it all?"

"I have studied these things for many years."

"You must know more than anyone in the world!"

Tiamak averted his face. Miriamele was fascinated. Was he blushing? "No," he said, "no, I am just a student." He looked up shyly, but with a hint of pride. "But someday I do hope that my studies will be known—that my name will be remembered."

"I'm sure that it will." She was still somewhat awed. This slender little man with his unruly mop of thinning black hair, dressed now like any other Wrannaman in nothing but a belt and a loincloth, seemed as learned as any of the writing-priests of the Hayholt! "No wonder Morgenes and Dinivan were your friends."

His pleased look abruptly evaporated, leaving behind a kind of sadness. "Thank you, Lady Miriamele. Now I will leave you to do what you will with those small fish. I have bored you long enough."

He turned and walked back across the marshy clearing,

stepping without visible attention from one tussock of
solid earth to another, so that when he reached the far side
and sat down on a log his feet were still dry. Miriamele,
who had mud up to her shins, was forced to admire his
sure-footedness.

But what did I say to upset him? She shrugged and
took her handful of marsh-blossoms back to the waiting
fish.

After supper—Tiamak's savory touches had proven
most welcome—the company stayed seated around the
fire. The air remained warm, but the sun had gone down
behind the trees and the marsh was filling with shadows.
An army of frogs that had begun booming and croaking
at the first onset of evening was contesting with a vast array of whistling, chirping, and screeching birds, so that
the twilight was as noisy as a holiday fair.

"How big is the Wran?" Miriamele asked.

"It is almost as large as the peninsula of Nabban," said
Tiamak. "But we will only have to cross a small part of
it, since we are already in the northernmost region."

"And how long will it take, O guide?" Cadrach was
leaning back against a log, trying to make a flute out of
a marsh reed. Several crumpled stalks, the victims of previous attempts, lay beside him.

The sad look that Miriamele had seen earlier returned
to the Wrannaman's face. "That depends."

Isgrimnur cocked a bushy eyebrow. "Depends on what,
little man?"

"On which way we go." Tiamak sighed. "Perhaps it is
best I share my worries with you. I suppose it is not a decision I should make alone."

"Speak, man," the duke said.

Tiamak told them of his dilemma. He made it plain that
it was not only the shame of returning to his village-folk
after having failed their errand that he feared, but that
even if the rest of the company were allowed to leave
again, Tiamak himself might not be, stranding them deep
in the Wran without a guide.

"Could we not hire another of the villagers?" Isgrimnur

asked. "Not that we want to see anything happen to you, of course," he added hastily.

"Of course." Tiamak's glance was cool. "As to your question, I do not know. Our clan has never been one to cause trouble for others, unless actual harm is done to someone of Village Grove, but that does not mean that the elders might not prevent anyone in the settlement from helping you. It is hard to say."

The company debated as night came on. Tiamak did his best to explain the distance and the dangers involved in a trip to any alternate settlement south of Village Grove. At last, as a troop of chittering apes scrambled past overhead, making the tree branches dip and waver, they arrived at a decision.

"It's hard, Tiamak," Isgrimnur said, "and we will not force you against your will, but it seems best we go to your village."

The Wrannaman nodded solemnly. "I agree. Even though I have done no wrong to the clanfolk of High Branch Houses or Yellow Trees, there is no certainty that they would take kindly to strangers. At least my people have been tolerant of the few drylanders that have come." He sighed. "I think I will walk for a short while. Please, stay near the fire." He rose and ambled down toward the waterway, quickly vanishing in the shadows.

Camaris, bored by the others' talk, had long since curled up with his head on a cloak and gone to sleep, his long legs drawn up like a small child's. Miriamele, Isgrimnur, and Cadrach faced each other over the flickering blaze. The hidden birds, who had quieted as Tiamak walked out of the campsite, swelled into raucous voice again.

"He seems very sad," Miriamele said.

Isgrimnur yawned. "He's been steady enough, in his way."

"Poor man." Miriamele lowered her voice, worried that the Wrannaman might return and hear them. No one liked to be pitied. "He knows a lot about plants and flowers. It's too bad that he has to live so far away from people who could understand him."

"He is not the only one with such a problem," said Cadrach, mostly to himself.

Miriamele was watching a small deer, white-spotted and round-eyed, that had come down to the watercourse to drink. She held her breath as it stilted along the sandy bank, a bare three cubits from the boat; her companions had all fallen silent in the afternoon heat, so there was nothing to frighten the deer away. Miriamele rested her chin on the railing of the boat, marveling at the creature's graceful movements.

As it dipped its nose to the muddy river, a toothy snout suddenly erupted from the water. Before it could leap back, the little deer was seized by the crocodile and dragged down thrashing into the brown darkness. Nothing remained but ripples. Miriamele turned away, revolted and more than a little frightened. How swiftly death had come!

The more she watched, the more fickle the Wran seemed, a place of waving fronds, shifting shadows, and constant movement. For every beauty—great bell-like scarlet flowers as heavily scented as any Nabbanai dowager, or hummingbirds like streaks of jeweled light— Miriamele saw what seemed to be a corresponding ugliness, like the great gray spiders, large as supper bowls, that clung to the overhanging branches.

In the trees she saw birds of a thousand colors, and mocking apes, and even dappled snakes that hung from the branches like swollen vines. At sunset, clouds of bats leaped out from the upper branches and turned the sky into a whirling storm of wings. Insects, too, were everywhere, buzzing, stinging, wings shimmering in the uneven sunlight. Even vegetation moved and shifted, the reeds and trees bending in the wind, the water plants bobbing with every ripple. The Wran was a tapestry in which every thread seemed to be in motion. Everything was alive.

Miriamele remembered the Aldheorte, which had also been a place of life, of deep roots and quiet power, but that forest had been old and settled. Like an ancient people, it seemed to have found its own stately music, its own measured and unchanging pace. She remembered thinking that the Aldheorte could easily remain just as it was until the end of time. The Wran seemed to be inventing itself every moment, as though it were a curl of foam on the boiling edge of creation. Miriamele could just as easily imagine returning in twenty years to find it a howling desert, or a jungle so thick that there would be no passage through it, a clot of green and black where the twining leaves would shut out the very light of the sun.

As the days passed and the boat and its small crew moved deeper into the marshlands, Miriamele felt a weight lift from her being. She felt anger still, at her father and his terrible choices, at Aspitis who had tricked her and violated her, at the supposedly kindly God that had so twisted her own life from her grasp . . . but it was an anger that did not bite so fiercely now. When all around her was so full of weirdly vibrant and changing life, it was hard to hold on to the bitter feelings that had ruled her in the weeks before. When the world was ceaselessly recreating itself on every side, it was almost impossible for her not to feel as though she, too, were being made anew.

"What are all these bones?" Miramele asked. On either side of the waterway, the shoreline was littered with skeletons, a jumble of spines and rib cages like the bleached staves of ruined ships, strangely white against the mud. "I hope they belong to animals."

"We are all animals," said Cadrach. "We all have bones."

"What are you trying to do, monk, frighten the girl?" Isgrimnur said angrily. "Look at those skulls. Those were cockindrills, not men."

"Ssshh." Tiamak turned from the prow of the boat. "Duke Isgrimnur is right. They are the bones of crocodiles. But you must be quiet for a while now. We are coming to the Pool of Sekob."

"What is that?"

"It is the reason for all these remains." The Wrannaman's eyes lit on Camaris, who was trailing his

veined hand in the water, watching the ripples with the
absorbed stare of childhood. "Isgrimnur! Do not let him
do that!"

The duke turned and lifted Camaris' hand out of the
water. The old man looked at him with mild reproach, but
kept his dripping hand in his lap.

"Now, please be quiet for a little while," said Tiamak.
"And row slowly. Do not splash."

"What is this all about?" Isgrimnur demanded, but at a
look from the Wrannaman he fell silent. He and
Miriamele did their best to make their touch on the oars
gentle and steady.

The boat floated down a waterway so draped with the
fronds of leaning willows that it seemed hung with a solid
green curtain. When they had passed the willows, they
discovered that the passage had suddenly opened before
them into a wide, still lake. Banyan trees grew down to
the water's edge, serpentine roots forming a wall of curling wood around most of the lake. On the far side the
banyans fell away and the lake floor sloped up into a
broad beach of pale sand. A few small islands, mere
bumps on the surface of the water near the beach, were
the only thing that marred the lake's glassy smoothness.
A pair of bitterns stalked along the water's edge at the
near end, bending to probe in the mud. Miriamele thought
that the wide strand looked like a wonderful place to
camp—the lake itself seemed an airy paradise after some
of the wet and tangled places they had stopped—and she
was about to say so when Tiamak's fierce look stilled her.
She supposed that this was some kind of sacred spot for
the Wrannaman and his folk. Still, there was no cause for
him to treat her like a misbehaving child.

Miriamele turned away from Tiamak and looked out
across the lake, memorizing it so that someday she would
be able to summon up the feeling of pure peace it represented. As she did, she had a sudden disquieting sensation
that the lake was moving, that the water was flowing
away to one side. A moment later she realized that it was
the small islands that were moving instead. Crocodiles!
She had been fooled before, seen other logs and sandbars

that abruptly lurched into life; she smiled at her own city-bred innocence. Perhaps it would not be such a wonderful choice for camp after all—still, a few crocodiles did not spoil the looks of the place. . . .

The moving bumps rose farther out of the water as they neared the beach. It was only when the immense, impossible thing finally crawled up onto the sand, dragging its bloated form into the clear light of the sun, that Miriamele finally realized that there was only one crocodile.

"God's mercy on us!" Cadrach said in a strangled whisper. Isgrimnur echoed him.

The great beast, long as ten men, wide as a mason's barge, turned its head to regard the little boat slipping across the lake. Both Miriamele and Isgrimnur ceased rowing, hands clammy and nerveless on the sweeps.

"Don't stop!" Tiamak hissed. "Slowly, slowly, but keep going!"

Even across the expanse of water, Miriamele thought she could see the creature's eye glitter as it watched them, feel its cold and ancient stare. When the immense legs shifted and the clawed feet dug briefly at the ground as though the giant would turn and re-enter the water, Miriamele feared her heart would stop. But the great crocodile did no more than send a few gouts of sand into the air, then the huge, knobby head dropped down to the beach and the yellow eye closed.

When they had made their way across to the waterway's outlet, Miriamele and Isgrimnur began rowing hard, as if by silent agreement. After a few moments they were breathing heavily. Tiamak told them to stop.

"We are safe," he said. "The time has long gone when he could follow us up this way. He has gotten far too big."

"What was it?" Miriamele gasped. "It was horrible."

"Old Sekob. My folk call him the grandfather of all crocodiles. I do not know if that is true, but he is certainly the master of all his kind. Year after year other crocodiles come to fight him. Year after year he feeds on these challengers, swallows them whole, so he never has to hunt

any more. The strongest of all sometimes escape the lake
and crawl as far away as the riverbank before they die.
Those were the bones you saw."

"I've never seen anything like it." Cadrach had gone
quite pale, but there was a quality of exhilaration in his
tone. "Like one of the great dragons!"

"He is the dragon of the Wran," Tiamak agreed. "There
is no doubt of that. But unlike drylanders, we marsh-folk
leave our dragons alone. He is no threat to us, and he kills
many of the largest man-eaters that would otherwise prey
on the Wran people. So we show him respect. Old Sekob
is far too well-fed to need to chase such a puny morsel as
we would make."

"So why did you want us to be quiet?" asked
Miriamele.

Tiamak gave her a dry look. "He might not need to eat
us, but you do not go into the king's throne room and
play children's games, either. Especially when the king is
old and quick to temper."

"Elysia, Mother of God." Isgrimnur shook his head.
Sweat beaded his forehead, although the day was not particularly warm. "No, we certainly would not want to get
that old fellow upset."

"Now come," said Tiamak. "If we keep on until first
dark, we should be able to reach Village Grove by tomorrow midday."

As they traveled, the Wrannaman became more talka-
tive. When they had reached waters so shallow that
rowing was no use, there was little else to do but listen
to each others' stories as Tiamak stood and poled the boat
along. Under Miriamele's questioning he told them much
about the life of the Wran, as well as about his own unusual choices which had marked him out from his fellow
villagers.

"But your people have no king?" she asked.

"No." The small man thought for a moment. "We have
elders, or we call them that, but some of them are no
older than I am. Any man can become one."

"How? By asking to?"

"No. By giving feasts." He smiled shyly. "When a man has a wife and children—and whatever other family lives with him—and can feed them all with some left over, he begins to give what is left to others. In return, he might ask for something like a boat or new fishing floats, or if he chooses he can say: 'I will ask payment when I give my feast.' Then, when he is owed enough, he 'calls for the crabs,' as we say, which means he asks all those who owe him things to pay him back; then he invites everyone in the village for a feast. If everyone is satisfied, that man becomes an elder. He must then give such a feast once every year, or he will not be an elder in that year."

"Sounds daft," Isgrimnur grumbled, scratching. He had been by far the greatest target for the local insect life; his broad face was covered in bumps. Miriamele understood, and forgave him his short temper.

"No more daft than passing land down from father to son." Cadrach's response was mild, but held an edge of sarcasm. "Or getting it in the first place by braining your neighbor with an ax—as your folk did until fairly recently, Duke."

"No man should have what he is not strong enough to protect," Isgrimnur responded, but he seemed more preoccupied with digging at a difficult spot between his shoulder blades than with continuing the debate.

"I think," Tiamak said quietly, "that it is a good way. It makes certain that no one starves and that no one hoards his wealth. Until I studied in Perdruin, I could not imagine that there was another way of doing things."

"But if a man doesn't wish to be an elder," Miriamele pointed out, "then there's nothing to make him give up the things he is gathering."

"Ah, but then no one in the village thinks very highly of him." Tiamak grinned. "Also, since the elders decide what is best for the village, they might just decide that the excellent fish pond beside which a rich and selfish man has built his house now belongs to all the village. There is little sense in being rich and not being an elder—it causes jealousy, you see."

Duke Isgrimnur continued to scratch. Tiamak and

Cadrach fell into a quiet conversation about some of the
more intricate points of Wran theology. Miriamele, who
had grown tired of talk, took the opportunity to watch old
Camaris.

Miriamele could stare without embarrassment: the tall
man seemed quite uncaring, no more interested in the
business of his fellows than a horse in a paddock might
be with the traders talking by the fence. Observing his
bland but certainly not stupid face, it was almost impossible to believe that she was in the presence of a legend.
The name of Camaris-sá-Vinitta was nearly as famous as
that of her grandfather Prester John, and both of them,
she felt sure, would be remembered by generations yet
unborn. Yet here he was, old and witless, when all the
world had thought him dead. How could such a thing
have come to pass? What secrets hid behind his guileless
exterior?

Her attention was drawn down to the old knight's
hands. Gnarled and callused by decades of toil at
Pelippa's Bowl and on countless battlefields, they were
still somehow quite noble, huge and long-fingered but
gentle. She watched him twisting aimlessly at the material
of his ragged breeches and wondered how such deft, careful hands could have dealt death as swiftly and terribly as
his legend said. Still, she had seen his strength, which
would have been impressive even in a man half his age,
and in the few moments of danger the little company had
experienced in the Wran, when the boat had threatened to
overturn or someone had fallen into a pit of sucking mud,
he had responded with amazing quickness.

Miriamele's eyes strayed back to Camaris' face once
more. Before encountering him at the inn, she had never
met him, of course—he had disappeared a quarter of a
century before her birth—but there was something trou-
blingly familiar about his face. It was something that she
only saw at certain angles, a phantom glint that left her
feeling as though she were on the verge of some revelation, of some profound recognition ... but the moment
would always pass and the familiarity would disappear.
Just now, for instance, the nagging sensation was not

present: at this moment, Camaris looked like nothing but a handsome old man with a particularly serene and other-worldly expression.

Perhaps it was only the paintings and tapestries, Miriamele reasoned—after all, she had seen so many pictures of this famous man! There were likenesses of him in the Hayholt, in the ducal palace at Nabban, even in Meremund . . . although Elias had only hung them when his father John was coming, to honor the old man's friendship with Osten Ard's greatest knight. Her father Elias, who had considered himself the paramount knight of his father's kingdom in latter days, had shown little patience with stories of the old times of the Great Table, and particularly with tales about the splendor of Camaris. . . .

Miriamele's thoughts were interrupted by Tiamak's announcement that they were nearing Village Grove.

"I hope you will forgive me if we stop and spend the night at my little house," he said. "I have not seen it for several months and I would like to make sure that my birds have survived. It would take us another hour or so to reach the village anyway, and it is later in the day than I thought it would be." He waved a hand toward the reddening western sky. "We may as well wait until morning to go see the elders."

"I hope your house has curtains to keep the bugs out," Isgrimnur said somewhat plaintively.

"Your birds?" Cadrach was interested. "From Morgenes?"

Tiamak nodded. "To begin with, although I have long since been raising my own. But Morgenes taught me the art, it is true."

"Could we use them to send a message to Josua?" Miriamele asked.

"Not to Josua," Tiamak said, frowning in thought. "But if you know of any Scrollbearers who might be with him we could try. These birds cannot find just anybody. Except for certain people whom they have been trained to seek out, they only know places, like any ordinary messenger birds. In any case, we will talk about this when we are under my roof."

* * *

Tiamak guided the boat through a succession of tiny streamlets, some so shallow that the whole company was forced to stand waist-deep in the water to lift the rowboat over the sandbars. At last they entered a slow-moving waterway that took them down a long alley of banyan trees. They drew up at last before a hut so cunningly hidden that they would surely have drifted past if its owner were not guiding the boat. Tiamak hooked down the ladder of twisted vines and one by one they climbed up into the Wrannaman's house.

Miriamele was disappointed to find the interior of the hut so spare. It was obvious that the little scholar was a man of humble means, but she had at least hoped in this, her first experience of a Wran dwelling, to find a little more in the way of exotic furnishings. There were neither beds, tables, nor chairs. Other than the firepit set into the floor of the house beneath a cleverly vented smoke hole, the only household belongings were a small chest of wickerwork, another much larger and sturdier wooden chest, a stretched-bark writing board, and a few other odds and ends. Still, it was dry, and that alone was such a change from the last few days that Miriamele was grateful.

Tiamak showed Cadrach the wood piled beneath the eaves outside one of the high windows, then left the monk to start a fire while he himself clambered up onto the roof to see to his birds. Camaris, whose height made him seem a giant in the small house—although Isgrimnur was not much shorter and was certainly a great deal heavier—squatted uncomfortably in the corner.

Tiamak appeared at the window, upside down. He was leaning over the edge of the roof, and he was clearly delighted. "Look!" He held up a handful of powdery gray. "It is Honey-Lover! She has come back! Many of the others, too!" He disappeared from sight as though jerked up by a string. After a moment, Camaris went to the window and climbed out after him with his usual surprising dexterity.

"Now if we could only find something to eat," Isgrimnur said. "I don't really trust Tiamak's marsh-muck—not that I'm not grateful." He wet his lips. "It's just that I wouldn't turn down a joint of beef or something like. Keep our strength up."

Miriamele could not help laughing. "I don't think there are many cows in the Wran."

"Can't be sure," Isgrimnur muttered distractedly. "It's a strange place. Could be anything here."

"We met the grandfather of all crocodiles," Cadrach said as he fumbled with the flints. "Could it be, Duke Isgrimnur, that somewhere in the dank shrubbery lurks the gigantic grandmother of all cows? With a brisket big as a wagon?"

The Rimmersman would not be baited. "If you mind your manners, sirrah, I might even leave you a bite or two."

There was no beef. Isgrimnur, along with the rest of the company, was forced to make do with a thin soup made from various kinds of marsh-grass and a few slivers from the one fish Tiamak was able to catch before dark. Isgrimnur made an offhand remark about the charm of an ember-roasted pigeon, but the Wrannaman was so horrified that the duke quickly apologized.

"It's just my way, man," he grumbled. "I'm damned sorry. Wouldn't touch your birds."

Even had he been serious, he might have found it more difficult than expected. Camaris had taken to Tiamak's pigeons as though to a long-lost family. The old knight spent most of the evening up on the roof of the house with his head stuck in the dovecote. He came down for only a few moments to drink his share of the soup, then climbed back to the roof again, where he sat in silent communion with Tiamak's birds until everyone else had curled up in their cloaks on the board floor. The old man returned at last and lay down, but even then he stared fixedly at the shadow-darkened ceiling as though he could see through the thatch to where his new friends roosted; his eyes were still open long after the sound of Isgrimnur and Cadrach snoring had filled the small room. Miriamele watched him until drowsiness began to send her own thoughts spinning slowly around like a whirlpool.

So Miriamele fell asleep in a house in a tree with the quiet slapping of water beneath her, the questioning cries of night birds above.

Different birds were shrilling when the tree-filtered sunlight awoke her. Their voices were coarse and repetitive, but Miriamele did not find it too distracting. She had slept astonishingly well—she felt as though she had gotten the first solid night's sleep since leaving Nabban.

"Good morning!" she said cheerily to Tiamak, who was huddled over the firepit. "Something smells nice."

The Wrannaman bobbed his head. "I found a pot of flour I had buried in the back. How it stayed dry I will never know. Usually my seals don't hold." He pointed his long fingers at the flat cakes bubbling on a hot stone. "It is not much, but I always feel better when I get hot food."

"Me, too." Miriamele took a deep, savoring sniff. How astonishing yet reassuring it was that someone raised around the groaning banquet tables of Erkynlandish royalty could still find herself so pleased by unleavened biscuits cooked on a rock—if only the circumstances were right. There was something profound in that, she knew, but it seemed a shame to brood so early in the morning. "Where are the others?" she asked.

"Trying to clear some rocks out of the narrow part of the waterway. If we can get the boat past this spot, we will have an easy time in to Village Grove. We will be there long before noon."

"Good." Miriamele considered for a moment. "I want to wash. Where should I go?"

"There is a rainwater pool not too far away," Tiamak said. "But I should take you there."

"I can go by myself," she said, a little briskly.

"Of course, but it is very easy to make a bad step here, Lady Miramele." The slender man was embarrassed to have to correct her, and Miriamele immediately felt ashamed.

"I'm sorry," she said. "It's very kind of you to take me, Tiamak. Whenever you're ready, we'll go."

He smiled. "Now. Just let me pull these cakes off, so they do not burn. The first crabs should go to the one who made the trap, don't you think?"

It was not easy to climb down from the house while juggling hot cakes. Miriamele almost fell off the ladder.

Their three companions were a little way up the estuary, waist-deep in green, scummy water. Isgrimnur straightened up and waved. He had doffed his shirt, and his great chest and stomach, covered with reddish-brown fur, were revealed in all their glory beneath the murky sun. Miriamele giggled. He looked just like a bear.

"There is food inside," Tiamak called to them. "And batter in the bowl to make more."

Isgrimnur waved again.

After wading through the thick, clinging underbrush for a few moments, skirting patches of sucking mud, Miriamele and Tiamak began to climb a short, low rise. "This is one of the little hills," Tiamak said. "There are a few in this part of the Wran—the rest is very flat." He pointed into the distance, which was just as tree-choked where he pointed as in any other direction. "You cannot see from here, but the highest point in the Wran is there, half a league away. It is called *Ya Mologi*—Cradle Hill."

"Why?"

"I don't know. I think that She Who Birthed Mankind is supposed to have lived there." He looked up, shy again. "One of our gods."

When Miriamele did not comment, the little man turned around and pointed along the rise a short distance to a place where the land folded in upon itself. A row of tall trees grew there—willows again, Miriamele noticed. They seemed far more robust than the surrounding vegetation. "There." Tiamak headed toward the spot where the land dipped down.

It was a tiny canyon, a mere wrinkle in the hillside, less than a stone's throw from end to end. The bottom was almost entirely filled with a standing pond choked with hyacinths and water lilies and long trailing grasses. "It is a rainwater pond," Tiamak said proudly. "It is the reason my father Tugumak built his house here, although we were far from Village Grove. There are a few other such ponds in this part of the Wran, but this is much the nicest."

Miriamele looked it over a little doubtfully. "I can bathe in it?" she asked. "No crocodiles or snakes or anything else?"

"A few water beetles, nothing more," the Wrannaman assured her. "I will go and leave you to your washing. Can you find your way back?"

Miriamele thought for a moment. "Yes. I'm close enough to shout if I get lost, in any case."

"True." Tiamak turned and made his way back up the shallow defile, then disappeared through the hedge of willows. When she heard his voice again, it was quite faint. "We will save some food for you, Lady!"

He did that to let me know he was far away, Miriamele thought, smiling. *So I wouldn't worry that he was staying to watch. Even in the swamp, there are gentlemen.*

She undressed, enjoying the morning warmth that was one of the few nice things about the swamp, then waded into the pond. She sighed with pleasure as the water reached her knees: it was quite comfortable, only a little cooler than a tub bath. Tiamak had given her a small gift, she realized; it was one of the nicest she had been given in a long while.

The bottom of the pond was covered with soft, firm mud that felt good beneath her toes. The willows that loomed so closely and drooped so low, as if greedy for the pondwater, made her feel almost as protected and private as if she had been in her chamber at Meremund. After wading partway around the rim of the pool, she found a spot where the grass grew thick beneath the surface. She sat on it as though it were a carpet, sinking down until the water almost reached her chin. She splashed water on her face, then wetted her hair and tried to loosen the tangles. Now that it was beginning to grow out again, she could not treat it as carelessly as she had of late.

After she had finished, she simply sat for a while, listening to the racket of birds and the warm wind moving the trees.

As Miriamele was belting her dirty and somewhat odoriferous monk's robe around her waist once more—and grumbling to herself as she did because she had not been foresighted enough to bring a change of clothing with her out of *Pelippa's Bowl*—the rustle of leaves overhead suddenly became louder. Miriamele looked up, expecting a large bird or perhaps even one of the marsh apes, but what she saw instead caused her to suck in her breath in shocked surprise.

The thing hanging from the branch was only as big as a young child, but that was still unpleasantly large. It looked something like a crab and something like a spider, but despite its crustacean exterior it had, as far as Miriamele could tell, only four limbs; each was jointed, ending in a recurved claw. The creature's body was covered in a horny, leathery shell, gray and brown splashed with inky black, crisscrossed with uneven trails of lichen. Its eyes were the worst part, though: their beady black glimmer—somehow so oddly intelligent, despite the malformed head and chitinous body—sent her stumbling backward until she was sure it could not reach her, no matter how prodigious a leaper it might be. The thing did not move. It seemed to watch her in a disturbingly human way, but the creature was otherwise not human in the least; it did not even have a mouth that she could see, unless the little clicking things in the cleft at the bottom of its blunt head served that purpose.

Miriamele shivered in disgust. "Go away!" she cried, waving her hands as she might try to shoo a dog. The glittering eyes stared at her with what almost seemed an attitude of amused malice.

But it has no face, she told herself. *How can it have feelings?!* It was an animal, and it was either dangerous or not. How could she think she saw feelings in something that was no more than a huge bug? Still, she found the creature terrifying. Although it made no hostile movement, she circled the tree widely as she made her way up out of the little canyon. The thing made no move to follow her, but it turned to watch her go.

"A ghant," Tiamak explained as they were all climbing back into the boat. "I am sorry it frightened you, Lady Miriamele. They are ugly things, but they seldom attack people, and almost never anyone larger than a child."

"But it looked at me like a person would!" Miriamele shuddered. "I don't know why, but it was dreadful."

Tiamak nodded his head. "They are not just low animals, Lady—or at least I do not think so, although others of my folk insist they are no cleverer than crayfish. I wonder, though: I have seen the huge nests they build, and the clever way they hunt for fish and trap birds."

"So you would suggest they are thinking creatures?" Cadrach asked dryly. "That would come as a disturbing thought to the hierarchy of Mother Church, I should think. Must they not then have souls? Perhaps Nabban will have to send missionary priests out to the Wran to bring them to the bosom of the True Faith."

"Enough of your mockery, Hernystirman," Isgrimnur grunted. "Help me get this damnable boat off the sandbar."

It was a short journey to Village Grove, or so Tiamak had said. The morning was bright and only comfortably warm, but even so, the ghant had darkened Miriamele's mood. It had reminded her of the terrible, alien nature of the marsh country. This was not her home. Tiamak might be able to live happily here—although she doubted that such was the case even with him—but she herself certainly never could.

The Wrannaman, poling now with the oar handle, directed them down an ever-turning succession of interwoven canals and streamlets, each one hidden from the next by the thick shield of vegetation that grew along its sandy, unstable banks—dense walls of pale reeds and dark, tangled growth festooned with bright but somehow feverish-looking flowers—so that every time that a side course took them from one waterway to the next, the previous one had vanished behind them almost as soon as the stern of the boat had crossed over to the new one.

Soon the first houses of Village Grove began to appear on either side of the waterway. Some were built in trees, like Tiamak's; others loomed on tree-trunk stilts. After they had floated past a few, Tiamak pulled the boat up beneath the landing of a large stilt-house and loudly hailed the occupants.

"Roahog!" he called. When there was no reply, he banged the oar handle against one of the pilings; the rattling drove a bevy of green and scarlet birds shrieking from the trees overhead, but brought no other response. Tiamak shouted again, then shrugged.

"The potter is not home," he said. "I saw no one in the other houses, either. Perhaps there is a gathering at the landing-place."

They poled on. The houses that now began to appear were closer together. Some of the dwellings seemed to be composed of many small houses of different shapes and sizes that had been grafted onto an original hut—clumps of muddled shapes pocked with irregular black windows, like the nests of cliff-dwelling owls. Tiamak stopped and called at several of them, but no one ever answered his hail.

"The landing-place," he said firmly, but Miriamele thought he looked worried. "They must be at the landing-place."

This proved to be a great, flat dock that protruded halfway out into the middle of the widest part of the watercourse. Houses gathered thickly around it on all sides, and parts of the landing-place itself were equipped with thatched roofs and walls. Miriamele guessed these areas might be used for market stalls. There were other signs of recent life—large decorated baskets set back in the leafy shade, boats bobbing at the end of their painters—but no people.

Tiamak was clearly shaken. "They Who Watch and Shape," he breathed, "what has happened here?"

"They're gone?" Miriamele looked around. "How could a whole village be gone?"

"You've not seen the north, my lady," Isgrimnur said dourly. "There are many towns on the Frostmarch that are empty as old pots."

"But those people have been chased out by war. Surely there's no war here. Not yet."

"Some in the north have been chased out by war," Cadrach murmured. "Some by fear of things more difficult to name. And fear is everywhere in these days."

"I do not understand." Tiamak wagged his head as though he still could not believe what he saw. "My people would not just run away, even if they were afraid of the war—which I doubt they have even heard about. Our life is here. Where would they go?"

Camaris stood up suddenly, setting the boat rocking and filling the other passengers with alarm; but when the old man had balanced himself, he merely reached up and plucked a long yellowish seedpod from one of the tree branches hanging overhead, then sat back down again to examine his prize.

"Well, there are boats here, anyway," Isgrimnur said. "They're what we need. I don't mean to be cruel, Tiamak, but we should pick one and be on our way. We'll leave our boat for trade, as you said." He made a face, trying to think of the knightly thing to do. "Maybe you can scratch a letter on one of your parchments or somesuch—let 'em know what we've done."

Tiamak stared for a moment as though he had suddenly forgotten the Westerling language. "Oh," he said at last. "A new boat. Of course." He shook his head. "I know we have need for haste, Duke Isgrimnur, but would you mind if we stopped here a little time? I must look around—see if my sisters or anyone else left word of where they have gone."

"Well . . ." Isgrimnur peered at the deserted dock. Miriamele thought the duke seemed a little reluctant. There was indeed something eerie about the empty village. The inhabitants seemed to have vanished quite suddenly, as though they had been swept away by a strong wind. "I suppose that's all right, certainly. We thought it might take us the whole day, after all. Certainly."

"Thank you." Tiamak nodded. "I would have felt . . ." He started again. "So far I have not done all that I could do for my people. It would not be right just to take a flatboat and float away without even looking about."

He caught hold of one of the tie posts and made their boat fast to the landing-place.

The people of Village Grove did seem to have left in a hurry. A cursory inspection showed that many useful things had been left behind, not least of which were several baskets of fruits and vegetables. While Tiamak went off to search for some indication of why and where his people had fled, Cadrach and Isgrimnur began to harvest this unexpected bounty, loading their new vessel—a large and well-constructed flatboat—until it floated rather lower in the water than Tiamak might think was best. On her own, Miriamele found some flower-colored dresses in one of the huts near the landing-place. They were baggy and shapeless, quite unlike anything she would ever have worn at home, but in these conditions they would serve nicely for a change of clothing. She also discovered a pair of leather slippers, thong-stitched, that seemed as though they might make a nice change from the boots she had been wearing almost continuously since leaving Naglimund. After a moment's hesitation over the propriety of taking someone's belongings without leaving anything in return, Miriamele steeled herself and appropriated the clothes. After all, what did she have to exchange?

As morning slid into afternoon, Tiamak returned occasionally to pass on his news, which was generally no news. He had discovered the same curious evidence of hasty retreat, but could find nothing to indicate why the flight had occurred. The only possible clue was that several spears and other weapons were missing from the hut where the village's elders met—weapons that Tiamak said were not the property of individuals but of the village as a whole, important weapons which were only taken down in time of battle or other conflict.

"I think I will go to Older Mogahib's house," said the

Wrannaman. "He is our chief elder, so anything important would be there. It is a good distance up the watercourse, so I will take a boat. I should be back before the sun hits the treeline." He pointed to indicate the sun's westward path.

"Do you want to eat before you go?" Isgrimnur asked. "I'll have the fire going in a moment."

Tiamak shook his head. "I can wait until I return. As I said, there will still be much of the day left when I get back."

But the afternoon waned and Tiamak did not return. Miriamele and the others ate turnips—or at least something that looked like turnips, bulbous, starchy things which Tiamak had assured them were safely edible—and a squishy yellow fruit that they wrapped in green leaves and baked in the coals of the fire. A brown, dovelike bird that Cadrach captured with a snare, when boiled for soup, helped to fill out the meal. As the shadows lengthened across the green water and the hum of insects began to rise, Miriamele became worried.

"He should have been back by now. The sun went below the trees a long time ago."

"The little fellow's fine," Isgrimnur assured her. "He's probably found something interesting—some damned marsh-man scroll or something. He'll be back soon."

But he did not come back, not even when the sun had gone and the stars came out. Miriamele and the others made their beds out on the landing dock—more than a little reluctantly, since they still had no idea what had happened to Village Grove's vanished citizens—and were glad for the embers of the fire. Miriamele did not fall asleep for a long time.

The morning sun was high when Miriamele awoke. One look at Isgrimnur's worried face was enough to confirm what she had feared.

"Oh, poor Tiamak! Where is he? What could have happened!? I hope he isn't hurt!"

"Not just poor Tiamak, Lady." Cadrach's studiedly sour tone did not entirely cover his deep unease. "Poor us

as well. How will we ever find our way out of this god-
less swamp by ourselves?"

She opened her mouth, then shut it again. There was
nothing to say.

"There's nothing else to do," Isgrimnur said on the second Tiamak-less morning. "We have to try and find our
way out by ourselves."

Cadrach made a bitter face. "We might as well give
ourselves to the grandfather crocodile, Rimmersman. At
least it would save time."

"Damn you," Isgrimnur snarled, "don't expect *me* to
crawl off and die! I've never given up in my life, and I've
been in some tight spots."

"You've never been lost in the Wran before," Cadrach
pointed out.

"Stop it! Stop it now!" Miriamele's head hurt. The
wrangling had been going on since the middle of the day
before. "Isgrimnur's right. We have no other choice."

Cadrach seemed about to say something unpleasant,
but shut his mouth instead and stared off at the empty
houses of Village Grove.

"We will go the same direction Tiamak went," declared
Isgrimnur. "That way, if something has happened to
him—I mean if he is hurt or holed his boat or something
like—at least we may chance upon him."

"But he said he was not going far—just to the other
end of his people's village," she said. "When we leave the
last houses, we will not know where he meant us to go
next, will we?"

"No, curse it, and I was too foolish to think to ask him
when I could have." Isgrimnur scowled. "Not that anything he said would have made much sense—this damnable place just turns my head around."

"But the sun is still the same, even over the Wran,"
Miriamele said, a touch of desperation now making itself
felt. "The stars, too. We should be able to decide which
direction is north toward Uncle Josua, at least."

Isgrimnur smiled sadly. "Aye. That's true, Princess. We will do our best."

Cadrach stood suddenly, then walked to the flatboat they had selected, stepping around the old man Camaris, who was dangling his feet off the dock into the green water. Earlier Miriamele had dangled her own feet similarly and been bitten by a turtle, but the old man seemed to have established more amicable relations with the river's inhabitants.

Cadrach bent and hefted one of the sacks piled on the dock. He heaved it to Camaris, who caught it with ease and dropped it into the boat. "I will not argue any further," the monk said as he stooped for a second sack. "Let us load what food and water we can. At least we will not die from hunger or thirst—although we soon may wish we had."

Miriamele had to laugh. "Elysia, Mother of God, Cadrach, could you be more gloomy if you tried?! Maybe we should just kill you now and put you out of your misery."

"I've heard worse ideas," grunted Isgrimnur.

Miriamele watched with apprehension as the center of Village Grove disappeared behind them. Although it had been empty, nevertheless it had clearly been a place where people had lived: the marks of their recent habitation were everywhere. Now she and her remaining friends were leaving this bastion of comparative familiarity and heading back into the unknowable swamps. She suddenly wished they had decided to wait a few more days for Tiamak.

They continued to float past deserted houses well into the morning, although the dwellings were becoming ever more widely separated from each other. The greenery was as dense as ever. Watching the endless mural of vegetation unroll on either side, Miriamele for the first time found herself wishing they had not followed Tiamak into this place. The Wran seemed so heedless in its vegetative enterprise, so busily unconcerned with anything as meaningless as people. She felt very small.

* * *

It was Camaris who saw it first, although he did not speak or make any noise; it was only by his stance, the sudden alertness like a hound on the point, that the others were drawn to squint down the waterway at the drifting speck.

"It's a flatboat!" Miriamele cried. "Someone's in it—lying down! Oh, it must be Tiamak!"

"It's his boat, all right," Isgrimnur said, "—the one with the yellow and black eyes painted on the front."

"Oh, hurry, Cadrach!" Miriamele almost toppled the monk into the waterway as she pushed at his arm. "Pole faster!"

"If we tip over and drown," Cadrach said through clenched teeth, "then we will do the marsh man little good."

They approached the flatboat. The dark-haired, brown-skinned figure lay curled in the bottom with one arm hanging over the side, as though he had fallen asleep trying to reach his hand down to the water. The boat was drifting in a slow circle as Miriamele and her companions pulled alongside. The princess was the first to cross over, setting both boats rocking as she hurried to the Wrannaman's aid.

"Careful, my lady," Cadrach said, but Miriamele had already lifted the small man's head onto her lap. She gasped at the blood that had dried on the dark face, then a moment later, gasped again.

"It's not Tiamak!"

The Wrannaman, who had obviously suffered much in recent days, was stouter and a little lighter-skinned than their companion. His skin was covered with some sticky substance whose odor made Miriamele wrinkle her nose in discomfort. Nothing else could be discovered, though, for he was completely insensible. When she lifted the water-skin to his cracked lips, Miriamele had to be very careful not to choke him. The stranger managed to down a few swallows without ever appearing to wake.

"So how did this blasted other marsh man wind up

with Tiamak's boat?" Isgrimnur grumbled, digging the mud from his bootheels with a stick. They had come ashore to make a temporary camp while they decided what to do; the ground in this spot was somewhat soggy. "And what's happened to Tiamak? Do you think this fellow waylaid him for his flatboat?"

"Look at him," Cadrach said. "This man could not strangle a cat, I am sure. No, the question is not how he got the boat, but why Tiamak isn't in it with him, and what happened to this unlucky fellow in the first place. Remember, this is the first of Tiamak's folk we've seen since we left Kwanitupul for the marshes."

"That's true." Miriamele stared at the stranger. "Maybe whatever happened to Tiamak's villagers happened to this man, too! Or maybe he was running away from it . . . or . . . or something." She frowned. Instead of finding their guide, they instead had discovered a new mystery to make things even more complicated and unpleasant. "What do we do?"

"Take him with us, I suppose," Isgrimnur said. "We will want to ask him questions when he wakes up—but the Aedon only knows how long that will be. We can't afford to wait."

"Ask him questions?" Cadrach murmured. "And how, Duke Isgrimnur, will we do that? Tiamak is a rarity among his people, as he told us himself."

"What do you mean?"

"I doubt this fellow can speak anything other than the Wran-tongue."

"Damn! Damn and damn and thrice damned!" The duke colored. "Begging your pardon, Princess Miriamele. He's right, though." He pondered a moment, then shrugged. "Still, what else can we do? We'll bring him."

"Maybe he can draw pictures, or maps," Miriamele offered.

"There!" Isgrimnur was relieved. "Maps! Clever, my lady, very clever. Maybe he can do that, indeed."

The unknown Wrannaman slept through the rest of the afternoon, not stirring even when the boat was scraped down the muddy bank and relaunched into the water-course. Before departure, Miriamele had cleaned his skin, discovering to her relief that most of his wounds were not serious—at least the ones she could see. She could think of nothing else to do.

Isgrimnur's thankless task of trying to find a safe passage through this treacherous and unfamiliar land was made easier by the relatively straightforward nature of this section of the waterway. Because there were few side streams and few forks, it had seemed easiest to simply remain in the center of the watercourse, and so far it was working. Although there had been a few junctures at which Isgrimnur could have gone a different way, they were still seeing occasional houses, so there seemed no cause yet for worry.

Somewhat after the sun had passed the midpoint of the sky, the strange Wrannaman suddenly woke up, startling Miriamele, who was shading his eyes with a broad leaf as she mopped his brow. The man's brown eyes widened in fear as he saw her, then darted from side to side as though he were surrounded by enemies. After a few moments his hunted look softened and he became calmer, although he still did not speak. Instead, he lay for a long while staring up at the canopy of branches sliding past overhead. He breathed shallowly, as though just to keep his eyes open and watching represented the farthest limit of his strength. Miriamele talked softly to him and continued moistening his brow. She was certain that Cadrach was right when he guessed that this man could not speak her tongue, but she was not trying to tell him anything important: a quiet and friendly voice, she hoped, might make him feel better even if he did not understand any of her words.

A little over an hour later the man was at last recovered enough to sit partway up and take a little water. He still seemed quite confused and ill, so it was no surprise when the first noises he made were moans of discomfort, but the unhappy sounds continued even as Miriamele offered him another drink. The Wrannaman pushed away the skin

bag, gesturing up the watercourse and showing every sign
of extreme disquiet.

"Is he mad?" Isgrimnur peered at the man suspiciously.
"Just what we need, some mad swamp fellow."

"I think he's trying to tell us to turn back," Miriamele
said, then realized with a sudden vertiginous drop in her
innards what she was saying. "He's telling us it's ... *bad*
to go the way we're going."

The Wrannaman at last found his words. "*Mualum
nohoa!*" he gabbled, obviously terrified. "*Sanbidub
nohoa yia ghanta!*" When he had said this again several
times, he tried to drag himself over the side and into the
water. He was weak and distracted; Miriamele was able to
restrain him with little difficulty. She was shocked when
he burst into tears, his round brown face as defenseless
and unashamed as a child's.

"What can it be?" she asked, alarmed. "He thinks it's
dangerous, whatever it is."

Isgrimnur shook his head. He was helping Cadrach
keep the boat off the tangled bank as they negotiated a
bend in the waterway. "Who knows? Could be some animal, or some other group of marsh men who are at war
with these fellows. Or it could be some heathen
superstition—a haunted pond or something like."

"Or it could be what emptied Tiamak's village,"
Cadrach said. "Look."

The Wrannaman sat up again, straining to escape
Miriamele's grip. "*Yia ghanta!*" he burbled.

"Ghanta," Miriamele breathed, staring across the waterway. "Ghants? But Tiamak said ..."

"Tiamak may have found out that he was wrong."
Cadrach's voice had dropped to a whisper.

On the far side of the watercourse, now revealed as the
flatboat made its way past the bend, sprawled a huge and
bizarre structure. It might almost have been built in parody of Village Grove, for like that place it was obviously
the dwelling place of many. But where the village had
clearly been the work of human hands, this lopsided ag-
glomeration of mud and leaves and sticks, although it
stretched up from the water's edge into the trees to many

times a man's height, and along the bank for what looked like well over a furlong, was just as clearly not built by human beings at all. A buzzing, clicking sound issued from it and out across the Wran, a great cloud of noise like an army of crickets in an echoing, high-arched room. Some of the builders of the huge nest could be seen clearly, even from the far side of the wide canal. They moved in their distinctive manner, dropping deftly from one stump of branch to a lower, scuttling swiftly in and out of the black doors of the nest.

Miriamele felt both terror and a certain disgusted fascination. A single ghant had been disturbing. From the size of the dwelling, she did not doubt that hundreds of the unpleasant creatures were sheltering in this pile of dirt and sticks.

"Mother of Usires," Isgrimnur hissed. He turned the boat and poled rapidly back up the waterway until the bend in the river shielded them once more from the alarming sight. "What kind of hell-thing is that?"

Miriamele squirmed as she remembered the mocking eyes that had watched her bathe, dots of jet pivoting in an inhuman face. "Those are the ghants Tiamak told us about."

The sick Wrannaman, who had fallen into deathly silence when the nest came into view, began to waggle his hands. *"Tiamak!"* he said hoarsely. *"Tiamak nib dunou yia ghanta!"* He pointed back to where the nest lay hidden from their view by a wall of greenery. Miriamele did not need to speak the Wran-tongue to know what the strange man was saying.

"Tiamak's in there. Oh, God help him, he's in that nest. The ghants have him."

14

Dark Corridors

The stairs were steep and the sack was heavy, but Rachel felt a certain joy, nevertheless. One more trip—just one more time that she would be forced to brave the haunted upper rooms of the castle—and then she would be finished.

Just off the shadowy landing, halfway down the stairs, she stopped and set down her burden, careful not to let the jars clank. The doorway was hidden by what Rachel the Dragon felt sure was the oldest, dustiest arras in the entire castle. It was a measure of the importance of her hiding hole remaining inconspicuous that she could pass it every day and leave it uncleaned. Her very soul rebelled each time she had to lay her hands on the moldering fabric, but there were circumstances when even cleaning had to take second place. Rachel grimaced. *Hard times make odd changes,* her mother had always said. Well, if that wasn't Aedon's holy truth, what was?

Rachel had taken great care to oil the ancient hinges, so when she lifted the tapestry and pushed at the handle, the door swung in almost silently. She lifted her bag over the low threshold, then let the heavy tapestry slip back into place behind her so it would again hide the door. She unshielded her lamp, set it in a high niche, and went to work unpacking.

When the last jar had been removed and Rachel had drawn a picture of the contents on its outside with a straw dipped in lamp-black, she stepped back to survey her larder. She had labored hard over the last month, surprising

even herself with her daring pilferage. Now she wanted
only the sack of dried fruit she had spotted on today's
raid, then she would be able to last out the entire winter
without risking capture. She needed that sack: a lack of
fruit to eat would mean the clenches, if not something
worse, and she could not afford to become ill with no one
to tend her. She had planned everything with great care so
that she could be alone: there was certainly no one left in
the castle she could trust.

Rachel had searched patiently for just the right place to
make her sanctuary. This monk's hole, far down in one of
the long-unused sections of the Hayholt's underground
rooms, had worked out perfectly. Now, thanks to her
ceaseless hunting, it was stocked with a larder that many
a lord of troubled Erkynland might envy. Also, just up a
few flights she had found another unused room—not as
well-hidden, but with a small slit window that protruded
just above ground level. Outside that window hung the
drain spout from one of the Hayholt's stone gutters. Rachel already had a full barrel of water in her cell; as long
as the snows and rains lasted, she would be able to fill a
bucket every day from the spout outside the room above,
and not have to touch her precious store of drinkable water at all.

She had also scavenged spare clothing and several
warm blankets, as well as a straw mattress, and even a
chair to sit in—a fancy chair, as she marveled, with a
back on it! She had wood for the tiny fireplace, and so
many rows of jars of pickled vegetables and meats and
wrapped piles of hard-baked bread were stacked along the
walls that there was scarcely room to walk from the door
to the bed. But it was worth it. Here, in her hidden room
filled with provender, she knew she could last the better
part of a year. What might happen by the time the provisions ran out, what event might take place that would allow her to leave her den and reemerge into daylight,
Rachel wasn't sure . . . but that was something she could
not worry about. She would spend her time staying safe,
keeping her nest clean, and waiting. That lesson had been

pounded into her since childhood: Do what you can. Trust
God for the rest.

She thought about her youth a great deal these days.
The constant solitude and the secretive nature of her daily
life conspired, limiting her activities and throwing her
back on her memories for entertainment and solace. She
had remembered things—an Aedonmansa when her father
had been feared lost in the snow, a straw doll that her sister had once made for her—that she had not thought of
for years. The memories, like the foodstuffs floating in
the briny darkness of the jars she was rearranging, were
only waiting to be taken out once more.

Rachel pushed the last jar back a little farther, so that
they made an even row. The castle might be falling apart,
but here in her haven she would have order! *Only one
more trip,* she thought. *Then I won't have to be afraid any
more. Then I can finally have a little rest.*

The Mistress of Chambermaids had reached the top of
the stairway and was reaching for the door when a feeling
of immense cold suddenly swept over her. Footsteps were
approaching on the other side of the door, a dull ticking
sound like water dripping on stone. Someone was coming! She would be caught!

Her heart seemed to be beating so swiftly she feared it
would climb right up out of her chest. She was gripped by
a nightmarish immobility.

Move, idiot woman, move!

The footsteps were growing louder. She finally pulled
back her hand, then, seeing that movement was possible
after all, forced herself to back down onto a lower step,
looking around wildly. Where to go, where to go?
Trapped!

She backed farther down the slippery steps. Where the
stairway bent around the corner there was a landing,
much like the one where she had discovered her new
home. This landing, too, was graced with a musty, ragged
arras. She grabbed at it, struggling as the heavy, dusty
cloth resisted her. It seemed too much to hope that a room
was hidden behind this one, too, but at least she could

press herself flat against the wall and hope that the person who was even now pulling at the door above her was shortsighted, or in a hurry.

There *was* a door! Rachel wondered momentarily if there hung a single tapestry in the sprawling castle that didn't shield some hidden portal. She tugged at the ancient handle.

Oh, Aedon on the Tree, she mouthed silently—surely the hinges would creak! But the hinges did not make a sound, and the door swung open quietly, even as the door at the top of the stairs above her scraped across the stone flags. The noise of bootheels grew louder as they descended the steps. Rachel pushed herself through and pulled the door after her. It swung most of the way closed, then stopped with a little less than a hand's width remaining. It would not shut.

Rachel looked up, wishing she dared to unshutter her lantern, but grateful that at least there was a torch burning fitfully in the stairwell outside. She forced herself to search carefully, even though black spots were swirling before her eyes and her heart was rabbiting in her breast. There! The top of the arras was caught in the door . . . but it was far above where she could reach. She grasped the thick, dust-caked velvet to shake it free, but the footsteps were almost on the landing. Rachel shrank back from the open crack of the doorway and held her breath.

As the noise came closer, so, too, did the sensation of cold—a bone-deep chill like walking out of a hot room into mid-winter winds. Rachel began shivering uncontrollably. Through the crack of the doorway she saw a pair of black-clad figures. The quiet noise of their conversation, which had just become audible, abruptly ceased. One of them turned so that its pale face was momentarily visible from Rachel's hiding place. Her heart lurched, seeming to lose its beat. It was one of those witch-things—the White Foxes! It turned away again, speaking to its companion in a low but oddly musical voice, then looked back up the steps they had just descended. Another clatter of footsteps came echoing down the stairwell.

More of them!

Rachel, despite a horror of moving or doing anything at
all that might make a noise, began to back away. As she
stared at the partially opened doorway, praying that the
things would not notice how it was ajar, Rachel kept feeling behind her for the rear wall. She took several steps
backward, until the doorway was only a thin vertical line
of yellowish torch-glow, but still her hand encountered no
resistance. She stopped at last and turned to look, terrified
by the sudden idea that she might stumble over something
stored in this room and send it clattering to the ground.

It was not a room. Rachel stood in the mouth of a corridor that led away into darkness.

She paused for a moment, forcing herself to think.
There was no sense in remaining here, especially with a
flock of those creatures just beyond the door. The stark
stone wall was devoid of hiding places, and she knew that
any moment now she might make an involuntary noise, or
worse, grow faint and fall noisily to the floor. And who
knew how long those things might stand there, murmuring to themselves like carrion birds on a branch? When
their fellows all arrived, they might next enter this very
passageway! At least if she went now she might find
some better place to hide or another way out.

Rachel tottered down the corridor, trailing one hand
along the wall—the horrible, grimy things that she felt
beneath her fingers!—and holding the darkened lantern in
front of her with the other, trying to make sure that it did
not bump against the stone. The thin sliver of light from
the doorway disappeared behind a bend in the hallway,
leaving her in utter darkness. Rachel carefully pulled
back the lantern's hood a little way, allowing a single
beam to leap out and shine on the flagstones before her,
then began to walk swiftly down the passageway.

Rachel held the lamp high, squinting down the featureless corridor into the unexplored darkness beyond the
pool of light. Was there no end to the castle's maze of
passageways? She had thought she knew the Hayholt as
well as anyone, yet the last few weeks had been a revela-

tion. There seemed to be another entire castle beneath the
basement storehouses that had once been the downward
limit of her experience. Had Simon known about these
places?

Thinking of the boy was painful, as always. She shook
her head and trudged forward. There had been no sound
of pursuit yet—she had finally caught her fear-shortened
breath—but there was no sense standing around waiting.

But there *was* a problem to be solved, of course: if she
dared not go back, what could she do? She had long
ceased trusting her ability to find her way in this warren.
What if she took a wrong turn and went wandering into
darkness forever, lost and starving. . . ?

*Fool woman. Just don't turn off from this hall—or at
least mark the turn if you do. Then you can always find
the landing and the stairs again.*

She snorted, the same chuff of sound that had reduced
many a novice chambermaid to whimpers. Rachel knew
discipline, even if it was she herself that needed it this
time.

No time for nonsense.

Still, it was strange to be wandering here in these
lonely, between-ish spaces. It was a little like what Father
Dreosan had said about the Waiting Place—that spot between Hell and Heaven where dead souls waited for judgment, where they remained for a timeless time if they
were not bad enough for the former but not ready for the
latter. Rachel had found this a rather uncomfortable idea:
she liked her distinctions clean and forthright. Do wrong,
be damned and burnt. Lead a life of cleanliness and
Aedonite rigor and you could fly up to heaven and sing
and rest beneath eternal blue skies. This middle place that
the priest had spoken of just seemed unpleasantly mysterious. The God that Rachel worshiped should not work in
such a way.

The lamp's light fell upon a wall before her: the corridor had ended in a perpendicular hallway, which meant
that if she wished to continue, she had to go right or left.
Rachel frowned. Here she was already, having to leave
the straight path. She didn't like it. The question was, did

she dare go back, or even remain in the hallway? She
didn't think she'd traveled very far since leaving the staircase.

The memory of the whispering, white-faced things
gathering on the steps decided her.

She dipped a finger in lampblack, then stood on tiptoe
to mark the left wall of the corridor in which she stood.
That would be what she would see on returning. She then
turned reluctantly down the right-hand side of the inter-
secting corridor.

The passageway wound on and on, crisscrossed by
halls, opening out from time to time into small,
unwindowed galleries, each as empty as a plundered
tomb. Rachel dutifully marked each turn. She was beginning to worry about the lamp—surely she would run out
of oil if she went much farther before turning back—
when the passageway ended abruptly at an ancient door.

The door had no markings, nor any bolt or lock. The
wood was old and warped and so waterstained that it was
splotched like the shell of a tortoise. The hinges were
great clumsy chunks of iron, fastened by nails that
seemed little more than shards of rough metal. Rachel
squinted at the floor to make sure that no recent footprints
other than her own were there, then made the Tree before
her breast and pulled at the stubby handle. The door gritted open partway before grinding to a halt, wedged by
what must have been a century's worth of dust and rubble
on the floor. Beyond lay another darkened space, but this
darkness was glazed with reddish light.

It's Hell! was Rachel's first thought. *Out of the Waiting
Place and through the door to Hell!* Then: *Elysia the
Mother! Old woman, you aren't even dead! Be sensible!*
She stepped through.

The passageway on the far side was different than
those through which she had come. Instead of being lined
with cut and fitted stone, it was walled with naked rock.
The glimmers of red light which writhed across the rough
walls seemed to be coming from farther up the corridor to
the left, as though somewhere just around a corner a fire
was burning.

Despite her uncertainty over this new development, Rachel was just about to take a few steps up the passage toward the source of the red glow when she heard a sudden noise from the opposite direction, down the new corridor to her right. She hurriedly stepped back into the doorway, but it was still stuck fast and would not close. She pushed herself back into the shadows and tried to hold her breath.

Whatever made the new noise did not move very quickly. Rachel cringed as the faint scraping slowly grew louder, but mixed with the fear was a deep anger. To think that she, the Mistress of Chambermaids, should be made to cower in her own home by ... by things! Trying to slow her racing heart, she relived the moment when she had struck out at Pryrates—the hellish excitement of it, the odd satisfaction of being able to actually do something after all those bleak months of suffering. But now? Her strongest blow had not seemed to affect the red priest at all, so what could she hope to do against a whole gang of demons? No, it was better to stay hidden and save the anger for when it might do her some good.

When the figure passed the stuck doorway, Rachel was at first tremendously relieved to see that it was only a mortal after all, a dark-haired man whose form was barely distinguishable against the red-lit rocks. A moment later her curiosity came rushing back, buoyed by the same fury she had felt earlier. Who felt so free to walk these dark places?

She poked her head out through the doorway to watch the retreating figure. He was walking very slowly, trailing his hand along the wall, but his head was back and waving from side to side, as though he tried to read something written on the corridor's shadowed ceiling.

Mercy, he's blind! she suddenly realized. The hesitation, the questing hands—it was obvious. A moment later, she realized that she knew the man. She flung herself back into the darkness of the doorway.

Guthwulf! That monster! What is he doing here? For a moment she had the dreadful certainty that Elias' henchmen were still looking for her, combing the castle hall by hall in meticulous search. But why send a blind man? And when had Guthwulf gone blind?

A memory came back, fragmented but still unsettling. That *had* been Guthwulf on the balcony with the king and Pryrates, hadn't it? The Earl of Utanyeat had grappled with the alchemist even as he, with Rachel's dagger standing in his back, rounded upon the Mistress of Chambermaids who lay stunned on the floor. But why would Guthwulf have done that? Everyone knew that Utanyeat was the High King's Hand, most hardhearted of Elias' minions.

Had he actually saved her life?

Rachel's head was whirling. She peered out through the open doorway again, but Earl Guthwulf had disappeared around a bend in the corridor, heading toward the red glow. A tiny shadow detached itself from the greater darkness and skittered past her feet, following him into the shadows. A cat? A gray cat?

The world beneath the castle had become altogether too confusingly dreamlike for Rachel. She unshuttered her lantern again and turned back in the direction she had come, leaving the door to the rough passageway ajar. For now, she wanted no dealings with Guthwulf, blind or not. She would follow her own careful marks back toward the staircase landing and pray that the White Foxes had gone on about their unholy business. There was much to think about—too much. Rachel wanted only to shut herself safely away in her sanctuary and go to sleep.

As Guthwulf trudged along, his head was full of seductive, poisonous music—a music that spoke to him, that summoned him, but that also frightened him as nothing else ever had.

For a long time in the endless darkness of his days and nights he had heard that song only in dreams, but today the music had come to him at last in his waking hours, summoning him up from the depths, driving even the whispering voices that were his regular companions out of his mind. It was the voice of the gray sword, and it was somewhere nearby.

A part of the Earl of Utanyeat knew perfectly well that the sword was only an object, a mute stem of metal that hung on the king's belt, and that the last thing in the world he should want to do was seek it out, since where it was, King Elias would also be. Guthwulf certainly did not want to be caught—he cared little for his safety, but he would rather die alone in the pits below the castle than be seen by the people who had known him before he had become such a pitiable wreck—but the presence of the sword was hugely compelling. His life was now little more than echoes and shadows, cold stone, ghostly voices, and the tapping and scraping of his own footsteps. But the sword was alive, and somehow its life was more powerful than his own. He wanted to be near it.

I will not be caught, Guthwulf told himself. *I will be clever, careful.* He would merely venture close enough to feel its singing strength. . . .

His thoughts were disrupted by something twining through his ankles—the cat, his shadow-friend. He bent to touch the animal, running his fingers along its bony back, feeling its lean muscles. It had come with him, perhaps to keep him out of trouble. He almost smiled.

Sweat dripped down his cheek as he straightened. The air was getting warmer. He could half-believe that after all the stairs he had climbed, all the long upward ramps he had trudged, he might be approaching the surface—but could things have changed so much in his time below-ground? Could the winter be fled, replaced by hot summer? It did not seem that so much time could have passed, but perpetual darkness was deceptive. Blind Guthwulf had already learned that while still in the castle. As for the weather . . . well, in such ill-omened and confusing times as these, anything was possible.

Now the stone walls were beginning to feel warm beneath his questing fingers. What was he walking into? He pushed the thought down. Whatever it was, the sword was there. The sword that was calling to him. Surely he should go just a little farther. . . .

That moment when Sorrow had sung inside him, filling him . . .

In the moment Elias had forced him to touch it, it had seemed that Guthwulf had become a part of the sword. He had been subsumed in an alien melody. For that moment at least, he and the blade were one.

Sorrow needed its brothers. Together they would make a music greater still.

In the king's throne room, despite his horror, Guthwulf had also yearned for that communion. Now, remembering, he ached for it again. Whatever the risks, he needed to feel the song that had haunted him. It was a kind of madness, he knew, but he did not have the strength to resist it. Instead, it would take all his reserves of cunning and self-restraint just to get closer without being revealed. It was so near now. . . .

The air in the narrow corridor was stifling. Guthwulf stopped and felt around. The little cat was gone, probably retreated to some place less injurious to its pads. When he put his hand back onto the corridor wall, he could only drag it for a short distance before he had to snatch it away once more. From somewhere ahead he could now hear a faint but continuous rush of sound, a near-silent roar. What could lie before him?

Once a dragon had made its lair beneath the castle—the red worm Shurakai, whose death had made Prester John's reputation and provided the bones for the Hayholt's throne, a beast whose fiery breath had killed two kings and countless castle-dwellers in an earlier century. Might there still be a dragon, some whelp of Shurakai, grown to adulthood in darkness? If so, let it kill him if it would— let it roast him to ashes. Guthwulf was beyond caring much about such things. All he wished was to bask first in the song of the gray sword.

The pathway took a sharp upward angle, and he had to lean forward to make any headway. The heat was fierce; he could imagine his skin blackening and shriveling like the cooked flesh of a holiday pig. As he struggled against the slope, the roaring noise became louder, a deep unsteady growl like thunder, or an angry sea, or the troubled breath of a sleeping dragon. Then the sound began to change. After a moment, Guthwulf realized that the passageway was widening. As he turned the corner, his blind man's senses told him that the hall had not only widened but grown higher as well. Hot winds billowed toward him. The grumbling noise echoed strangely.

Another few steps and he knew the reason. There was some much larger chamber beyond this one, something vast as the great dome of Saint Sutrin's in Erchester. A fiery pit? Guthwulf felt his hair wafting in the hot breeze. Had he somehow arrived at the fabled Lake of Judgment where sinners were cast into a pool of flame forever? Was God Himself waiting down here in the rocky fastnesses? In these confused, distracted days Guthwulf did not remember much of his life before the blinding, but what he did remember now seemed full of foolish, meaningless actions. If there was such a place, such a punishment, he doubtless deserved it, but it would be a pity never to feel the strong magic of the gray sword again.

Guthwulf began taking smaller steps, dragging each foot in a careful side-to-side arc before setting it down. His progress slowed as he devoted all his attention to feeling his way forward. At last his foot touched air. He stopped and squatted, tapping his fingers along the hot passage floor. A lip of stone lay before him, stretching on either side farther than he could reach. Beyond that was nothing but emptiness and scorching winds.

He stood, shifting from foot to foot as the heat worked its way through his boot soles, and listened to the great roaring. There were other sounds, too. One was a deep, irregular clanging, as of two massive pieces of metal crashing together; the other was that of human voices.

The sound of metal on metal came again, and the noise finally pushed up a memory from his life in the castle of old. The thunderous clanging was the great forge doors being opened and closed. Men were throwing fuel into the blaze—he had seen it many times when he had inspected the foundries in his role as King's Hand. He must be standing at one of the tunnel mouths almost directly above the huge furnace. No wonder his hair was about to catch fire!

But the gray sword was here. He knew that as certainly as a foraging mouse knows when an owl is on the wing overhead. Elias must be down among the forges, the sword at his side.

Guthwulf backed away from the edge, thinking frantically of ways he could descend to the foundry floor without being observed.

When he had stood in one place long enough to burn his feet, he had to move farther away. He cursed as he went. There was no way to approach the thing. He might wander through these tunnels for days without finding another route down, and surely Elias would be gone by then. But neither could he simply give up. The sword called to him, and it did not care what stood in his way.

Guthwulf stumbled farther down the passageway, away from the heat, although the sword called to him to come back, to leap down into fiery oblivion.

"Why have you done this to me, sweet God?!" he shouted, his voice swiftly disappearing in the roar of the furnace. "Why have you hung me with this curse?!"

The tears evaporated from his eyelids as swiftly as they emerged.

Inch bowed before King Elias. In the flickering forge light, the huge man looked like an ape from the southern jungles—an ape dressed in clothes, but still a poor mockery of a man. The rest of the foundrymen had cast themselves to the floor upon the king's entrance; the scatter of bodies all round the great chamber made it seem as though his very presence had struck a hundred men dead.

"We are working, Highness, working," Inch grunted. "Slow work, it is."

"Working?" Elias said harshly. Though the foundrymaster dripped with sweat, the king's pale skin was dry. "Of course you are working. But you are not finished with the task I have set, and if I do not hear a reason quickly, your filthy skin will be flayed and hung to dry over your own furnace."

The large man dropped to his knees. "We work as fast as we can."

"But it is not fast enough." The king's gaze wandered across the cavern's shadowy roof.

"It is hard, master, hard—we only have parts of the plans. Sometimes we must make everything over when we see the next drawing." Inch looked up, his single eye keen in his dull face as he watched for the king's reaction.

"What do you mean, 'parts of the plans'?" Something was moving in a tunnel mouth, high on the wall above the great furnace. The king squinted, but the flirt of pale color—a face?—was obscured by risking smoke and heat-jumbled air.

"Your majesty!" someone called. "Here you are!"

Elias turned slowly toward the scarlet-robed figure. He lifted an eyebrow in mild surprise, but said nothing.

Pryrates hurried up. "I was surprised to find you gone." His raspy voice was sweeter, more reasonable than usual. "Can I assist you?"

"I do not need you every moment, priest," Elias said curtly. "There are things I can do by myself."

"But you have not been well, Majesty." Pryrates lifted his hand, the red sleeve billowing. For a moment it seemed he might actually take Elias' arm and try to lead him away, but he lifted his fingers to his own head instead, brushing at his hairless scalp. "Because of your weakness, Majesty, I only feared you might stumble on these steep stairs."

Elias looked at him, narrowing his eyes until they were scarcely more than black slits. "I am not an old man, priest. I am not my father in his last years." He flicked a glance at the kneeling Inch, then turned back to Pryrates again. "This clod says that the plans for the castle's defense are difficult."

The alchemist darted a murderous look at Inch. "He lies, Majesty. You approved them yourself. You know that is not so."

"You give us only part at a time, priest." Inch's voice

was deep and slow, but the anger prisoned behind it was more apparent than ever.

"Do not bandy words before the king!" Pryrates snarled.

"I tell truth, priest!"

"Silence!" Elias drew himself up. His knob-knuckled hand fell onto the hilt of the gray sword. "I will have silence!" he shouted. "Now, what does he mean? Why does he get the plans only in pieces?"

Pryrates took a deep breath. "For secrecy, King Elias. You know that several of these foundrymen have run away already. We dare not let anyone see all the plans for defense of the castle. What would prevent them running straight to Josua with what they knew?"

There was a long moment of silence as Pryrates stared at the king. The air in the forge seemed to change slightly, thickening, and the roar of the fires grew strangely muffled. The flickering lights threw long shadows.

Elias suddenly seemed to lose interest. "I suppose." The king's gaze went drifting back to the spot along the cavern wall where he thought he had seen movement. "I will send a dozen more men here to the forges—there are at least that many mercenaries whose looks I do not care for." He turned to the overseer. "Then you will have no excuse."

A tremor ran through Inch's wide frame. "Yes, Highness."

"Good. I have told you when I wish the work on walls and gate to be done. You *will* have it finished."

"Yes, Highness."

The king turned toward Pryrates. "So. I see it takes the king to make certain things go as they should."

The priest bowed his shiny head. "You are irreplaceable, sire."

"But I am also a little tired, Pryrates. Perhaps it is as you said—I have not been well, after all."

"Yes, Highness. Perhaps your healing drink, then a little sleep?" And now Pryrates did insinuate his hand beneath Elias' elbow, turning him gently toward the staircase leading back up to the castle proper. The king went, docile as a child.

"I might lie down for a while, Pryrates, yes ... but I do not think I will sleep just now." He stole a look back at the wall above the furnace, then shook his head dreamily.

"Yes, sire, an excellent idea. Come, we will let the forgemaster get on with his work." Pryrates stared pointedly at Inch, whose one eye looked fixedly back, then the red priest turned away, his face expressionless, and led the king out of the cavern.

Behind them, the prostrated workers slowly began clambering to their feet, too beaten and exhausted even to whisper about such an unusual happening. As they trudged back to their tasks, Inch remained kneeling for some time, his features as frozen as the priest's had been.

Rachel carefully retraced her steps and found the original landing once more. To her even greater relief, when she stared out through the crack, the stairwell was empty. The White Foxes had gone.

Off to work some kind of deviltry, no doubt. She made the sign of the Tree.

Rachel pushed a strand of graying hair out of her eyes. She was exhausted, not only by the dreadful corridor-tramping—she had walked for what seemed like hours—but by the shock of near-discovery. She was not a girl anymore, and she did not like to feel her heart beating as it had beat today: that was not the racing blood of good honest work.

Old—you're getting old, woman.

Rachel was not so foolish as to lose all caution, so she kept her footsteps light and quiet as she made her way down the stairs, peering cautiously around each corner, holding her shuttered lantern behind her so it would not give her away. Thus she saw the king's cupbearer Brother Hengfisk standing on the stairway below her a moment before she would have otherwise run into him in the shadows between wall-torches. As it was, her surprise was

still so great that she gave a startled shriek and dropped
her lantern. It rolled thumping down to the landing—her
landing, the location of her sanctuary!—to lie at the
monk's sandal-shod feet as it dripped blazing oil onto the
stone. The pop-eyed man looked down at the flames burning around his feet with calm interest, then lifted his gaze
to Rachel once more, mouth stretched in a wide grin.

"Merciful Rhiap," Rachel gasped. "Oh, God's mercy!"
She tried to retreat back up the stairwell, but the monk
moved as swiftly as a cat; he was past her in a moment,
then turned to block her passage, still smiling his horrid
smile. His eyes were empty pools.

Rachel took a few tottering steps back down toward the
landing. The monk moved with her, one step at a time,
absolutely silent as he matched his movements to hers.
When Rachel stopped, he stopped. When she tried to
move more swiftly, he headed her off, forcing her
to shrink back against the stone walls of the stairwell to
avoid contact with him. He gave off a feverish warmth,
and there was a strange, alien stink about him, like hot
metal and decaying plants.

She began to cry. Shoulders quivering, unable to hold
up a moment longer, Rachel the Dragon slid down the
wall into a crouch.

"Blessed Elysia, Mother of God," she prayed aloud,
"pure vessel that brings forth the Ransomer, take mercy
on this sinner." She squeezed her eyes shut and made the
Tree sign. "Elysia, raised above all other mortals, Queen
of the Sky and Sea, intercede for your supplicant, so that
mercy may smile upon this sinner."

To her horror, she could not remember the rest of the
words. She huddled, trying to think—oh, her heart, her
heart, it was beating so swiftly!—and waited for the thing
to take her, to touch her with its foul hands. But when
long moments had passed and nothing had happened, her
curiosity overcame even her fear. She opened her eyes.

Hengfisk still stood before her, but the grin was gone.
The monk was leaning against the wall, tugging at his
garments as though surprised to find himself wearing
them. He looked up at her. Something had changed. There

was a new sort of life in the man—cloudy, muddled, but somehow more human than what had stood before her moments earlier.

Hengfisk looked down at the pool of burning oil, at the blue flames licking at his feet, then leaped back, startled. The flames flickered. The monk's lips moved, but at first nothing came out.

"... *Vad es*... ?" he said at last. "... *Uf nammen Hott, vad es*... ?"

He continued to stare at Rachel as if bewildered, but now something else was working behind his eyes. A tightness came to his features, like an invisible hand clutching the back of his tonsured head. The lips pulled taut, the eyes emptied. Rachel gave a little squeak of alarm. There was something going on that she could not understand, some struggle inside the pop-eyed man. She could only stare, terrified.

Hengfisk shook his head like a dog emerging from the water, looked at Rachel once more, then all around the stairwell on either side. The expression on his face had changed again: he looked like a man trapped beneath a crushing weight. A moment later, without warning, Hengfisk turned and stumbled up the stairs. She heard his uneven footfalls winding away into darkness.

Rachel lurched to the tapestry and pulled it aside with clumsy, shaking fingers. When she had fumbled open the door, she fell through and pushed it closed behind her. She shot the bolt before throwing herself onto her mattress and pulling her blanket all the way over her head, then lay trembling as though she had a fever.

The song that had tempted him up from the safer depths was growing more faint. Guthwulf cursed weakly. He was too late. Elias was going, taking the gray sword back up to his throne room, back to that dusty, bloodless tomb of malachite statues and dragon's bones. Where the sword's music had been there was now only emptiness, a gnawing hollow in his being.

Hopelessly, he chose the next corridor that seemed to slope downward, retreating from the surface like a worm unearthed by a shovel. There was a hole in him, a hole through which the wind would blow and the dust sift. He was empty.

As the air became more breathable and the stones grew cool beneath his touch, the little cat found him again. He could feel its buzzing purr as it wound itself around his feet, but he did not stop to give it comfort: at that moment, there was nothing in him to give. The sword had sung to him, then it had gone away once more. Soon the idiot voices would return, the ghost-voices, meaningless, meaningless. . . .

Feeling his way, slow as Time's great wheel, Guthwulf trudged back down into the depths.

15

Lake of Glass

The noise of their coming was like a great wind, a roaring of bulls, a wildfire sweeping through dry lands. Although they ran on roads unused for centuries, the horses did not hesitate, but sped along the secret paths that twined through forest and dale and fen. The old ways, untraveled for scores of mortal generations, were on this day opened again, as though Time's wheel had been stopped in its rut and turned back on itself.

The Sithi had ridden out of summer into a country shackled by winter, but as they passed through the great forest and across the places of their ancient sovereignty—hilly Maa'sha, cedar-mantled Peja'ura, Shisae'ron with her streams, and the black earth of Hekhasór—the land seemed to move restlessly beneath the tread of their hooves, as though struggling to awaken from a cold dream. Birds flew startled from their winter nests and hung in the air like bumblebees as the Sithi thundered past; squirrels clung, transfixed, on frozen boughs. Deep in their dens in the earth, the sleeping bears groaned with hungry anticipation. Even the light seemed to change in the wake of the bright company, as beams of sunlight came needling down through the shrouded sky to sparkle on the snows.

But winter's grip was strong: when the Sithi had passed by, its fist soon closed on the forest once more, dragging everything back down into chill silence.

*   *   *

The company did not stop to rest even as the red glow of sunset drained from the sky and stars glistened between the tree branches overhead. Nor did the horses need more than starlight to find their way along the old roads, though all those tracks were covered with the growth of years. Mortal and earthly the horses were, made only of flesh and blood, but their sires had been of the stock of Venyha Do'sae, brought out of the Garden in the great flight. When the native horses of Osten Ard still ran untamed and frightened on the grasslands, ignorant of hand or bridle, the forebears of these Sithi steeds had ridden to war against the giants, or carried messengers along the roads that spanned from one end to the other of the bright empire. They had borne their riders as swiftly as a sea breeze, and so smoothly that Benayha of Kementari was said to have painted meticulous poems while in the saddle, with never a smeared character. The mastery of these roads was bred into them, a knowledge carried in their wild blood—but their endurance seemed almost a kind of magic. On this endless day, when the Sithi rode once more, their steeds seemed to grow stronger as the hours wore by. As the company sped onward and the sun began to warm beyond the eastern horizon, the tireless horses still ran like a surging wave rushing toward the forest's edge.

If the horses carried ancient blood, their riders were the history of Osten Ard in living flesh. Even the youngest, born since the exile from Asu'a, had seen centuries pass. The eldest could remember many-towered Tumet'ai in its springtime, and the glades of fire-bright poppies, miles of blazing color, that had surrounded Jhiná-T'seneí before the sea swallowed her.

Long the Peaceful Ones had hidden from the eyes of the world, nursing their sadnesses, living only in the memories of other days. Today they rode in armor as brilliant as the plumage of birds, their spears shining like frozen lightning. They sang, for the Sithi had always sung. They rode, and the old ways unfolded before them, forest glades echoing to their horses' hoofbeats for the first time since the tallest trees had been seedlings. After a sleep of centuries, a giant had awakened.

The Sithi were riding.

Although he had been battered and bruised to exhaustion during the day's fighting, and had then spent over an hour after sunset helping Freosel and others to hunt loose arrows in the icy mud—a chore that would have been hard in daytime and was cruelly difficult by torchlight—Simon still did not sleep well. He awoke after midnight with his muscles aching and his mind running in circles. The camp was quiet. Wind had swept the skies clean, and the stars glittered like knife-points.

When it became obvious that sleep was indeed lost, at least for a while, he got up and made his way to the watchfires that burned on the hillside above the great barricades. The largest blazed beside one of the weathered Sithi monument stones, and there he found Binabik and a few others—Geloë, Father Strangyeard, Sludig, and Deornoth—sitting with the prince, talking quietly. Josua was drinking soup from a steaming bowl. Simon guessed that it was the first nourishment the prince had taken that day.

The prince looked up as Simon stepped into the circle of light. "Welcome, young knight," he said. "We are all proud of you. You fulfilled my trust today, as I knew you would."

Simon inclined his head, unsure of what to say. He was glad of the praise, but troubled by the things he had seen and done on the ice. He did not feel very noble. "Thank you, Prince Josua."

He sat huddled in his cloak and listened as the others discussed the day's battle. He sensed that they were talking around the central point, but he also guessed that everyone at the fire knew it as well as he did: they could not win a battle of attrition with Fengbald. They were too badly outnumbered. Sesuad'ra was not a castle to be defended against a long siege—there were too many places where an invading army could gain a foothold. If they could not stop the earl's forces upon the frozen lake, there was little else to do but sell their lives as dearly as they could.

As Deornoth, his head bandaged with a strip of cloth, told of the fighting tendencies he had seen in the Thrithings mercenaries, Freosel strode up to the fire. The constable was still wearing his battle-stained gear, his hands and wide face dirt-smeared; despite the freezing temperatures, his forehead was dotted with sweat, as though he had run all the way down the hill-trail from New Gadrinsett.

"I come from the settlement, Prince Josua," Freosel panted. "Helfgrim, Gadrinsett's mayor, is gone."

Josua looked at Deornoth for a moment, then at Geloë. "Did anyone see him go?"

"He was with others, watching the fighting. No one saw what happened to him."

The prince frowned. "I do not like that. I hope no harm has befallen him." He sighed and put down his bowl, then stood up slowly. "I suppose we must see what we can find out. There will be scant chance in the morning."

Sludig, who had come up behind Freosel, said: "Your pardon, Prince Josua, but there is no need to bother yourself with it. Let others do this so you can rest."

Josua smiled thinly. "Thank you, Sludig, but I have other tasks up at the settlement as well, so it is no great effort. Deornoth, Geloë, perhaps you would accompany me. You, too, Freosel. There are things I would finish discussing with you." He pushed absently at one of the fire logs with the toe of his boot, then drew his cloak about him and moved to the path. Those he had summoned followed, but Freosel turned back for a moment and came and put his hand on Simon's shoulder.

"Sir Seoman, I spoke quick the other day, without thinking."

Simon was confused, and more than a little embarrassed to hear his title in the mouth of this powerful and competent young man. "I don't know what you mean."

"About the fairy-folk." The Falshireman fixed him with a serious look. "You may think I made fun, or showed disrespect. See now, I fear the Peaceful Ones like any God-fearing Aedonite man, but I know they can be powerful friends, for all that. If summon 'em you can, go to it. We need any help we can get."

Simon shook his head. "I have no power over them, Freosel—none at all. You don't know what they're like."

"Nor do I, that's true. But if they be your friends, tell 'em we be in hard straits. That's all I have to say." He turned and went up the path, hurrying to catch the prince and the others.

Sludig, who had remained, made a face. "Summon the Sithi. Hah! It would be easier to summon the wind."

Simon nodded in sad agreement. "But we do need help, Sludig."

"You are too trusting, lad. We mean little to the Sithi-folk. I doubt we will see Jiriki again." The Rimmersman frowned at Simon's expression. "Besides, we have our swords and our brains and our hearts." He hunkered down before the flames and warmed his hands. "God gives a man what he deserves, no more, no less." A moment later he straightened up, restless. "If the prince has no need of me, I will go and find a place to sleep. Tomorrow will be bloodier work than today." He nodded at Simon and Binabik and Strangyeard, then walked down toward the barricade, the chain on his sword belt clinking faintly.

Simon sat watching him go, wondering if Sludig was right about the Sithi, dismayed because of the feeling of loss that idea brought.

"The Rimmersman is angry." The archivist sounded surprised by his own words. "I mean, that is, I scarcely know him . . ."

"It is my thinking you speak the truth, Strangyeard." Binabik looked down at the piece of wood he had been carving. "Some folk there are who are not liking much to be beneath others, especially when it was once being otherwise. Sludig has become again a foot-soldier, after being chosen for questing and bringing back a great prize." The troll's words were thoughtful, but his face was unhappy, as though he shared the Rimmersman's pain. "I am afraid for him to be fighting in battle with that feeling in his heart—we have shared a friendship since our trav-

els in the north, but he has seemed dark and sad-hearted
to me since coming here."

A silence fell on the little gathering, broken only by the
crackle of the flames.

"What about what he said?" Simon asked abruptly. "Is
he right?"

Binabik looked at him inquiringly. "What are you
meaning, Simon? About the Sithi?"

"No. 'God gives a man what he deserves, no more, no
less,' that's what Sludig said." Simon turned to
Strangyeard. "Is that true?"

The archivist, flustered, looked away; after a moment,
though, he turned back and met Simon's gaze. "No, Simon. I don't think that is true. But I cannot know the
mind of God, either."

"Because my friends Morgenes and Haestan certainly
didn't get what they deserved—one burned and one
crushed by a giant's club." Simon could not keep the bitterness from his voice.

Binabik opened his mouth as though he would say
something, but seeing Strangyeard had done the same, the
troll stayed silent.

"I believe that God has plans, Simon." The archivist
spoke carefully. "And it may be that we simply do not understand them . . . or it may be that God Himself does not
quite know how His plans will work out."

"But you priests are always saying that God knows everything!"

"He may have chosen to forget some of the more painful things," Strangyeard said gently. "If you lived forever,
and experienced every pain in the world as though it were
your own—died with every soldier, cried with every
widow and orphan, shared every mother's grief at the
passing of a beloved child—would you not perhaps yearn
to forget, too?"

Simon looked into the shifting flames of the fire. *Like
the Sithi,* he thought, *trapped with their pain forever.*
Craving an ending, as Amerasu had said.

Binabik carved a few more chips from the piece of
wood. It was beginning to take a shape that might be a

wolf's head, prick-eared and long of muzzle. "If I am allowed the asking, friend Simon, is there a reason that Sludig's saying struck you with such strongness?"

Simon shook his head. "I just don't know how to . . . to be. These men have come to kill us—I want them all to die, painfully, horribly. . . . But Binabik, these are the Erkynguard! I knew them at the castle. Some of them used to give me sweets, or lift me up on their horses and tell me I reminded them of their own sons." He fidgeted with a stick, scuffing at the muddy soil. "Which is right? How could they do these things to us, who never did them any harm? But the king is making them, so why should they be killed, any more than us?"

Binabik's lips curled in a tiny smile. "I notice you are not having worries about the mercenaries—no, say nothing, there is no need! It is hard to feel sorry for those who are searching out war for gold." He slipped the half-finished carving into his jacket and began to reassemble his walking-stick, socketing the knife back into the long handle. "The questions you are asking are important ones, but they are also questions without answers. This is what being a man or woman means, I am thinking, instead of a boy or girl child: you must be finding your own solution to questions that are having no true answers." He turned to Strangyeard. "Do you have Morgenes' book somewhere that is near, or is it now up in the settlement?"

The archivist had been staring into the flames, lost in thought. "What?" he said, suddenly rousing. "The book, you say? Oh, heavenly pastures, I carry it with me everywhere! How could I trust it left in some place unwatched?" He turned abruptly and looked shyly at Simon. "Of course, it is not mine—please do not think I have forgotten your kindness, Simon, in letting me read it. You cannot imagine how wonderful it has been, having Morgenes' words to savor!"

Simon felt an almost pleasurable twinge of regret at the memory of Morgenes. How he missed that good old man! "It is not mine, either, Father Strangyeard. He merely gave it to me for safekeeping so that eventually people like you and Binabik would be able to read it." He smiled

gloomily. "I think that is what I am learning these days—
that nothing is really mine. I thought for a time that Thorn
was meant for me, but I doubt it now. I have been given
other things, but none of them quite do what they are supposed to. I'm glad someone is getting good use of Morgenes' words."

"We all are getting such use." Binabik smiled back, but
his tone was serious. "Morgenes planned for us all in this
dark time."

"Just a moment." Strangyeard scrambled to his feet. He
returned a moment later with his sack, inadvertently spilling its contents—a Book of the Aedon, a scarf, a water
skin, a few small coins and gewgaws—in his effort to get
to the manuscript lodged firmly at the bottom. "Here it
is," he said in triumph, then paused. "Why was I looking
for it?"

"Because I was asking if you had it," Binabik explained. "There is a passage I think Simon would find of
great interestingness."

The troll took the proffered manuscript and leafed
through it with delicate care, frowning as he tried to read
by the uncertain light of the campfire. It did not seem that
it would be a very swift process, so Simon got up to
empty his bladder. The wind was chilly along the hillside,
and the white lake below, which he glimpsed through a
break in the trees, looked like a place for phantoms.
When he got back to the fire he was shivering.

"Here, I have found it." Binabik waved the page.
"Would you prefer reading for yourself, or should I go to
reading it for you?"

Simon smirked at the troll's solicitousness. "You love
to read things at me. Go ahead."

"It is in the interest of your continuing education,
only," Binabik said mock-severely. "Listen: *'In fact,'*
Morgenes writes,

> *'the debate as to who was the greatest knight in
> Aedondom was for many years a source of argu-
> ment everywhere, in both the corridors of the
> Sancellan Aedonitis in Nabban and the taverns of*

Erkynland and Hernystir. It would be difficult to claim that Camaris was the inferior of any man, but he seemed to take so little joy in combat that for him warfare might have been a penance, his own great skills a form of punishment. Often, when honor compelled him to fight in tournaments, he would hide the kingfisher-crest of his house beneath a disguise, thus to prevent his foes from being overmatched simply by awe. He was also known to give himself incredible handicaps, such as fighting with his left hand only, not out of bravado, but out of what I myself guess was a dreadful desire to have someone, somewhere, finally best him, thus removing from his shoulders the burden of being Osten Ard's preeminent knight—and hence a target for every drunken brawler as well as the inspiration of every balladeer. When fighting in war, even the priests of Mother Church agreed, his admirable humility and mercy to a beaten foe seemed almost to stretch too far, as though he longed for honorable defeat, for death. His feats of arms, which were talked about across the length and breadth of Osten Ard, were to Camaris acts almost shameful.

'Once Tallistro of Perdruin had been killed by ambush in the first Thrithings War—a treachery made famous in almost as many songs as tell of Camaris' exploits—it was only John himself who could ever be considered a rival to Camaris for the title of Aedondom's greatest warrior. Indeed, none would have suggested that even Prester John, as mighty as he was, could have defeated Sir Camaris in an open fight: after Nearulagh, the battle in which they met, Camaris was careful never even to spar with John again, for fear of upsetting the delicate balance of their friendship. But where Camaris' skills were to him an onerous burden, and the prosecution of war—even those wars that Mother Church sanctioned and,

*some might say, occasionally encouraged—was
for Nabban's greatest knight a trial and a source
of grief, Prester John was a man who never
seemed happier than on the battlefield. He was
not cruel—no defeated foe was ever shown less
than fairness by him, except for the Sithi, against
whom John held some private but powerful ill-
feelings, and whom he persecuted until they have
all but vanished from the sight of mortal men. But
since some would argue that the Sithi are not
men, and therefore do not have souls—although I
myself would not so argue—it could then be said
that all John's enemies were treated in a way that
even the most scrupulous churchman would have
to call just and merciful. And to his subjects, even
the pagan Hernystiri, John was a generous king.
It was only in those times when the carpet of war
was spread before him that he became a dangerous weapon. Thus it was that Mother Church, in
whose name he conquered, named him—in gratitude and perhaps a bit of quiet fear—the Sword
of the Lord.*

   *'So the argument raged, and does to this day:
who was the greater? Camaris, the most skillful
man to lift a sword in human memory? Or John,
only slightly less proficient, but a leader of men,
and himself a man who welcomed a just and
godly war. . . ?' "*

Binabik cleared his throat. "And, as he is telling that
the argument went on, so Morgenes himself is going on
for several pages more, talking in greater depth of this
question, which was of great importantness in its day—or
was anyway *thought* to be of such importantness."

"So Camaris killed better but liked it less than King
John did?" Simon asked. "Why did he do it, then? Why
not become a monk, or a hermit?"

"Ah, that is being the nub of what you were earlier
wondering, Simon," Binabik said, his dark eyes intent.
"That is why the writing of great thinkers is being such a

help to the rest of us in our own thinking. Here Morgenes has put the words and names in a different way, but it is the same questioning as yours: is it right to be killing, even if it is what your master or country or church wishes? Is it better to kill but not to enjoy it, or to not kill at all, and then perhaps be seeing bad things happen to those who you are loving?"

"Does Morgenes give an answer?"

"No." Binabik shook his head. "As I said, the wise know that these questions have no true answers. Life is made from these wonderings, and from the answers that we each and every one are finding for ourselves."

"Just for once, Binabik, I want you to tell me there *is* an answer for something. I'm tired of thinking so much."

The troll laughed. "The punishment for being born ... no, perhaps that is too much to be calling that. The punishment for being truly alive—that is fair to say. Welcome, Simon, to the world of those who are every day condemned to thinking and wondering and never ever knowing with certainness."

Simon snorted. "Thank you."

"Yes, Simon," There was strange, somber earnestness in Strangyeard's voice. "Welcome. I pray that someday you will be glad that your decisions were not simple ones."

"How could that be?"

Strangyeard shook his head. "Forgive me for saying the kind of things that old men say, Simon, but ... you will see."

Simon stood up. "Very well. Now that you have made my head spin, I will do as Sludig did: go away in disgust and try to sleep." He put his hand on Binabik's shoulder, then turned to the archivist, who was reverently placing Morgenes' book back in his bag. "Good night, Father Strangyeard. Be well. Good night, Binabik."

"Good night, friend Simon."

He heard the troll and the priest talking quietly as he walked back to his sleeping spot. It made him feel a little safer, for some reason, to know that such folk were awake.

In the last moments before dawn, Deornoth had run out of tasks. His sword had been sharpened, then sharpened again. He had reattached several buckles that had been torn from his byrnie, which had required hard, finger-cramping work with a tack-needle, and then laboriously cleaned the mud from his boots. Now he would either have to remain barefoot but for the rags that wrapped his feet—a cold, cold condition—until it was time to move out onto the ice, or put his boots back on and stay where he was. A single step across the muddy ruin that was the encampment would certainly undo his careful work. The footing was going to be bad enough without slick mud on his boot soles to make it worse.

As the sky began to pale, Deornoth listened to some of his men singing quietly. He had never fought beside any of them before yesterday. They were a tattish army, no doubt: many of them had never wielded a sword before, and of those who had, more than a few were so old that back in their shareholdings they had not come to the seasonal muster for years. But fighting in defense of home could turn even the mildest farmer into an enemy to be reckoned with, and this bare stone was home now to many. Deornoth's men, under the leadership of those few of their number who had actually served under arms, had acquitted themselves bravely—very bravely indeed. He only wished he had something better to offer them in the way of reward than this coming day's slaughter.

He heard the sucking noise of horses' hooves in mud; the quiet murmur of the men around him died away. He turned to see a small group of riders winding their way down the trail that ran through the camp. Foremost among them was a tall, slender figure mounted on a chestnut stallion, his cloak rippling in the strong wind. Josua was ready at last. Deornoth sighed and stood up, waving for the rest of his troops as he grabbed his boots. The time for woolgathering was past. Still unshod, still postponing that inevitable moment, he went to join his prince.

At first there were few surprises in the second day's fighting. It was bloody work, as Sludig had prophesied, breast to breast, blade against blade; by mid-morning the ice was washed in red and ravens were feasting on the outskirts of combat.

Those who survived this battle would call it by many names: to Josua and his closest company, it was the Siege of Sesuad'ra. For the captains of Fengbald's Erkynlandish troops, it was Stefflod Valley; to the mercenary Thrithings-men, the Battle of the Stone. But for most who remembered it, and few did without a shudder, the name that was most evocative was the Lake of Glass.

War surged back and forth across Sesuad'ra's icy moat all morning long as first one side and then the other gained a momentary advantage. At first the Erkynguard, embarrassed by their showing the day before, pressed the attack so strongly that the Stone's defenders were driven back against their own barricades. They might have been cut down then, overwhelmed by superior numbers, but Josua rode forth on fiery Vinyafod, leading a small mounted group of Hotvig's Thrithings-men, and caused enough dismay in the flanks of the king's soldiers that they could not push their advantage to its fullest extent. The arrows that Freosel and the other defenders had scavenged flew down from the hillside, and the green-liveried Erkynguard were forced to draw back out of range, waiting until the missiles were spent. Red-cloaked Duke Fengbald rode back and forth in a clear section of ice at mid-lake, waving his sword and gesticulating.

His troops attacked again, but this time the defenders were ready and the wave of mounted Erkynguard broke against the great log walls. A sallying force from the hillside then pierced the green line and stabbed deep into the middle of Fengbald's forces. They were not strong enough to split the duke's army, or the battle might have gone very differently, but even when they were thrown back with heavy losses, it was clear that Deornoth's farmer-soldiers had found a renewed determination. They knew they could fight on this field as near-equals; it was clear that they would not give up their home to the king's swords without exacting a bloody price.

The sun reached the tips of the treeline, morning light just spilling onto the far side of the valley. The ice was again thick with mist. Down in the murk, the fighting grew desperate as men struggled not just with each other but with the treacherous battlefield as well. Both sides seemed determined that things would be finished by nightfall, the issue settled forever. From the number of unmoving shapes that already lay sprawled across the frozen lake, there seemed little doubt that by afternoon, there would be few of Sesuad'ra's defenders left to contest the matter.

Within the first hour after dawn, Simon had forgotten about Camaris, about Prester John, even about God. He felt like a boat caught in a terrible storm, but the waves that threatened to drown him had faces and carried sharp blades. There was no attempt today to hold the trolls in reserve. Josua had felt sure that Fengbald would simply throw his men against Sesuad'ra's defenders until they were beaten down, so there was little point in trying to surprise anyone. There was no order of battle, only a skeleton of battlefield command, tattered banners and distant horns. The opposing armies rushed together, hit, and clung to each other like drowning men, then withdrew again to rest before the next surge, leaving the bodies of the fallen splayed across the misty lake.

As the Erkynguard's assault pressed the defenders back against the barricades, Simon saw the troll-herder Snenneq skewered by an Erkynguardsman's lance, lifted completely out of his ram-saddle and pinned against one of the barricade tree trunks. Although the troll was undoubtedly dead or dying, the armored guardsman jerked his weapon free and pierced the small body again as it slid down the wall, twisting the lance as though killing an insect. Simon, maddened, spurred Homefinder through a gap in the crush of men and brought his sword around with all the strength he could muster, nearly beheading the guardsman, who crashed off his horse and fell to the frozen lake, fountaining blood. Simon bent and caught at Snenneq's hide jacket, pulling him up from the ground with one hand without even feeling the weight. The troll's head bobbed; his brown eyes stared sightlessly. Simon cradled the small, stocky form against his own body, heedless of the blood that soaked his breeches and saddle.

Sometime later he found himself on the edge of the battle. Snenneq's body was gone. Simon did not know if he had put it down or dropped it; he did not remember anything but the dead troll's astonished, frightened face. There had been blood on the little man's lips and between his teeth.

It was easy to hate if he did not think, Simon discovered. If he saw the faces of enemies only as pale smears within their helmets, if he saw their open mouths as horrid black holes, it was easy to ride at them and smash them with all his strength, to try and separate the knobby heads and flailing limbs from the bodies until the hated things were dead. He also found that if he was not afraid of dying—and at this moment he was not: he felt as though all his fear had been charred away—it was easy to survive. The men against whom he rode, even though they were trained fighting men, many of them veterans of several battles, seemed frightened by Simon's single-minded assaults. He swung and swung, each blow as hard or harder than the last. When they lifted their own weapons, he swung at their arms and hands. If they fell back to try to lure him off-balance, he rode Homefinder full into their sides and battered away as Ruben the Bear had once pounded red-hot metal in the Hayholt's stables. Sooner or later, Simon discovered, the look of fear would creep into their eyes, the whites flashing in the depths of their helmets. Sooner or later they would shy back, but Simon would hammer on, slashing and hewing, until they fled or fell. Then he would suck air deep into his lungs, hearing little but the impossibly fast drumbeat of his own heart, until anger rebirthed his strength and he went riding on in search of something else to hack.

Blood spurted, hovering for long moments like a red

mist. Horses fell, legs kicking convulsively. The noise of battle was so loud as to be virtually unhearable. As he pushed through the carnage, Simon felt his arms turn to iron—rigid, hard as the blade he held in his hand; he had no horse, but rather four strong legs that took him where he wished to go. He was spattered in red, some of it his own, but he felt nothing but fire inside his chest and a spastic need to beat down the things that had come to steal his new home and slaughter his friends.

Simon did not know it, but beneath his helm, his face was wet with tears.

A curtain seemed to draw away at last, letting light into the dark room of Simon's bestial thoughts. He was somewhere near the middle of the lake and someone was calling his name.

"Simon!" It was a high voice, yet strange. For a moment he was not quite sure where he was. "Simon!" the voice called again.

He looked down, searching for the one who had spoken, but the foot-soldier who lay crumpled there would never call to anyone again. Simon's horrifying numbness melted a little further. The corpse belonged to one of Fengbald's soldiers. Simon turned away, unwilling to look at the man's slack face.

"Simon, come!" It was Sisqi, followed by two of her troll-kin, riding toward him. Even as he brought Homefinder around to face the new arrivals, he could not help looking at the yellow slot-eyes of their saddle-rams. What were they thinking? What could animals think of such a thing as this?

"Sisqi." He blinked. "What. . . ?"

"Come, come fast!" She gestured with her spear toward a place closer to the barricades. The battle was still swirling, and although Simon stared hard, he knew it would take someone like old Jarnauga to make any sense out of such chaos.

"What is it?"

"Help your friend! Your *Croohok!* Come!"

Simon kicked his heels against Homefinder's ribs and

followed the trolls as they neatly wheeled their rams about. Homefinder lurched as she struggled across the slippery lake surface after them. Simon could tell that the horse was tired, dreadfully tired. Poor Homefinder! He should stop and give her water ... let her sleep ... sleep ... Simon's own head was pounding, and his right arm felt as though it had been beaten with clubs.

Aedon's mercy, what have I done? What have I done to-day?

The trolls led him back into the knot of battle. The men he saw around him were exhausted almost to heedlessness, like South Islander slaves sent to fight in the old Nabbanai arenas. Foes seemed to hold each other up as they struck, and the clang of weaponry had a dolorous, off-key sound, like a hundred cracked bells pealing.

Sludig and a knot of defenders were surrounded by Thrithings mercenaries. The Rimmersman had an ax in each hand. He had been unhorsed, but even as he struggled to keep his footing on the ice he held two scarfaced Thrithings-men at bay. Simon and the trolls came on as swiftly as the footing would allow, falling on Sludig's attackers from behind. Although Simon's cramping arm failed to strike a clean blow, his blade struck near the unprotected tail of one of the Thrithings-men's horses, making the creature rear suddenly. Its rider crashed to the ice, where he was quickly savaged by Sludig's companions. The Rimmersman used the skidding, riderless horse as a shield against his other enemy, then was able to get a foot into the stirrup and clamber into the saddle, bringing one of his axes up just in time to ward a blow from the Thrithings-man's curved sword. Their weapons clanked together twice more, then Sludig, roaring wordlessly, hooked the man's blade from his grip with one ax and buried the other in the mercenary's head, smashing down through the stiff leather helmet as though it were an eggshell. He put his boot in the man's chest and wrenched the ax free; the mercenary flopped over his horse's neck, then slid heavily to the ground.

Simon shouted to Sludig, then turned quickly as another surge of the struggle pushed a riderless horse heav-

ily against Homefinder's shoulder, almost jarring him out
of his seat. He clutched at the reins, then righted himself
and kicked at the panicking creature, which whinnied and
scrambled for purchase on the ice before scrambling
away.

The Rimmersman stared at Simon for a moment as
though he did not recognize him. His yellow beard was
spattered with drops of blood, and his chain mail was broken and torn in several places. "Where is Deornoth?"

"I don't know! I just got here!" Simon lifted himself
higher in the saddle to look around, clutching Homefinder
with his knees.

"He was cut off." Sludig stood in his own stirrups.
"There! I see his cloak!" He pointed into a clot of
Thrithings-men nearby, in whose midst there was a flash
of blue. "Come!" Sludig spurred the mercenary's horse
ahead. The beast, fitted with no special iron spikes,
slipped and skidded.

Simon called for Sisqi and her friends, who were
calmly spearing wounded Thrithings-men. The daughter
of the Herder and Huntress barked something to her companions in the Qanuc tongue and they all cantered after
Simon and Sludig.

The sky had grown darker overhead as clouds had covered the sun. Now a flurry of tiny snowflakes began to fill
the air. The mist seemed to be growing thicker, too. Simon thought he saw a flash of crimson moving in the
dark sea of struggling men not far beyond Sludig. Could
it be Fengbald? Here, in the middle of things? It seemed
impossible the duke would take such a risk when numbers
and experience were on his side.

Simon had less than a moment to ponder this unlikely
possibility before Sludig had crashed into the clump of
Thrithings-men, laying about indiscriminately with his
axes. Although two men fell wounded before the
Rimmersman, opening his way, Simon saw that others
were moving into the gap, several of them still on horseback: Sludig would be surrounded. Simon's sense of unreality became even stronger. What was he doing here?
He was no soldier! This was madness. Yet what else

could he do? His friends were being hurt and killed. He spurred forward, slashing at the bearded mercenaries. Each blow now leaped up his arm, a pain like a tongue of fire that he felt through his shoulders into the base of his skull. He heard the strange yipping cries of Sisqi and her Qanuc behind him, then suddenly he was through.

Sludig had climbed down off his horse. He was kneeling beside a figure in a cloak the color of an early evening sky. It was Deornoth, and his face was very pale. Beneath Josua's knight, half-covered by his blue cloak, a hugely-muscled Thrithings-man lay on his back, staring sightlessly at the cloudy sky, a crust of blood on his lips. With the sharpened clarity of near-madness, Simon saw a snowflake flutter down to land on the mercenary's opened eye.

"It is the leader of the mercenaries," Sludig shouted over the clamor. "Deornoth has killed him."

"But Deornoth, is he alive?"

Sludig was already struggling to lift the knight from the ice. Simon looked around to see if they were in immediate danger, but the mercenaries had been lured away to some other pocket of the shifting chaos. Simon quickly dismounted and helped Sludig lift Deornoth onto the saddle. The Rimmersman climbed up and clutched at the knight, who sagged like an understuffed doll.

"Bad," Sludig said. "He is bad. We must get him back to the barricades."

He set out at a trot. Sisqi and the other two trolls fell in behind him. The Rimmersman steered his horse in a wide arc, heading for the outer fringe of the killing ground and comparative safety.

Simon could only lean against Homefinder's side, panting, staring at Sludig's back and Deornoth's slack face bouncing beside the Rimmersman's shoulder. Things were as bad as could be imagined. Jiriki and his Sithi were not coming. God had not seen fit to rescue the virtuous. If only this whole nightmarish day could be wished away. Simon shivered. It seemed almost that if he closed his eyes this would all be gone, that he would wake in his bed in the Hayholt's serving quarters, the spring sunlight crawling across the flagstones outside. . . .

He shook his head and struggled into the saddle, legs trembling. He spurred Homefinder forward. No time to let the mind wander. No time.

There was the flash of red again, just to his right. He turned and saw a figure in crimson, sitting on a white horse. The mounted man's helm was furnished with silver wings.

Fengbald!

Slowly, as though the ice had turned to sticky honey beneath his horses' hooves, Simon reined up and turned toward the armored man. Surely this was a dream! The duke was behind a small knot of Erkynguardsmen, but his attention seemed fixed on the fighting just before him. Simon, at the outer edge of the battle, had a clear path. He spurred Homefinder forward.

As he moved closer, picking up speed, the silver helmet seemed to grow before him, dazzling even in the murky light. The crimson cloak and bright chain mail were like a wound on the dim darkness of the far-away trees.

Simon shouted, but the figure did not turn. He kicked his boot-irons against Homefinder's side. She made a huffing noise and increased her pace; foam flew from her lips. "Fengbald!" Simon screamed again, and this time the duke seemed to hear. The closed helm swiveled toward Simon, the eye-slit blankly inscrutable. The duke lifted his sword with one hand and tugged at his reins to bring his horse around to face this attacker. Fengbald seemed slow, as if underwater, as though he, too, found himself in some terrible dream.

Beneath his own helm, Simon's lips skinned back from his teeth. A nightmare, then. He would be Fengbald's nightmare, this time. He swung his own sword back, feeling the muscles in his shoulders jump and strain. As Homefinder swept down on the duke, Simon brought his sword around with both hands. It met the duke's blade with a shivering impact that nearly pushed Simon backward out of the saddle, but something yielded at the blow. When he was past, and had straightened himself in the saddle, he turned Homefinder around in a careful half-circle. Fengbald had fallen from his horse and his sword had been knocked from his hand. The duke lay on his back, struggling to rise.

Simon vaulted from the saddle and promptly slipped, falling forward to land painfully on elbows and knees. He crawled to where the duke still fought for balance, then rose on his knees and brought the flat of his sword against the shining helm as hard as he could. The duke fell back, arms spread wide like the wings of the silver eagle on his surcoat. Simon clambered on top of him and squatted on his chest. He, Simon, had beaten Duke Fengbald! Had they won, then? Panting, he darted a quick look around him, but no one seemed to have seen. Neither was there any sign that the fighting had been resolved—clots of figures still thrashed in the mist all across the lake. Could he have won the battle without anyone noticing?

Simon pulled his Qanuc knife from the sheath and pressed it against Fengbald's throat, then fumbled at the duke's helm. He worked it free at last, tugging it loose with little regard for its owner's comfort. He tossed it aside. It spun on the ice as Simon leaned forward.

His prisoner was a middle-aged man, bald where he was not gray. His bloodied mouth was missing most of its teeth. He was not Fengbald.

" 'S Bloody Tree!" Simon swore. The world was collapsing. Nothing was real. He stared at the surcoat, at the falcon-winged helmet lying just inches away. They were Fengbald's, there was no question. But this was not the duke.

"Tricked!" Simon groaned. "Oh, God, we have been tricked like children." There was a cold knot in his stomach. "Mother of Aedon—*where is Fengbald!?*"

Far across Osten Ard to the west, far from the concerns of Sesuad'ra's defenders, a small procession emerged from a hole in the Grianspog mountainside like a troop of white mice released from a cage. As they left the shadowy tunnels they stopped, blinking and squinting in the snow-glare.

The Hernystiri, only a few hundred all told, most of them women, children, and old men, milled in confusion on the rocky shelf outside the cavern. Maegwin sensed that with any prompting at all they would quickly dash back into the safety of the caves once more. The balance was very delicate. It had taken a great effort on Maegwin's part, all her powers of persuasion, to convince her people even to set out on this seemingly doomed journey.

Gods of our forefathers, she thought, *Brynioch and Rhynn, where is our backbone!?* Only Diawen, breathing deeply of the cold air with her arms lifted as if in ritual celebration, seemed to understand the glory of this march. The expression on the lined face of Old Craobhan left no doubt as to what *he* thought of this foolishness. But the rest of her subjects seemed mostly fearful, looking for some portent, some excuse to turn back again.

They needed prodding, that was all. It was frightening for mortals to live as their deities wished them to—it was a greater responsibility than most wished to bear. Maegwin took a deep breath.

"Great days are before us, people of Hernystir," she cried. "The gods wish us to go down the mountain to face our enemies—the enemies who have stolen our houses, our farms, our cattle and pigs and sheep. Remember who you are! Come with me!"

She strode forward onto the path. Slowly, reluctantly, her followers fell into step behind her, shivering despite being wrapped in the warmest clothing they had been able to find. Many of the children were crying.

"Arnoran," she called. The harper, who had been walking a little distance behind—perhaps hoping that he could fall far enough back that his presence would not be missed—came forward, leaning against the force of the wind.

"Yes, my lady?"

"Walk beside me," she directed. Arnoran took a look

down at the mountain's sheer, snowy face just beyond the narrow path, then quickly looked away again. "I want you to play a song," Maegwin said.

"What song, Princess?"

"Something that everyone knows the words to. Something that lifts the heart." She pondered as she walked. Arnoran looked nervously down at his feet. "Play 'The Lily of the Cuimnhe.' "

"Yes, my lady." Arnoran lifted his harp and began to pick out the opening strains, working it through a few times to let his chilled fingers warm. Then he began in earnest, playing loudly so that those behind could easily hear.

"The Hernysadharc rose is fair."

he sang, lifting his voice above the wind that prowled the mountainside and stirred the trees,

"As red as blood, as white as snow,
But still unplucked I'll leave it there
For I have somewhere else to go."

One by one at first, then in bunches, others of Maegwin's band began to pick up the verses of the familiar song.

"At Inniscrich the violets grow
As dark as skies of early night,
But I'll not have them, even so
For I prefer my beauties bright.

"Near Abaingeat the daisies bloom
Like stars a-twinkle in the sky,
But I will leave them in the coomb
I cannot stop; I must pass by.

"The sweetest flower of all, she grows
Where river past sweet meadow flows,

And where she blossoms I will go:
The Lily of the Cuimhne.

"When someday winter's winds shall blow
When leaves are withered, sap is slow,
I will recall this love, I know:
The Lily of the Cuimhne ..."

By the refrain, scores of people had joined in. The pace
of the marching feet seemed to increase, to match itself to
the rhythm of the old song. The voices of Maegwin's people rose until they outshouted the wind—and strangely,
the wind grew weaker, as if acknowledging defeat.

The remnants of Hernysadharc marched down from
their mountain retreat, singing.

They stopped on a shelf of snow-swept rock, and ate
their midday meal beneath the dim and straining sun.
Maegwin walked among her people, paying special attention to the children. She felt happy and fulfilled for the
first time in long memory: Lluth's daughter was finally
doing what she was meant to do. Satisfied at last, she felt
her love for the people of Hernystir come bubbling up—
and her people felt it, too. Some of the older folk might
still have misgivings about this mad undertaking, but to
the children it was a wonderful lark; they followed
Maegwin through the camp, laughing and shouting, until
even the worried parents were able to forget for a while
the danger into which they were traveling, to put aside
their doubts. After all, how could the princess be so full
of light and truth if the gods were not with her?

As for Maegwin, virtually all her own doubts had been
left on Bradach Tor. She had the entire company singing
again and on their way before the noon hour had passed.

When they reached the bottom of the mountain at last,
her people seemed to gain hope. For all but a few of
them, this was the first time they had touched the meadows of Hernystir since the Rimmersgard troops had
driven them into the high places half a year before. They
were returning home.

The first of Skali's pickets came forward in a rush as they saw a small army descending from the Grianspog, but reined up in surprise, the hooves of their horses digging up great gouts of powdery snow, when they saw that the army bore no weapons—in fact, carried nothing at all in their arms but swaddled infants. The Rimmersmen, hardened warriors every one, undaunted by the confusion and horror of battle, stared in consternation at Maegwin and her troop.

"Stop!" the leader cried. He was all but hidden in his helmet and fur-lined cloak, and for a moment seemed a startled badger blinking in the door of its sett. "Going where are you?"

Maegwin made a haughty face at his poor command of the Westerling tongue. "We are going to your master, Skali of Kaldskryke."

The soldiers looked, if possible, even more bewildered. "So many to surrender are not needed," the leader said. "Tell the women and children for waiting here. Men with us will come."

Maegwin scowled. "Fool. We do not come to surrender. We come to take our land back." She waved. Her followers, who had stopped while she spoke to the soldiers, surged forward once more.

The Rimmersmen fell in beside them like dogs trying to herd a flock of unimpressed and hostile sheep.

As they made their way across the snowy meadowlands between the foothills and Hernysadharc, Maegwin felt anger growing within her once more, anger that for a while had been overwhelmed by the glory of positive action. Here stand after stand of ancient trees, oak and beech and alder, had been leveled by Rimmersgard axes, their carcasses stripped of bark and dragged away across the rutted ground. Skali's soldiers and their horses had churned the earth around their camps to frozen mud, and the ashes of their countless fires blew across the gray snow. The very face of the land was wounded and suffering—no wonder the gods were unhappy! Maegwin looked around and saw her own fury mirrored in the faces of her followers, their few lingering doubts now vanishing like water drops on a hot stone. The gods would make this place clean again, with their help. How could anyone doubt that it would be so?

At last, as the afternoon sun hung swollen in the gray sky, they reached the outskirts of Hernysadharc itself. They were now part of a much larger crowd: during the slow approach of Maegwin's folk, many of the Rimmersmen had drifted in from the encampments to watch this odd spectacle, until it seemed that the whole occupying army trailed along after them. The combined company, nearing perhaps a thousand souls, made its way through the narrow, spiraling streets of Hernysadharc toward the king's house, the Taig.

When they reached the great cleared place atop the hillock, Skali of Kaldskryke was waiting for them, standing before the Taig's vast oaken doors. The Rimmersman was dressed in his dark armor as though waiting for a fight, and he carried his raven-helm under his arm. He was surrounded by his household guard, a legion of grim, bearded men.

Many of Maegwin's people now, at this late moment, felt their courage suddenly falter. As Skali's own Rimmersmen kept to a respectful distance, so, too, did many of Maegwin's company slow and begin to hang back. But Maegwin and a few others—Old Craobhan, always the loyal servant, was one of them—strode forward. Maegwin moved without fear or hesitation toward the man who had conquered and brutally subjugated her country.

"Who are you, woman?" Skali demanded. His voice was surprisingly soft, with a suggestion of a stutter. Maegwin had only heard him once before—Skali had shouted up at the Hernystiri's hiding place on the mountain side, trumpeting the gift of her brother Gwythinn's mutilated body—but that one horrid time was enough: shouting or whispering, Maegwin knew that voice and loathed it. The nose that had given Skali his nickname stood out starkly from a broad, wind-burned face. His eyes were intent and clever. She did not see a hint of any sort of kindness in their depths, but she had not expected to.

Face-to-face at last with the destroyer of her family, she was pleased by her own icy calm. "I am Maegwin," she proclaimed. "Daughter of Lluth-ubh-Llythinn, the king of Hernystir."

"Who is dead," Skali said shortly.

"Whom you killed. I have come to tell you that your time is over. You are to leave this land now, before the gods of Hernystir punish you."

Skali stared at her carefully. His guardsmen were smirking at the ridiculousness of the situation, but Sharp-nose was not. "And if I do not, king's daughter?"

"The gods will decide your fate." She spoke serenely despite the hatred boiling within her. "It will not be a kind one."

Skali looked at her a moment longer, then gestured to some of his guardsmen. "Pen them. If they resist, kill the men first." The guards, laughing openly now, moved to surround Maegwin's people. One of the children began to cry, then more joined in.

As the guards began to lay rough hands on her folk, Maegwin felt her confidence waver. What was happening? When would the gods make things right? She looked around, expecting deadly lightnings to leap from the skies, or the ground to heave and swallow the defilers, but nothing happened. She sought frantically for Diawen. The scryer's eyes were closed in rapt concentration, her lips soundlessly moving.

"No! Do not touch them!" Maegwin cried as the guardsmen prodded with their spears at some of the crying children, trying to round them back into line with the others. "You must quit this land!" she shouted with all the authority she could summon. "It is the will of the gods!"

But the Rimmersmen paid no attention. Maegwin's heart was racing as though it would burst. What was happening? Why had the gods betrayed her? Could this have all been some incomprehensible trick?

"Brynioch!" she cried. "Murhagh One-Arm! Where are you!?"

The skies did not answer.

The light of early dawn was filtering through the tree-tops, shimmering faintly on the crumbling stones. The company of fifty mounted knights and twice that many foot-soldiers passed yet another ruined wall, a precarious stack of eroded, snow-dusted blocks glazed with brilliant rose and shining lavender which seemed more alive than any mere stones should. They rode by in silence, then began to wind down the hillside toward the icy lake, an expanse of white streaked with blue and gray hanging behind the outermost trees like a painter's catch-cloth.

Helfgrim, the Lord Mayor, craned his head to look back at the ruins, although it was no little strain to do so with his hands tied to the pommel of a saddle.

"So that is it," he said softly. "The fairy city."

"I may need you to lead me to the path," Fengbald snapped, "but that doesn't mean I can't break your arm. I will hear no more about any 'fairy cities.' "

Helfgrim turned, a hint of a smile curling his puckered mouth. "It is a shame to pass so near such a thing and not look, Duke Fengbald."

"Look all you want. Just keep your mouth shut." And he glared at the mounted soldiers, as if daring any of them to share Helfgrim's interest.

When they reached the shore of the frozen lake, Fengbald looked up, smoothing his unbound black hair away from his face. "Ah. The clouds are gathering. Good." He turned to Helfgrim. "It would be best of all to have done this in darkness, but I am not such a fool as to trust an old dotard to find his way by night. Besides, Lezhdraka and the rest should be making enough of a ruckus on the far side of the hill by now to keep Josua nicely occupied."

"I'm sure." Helfgrim gave the duke a wary glance. "My lord, could we at least have my daughters to ride here beside me?"

Fengbald stared at him suspiciously. "Why?"

The old man paused a moment. "It is hard for me to say it, my lord. I trust your word, please don't believe I don't. But I fear that your men—well, if they're out of your sight, Duke Fengbald, they might perform some mischief."

The duke laughed. "Surely you do not fear for the virtue of your daughters, old fellow? Unless I miss my guess, their maiden days are far behind them."

Helfgrim could not conceal a flinch. "Even so, my lord, it would be a kindness to put a father's heart at ease."

Fengbald considered for a moment, then whistled for his page. "Isaak, tell the guardsmen who carry the women to come ride nearer to me. Not that any should complain at being asked to ride beside their liege-lord," he added for the old man's benefit.

Young Isaak, who seemed to wish that he himself had the option of riding anything at all, bowed and went sloshing back up the muddy trail.

A few moments later the guardsmen appeared. Helfgrim's two daughters were not bound, but each one sat in the saddle before an armored man, so that they looked not unlike Hyrka brides—who, it was reputed in the cities, were frequently stolen in midnight raids and unceremoniously carried away, draped across their captor's saddles like sacks of meal.

"Are you well, daughters?" Helfgrim asked. The younger of the two, who had been crying, wiped her eyes with the hem of her cloak and tried to smile bravely.

"We are quite well, Father."

"That is good. No tears, then, my little coney. Be like your sister. There is nothing to fear—you know that Duke Fengbald is a man of his word."

"Yes, Father."

The duke smiled beneficently. *He* knew what sort of man he was, but it was good to see that the common folk knew it, too.

The wind blew harder as the first horses stepped out onto the ice. Fengbald cursed as his mount misstepped and had to splay its legs to stay afoot. "Even had I no other reasons," he hissed, "I would kill Josua just for bringing me to this godforsaken spot."

"Men must run far to elude your long arm, Duke Fengbald," said Helfgrim.

"There is no place that far."

Snow came flurrying around the great hill's northern flank, moving almost horizontally in the strong wind. Fengbald squinted and pulled up his hood. "Are we almost there?"

Helfgrim squinted, too, then nodded and pointed to a blot of deeper shadow ahead. "There is the foot of the hill, Lord." He continued to stare into the darting snow.

Fengbald smiled. "You look very glum," he called over the noise of the wind. "Can it be that you still do not trust my word?"

Helfgrim looked down at his bound wrists and pursed his lips before speaking. "No, Duke Fengbald, but surely I must feel some grief that I am betraying folk who were kind to me."

The duke waved his hand at the nearest riders. "To save your daughters—a noble enough reason. Besides, Josua was doomed to lose in any case. You are no more to blame for his fall than the worm that devours the corpse is to blame for Death's reaping." He grinned, pleased with his turn of phrase. "No more to blame than a worm, do you see?"

Helfgrim looked up. His wrinkled skin, speckled by snow, seemed gray. "Perhaps you are right, Duke Fengbald."

The hill now loomed overhead like a finger raised in warning. The company was only a few hundred ells from the edge of the ice when Helfgrim pointed again.

"There is the path, Duke Fengbald."

It was a tiny break in the vegetation, barely visible even from their near vantage point. Still, Fengbald could see enough to be satisfied that Helfgrim told the truth.

"Now, then . . ." the duke said, when suddenly a voice came rolling down from the mountainside.

"Stop, Fengbald! You may not pass!"

The duke pulled up, startled. A small group of shadowy figures had appeared at the lip of the path. One of them raised his hands to cup his mouth. *"Go back,*

*Fengbald—go away and leave this place. Ride away back
to Erkynland and we will let you live."*

The duke turned suddenly and slapped Helfgrim on the
side of the head. The old man swayed and almost fell, but
his bound wrists held him in the saddle. "Traitor! You
said there would be only a few guards!"

Helfgrim's face sagged in fear. Fengbald's mark
showed red on his pale cheek. "I did not lie, my lord!
Look, they are a few only."

Fengbald waved for his troops to hold their position,
then rode a little distance forward, staring. "I see only a
handful of you," he shouted up at the men on the path.
"How will you stop me?"

The man nearest the edge stepped forward. "We will,
Fengbald. We will give our lives and more to stop you."

"Very well." The duke had evidently decided it was a
bluff after all. "Then I will let you hurry and give them."
He raised his arm to order his troops forward.

"Stop!" the figure called. "I will give you one last
chance, damn you! You don't recognize my face I know,
but how about my name? I am Freosel, Freobeorn's son."

"What do I care, you madman?" Fengbald shouted.
"You are nothing to me!"

"Nor were my wife and children, my father and
mother, nor any of the others you murdered!" The stocky
figure had stepped out onto the ice with the rest of his
companions. They were less than a dozen all told. "You
burned half of Falshire, you great whoreson bastard! Now
the time has come for you to pay!"

"Enough!" Fengbald turned to wave his men forward.
"Up now and clean the madmen out. It is a rat's nest!"

Freosel and his companions bent and lifted what at first
seemed like axes, or swords, or some other weapons with
which to defend themselves. A moment later, as his men
began to guide their slipping mounts past him, Fengbald
saw to his astonishment that the hill's defenders were
swinging heavy mallets. Freosel brought his own down
first, smashing it onto the ice as though in idiot frustration. His companions on either side strode forward and
joined him.

"What are they doing!?" Fengbald bellowed. The furthermost of his soldiers were still a hundred ells from the shore. "Have all of Josua's people gone starvation-mad?"

"They are killing you," a calm voice said beside him.

The duke whirled to see Helfgrim, still lashed to the saddle of his horse. His daughters and their guards were close by, the soldiers looking both excited and confused.

"What are you babbling about?" Fengbald snarled, lifting his sword as if to swipe off the old man's head. Before he could move a pace closer, there was a horrible, deafening crack, like the splitting of a giant's bones. A moment later it sounded again. Somewhere at the foremost edge of Fengbald's company there was a sudden roar of men's voices and, even more chillingly, the almost human screaming of terrified horses.

"What is happening?" the duke demanded, straining to see past the crush of mounted men.

"They prepared the ice for you, Fengbald. I helped them plan it. You see, *we* are of Falshire, too." Helfgrim spoke just loudly enough to be heard above the wind. "My brother was its Lord Mayor, as you would have known instantly if you had ever bothered to come there except to steal our bread, our gold, even our young women for your bed. Surely you did not think we would stand by and let you also destroy the few of our people who had escaped your brutality?"

There was another jarring crack, and suddenly, just yards away from the Lord Mayor and the duke, a crevice foamed with black water where there had been ice a moment before. More ice crumbled along the opening and sheared loose; a pair of horsemen toppled in, flailing for an instant until they were sucked down into darkness.

"But you will die, too, damn you!" Fengbald shouted, urging his horse toward the old man.

"Of course I will. It is enough that my daughters and I avenge the others—their souls will welcome us." And then Helfgrim smiled, a cold smile without a scintilla of mirth.

Fengbald suddenly found himself flung sideways as the white surface erupted beneath him, snapping upward like dragon's jaws. A moment later the duke's horse was gone and he was clutching a jagged-edged sheet of ice which rocked precariously. His boots and breeches were already submerged in freezing water. "Help me!" he shrieked.

Eerily, Helfgrim and his daughters were still upright, seated on their frantic horses just cubits away. Their guards were scrambling away across the remaining sheet of unbroken ice, struggling toward the shelter of the standing stone. "Too late," the old man cried. The two women stared down at the duke, eyes wide as they struggled to contain their terror. "Too late for you, Fengbald," Helfgrim repeated. A moment later, with a sudden grinding crunch, the entire section on which the trio and their mounts stood broke and collapsed into the choppy black waters. The Lord Mayor and his daughters vanished like ghosts chased by the dawn-knell.

"Help!" Fengbald screamed. His fingers were slipping. As he slid, the piece of ice to which he clung began to tilt, the far end reaching for the gray sky even as his own end plunged inexorably downward. Fengbald's eyes bulged. "No! I can't die! I *can't!*"

The ragged pane of ice, almost vertical now, overbalanced and abruptly flipped over. The duke's gloved hand snatched briefly at the air, then was gone.

The sun was in Maegwin's eyes. Doubt dug into her heart, sending black rays of pain through all her limbs. Around her, Skali's Rimmersmen were rounding up her people, prodding them at spear-point, herding them as though they were beasts.

"Gods of our people!" Her voice tore in her throat. "Save us! *You promised!"*

Skali Sharp-nose approached, laughing, his hands tucked into his belt. "Your gods are dead, girl. Like your father. Like your kingdom. But I may find a use for you yet." Maegwin could smell the stink of him, like the tangy, rotten scent of over-aged venison. "You are plain, *haja,* but your legs are long . . . and I like long legs. Better than being a whore to my men, eh?"

Maegwin stepped back, raising her arms as though to ward a blow. Before she could say anything, the air was ripped by the sound of a distant horn. Skali and some of his men turned, surprised. The horn sounded again, louder now, clear and shrill and powerful. It played a cascade of notes that echoed around the Taig and out over the fields of Hernysadharc. Maegwin stared.

It was only a gleam at first, a rippling shimmer out of the east. The hooves made a rushing sound, like a river after strong rains. Skali's men began to scramble for the helmets they had tossed aside when they had discovered the nature of Maegwin's company of partisans; Skali himself began screaming for his horse.

It was an army, Maegwin realized—no, it was a dream, a dream made flesh and unleashed upon the snowy meadows. They were coming at last!

The horn echoed again. The riders were thundering toward Hernysadharc, impossibly swift. Their armor shone in every color the rainbow had—sky-blue, ruby-crimson, leaf-green, the orange and vermilion of sunset fog. She could hear them singing now as they rode, a high, brilliant keening like a flock of impossibly musical birds. They could have been a hundred riders or ten thousand: Maegwin could not even try to guess, for in the beautiful terror of their coming it was almost impossible to stare at them too long. They streamed with color and noise and light, as though the world had been torn open and the raw stuff of dream allowed to spill through.

Again the horn sounded. Maegwin, suddenly all alone, stumbled toward the Taig, not even conscious at that moment that this was the first time she had touched its wooden walls since Skali had put her people to flight. The Rimmersmen, dismayed, were gathering on the hillside below her father's great hall, milling and shouting as they struggled to make their horses face this incomprehensible enemy. The horns of the oncoming army sounded again.

The gods have come! Maegwin turned in the doorway

TO GREEN ANGEL TOWER

to watch. The culmination of all her agonies and hope was here at last, burning across the snowy fields to rescue her people. The gods! The gods! She had brought the gods!

There was a clatter from within the Taig. More of Skali's men came streaming forth, pulling on helmets, fumbling with sword belts. One of them pushed into Maegwin and sent her spinning into the path of another, who raised his mailed fist and brought it crashing against her head.

Maegwin's world abruptly vanished.

It was Binabik who found Simon at last, with Sisqi helping him search—or rather it was Qantaqa, whose nose could discern the proper scent even in the madness that surrounded Sesuad'ra. They found him sitting cross-legged on the ice beside a motionless figure wearing Fengbald's armor. Homefinder stood over him, shivering in the terrible wind, her muzzle near Simon's ear. Qantaqa pawed at the young man's leg and made a soft sound as she waited for her master.

"Simon!" Binabik scrambled toward him across the rough surface of the lake. There were bodies scattered all about, but the troll did not stop to look at any of them. "Are you injured?"

Simon lifted his head slowly. His throat was so rough that his voice was barely a whisper. "Binabik? What happened?"

"Are you safe, Simon?" The little man bent to examine his friend, then straightened. "You have many wounds. We must get you back."

"What happened?" Simon asked again. Binabik was pulling at his shoulders, trying to help him stand, but Simon could not seem to gather the strength. Sisqi approached and stood nearby, waiting to see if Binabik would need her help.

"We have won," said Binabik. "The price we have been paying is great, but Fengbald is dead."

"No." A look of concern flitted across Simon's haggard face. "It wasn't him. It was someone else."

Binabik darted a look at the figure lying nearby. "I know, Simon. It is elsewhere that Fengbald is being dead—a horrible death, and for many others than him only. But come. You are needing a fire, and food, and some attending to your wounds."

Simon let out a deep groan as he let the little man urge him to his feet, a hollow noise that drew another worried look from Binabik. Simon limped a few steps, then stopped and caught at Homefinder's reins. "I can't get into the saddle," he murmured sadly.

"Walk, then, if you can," Binabik said. "With slowness. Sisqi and I will be walking with you."

With Qantaqa in the lead once more, they turned and trudged toward the Stone, whose summit was painted with rosy light from the dying sun. Thickening mist hung over the icy lake, and all around the ravens hopped and scuttled from body to body like tiny black demons.

"Oh, God," Simon said. "I want to go home."

Binabik only shook his head.

16

Torches in the Mud

"Stop." Cadrach's voice was nearly a whisper, but the straining tone was evident. "Stop now."

Isgrimnur pushed the pole down until it touched the muddy bottom of the watercourse, arresting their progress. The boat floated gently back into the reeds once more. "What is it, man?" he said irritably. "We have gone over everything a dozen times. Now it's time to move."

In the bow of the boat, ancient Camaris fingered a long spear Isgrimnur had made from a stiff swamp reed. It was thin and light, and the point had been scraped against a stone until it was sharp as an assassin's dirk. The old knight, as usual, seemed oblivious to the conversation of his fellows. He hefted the spear and made a slow, mock stab, slipping the point into the still water.

Cadrach took a deep, shaky breath. Miriamele thought he looked as though he were on the brink of tears. "I cannot go."

"Cannot?" Isgrimnur almost shouted. "What do you mean, cannot? It was your idea we wait for morning before going into the nest! What are you talking about now!?"

The monk shook his head, unable to meet the duke's eyes. "I tried to nerve myself all night. I have been saying prayers all the morning—me!" He turned to Miriamele with a look of bleak irony. "Me! But I still cannot do it. I am a coward, and I cannot go into . . . that place."

Miriamele reached out a hand and touched his shoulder. "Even to save Tiamak?" She let the hand rest gently, as though the monk had turned to fragile glass. "And as you said, even to save ourselves? For without Tiamak, we may never get out of this place at all."

Cadrach buried his face in his hands. Miriamele felt a hint of her old distrust come sneaking back. Could the monk be play-acting? What else could he have in mind?

"God forgive me, Lady," he moaned, "but I simply cannot go down into that hole with those creatures. I *cannot*." He shuddered, a convulsive movement so uncontrolled that Miriamele doubted it could be trickery. "I have given over my right to be called a man long ago," Cadrach said through his splayed fingers. "I do not even care for my life, believe me. But—I—cannot—go."

Isgrimnur grumbled his frustration. "Well, damn you, that is the end. I should have broken your skull when we met, as I wanted to." The duke turned to Miriamele. "I should never have let you talk me out of it." He shifted his scornful gaze back to Cadrach. "A kidnapper, a drunkard, and a coward."

"Yes, you probably should have killed me when you first had the chance," Cadrach agreed tonelessly. "But I promise you would still be better off doing it now than dragging me down into that mud nest. I will not go in there."

"But why, Cadrach?" Miriamele asked. "Why won't you?"

He looked at her. His sunken eyes and sun-reddened face seemed to plead for understanding, but his grim smile suggested he expected none. "I simply cannot, Lady. It . . . it reminds me of a place I was in before." Again he shuddered.

"What place?" she prodded, but Cadrach would not answer.

"Aedon on the Holy Tree," Isgrimnur swore. "So what do we do now?"

Miriamele stared at the waving reeds, which at this moment hid them from the sight of the ghant nest a few hundred ells up the waterway. The muddy bank nearby had a low-tide smell. She wrinkled her nose and sighed. What could they do, indeed?

*   *   *

They had not even been able to make a plan until late the afternoon before. There was a strong chance that Tiamak was already dead, which made any decision more difficult. Although no one had wanted to say it directly, there was some sentiment that the best thing to do would be to go on, hoping that the Wrannaman they had found floating in Tiamak's boat might recover enough to guide them. Failing that, they might discover another swamp native who would help them find their way out of the Wran. No one had been comfortable with the idea of abandoning Tiamak, although it seemed by far the least risky course, but it was dreadful to think about what it would take to find out if he still lived, and to save him if he did.

Still, when Isgrimnur at last said that leaving Tiamak would not be the Aedonite thing to do, Miriamele had been relieved. She had not wanted to run away without at least trying to save the Wrannaman, however terrifying the idea of entering that nest. And, she reminded herself, she had faced at least as bad in the past months. In any case, how could she live with herself if she made it to safety and had to remember the shy little scholar left to those clicking monstrosities?

Cadrach—even then he had seemed more frightened of the nest than the rest of them—had argued strenuously for waiting until morning. His reasons had seemed good: there was little sense in trying such a foolhardy thing without a battle plan, and even less sense starting when it would soon be dark. As it was, Cadrach had said, they would need not just weapons but torches, because even though the nest seemed to have holes that let in the light, who knew what dark passages might run through the heart of the thing? So it had been agreed.

They found a rattling grove of heavy green reeds along the edge of the watercourse and made camp near it. The site was muddy and wet, but it was also a good distance from the nest, which was recommendation enough. Isgrimnur took his sword Kvalnir and cut a great bundle of the reeds, then he and Cadrach hardened them over the

embers of the campfire. Some of the stalks they had cut
and sharpened to make short stabbing spears; they split
the ends of others and forced stones between the halves,
then tied the stones in place with thin vines to make
clubs. Isgrimnur lamented the lack of good wood and
rope, but Miriamele admired the job. It was much more
reassuring to go into the nest with even such primitive
arms than to walk in empty-handed. Lastly, they sacrificed some of the clothes Miriamele had brought out of
Village Grove, shredding them for rags which they wound
tightly around the remaining reeds. Miriamele crushed
one of the leaves of a tree which Tiamak had named as an
oil palm during his botanical tour a few days before, then
dabbed a rag in it and held the cloth to the campfire. It
held a flame, she discovered, although nothing like true
lamp oil; the scent of its burning was acrid and foul. Still,
it would keep the torches blazing a little while longer, and
she had a feeling that they would need all the time they
could buy. She plucked an armful of fronds and rubbed
crushed pulp on the torch rags until her hands were so
coated with sap that her fingers stuck together.

When the night sky had at last begun to lighten, just
before dawn, Isgrimnur had awakened the company. They
had decided to leave the wounded Wrannaman in camp:
there was little sense in bringing him into further danger,
since he seemed already to be exhausted and starved
nearly to death. If they survived their attempt to rescue
Tiamak, they could always come back for him; if they did
not, at least he would have a small chance to survive and
make his own escape.

Isgrimnur lifted his pole to the surface of the water and
swished off the mud that clung to the end. "So, then?
What do we do? The monk is worthless."

"There may still be a way he can help." Miriamele
looked meaningfully at Cadrach. He kept his face averted.
"In any case, we can certainly go on with the first part of
what we planned, can't we?"

"I suppose." Isgrimnur stared at the Hernystirman as
though he would have liked to test one of the reed clubs

on him. He thrust the pole into the monk's hands. "Let's get to it. You can damn well make yourself useful."

Cadrach poled the boat out of the waving forest of reeds and onto the wide part of the watercourse. The morning sun was not very bright today, hidden behind a smudgy sheet of clouds, but the air was even hotter than it had been the day before. Miriamele felt a sheen of sweat on her forehead and wished that she dared to flout the crocodiles by taking off her boots and dangling her feet in the murky water.

They slipped along the waterway until they finally came into view of their objective, then moved close to the bank and slowly and cautiously up the canal, trying to use the cover of reeds and trees to stay out of direct sight. The nest looked just as sinister as it had the day before, although there seemed to be fewer ghants scuttling about outside. When they had gotten as close as they dared, Isgrimnur let the boat drift toward the outer edge of the waterway until a tree-lined bend in its course blocked them completely from view of the nest.

"Now we wait," he said quietly.

They sat in silence for no little time. The insects were a misery. Miriamele, afraid to slap at them because of the noise, tried to pick them off with her fingers as they landed, but they were too numerous and too persistent: she was bitten many times. Her skin itched and throbbed so completely that she felt she would go mad, and the idea of leaping into the river and drowning all the bugs at once grew stronger and stronger, until it seemed that any moment she would be able to hold it off no longer. Her fingers clutched the wales of the boat. It would be cool. It would stop the stinging. Let the crocodiles come, damn them. . . .

"There," Isgrimnur whispered. Miriamele looked up.

Not twenty cubits from where they sat, a lone ghant was coming down a long tree branch that snaked out over the water. Because of its jointed legs, its movements seemed strangely awkward, but it traveled swiftly and confidently on the thin, swaying branch. From time to time it would stop suddenly, becoming so utterly motionless that, gray and lichen-streaked as it was, it seemed part of the bark, just a particularly large tree gall.

"*Push,*" Isgrimnur mouthed, gesturing at Cadrach. The monk prodded the boat away from the bank and sent it idling down the watercourse toward the branch. Miriamele and all the company remained as still as they could.

The ghant did not seem to notice them at first. As they drew closer, it continued to creep out along the bough, moving patiently toward a trio of small birds that had lit at the end. Like the thing that hunted them, the birds seemed oblivious to the presence of danger.

Isgrimnur replaced Camaris in the prow of the boat, then leaned forward, steadying himself as well as he could. The ghant finally seemed to see the boat floating toward it; black eyes glittered as it swayed in place, trying to decide whether the approaching object was a menace or a potential meal. As Isgrimnur raised the reed spear, the ghant seemed to come to a conclusion: it turned and began to shinny back toward the tree trunk.

"Now, Isgrimnur!" cried Miriamele. The Rimmersman flung the spear as hard as he could; the boat rocked treacherously with the force of his throw. The birds lifted from the branch, squawking and flapping. The spear hissed through the air, a length of Tiamak's precious rope falling away behind it, and struck the ghant but did not pierce its shell; the spear bounced away and fell to the water, but the force of the blow was enough to knock the animal from the bough. It splashed into the green water and surfaced a moment later with legs flexing wildly, then righted itself and began a strange, jerky swim toward the bank.

Cadrach swiftly poled the boat forward until they were beside the creature. Isgrimnur leaned low and struck it hard twice with the flat of his sword. When it floated back up, clearly beyond struggling, he looped a bit of Tiamak's rope around one clawed leg so they could tow it back to shore.

"Don't want to put the thing in the boat," he said. Miriamele could not have agreed more.

The ghant seemed dead—the carapace of its lumpish head was cracked, oozing gray and blue fluids—but no one stood too near as they used the steering pole to turn it onto its back on the sandy bank. Camaris remained in the boat, although he seemed to be watching as curiously as the rest of the company.

Isgrimnur scowled. "God help us. They are ugly bastards, aren't they?"

"Your spear couldn't kill it." Miriamele's feelings about their chances had sunk even lower.

Isgrimnur waved his hand reassuringly. "Got thick armor, these things. Have to make the spears a little heavier. A stone spliced in the end should do it. Don't worry yourself more than you need, Princess. We'll be able to do what we need to."

Strangely, she believed him and felt better. Isgrimnur had always treated her like a favorite niece, even when his relations with her father had become strained, and she in turn treated him with the loving, mocking familiarity she had never been able to use on Elias. She knew he would do his best to keep them all safe—and the Duke of Elvritshalla's best was usually very good. Although he allowed his comrades and even his house-carls to make fun of his fierce but short-lived temper and his underlying softheartedness, the duke was a tremendously capable man. Miriamele was again grateful that Isgrimnur was with her.

"I hope you're right." She reached out and squeezed his broad paw.

They all stared at the dead ghant. Miriamele could now see that it did have six legs, just like a beetle, not four as she had thought. The two she had missed on her first ghant were tiny, withered things tucked just below the place where the neckless head met the rounded body. The thing's mouth was half-hidden behind an odd featherlike fringe and its shell was dull and leathery as a sea-turtle's egg.

"Turn away, Princess," Isgrimnur said as he lifted Kvalnir. "You won't want to see this."

Miriamele suppressed a smile. What did he think she

had been doing the last half year? "Go ahead. I'm not squeamish."

The duke lowered his sword and placed it against the creature's abdomen, then pushed. The ghant slid across the mud a little way. Isgrimnur grunted, then held the carcass steady with his foot before pushing again. This time, after a moment of effort, he was able to push the blade through the shell, which gave with a faint popping noise. A salty, sour smell wafted up and Miriamele took a step back.

"The shells are tough," Isgrimnur said thoughtfully, "but they can be pierced." He tried to smile. "I was worried that we might have to besiege a castle of armored soldiers."

Cadrach had gone quite pale, but continued to stare at the ghant, fascinated. "It is disturbingly manlike, as Tiamak said," he murmured. "But I will not be too sorry about this one or any others we kill."

"*We* kill?" Isgrimnur began angrily, but Miriamele gave him another hand-squeeze.

"What else can this tell us?" she asked.

"I don't see any poison stingers or teeth, so I suppose they don't bite like spiders do—that's a relief." The duke shrugged. "They can be killed. Their shells are not as hard as tortoise shells. That is enough, I think."

"Then I suppose it's time to go," Miriamele said.

Cadrach poled the flatboat in to the bank. They were only a few hundred steps from the edge of the nest now. So far, they seemed to be unnoticed.

"But what about the boat?" Isgrimnur whispered. "Can we leave it so we can get back to it in a hurry?" His expression soured. "And what about this damnable monk?"

"That's my idea," Miriamele whispered back. "Cadrach, if you keep the boat in the middle of the waterway until we come out, you can land right at the front of the nest and get us. We'll probably be in a hurry," she added wryly.

"What!?" Isgrimnur struggled to keep his voice soft, with only partial success. "You're going to leave this coward in our boat, free to paddle away if he wants to? Free to strand us here? No, by the Aedon, we will take him with us—bound and gagged if need be."

Cadrach clutched the steering pole, his knuckles white. "You might as well kill me first," he said hoarsely. "Because I will die if you drag me in there."

"Stop it, Isgrimnur. He may not be able to go into the nest, but he would never leave us here. Not after all he and I have been through." She turned and gave the monk a purposeful glance. "Would you, Cadrach?"

He looked at her carefully, as though he suspected a trick. A moment passed before he spoke. "No, my lady, I would not—whatever Duke Isgrimnur thinks."

"And why should I let you make such a decision, Princess?" Isgrimnur was angry. "Whatever you think you know of this man, you also said yourself that he stole from you and sold you out to your enemies."

Miriamele frowned. It was true, of course—and she had not told Isgrimnur everything. She had never mentioned Cadrach's attempt to escape and leave her behind on Aspitis' ship, which would certainly not argue in his favor. She found herself wondering why she *was* so certain that Cadrach could be trusted to wait for them, but it was no use: there was no answer. She just believed that he would be there when they got out . . . *if* they got out.

"We really have very little choice," she told the duke. "Unless we force him to go along—and it will be hard enough to find our way and do what we must without also dragging a prisoner with us—we would have to tie him up somewhere to prevent him taking the boat if he wanted to. Don't you see, Isgrimnur, it's just the best way! If we leave the boat untended, even if we try to hide it from the ghants . . . well, who knows what could happen?"

Isgrimnur pondered for a long moment, his bearded jaws working as though he chewed on the various possibilities. "So," he said at last. "I suppose that is true. Very well—but if you are *not* there when we need you," he whirled on Cadrach menacingly, "I will find you some day and crush your bones. I will eat you like a game hen."

Cadrach smiled sadly. "I'm sure you would, Duke Isgrimnur." The monk turned to Miriamele. "Thank you for trusting me, my lady. It is not easy to be a man like myself."

"I should hope not," Isgrimnur growled. "Otherwise there'd be more of you."

"I think it will all be well, Cadrach," said Miriamele. "But pray for us."

"Every god I know."

The duke, still muttering angrily, struck a spark with his flint and lit one of the torches. The rest he and Miriamele stuck in their belts until they were both spined like hedgehogs. Miriamele carried a club and one of the weighted spears, as did Camaris, who handled his weapons distractedly while the other two prepared. Isgrimnur had Kvalnir sheathed on his belt, and a pair of short spears clutched in his free hand.

"Going into battle armed with sticks," he growled. "Going to fight bugs."

"It will make a wretched song," Miriamele whispered. "Or a glorious one, perhaps. We'll see." She turned to the old man. "Sir Camaris, we're going to help Tiamak. Your friend—do you remember? He's in there." She pointed with her spear at the dark bulk of the nest looming behind the trees. "We have to find him and bring him out." She stared at his unexcited expression. "Do you think he understands, Isgrimnur?"

"He has become simple . . . but not as simple as he seems, I think." The duke grabbed at a low branch and helped himself over the side of the boat and into the shin-deep water. "Here, Princess, let me help you." He lifted her and set her on the bank. "Josua will never forgive me if anything happens to you. I still think it is foolish to bring you along—especially when *that* one is staying behind, cozy and safe."

"You need me," she said. "It will be difficult enough with three."

Isgrimnur shook his head, unconvinced. "Just stay near me."

"I will, old uncle."

As Camaris sloshed to shore, Cadrach began to push the boat out into deeper water.

"Hold," said Isgrimnur. "Wait until we are inside at least. We don't need to attract their attention until we're ready."

Cadrach nodded and used the pole to stop the boat.

"Bless you all," he said softly. "Good luck to you."

The duke snorted and moved away into undergrowth, boots squelching in the mud. Miriamele nodded to Cadrach, then took Camaris' hand and led him after the duke.

"Good luck," Cadrach said again. He spoke in a whisper, and none of the others seemed to hear him.

"See!" Miriamele hissed. "There's one that's big enough!"

A soft humming filled the air. They were very close to the nest, so close that had Miriamele dared to stretch her hand out from where they hid in a tangle of flowering brush, she could almost have touched it. Upon approaching the huge mud structure, they had quickly realized that many of the doors—mere holes in the walls, actually— were far too small for even the princess to enter, let alone broad Isgrimnur.

"Right," said the duke. "Let's get to it, then." He started to reach for his torch, then stopped and waved for his companions to do the same. A few cubits away, a pair of ghants came creeping along the perimeter of the nest. Although they walked in file, one behind the other, they were clicking and hissing back and forth as though they conversed. Again Miriamele wondered how smart the things were. The ghants walked past on all fours, jointed legs ticking as they went. The trio watched them until they were gone around the curve of the huge nest.

"Now." Isgrimnur plucked his torch out of the mud; he had set it behind him so that his broad frame masked its light. Even in the morning sun, its flame made Miriamele feel a little safer.

After looking cautiously in all directions, the duke crossed the short distance to the nest and leaned into the

ragged opening. He stepped through, then reached back to
beckon to Miriamele and Camaris.

Increasingly reluctant as the actual moment approached, Miriamele hesitated before following the duke
inside, taking a deep breath as if to dive into water. She
understood Cadrach's decision better than she did her
own. The place would be full of those crawling, clicking,
many-legged things. . . . Her knees grew weak. How
could she walk into that black hole? But Tiamak was already there, alone with the ghants. He might be screaming
for help down in the darkness.

Miriamele swallowed, then stepped into the nest.

She found herself in a circular passageway as wide as
her outstretched arms and only a little taller than her own
height. Isgrimnur had to hunch down, and Camaris, who
followed Miriamele, had to bend even lower. The mud
walls were spiky with loose stones and bits of splintered
sticks, all covered with pale froth that looked like spittle.
The tunnel was dark and steamily humid and smelled of
rotting vegetation.

"Ugh." Miriamele wrinkled her nose. Her heart was
pounding. "I don't like this at all."

"I know," Isgrimnur whispered. "It's foul. Come on,
let's see what we can see."

They followed the winding passageway, struggling for
footing on the slippery mud. Isgrimnur and Camaris had
to lean forward, which made balancing even more difficult. Miriamele felt her courage beginning to fail. Why
had she been so anxious to prove herself? This was no
place for a girl. This was no place for anyone.

"I think Cadrach was right." She tried to keep the quaver out of her voice.

"No sensible person would want to come in here," the
duke said quietly, "but that's not the question. Besides, if
this is as bad as it gets, I'll be happy. I'm afraid we might
find ourselves in a smaller tunnel and have to go on our
knees."

Miriamele thought of being chased by the scuttling
ghants but not being able to run. She stared at the slickly
glistening tunnel floor and shuddered.

The light from the entrance began to dim as they put several bends of the tunnel behind them. The rotten smell grew stronger, accompanied now by a strange spicy odor, musty and cloyingly sweet. Miriamele slipped her club into her belt and lit one of her brands from Isgrimnur's, then lit another and gave it to Camaris, who took it as placidly as an infant handed a crust of bread. Miriamele envied his idiot calm. "Where are the ghants?" she whispered.

"Don't look for trouble." Isgrimnur made the Tree sign in the air with his torch before moving on.

The uneven passage turned and turned again, as though they clambered through the guts of some vast animal. After a few more squishing steps, they reached a point where a new tunnel crossed theirs. Isgrimnur stood and listened for a moment.

"I think I hear more noise from this one." The duke pointed down one of the side branches. Indeed, the dull humming did seem stronger there.

"But should we go toward it or away from it?" Miriamele tried to wave the choking torch smoke away from her face.

Isgrimnur's expression was fatalistic. "I think that Tiamak or any other prisoners would be at the heart of the thing. I say, follow the noise. Not that I like it," he added. He reached up and scraped a circle in the froth with one of his reed spears, exposing the muddy wall beneath. "We have to remember to mark our way."

The froth on the walls was thicker in the new passage; in places it hung from the tunnel roof in viscous, ropy strands. Miriamele did her best to avoid touching the stuff, but there was no way to avoid breathing. She could almost feel the damp, unpleasant air of the tunnels congealing inside her chest. Still, Miriamele told herself, she had no real cause for complaint: they had been in the nest for no little time, and still had not met any of the inhabitants. That alone was an incredible piece of luck.

"This place doesn't look nearly so big from outside," she said to Isgrimnur.

"We never saw the back of it, for one thing." He

stepped carefully over a glob of pale muck in the passageway. "And I think that these tunnels may be looping back on themselves. I'd wager that if you broke through this . . ." he prodded at the wall with his torch; the froth hissed and bubbled, ". . . you'd find another tunnel just on the other side of it."

"Round and round. Farther and farther in. Like a chamber-shell," Miriamele whispered. It was more than a little dizzying to think of such an endless spiral of mud and shadows. Again she fought down rising panic. "Still . . ." she began.

There was a scuttling movement in the tunnel before them.

The ghant had apparently stepped out of another side tunnel; it crouched motionless in the middle of the passage as though stunned. Isgrimnur also froze for a moment, then slowly walked forward. The ghant, devoid of anything that could truly be called a face, stared at their approach, the tiny legs below its head straightening and contracting. Suddenly it turned and scuttled away up the tunnel. Isgrimnur hesitated for a moment, then ran heavily after it, struggling to keep his balance. He stopped and hurled his spear, then pulled up suddenly with a hiss of pain that made Miriamele's heart race.

"*Damn!* I've hit my head. Careful, the cursed roof is low here." He rubbed at his forehead.

"Did you get it?"

"I think so. I can't quite see it yet." He went forward a little way. "Yes. It's dead—or it looks it, anyway."

Miriamele came up beside him, peering around the duke's wide shoulders at the thing in the pool of torchlight. The ghant lay in the mud of the passageway with Isgrimnur's spear protruding from the armor of its back; the wound oozed a thin fluid a shade paler than blood. The jointed legs twitched a few times, then slowly came to rest as Camaris stepped forward and reached out his long arm to turn the creature over. The ghant's face was as blank in death as in life. The old man, with a contemplative look, scooped a handful of mucky earth from the tunnel floor and dropped it onto the dead thing's chest. It was a strange gesture, Miriamele thought.

"Come," Isgrimnur muttered.

The new tunnel did not twist as much as the first had. It ran steeply downward, bumpy and sodden, the walls as uneven as if they had been chewed out of the mud by monstrous jaws: looking at the gleaming strands of foam, Miriamele decided that was not a pleasant thought to pursue.

"Curse it," Isgrimnur said suddenly. "I'm stuck."

His boot had sunk deep into the squelching mud of the tunnel floor. Miriamele held out her arm to him so he could balance as he pulled. A terrible odor rose from the disturbed mud, and tiny wet things brought to light by Isgrimnur's struggles quickly buried themselves again. The Rimmersman, for all his efforts, only seemed to sink deeper.

"It's like that sucking sand Tiamak said they have in the swamp. Can't get free." There was an edge of panic in Isgrimnur's voice.

"It's just mud." Miriamele tried to sound calm, but she could not help wondering what would happen if the ghants came upon them suddenly. "Leave the boot if you have to."

"It's my whole leg, not just the boot." Indeed, one leg had now sunk to the knee, and the foot of the other boot was also lodged in the slime. The carrion smell grew worse.

Camaris stepped forward, then braced his own legs to either side of Isgrimnur's foot before taking the Rimmersman's leg in his hands; Miriamele prayed there was only one patch of treacherous mud. If not, they might both become trapped. What would she do then?

The old knight heaved. Isgrimnur grunted in pain, but his foot did not come loose. Camaris pulled again, so strenuously that the cords on his neck grew taut as ropes. With a sucking gasp, Isgrimnur's leg came free; Camaris tugged him away to a firmer patch of ground.

The duke stood bent over for a moment, examining the glob of mud below his knee. "Just stuck," he said. He

was breathing heavily. "Just stuck. Let's keep moving."
The fear was not entirely gone from his voice.

They sloshed on, trying to find the driest spots to walk.
The smoke of the torches and the stench of the mud was
making Miriamele feel ill, so she was almost heartened
when the narrow passage opened at last into a wider
room, a sort of grotto in which the white froth hung like
stalactites. They entered it cautiously, but it seemed as deserted as the tunnel had been. As they made their way
across the chamber, stepping around the larger puddles,
Miriamele looked up.

"What are those?" she asked, frowning. Large, faintly
luminous sacs sagged from the ceiling, hanging unpleasantly close overhead. Each was as long as a crofter's
hammock, with thin, cobwebby white tendrils depending
from its center, a wispy fringe that drifted lazily in the
warm air rising from the torches.

"I don't know, but I don't like them," Isgrimnur said
with a grimace of distaste.

"I think they're egg pouches. You know, like the spider
eggs you see on the bottoms of leaves."

"Haven't looked much at the bottoms of leaves," the
duke muttered. "And I don't want to look at these any
longer than I have to."

"Shouldn't we do something? Kill them or something?
Burn them?"

"We're not here to kill all these bugs," said Isgrimnur.
"We're here to get in and find that poor little marsh fellow, then get out. God only knows what would happen if
we started mucking around with these things."

With mud sucking at their bootheels, they made their
way quickly to the other side of the chamber, where the
tunnel resumed its former size. Miriamele, drawn by a
horrid sort of interest, turned back for a last glance. In the
fading light of the torch, she thought she saw a shadowy
movement in one of the sacs, as though something was
pawing at the maggot-white membrane, seeking a way
out. She wished she hadn't looked.

Within a few steps the passageway turned and they
found themselves facing a half-dozen ghants. Several had

been climbing up the tunnel wall and now hung in place, clicking in apparent surprise. The others squatted on the floor, mud-smeared shells glimmering dully in the torchglow. Miriamele felt her heart turn over.

Isgrimnur stepped forward and wagged Kvalnir from side to side. Swallowing hard, Miriamele moved up behind him and lifted her torch. After a few more seconds of chittering indecision, the ghants turned and scrambled away down the tunnel.

"They're afraid of us!" Miriamele was exhilarated.

"Perhaps," said Isgrimnur. "Or perhaps they're going for their friends. Let's get on." He began walking swiftly, head hunched beneath the low ceiling.

"But that's the direction *they* went," Miriamele pointed out.

"I said, it's the heart of this wretched place we want."

They passed numerous side tunnels as they traveled downward, but Isgrimnur seemed certain of where he was going. The humming continued to grow louder; the stench of putrefaction grew stronger, too, until Miriamele's head ached. They passed through two more of the egg chambers—if that was indeed what they were—hurrying through both. Miriamele no longer felt any urge to linger and stare.

They came upon the central chamber so suddenly that they almost fell through the tunnel mouth and tumbled down the sloping mud into the vast swarm of ghants.

The room was huge and dark; the torches of Miriamele and her companions cast the only light, but it was enough to reveal the great crawling horde, the faint wink of their shells as they clambered over each other in the darkness at the bottom of the chamber, the muted glimmering of their countless eyes. The chamber was a long stone's throw in width, with walls of piled and smoothed mud. The entire floor was covered with many-legged things, hundreds and hundreds of ghants.

The humming sound that arose from the squirming mass was stronger here, a pulsing throb of sound so powerful that Miriamele could feel it in her teeth and the bones of her head.

"Mother of Usires," Isgrimnur swore brokenly.

Miriamele felt chilly and light-headed. "W—what . . ." She swallowed bile and tried again. "What . . . do we do?"

Isgrimnur leaned forward, squinting. The swarm of ghants did not appear to have noticed them, though the nearest was only a dozen cubits away: they seemed enmeshed in some dreadful and all-consuming activity. Miriamele fought to catch her breath. Maybe they were laying their eggs here and, caught up in the grip of Nature, would not notice the interlopers.

"What's that at the middle?" Isgrimnur whispered. The duke was having trouble keeping his voice from breaking. "That thing they're all gathered around?"

Miriamele strained to see, although at that moment there was nothing she would less rather look at. It was like the worst vision of hell, a writhing pile of muddy things without hope or joy, legs kicking pointlessly, shells scraping as they rubbed against each other—and always the terrible droning, the ceaseless grinding sound of the assembled ghants. Miriamele blinked and forced herself to concentrate. At the center, where the activity seemed the most fervid, stood a row of pale, shining lumps. The nearest had a dark spot at the top which seemed to be moving. It took her a moment to realize that the spot atop the gleaming mass was a head—a human head.

"It's Tiamak," she gasped, horrified. Her stomach heaved. "He's stuck in something terrible—it's like a pudding. Oh, Elysia Mother of God, we have to help him!"

"Ssshhh." Isgrimnur, who looked as sickened as Miriamele felt, gestured her to silence. "Think," he murmured. "Got to think."

The tiny ball that was Tiamak's head began to wiggle back and forth atop the gelatinous mound. As Miriamele and Isgrimnur stared in amazement, the mouth opened and Tiamak began to shout in a loud voice. But instead of words, what roared out was the tormented sound of buzzing, clicking ghant-speech—something that sounded so cruelly wrong coming from the little Wrannaman's mouth that Miriamele burst into tears.

"What have they done to him!?" she cried. Suddenly there was movement beside her, a rush of hot air as a torch swished past, then the flame was bobbing down the slope toward the floor and the squirming congregation of ghants.

"Camaris!" Isgrimnur shouted, but the old man was already forcing his way through the outermost ghants, swinging his torch like a scythe. The great humming sound faltered, leaving echoes in Miriamele's ears. The ghants around Camaris started to buzz shrilly, and others in the vast gathering took up the cries of alarm. The tall old man waded through them like a master of hounds come to take the fox away. Agitated creatures swirled around his legs, some clutching at his cloak and breeches even as he knocked others away with his club.

"Oh, God help me, he can't do it himself," Isgrimnur groaned. He began making his way down the slippery mud, spreading his arms for balance. "Stay there," he called to Miriamele.

"I'm coming with you," she shouted back.

"*No,* damn it," the duke cried. "Stay there with the torch so we can find our way back to this tunnel! If we lose the light, we're done for!"

He turned, lifting Kvalnir over his head, and swung it at the nearest ghants. There was an awful hollow smack as he struck the first one. He took a few steps forward into the swarm and the noise of his struggle was lost in the greater uproar.

The humming had completely died out. The great chamber was now filled instead with the staccato cries of angry ghants, a dreadful chorus of wet clicking. Miriamele tried to make out what was happening, but Isgrimnur had already lost his torch and was now little more than a dark shape in the middle of a seething mass of shells and twitching legs. Somewhere closer to the center, Camaris' torch still cut the air like a banner of fire, swinging back and forth, back and forth, as he waded toward the spot where Tiamak was prisoned.

Miriamele was terrified but furious. Why should she wait while Isgrimnur and Camaris risked their lives? They were her friends! And what if they died or were captured? Then she would be alone, forced to try and find her way out, pursued by those horrible things. It was stupid. She wouldn't do it. But what else could she do?

Think, girl, think, she told herself, even as she hopped up and down anxiously, trying to see if Isgrimnur was still on his feet. *Do what? What?*

She couldn't stand waiting. It was too horrible. She took the two remaining torches from her belt and lit them. When they were burning, she thrust them down into the mud on either side of the tunnel mouth, then took a deep breath and followed Isgrimnur's track down the slope, her legs so wobbly she feared she might fall down. Unreality gripped her: she couldn't be doing this. Her skin was pricklingly cold. No one with their wits left would go down into that pit. But somehow her booted feet kept moving.

"Isgrimnur!" she shrieked. "Where are you?"

Cold muddy legs clutched at her, chitinous things like animate tree branches. The hissing creatures were all around; knobby heads butted at her legs and she felt her stomach thrash again. She kicked out like a horse, trying to drive them back. A claw caught at her leg and hooked itself into her boot top; the torch momentarily illuminated her target, which gleamed like a wet stone. She lifted her short spear, almost dropping the torch, which was clutched awkwardly in the same hand, and stabbed down as hard as she could. The spear thumped into something which gave satisfyingly. When she jerked it back, the claw let go.

It was easier to swing the club, but it did not seem to kill the things. At every blow they fell and tumbled, but a moment later they were back again, scratching, clasping, worse than any nightmare. After a few moments she pushed the cudgel into her belt and took up the torch in her free hand, which seemed at least to keep them at bay. She hit one of the ghants full in its empty face, and some of the burning palm oil spattered and stuck. The thing shrieked like a fool's whistle and dove forward, digging itself into the mud, but another clambered over its quivering shell to take its place. She shouted in fear and disgust as she kicked it aside. The army of ghants was never-ending.

"Miriamele!" It was Isgrimnur, somewhere ahead of her. "Is that you!?"

"Here!" she cried, her voice tearing along the edge, threatening to become a shriek that would never stop. "Oh, hurry, hurry, hurry!"

"I told you to stay!" he shouted. "Camaris is coming back! See the torch!"

She stabbed at one of the things before her, but her spear only scraped along the shell. Out in the churning mass there was suddenly a glint of flame. "I see it!"

"We're coming!" The duke was barely audible above the rattling voices of the ghants. "Stay where you are and wave your torch!"

"I'm here," she howled, "I'm here!"

The sea of writhing creatures seemed to pulse as though a wave rolled through it. The light of the torch jiggled above them, moving closer. Miriamele fought desperately—there was still a chance! She swung her torch in as wide an arc as she could, trying to keep her attackers at a distance. A clawing leg caught at the brand and suddenly it was gone, sizzling into the mud and leaving her in darkness. She thrust out wildly with the spear.

"Here!" she screamed. "My torch is gone!"

There was no reply from Isgrimnur. All was lost. Miriamele wondered briefly if she would be able to use the spear on herself—certainly she could never let them have her alive. . . .

Something grasped her arm. Shrieking, she struggled but could not break free.

"It's me!" cried Isgrimnur. "Don't stick me!" He pulled her against his broad side and shouted to Camaris, who was still some distance away. The torch came closer, the ghants dancing around it like water drops on a hot stone. "How will we find our way out?" Isgrimnur bellowed.

"I left torches by the door." Miriamele turned to look,

even as something snatched at her cloak. "There!" She realized Isgrimnur could not see her pointing. She kicked
and the snagging claw fell away. "Behind you."

Isgrimnur lifted her bodily and carried her for a few
steps, clearing the way with Kvalnir until they had pushed
through a clump of buzzing creatures and found their feet
on the upward slope.

"We have to wait for Camaris."

"He's coming," Isgrimnur bellowed. "Move!"

"Did he get Tiamak?"

"Move!"

Slipping back half as far as each step took her forward,
Miriamele struggled up the muddy incline toward the
light of the twin torches. She could hear Isgrimnur's
grunting breath behind her, and at intervals the muffled
crack of Kvalnir's steel against the shells of their pursuers. When she reached the top she grasped the two
torches and pulled them from the mud, then turned, ready
to fight again. Isgrimnur was right behind her, and the
flickering brand that she knew must belong to Camaris
was at the bottom of the slope.

"Hurry!" she called down. The torch paused, then
waved from side to side, as though Camaris used it to
keep the swarm away as he climbed. Now she could see
his hair gleaming silver-yellow in the torchlight. "Help
him," she pleaded with Isgrimnur. The duke took a few
steps down, Kvalnir moving in a blurry arc, and in a moment Camaris had broken free and the two of them came
tripping and sliding up the slope to the tunnel mouth.
Camaris had lost his club. Tiamak, covered with white
jelly and apparently senseless, hung over his shoulder.
Miriamele stared at the Wrannaman's slack features in
dismay.

"Go, damn it!" Isgrimnur pushed Miriamele toward the
tunnel. She tore her eyes from Tiamak's sticky form and
began to run, waving her burning brand as she went, making shadows leap and streak madly across the dun walls.

The floor of the chamber behind them seemed to erupt
as the ghants came scurrying in pursuit. Isgrimnur pushed
through into the tunnel; a mass of angrily clicking shapes

followed him, a wave of armored flesh. The pursuing ghants might have caught the duke and his companions within moments, but their numbers were so great that they filled the passage almost completely, tangling themselves. Those following tried to force their way past; within instants the tunnel mouth was clogged with writhing, leg-waving bodies.

"Lead the way!" the duke cried.

It was difficult to move quickly with her head hunched down and her back bent, and the muddy floor had been difficult to traverse even at walking speed. Miriamele fell down several times, once giving her ankle a nasty twist. She scarcely felt the pain, but a dim part of her thoughts knew that if she survived, she would certainly feel it later. She did her best to look for the marks Isgrimnur had so conscientiously scraped in the foamy walls, but by the time they had gone a few hundred paces from the great chamber Miriamele realized in horror that she had missed a turning. She knew that they should have passed through at least one of the egg-chambers by now, but instead they were still in one of the featureless tunnels—and this one was sloping downward, when the return trip should have led up.

"Isgrimnur, I think we're lost!" She slowed to a trot, holding her torch close to the dripping walls as she looked desperately for something that she recognized. She could hear Camaris' heavy tread just behind.

The Rimmersman swore floridly. "Just keep running, then—can't be helped!"

Miriamele sped her pace again. Her legs were aching, and each breath pushed at her lungs with sharp needles. Positive now that they had lost their course, she chose the next of the cross tunnels that seemed to lead upward. The slope was not steep, but the slippery mud made climbing difficult. Above the sound of her own ragged breath she could hear the clatter of the ghants rising again behind them.

The top of the rise came into view, another tunnel running perpendicularly to theirs, about a hundred ells above; but even as Miriamele's heart lightened a little, a swarm of ghants came scuttling into the tunnel below them. Moving low to the ground and traveling on four legs instead of two, the creatures were making much swifter time up the sloping pathway. Miriamele dug harder, forcing herself up the final slope. She only hesitated an instant before choosing the right-hand side of the cross-tunnel. Even Camaris' breathing was loud and harsh now. A few of the fastest ghants reached Isgrimnur, who was bringing up the rear. Bellowing with anger and disgust, the duke made a broad sweep with Kvalnir; hissing, the ghants tumbled back down into the boiling mass of their fellows.

Before Miriamele and her companions had gone fifty paces down the new passage, the ghants reached the top of the rise behind them and spilled out into the tunnel. On flat ground they traveled even more swiftly, hopping forward at a terrifying pace. Some ran directly up the walls before swiveling to pursue the fleeing company.

"We must turn and fight," Isgrimnur gasped. "Camaris! Put the marsh man down!"

"Oh, God love us, no!" cried Miriamele, "I hear more of them ahead!" It was a nightmare, a dreadful, endless nightmare. "Isgrimnur, we're trapped!"

"Stop, damn it, stop! We'll fight here!"

"No!" Miriamele was horrified. "If we stop here, we'll have to fight both swarms, front and back. Keep running!"

She took a few steps farther down, but she could tell no one was following her. She turned to see Isgrimnur staring grimly at the ghants behind them, who had slowed when their prey did and now came forward with deliberate caution, their numbers swelling as dozens more scrambled up from the tunnel below. Miriamele turned and saw jiggling spots down the corridor before her as the glossy, dead eyes of the ghants there began to catch the torchlight.

"Oh, Merciful Elysia," Miriamele breathed, utterly defeated. Camaris, who stood beside her, was staring at the floor as though musing on some odd but not terribly important thought. Tiamak lay against his shoulder, eyes closed and mouth open like a sleeping child. Miriamele felt a moment of sadness. She had wanted to save the marsh man ... it would have been so lovely to save him. ...

With a bellow, Isgrimnur abruptly turned. To Miriamele's complete astonishment, he kicked the wall behind him as hard as he could. Caught up in what must be some fit of insane frustration, he slammed his boot sole against it again and again.

"Isgrimnur. . . !" Miriamele began, but at that moment the duke's boot smashed through the wall, making a hole the size of his head in the crumbling mud. He lashed out again and another section fell through.

"Help me!" he grunted. Miriamele stepped forward, but before she could lend any aid, Isgrimnur's next blow knocked out a large section. There was now a hole in the wall almost two cubits high, with nothing beyond but blackness.

"Go on!" the duke urged her. A dozen paces away the ghants were clicking madly. Miriamele pushed the torch through the gap, then forced her head and shoulders after it, half-certain she would feel jointed claws reach down and clutch her. Slipping and struggling, she scrambled through, praying that there was some solid ground there, that she would not fall into nothingness. Her hands touched the muck of another tunnel floor; she caught a momentary glimpse of the empty passage that surrounded her before she turned back to help the others. Camaris pushed Tiamak's limp form through to her. She nearly dropped him—the slender Wrannaman did not weigh much, but he was sagging dead weight covered with slippery ooze. The old knight followed, then Isgrimnur squeezed his own broad body through a moment later. Almost on his heels, the hole filled with the reaching arms of ghants, hard and shiny as polished wood.

Kvalnir slashed out, bringing fizzing squeals of pain from the far side of the hole. The arms were quickly withdrawn, but the chittering of the ghants continued to grow.

"They'll decide to come through in a moment, sword or no sword," the duke panted.

Miriamele stared at the gap for a moment. The stench of the ghants was strong, as was the coarse noise they made as they rubbed against each other. They were gathering for another attack, and they were only a few scant inches away.

"Give me your shirt," she told Isgrimnur suddenly. "And his, too." She pointed at Camaris.

The duke looked at her for a moment in alarm, as though she might have suddenly lost her wits, then quickly stripped off his tattered shirt and handed it to her. Miriamele held it to the flame of her torch until it caught—it was a maddeningly slow process, since that shirt was damp and mud-streaked—then used her spear-point to push the burning cloth into the gap in the wall. Surprised hisses and quiet snicking noises came from the ghants on the other side. Miriamele pushed Camaris' shirt in beside it; when it had caught fire and both garments were burning steadily, she took Isgrimnur's heavy cloak as well and crammed it into the remaining space.

"Now we run again," she said. "I don't think they like fire." She was surprised at how calm she suddenly felt, despite a certain light-headedness. "But it won't hold them long."

Camaris scooped up Tiamak and they all hastened on. At each turning they chose the tunnel that seemed to lead upward. Two more times they broke through sections of the passageway walls and sniffed at the holes like dogs, hunting for outside air. At last they found a tunnel that, although lower and narrower than many through which they had passed, seemed somehow fresher.

The clamor of pursuit had begun again, although as yet none of the creatures had come into view. Miriamele ignored the gelatinous froth beneath her hands as she half-walked, half-crawled through the low tunnel. Strands of pale foam fell wetly across her face and fouled her hair. A curl of it touched her open lips, and before she could spit it out, she tasted bitter musk. At the next bend in the passage the tunnel suddenly became larger. After a few more lurching steps, they turned another corner and found light splashed across the mud.

"Daylight!" Miriamele shouted. She had never been happier to see it.

They stumbled along until the tunnel turned again, then found themselves facing a round but ragged hole in the tunnel wall, beyond which hung the sky—gray and dim, but the sky nonetheless, the glorious sky. She threw herself forward, clambering through the hole and out onto a rounded floor of lumpy mud.

Treetops waved below them, so green and intricate that Miriamele's muck-deadened mind almost could not take them in. They were standing atop one of the upper parts of the nest; a scant two hundred cubits away lay the watercourse, tranquil as a great snake. There was no flatboat waiting.

Camaris and Isgrimnur followed her out onto the roof of the nest.

"Where is the monk?" Isgrimnur howled. "Damnation! Damnation! I knew he couldn't be trusted!"

"Never mind that now," said Miriamele. "We have to get off this thing."

After a quick search they found a way down onto a lower roof. They teetered across a slender ridge of mud for some dozen paces before reaching the safety of the next level, then continued from flat spot to flat spot, moving always toward the front of the nest and the waiting watercourse. As they reached the outermost point, from which it was only a leap of three or four ells down to the ground, a company of ghants surged out of the hole near the top of the nest.

"Here they come," Isgrimnur wheezed. "Jump down!"

Before Miriamele could do so, another, larger swarm of the creatures came spilling out of one of the nest's large front entrances, gathering quickly into an agitated mass directly below them. Miriamele felt a deathly, terrible weariness settle over her. To be so close—it wasn't fair!

"Holy Aedon, save us now." There was little strength left in the duke's voice. "Move back, Miriamele. I'll jump first."

"You can't!" she cried. "There are too many of them."

"We can't stay here." Indeed, the other ghants were

moving rapidly down across the uneven upper levels of
the nest, leggy as spiders, nimble as apes. They were
clicking in anticipation and their black eyes glittered.

A bright streak abruptly flashed across the beach. Startled, Miriamele looked down at the ghants below, who
were milling wildly. Their percussive cries were even wilder and more shrill than they had been, and several of
them seemed to have caught fire. Miriamele looked out to
the watercourse, trying to make sense of what was happening. The flatboat had floated into view. Cadrach, who
stood spread-legged in the square bow, held something in
his hand that looked like a large torch, its upper end burning brightly.

As Miriamele stared in numb astonishment, the monk
swung the thing forward and a ball of fire seemed to leap
from the end, arcing across the water to land amid the
ghants clustered on the sand below her. The fiery blob
burst, scattering great splashes of flame which stuck to
the creatures like burning glue. Some of those who were
struck fell to the ground with their shells bubbling from
the heat and began to pipe like boiling lobsters, while others ran back and forth, tearing ineffectually at their own
armor, clacking and clattering like broken wagon wheels.
Out on the flatboat, Cadrach bent; when he straightened,
another flame had blossomed at the end of his strange
stick. He threw once more and another gout of liquid fire
spattered across the shrieking ghants. The monk raised his
hands to his mouth.

"Jump now!" he cried, his voice echoing faintly.
"Hurry!"

Miriamele turned and looked briefly at Isgrimnur. The
duke's face was slack with wonder, but he drew himself
together long enough to give Miriamele a gentle but purposeful shove.

"You heard him," he growled. *"Jump!"*

She did, then landed hard in the sand and rolled. A fiery bit of something caught in her cloak, but she thumped
it out with her hands. A moment later, with a *whoof* of
outrushing breath, Isgrimnur crashed down beside her.
The ghants, who were squealing and dashing madly back

and forth across the grass-strewn beach, paid little attention to their former quarry. The duke turned and climbed
to his feet, then reached up his hands. Camaris, leaning
far over the uneven edge of the nest, dropped Tiamak
down to him. The duke was knocked back to the sand, but
cradled the unmoving Wrannaman; a moment later
Camaris had vaulted down as well. The company dashed
across the strand. A few ghants who had not been struck
by Cadrach's fiery attack scuttled toward them but
Miriamele and Camaris kicked them out of the way. The
fleeing company stumbled down the bank and waded out
into the sluggish green water.

Miriamele sprawled in the bottom of the flatboat, gasping for air. With a few shoves of the pole, the monk sent
the boat bobbing out toward the middle of the waterway,
well out of reach of the capering ghants.

"Are you hurt?" Cadrach's face was pale, his eyes almost feverishly bright.

"What . . . what did you. . . ?" She could not find the
breath to finish her sentence.

Cadrach dipped his head, shrugging. "The oil-palm
leaves. I had an idea after you went into . . . that place. I
cooked them. There are things I know how to do." He
held up the tube he had made from a large reed. "I used
this to throw the fire." The hand that clutched the tube
was covered with angry blisters.

"Oh, Cadrach, look what you've done."

Cadrach turned to look at Camaris and Isgrimnur, who
were huddled over Tiamak. Behind them on the shoreline,
the ghants were leaping and hissing like damned souls
made to dance. Smears of flame still burned along the
nest's front walls, sending knots of inky smoke into the
late afternoon sky.

"No, look what *you've* done," the monk said, and
smiled a grim but not entirely unhappy smile.

PART TWO

The
Winding Road

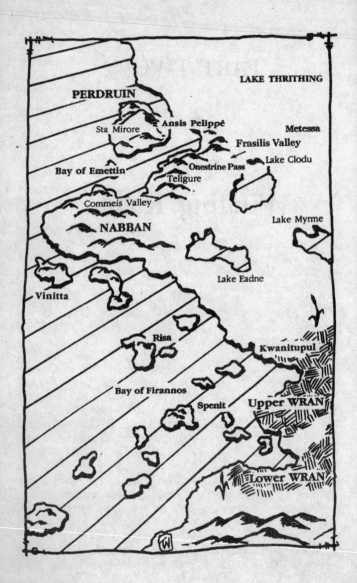

LAKE THRITHING

PERDRUIN

Sta Mirore   Ansis Pelippé   Metessa

Frasilis Valley

Bay of Emettin   Onestrine Pass   Lake Clodu
                      Teligure

Commeis Valley

NABBAN   Lake Myrme

                        Lake Eadne

Vinitta

        Risa   Kwanitupul

Bay of Firannos   Upper WRAN

                Spenit

                        Lower WRAN

17

Bonfire Night

"I don't think I want to go, Simon." Jeremias was doing his best, with a rag and a smoothing stone, to clean Simon's sword.

"You don't have to." Simon grunted in pain as he pulled on his boot. Three days had passed since the battle on the frozen lake, but every muscle still felt as though it had been pounded on a blacksmith's anvil. "This is just something he wants me to do."

Jeremias seemed relieved, but was unwilling to accept his freedom so easily. "But shouldn't your squire go along when the prince calls for you? What if you need something that you've forgotten—who would go back for it?"

Simon laughed, but broke off as he felt a band of pain tighten around his ribs. The day after the battle he had barely been able to stand. His body had felt like a bag of broken crockery. Even now, he still moved like an old, old man. "I'll just have to go and get it myself—or I'll call for you. Don't worry. It's not like that here, which you should know as well as anybody. It's not a royal court, like at the Hayholt."

Jeremias peered closely at the blade's edge, then shook his head. "You say that, Simon, but you never can tell when princes will get squinty on you. You can never tell when they might suddenly feel their blood and go all royal."

"It's a risk I'll have to take. Now give me that damned sword before you polish it away to a sliver."

Jeremias looked up anxiously. He had regained a little weight since coming to New Gadrinsett, but provisions were scarce and he was still far from being the chubby boy Simon had grown up with; he had a drawn look that Simon doubted would ever completely go away. "I would never harm your sword," he said seriously.

"Oh, God's Teeth," Simon growled, swearing with the practiced indifference of a blooded soldier. "I was joking. Now give it here. I've got to go."

Jeremias gave him a haughty look. "One thing about jokes, Simon—they're supposed to be funny." Despite the grin that was beginning to crinkle his lips, he handed the blade over carefully. "And I'll let you know if you're ever actually funny, I promise."

Simon's witty reply—which in truth he had not yet formulated—was forestalled by the opening of the tent flap. A small figure appeared in the doorway, silent and solemn.

"Leleth!" Jeremias said. "Come in. Would you like to go for a walk with me? Or I could finish telling you that story about Jack Mundwode and the bear."

The little girl moved a few steps into the tent, which was her way of showing assent. Her eyes, as they turned momentarily to Simon's, were disturbingly adult. He remembered how she had looked on the Dream Road—a free creature in its element, flying, exulting—and felt an obscure sense of shame, as if he were somehow helping to keep a beautiful thing prisoned.

"I'll be on my way," he said. "Take care of Jeremias, Leleth. Don't let him handle anything sharp."

Jeremias flung the polishing cloth at him as he stepped through the tent flap.

Outside, Simon took a deep breath. The air was chill, but he thought it felt subtly warmer than it had a few days before, as though somewhere nearby Spring was looking for a way in.

We only beat Fengbald, he cautioned himself. *We didn't hurt the Storm King at all. So there's not much chance we've driven the winter away.*

But the thought raised another question. Why hadn't

the Storm King sent help to Fengbald as he had to Elias at the siege of Naglimund? Survivors' stories of the horror of the Norns' attack were almost as vivid in Simon's mind as the memories of his own strange adventures. If the swords were so important, and if Josua was known by the Hikeda'ya to have one of them—which, according to the prince and Deornoth, was almost certainly the case—why hadn't Sesuad'ra's defenders found themselves staring down at an army of ice-giants and armored Norns? Was it something about the Stone itself?

Perhaps because it is a Sithi place. But they weren't afraid to attack Jao é-Tinukai'i, finally.

He shook his head. It was something to share with Binabik and Geloë, although he was sure it had already occurred to them. Or had it? It might be almost too overwhelming to add another unsolvable puzzle to the pile they already faced. Simon was so tired of questions without answers.

His boots crunched in the thin snow as he made his way across the Fire Garden toward Leavetaking House. He had gladly played the fool with Jeremias, since it seemed to bring his friend out of his worries and evil memories, but Simon was not in a particularly cheerful frame of mind. His last nights had been filled with dreams of the battle's carnage, of madness and blood and screaming horses. Now he was going to see Josua, and the prince was in an even blacker mood than he was. Simon was not looking forward to this at all.

He stopped, his frosty breath rising around his head in a cloud, and stared at the broken dome of the Observatory. If only he dared take the mirror and try to speak with Jiriki again! But the fact that the Sithi had not come, despite the defenders' great need, made it clear that Jiriki had more important things on his mind than the doings of mortals. Also, the Sitha had expressly warned Simon that this was a perilous time to walk the Road of Dreams. Perhaps if he tried, he would somehow bring the Storm King's attention to Sesuad'ra—Simon might shatter the very indifference that seemed to have been the single greatest reason for their unbelievable victory.

He was a man now, or might as well be. There could be
no more mooncalf tricks, he decided. The stakes were far
too high.

Leavetaking House was poorly lit: only a few torches
burned in the sconces, so that the great room seemed half-
dissolved in shadow. Josua was standing by the bier.

"Thank you for coming, Simon." The prince barely
raised his eyes before returning his gaze to Deornoth's
body, which was laid out on the slab of stone with the
Tree and Drake banner draped across it, as though the
knight were only sleeping beneath a thin blanket.
"Binabik and Geloë are there," the prince said, gesturing
to a pair of figures sitting beside the firepit near the far
wall. "I will join you in a moment."

Simon walked to the fire with a careful tread, trying to
avoid disrespectful noise. The troll and the witch woman
were talking quietly.

"Greetings, friend Simon," said Binabik. "Come, sit
and be warm."

Simon sat cross-legged on the stone floor, then moved
forward to a warmer spot. "He seems even sadder than
yesterday," he whispered.

The troll looked at Josua. "It has struck him with a
great weightiness. It is as though all the people he was
loving, and for whose safety he was fearing, were all
killed with Deornoth."

Geloë made a noise of mild exasperation. "You cannot
fight battles without losses. Deornoth was a good man,
but others died, too."

"Josua is now mourning for all of them, I am
thinking—in his way." The troll shrugged. "But I have
certainty he will recover."

The witch woman nodded. "Yes, but we have little
time. We must strike while the advantage is ours."

Simon looked at her curiously. Geloë seemed as age-
less as ever, but she seemed to have lost a little of her
vast assurance. Not that it would be surprising if she had:
the past year had been a dreadful one. "I wanted to ask

you something, Geloë," he said. "Did you know about Fengbald?"

She turned her yellow eyes on him. "Did I know he would send someone onto the field wearing his armor, to fool us? No. But I did know that Josua had conspired with Helfgrim, the Lord Mayor. I did *not* know whether Fengbald would take the bait."

"I am afraid that I was also knowing, Simon," said Binabik. "My help was needed for planning how to split the ice. It was done with the helping of some of my Qanuc fellows."

Simon felt a little warmth rise to his cheeks. "So everybody knew but me?"

Geloë shook her head. "No, Simon. Besides Helfgrim, Josua and myself, there were only Binabik, Deornoth, Freosel, and the trolls that helped prepare the trap—that was all who knew. It was our last hope, and we dared not take a chance of it being even rumored to Fengbald."

"Didn't you trust me?"

Binabik laid a calming hand on his shoulder. "Trust was not the thing that was mattering, Simon. You and any others who were fighting on the ice could have been captured. Even the bravest will tell all they know if they are under torturing—and Fengbald was not being the sort for scruples in such things. The fewer who knew, the better were being chances that the secret would hold. If there had been need to tell you, as there was with those others, we would have told you with no hesitating."

"Binabik is right, Simon." Josua had come up silently as they spoke and now stood over them. The firelight threw his shadow across the ceiling, a long empty stripe of darkness. "I trust you as fully as I trust anyone— anyone living, that is." A hint of something darted across his face. "I ordered that only those necessary to the plan should know. I am sure you can understand."

Simon swallowed. "Of course, Prince Josua."

Josua lowered himself down onto a stone and gazed absently at the wavering flames. "We have won a great victory—it is a miracle, truly. But the price was so very high. . . ."

"No price that kept innocent people alive could be too high," Geloë replied.

"Perhaps. But there is a possibility that Fengbald would have let the women and children go. . . ."

"But now they are alive and *free*," said Geloë shortly. "And a good number of the men are, too. And we have had an unexpected victory."

The ghost of a smile flickered on Josua's lips. "Are you to take Deornoth's place, then, Valada Geloë? For that is what he always did for me—reminded me when I began to brood."

"I cannot take his place, Josua, but I do not think we need to apologize for winning. Mourning is honorable, of course. I do not seek to take that away from you."

"No, of course not." The prince looked at her for a moment, then pivoted slowly and surveyed the long hall. "We must honor the dead."

There was a scrape of leather in the doorway. Sludig stood there, a pair of saddlebags draped over his brawny arm. Looking at the strain on the Rimmersman's face, Simon wondered if they were packed full of stones. "Prince Josua?"

The prince turned. "Yes, Sludig?"

"These are all that were found. They have Fengbald's crest on them. They are soaking wet, though. I have not opened them."

"Put them down here by the fireside. Then please sit and speak with us. You have been a great help, Sludig."

The Rimmersman bobbed his head. "Thank you, Prince Josua. But I also have another message for you. The prisoners are ready to talk now—or so Freosel says."

"Ah." Josua nodded. "And Freosel is no doubt right. He is rough, but very clever. Not unlike our old friend Einskaldir, eh, Sludig?"

"Just as you say, Highness." Sludig seemed uncomfortable talking to the prince. He was finally getting the attention and credit he seemed to have wanted, Simon noted, but did not seem completely happy with it.

Josua laid his hand on Simon's shoulder. "I suppose I

must go and do my duty, then," he said. "Would you come with me, Simon?"

"Of course, Prince Josua."

"Good." Josua made a gesture toward the others. "If you would be so good, attend me after supper. There is much to speak about."

As they approached the door, Josua put the stump of his right wrist beneath Simon's elbow and led him toward the bier where Deornoth lay. Simon could not help noticing that he was a little taller than the prince. It had been a long time since he had stood so close to Josua, but he was still surprised. He, Simon, was tall—and not just for a youth, but for a man. It was a strange thought.

They stopped before the bier. Simon stood on the balls of his feet, respectfully silent but anxious to move on. Being so close to the knight's body made him uncomfortable. The pale, angular face that lay upon the stone slab looked less like the Deornoth he remembered than like something carved in soap. The skin on his face, especially on his eyelids and nostrils, was bloodlessly translucent.

"You did not know him well, Simon. He was the best of men."

Simon swallowed. His mouth felt dry. The dead were . . . so *dead*. And someday Josua, Binabik, Sludig, everyone in New Gadrinsett would be that way. Even he would be that way, Simon realized with a feeling of distaste. What was it like? "He was always very kind to me, Highness."

"He knew no other way. He was the truest knight I have ever known."

The more Josua had spoken of Deornoth in the last few days, the more Simon had come to realize that he had apparently not known the man at all. He had seemed a simple man, kind and quiet, but hardly an exemplar of knightliness as Josua seemed to think him, a modern Camaris.

"He died bravely." It seemed a lame sort of condolence to offer, but Josua smiled.

"He did. I wish you and Sludig could have reached his side sooner, but you did your best." Josua's face changed abruptly, like clouds blowing across a spring sky. "I do not mean to suggest that you two failed in some way, Simon. Please forgive me—I have grown thoughtless in my grief. Deornoth could always chivvy me out of my self-indulgence. Ah, God, I will miss him. I think he was my best friend, although I never knew it until he was dead."

Simon was further discomfited to see tears forming in Josua's eyes. He wanted to look away, but was suddenly reminded of the Sithi, and of what Strangyeard had said. Perhaps it was the highest and the greatest who always bore the largest griefs. How could there be shame in such sadness?

Simon reached up and took the prince's elbow. "Come, Josua. Let's walk. Tell me about Deornoth, since I never had the chance to know him properly."

The prince tore his gaze away from Deornoth's alabaster features. "Yes, of course. We will walk."

He let Simon lead him out the door and into the hilltop wind.

". . . And he actually came to me and apologized!" Josua was laughing now, although there seemed little joy in it. "As though he himself had transgressed. Poor, loyal Deornoth." He shook his head and wiped at his eye. "Aedon! Why is it that this cloud of regret seems to surround me, Simon? Either I am pleading forgiveness, or those around me are—it is no wonder that Elias thought I was soft-headed. Sometimes I think he was right."

Simon suppressed a grin. "Perhaps the problem is only because you are too quick to share your thoughts with people you do not know well—like escaped scullions."

Josua looked at him narrowly for a moment, then laughed, but this time his mirth seemed less constrained. "Perhaps you are right, Simon. People like their princes strong and unswerving, don't they?" He chuckled. "Ah, Usires the Merciful, could they ever have a prince less like that than me?" He looked up, squinting across the field of tents. "God help me, I have wandered. Where is the cave where the prisoners are kept?"

"There." Simon pointed to a rocky outcropping just inside Sesuad'ra's outer barrier, barely visible behind the wind-shimmied walls of the tent city. Josua altered his course and Simon followed, moving slowly to ease the ache of his several wounds.

"I have let myself run far afield," Josua said, "and not only in my search for the prisoners. I asked you to come to me so I could ask you a question."

"Yes?" Simon could not help but be interested. What could the prince possibly want of him?

"I wish to bury our dead on this hill." Josua waved his arm, spanning the breadth of Sesuad'ra's grassy summit. "You of all the people here know the Sithi best, I think—or at least the most intimately, for certainly Binabik and Geloë have studied them. Do you think that it would be allowed? This is their place, after all."

Simon thought about this for a moment. "Allowed? I can't imagine the Sithi preventing it, if that's what you mean." He smiled wryly. "They didn't even show up to defend it, so I don't think that they would suddenly arrive with an army to keep us from burying our dead."

They walked on a short way in silence. Simon pondered before speaking again. "No, I don't think they would object—not that I could ever claim to speak for them," he added hurriedly. "After all, Jiriki buried his kinsman An'nai with Grimmric, back on Urmsheim." The days on the dragon-mountain seemed so far away now, as though they had been spent there by another Simon, a distant relative. He kneaded the muscles of his painfully stiff arm and sighed. "But, as I said, I cannot speak for the Sithi. I was there for—what, months? And I still could never hope to understand them."

Josua looked at him keenly. "What was it like to live with them, Simon? And what was their city like—Jao . . . Jao. . . ?"

"*Jao é-Tinukai'i.*" Simon was more than a little proud at how easily the difficult syllables fell from his lips. "I wish I could explain, Josua. It's sort of like trying to describe a dream—you can tell what happened, but you can't quite make someone understand how it felt. They are old, Highness, very, very old. But to look at them,

they are young and healthy and . . . and beautiful." He remembered Jiriki's sister Aditu, her lovely, bright, predatory eyes, her smile full of secret amusement. "They have
every right to hate us, Josua—at least I think they do—
but instead they seem . . . puzzled by us. As we would
feel if sheep became mighty and drove us out of our cities."

Josua laughed. "Sheep, Simon? Are you saying that the
Imperators of Nabban and King Fingil of Rimmersgard
. . . and my father, for that matter . . . were woolly, harmless creatures?"

Simon shook his head. "No, I only mean that we are
that *different* from the Sithi. They don't understand us any
more than we understand them. Jiriki and his grandmother Amerasu might not be as different as some—they
certainly treated me with kindness and understanding—
but the other Sithi . . ." He stopped, at a loss. "I don't
know how to explain it."

Josua looked at him kindly. "What was the city like?"

"I tried to describe it before, when I came here. I said
then that it was like a huge boat, but that it was also like
a rainbow in front of a waterfall. That's terrible, but I still
can't describe it any better than that. It's all made of cloth
strung between the trees, but it seems as solid as any city
I've ever seen. But it looks as though they could pack it
up any moment and take it somewhere else." He laughed
despairingly. "You see, I keep running out of words!"

"I think you explain it very well, Simon." The prince's
thin features were pensive. "Ah, how I would like to truly
know the Sithi someday. I cannot understand what made
my father fear and hate them so. What a storehouse of
history and lore they must possess!"

They had reached the cave entrance, which was barred
with a makeshift portcullis of heavy, rough-cut timbers. A
guard posted there—one of Hotvig's Thrithings-men—
left the jug of coals over which he had been warming his
hands to raise the gateway and let them in.

Several more guards, an even mix of Thrithings-men
and Freosel's Erkynlanders, stood in the antechamber.
They saluted both the prince and Simon respectfully,

much to the bemused chagrin of the latter. Freosel, rubbing his hands together, appeared from the depths of the cavern.

"Your Highness . . . and Sir Seoman," he said, inclining his head. "I think time has come. They be starting to get frisky-like. If we wait longer, we may have trouble—if you pardon my saying so."

"I trust your judgment, Freosel," said Josua. "Take me to them."

The inner part of the wide cavern, which was separated from the front by a bend in the stone walls and thus hidden from the sun, had been divided by the use of more stout timbers into two stockades with a sizable open space between them.

"They do shout at each other 'cross the cave." Freosel's grin revealed the gap in his teeth. "Blaming each other, like. Take turns keeping each other awake nights. Do our job for us, they do."

Josua nodded as he approached the left-hand stockade, then turned to Simon. "Say nothing," he said firmly. "Just listen."

In the dim, torchlit cavern, Simon at first had trouble making out its occupants. The smell of urine and unwashed bodies—something Simon had thought he could no longer notice—was strong.

"I wish to speak with your captain," Josua called. There was slow movement in the shadows, then a figure in the tattered green surcoat of an Erkynguardsman stepped up to the rough bars.

"That is me, your Highness," the soldier said.

Josua looked him over. "Sceldwine? Is that you?"

The man's embarrassment was plain in his voice. "It is, Prince Josua."

"Well." Josua seemed to be taken aback. "I never dreamed to see you in a place like this."

"Nor did I, Highness. Nor expected to be sent to fight against you either, sire. It's a shame . . ."

Freosel abruptly stepped forward. "Don't you listen to him, Josua," he sneered. "He and his murdering cronies will say anything to save their lives." He thumped his powerful hand against the stockade wall hard enough to make the wood quiver. "The rest of us haven't forgot what your kind did to Falshire."

Sceldwine, after drawing back in alarm, leaned forward to see better. His pale face, exposed now by the torchlight, was drawn and worried. "None of us were happy about that." He turned to the prince. "And we did not want to come against you, Prince Josua. You must believe us."

Josua started to say something, but Freosel, astonishingly, interrupted him. "Your people won't have it, Josua. This ben't the Hayholt or Naglimund. We don't trust these armored louts. If you let them live, there'll be trouble."

A mumbling growl ran through the prisoners, but there was more than a little fear in it.

"I don't want to execute them, Freosel," Josua said unhappily. "They were sworn to my brother. What choice did they have?"

"What choice have any of us got?" the Falshireman shot back. "They made the wrong one. Our blood be on their hands. Kill them and have done. Let God worry about choices."

Josua sighed. "What do you say, Sceldwine? Why should I let you live?"

The Erkynguardsman seemed momentarily at a loss. "Because we are just fighting men, serving our king, Highness. There is no other reason." He stared out between the bars.

Josua beckoned for Freosel and Simon and walked away from the stockade to the center of the cavern, out of earshot.

"Well?" he said.

Simon shook his head. "Kill them, Prince Josua? I don't . . ."

Josua raised his hand. "No, no. Of course I won't kill them." He turned to the Falshireman, who was grinning. "Freosel has been working on them for two days. They are convinced he wants their hides, and that the citizens of New Gadrinsett are demanding they be hung before

Leavetaking House. We just want them in the proper mood."

Simon was again embarrassed: he had misjudged. "What are you going to do, then?"

"Watch me." After stalling for a few moments more, Josua assumed an air of solemnity and walked slowly back to the stockade and the nervous prisoners. "Sceldwine," he said, "I may regret this, but I am going to let you and your men live."

Freosel, scowling, snorted a great angry snort and marched away. An audible sigh of relief rose from the prisoners.

"But," Josua raised his finger, "we will not keep you and feed you. You will work to earn your lives. My people would hang *me* if I did any less—they will already be very displeased to be cheated of your executions. If you prove yourselves trustworthy, we may let you fight at our side when we push my mad brother from the Dragonbone Chair."

Sceldwine gripped the wooden bars with both his hands. "We will fight for you, Josua. No one else would show us such mercy in these mad times." His comrades gave ragged shouts of agreement.

"Very well. I will think further on how this is to be accomplished." Josua nodded stiffly, then turned his back on the prisoners. Simon followed him out into the middle of the room once more.

"By the Ransomer," said Josua, "if they *will* fight for us, what a boon! A hundred more disciplined soldiers. They may be the first of many more defections, when word begins to spread."

Simon smiled. "You were very convincing. Freosel, too."

Josua looked pleased. "I think that there may be a few strolling players in the constable's family history. As for me—well, all princes are born liars, you know." His expression turned serious. "And now I must deal with the mercenaries."

"You will not make them the same offer, will you?" Simon asked, suddenly worried.

"Why not?"

"Because ... because someone who fights for gold is different."

"All soldiers fight for gold," Josua said gently.

"That's not what I mean. You heard what Sceldwine said. They fought because they thought they must—that's at least partly true. Those Thrithings-men fought because Fengbald paid them. *You* can't pay them with anything but their lives."

"That's not an inconsiderable sum," Josua pointed out.

"But after they're armed again, how much weight will that have? They're different than the Erkynguard, Josua, and if you want to make a kingdom that's different than your brother's, you can't build it on men like the mercenaries." He stopped abruptly, horrified to discover he was lecturing the prince. "I'm sorry," he blurted. "I have no right to speak this way."

Josua was watching him, eyebrow raised. "They are right about you, young Simon," he said slowly. "There is a good head under that red hair of yours." He laid his hand on Simon's shoulder. "I had not planned to deal with them until Hotvig could join me, in any case. I will think carefully on what you have said."

"I hope you can forgive me my forwardness," Simon said, abashed. "You have been very kind with me."

"I trust your thoughts, Simon, as I do Freosel's. A man who will not listen carefully to advice honestly given is a fool. Of course, a man who blindly takes any advice he receives is a bigger fool." He gave Simon's shoulder a squeeze. "Come, let us walk back. I would like to hear more about the Sithi."

It was strange to use Jiriki's mirror for such a mundane purpose as trimming his beard, but Simon had been told by Sludig—and none too subtly—that he was looking rather straggly. Propped on a rock, the Sithi glass winked in the failing afternoon light. There was a faint mist in the air which continually forced Simon to clean the mirror with his sleeve. Unfamiliar with the art of grooming with a bone knife—he could have borrowed a sharper steel blade from Sludig, but then the Rimmersman probably would have stood by and made comments—Simon had accomplished little more than causing himself a few twinges of pain when the three young women approached.

Simon had seen all three of them around New Gadrinsett—he had even danced with two of them the evening he had become a knight, and the thinnest one had made him a shirt. They seemed terribly young, even though he was probably no more than a year older than any of them. One of them, though, a dark-eyed girl whose round figure and curly brown hair was a little reminiscent of the chambermaid Hepzibah, he thought was rather fetching.

"What are you doing, Sir Seoman?" the thin one asked. She had large, serious eyes which she hooded with her lashes whenever Simon looked at her too long.

"Cutting my beard," he said gruffly. Sir Seoman, indeed! Were they making fun of him?

"Oh, don't cut it off!" the curly-haired girl said. "It makes you look so grand!"

"No, don't," her thin friend echoed.

The third, a short girl with straight yellow hair and a few spots on her face, shook her head. "Don't."

"I'm just trimming it." He marveled at the silliness of women. Just days before, people had been killed defending this place! People that these girls knew, most likely. Yet here they were, bothering him about his beard. How could they be so flittery? "Do you really think it looks . . . grand?" he said.

"Oh, yes," Curly-Hair blurted, then reddened. "That is, it makes you . . . it makes a man look older."

"So you think I need to look older?" he asked in his sternest voice.

"No!" she said hurriedly. "But it looks nice."

"They say you were very brave in the battle, Sir Seoman," said the thin girl.

He shrugged. "We were fighting for our home . . . for our lives. I was just trying not to be killed."

"Just like Camaris would have said," the thin girl sighed.

Simon laughed aloud. "Nothing like Camaris. Nothing at all."

The small girl had sidled around and was now looking intently at Simon's mirror. "Is that the Fairy Glass?" she asked.

"Fairy Glass?"

"People say . . ." She faltered and looked to her friends for help.

Thin One jumped in. "People say that you are a fairy-friend. That the fairies come when you call them with your magic looking-glass."

Simon smiled again, but hesitantly. Bits of truth mixed up with silliness. How did that happen? And who was talking about him? It was odd to think about. "No, that's not quite right. This was given to me by one of the Sithi, yes, but they do not simply come when I call. Otherwise, we would not have fought by ourselves against Duke Fengbald, now would we?"

"Can your looking-glass grant wishes?" Curly-Hair asked.

"No," Simon said firmly. "It's never granted any of mine." He paused, remembering his rescue by Aditu in Aldheorte's wintery depths. "I mean, that's not really what it does," he finished. So he, too, was mixing truth with lies. But how could he possibly explain the madness of this last year so that they could understand it?

"We were praying that you would bring us allies, Sir Seoman," the thin girl said seriously. "We were so frightened."

As he looked at her pale face, he saw that she was telling the truth. Of course they had been upset—did that mean that they could not be glad that they were alive? That wasn't the same as being flittery, really. Should they brood and mourn like Josua?

"I was frightened, too," he said. "We were very lucky."

There was a pause. The curly-haired girl arranged her cloak, which had fallen open to reveal the soft skin of her throat. The weather *was* getting warmer, Simon realized. He had been standing motionless here for some time, but had not shivered once. He looked up at the sky, as if hoping to find some confirmation of winter's dwindling.

"Do you have a lady?" the curly-haired girl said suddenly.

"Do I have a what?" he asked, although he had heard her perfectly well.

"A lady," she said, blushing furiously. "A sweetheart."

Simon waited for a moment before replying. "Not really." The three girls were staring at him raptly, expectant as puppies, and he felt his own cheeks grow hot. "No, not really." He had been clutching his Qanuc knife so long that his fingers had begun to ache.

"Ah," said Curly-Hair. "Well, we should leave you to your work, Sir Seoman." Her slender friend pulled at her elbow, but she ignored her. "Will you be coming to the bonfire?"

"Bonfire?" Simon furrowed his brow.

"The celebration. Well, and the mourning, too. In the middle of the settlement." She pointed toward the massed tents of New Gadrinsett. "Tomorrow night."

"I didn't know. Yes, I suppose I might." He smiled again. These were really quite sensible young women when you talked with them a while. "And thank you again for the shirt," he told Thin One.

She blinked rapidly. "Maybe you will wear it tomorrow night."

After saying good-bye, the three girls turned and walked off across the hillside, leaning their heads very close together, wriggling and laughing. Simon felt a moment's indignation at the thought that they might be laughing at him, but then he let it pass. They seemed to like him, didn't they? That was just the way that girls were, as far as he could tell.

He turned to his mirror once more, determined to finish with his beard before the sun began to set. A bonfire, was it. . . ? He wondered if he should wear his sword.

*   *   *

Simon pondered his own words. It was true, of course, that he had no lady love, as he supposed knights should—even the ragtag sort of knight he had become. Still, it was hard not to think about Miriamele. How long had it been since he had seen her? He counted the months on his hand: Yuven, Anitul, Tiyagaris, Septander, Octander . . . almost half a year! It was easy to believe she had forgotten him entirely by now.

But he had not forgotten her. There had been moments, strange and almost frightening moments, when he had been certain that she felt as drawn to him as he was to her. Her eyes had seemed so large when she looked at him, so careful to take him in, as though she memorized his every line. Could it be only his imagination? Certainly they had shared a wild and almost unbelievable adventure together, and almost equally certainly, she considered him a friend . . . but did she think anything more of him than that?

The memory of how she had looked at Naglimund swept over him. She had been dressed in her sky-blue gown and had been suddenly almost terrible in her completeness—so different from the ragged serving girl who had slept on his shoulder. And yet, the very same girl had been inside that blue dress. She had been almost hesitant when they had met in the castle courtyard—but was it out of shame at the trick she had played him, or worry that her resumption of station might have separated them?

He had seen her on a Hayholt tower top: her hair had been like golden floss. Simon, a poor scullion, had watched and felt like a mud-beetle catching a glimpse of the sun. And her face, so alive, so quick to change, full of anger and laughter, more mercurial and unpredictable than that of any woman he had ever met . . .

But it was fruitless to go on mooning this way, he told himself. It was unlikely in the extreme that she even thought of him as anything more than a friendly scullion, like the servants' children with whom the nobility were raised, but who they quickly forgot upon reaching adulthood. And of course, even if she did care for him at all, there was no chance that anything could ever come of it.

That was just the way of things, or at least so he had been taught.

Still, he had been out in the world long enough now and had seen enough oddities that the immutable facts of life Rachel had taught him seemed much less believable. How were common folk and those of royal blood different, anyway? Josua was a kind man, a clever and earnest man—Simon had little doubt that he would make a fine king—but his brother Elias had proved to be a monster. Could any peasant dragged from the barley fields do any worse? What was so sacred about royal blood? And, now that he thought about it, hadn't King John himself come from a family of peasants—or as good as peasants?

A mad thought suddenly occurred to him: what if Elias should be defeated, but Josua died? What if Miriamele never returned? Then someone else must be king or queen. Simon knew little of the affairs of the world—at least those outside his own tangled journey of the past half year. Were there others of royal blood who would step forward and claim the Dragonbone Chair? That fellow in Nabban, Bigaris or whatever his name was? Whoever was the heir of Lluth, dead king of Hernystir? Or old Isgrimnur, perhaps, if he should ever come back. He, at least, Simon could respect.

But now the fleeting thought was glowing like a hot coal. Why shouldn't he, Simon, be as likely as anyone else? If the world were turned upside down, and if all those with claims were gone when the dust settled, why not a knight of Erkynland—one who had fought a dragon just as John had, and who had been marked by the dragon's black blood? One who had been to the forbidden world of the Sithi, and who was a friend of the trolls of Yiqanuc? Then he would be fit for a princess or anyone else!

Simon stared at his reflection, at the curl of white hair like a dab of paint, at his long scar and his disconcertingly fuzzy beard.

Look at me, he thought, and suddenly laughed aloud. *King Simon the Great! Might as well make Rachel the Duchess of Nabban, or that monk Cadrach the Lector of*

Mother Church. Might as well wait for the stars to shine in the middle of the day!

And who would want to be the king, anyway?

For that was it, after all: Simon saw little but pain in store for whoever replaced Elias on the chair of bones. Even if the Storm King could be defeated, which seemed a possibility small to the point of nonexistence, the whole of the land was in ruins, the people starved and frozen. There would be no tournaments, no processions, no sunlight gleaming on armor, not for many years.

No, he thought bitterly, *the next king should be some-one like Barnabas, the sexton of the Hayholt's chapel—someone good at burying the dead.*

He pushed the mirror back into the pocket of his cloak and sat down on a rock to watch the sun slipping behind the trees.

Vorzheva found her husband in Leavetaking House. The long hall was empty but for Josua and the pale form of Deornoth. The prince himself scarcely seemed like one of the living, standing motionless as a statue beside the altar that bore his friend's body.

"Josua?"

The prince turned slowly, as though waking from a dream. "Yes, lady?"

"You are here too much. The day is ending."

He smiled. "I have only just returned. I was walking with Simon, and I had some other duties."

Vorzheva shook her head. "You returned long ago, even if you do not remember. You have been in this place most of the afternoon."

Josua's smile faltered. "Have I?" He turned to look at Deornoth. "I feel, I don't know, that it is wrong to leave him alone. He was always looking after me."

She stepped forward and took his arm. "I know. Come, walk with me."

"Very well." Josua reached out and touched the shroud draped across Deornoth's chest.

Leavetaking House had been little more than a shell when Josua and his company had first come to Sesuad'ra. The settlers had built shutters for the gaping windows and stout wooden doors to make it a place where the business of New Gadrinsett could take place in warmth and privacy. There was still something of the makeshift about it, though—the crude contrivances of the latest residents made an odd contrast when set against the graceful handiwork of the Sithi. Josua let his fingers trail across a bloom of carvings as Vorzheva led him toward one of the doors in the back wall and out into the failing sunlight.

The garden's walls were crumbled, the stone walkways broken and upended. A few hardy old rosebushes had survived winter's onslaught, and although it might be months or years before they would bloom again, their dark leaves and gray, thorny boughs looked strong and vigorous. It was hard not to wonder how long they had grown there, or who had planted them.

Vorzheva and Josua walked past the knotted trunk of a huge pine tree which grew in the breach of one of the walls. The dying sun, a blur of burning red, seemed hung in its branches.

"Do you still think of her?" Vorzheva asked suddenly.

"What?" Josua's mind seemed to have been wandering. "Who?"

"That other one. The one you loved, your brother's wife."

The prince inclined his head. "Hylissa. No, not often. There are far more important things to think on these days." He put his arm about his wife's shoulders. "I have a family now which needs my care."

Vorzheva looked at him suspiciously for a moment, then nodded her head with quiet satisfaction. "Yes," she said. "You do."

"And not just a family, but a whole people, it seems."

She made a quiet noise of despair. "You cannot be everyone's husband, everyone's father."

"Of course not. But I must be the prince, whether I wish to or not."

They walked on for a while without talking, listening

to the irregular music of a lone bird perched high in the swaying branches. The wind was chilly, but the edge seemed a little less than it had been in the days before, which might have been why the bird sang.

Vorzheva pressed her head against Josua's shoulder so that her black hair fluttered around his chin. "What will we do now?" she asked. "Now the battle is ended?"

Josua led her toward a stone bench, fallen to shards at one end, but still with much of its surface unbroken. They brushed off a few melting spatters of snow and sat down. "I do not know," he said. "I think it is time for another Raed—a council. We have much to decide. I have many doubts about what is the wisest course. We should not wait long after . . . after we have buried our fallen."

Vorzheva looked at him, surprised. "What do you mean, Josua? Why such hurry to have this thing?"

The prince raised his hand and examined the lines on his palm. "Because there is a possibility that if we do not strike now, an important chance will be lost."

"Strike?" She seemed astounded. "Strike what? What madness is this? We have lost one of every three! You would take these few hundred against your brother!?"

"But we have won an important victory. The first anyone has had against him since he began his mad campaign. If we strike out now, while memory is fresh and Elias is unaware of what has happened, our people here will take heart; when others see we are moving, they will join us, too."

Vorzheva stood, her eyes wide. She held an arm around her middle as if to protect their unborn child. "No! Oh, Josua, that is too stupid! I thought you were to wait at least until the winter had passed! How can you go off to fight now?"

"I never said I was going to do anything," he said. "I have not decided yet—nor will I, until I have called a Raed."

"Yes, you men will sit around and talk of the great battle you fought. Will the women be there?"

"Women?" He looked at her quizzically. "Geloë will be a part of it."

"Oh, yes, Geloë," she said with scorn. "Because she is called a 'wise woman.' That is the only sort of woman you will listen to—one who has a name for it, like a fast horse or a strong ox."

"What should we do—invite everyone from all of New Gadrinsett?" He was growing annoyed. "That would be foolish."

"No more foolish than listening to only men." She stared at him for a moment, then visibly forced herself to become calm. She took several breaths before speaking again. "There is a story the women of the Stallion Clan tell. It is about the bull who would not listen to his cows."

Josua waited. "Well," he said at last. "What happened to him?"

Vorzheva scowled and moved away down the broken path. "Go on as you are doing. You will find out."

Josua's expression seemed half-amusement, half-displeasure. "Wait, Vorzheva." He rose and followed her. "You are right to chide me. I should listen to what you have to say. What happened to the bull?"

She looked him over carefully. "I will tell you some other time. I am too angry now."

Josua took her hand and fell into step beside her. The path curled through the disarranged stones, bringing them close to the tumbled blocks of the outer garden wall. There was a noise of voices from beyond.

"Very well," she said abruptly. "The bull was too proud to listen to his cows. When they told to him that a wolf was stealing the calves, he did not believe, because he did not see it himself. When all the calves were stolen, the cows drove the bull away and found a new bull." Her stare was defiant. "Then the wolves ate the old bull, since he had no one to protect him while he slept."

Josua's laugh was harsh. "And is that a warning?"

She squeezed his arm. "Please, Josua. The people are tired of the fighting. We make a home here." She pulled him closer to the breach in the stone. From the far side rose the noise of the ragtag marketplace that had sprung up in the shelter of Leavetaking House's outer walls. Several dozen men, women, and children were bartering with old possessions carried out of their former homes and new things gathered on and about Sesuad'ra. "See," Vorzheva said, "they make a new life. You told them they fought for their home. How can you make them move again?"

Josua stared at a group of bundled children playing tug-o-war with a colorful rag. They were shrieking with laughter and kicking up puffs of snow; nearby, someone's mother was calling angrily for her child to come in out of the wind. "But this is not their true home," he said quietly. "We cannot stay here forever."

"Who is staying forever?" Vorzheva demanded. "Until spring! Until our child is born!"

Josua shook his head. "But we may never have a chance like this again." He turned away from the wall, his face grave. "Besides, I owe it to Deornoth. He gave his life, not for us to quietly disappear, but so that we could pay back the wrongs my brother has done."

"Owe it to Deornoth!" Vorzheva sounded angry, but her eyes were sad. "What a thing to say! Only a man would say such a thing."

Josua turned and caught her up, pulling her toward him. "I do love you, Lady. I only try to do what is right."

She averted her eyes. "I know. But . . ."

"But you do not think I am making the best decision." He nodded, stroking her hair. "I am listening to everyone, Vorzheva, but the final word must be mine." He sighed and held her for a while without speaking. "Merciful Aedon, I would not wish this on anyone," he said at last. "Vorzheva, promise me something."

"What?" Her voice was muffled in his cloak.

"I have changed my mind. If something happens to me . . ." He thought. "If something happens to me, take our child away from this. Do not let anyone put him on a throne, or use him as the rallying symbol for some army."

"Him?"

"Or her. Do not let our child be forced into this game as I was."

Vorzheva shook her head fiercely. "No one will take my baby away from me, not even your friends."

"Good." He looked out through the blowing tendrils of her hair. The sun had fallen behind Leavetaking House, reddening the entire western sky. "That makes whatever will come easier to bear."

Five days after the battle, the last of Sesuad'ra's dead were buried—men and women of Erkynland, Rimmersgard, Hernystir and the Thrithings, of Yiqanuc and Nabban, refugees from half a hundred places, all laid to rest in the shallow earth on the summit of the Stone of Farewell. Prince Josua spoke carefully and seriously about their suffering and sacrifice as his cloak billowed in the winds that swirled around the hilltop. Father Strangyeard, Freosel, and Binabik all rose in turn to say words of one sort or another. The citizens of New Gadrinsett stood, hard-faced, and listened.

Some of the graves had no markers, but most had some small monument, a carved board or rough-chiseled piece of stone that bore the name of the fallen one. After great labors to hack into the icy ground, the Erkynguard had buried their own dead in a mass grave beside the lake, crowning it with a single slab of rock that bore the legend: "Soldiers of Erkynland, killed in the Battle of Stefflod Valley. *Em Wulstes Duos.*" By God's will.

Only the fallen Thrithings mercenaries were unmourned and unmarked. Their living comrades dug a vast barrow for them on the grasslands below Sesuad'ra—half believing it would be their own, that Josua planned to execute them. Instead, when the labor was finished they found themselves escorted by armed men far out onto the open lands and then set free. It was a terrible thing for a Thrithings-man to lose his horse, but the surviving mercenaries decided quickly that walking was better than dying.

So, at last, all the dead were buried and the ravens were cheated of their holiday.

As solemn music played, vying with the harsh wind to be heard, the thought came to many of those who watched that although Sesuad'ra's defenders had won an improbable and heroic victory, they had paid dearly for it. The fact that they had defeated only the tiniest portion of the forces arrayed against them, and had lost nearly half their number in doing so, made the winter-shrouded hillcrest seem an even colder and lonelier place.

Someone caught Simon's arm from behind. He turned swiftly, tugging his arm loose, and raised it to strike.

"Here, lad, here, don't be so hasty-quick!" The old jester cowered, hands held over his head.

"I'm sorry, Towser." Simon rearranged his cloak. The bonfire was glowing in the near distance and he was impatient to be going. "I didn't know who it was."

"No offense taken, laddie." Towser swayed slightly. "The thing is ... well, I was just wondering if I could walk with you a way. Over to the celebration. I'm not as steady on my feet as I was."

Not surprising, Simon thought: Towser's breath was heavily scented with wine. Then he remembered what Sangfugol had said and fought down his urge to hurry on. "Of course." He extended a discreet arm for the old man to lean on.

"Kind, lad, very kind. Simon, isn't it?" The old man looked up at him, his shadowed face a puzzle of wrinkles.

"That's right." Simon smiled in the darkness. He had reminded Towser of his name a dozen different times.

"You'll do well, you will," the old man said. They moved toward the flickering light, walking slowly. "And I've met them all."

Towser did not stay with him long once they reached the celebration. The old jester quickly found a group of drunken trolls and went off to reintroduce them to the glories of Bull's Horn—and himself to the glories of *kangkang,* Simon suspected. Simon wandered for a while on the periphery of the gathering.

It was a true feast night, perhaps the first that Sesuad'ra had seen. Fengbald's camp had proven to be groaningly full of stocks and stores, as though the late duke had plundered all Erkynland to insure he would be as comfortable in the Thrithings as if he had remained at the Hayholt. Josua had wisely made sure that most of the food and other useful things were hidden away for later—even if the company was to leave the Stone, it would not be tomorrow—but a generous portion had been made available for the celebration, so that tonight the hilltop had a genuinely festive air. Freosel, in particular, had derived no little pleasure from breaching Fengbald's casks, draining off the first mug of Stanshire Dark himself with as much pleasure as if it had been the duke's blood instead of only his beer.

Wood, one of the other things not in short supply, had been piled high in the center of the vast flat surface of the Fire Garden. The bonfire was burning brightly, and most of the people were gathered on the wide field of tiles. Sangfugol and some of the other musical citizens of New Gadrinsett were strolling here and there, playing for knots of appreciative listeners. Some of the listeners were more enthusiastic than others. Simon had to laugh as a particularly sodden trio of celebrants insisted on joining the harper in his rendition of "By Greenwade's Shore." Sangfugol winced but gamely played on; Simon silently congratulated the harper on his fortitude before wandering away.

The night was chilly but clear, and the wind that had bedeviled the hilltop during the burial rites was all but gone. Simon, after pondering for a moment, decided that considering the time of the year, the weather was actually rather nice. Again he wondered if the Storm King's power might somehow be slipping, but this time the thought was followed by an even more worrisome question.

What if he's only gathering his strength? What if he's going to reach out now and do what Fengbald couldn't?

That was not a line of thought Simon wished to pursue. He shrugged and readjusted his sword belt.

The first cup of wine offered to him went down very nicely, warming his stomach and loosening his muscles. He had been part of the small army put to work burying the dead—a ghastly task made worse by the occasional familiar face glimpsed beneath a mask of hoarfrost. Simon and the others had worked like demons to breach the stony ground, digging with whatever they could find— swords, axes, limbs of fallen trees, but as difficult as it had been to scrape in the frozen earth, the cold had slowed putrefaction, making a horrible job just a little more bearable. Still, Simon's sleep had been raddled by nightmares the past two nights—endless visions of stiffened bodies tumbling into ditches, bodies rigid as statues, contorted figures that might have been carved by some mad sculptor obsessed by pain and suffering.

War's rewards, Simon thought as he walked through the noisy throng. And if Josua were to be successful, the battles to come would make this look like an Yrmansol dance. The corpses would be piled higher than Green Angel Tower.

The thought made him feel cold and sick. He went in search of more wine.

The festival had a certain air of heedlessness, Simon noted. Voices were too loud, laughter too swift, as though those who talked and made merry were doing so for the benefit of others more than themselves. With the wine came fighting, too, which seemed to Simon as though it should be the last thing anyone would desire. Still, he passed more than a few clumps of people gathered around a pair or more of swearing, shouting men, calling encouragement and mockery as the combatants rolled in the mud. Those in the crowd who were not laughing looked disturbed or unhappy.

They know we are not saved, Simon thought, regretting his own mood on what should be a wonderful night. *They are happy to be alive, but they know the future may be worse.*

He wandered on, taking a drink when it was offered. He stopped for a while near Leavetaking House to watch Sludig and Hotvig wrestle—a friendlier kind of combat than he had seen elsewhere. The northerner and the Thrithings-man were stripped to the waist and grappling fiercely, each trying to throw the other out of a circle of rope, but both men were laughing; when they stopped to rest, they shared a wineskin. Simon called out a greeting to them.

Feeling like a lonely seagull circling the mast of a pleasure boat, he walked on.

Simon was not sure what time it was, whether it was just an hour or so after dark or approaching midnight. Things had begun to grow a little blurry somewhere after his half-dozenth drink of wine.

However, at this exact moment, time did not seem very important. What *did* seem that way was the girl who walked beside him, the light of the fading bonfire glinting in her dark, wavy hair. She wasn't named Curly-Hair, but Ulca, as he had recently learned. She stumbled and he put his arm around her, amazed at how warm a body could feel, even through thick clothing.

"Where are we going?" she asked, then laughed. She did not seem terribly worried about possible destinations.

"Walking," Simon replied. After a moment's thought he decided he should make his plan more clear. "Walking around."

The noise of the celebration was a dull roar behind them, and for a moment Simon could almost imagine that he was in the middle of the battle once more, on the frozen lake, slick with blood. . . .

His hackles rose. Why would he want to think about something like that!? He made a noise of disgust.

"What?" Ulca swayed, but her eyes were bright. She had shared the wineskin Sangfugol had given to him. She seemed to have a natural talent for holding her wine.

"Nothing," he replied gruffly. "Just thinking. About the fighting. The battle. Fighting."

"It must have been . . . horrible!" Her voice was full of wonder. "We watched. Welma 'n' me. We were crying."

"Welming you?" Simon glared at her. Was she trying to confuse him? "What does that mean?"

"Welma. I said 'Welma an' me.' My friend, the slender one. You met her!" Ulca squeezed his arm, amused by his clever jest.

"Oh." He reflected on the recent conversation. What had they been talking about? Ah. The battle. "It was horrible. Blood. People killed." He tried to find some way to sum up the totality of the experience, to let this young woman know what he, Simon, had experienced. "Worse than anything," he said heavily.

"Oh, Sir Seoman," she cried, and stopped, losing her balance for a moment on the slippery ground. "You must have been frightened!"

"Simon. Not Seoman—Simon." He considered what she had said. "Little. A little." It was hard not to notice her proximity. She had a very nice face, really, full-cheeked and long-lashed. And her mouth. Why was it so close, though?

He refocused his eyes and discovered that he was leaning forward, toppling toward Ulca like a felled tree. He put his hands on her shoulders for balance, and was interested by how small she felt beneath his touch. "I'm going to kiss you," he said suddenly.

"You shouldn't," Ulca said, but closed her eyes and did not move away.

He kept his own eyes open for fear of missing his mark and tumbling to the snow-flecked ground. Her mouth was strangely firm beneath his, but warm and soft as a blanketed bed on a winter's night. He let his lips stay there for a moment, trying to remember if he had ever done this before and if so, what to do next. Ulca did not move, and they stood in place, breathing air gently scented with wine into each other's mouths.

Simon discovered soon enough that kissing was more than just standing lip to lip, and after a short while the cold air, the horrors of battle, even the ruckus of the bonfire a short distance away had disappeared from his mind. He stretched his arms around this wonderful creature and pulled her close, enjoying the feeling of sweetly yielding girl pressed against him, never wanting to do anything else in his whole life, however long it might be.

"Ooh, Seoman," Ulca said at last, pulling back to catch her breath, "you could make a girl faint."

"Mmmm." Simon drew her back again, bending his

neck so that he could nibble at her ear. If only she were a little taller! "Sit down," he said. "I want to sit down."

They struggled along for a few joined steps, clumsy as a crab, until Simon found a chunk of fallen masonry of appropriate height. He wrapped his cloak around both of them as they sat down, then pulled Ulca close once more, squeezing and kneading even as he continued to kiss her. Her breath was warm against his face. She was soft in some places, firm in others. What a wonderful world this was!

"Ooh, Seoman." Her voice was muffled as she spoke into his cheek. "Your beard, it scratches so!"

"Yes, it does, doesn't it?"

It took Simon a moment to realize that someone other than himself had answered Ulca. He looked up.

The figure standing before them was dressed all in white—jacket, boots, and breeches. It had long hair that streamed in the light breeze, a mocking smile, and up-turned eyes no more human than those of a cat or a fox.

Ulca stared for a moment, her mouth open. She let out a tiny squeak of amazement and fear.

"Who. . . ?" She rose unsteadily from their seat. "Seoman, who. . . ?"

"*I* am a fairy woman," said Jiriki's sister, her voice suddenly stony. "And *you* are a little mortal girl . . . who is *kissing my husband-to-be!* I think I shall have to do something dreadful to you."

Ulca gasped for breath and screamed in earnest this time, pushing herself away from Simon so strongly that he was almost toppled from the rock. Curly hair unbound and flying behind her, she ran back toward the bonfire.

Simon stared after her stupidly for a moment, then turned back to the Sitha-woman. "Aditu?"

She was watching the disappearing form of Ulca. "Greetings, Seoman." She spoke calmly, but with a hint of amusement. "My brother sends his regards."

"What are you doing here?" Simon could not understand what had just happened. He felt as though he had fallen out of bed during a wonderful dream and landed on his head in a bear pit. "Merciful Aedon! And what do you mean, 'husband-to-be'?!"

Aditu laughed, her teeth flashing. "I thought it would be a good story to add to the other Tales of Seoman the Bold. I have been haunting the shadows all evening and have heard many people mention your name. You slay dragons and wield fairy-weapons, so why not have a fairy-wife?" She reached out a hand, enclosing his wrist with cool, supple fingers. "Now come, we have much to talk about. You can rub faces with that little mortal girl some other time."

Simon followed, stunned, as Aditu led him back toward the light of the bonfire. "Not after this I can't," he mumbled.

18

The Fox's Bargain

Eolair's sleep had been shallow and troubled, so he woke instantly when Isorn touched his shoulder.

"What is it?" He fumbled for his sword, fingers scrabbling through the damp leaves.

"Someone coming." The Rimmersman was tense, but there was an odd look on his face. "I don't know," he muttered. "You had better come."

Eolair rolled over and clambered to his feet, then paused to buckle on his sword belt. The moon hung solemnly above the Stagwood; from its position, Eolair guessed that dawn could not be far away. There *was* something odd in the air: the count could feel it already. This forest the Hernystiri called *Fiathcoille*, which spread in a contented clump a few leagues southeast of Nad Mullach beside the river Baraillean, was a place he had hunted every spring and fall as a young man, a spot he knew like his own hall. When he had rolled himself in his cloak and blanket to sleep, it had been familiar as an old friend. Now, suddenly, it seemed different in a way he could not understand.

The camp was stirring into wakefulness. Already most of Ule's men were pulling on their boots. Their numbers had almost tripled since he and Isorn had found them—there were quite a few masterless men wandering the edges of the Frostmarch who were happy to join an organized band, regardless of its purpose—and Eolair doubted that anything but a major force of arms could threaten them.

But what if Skali had received word of their presence? They were a sizable company, but against an army like Kaldskryke's they could not hope to be more than a brief annoyance.

Isorn stood just ahead at the forest fringe, beckoning. Eolair moved toward him, trying to move as quietly as he could, but even as he listened to the soft crunching of his own footfalls, he became aware of . . . something else.

At first he thought it was the wind, wailing like a chorus of spirits, but the trees around him were still, clumps of soft snow balanced delicately at the ends of the branches. No, it was not the wind. The sound had a regular quality, rhythmic, even musical. It sounded, Eolair thought, like . . . singing.

"Brynioch!" he swore as he moved up beside Isorn. "What is it?"

"The sentries heard that an hour gone," the duke's son muttered. "How loud must it be, that we have not seen them yet?"

Eolair shook his head. The snow-dappled plain of the lower Inniscrich lay before them, pale and uneven as rumpled silk. Men were moving up on either side, crawling to the edge of the trees to look out, until Eolair felt as though he were surrounded by a crowd awaiting a royal procession. But the anticipatory looks of the hard-faced men around him were more than a little fearful. Many sword-hilts were already clutched in damp palms.

The singing rose in pitch, then abruptly stopped. In its wake, the sound of many hoofbeats echoed along the Stagwood's fringe. Eolair, still wiping sleep from his eyes, drew breath to say something to Isorn. As it turned out, he held that breath for a long time, and when he let it go, it was only to suck in another.

They appeared from the east, as though they had come out of northern Erkynland—or, Eolair thought distractedly, out of the depths of Aldheorte Forest. They were little more than a shimmer of moonlight on metal at first, a distant cloud of silvershine in the darkness. Hoofbeats rumbled like heavy rain on a wooden roof, then a horn winded, an oddly haunting note that pierced the night, and suddenly they seemed almost to burst into full view. One of Ule's men went mad when he saw them. He ran shouting into the forest, slapping at his head as though it burned, and was not seen again by any of his fellows.

Although none of the others were so badly afflicted, no one who passed that night in the Stagwood was ever after the same, nor could any of them quite say why. Even Eolair was stunned, Eolair who had traveled most of the length and breadth of Osten Ard, who had seen sights that reduced most men to tongue-tied awe. But even the worldly count would never be able to explain just how it had felt to watch the Sithi ride.

As the wild company thundered past, the very quality of the moonlight seemed to change. The air became pale and crystalline; objects seemed to glitter at the edges, as though every tree and man and blade of grass was limned in diamond. The Sithi rolled past like a great ocean wave capped with gleaming spear-points. Their faces were hard and fierce and beautiful as the faces of hunting hawks, and their hair streamed in the wind of their passage. The immortals' steeds seemed to race more swiftly than any horses could run, but they moved in a way that seemed fit only for dreams, pace smooth as melting honey, hooves carving the darkness into pale streaks of fire.

Within moments the bright company had dwindled to a dark mass vanishing in the west, their hoofbeats a fading murmur. They left behind them silence and, in some of the watchers, tears.

"The Fair Ones . . ." Eolair breathed at last. His own voice seemed as thick and hoarse as the croaking of a frog.

"The . . . Sithi?" Isorn shook his head as though he had been struck a blow. "But . . . but why? Where are they going?"

And suddenly Eolair knew. "The Fox's Bargain," he said, and laughed. His heart felt buoyant in his chest.

"What do you mean?" Isorn watched in bewilderment as the Count of Nad Mullach turned and headed back into the forest.

"An old song," he called back. "The Fox's Bargain!"

He laughed again and sang, feeling the words leap out as though they sought the night air of their own accord.

> " 'We never forget,' the Fair Ones said,
> 'Though Time may ancient run.
> You will hear our horns beneath the moon,
> You will see our spears shine in the sun . . .' "

"I do not understand!" Isorn cried.

"Never mind!" Eolair was almost out of sight, moving rapidly toward the camp. "Get the men! We must ride to Hernysadharc!"

As if to echo him, a silvery horn sounded in the distance.

"It is an old song of our people," Eolair called across to Isorn. Although they had been riding at speed since before the sun had risen, there was no sign of the Sithi but for a trample of hoofprints on the snowy grass, hoofprints already fading as the grass sprang back and the snow liquefied in the morning's warmth. "It tells of the promise the Fair Ones made to the Red Fox—Prince Sinnach— before the battle of Ach Samrath: they swore they would never forget the faithfulness of Hernystir."

"So you think they are riding against Skali?"

"Who can say? But look where they are bound!" The count stood in the saddle and pointed out across the broad grasslands at the tracks disappearing into the west. "True as an arrow's flight to the Taig!"

"Even if that is where they are going, we cannot ride all the way there at this pace," said Isorn. "The horses are flagging already, and we have only traveled a few leagues."

Eolair looked around. The company was beginning to slide apart, some of the riders falling well back. "Perhaps. But, Bagba bite me, if they are going to Hernysadharc, I want to be there!"

Isorn grinned, his wide face crinkling. "Not unless

your fairy-folk left us some of their fairy-horses, with wings on their feet. But we will get there eventually."

The count shook his head, but pulled gently back on the reins, slowing his gray horse to a canter. "True. We'll do no one any good if we kill our mounts."

"Or ourselves." Isorn waved his hand to slow the rest of the company.

They stopped for a midday meal. Eolair balanced his impatience against what he knew to be the wisdom of having his troop at least somewhat rested: if there was to be fighting, men who were ready to drop in their tracks and horses who could not walk another step would make a very indifferent contribution.

After an hour's rest they were back in the saddle again, but Eolair now kept the pace more reasonable. By the time darkness arrived, they had crossed the Inniscrich to the outskirts of the territory of Hernysadharc, although they were still several hours' ride from the Taig. They had passed some encampments that Eolair guessed had belonged to Skali's men. All were deserted, but signs indicated that the tenancy had been recent: in one of them the cookfires still smoldered. The count wondered if the Rimmersmen had fled before the onrushing Sithi, or had suffered some other, stranger fate.

At Isorn's insistence, Eolair finally brought the company to a halt near Ballacym, a walled town on a low hillside that looked back over the western edge of the Inniscrich. Much of the town had been destroyed during Lluth's losing battle with Skali nearly a year before, but enough of the walls remained to offer some shelter.

"We do not want to arrive in the midst of any struggle at night," Isorn said as they rode through the shattered gates. "Even if you are correct and your fairy-folk have come to fight for Hernystir, how will they know the difference between the right and wrong sort of mortal in the dark?"

Eolair was not pleased, but he could not dispute the wisdom of Isorn's words. As he had already known, there was little his small band could do against a large army like Skali's, but the thought of having to wait was still infuriating. His heart had sung to match the Sithi themselves as he had watched them ride. To do something—to finally strike a blow at those who had devastated his land! The idea had pushed at him like a strong wind. And now he must wait until morning.

Eolair drank more than his usual modest portion of wine that night, though it was in short supply, then lay down early, uninterested in talking about what they all had seen and what they might be riding toward. He knew that even with the wine-fumes in his head, sleep would be a long time coming. It was.

"I do not like this," Ule Frekkeson growled, drawing back on his reins. "Where have they gone? And, by the Holy Aedon, what has happened here?"

The streets of Hernysadharc were strangely deserted. Eolair knew that few of his people had remained after Skali's conquest, but even if all the Rimmersmen had been driven out by the Sithi—which seemed impossible, since scarcely more than a day had passed since the Fair Ones rode past, half a hundred leagues west—there should still be at least a few of the native Hernystir-folk.

"I do not like it any more than you do," the count replied, "but I cannot imagine Skali's entire army would be hiding in ambush for our seven or eight score."

"Eolair is right." Isorn shaded his eyes. The weather was still cold, but the sun was surprisingly bright. "Let's ride in and take our chances."

Ule bit back a rejoinder, then shrugged. The trio rode in through the crude gates the Rimmersmen had built; the men followed, talking among themselves.

It was disturbing enough to see a wall around Hernysadharc. Never in Eolair's memory had there been one, and even the ancient wall that circled the Taig remained only out of the Hernystiri reverence for past days. Most of the older wall had collapsed long ago, so that the remaining sections stood vastly separated, like the few remaining teeth in an old man's jaw. But this rough yet sturdy barrier around the innermost section of the city had been built very recently.

What was Skali afraid of? Eolair wondered. *The re-*

maining Hernystiri, a beaten people? Or perhaps it was his own ally, the High King Elias, that he did not trust.

Disturbing as it was to see the new wall, it was even more so to see what had happened to it. The timbers were scorched and blackened as though they had been lightning-struck, and a section wide enough for a score of riders to pass through abreast had been blasted away entirely. A few wisps of smoke still curled above the wreckage.

The mystery of what had happened to Hernysadharc's inhabitants was partially solved as Eolair's company swung out onto the wide road that had once been named Tethtain's Way. That name had passed not long after the great Hernystiri King, and people usually called it the Taig Road, for it led directly up the hill to the great hall. Now, as the company entered the muddy thoroughfare, they saw a great crowd of people standing at the summit of the hill, clustered around the Taig like sheep at a salt lick. Curious but still careful, Eolair and the others rode forward.

When Eolair saw that most of the crowd swarming on the lower slopes of Hern's Hill seemed to be Hernystiri, his heart rose. When a few of the outermost people turned, alarmed at the sight of a troop of mounted and armored men, he hastened to reassure them.

"People of Hernysadharc!" he cried, standing in his stirrups. Several more members of the crowd turned at the sound of his voice. "I am Eolair, Count of Nad Mullach. These men are my friends and will do you no harm."

The reaction was surprising. While several of those nearest cheered and waved to him, they seemed little moved. After staring for a moment, they turned their attention back to the hilltop again, despite the fact that none of them had a better vantage point than mounted Eolair, and he himself could see nothing before him but the stretching crowd.

Isorn was puzzled, too. "What are you doing here?" he shouted to the people standing nearby. "Where is Skali?"

Several shook their heads as though they did not understand, and several others made joking remarks about Skali being headed back to Rimmersgard, but no one seemed inclined to waste too much time or energy enlightening the duke's son and his companions.

Eolair cursed quietly and spurred his horse forward, letting the beast make room for him. Although no one actively contested his passage, it was slow going to push through the crush of people, and no short while before they passed between two of the standing remnants of ruined fortress wall and onto the ancient grounds of the Taig. Eolair squinted, then whistled with astonishment.

"Bagba bite me," he said, and laughed, although he could not have said why.

The Taig and its outbuildings still stood on the hilltop, solid and impressive, but now all the fields across the summit of Hern's Hill were covered with wildly colorful tents. They were every shade imaginable and a hundred different sizes and shapes; someone might have emptied a giant basket of quilt-squares across the snowy grass. What had been the capital of the Hernystiri nation, the royal seat, had suddenly become a village constructed by wild, magical children.

Eolair could see movement among the tents—slender shapes in garb as colorful as the newly-erected dwellings. He spurred forward, passing the last of the Hernystiri onlookers as he climbed the hill. These stared hungrily at the bright cloth and the strange visitors, but seemed reluctant to cross the last open space and draw too close. Many watched the count and his company with something like envy.

As they rode into the wind-billowed city of tents, a lone figure came toward them. Eolair reined up, prepared for anything, but was astonished to find that the one who came forward to greet them was Craobhan, the royal family's most elderly but also most loyal advisor. The old man seemed almost thunderstruck to see them; he stared at Eolair for a long time without speaking, but at last tears came to his eyes and he opened his arms wide.

"Count Eolair! Mircha's wet blessing upon us, it's good to see you."

The count scrambled down from his horse and embraced the counselor. "And you, Craobhan, and you. What has happened here?"

"Ha! More than I can tell you standing in the wind." The old man chuckled strangely. He seemed genuinely befuddled, a state in which Eolair had never thought to find him. "By all the gods, more than I can tell you. Come to the Taig. Come in and have something—food, drink."

"Where is Maegwin? Is she well?"

Craobhan looked up, his watery gaze suddenly intent. "She is alive and happy," he said. "But come. Come see . . . well, as I said, more than I can tell you now." The old man took his elbow and tugged.

Eolair turned and waved to the others. "Isorn, Ule, come!" He patted Craobhan's shoulder. "Can our men have something to eat?"

Beyond worrying, Craobhan waved his bony hand. "Somewhere. Some of the people from the town have probably hoarded a few things. There's much to do, though, Eolair, much to do. Hardly know where to start."

"But what's happened? Did the Sithi drive off Skali?"

Craobhan pulled at his arm, leading him toward the great hall.

The Count of Nad Mullach got scarcely more than a glance at the score or so of Sithi who were on the hilltop. Those he saw seemed absorbed in the task of building their camp, and did not even look up as Eolair and the others walked by, but even from a distance he could see the strangeness of them, their odd but graceful motions, their quiet serenity. Although in some places more than a few Sithi were working together, men and women both, they uttered no words that he could hear, going about their tasks with a smooth uniformity of purpose that was somehow as unsettling as their alien faces and movements.

As they drew closer to the Taig, it was easy to see the marks of Skali's occupation. The carefully cultivated gardens had been dug up, the stone pathways torn apart. Eolair cursed Sharp-nose and his barbarians, then wondered again what had happened to the occupiers.

Inside the Taig's great doors things were no different. The walls had been denuded of tapestries, relics had been stolen from their niches, and the floors were scarred with the ruts of countless booted feet. The Hall of Carvings, where King Lluth had held court, was in better condition—Eolair guessed it had been Thane Skali's seat—but still there were signs that the northern reavers had not been overly reverent. Many scores of arrows bristled in the high-arched ceilings, where the hanging wooden carvings · had proven tempting targets for Kaldskryke's winter-bound soldiers.

Craobhan, who seemed to wish to avoid talking, seated them in the hall and went to find something to drink.

"What do you suppose has happened, Eolair?" Isorn shook his head. "It makes me feel ashamed to be a Rimmersman when I see what Skali and his cutthroats have done to the Taig." Beside him, Ule was peering suspiciously into the corners of the hall, as though Kaldskrykemen might be hiding there.

"You have nothing to be ashamed of," said Eolair. "They did not do this because they were Rimmersmen, but because they were in someone else's country in a bad time. Hernystiri or Nabbanai or Erkynlanders might do the same."

Isorn was not mollified. "It is wrong. When my father has his dukedom back, we will see that the damage is repaired."

The count smiled. "If we all survive and this is the worst we have to deal with, then I will gladly sell my own home at Nad Mullach stone by stone to make it right again. No, this will be mild, I'm afraid."

"I fear you are right, Eolair." Isorn frowned. "God knows what has happened in Elvritshalla since *we* were driven out. And after the terrible winter, too."

They were interrupted by Craobhan, who tottered back in with a young Hernystiri woman who carried four large hammered silver tankards decorated with the leaping stag of the royal house.

"Might as well use the best," Craobhan said with a crooked smile. "Who's to say no in these strange days?"

"Where is Maegwin?" Eolair's apprehension had grown when she had not appeared to greet them.

"Sleeping." Again Craobhan made a dismissive gesture. "I'll take you when you've finished. Drink up."

Eolair stood. "Forgive me, old friend, but I'd like to see her now. I'll be better able to enjoy my beer."

The old man shrugged. "In her old room. There's a woman seeing to her." He seemed more interested in his tankard than in the fate of the king's only living child.

The count looked at him for a moment. What had happened to the Craobhan he knew? The old man seemed muddle-headed, as though he'd been struck with a club.

There were far too many other things that needed worrying over. Eolair walked out of the hall, leaving the others to drink and stare up at the shattered carvings.

Maegwin was indeed sleeping. The wild-haired woman who sat beside the bed looked slightly familiar, but Eolair gave her scarcely more than a glance before he kneeled down and took Maegwin's hand. A wet cloth lay across her forehead.

"Has she been wounded?" There seemed to be something Craobhan was keeping from him—perhaps she was badly hurt.

"Yes," the woman said. "But it was a glancing blow only, and she has already recovered." The woman lifted the cloth to show Eolair the bruise on Maegwin's pale brow. "She is merely resting now. It has been a great day."

Eolair turned sharply at the sound of her voice. She looked as distracted as Craobhan, her eyes wide and fey, her mouth twitching.

Has everyone here gone mad? he wondered.

Maegwin stirred at the sound of his voice. As he turned back, her eyes fluttered open, closed again, then opened once more and stayed that way.

"'Eolair... ?" Her voice was groggy with sleep. She smiled like a young child, with no trace of the fretfulness he had seen the last time they had spoken. "Is that you, truly? Or just another dream. . . ."

"It is me, Lady." He squeezed her hand again. She

looked little different at that moment than when she had
been a girl and he had first felt his heart stirring with interest. How could he have ever been angry with her, no
matter what she had said or done?

Maegwin tried to sit up. Her sorrel hair was disarranged, her eyes still heavy-lidded. She seemed to have
been put to bed fully dressed; only her feet, which protruded from beneath the blanket, were bare. "Did . . . did
you see them?"

"Did I see who. . . ?" he asked gently, although he felt
sure he knew. Her answer, though, surprised him.

"The gods, silly man. Did you see the gods? They were
so beautiful. . . ."

"The . . . gods?"

"I made them come," she said, and smiled sleepily.
"They came for me. . . ." She let her head fall back into
the pillow and closed her eyes. "For me," she murmured.

"She needs sleep, Count Eolair," the woman said from
behind him. There was something peremptory in her
voice that lifted Eolair's hackles.

"What is she talking about, the gods?" he demanded.
"Does she mean the Sithi?"

The woman smiled, a smugly knowing smile. "She
means what she says."

Eolair stood, holding back his anger. There was much
to discover here. He would bide his time. "Take good
care of Princess Maegwin," he said as he moved toward
the door. It was more of an order than a request. The
woman nodded.

Musing, Eolair had just re-entered the Hall of Carvings
when there was a clatter of boots at the front doors behind him. He stopped and turned, his hand reflexively
dropping to his sword-hilt. A few paces away, Isorn and
husky Ule also rose, alarm plain on their faces.

The figure that appeared in the door of the hall was tall
but not overly so, dressed in blue armor that, strangely,
had the look of painted wood—but the armor, an intricate
collection of plates held together by shiny red cords, was
not the strangest thing about him. His hair was white as
a snow-drift; bound in a blue scarf, it fell past his shoul-

ders. He was slender as a young birch tree, and despite the color of his hair, looked to be scarcely into his manhood, insofar as Eolair could read a face so angular, so different from a human face. The stranger's upturned eyes were golden, bright as noon sun reflected in a forest pond.

Surprised into immobility, Eolair stared. It was as though some creature out of elder days stood before him, one of his grandmother's stories appearing in flesh and bone. He had expected to meet the Sithi, but he was no more prepared than someone told about a deep canyon could be when they suddenly discovered they were standing on its rim.

When the count had stood frozen for some seconds, the newcomer took a step backward. "Forgive me." The stranger made an oddly-articulated bow, sweeping his long-fingered hand past his knees, but although there was something light in his movements, there was no mockery. "I forget my manners in the heat of this memorable day. May I enter here?"

"Who ... who are you?" Eolair asked, startled out of his normal courtesy. "Yes, come in."

The stranger did not seem offended. "I am Jiriki i-Sa'onserei. At this moment I speak for the Zida'ya. We have come to repay our debt to Prince Sinnach of Hernystir." After this formal speech, he suddenly flashed a cheerfully feral grin. "And who are you?"

Eolair hastily introduced himself and his companions. Isorn was staring, fascinated, and Ule was pale and unsettled. Old Craobhan wore an odd, mocking smile.

"Good," Jiriki said when he had finished. "This is very good. I have heard your name mentioned today, Count Eolair. We have much to talk about. But first, who is the master here? I understand that the king is dead."

Eolair looked dazedly to Craobhan. "Inahwen?"

"The king's wife is still up in the caves in the Grianspog." Craobhan wheezed with what might have been laughter. "Wouldn't come down with the rest of us. I thought she was being sensible at the time. Then again, perhaps she was."

"And Maegwin, the king's daughter, is asleep." Eolair shrugged. "I suppose then I am the one with whom you must speak, at least for the present."

"Would you be kind enough to come with me to our camp? Or would you rather we came here to talk?"

Eolair was not sure exactly who "we" might be, but he knew he would never forgive himself if he did not experience this moment to its fullest. Maegwin, in any case, obviously needed her rest, which would not be best accomplished with the Taig full of men and Sithi.

"We will be pleased to accompany you, Jiriki i-Sa'onserei," the count said.

"Jiriki, if it is acceptable." The Sitha stood waiting.

Eolair and his companions walked with him out the Taig's front doors. The tents billowed before them like a field of oversized wildflowers. "Do you mind my asking," Eolair ventured, "what happened to the wall Skali built around the city?"

Jiriki seemed to ponder for a moment. "Ah. That," he said at last, and smiled. "I think you probably are speaking of the handiwork of my mother, Likimeya. We were in a hurry. The wall was in our way."

"Then I hope *I* am never in her way," Isorn said earnestly.

"As long as you do not come between my mother and the honor of Year-Dancing House," said Jiriki, "you need not worry."

They continued across the wet grass. "You mentioned the bargain with Sinnach," the count said. "If you can defeat Skali in a day ... well, forgive me, Jiriki, but how was the battle at Ach Samrath ever lost?"

"First, we have not quite defeated this Skali. He and many of his men have fled into the hills and out onto the Frostmarch, so there is work still to be done. But your question is a good one." The Sitha's eyes narrowed as he considered. "I think we are, in some ways, a different people from what we were five centuries gone. Many of us were not born then, and we children of the Exile are not as cautious as our elders. Also, we feared iron in those days, before we learned how to protect ourselves from it." He smiled, that same fierce cat-grin, but then his face grew somber. He brushed a strand of his pale hair from his eyes. "And these men, Count Eolair, these Rimmersmen here, they were not prepared for us. Surprise was on our side. But in the battles ahead—and there will be many, I think—no one will be so unprepared. Then it will be like Ereb Irigú all over again—what you men call 'the Knock.' There will be much killing, I fear ... and my people can afford it even less than yours."

As he spoke, the wind that rippled the tents changed direction, swinging around until it blew from the North. It was suddenly much colder on Hern's Hill.

Elias, High King of all Osten Ard, staggered like a drunkard. As he made his way across the Inner Bailey courtyard he lurched from one shadowy spot to another as though the direct light of the sun made him ill, even though it was a gray, cold day and the sun itself, even at noon, was invisible behind a choke of clouds. The Hayholt's chapel dome loomed behind him, strangely asymmetrical; a mass of dirty snow, long uncleared, had dimpled several of the leaded panes inward so that the great dome looked like an old, rumpled felt hat.

Those few shivering peasants who were compelled to live within the Hayholt's walls and tend the castle's crumbling facilities seldom left their quarters unless forced by duty, which usually appeared in the form of a Thrithingsman overseer, whose commands were upheld by the possibility of sudden and violent retribution. Even the remainder of the king's army now barracked itself in the fields outside Erchester. The story given out was that the king was unwell and wished his peace, but it was commonly whispered that the king was mad, that his castle was haunted. As a result, only a handful of people were creeping about the Inner Bailey this gray, murky afternoon, and of those few—a soldier bearing a message for the Lord Constable, a pair of fearful rustics carting a wagon full of barrels away from Pyrates' chambers—not a one watched Elias' uneven passage for more than a moment before looking away. Not only would it be dangerous, possibly even fatal, to be caught staring at the king in his infirmity, but there was something so dreadfully *wrong* in his stiff-legged gait, some quality so terrifyingly unnatural, that those who saw him felt compelled to turn aside and furtively make the sign of the Tree before their breasts.

Hjeldin's Tower was gray and squat. With the red windows in its upper story gleaming dully, it might have been some ruby-eyed pagan god of the Nascadu wastes. Elias came to a stop before the heavy oak doors, which were three ells high and painted an unglossy black, studded with bronze hinges going splotchily green. On either side of the entrance stood a figure hooded and robed in a black even darker and flatter than the door. Each bore a lance of strange, filigreed design, a fantastic weave of curlicues and whorls, sharp as a barber's razor.

The king swayed in place, staring at the twin apparitions. It was clear that the Norns filled him with unease. He moved another step closer to the door. Although neither of the sentries moved, and their faces were invisible in the depths of their hoods, they seemed to become suddenly more intent, like spiders feeling the first trembling steps of a fly on the outskirts of a web.

"Well?" Elias said at last, his voice surprisingly loud. "Are you going to open the damned door for me?"

The Norns did not reply. They did not move.

"Blast you to hell, what ails you?!" he growled. "Don't you know me, you miserable creatures? I'm the king! Now open the door!" He took a sudden step forward. One of the Norns allowed his lance to sag a handspan into the doorway. Elias stopped and leaned back as though the point had been waved in his face.

"So this is the game, is it?" His pale face had begun to take on a gleam of madness. "This is the game? In my own house, eh?" He began to rock back and forth on his heels as though preparing to fling himself toward the door. One of his hands slithered down to clutch at the double-guarded sword which hung at his belt.

The sentry turned slowly and thumped twice on the heavy doors with the butt of his lance. After a moment's pause, he banged three more times before resuming his settled stance.

As Elias stood staring, a raven screeched on one of the tower's parapets. After what seemed like only a few heartbeats, the door grated open and Pyrates stood in the gap, blinking.

"Elias!" he said. "Your Majesty! You honor me!"

The king's lip curled. His hand was still tightening and loosening on Sorrow's hilt. "I don't honor you at all, priest. I came to talk to you—and *I* am dishonored."

"Dishonored? How?" Pyrates' face was full of shocked concern, but there was an unmistakable trace of mirth as well, as though he played mocking games with a child. "Tell me what has happened and what I can do to make it up to you, my king."

"These . . . things wouldn't open the door." Elias jerked his hand toward the silent warders. "When I tried to do it myself, one of them blocked my path."

Pyrates shook his head, then turned and conversed with the Norns in their own musical speech, which he seemed to speak well if somewhat haltingly. He faced the king again. "Please do not blame them, Highness, or even me. You see, some of the things I do here in the pursuit of knowledge can be hazardous. As I told you before, I fear that someone coming in suddenly might find himself endangered. You, my king, are the most important man in the world. Therefore I have asked that *no one* be allowed to walk in until I am here to escort them." Pyrates smiled, an unmodified baring of teeth that would have seemed appropriate on the face of an eel. "Please understand that it was for your safety, King Elias."

The king looked at him for a moment, then peered at the two sentries; they had returned to their positions and were stiff as statues once more. "I thought you were using mercenaries to stand guard. I thought these things didn't like the daylight."

"It does not harm them," said Pyrates. "It is just that after several score centuries living in the great mountain

Stormspike, they prefer shade to sun." He winked, as though over the foibles of some eccentric relative. "But I am at an important point in my studies, now—*our* studies, Majesty—and thought they would be better warders."

"Enough of this," Elias said impatiently. "Are you going to let me in? I came here to talk to you. It can't wait."

"Of course, of course," Pryrates assured him, but the priest seemed suddenly distracted. "I always look forward to speaking with you, my king. Perhaps you would prefer it if I came to your apartments. . . ?"

"Damn it, priest, let me in. You don't make a king stand on the doorstep, curse you!"

Pryrates shrugged and bowed. "Of course not, sire." He stepped aside, extending his arm toward the staircase. "Come up to my chambers, please."

Inside the great doors, in the high-ceilinged anteroom, a single torch burned fitfully. The corners were full of shadows that leaned and stretched as though struggling to free themselves. Pryrates did not pause, but went immediately up the narrow staircase. "Let me go ahead and make sure things are ready for you, Majesty," he called back, his voice echoing in the stairwell.

Elias stopped on the second landing to catch his breath. "Stairs," he said direly. "Too many stairs."

The door to the chamber was open, and the light of several torches spilled out into the passageway. As he entered, the king looked up briefly at the windows, which were masked by long draperies. The priest, who was closing the lid of a large chest on what seemed to be a pile of books, turned and smiled. "Welcome, my king. You have not favored me with a visit here in some time."

"You have not invited me. Where can I sit down—I am dying."

"No, my lord, not dying," Pryrates said cheerfully. "The opposite, if anything—you are being reborn. But you have been very sick of late, it's true. Forgive me. Here, take my chair." He ushered Elias to the high-backed chair; it was innocent of any decorations or carvings, yet somehow carried an air of great antiquity. "Would you like some of your soothing drink? I see Hengfisk has not accompanied you, but I could arrange to have some made." He turned and clapped his hands. *"Munshazou!"* he called.

"The monk is not here because I have knocked in his head, or near to," Elias growled, shifting uncomfortably on the hard seat. "If I never see his pop-eyed face again, I will be a happy man." He coughed, his fever-bright eyes blinking closed. At this moment, he did not look in the least like a happy man.

"He caused you some trouble? I am so unhappy to hear that, my king. Perhaps you should tell me what happened, and I will see that he is . . . dealt with. I am your servant, after all."

"Yes," Elias said dryly. "You are." He made a noise in his throat and shifted again, trying to find a better position.

There was a discreet cough from the doorway. A small dark-haired woman stood there. She did not look particularly aged, but her sallow face was lined with deep wrinkles. A mark of some kind—it might have been a letter from some foreign script—was scribed on her forehead above her nose. She moved ever so slightly as she stood, weaving in a slow, circular motion so that the hem of her shapeless dress brushed against the floor and the tiny bone-colored charms she wore at waist and neck tinkled gently.

"Munshazou," Pryrates said to Elias, "my servant from Naraxi, from my house there." He told the dark woman: "Bring something the king can drink. And for me—no, I need nothing. Go now."

She turned with a rattle of ivory and was gone. "I apologize for the interruption," said the alchemist. "You were telling me of your problem with Hengfisk."

"Don't worry about the monk. He is nothing. I just woke suddenly and found him standing over me, staring. Standing over my bed!" Remembering, the king shook himself like a wet dog. "God, but he has a face only a mother could bear. And that cursed smile always . . ." Elias shook his head. "I struck him—gave him my fist. Knocked him right across the bedchamber." He laughed and then coughed. "Teach him to come spying on me while I sleep. I *need* my sleep. I've been getting precious little. . . ."

"Is that why you came to me, Lord?" Pryrates asked. "For your sleep? I could perhaps make something for you—there is a sort of wax I have that you could burn in a dish by your bedside. . . ."

"No!" Elias said angrily. "And it's not the monk, either. I came to you because I had a dream!"

Pryrates looked at him carefully. The patch of skin above his eye—a spot where others had eyebrows—rose in a questioning look. "A dream, lord? Of course, if that is what you wish to speak with me about . . ."

"Not that sort of dream, damn you! You know what kind I mean. I had a *dream!*"

"Ah." The priest nodded. "And it disturbed you."

"Yes it bloody well did, by the Sacred Tree!" The king winced and laid his hand on his chest, then burst into another round of wracking coughs. "I saw the Sithi riding! The Dawn Children! They were riding to Hernystir!"

There was a faint clicking noise from the door. Munshazou had reappeared, bearing a tray on which stood a tall goblet glazed in a deep rust-red. It steamed.

"Very good." Pryrates strode forward to take it from the woman's hand. Her small, pale eyes watched him, but her face remained expressionless. "You may go now," he told her. "Here, Majesty, drink this. It will help your clouded chest."

Elias took the goblet suspiciously and sipped. "It tastes like the same swill you always give me."

"There are . . . similarities." Pryrates moved back to his position near the trunk full of books. "Remember, my king, you have special needs."

Elias took another swallow. "I saw the immortals—the Sithi. They were riding against Skali." He looked up from his cup to fix his green gaze on Pryrates. "Is it true?"

"Things seen in dreams are not always wholly true or wholly false . . ." Pryrates began.

"God damn you to the blackest circles of hell!" Elias shouted, half-rising from the chair. *"Is it true?!"*

Pryrates bowed his hairless head. "The Sithi have left their home in the fastness of the forest."

Elias' green eyes glittered dangerously. "And Skali?"

Pryrates moved slowly toward the door, as though preparing to flee. "The thane of Kaldskryke and his Ravens have . . . decamped."

The king hissed out a long breath and his hand tugged at Sorrow's hilt, sinews jumping in his pale arm. A length of the gray sword appeared, mottled and shiny as a pikefish's back. The torches in the room seemed to bend inward, as though drawn toward it. "Priest," Elias growled, "you are listening to your last few heartbeats if you don't speak quickly and plainly."

Instead of cringing, Pryrates drew himself upright. The torches fluttered again, and the alchemist's black eyes lost their luster; for a moment, the whites seemed to vanish, almost as though they had drawn back into his head, leaving only holes in a darkened skull. An oppressive tension filled the tower room. Pryrates raised his hand and the king's knuckles tightened on the sword's long hilt. After a moment's stillness the priest lifted his fingers to his neck, carefully smoothed the collar of his red robe as though adjusting the fit, then let the hand drop again.

"I am sorry, Highness," he said, and allowed himself a small, self-mocking smile. "It is often a counselor's wish to shield his liege from news that might be upsetting. You have seen rightly. The Sithi have come to Hernystir and Skali has been driven out."

Elias stared at him for a long moment. "What does this mean to all your plans, priest? You said nothing about the Dawn Children."

Pryrates shrugged. "Because it *means* nothing. It was inevitable once things reached a certain point. The increasing activity of . . . of our benefactor was bound to draw them in. It should not disrupt any of our plans."

"*Should* not? Are you saying that what the Sithi do doesn't matter to the Storm King?"

"That one has planned long. There is nothing that will surprise him in any of this. In truth, the Norn Queen told me to expect it."

"She did, did she? You seem very well informed, Pryrates," Elias' voice had not lost its edge of fury. "Then tell me: if you knew this, why can you not tell me what is happening with Fengbald? Why have we no knowledge of whether he has driven my brother from his lair?"

"Because our allies deem it of little account." Pryrates lifted his hand again, this time to forestall the king's angry reply. "Please, majesty, you asked for candor and so I give it to you. They feel that Josua is beaten and that you waste your time with him. The Sithi, on the other hand, have been the enemies of the Norns since time out of mind."

"But still of no account, apparently, if what you said before is correct." The king glowered. "I do not understand how they can be more important than my treacherous brother and yet not important enough for us to worry about—even when they have destroyed one of my chief allies. I think you are playing a double game, Pryrates. God help you if I find that to be true!"

"I serve only my master, Highness, not the Storm King, not the Norn Queen. It is all a matter of timing. Josua was a threat to you once, but you defeated him. Skali was needed to protect your flank, but he is no longer necessary. Even the Sithi are no threat, because they will not come against us until they have saved Hernystir. They are cursed by ancient loyalties, you see. That will be far too late for them to be any hindrance to your ultimate victory."

Elias stared into his steaming cup. "Then why did I see them riding in my dreams?"

"You have grown close to the Storm King, sire, since you accepted his gift." Pryrates gestured to the gray sword, now sheathed once more. "He is of the Sithi blood—or was when he still lived, to speak rightly. It is only natural that the mustering of the Zida'ya should draw his attention and thus make its way to you." He moved a few steps closer to the king. "You have had other ... dreams ... before this, have you not?"

"You know I have, alchemist." Elias drained the cup, then made a face as he swallowed. "My nights, those few

when sleep actually comes, are full of him. Full of him!
Of that frozen thing with the burning heart." His eyes
wandered across the shadowed walls, suddenly full of
fear. "Of the dark spaces between . . ."

"Peace, your Majesty," Pryrates said. "You have suffered much, but the reward will be splendid. You know
that."

Elias shook his head heavily. His voice, when he spoke,
was a straining rasp. "I wish I had known the way this
would feel, the things . . . the things it would do to me. I
wish I had known before I made that devil's bargain. God
help me, I wish I had known."

"Let me get my sleeping-wax for you, Highness. You
need rest."

"No." The king lifted himself awkwardly from the
chair. "I do not want any more dreams. It would be better
never to sleep again."

Elias moved slowly toward the door, waving away
Pryrates' offer of assistance. He was a long time going
down the stairs.

The red-robed priest stood and listened to his entire descent. When the great outer doors creaked open and then
crashed closed, Pryrates shook his head once, as if dismissing an irritating thought, then went to retrieve the
books he had hidden.

Jiriki had gone ahead, his smooth strides carrying him
deceptively quickly. Eolair, Isorn, and Ule followed at a
slower pace, trying to take in the strange sights.

It was particularly unsettling for Eolair, to whom
Hernysadharc and the Taig had been a second residence.
Now, following the Sitha across Hern's Hill, he felt like
a father come home to find that all his children were
changelings.

The Sithi had built their tent city so swiftly, the billowing cloths stretched artfully between the trees that
ringed the Taig, that it almost seemed it had always been
there—that it belonged. Even the colors, which had been

so jarringly bright when seen from a distance, now seemed to him more muted—tones of summer sunset and dawn more in keeping with a king's house and gardens.

If their lodgings already seemed like a natural part of the hilltop, the Zida'ya themselves seemed scarcely less at home. Eolair saw no sign of diffidence or meekness in those Sithi who surrounded him; they paid scant attention to the count and his companions. The immortals walked proudly, and as they worked they sang lilting songs in a language that, although strange to him, seemed oddly familiar in its swooping vowels and birdlike trills. Although they had been in the place scarcely a day, they seemed as comfortable on the snowy grass and beneath the trees as swans scudding across a mirror-still pond. Everything they did seemed to speak of immense calm and self-knowledge; even the act of looping and knotting the many ropes that gave their tent city its shape became a kind of conjuror's trick. Watching them, Eolair—who had always been judged a nimble, graceful man—felt bestial and clumsy.

The new-made house into which Jiriki had vanished was little more than a ring of blue and lavender cloth which hemmed one of the hilltop's magisterial oak trees like a paddock around a prize bull. As Eolair and the others stood, uncertain, Jiriki reemerged and beckoned them forward.

"Please understand that my mother may stray a little beyond the bounds of courtesy," Jiriki murmured as they stood at the opening. "We are mourning for my father and First Grandmother." He ushered them forward into the enclosure. The grass was dry, swept clean of snow. "I bring Count Eolair of Nad Mullach," he said, "Isorn Isgrimnurson of Elvritshalla, and Ule Frekkeson of Skoggey."

The Sitha-woman looked up. She was seated on a cloth of pale, shining blue, surrounded by the birds which she had been feeding. Despite the soft feathered bodies perched on her knees and arms, Eolair had the immediate impression that she was hard as sword-steel. Her hair was flaming red, bound by a gray scarf across her forehead;

several long, soot-colored feathers hung in her braids. Like Jiriki, she was armored in what looked to be wood, but hers was shiny and black as a beetle's shell. Beneath the armor she wore a kirtle of dove-gray. Soft boots of the same color rose above her knees. Her eyes, like her son's, were molten gold.

"Likimeya y'Briseyu no'e-Sa'onserei," Jiriki intoned. "Queen of the Dawn Children and Lady of the House of Year-Dancing."

Eolair and the rest dropped to a knee.

"Get up, please." She spoke in a throaty murmur, and seemed less comfortable with the mortal tongue than Jiriki. "This is your land, Count Eolair, and it is the Zida'ya who are guests here. We have come to pay our debt to your Sinnach."

"We are honored, Queen Likimeya."

She waved a long-nailed hand. "Do not say 'queen.' It is a title, only—it is the nearest mortal word. But we do not call ourselves such things except at certain times." She cocked an eyebrow at Eolair as he and his companions rose. "You know, Count Eolair, there is an old story that Zida'ya blood is in the House of Nad Mullach."

For a moment the count was confused, thinking she meant some kind of injustice had been done against the Sithi in his ancestral home. When he realized what she had truly said, he felt his own blood turn cold and the hairs lift on the back of his arms. "An old story?" Eolair felt as though his head was about to float away. "I'm sorry, my lady, I am not sure I understand. Do you mean to say that there was Sithi blood among my ancestors?"

Likimeya smiled, a sudden, fierce gleam of teeth. "It is an old story, as I said."

"And do the Sithi know whether it is true?" Was she playing some sort of game with him?

She fluttered her fingers. A cloud of birds leaped up and into the tree branches overhead, momentarily hiding her from view with the blur of their wings. "Long ago, when mortals and Zida'ya were closer . . ." She made a strange gesture. "It could be. We know it *can* happen."

Eolair definitely felt himself on shaky ground, and was

surprised at how swiftly his training in diplomacy and politicking had deserted him. "It has happened, then? The Fair Folk have . . . mingled with mortals?"

Likimeya seemed to lose interest in the subject. "Yes. Long ago, for the most part." She motioned to Jiriki, who came forward with more of the shimmery, silken cloths, which he spread for the count and his companions before gesturing for them to sit. "It is good to be on *M'yin Azoshai* again."

"That is what we call this hill," Jiriki explained. "It was given to Hern by Shi'iki and Senditu. It was, I suppose you would say, a sacred place for our folk. That it was granted to a mortal for his steading is a mark of the friendship between Hern's people and the Dawn Children."

"We have a legend that says something much like that," Eolair said slowly. "I had wondered if there was truth to it."

"Most legends have a kernel of truth at their center." Jiriki smiled.

Likimeya had turned her cat-bright eyes from Eolair to his two comrades, who almost seemed to flinch beneath the weight of her gaze. "And you are Rimmersmen," she said, looking at them intently. "We have little cause to love your folk."

Isorn hung his head. "Yes, Lady, you do." He took a deep breath, steadying his voice. "But please, do not forget that we live short lives. That was many years ago—a score of generations. We are not much like Fingil."

Likimeya's smile was brief. "You may not be, but what about this kinsman of yours we have put to flight? I have seen his handiwork here on M'yin Azoshai, and it looks little different than what your Fingil Bloodfist did to the Zida'ya lands five centuries ago."

Isorn shook his head slowly, but did not reply. Beside him, Ule had turned quite pale and looked as though he might bolt at any moment.

"Isorn and Ule fought *against* Skali," Eolair said hurriedly, "and we were bringing more men here to take up the battle when you and your folk passed us by. You have done these two as great a favor by putting the murderer to flight as you have done for my own people. Now there is hope that someday Isorn's father can retain his rightful dukedom."

"Ah." Likimeya nodded. "Now we come to it. Jiriki, have these men eaten?"

Her son looked at the count inquiringly. "No, my lady," Eolair replied.

"Then you will eat with us, and we will talk."

Jiriki got up and vanished through a gap in the rippling walls. There followed a long and, for Eolair, uncomfortable silence which Likimeya seemed uninclined to break. They sat and listened to the wind in the oak tree's upper branches until Jiriki returned bearing a wooden tray piled with fruit, bread, and cheese.

The count was astonished. Didn't these creatures have servants to perform such humble tasks? He watched while Jiriki, as commanding a presence as he had ever encountered, poured something from a blue crystal flask into drinking cups carved from the same wood as the tray, then handed the cups to Eolar and his companions with a simple but elegant bow. The queen and prince of the eldest folk, yet they waited on themselves? The gap between Eolair and these immortals seemed broader than ever.

Whatever was in the crystal flask burned like fire but tasted like clover-honey and smelled like violets. Ule sipped his cautiously, then drained it at a swallow and gladly let Jiriki refill his cup. As he drank his own cup dry, Eolair felt the pain of two days' hard riding dissolve in the warm glow. The food was excellent as well, each piece of fruit at the peak of ripeness. The count wondered briefly where the Sithi could have found such delicacies in the middle of a year-long winter, but dismissed it as only another small miracle in what was rapidly becoming a vast catalog of wonders.

"We have come to war," Likimeya said suddenly. Of all, only she had not eaten, and she had taken no more than a sip of the honey cordial. "Skali eludes us for a moment, but the heart of your kingdom is free. We have made a start. With your help, Eolair, and those of your people whose wills are still strong, we will soon lift the yoke from the neck of our old allies."

"There are no words for our gratitude, Lady," Eolair replied. "The Zida'ya have shown us today that they honor their promises. Few mortal tribes can say the same."

"And what then, Queen Likimeya?" Isorn asked. He had drunk three glasses of the pale elixir, and his face had gone a bit red. "Will you ride with Josua? Will you help him take the Hayholt?"

The look she turned on him was cool and austere. "We do not fight for mortal princes, Isorn Isgrimnurson. We fight to honor our debts, and to protect ourselves."

Eolair felt his heart sink. "So you will stop here?"

Likimeya shook her head, then lifted her hands and wove her fingers together. "It is nothing like that simple. I spoke too quickly. No, there are things that threaten both your Josua Lackhand and the Dawn Children as well. Lackhand's enemy has made a bargain with our enemy, it seems. Still, we will do what we alone are fit for: once Hernystir is free, we will leave the wars of mortals to mortals—at least for now. No, Count Eolair, we owe other debts, but these are strange times." She smiled, and this time the smile was a little less predatory, a little more like something that might stretch across a mortal face. Eolair was struck by her angular beauty. At the same moment, in lightning juxtaposition, he realized that he sat before a being who had seen the fall of Asu'a. She was as old as the greatest cities of men—older, perhaps. He shivered.

"Yet," Likimeya continued, "although we will not ride to the aid of your embattled prince, we *will* ride to the aid of his fortress."

There was a moment of confused silence before Isorn spoke. "Your pardon, Lady. We do not understand what you mean."

It was Jiriki who answered. "When Hernystir is free, we will ride to Naglimund. It is the Storm King's now, and it stands too close to the house of our exile. We will take this place back from him." The Sitha's face was grim. "Also, when the final battle comes—and it is coming, mortal men, do not doubt it—we wish to be sure that the Norns have no bolt hole left in which to hide themselves."

Eolair watched Jiriki's eyes as the Sitha spoke, and fancied that he saw a hatred there that had smoldered for centuries.

"A war unlike any the world has seen," Likimeya said. "A war in which many matters will be settled for once and all." If Jiriki's eyes smoldered, hers blazed.

19

A Broken Smile

"I **have done** all I can do for either of them—
unless . . ." Cadrach rubbed fretfully at his damp forehead, as though to bring out some idea hiding there. He
was obviously exhausted, but just as obviously—with the
duke's slurs still fresh in his mind—he was not going to
let that stop him.

"There is nothing else to be done," Miriamele said
firmly. "Lie down. You need some sleep."

Cadrach looked up at Isgrimnur, who stood at the bow
of the flatboat with the pole clasped firmly in his broad
hands. The duke only tightened his lips and returned to
his inspection of the watercourse. "Yes, then, I suppose I
should." The monk curled up beside the still forms of
Tiamak and the other Wrannaman.

Miriamele, recently awakened from her own evening-
long nap, leaned forward and draped her cloak across the
three of them. There was little use for the garment anyway, except to keep off bugs. Even near midnight, the
marsh was warm as a midsummer day.

"If we snuff the lamp," Isgrimnur rumbled, "maybe
these creepy-crafties will go make a meal on something
else for a change." He slapped at his upper arm and held
the resultant smear up for inspection. "The damnable
light draws them. You'd think a lamp that comes from
that marsh-man town would keep 'em away." He snorted.
"How people can live here year-round is a puzzle to me."

"If we're going to do that, we should drop the anchor."
Miriamele did not much like the idea of floating along in

the dark. So far, they seemed to have left the ghants behind, but she still looked carefully at every low-hanging branch or dangling vine. But Isgrimnur had gone long without sleep; it only seemed fair to try to bring him some relief from the flying insects.

"That's good. I think this bit is wide enough to make us as safe as we'd be anywhere else," Isgrimnur said. "Don't see any branches. The little bugs are bad enough, but if I never see one of those Aedon-cursed big ones again . . ." He did not need to finish. Miriamele's shallow sleep had been full of dreams of clacking, scuttling ghants and sticky tendrils that held her in place when she wanted only to run.

"Help me with the anchor." Together they heaved the stone up and dumped it over the side. When it had struck bottom, Miriamele tested the rope to make sure there was not too much slack. "Why don't you sleep first," she told the duke. "I'll watch for a little while."

"Very well."

She glanced quickly at Camaris, sleeping soundlessly in the stern with his white head propped on his cloak, then she reached out and shuttered the lamp.

At first, the darkness was frighteningly complete. Miriamele could almost feel jointed legs reaching silently toward her, and fought the impulse to turn around and wave her hands in the blackness to keep the phantoms at bay.

"Isgrimnur?"

"What?"

"Nothing. I just wanted to hear your voice."

Her sight began to come back. There was little enough light—the moon was gone, either blocked by clouds or by the close-tangled trees that roofed the watercourse, and the stars were only faint specks—but she could make out forms around her, the dark bulk of the duke, the patchy shadows of the river banks on either side.

She heard Isgrimnur rattling the pole around until he got it well-situated, then his shadowy form sank down. "Are you sure you don't need to sleep more yourself?" he asked. Weariness was making his voice muddy.

"I'm rested. I'll sleep a little later. Go on now, put your head down."

Isgrimnur did not protest further—a sure sign of his exhaustion. Within moments he was snoring noisily. Miriamele smiled.

The boat moved so smoothly that it was not hard to imagine they were floating like a cloud through the night sky. There was no tide and no discernible current, only the minute push of the swamp breezes that sent them slowly circling around the anchor, moving smoothly as quicksilver on a tilted pane of glass. Miriamele sat back and stared up at the murky sky, trying to make out a familiar star. For the first time in some days, she could afford the luxury of homesickness.

I wonder what my father is doing now? Does he think about me? Does he hate me?

Thoughts of Elias set other things to stirring inside her head. Something Cadrach had mentioned their first night after escaping the *Eadne Cloud* had been nagging at her. During his long and difficult confession, the monk had said that Pryrates had seemed particularly interested in communicating with the dead—"speaking through the veil," Cadrach had said it was called—and that those were the parts of Nisses' book on which he had been most fixated. For some reason, that phrase had made her think of her father. But why? Was it something Elias had said?

Try as she might to summon the idea that had snagged at the back of her mind, it remained elusive. The boat spun slowly, silent beneath dim stars.

She had drowsed a little. The first light of morning was creeping into the skies above the marsh, turning them pearly gray. Miriamele straightened, groaning quietly. Her bruises and aches from the ghant nest had begun to stiffen: she felt as though she had been rolled down a hill in a bag of rocks.

"L–L–Lady?" It was a breathy sound, little more than a sigh.

"Tiamak?!" She turned abruptly, causing the boat to

pitch. The Wrannaman's eyes were open. His face, though pale and slack-featured, held the spark of intelligence once more.

"Y—yes. Yes, Lady." He took a deep breath, as though even those few words had tired him out. "Where . . . are we?"

"We are on the waterway, but I have no idea where. We poled for most of a day after leaving the ghant nest." She looked at him carefully. "Are you in pain?"

He tried to shake his head, but could only move it slightly. "No. But water. Would be kind."

She leaned across the boat to take the water skin lying near Isgrimnur's leg. She unstoppered it and gave the Wrannaman a few careful swallows.

Tiamak turned a little to eye the still form next to him. "Younger Mogahib," he whispered. "Is he alive?"

"Barely. At least he seems very close to . . . he seems very sick, although Cadrach and I couldn't find any wounds on him."

"No. You would not. Nor on me." Tiamak let his head fall back and closed his eyes. "And the others?"

"Which others?" she asked cautiously. "Cadrach, Isgrimnur, Camaris, and I are all here, and all more or less well."

"Ah. Good." Tiamak's eyes remained closed.

In the prow, Isgrimnur sat up groggily. "What's this, then?" he mumbled. "Miriamele . . . what?"

"Nothing, Isgrimnur. Tiamak's woken up."

"Has, has he?" The duke settled back, already sliding down into slumber once more. "Brains not scrambled? Talks like himself? Damnedest thing I ever saw . . ."

"You were speaking another language in the nest," Miriamele told Tiamak. "It was frightening."

"I know." His face rippled, as though he fought down revulsion. "I will talk about it later. Not now." His eyes opened partway. "Did you bring anything out with me?"

Miriamele shook her head, thinking. "Just you. And the muck you were covered with."

"Ah." Tiamak looked disappointed for a moment, but

then relaxed. "Just as well." A moment later, his eyes opened wide. "And my belongings?" he demanded.

"Everything you had in the boat is still here." She patted the bundle.

"Good . . . good." He sighed his relief and slid down into the cloak.

The sky was growing paler, and the foliage on either side of the river was beginning to emerge from shadow into color and life.

"Lady?"

"What?"

"Thank you. Thank you all for coming after me."

Miriamele listened as his breathing grew slower. Soon the little man was asleep again.

"As I told Miriamele last night," Tiamak said, "I wish to thank you all. You have been better friends to me than I could have hoped—certainly better than I have earned."

Isgrimnur coughed. "Nonsense. Couldn't have done anything else." Miriamele thought the duke looked a little shamefaced. Perhaps he was remembering the debate on whether to try to save the Wrannaman or to leave him behind.

The company had set up a makeshift camp near the watercourse. The small fire, its flames almost invisible in the bright late-morning light, was burning merrily, heating water for soup and yellowroot tea.

"No, you do not understand. It was not merely my life you saved. If I have a *ka*—a soul, you would call it—it would not have survived another day in that place. Perhaps not another hour."

"But what were they doing to you?" Miriamele asked. "You were babbling away—you sounded almost like a ghant yourself!"

Tiamak shuddered. He was sitting up, wrapped in her cloak, but he had so far moved very little. "I will tell you as best I can, although I do not understand much myself. But you are certain that you brought nothing out of that place with me?"

The rest of the company shook their heads.

"There was ..." he began, then stopped, thinking. "It was a piece of what looked like a mirror—a looking glass. It was broken, but there was still a bit of the frame in place, carved with great art. They ... the ghants ... they put it in my hands." He lifted his palms to show them the healing cuts. "As soon as I held it, I felt cold running through me, from my fingers right into my head. Then some of the creatures vomited forth that sticky substance, covering me with it." He took a deep breath but could not immediately continue. For a moment he just sat, tears shining in his eyes.

"You don't have to talk about it, Tiamak," Miriamele said. "Not now."

"Or at least just tell us how they got hold of you," Isgrimnur said. "If that's not so bad, I mean."

The Wrannaman looked down at the ground. "They caught me as easily as if I were a just-hatched crablet. Three of them dropped on me out of the trees," he looked up quickly, as though it might happen again, "and while I struggled with them, a dozen more came swarming down and overwhelmed me. Oh, they are clever! They wrapped me in vines, just as you or I would bind a prisoner, although they did not seem able to tie knots. Still, they held the vines tight enough that I could not escape. Then they tried to lift me into the trees, but I suppose I was too heavy. Instead, they were forced to grab at vines and sunken branches and pull the flatboat against the sandbank. Then they took me to the nest. I cannot tell you how many times I wished that they would kill me, or at least knock me senseless. To be carried alive and awake through that horrible pitch-black place by those chattering *things*... !" He had to pause for a moment to regain his composure.

"What they did with me, they had already done with Younger Mogahib." He nodded toward the other Wrannaman, who lay on the ground nearby, still locked in feverish slumber. "I think he lived because he had not been there long: perhaps he had not proved as useful a tool as they thought I would. In any case, they must have had to free him to get the mirror-shard for me. When they dragged him past, I cried out. He was half-mad, but he heard my voice and called back. I recognized him then, and shouted that my boat was still on the bank outside, that he should escape if he could and take it."

"Did you tell him to find us?" Cadrach asked. "It was an unbelievable stroke of luck if he was trying to."

"No, no," Tiamak said. "There were only moments. Later, though, I hoped that if he did get free and made his way back to Village Grove, he might find you there. But even then, I only hoped that you would find out I had not deserted you by choice." He frowned. "It was too much to hope that someone would come into that place after me. . . ."

"Enough of that, man," Isgrimnur said quickly. "What were they doing to you?"

Miriamele was certain now that the duke wished to avoid the subject of their decision. She almost smiled. As if anyone would ever doubt his good will and bravery! Still, after what he had said about Cadrach, perhaps Isgrimnur was a little sensitive.

"I am still not sure." Tiamak squinted, as if trying to summon an image to his mind's eye. "As I said, they . . . put the mirror in my hand and covered me with that ooze. The feeling of cold grew stronger and stronger. I thought I was dying—smothering and freezing at the same moment! Then, just when I was certain I had breathed my last, something even stranger happened." He looked up, meeting Miriamele's eyes as though to make sure that she would believe him. "Words began to come into my head—no, not words. There were no words to it at all, merely . . . visions." He paused. "It was as though a door had been opened—as though someone pushed an entrance through into my head and other thoughts came flooding in. But, worst of all, they . . . they were not *human* thoughts."

"Not human? But how could you know such a thing?" Cadrach was interested now, leaning forward, his gray eyes intent on the Wrannaman.

"I cannot explain, but just as you could hear a red knifebill squawk in the trees and know it was not a human voice, so I could tell that these were thoughts that had never known a mortal mind. They were ... cold thoughts. Slow and patient and so hateful to me that I would have torn my head from my shoulders if I had not been imprisoned in that muck. If I did not quite believe in They Who Breathe Darkness before, I do now. It was h–horrible to have them inside of my sk–skull."

Tiamak was shaking. Miriamele reached forward to pull the cloak up around his shoulders. Isgrimnur, nervous and fidgeting, threw more sticks onto the flames. "Perhaps you have told enough," she said.

"I am almost f–f–finished. F–forgive me, my t–t–teeth are banging together."

"Here," Isgrimnur said, relieved to have something to do. "We'll move you closer to the fire."

When Tiamak was relocated, he began again.

"I half-knew that I was speaking like a ghant, although it did not feel like that. I felt as though I was taking the terrible, crushing thoughts inside my head and speaking them aloud, but somehow it came out as clicks and buzzing and all the noises those creatures make. Yet it made sense, somehow—it was what I wanted to do, to talk and talk, to let all the thoughts of the cold thing inside me just bleed out for the ghants to understand."

"What were the thoughts about?" Cadrach asked. "Can you remember?"

Tiamak scowled. "Some. But as I said, they were not words, and they were so unlike the things I think or you think that I find it difficult even to explain what I *do* remember." He snaked a hand out from the folds of the cloak to take a bowl of yellowroot tea. "They were visions, really, just pictures as I told you. I saw ghants swarming out of the swamps into the cities—thousands upon thousands, like flies on a sugar-bulb tree. They were just ... just swarming. And they were all singing in their buzzing voices, all singing the same song of power and food and never dying."

"And this was what the ... the cold thing was telling them?" Miriamele asked.

"I suppose. I was speaking as a ghant, I was seeing

things as they did—and that was terrible, too. He Who
Always Steps on Sand, preserve me from ever seeing
such a thing again! The world through their eyes is
cracked and skewed, the only colors are blood-red and
tar-black. Shimmery, too, as though everything were covered in grease, or as if one's eyes were full of water.
And—this is the hardest to explain—nothing had a face,
not the other ghants, not the people running screaming
from the invaded cities. Every living th–thing was just a
muddy l–l–lump with l–legs."

Tiamak fell silent, sipping his tea, the bowl trembling
in his hands.

"That is all." He took a deep, shaky breath. "It seemed
as though it lasted for years, but it cannot have been more
than a few days."

"Poor Tiamak!" Miriamele said with feeling. "How did
you keep your wits!?"

"I would not have if you had been any longer in coming," he said firmly. "I am sure of that. I could feel my
own mind straining and slipping, as though I hung by my
fingertips over a long drop. A drop into darkness without
end." He looked down into his tea-bowl. "I wonder how
many of my fellow villagers besides Younger Mogahib
served them as I did, but were *not* rescued?"

"There were lumps." Isgrimnur spoke slowly. "Other
lumps in a row beside you—but bigger, with no heads
sticking out. I came close to them." He hesitated. "There
were . . . there were shapes under that white ooze."

"Others of my tribe, I am sure," Tiamak murmured.
"Ah, it is horrible. They must have been used up like can-
dles, one at a time." His face sagged. "Horrible."

No one said anything for a while.

Miriamele finally spoke. "You said that the ghants had
never been dangerous before."

"No. Although I am sure now that they became dangerous enough after I left that the villagers made a raid on
the nest. That is why the weapons were missing from
Older Mogahib's house, almost certainly. And the things
Isgrimnur saw tells what happened to the raiders." He

looked over to the other Wrannaman. "This one was probably the last of the prisoners."

"But I still don't understand all this about a mirror," the duke said. "Ghants don't use mirrors, do they?"

"No. Nor do they make anything so fine." Tiamak offered the duke a weak smile. "I wonder too, Isgrimnur."

Cadrach, who had been pouring out a bowlful of tea for silent Camaris, turned to look over his shoulder. "I have some ideas, but I must think on them. However, one thing is sure. If some sort of intelligence does guide those creatures, or is capable of guiding them sometimes, then we cannot afford to tarry. We must escape the Wran as swiftly as we possibly can." His tone was cold, as though he spoke of events that barely concerned him. Miriamele did not like the distant look in his eyes.

Isgrimnur nodded. "The monk's right, for once. I don't see that we have any time to waste."

"But Tiamak is sick!" Miriamele said angrily.

"There is nothing to be done, Lady. They are right. If I can be propped up with something to lean against, I can give directions. I can at least take us far enough from the nest by nightfall that we might risk sleeping on land."

"Let's to it, then." Isgrimnur rose. "Time is short."

"It is indeed," said Cadrach. "And growing shorter every day."

His tone was so flat and somber that the others turned to look at him, but the monk only sloshed to the water's edge and began loading their belongings back into the flatboat.

By the next day, Tiamak was much recovered, but Younger Mogahib was not. The Wrannaman slid in and out of fever-madness. He thrashed and raved, shouting things that, when Tiamak translated them, sounded much like the nightmarish visions he himself had experienced; when he was quiet, Younger Mogahib lay like one dead. Tiamak fed him concoctions made from healing herbs gathered along the banks of the watercourse, but they seemed little use.

"His body is strong. But I think his thoughts are

wounded, somehow." Tiamak sadly shook his head. "Perhaps they had him longer than I suspected."

They sailed on through the Wran, bearing north in the large part, but going there by a circuitous route that only Tiamak could follow. It was clear that without him they would indeed have been doomed to wander the swamp's backwaters for a long time. Miriamele did not like to think about what their end might have been.

She was growing tired of the swamp. The descent into the nest had filled her with a disgust for mud and stench and odd creatures that now spread to include all the wild Wran. It was stunningly alive, but so was a tub full of worms. She would not want to spend a moment longer than necessary in either of them.

On the third night after their escape from the nest, Younger Mogahib died. He had been shouting, according to Tiamak, about "the sun running backward" and about blood pouring through the drylander cities like rainwater, when suddenly his face darkened and his eyes bulged. Tiamak tried to give him water to drink, but his jaws were clamped shut and could not be opened. A moment later, the Wrannaman's entire body went rigid. Long after the gleam of life had faded from his wide eyes he remained as stiff as a wooden post.

Tiamak was upset, although he tried to maintain his composure. "Younger Mogahib was not a friend," he said as they drew a cloak over the staring face, "but he was the last link to my village. Now I will not know if they were all captured—taken to the nest . . ." his lip quivered, ". . . or fled to another, safer village when the raiding party failed."

"If there *are* safer villages," said Cadrach. "You say there are many ghant nests in the Wran. Could this be the only one that has become so dangerous?"

"I do not know." The small man sighed. "I will have to come back and search for an answer to that."

"Not by yourself," Miriamele said firmly. "Stay with us. When we find Josua, he will help you find your people."

"Now, Princess," Isgrimnur cautioned, "you can't know that for certain. . . ."

"Why not? Am I not of the royal blood as well? Doesn't that count for anything? Besides, Josua will need all the allies he can find, and the Wrannamen are nothing to scoff at—as Tiamak has proven to us time and again."

The marsh man was dreadfully embarrassed. "You are kind, Lady, but I could not hold you to such a promise." He looked down at Younger Mogahib's shrouded form and sighed. "We must do something with his body."

"Bury him?" Isgrimnur asked. "How do you, when the ground's so wet?"

Tiamak shook his head. "We do not bury our dead. I will show you in the morning. Now, if you will forgive me, I need to walk for a while." He limped slowly out of the campground.

Isgrimnur looked uncomfortably at the body. "I wish he hadn't left us with this."

"Do you fear ghosts, Rimmersman?" Cadrach asked with an unpleasant smile.

Miriamele frowned. She had hoped that when the monk's oil-fire missiles had helped them escape, the hostility between Cadrach and Isgrimnur would diminish. Indeed, the duke seemed ready to call a truce, but Cadrach's anger had hardened into something cold and more than a little unpleasant.

"There's nothing wrong with caution . . ." Isgrimnur began.

"Oh, be quiet, both of you," Miriamele said irritably. "Tiamak has just lost his friend."

"Not a friend," Cadrach pointed out.

"His clansman, then. You heard him: this man was the only one of his village he's found since he returned. This is the only other Wrannaman he's seen! And now he's dead. You'd want a little time alone, too." She turned on her heel and walked over to sit next to Camaris, who was twining grasses to make a sort of necklace.

"Well . . ." Isgrimnur said, but then fell silent, chewing his beard. Cadrach, too, said no more.

*   *   *

When Miriamele awoke the next morning, Tiamak was gone. Her fears were allayed a short while later when he returned to the camp bearing a huge sheaf of oil-palm fronds. As she and the others watched, he wrapped Younger Mogahib with them, layer after layer, as if in parody of the priest of Erchester's House of Preparing; soon there was nothing to be seen but an oblong bundle of oozing green leaves.

"I will take him now," Tiamak said quietly. "You need not come with me if you do not wish it."

"Would you like us to?" Miriamele asked.

Tiamak looked at her for a moment, then nodded. "I would like that, yes."

Miriamele made sure that the others came along—even Camaris, who seemed far more interested in the fringe-tailed birds in the branches overhead than in corpses and funeral parties.

With Isgrimnur's help, Tiamak carefully laid Younger Mogahib's leaf-wrapped body in the flatboat. A short way up the watercourse, he poled against a sand bank and led them ashore. He had built a sort of frame of thin branches in a flat clearing. Beneath the frame, wood and more oil-palm leaves had been stacked. Again with Isgrimnur's assistance, Tiamak lifted the bundle up onto the slender frame, which swayed gently beneath the weight of the corpse.

When everything had been arranged to his satisfaction, Tiamak stepped back and stood beside his companions, facing the frame and the unlit pyre.

"She Who Waits to Take All Back," he intoned, "who stands beside the last river, Younger Mogahib is leaving us now. When he drifts past, remember that he was brave: he went into the ghant nest to save his family, his clansmen and clanswomen. Remember also that he was good."

Here Tiamak had to pause and think for a moment. Miriamele remembered that he had said he and the other Wrannaman had not been friends. "He always respected his father and the other elders," Tiamak declared at last. "He gave his feasts when they were allotted, and did not stint." He took a deep breath. "Remember your agreement with She Who Birthed Mankind. Younger Mogahib had his life and lived it; then, when They Who Watch and Shape touched his shoulder, he gave it up. She Who Waits to Take All Back, do not let him drift by!" Tiamak turned to his companions. "Say it with me, please."

"Do not let him drift by!" they all cried together. In the tree overhead, a bird made a sound like a squeaky door.

Tiamak went and kneeled beside the pyre. With a few strokes of flint and steel, he set a spark among the scraps of oil palm. Within moments, the fire was burning strongly, and soon the leaves wrapped around Younger Mogahib's body began to blacken and curl.

"You do not need to watch," said Tiamak. "If you wait for me a little downstream, I will join you soon."

This time, Miriamele sensed, the Wrannaman did not want company. She and the others boarded the boat and poled a little way along the watercourse, until a bend in the stream hid from their view all but the growing plume of dark gray smoke.

Later, when Tiamak came wading through the water, Isgrimnur helped him aboard. They poled the short distance back to camp. Tiamak said little that night, but sat and stared at the campfire long after the others had bedded down.

"I think I understand something of Tiamak's story, now," Cadrach said.

It was late morning, six days since they had left the ghant nest behind. The weather was warm, but a breeze made the watercourse more pleasant than it had been in days. Miriamele was beginning to believe they might actually see the last of it soon.

"What do you mean, understand?" Isgrimnur tried to keep the surliness out of his voice, but without complete success. Relations between the Rimmersman and the monk had continued to worsen.

Cadrach favored him with a magisterial stare, but directed his reply to Miriamele and Tiamak, who sat in the middle of the boat. Camaris, watching the banks intently, was poling in the stern. "The shard of mirror. The ghant speech. I think I may know what they mean."

"Tell us, Cadrach," Miriamele urged.

"As you know, Lady, I have studied many ancient matters." The monk cleared his throat, not entirely averse to having an audience. "I have read of things called Witnesses. . . ."

"Was that in Nisses' book?" Miriamele asked, then was startled to feel Tiamak cringe beside her as if dodging a blow. She turned to look at him, but the slender man was staring at Cadrach with what looked oddly like suspicion—a fierce, intent suspicion, as if it had just been revealed that the Hernystirman was half-ghant.

Puzzled, she looked at the monk to find that *he* was looking at *her* with fury.

I suppose he doesn't much want to think about that, Miriamele realized, and felt bad that she had not kept quiet. Still, Tiamak's reaction was what truly puzzled her. What had she said? Or what had Cadrach said?

"In any case," Cadrach said heavily, as if unwillingly forced to continue, "there were once things called Witnesses, which were made by the Sithi in the depths of time. These things allowed them to speak to each other over great distances, and perhaps even let them show dreams and visions to each other. They came in many forms—'Stones and Scales, Pools and Pyres,' as the old books say. 'Scales' are what the Sithi called mirrors. I do not know why."

"Are you saying that Tiamak's mirror was . . . one of those things?" Miriamele asked.

"That is my guess."

"But what would the Sithi have to do with the ghants? Even if they hate men, which I have heard, I can't believe they would like those horrid bugs any better."

Cadrach nodded. "Ah, but if these Witnesses still exist, it could be that others beside the Sithi can use them. Remember, Princess, all the things you heard at Naglimund. Remember who plans and waits in the frozen north."

Miriamele, thinking of Jarnauga's strange speech, suddenly felt a chill quite unrelated to the mild breeze.

Isgrimnur leaned forward from his seat before Camaris' knees. "Hold, man. Are you saying that this Storm King fellow is doing some magic with the ghants? Then what did they need Tiamak for? Doesn't make sense."

Cadrach bit back a sharp reply. "I don't claim to know anything with certainty, Rimmersman. But it could be that the ghants are too different, too . . . simple, perhaps . . . for those who now use these Witnesses to be able to speak with them directly." He shrugged. "It is my guess that they needed a human as a sort of go-between. A messenger."

"But what could the Stor . . ." Miriamele caught herself. Even though Isgrimnur had uttered the name, she had no desire to do the same. "What could someone like that want with the ghants down in the Wran?"

Cadrach shook his head. "It is far beyond me, Lady. Who could hope to know the plans of . . . someone like that?"

Miriamele turned to Tiamak. "Do you remember anything else of what you were being made to say? Could Cadrach be right?"

Tiamak appeared reluctant to talk about it. He stared cautiously at the monk. "I do not know. I know little about . . . about magic or ancient books. Very little." The Wrannaman fell into silence.

"I thought I disliked the ghants before," Miriamele said finally. "But if that's true—if they're somehow part of . . . of what Josua and the others are fighting against . . ." She wrapped her arms around herself. "The sooner we leave here, the better."

"That's something we all agree on," Isgrimnur rumbled.

In Miriamele's dreams that night, as the boat gently rocked on the slow-moving waters, voices spoke to her from behind a veil of shadow—thin, insistent voices that whispered of decay and loss as though they were things to be desired.

She woke up beneath the faint stars and realized that even surrounded by friends, she was terribly lonely.

Tiamak's recovery proved to be incomplete. Within a day after Younger Mogahib's ceremonial burning, he had fallen back into a kind of fever that left him weak and listless. When darkness fell, the Wrannaman had terrible dreams, visions that he could not remember in the morning but which made him writhe in his sleep and cry out. With Tiamak suffering his nightly tortures, the remainder of the company was nearly as ill-rested as he was.

More days passed, but the Wran lingered like a guest that had outstayed his welcome: for every league of marshy tangle they crossed—floating beneath the steamy sky or wading through clinging, foully-scented mud as they struggled with the heavy flatboat—another league of swamp appeared before them. Miriamele began to feel that some sorcerer was playing a cruel trick on them, spiriting them back to their starting place each night while they lay in shallow sleep.

The hovering insects who seemed to delight in finding each person's tenderest spot, the shrouded but potent sun, the air as hot and damp as the steam over a soupbowl, all helped bring the travelers' tempers close to the snapping point—and many times to push them past it. Even the arrival of rain, which at first seemed like such a blessing, turned out to be another curse. The monotonous, blood-warm downpour persisted for three whole days, until Miriamele and her companions began to feel that demons were pounding on their heads with tiny hammers. The unpleasant conditions were even beginning to affect old Camaris, who had previously been unmoved and untouched by almost everything, so calm that he allowed the biting bugs to crawl across his skin without reprisal—something that made Miriamele itch uncontrollably just watching. But the three days and nights of unbroken rain reached even the old knight at last. As they poled along through the third day's storm, he pulled a hat he had

made from fronds lower over his white brows and stared
miserably out at the rain-pocked watercourse, his long
face so sorrowful that Miriamele finally went and put her
arm around him. He gave no clear sign of it, but something in his posture suggested he was grateful for the contact; whether that was true or not, he stayed in place for
some time, seemingly a little more content. Miriamele
marveled at his broad back and shoulders, which seemed
almost indecently solid on an old man.

Tiamak found it a labor just to sit upright in the stern
of the boat, wrapped in a blanket, and call directions
through his chattering teeth. He told them they had nearly
reached the Wran's northern fringe, but he had already
told them that many days earlier, and the Wrannaman's
eyes now had an odd, glazed look. Miriamele and
Isgrimnur were being careful not to let each other see
they were worrying. Cadrach, who more than once
seemed on the verge of coming to blows with the duke,
was openly scornful about their chances of finding the
way out. Isgrimnur at last told him that if he made any
more pessimistic predictions he would be thrown over the
side, so that if he wished to make the rest of the journey
it would have to be by swimming. The monk ceased his
carping, but the looks he directed at the duke when
Isgrimnur's back was turned made Miriamele uneasy.

It was clear to her that the Wran was finally wearing
them all down. It was not a place for people, ultimately—
especially drylanders.

"Over here should do well," she said. She took a few
more awkward steps, struggling to stay upright as the
mud squelched beneath her bootsoles.

"If you say so, Lady," Cadrach murmured.

They had moved a little way from their camp to bury
the remains of their meal, mostly fish bones and scaly
skin and fruit pits. During the long course of their journey, the inquisitive Wran apes had proved all too willing
to come into camp in search of leavings, even if one of
the human company stayed up and sat sentry. The last
time the offal had not been removed to at least a few

score yards from the campsite, the travelers had spent all night in the middle of what seemed a festival of brawling, screeching apes, all in mad competition for the rights to the finest scraps.

"Go to, Cadrach," she said crossly. "Dig the hole."

He gave her a quick sidelong look, then bent and began scraping at the moist soil. Pale wriggling things came up with each stroke of the hollowed reed spade, gleaming in the torchlight. When he had finished, Miriamele dropped in the leaf-wrapped bundle and Cadrach pushed the mud over it, then turned and began to make his way back toward the glow of the camp fire.

"Cadrach."

He turned slowly. "Yes, Princess?"

She took a few steps toward him. "I . . . I am sorry that Isgrimnur said what he did to you. At the nest." She lifted her hands helplessly. "He was worried, and he sometimes speaks without thinking. But he is a good man."

Cadrach's face was expressionless. It was as though he had drawn some curtain across his thoughts, leaving his eyes curiously flat in the torchlight. "Ah, yes. A good man. There are so few of those."

Miriamele shook her head. "That is not an excuse, I know. But please, Cadrach, surely you can understand why he was upset!"

"Of course. I can well understand it. I have lived with myself for many years, Lady—how can I fault someone else for feeling the same way, someone who doesn't even know all that I know?"

"Damn you," Miriamele snapped. "Why must you be this way? I don't hate you, Cadrach! I don't loathe you, even though we have caused trouble for each other!"

He stared at her for a moment, seeming to struggle with conflicting emotions. "No, my lady. You have treated me better than I deserve."

She knew better than to argue. "And I don't blame you at all for not wanting to go into that nest!"

He shook his head slowly. "No, Lady. Nor would any man, even your duke, if they knew . . ."

"Knew what?" she said sharply. "What happened to

you, Cadrach? Something more than what you told me about Pryrates—and about the book?"

The monk's mouth hardened. "I do not wish to speak of it."

"Oh, by Elysia's mercy," she said, frustrated. She took a few steps forward and reached out and grasped his hand. Cadrach flinched and tried to pull back, but she held him tightly. "Listen to me. If you hate yourself, others will hate you. Even a child knows that, and you are a learned man."

"And if a child is hated," he spat, "that child will grow to hate itself."

She did not understand what he meant. "But, please, Cadrach. You must forgive, starting with yourself. I cannot bear to see a friend so mistreated, even by himself."

The steady pressure with which the monk had tried to pull away suddenly slackened. "A friend?" he said roughly.

"A friend." Miriamele squeezed his hand and then released it. Cadrach pulled back a step, but went no further. "Now please, we must try to be kind to each other until we reach Josua, or we shall all go mad."

"Reach Josua . . ." The monk repeated her words without inflection. He was suddenly very distant.

"Of course." Miriamele started to walk toward the camp, then stopped again. "Cadrach?"

He did not reply for a moment. "What?"

"You know magic, don't you?" When he remained silent, she plunged on. "I mean, you know a great deal about it, at least—you've made that clear. But I think that you actually know how to do it."

"What are you talking about?" He sounded irritated, but there was a trace of fear in his words. "If you are talking about the fire-missiles, that was no magic at all. The Perdruinese invented that long ago, although they made it with a different sort of oil. They used it for sea-battles. . . ."

"Yes, it was a clever thing to do. But there is more than that to you, and you know it. Why else would you study things like . . . like that book. And I know all about Doctor Morgenes, so if you were part of his—what did you call it? The Scroll League. . . ?"

Cadrach made a gesture of annoyance. "The Art, my lady, is not some bag of wizard's tricks. It is a way of understanding things, of seeing how the world works just as surely as a builder understands a lever or a ramp."

"You see! You *do* know about it!"

"I do not 'do magic,' " he said firmly. "I have, once or twice, used the knowledge I have from my studies." Despite his straightforward tone, he could not meet her eyes. "But it is not what you think of as magic."

"But even so," Miriamele said, still eager, "think of the help you could be to Josua. Think of the aid we could give him. Morgenes is dead. Who else can advise the prince about Pryrates?"

Now Cadrach did look up. He looked hunted, like a cur backed into a corner. "Pryrates?" He laughed hollowly. "Do you think that I can be any help against Pryrates? And he is the smallest part of what is arrayed against you."

"All the more reason!" Miriamele reached out for his hand again, but the monk pulled it away. "Josua needs help, Cadrach. If you fear Pryrates, how much more do you fear the kind of world he will make if he and this Storm King are not defeated?"

At the sound of that terrible name, a muffled purr of thunder could be heard in the distance. Startled, Miriamele looked around, as though some vast, shadowy thing might be watching them. When she turned back, Cadrach was stumbling across the mud, headed back toward camp.

"Cadrach!"

"No more," he shouted. He kept his head lowered as he vanished into the shadowy undergrowth. She could hear him cursing as he made his way back across the treacherous mud.

Miriamele followed him to camp, but Cadrach refused all her attempts at conversation. She berated herself for having said the wrong thing, just when she had thought she was reaching him. What a mad, sad man he was! And, equally infuriating, in the confusion of their talk she had forgotten to ask him about her Pryrates-thought, the

one that had been tugging at her mind the other night—
something about her father, about death, about Pryrates
and Nisses' book. It still seemed important, but it might
be a long time until she could bring up the subject with
Cadrach again.

Despite the warm night, Miriamele rolled herself
tightly in her cloak when she lay down, but sleep would
not come. She lay half the night listening to the swamp's
strange, incessant music. She also had to put up with the
continual misery of crawling and fluttering things, but the
bugs, annoying as they might be, were as nothing compared to the irritation of her restless thoughts.

To Miriamele's surprise and pleasure, the next day
brought a marked change in their surroundings. The trees
were less thickly twined, and in places the flatboat slid
out from the humid tangle onto wide shallow lagoons,
mirrors compromised only by the faint rippling of the
wind and the forests of swaying grasses which grew up
through the water.

Tiamak seemed pleased with their progress, and announced that they were very close to the Wran's outermost edge. However, their approaching escape did not
cure his weakness and fever, and the thin brown man
spent much of the morning slipping in and out of uncomfortable sleep, waking occasionally with a startled movement and a mouthful of wild jabber before slowly coming
back to his ordinary self.

In late afternoon, Tiamak's fever became stronger, and
his discomfort increased to the point where he sweated
and babbled continuously, experiencing only short spans
of lucidity. During one of these, the Wrannaman regained
his wits enough to play apothecary for himself. He asked
Miriamele to prepare for him a concoction of herbs, some
of which he pointed out where they grew along the watercourse, a flowering grass called quickweed and a ground-
hugging, oval-leafed creeper which, in his weakened
state, he could not name.

"And yellowroot, too," Tiamak said, panting shallowly.
He looked dreadful, his eyes red, his skin shiny with per-

spiration. Miriamele tried to keep her hands steady as she ground the ingredients already gathered on a flat stone she held in her lap. "Yellowroot, to speed the binding," he mumbled.

"Which is that?" she asked. "Does it grow here?"

"No. But it does not matter," Tiamak tried to smile, but the effort was too much, and instead he gritted his teeth and groaned quietly. "Some in my bag." He rolled his head ever so slightly in the direction of the sack he had appropriated in Village Grove, which now held all the belongings he had guarded so zealously.

"Cadrach, would you find it?" Miriamele called. "I'm afraid I'll spill what I have here."

The monk, who had been sitting at Camaris' feet while the old man poled, stepped gingerly across the rocking flatboat, avoiding Isgrimnur without a glance. He kneeled and began to lift out and examine the contents of the bag.

"Yellowroot," Miriamele said.

"Yes, I heard, Lady," Cadrach replied with a little of his old mocking tone. "A root. And I know that it is yellow, too ... thanks to my many years of study." Something that he felt beneath his fingers made him pause. His eyes narrowed, and he pulled from Tiamak's bag a package wrapped in leaves and tied with thin vines. Some of the covering had dried and peeled away. Miriamele could see a flash of something pale inside. "What is this?" Cadrach eased the wrappings back a little further. "A very old parchment ..." he began.

"No, you demon! You witch!"

The loud voice startled Miriamele so much that she dropped the blunt rock she had been using as a pestle; it bounced painfully on her boot and thumped down into the bottom of the boat. Tiamak, his eyes bulging, was struggling to lift himself.

"You won't have it!" he shouted. Flecks of spittle gathered at the corners of his mouth. "I knew you would come after it!"

"He's fever-mad!" Isgrimnur was more than a little alarmed. "Don't let him tip the boat over."

"It's just Cadrach, Tiamak," Miriamele said soothingly,

but she, too, was startled by the look of hatred on the Wrannaman's face. "He's just trying to find the yellowroot."

"I know who it is," Tiamak snarled. "And I know just what he is, too, and what he wants. Curse you, demonmonk! You wait until I am ill to steal my parchment! Well, you may not have it! It is mine! I bought it with my own coin!"

"Just put it back, Cadrach," Miriamele urged. "It will make him stop raving."

The monk, whose initial look of startlement had changed to something even more unsettled—and, to Miriamele, unsettling as well—slowly eased the leaf-wrapped bundle back into the sack, then handed the whole thing to Miriamele.

"Here." His voice was once again strangely flat. "You take out what he wants. I cannot be trusted."

"Oh, Cadrach," she said, "don't be foolish. Tiamak is ill. He doesn't know what he's saying."

"I know." The Wrannaman's wide eyes were still fixed on the monk. "He gave himself away. I knew then that he was after it."

"For the love of Aedon," Isgrimnur growled, disgusted. "Just give him something to make him sleep. Even *I* know the monk wasn't trying to steal anything."

"Even you, Rimmersman?" Cadrach murmured, but with none of his usual sharpness. Rather, there was an echo of some great hopelessness in the monk's voice, and something else, too—some peculiar edge that Miriamele could not identify.

Worried and confused, she turned her concentration onto the search for Tiamak's yellowroot. The Wrannaman, his hair damp and tousled by sweat, continued to glare at Cadrach like a maddened blue jay who had found a squirrel sniffing about his nest.

Miriamele had thought the entire incident merely the product of Tiamak's illness, but that night she woke up suddenly in the camp they had made on a rare dry sandbank, and saw Cadrach—who had been delegated the first watch—rummaging through Tiamak's bag.

"What are you doing?!" She crossed the camp in a few swift paces. Despite her anger, she kept her voice low so as not to wake any of the rest of her companions from their sleep. She could not escape the feeling that somehow Cadrach was her responsibility alone, and that the others should not be brought in if she could avoid it.

"Nothing," the monk grumbled, but his guilty face belied him. Miriamele reached forward and plunged her hand into the sack, closing her fingers on his own and the leaf-wrapped parchment.

"I should have known better," she said, full of fury. "Is there truth to what Tiamak said? Have you been trying to steal his belongings, now that he is too sick to protect them?"

Cadrach snapped back like a wounded animal. "You are no better than all the rest, with your talk of friendship! At the first moment, you turn on me, just like Isgrimnur."

His words stung, but Miriamele was still angry to find him doing this low thing after she had given him her trust. "You haven't answered my question."

"You are a fool," he snarled. "If I wanted to steal something from him, why would I wait until he had been saved from the ghant's nest?!" He pulled his hand from the sack, bringing hers with it, then took the package and thrust it into her hands. "Here! I was merely interested in what it could be, and why he turned *goirach* . . . why he became so angry. I had never seen it before—didn't even know that it was there! You keep it, then, Princess. Safe from grubby little thieves like me!"

"But you could have asked him," she said, more than a little ashamed now that the heat had passed, and angry to feel that way. "Not come creeping after it when everyone was asleep."

"Oh, yes, asked him! You saw the kindly way he looked at me when I merely touched it! Do you have any idea what it is, my headstrong lady? Do you?"

"No. Nor will I until Tiamak tells me." Hesitantly, she stared at the cylindrical object. In other circumstances, she knew, she would have been the first to try to find out what the Wrannaman was protecting. Now, she was caught by her own high-handedness, and she had offended the monk as well. "I will keep it safe, and I will not look at it," she said slowly. "When Tiamak is well, I will ask him to show it to us."

Cadrach stared at her for a long moment. His moonlit features, touched with crimson by the last few embers of the fire, were almost frightening. "Very well, my lady," he whispered. She thought she could hear his voice hardening like ice. "Very well. By all means keep it out of the hands of thieves." He turned and walked to his cloak, then dragged it to the edge of the sand, far from the others. "Keep watch, then, Princess Miriamele. Make sure no evil men come near. I am going to sleep." He lay down, becoming only another lump of shadow.

Miriamele sat listening to the night noises of the swamp. Although the monk did not speak again, she could almost feel his unsleeping presence in the darkness a few short steps away. Something raw and painful in him had been exposed again, something that, for the last few weeks, had been almost completely hidden. Whatever it was, she had thought it might have been exorcised after Cadrach's long revelatory night on Firannos Bay. Now Miriamele found herself wishing desperately that she had slept through the night tonight and not awakened until morning, when the light of day would have made everything safe and ordinary.

The Wran fell away at last, not in a single broad stroke, but with the gradual dwindling of trees and narrowing of waterways, until finally Miriamele and her companions found themselves floating across an open scrubland crisscrossed with small channels. The world was wide again, something that spread from horizon to horizon. She had grown so used to the hemming-in of her vision that she found it almost uncomfortable to be confronted with so much space.

In some ways, the last stage of the Wran was the most treacherous, since they had to carry the boat over land more frequently than before. Once, Isgrimnur became stuck in a waist-deep sandhole, and was only rescued by the combined efforts of Miriamele and Camaris.

The Lake Thrithing lay before them, a vast expanse of low hills and, except for the ever-present grass, sparse vegetation. Trees clung near to the hillsides; but for a few copses of tall pines, they were dwarfish, barely distinguishable from bushes. In the late afternoon light it seemed a lonely, windswept land, a place where few creatures and no people would live by choice.

Tiamak had at last brought them beyond the bounds of his territorial knowledge, and they found increasing difficulty in choosing streams wide enough to carry the boat. When the latest channel narrowed beyond the point of navigability, they clambered from the boat and stood silent for a while, collars lifted against the cold breeze.

"It looks as though it's time to walk." Isgrimnur gazed out across the wilderness to the north. "This is the Lake Thrithing, after all, so at least there'll be drinking water, especially after this year's weather."

"But what about Tiamak?" Miriamele asked. The potion she had brewed for the Wrannaman had certainly helped, but it had not provided a miraculous cure: although he was standing, he was weak and his color was not good.

Isgrimnur shrugged. "Don't know. I suppose we could wait a few days until he gets better, but I hate to spend any more time than we need to out here. P'raps we could make some kind of sling."

Camaris abruptly stooped and put his long hands under Tiamak's armpits, startling the Wrannaman into a whoop of surprise. With an astounding absence of effort, the old man lifted Tiamak high and lowered him onto his shoulders; the Wrannaman, who began to understand in midair, spread his knees to either side of Camaris' neck, settling like a pickaback child.

The duke grinned. "There's your answer, looks like. I don't know how long he can go, but maybe at least until we can find better shelter. That would be more than fine."

They took their belongings from the boat, packing them in the few cloth sacks they had brought out of Village Grove. Tiamak took his own bag and clutched it in the arm he was not using to hold onto Camaris. He had not spoken of the bag and its contents again since the incident in the boat, and Miriamele had not yet felt inclined to press him to reveal what he carried.

With more regret than she had expected, Miriamele and the others bade a silent farewell to the flatboat and marched out onto the fringes of the Lake Thrithing.

Camaris proved more than equal to the task of carrying Tiamak. Although he stopped to rest when the others did, and moved very slowly through the few patches of swampy ground that still remained, he kept the same pace as the less burdened members of the company and did not seem inordinately tired. Miriamele could not help staring at him from time to time, full of awe. If he was like this as an old man, what prodigious feats must he have performed when he was in the bloom of youth? It was enough to make one believe that all the old legends, even the wildest ones, might be true after all.

Despite the old man's uncomplaining strength, Isgrimnur insisted on taking the Wrannaman onto his own shoulders for the last hour until sunset. When they stopped at last to make their camp, the duke was puffing and blowing, and looked as though he regretted his decision.

They made camp while the light was still in the sky, finding a spot in a grove of low trees and building a fire from deadwood. The snow that had covered much of the north had apparently not lingered on the Lake Thrithing, but as the sun finally dipped below the horizon, the evening grew cold enough to keep them all huddled by the fire. Miriamele was suddenly grateful she had not discarded her tattered, travel-stained acolyte's habit.

Chill wind sawed in the branches close over their heads. The surrounded feeling of the Wran had been replaced by a sensation of being dangerously exposed, but at least the ground beneath them was dry: that, Miriamele decided, was something to be thankful for, anyway.

*   *   *

Tiamak was a little better the next day, and was able to walk most of the morning before having to be hoisted onto Camaris' broad shoulders again. Isgrimnur, out of the confining and confusing swamps, was almost his old self, full of songs of questionable taste—Miriamele enjoyed counting how many verses he finished of each before stopping, flustered, to beg her pardon—and stories of battles and wonders he had seen. Cadrach, on the other hand, was as silent as he had been since they had escaped the *Eadne Cloud.* When spoken to, he responded, and he was strangely courteous to Isgrimnur, acting almost as if they had never had harsh words, but the rest of the day's trip he might have been as mute as Camaris for all he contributed. Miriamele did not like the hollow look of him, but nothing she said or did changed his calm, withdrawn manner, and at last she gave up.

The low-lying ravel of the Wran had long since disappeared behind them: even from the highest of the hills, there was little to see back on the southern horizon but a dark smear. As they set up camp in another copse of trees, Miriamele wondered how far they had come—and, more important, how long a journey still awaited them.

"How far are we going to have to walk?" she asked Isgrimnur as they shared a bowl of stew made with dried Village Grove fish. "Do you know?"

He shook his head. "Not sure, my lady. More than fifty leagues, perhaps sixty or seventy. A long, long hike, I'm afraid."

She made a worried face. "That could take weeks."

"What else can we do?" he said, then smiled. "In any case, Princess, we are far better off than we were—and closer to Josua."

Miriamele felt a momentary pang. "If he is really there."

"He is, young one, he is." Isgrimnur squeezed her hand in his broad paw. "We've come through the worst."

Something awakened Miriamele abruptly in the bruised light just before dawn. She had scarcely an instant to gather

her wits before she was grabbed by the arm and jerked up-right. A triumphant voice spoke in rapid Nabbanai.

"Here she is. Dressed like a monk, Lord, as you said."

A dozen men on horseback, several of them carrying torches, had surrounded them. Isgrimnur, who was sitting on the ground with one of the horsemen's lances at his throat, groaned.

"It was my watch!" the duke said bitterly. "My watch . . ."

The man who held Miriamele's arm pulled her a few steps across the copse toward one of the riders, a tall fig-ure in a capacious hood, his face invisible in the gray of night's end. She felt a claw of ice clutch at her.

"So," the rider said in accented Westerling. "So." De-spite the strange mushiness of his speech, his voice was unmistakably smug.

Miriamele's horror was warmed a little by anger. "Take off your hood, my lord. You have no need to play such a game with me."

"Truly?" The rider's hand rose. "Do you wish to see what you have done, then?" He pushed the hood back with a sweeping gesture like a traveling player's. "Am I as beautiful as you remember me?" asked Aspitis.

Miriamele, despite the soldier's restraining hand, stepped back. It was hard not to. The earl's face, once so handsome that, after their first meeting, it had haunted her dreams for days, was now a distorted ruin. His fine nose was a blob of flesh skewed to one side like a lump of ill-handled clay. His left cheekbone had been cracked like an egg and dented in-ward, so that the torchlight made a shadow in the deep hol-low. All around his eyes black blood had gathered beneath the skin and the rumple of scars, as though he wore a mask. His hair was still beautiful, still golden.

Miriamele swallowed. "I have seen worse," she said quietly.

Half of Aspitis Preves' mouth curled in an eerie grin, displaying the stumps of teeth. "I am glad to hear it, my sweet lady Miriamele, since you will be waking up to it the rest of your life. Bind her!"

"No!" It was Cadrach who shouted, lurching up from

where he lay in the darkness. A moment later, an arrow shivered in the gnarled trunk of a tree, a handspan from his face.

"If he moves again, kill him," said Aspitis calmly. "Perhaps I should let you kill him anyway—he was as responsible as she for what happened to me, to my ship." He shook his head slowly, savoring the moment. "Ah, you are such fools, Princess, you and your monk. Once you had slipped away into the Wran, what did you think? That I would let you go? That I would forget what you had done to me?" He leaned forward, fixing her with bloodshot eyes. "Where else would you go but north, back to the rest of your friends? But you forget, my lady, that this is *my* fiefdom." He chuckled. "My castle on Lake Eadne is only a few leagues away. I have been combing these hills, hunting you for days. I knew you would come."

She felt miserably numb. "How did you get off the ship?"

Aspitis' crooked smirk was horrible. "I was slow to realize what had happened, it is true, but after you had gone and my men found me, I had them kill the treacherous Niskie—Aedon burn her! She had finished her devil's work. She did not even try to escape. After that, the rest of the kilpa went back over the side—I do not think they would have had the courage to attack without the sea witch's spell. We had enough men to row my poor damaged *Eadne Cloud* to Spenit." He slapped his hands on his thighs. "Enough. You are mine again. Save your prattling questions until I ask for them."

Full of anger and sorrow over Gan Itai's fate, Miriamele struggled toward him, dragging the soldier who gripped her arm a full pace forward. "God's curse on you! What kind of man are you? What kind of knight? You, with all your talk about the fifty noble families of Nabban."

"And you, a king's daughter, who willingly gave herself to me—who brought me to her bed? Are you so high and pure?"

She was ashamed that Isgrimnur and the others should hear, but a sort of high, clear anger followed, sharpening her thoughts. She spat on the ground. "Will you fight for me?" she demanded. "Here, before your people and mine? Or will you take me as a sneak thief, as you tried to take me before—with lies, and with force used against those who were your guests?"

The earl's eyes narrowed to slits. "Fight for you? What nonsense is this? Why should I? You are mine, by capture and maidenhead."

"I will never be yours," she said in her haughtiest tones. "You are lower than the Thrithings-men, who at least fight to claim their brides."

"Fight, fight, what trick is this?" Aspitis glared. "Who would fight for you? One of these old men? The monk? The little swamp boy?"

Miriamele let her eyes fall closed for a moment, struggling to contain her fury. He was vile, but this was not the moment to let emotions rule her. "Anyone in this camp can beat you, Aspitis. You are not a man at all." She looked around, making sure that she had the attention of the earl's soldiers. "You are a stealer of women, but you are no man."

Aspitis' osprey-hilted blade slid from its sheath with a metallic hiss. He paused. "No, I see your game, Princess. You are a clever one. You think to make me so maddened that I kill you here." He laughed. "Ah, to think that a woman exists who would rather die than wed the Earl of Eadne." He lifted his hand and touched his shattered face. "Or rather, to think that you felt that way even *before* you did this to me." He held his sword out; the point wavered in the air not a cubit from her neck. "No, I know what punishment will best pay you back, and that is marriage. My castle has a tower that will keep you well. Within the first hour, you will know its every stone. Think how it will feel when years have passed."

Miriamele lifted her chin. "So you will not fight for me."

Aspitis slapped his fist on his thigh. "Enough of this! I grow weary of the joke."

"Do you hear?" Miriamele turned toward the rest of Aspitis' company, who sat, waiting. "Your master is a coward."

"Silence!" Aspitis shouted. "I will whip you myself."

"That old man can thrash you," she said, pointing to

Camaris. The old knight sat wrapped in his blanket, watching wide-eyed. He had made no move since Aspitis and his soldiers had arrived. "Isgrimnur," she called, "give the old man your sword."

"Princess . . ." Isgrimnur's voice was rough with worry. "Let me . . ."

"*Do it!* Let the earl's men see him cut to ribbons by an old, old man. Then they will know why their master has to steal women."

Isgrimnur, keeping a careful eye on the watching soldiers, pulled Kvalnir out from beneath his sack of belongings. The buckles of the sword belt clinked as he slid it across the ground toward Camaris. For a moment, that was the only sound.

"My lord?" the soldier who held Miriamele said hesitantly. "What. . . ?"

"Shut your mouth," Aspitis snapped as he dismounted. He walked to Miriamele and grabbed her face with his hand, staring at her intently for a moment. Then, before she had a chance to react, he leaned forward suddenly and kissed her with his broken mouth. "We will have many interesting nights." The earl then turned to Camaris. "Go on, put it on so I can kill you. Then I will finish the rest of you, too. But I will allow you to defend yourselves or run as you choose." He turned and looked at Miriamele. "I am, after all, a gentleman."

Camaris stared at the sword by his feet as though it were a serpent.

"Put it on!" Miriamele urged.

Elysia's mercy, she thought frantically, *what if he won't do it! What if, after all this, he won't do it?*

"For the love of God, man, put it on," Isgrimnur shouted. The old man looked at him, then bent and picked up the sword belt. He withdrew Kvalnir and let the belt and sheath slide back to the ground. He held it loosely, unwillingly.

"*Matra sá Duos,*" Aspitis said disgustedly, "he does not even know how to swing a sword." He unbelted his robe and let it fall, revealing a surcoat of yellow-gray trimmed in black, then took a few steps toward Camaris, who looked up bemusedly. "I will kill him quickly,

Miriamele," the earl declared. "*You* are the cruel one, to make an old man fight." He raised his weapon, which gleamed beneath the white dawn sky, then aimed a cut at Camaris' unprotected neck.

Kvalnir rose awkwardly and Aspitis' blade rebounded. The earl, with a noise of irritation, swung again. Once more his steel clanked against the duke's sword and flew back. Miriamele heard her warder grunt in soft surprise at his master's frustration.

"You see!" she said, and forced herself to laugh, though there was no mirth in her. "The coward earl cannot even best a man in his dotage."

Aspitis attacked more strongly. Camaris, moving almost like a man sleepwalking, kept Kvalnir weaving before him in deceptively slow arcs. Several more wicked blows were deflected.

"I see your old man *has* wielded a sword." The earl was beginning to breathe a little more heavily. "That is good. I will not feel that I have been forced to kill one who cannot defend himself."

"Fight back!" Miriamele shouted, but Camaris would not. Instead, as his movements became more fluid, ancient reflexes gradually awakening after a long sleep, he merely defended himself more diligently, blocking every thrust, guiding every slash away, spinning a web of steel that Aspitis could not breach.

The fighting was in deadly earnest now. It was plain that the Earl of Eadne and Drina was a very good swordsman, and he in turn had quickly grasped the fact that his opponent was something unusual. Aspitis eased his attack, pursuing a more cautious, probing strategy, but he did not back down from the challenge. Something, whether pride or some deeper, more animalistic urge, had caught him up. Camaris, meanwhile, seemed to fight only because he was forced to. Miriamele thought she saw several times when he could have pressed his own attack but chose not to, waiting until his enemy came at him once more.

Aspitis feinted, then slid in a thrust beneath Camaris' guard, but somehow Kvalnir was there to push the earl's blade aside. Aspitis cut at the old man's feet, but Camaris shuffled back without visible haste, keeping his balance firm and his shoulders level even as he avoided the earl's blow. He was like water, flowing always to where there was an opening, giving way but never breaking, absorbing every blow from Aspitis and directing its force up or down, to one side or the other. A thin film of sweat broke on the old man's forehead, but his face remained calmly regretful, as though he were being forced to sit and watch two of his friends trade unpleasant words.

The duel went on for what seemed to Miriamele a dreadfully long time. Although she knew that her heart was racing, each beat seemed to come long moments apart. The two men, the crack-faced earl and the tall, long-legged Camaris, worked their way out from the stand of pine trees and down onto the hillside, circling their way along the weedy slope like two moths revolving around a candle, their blades whirling and flickering beneath the gray sky. As the earl pressed forward once again, Camaris stepped in a hole and lost his balance; Aspitis took advantage of the opportunity and landed a swipe across the old man's arm, drawing a streak of blood. Behind her, Miriamele heard Isgrimnur curse in heartbreaking impotence.

The cut seemed to awaken something in Camaris. Although he still would not attack aggressively, he began to beat back the earl's attacks with greater strength, striking hard enough to make the rattle of steel echo across the plains of the Lake Thrithing. Miriamele worried that it would not be enough, since despite his almost unbelievable fortitude, he seemed to be tiring at last. He stumbled again, this time with no hole to blame, and Aspitis brought home a thrust that skimmed off Kvalnir and found Camaris' shoulder, freeing more blood. But the earl was flagging, too: after a swift flurry in which several of his strokes were blocked, he took a few steps back, panting, and bent low to the ground as if he might collapse. Miriamele saw him pick something from the ground.

"Camaris! Watch out!" she screamed.

Aspitis flung the handful of dirt in the old man's face and followed it with a swift and aggressive attack, seeking to end the combat with a single stroke. Camaris staggered backward, clawing at his eyes as Aspitis closed with him. A moment later, the earl fell to his knees, yowling.

Camaris, his greater reach enabling him to extend past the earl's outstretched blade, had struck his opponent a flat blow across the upper arm, but the blade had bounced and continued upward, slashing diagonally across the earl's forehead. Aspitis, his face quickly vanishing behind a sheet of blood, scrabbled across the ground toward Camaris, still waving his blade before him. The old man, who was rubbing the dirt from his watering eyes, stepped aside and brought the hilt of his sword down atop the earl's head. Aspitis dropped like a maul-slaughtered ox.

Miriamele pulled free from the grip of her thunderstruck guard and dashed down the hillside. Camaris sank to the ground, gasping for breath. He looked tired and vaguely unhappy, like a child asked to do too much. Miriamele glanced at him quickly to make sure his wounds were not dangerous, then took Kvalnir from his unresisting grasp and kneeled down beside Aspitis. The earl was breathing, too, although shallowly. She turned him over, staring for a moment at his bloody, shattered-doll face . . . and something changed inside of her. A bubble of hatred and fear that had been in her since the *Eadne Cloud,* a bubble that had grown chokingly large at finding Aspitis still pursuing her, abruptly burst. Suddenly, he seemed so small. He was nothing important at all, just a tattered, damaged thing—no different than the cloak draped over a chair-back that had given her the screaming night-terrors when she was a small child. Morning's light had come, and the demon had become a rumpled cloak again.

A sort of smile crossed Miriamele's face. She pressed the sword blade against the earl's throat.

"You men!" she shouted at Aspitis' soldiers. "Do you want to explain to Benigaris how his best friend was killed?"

Isgrimnur stood, pushing away the lance-point of the soldier who had held him.

"Do you?" Miriamele demanded.

None of the earl's men spoke.

"Then give us your bows—all of them. And four horses."

"We will not give you any horses, witch!" one of the soldiers shouted angrily.

"So be it. Then you can take Aspitis back with his gullet slit and tell Duke Benigaris it was done by an old man and a girl, while you stood watching—that is, if you get away unharmed, and you will have to kill us all to do that."

"Do not bargain with them," Cadrach shouted suddenly. There was desperation in his tone. "Kill the monster. Kill him!"

"Be quiet." Miriamele wondered if the monk was trying to convince the soldiers that the danger to their master was real. If so, he was a fine actor: he sounded remarkably sincere.

The soldiers looked at each other worriedly. Isgrimnur took advantage of the moment's confusion to begin relieving them of their bows and arrows. After the Rimmersman growled at him, Cadrach scrambled forward to help. Several of the men cursed them and looked as though they wished to resist, but no one made the move that would have sparked open conflict. When Isgrimnur and the monk each had an arrow nocked on a bow, the soldiers began to talk angrily among themselves, but Miriamele could see that the fight had gone out of them.

"Four horses," she said calmly. "I will do you a favor and ride with the man that *this* scum," she prodded Aspitis' still form, "called a 'swamp boy.' Otherwise you would be leaving us five."

After more arguing, Aspitis' troop turned over four horses, first removing the saddlebags. When riders and baggage were redistributed upon the remaining horses, two of the earl's household guard came forward and lifted their liege-lord from the ground, then draped him unceremoniously across the saddle of one of the remaining horses. His soldiers had to ride two-to-a-mount, and looked positively embarrassed as the little caravan rode off.

"And if he lives," Miriamele shouted after them, "remind him of what happened!"

The mounted company vanished quickly, riding east into the hills.

Wounds were tended, the newly-acquired horses were loaded with the travelers' scant baggage, and by the middle of the day they were on their way once more. Miriamele felt curiously light-headed, as though she had just woken up from a terrible dream to find a sunny spring morning outside her window. Camaris had returned to his normal placidity; the old man seemed scarcely the worse for his experience. Cadrach did not speak much, but that was no different than any day of the last few.

Aspitis had been a shadow at the back of Miriamele's mind since the night of the storm and her escape from the earl's ship. Now that shadow was gone. As she rode across the hilly Thrithings-country with Tiamak nodding in the saddle before her, she almost felt like singing.

They covered several leagues that afternoon. When they stopped for the night, Isgrimnur, too, was in an excellent mood.

"We shall make far better time now, Princess." He was grinning in his beard. If he thought less of her now that Aspitis had revealed her shame, he was too much a gentleman to show it. "By Dror's Mallet, did you see Camaris? Did you see him? Like a man half his age."

"Yes." She smiled. The duke was a good man. "I saw him, Isgrimnur. It was like an old song. No, it was better."

He woke her in the morning. She could tell by his face that something was wrong.

"Is it Tiamak?" She had a sickened feeling. They had come through so much! Surely the little man had been getting better?

The duke shook his head. "It's the monk. He's gone."

"Cadrach?" Miriamele was not prepared for that. She rubbed her head, fighting to wake up. "What do you mean, gone?"

"Gone away. Took one of the horses. He left a note." Isgrimnur pointed to a piece of the Village Grove cloth which lay on the ground near where she had been sleep-

ing; the furl of cloth had been anchored by a rock against
the stiff hillside breeze.

Where Miriamele's feelings about Cadrach's flight should
have been, there was nothing. She lifted the stone and
spread the sheet of pale fabric. Yes, he had written this: she
had seen Cadrach's hand before. It looked as though he had
done his writing with the burned tip of a twig.

What could have been so important to say, she wondered, *that he spent so much time writing a note before he
left?*

> *Princess,*

it said,

> *I cannot go with you to Josua. I do not belong
> with those people. Do not blame yourself. No one
> has been kinder to me than you, even after you
> knew me for what I am.
> I fear that things are worse than you know, much
> worse. I wish there was something more that I
> could do, but I am unable to help anyone.*

He had not signed it.

"What 'things'?" Isgrimnur asked, irritated. He was
reading over her shoulder. "What does he mean, 'things
are worse than you know'?"

Miriamele shrugged helplessly. "Who can say?" *Deserted again,* was all she could think.

"Maybe I was too hard on him," the duke said gruffly.
"But that's no cause to steal a horse and ride off."

"He was always afraid. Ever since I have known him.
It's hard to live with fear all the time."

"Well, we can't waste tears on him," Isgrimnur grumbled. "We have troubles of our own."

"No," Miriamele said, folding the note, "we shouldn't
waste tears."

20

Travelers and Messengers

"I **have not** been here for many seasons," Aditu said. "Many, many seasons."

She stopped and raised her hands, circling the fingers in a complicated gesture; her slim body swayed like a dowser's rod. Simon watched in wonder and more than a little apprehension. He was quickly becoming sober.

"Shouldn't you come down?" he asked.

Aditu only glanced down at him, a moonlit smile playing around the corners of her mouth, then turned her eyes upward to the sky once more. She took a few more steps along the Observatory's slender, crumbling parapet. "Shame to the House of Year-Dancing," she said. "We should have done more to preserve this place. It grieves me to see it fallen to pieces."

Simon did not think she sounded very grieved. "Geloë calls this place the Observatory," Simon said. "Why is that?"

"I do not know. What is 'observatory'? It is not a word that I know in your tongue."

"Father Strangyeard said it's a place like they used to have in Nabban in the days of the Imperators—a tall building where they look at the stars and try to figure out what will happen."

Aditu laughed and raised one foot in the air to take off her boot, then lowered it and did the same with the other, as calmly as though she stood on the ground beside Simon instead of twenty cubits in the air on a thin cornice of stone. She tossed the boots down. They thumped softly on the damp grass. "Then she is making fun, I think, although there is some meaning behind her jest. No one looked at the stars here, except as one would look at them anywhere. This was the place of the *Rhao iye-Sama'an*— the Master Witness."

"Master Witness?" Simon wished she wouldn't move along the slippery parapet so quickly. For one thing, it forced him to walk briskly just to stay within hearing. For another . . . well, it *was* dangerous, even if she didn't think so. "What's that?"

"You know what a Witness is, Simon. Jiriki gave you his mirror. That is a minor Witness, and there are many of those still in existence. There were only a few Master Witnesses, each more or less bound to a place—the Pool of Three Depths in Asu'a, the Speakfire in Hikehikayo, the Green Column in Jhiná-T'seneí—and most of those are broken or ruined or lost. Here at Sesuad'ra it was a great stone beneath the ground, a stone called the Earth-Drake's Eye. Earth-Drake is another name—it is difficult to explain the differences between the two in your tongue—for the Greater Worm who bites at his own tail," she explained. "We built this entire place on top of that stone. It was not quite a Master Witness—in fact, it was not even a Witness by itself, but such was its potency that a minor Witness like my brother's mirror would be a Master Witness if used here."

Simon's head was whirling with names and ideas. "What does that *mean,* Aditu?" he asked, trying to keep from sounding cross. He had been doing his best to remain calm and well-spoken once the wine had begun to wear off. It seemed important that she see how much he had grown in the months since they had last met.

"A minor Witness will lead you onto the Road of Dreams, but will usually show you only those you know, or those who are looking for you." She raised her left leg and leaned backward, her back arched like a drawn longbow as she bent gracefully into balance, looking for all the world like a little girl playing on a waist-high fence. "A Master Witness, if used by someone who knew the ways of it, could look on anyone or anything, and sometimes into other times and . . . *other* places."

Simon could not help remembering the night-visions of his vigil, as well as what he had seen when he had brought Jiriki's mirror to this place on a later night. He pondered this as he watched Aditu tilt backward until her palms touched the crumbling stone. A moment later, both her feet were in the air as she swayed upside down, standing on her hands.

"*Aditu!*" Simon said sharply, then tried to make his voice calm. "Shouldn't we go see Josua now?"

She laughed again, a swift sound of pure animal pleasure. "My frightened Seoman. No, there is no need to hurry to Josua, as I told you on the way here. The tidings from my folk can wait until morning. Give your prince a night of rest from worries. From what I saw of him, he needs some relief from woe and care." She inched along on her hands. Her hair, unbound, hung down over her face in a white cloud.

Simon felt sure she could no longer see what she was doing. It frustrated him and made him more than a little angry. "Then why did you come all the way from Jao é-Tinukai'i, if it wasn't important?" He stopped following. "Aditu! What are you doing this for?! If you've come to talk to Josua, then let's go and talk to Josua!"

"I did not say it was not important, Seoman," she replied. There was something of her old mocking tone, but there was a hint of something sharper, almost angry. "I merely said that it would best wait until tomorrow. And that is what will happen." She brought her knees down between her elbows and delicately placed her feet between her hands. Then she lifted her arms and stood up all in one motion, as though preparing to dive out into empty space. "So until then I will spend my time as *I* please, no matter what a young mortal might think."

Simon was stung. "You've been sent to bring news to the prince, but you'd rather do tumbling tricks."

Aditu was wintery-cool. "In fact, if I had been given my choice, I would not be here at all. I would have ridden with my brother to Hernystir."

"Well, why didn't you?"

"Likimeya willed otherwise."

So quickly that Simon barely had time to draw in a surprised breath, she bent, catching the parapet in one long-fingered hand, then dropped over the edge. She found a grip on the pale stone wall with her free hand and lodged the toe of one bare foot while probing with the other. She descended the rest of the way as quickly and effortlessly as a squirrel skittering down a tree trunk.

"Let us go inside," she said.

Simon laughed and felt his anger ease.

Standing beside the Sitha made the Observatory seem even eerier. The shadowed staircases which wound up the walls of the cylindrical room made him think of the insides of some huge animal. The tiles, even in the near-darkness, glimmered faintly, and seemed to be assembled in patterns that would not quite lie still.

It was odd to realize that Aditu was almost as much a youngling as he, since the Sithi had built this place long before her birth. Jiriki had once said that he and his sister were "children of the Exile," which Simon understood to mean that they had been born after the fall of Asu'a five centuries ago—a short time indeed in Sithi terms. But Simon had also met Amerasu, and *she* had come to Osten Ard before a single stone had been set on another stone anywhere in the land. And if his own vigil-night dream had been correct, Amerasu's elder Utuk'ku had stood in this very building when the two tribes had separated. It was disturbing to think of anything living as long as First Grandmother or the Norn Queen.

But the most disturbing thing of all was that the Norn Queen, unlike Amerasu, was *still* alive, still powerful ... and she seemed to have nothing but hatred for Simon and his mortal kind.

He did not like thinking about that—did not, in fact, like thinking about the Norn Queen at all. It was almost easier to understand crazed Ineluki and his violent anger than the spiderlike patience of Utuk'ku, someone who would wait a thousand years or more, full of brooding malice, for some obscure revenge. . . .

"And what did you think of war, Seoman Snowlock?" Aditu asked suddenly. He had sketched for her the bare outlines of the recent struggle as they exchanged news during their walk to the Observatory.

He considered. "We fought hard. It was a wonderful victory. We didn't expect it."

"No, what did *you* think?"

Simon took a moment before replying. "It was horrible."

"Yes, it is." Aditu took a few steps away from him, sliding into a spot beneath the wall where the moonlight did not penetrate, vanishing into shadow. "It is horrible."

"But you just said you wanted to go to war in Hernystir with Jiriki!"

"No. I said I wanted to be with them. That is not the same thing at all, Seoman. I could have been one more rider, one more bow, one more set of eyes. We are very few, we Zida'ya—even mustered together riding out of Jao é-Tinukai'i, with the Houses of Exile reunited. Very few. And none of us wished to go into battle."

"But you Sithi have been in wars," Simon protested. "I know that's true."

"Only to protect ourselves. And once or twice in our history, as my mother and brother are doing in the west now, we have fought to protect those who stood by us in our own need." She sounded very serious now. "But even now, Seoman, we have only taken up our arms because the Hikeda'ya brought the war to *us*. They entered our home and killed my father and First Grandmother, and many more of our folk as well. Do not think that we rush out to fight for mortals at the waving of a sword. These are strange days, Seoman—and you know that as well as I."

Simon took a few steps forward and tripped on a piece of broken stone. He bent to rub his toe, which throbbed painfully. "S'Bloody Tree!" he cursed under his breath.

"It is hard for you to see here at night, Seoman," she said. "I am sorry. We will go now."

Simon did not want to be babied. "In a moment. I'm

well." He gave the toe a final squeeze. "Why is Utuk'ku helping Ineluki?"

Aditu appeared from out of the moon-shadow and took his hand in her cool fingers. She seemed troubled. "Let us talk outside." She led him out the door. Her long hair lifted and fluttered in the wind, caressing his face as he walked beside her. It had a strong but pleasing scent, savory-sweet as pine bark.

When they were out on open ground once more, she took his other hand in hers and fixed him with her bright eyes, which seemed to gleam amber in the moonlight. "That is most certainly not the place to name their names, nor to think of them too much," she said firmly, then smiled a wicked smile. "Besides, I do not think I should let as dangerous a mortal boy as you be alone with me in a dark place. Oh, the tales they tell of you around your camp, Seoman Snowlock."

He was irritated but not altogether displeased. "Whoever 'they' are, they don't know what they're talking about."

"Ah, but you are a strange beast, Seoman." Without another word, she leaned forward and kissed him—not a short, chaste touch as she had given him at their parting many weeks ago, but a warm lover's kiss that sent a shiver of amazement running up his back. Her lips were cool and sweet as morning rose petals.

Far before he would have wished to stop, Aditu gently pulled away. "That little mortal girl liked kissing you, Seoman." Her smile returned, mocking, insolent. "It is an odd thing to do, is it not?"

Simon shook his head, at a loss.

Aditu took his arm and tugged him into motion, falling into step beside him. She bent to pick up the boots she had discarded, then they walked a little farther through the wet grass beside the Observatory wall. She hummed a brief snatch of melody before speaking. "What does Utuk'ku want, you asked?"

Simon, confused by what had happened, did not respond.

"That I could not tell you—not with certainty. She is

the oldest thinking creature in all of Osten Ard, Seoman, and she is far more than twice as old as the next most ancient. Be assured, her ways are strange and subtle beyond even the understanding of anyone except perhaps First Grandmother. But if I had to guess, I would say this: she longs for Unbeing."

"What does that mean?" Simon was beginning to wonder if he was truly sober after all, for the world was slowly spinning and he wanted to lie down and sleep.

"If she wished death," Aditu said, "then that would be oblivion just for herself. She is tired of living, Seoman, but she is *eldest*. Never forget that. As long as songs have been sung in Osten Ard, and longer, Utuk'ku has lived. She alone of any living thing saw the lost home that birthed our kind. I do not think she can bear to think of others living when she is gone. She cannot destroy everything, much as she might desire to, but perhaps she hopes to help create the greatest cataclysm possible—that is, to assure that as many living folk accompany her into oblivion as she can drag with her."

Simon stopped, horrified. "That's terrible!" he said with feeling.

Aditu shrugged, a sinuous gesture. She had a lovely neck. "Utuk'ku *is* terrible. She is mad, Seoman, although it is a madness as tightly woven and intricate as the finest *juya'ha* ever spun. She was perhaps the cleverest of all the Gardenborn."

The moon had freed itself from a bank of clouds; it hung overhead like a harvester's scythe. Simon wanted to go to sleep—his head felt very heavy—but at the same time he was loath to give up this chance. It was so rare to find one of the Sithi in a mood to answer questions, and even better, to answer them directly, without the usual Sithi vagueness.

"Why did the Norns go into the north?"

Aditu bent and picked a sprig of some curling vine, white-flowered and dark-leaved. She knotted it in her hair so that it hung against her cheek. "The two families, Zida'ya and Hikeda'ya, had a disagreement. It concerned mortals. Utuk'ku's folk felt your kind to be animals—

worse than animals, actually, since we of the Garden do not kill any creature if we can avoid doing so. The Dawn Children did not agree with the Cloud Children. There were other things, too." She lifted her head to the moon. "Then Nenais'u and Drukhi died. That was the day the shadow fell, and it has never been lifted."

No sooner had he congratulated himself on catching Aditu in a forthright mood than she had begun to grow obscure.... Still, Simon did not linger over her unsatisfying explanation. He did not really want any more names to learn—he was already overwhelmed with all the things she had told him tonight; in any case, he had another purpose in asking. "And when the two families parted," he said eagerly, "it was here, wasn't it? All the Sithi came to the Fire Garden with torches. And then in Leavetaking House they stood around some thing built of glowing fire and made their bargain."

Aditu lowered her eyes from the sliver of moon, fixing him with her cat-bright stare. "Who told you this tale?"

"I saw it!" He was almost sure by the look on her face that he had been right. "I saw it when I had my vigil. The night I became a knight." He laughed at his own words. Fatigue was making him feel silly. "My knight-night."

"Saw it?" Aditu folded her hand around his wrist. "Tell me, Seoman. We will walk a little while longer."

He described his dream-vision for her—then, for good measure, he told her of what had happened later when he used Jiriki's mirror.

"What happened when you brought the Scale here shows that there is still potency in *Rhao iye-Sama'an*," she said slowly. "But my brother was right to warn you off the Dream Road. It is very dangerous now—otherwise I would take the glass and try to find Jiriki myself, tonight, and tell him of what you told me."

"Why?"

She shook her head. Her hair drifted like smoke. "Because of the thing you saw during your vigil. That is fearful. For you to see something from the Elder Days, *without* a Witness ..." She made another of her strange finger gestures, this one tangled and complex as a basket of wriggling fish. "Either you have things in you that Amerasu did not see—but I cannot believe that First Grandmother, even in her preoccupation, would fail so abjectly—or there is something happening beyond anything we suspected. That worries me greatly. For the Earth-Drake's Eye to show a vision of the past that way, unbidden . . ." She sighed. Simon stared. She *looked* worried—something he would not have believed possible.

"Maybe it was the dragon's blood," Simon offered. He raised his hand to indicate his scar and shock of white hair. "Jiriki said I was marked somehow."

"Perhaps." Aditu did not seem convinced. Simon felt slightly insulted. So she didn't think he was special enough, did she?.

They walked on until they had crossed back over the ruptured tiles of the Fire Garden and were approaching the tent city. Most of the merrymakers had gone to their beds; only a few fires still burned. Beside them, a few shadowy shapes still talked and laughed and sang.

"Go and rest, Seoman," Aditu said. "You are staggering."

He wanted to argue, but knew that what she said was true. "Where will you sleep?"

Her serious expression changed to one of genuine amusement. "Sleep? No, Snowlock, I will walk tonight. I have much to think about. In any case, I have not seen the moon on Sesuad'ra's broken stones for almost a century." She reached out and squeezed his hand. "Sleep well. In the morning we will go to Josua." She turned and walked away, silent as dew. Within moments she was only a slender shadow disappearing across the grassy hilltop.

Simon rubbed at his face with both hands. There was so much to think about. What a night this had been! He yawned and headed toward the tents of New Gadrinsett.

"A strange thing has happened, Josua."

Geloë stood in the door of his tent, unusually hesitant. "Come in, please." The prince turned to Vorzheva, who was sitting up in bed beneath a mound of blankets. "Or perhaps you would prefer we go elsewhere?" he asked his wife.

Vorzheva shook her head. "I do not feel well today, but if I must lie here this morning, at least there will be some people to keep me company."

"But perhaps Valada Geloë's news will distress you," the prince said worriedly. He looked to the wise woman. "Can she hear it?"

Geloë's smile was sardonic. "A woman with a baby inside her is not like someone who is dying of old age, Prince Josua. Women are strong—bearing a child is hard work. Besides, this news should not frighten anyone ... even you." She softened her expression to let him know she was joking.

Josua nodded. "I deserved that, I suppose." His own answering smile was wan. "What strange thing has happened? Please, come in."

Geloë shrugged off her dripping cloak and dropped it just inside the doorway. A light rain had begun to fall soon after dawn, and had been pattering on the tent roof for the better part of an hour. Geloë ran her hand through her wet, cropped hair, then seated herself on one of the stools Freosel had built for the prince's residence. "I have just received a message."

"From whom?"

"I do not know. It came to me with one of Dinivan's birds, but the writing is not his hand." She reached into her jacket and pulled forth a bundle of damp feathers, which softly cheeped; its black eye gleamed through the gap between her fingers. "Here is what it bore." She held up a small curl of oilcloth. With some difficulty, she managed to pull a twist of parchment from the cloth and open it without unduly discommoding the bird.

"Prince Josua."

she read,

"Certain signs tell me that it may be propitious for you to begin thinking about Nabban. Certain

mouths have whispered in my ear that you might find more support there than you suspect. The kingfishers have been taking too much of the boatmen's catch. A messenger will arrive within a fortnight, bearing words that will speak more clearly than this brief message can. Do nothing until that one has arrived, for your own fortune's sake."

Geloë looked up as she finished reading, her yellow eyes wary. "It is signed only with the ancient Nabbanai rune for 'Friend.' Someone who is either a Scrollbearer or of equivalent learning wrote this. Perhaps someone who would wish us to *believe* that a Scrollbearer wrote it."

Josua gave Vorzheva's hand a gentle squeeze before he stood up. "May I see it?" Geloë gave him the note, which he scrutinized for a moment before handing it back. "I do not recognize the hand, either." He took a few steps toward the tent's far wall, then turned and paced back toward the door. "The writer is obviously suggesting that there is unrest in Nabban, that the Benidrivine House is not as loved as it once was—not surprising with Benigaris in the saddle and Nessalanta pulling the reins. But what could this person want of me? You say it came to you with Dinivan's bird?"

"Yes. And that is what most worries me." Geloë was about to say more when there was an apologetic cough from the doorway. Father Strangyeard stood there, the wisp of red hair atop his head plastered to his skull by rainwater.

"Your pardon, Prince Josua." He saw Vorzheva and colored. "Lady Vorzheva. Goodness. I hope you can forgive my . . . my intrusion."

"Come in, Strangyeard." The prince beckoned as though to summon a skittish cat. Behind him, Vorzheva smiled to show she did not mind.

"I asked him to come, Josua," said Geloë. "Since it was Dinivan's bird—well, you can understand, I think."

"Of course." He waved the archivist to one of the vacant stools. "Now, tell me about the birds. I remember what you told me about Dinivan himself—although I can still scarcely credit that the lector's secretary would be part of such a company."

Geloë looked a little impatient. "The League of the Scroll is a thing that many would be proud to be part of, and Dinivan's master would never have been troubled by anything that he did on its behalf." Her eyelids lowered as some new thought came to her. "But the lector is dead, if the rumors that have come to us here are true. Some say that worshipers of the Storm King murdered him."

"I have heard of these Fire Dancers, yes," Josua said. "Those of New Gadrinsett who fled here from the south can talk of little else."

"But the troubling thing is that since this rumored event, I have heard nothing from Dinivan," Geloë continued. "So who would have his birds, if not him? And if he survived the attack on the lector—I am told there was a great fire in the Sancellan Aedonitis—then why would he not write himself?"

"Perhaps he was burned or injured," Strangyeard said diffidently. "He might have had someone else write on his behalf."

"True," Geloë mused, "but then I think he would have used his name, unless he is somehow so frightened of discovery that he cannot even send a message by bird that bears his rune."

"So if it is not Dinivan," said Josua, "then we must accept that this could be a trick. The very ones who were responsible for the lector's death may have sent this."

Vorzheva raised herself a little higher in the bed. "It could be *not* either of those things. Someone who found Dinivan's birds could send it for their own reasons."

Geloë nodded slowly. "True. But it would have to be someone who knew who Dinivan's friends were, and where they might be: this message has your husband's name at the top of it, as though whoever sent it knew it would come straight to him."

Josua was pacing again. "I have thought about Nabban," he muttered. "So many times. The north is a wasteland—I doubt Isorn and the others will find more than a token force at best. The people have been scattered by war and weather. But if we could somehow drive Benigaris out of Nabban ..." He stopped and stared up at the tent ceiling, frowning. "We could raise an army, then, and ships. ... We would have a real chance to thwart my brother." His frown deepened. "But who can know whether this is real or not? I do not like to have someone pull at my strings like this." He slapped his hand against his leg. "Aedon! Why can nothing be simple?"

Geloë shifted on her stool. The wise woman's voice was surprisingly sympathetic. "Because nothing *is* simple, Prince Josua."

"Whatever it is," Vorzheva pointed out, "whether it is a true thing or a lie, it says that a messenger will be sent. Then we will learn more."

"Perhaps," Josua said. "If it is not just a ploy to keep us hesitant, to make us delay."

"But that does not seem likely, if you will pardon my saying so," Strangyeard piped up. "Which of our enemies is so powerless that they would stoop that low. . . ?" He trailed off, looking at Josua's hard, distracted face. "I mean ..."

"I think that makes sense, Strangyeard," Geloë agreed. "It is a weak play, and I think Elias and his ... ally ... are beyond such things."

"Then you should not hurry to have your Raed, Josua." There was something like triumph in Vorzheva's voice. "It would not make sense to have plans until you know if this is true or not. You must wait for this messenger. At least a little while."

The prince turned to her; a look passed between them, and although the others did not know what the silence between husband and wife meant, they waited. At last Josua nodded stiffly.

"I suppose that is true," he said. "The note says a fortnight. I will wait that long before calling the Raed."

Vorzheva smiled in satisfaction.

"I agree, Prince Josua," said Geloë. "But there is still much that we do not ..."

She stopped as Simon appeared in the doorway. When

he did not immediately enter, Josua beckoned to him impatiently. "Come in, Simon, come in. We are discussing a strange message, and what may be an even stranger messenger."

Simon started. "Messenger?"

"A letter was sent to us, perhaps from Nabban. Come in. Do you need something?"

The tall youth swallowed. "Perhaps now is not the best time."

"I can assure you," Josua said dryly, "there is nothing that you could ask me that would not seem simple when set beside the quandaries I have already discovered today."

Simon still seemed hesitant. "Well . . ." he said, then stepped inside. Someone followed him in.

"Blessed Elysia, Mother of our Ransomer," Strangyeard said in a curiously choked voice.

"No. My mother named me Aditu," replied Simon's companion. For all her fluency, her Westerling was strangely accented; it was hard to tell whether she meant mockery or not.

She was slender as a lance, with hungry golden eyes and a great spilling froth of snowy white hair tied with a gray band. Her clothes were white, too, so that she seemed almost to glow in the shadowed tent, as though a little piece of the winter sun had rolled through the doorway.

"Aditu is my friend Jiriki's sister. She's a Sitha," Simon added unnecessarily.

"By the Tree," Josua said. "By the Holy Tree."

Aditu laughed, a fluid, musical noise. "Are these things you all say magical charms to chase me away? If so, they do not seem to be working."

The witch woman stood. Her weathered face worked through an unreadable mixture of emotions. "Welcome, Dawn Child," she said slowly. "I am Geloë."

Aditu smiled, but gently. "I know who you are. First Grandmother spoke of you."

Geloë lifted her hand as if to touch this apparition. "Amerasu was dear to me, although I never met her face-

to-face. When Simon told me what had happened . . ."
Astonishingly, tears formed and trembled on her lashes.
"She will be missed, your First Grandmother."

Aditu inclined her head for a moment. "She *is* missed.
All the world mourns her."

Josua stepped forward. "Forgive me my discourtesy,
Aditu," he said, pronouncing the name carefully. "I am
Josua. Besides Valada Geloë, these others are my wife,
the lady Vorzheva, and Father Strangyeard." He ran his
hand across his eyes. "Can we offer you something to eat
or drink?"

Aditu bowed. "Thank you, but I drank from your
spring just before dawn and I am not hungry. I have a
message from my mother, Likimeya, Lady of the House
of Year-Dancing, which you may be interested to hear."

"Of course." Josua could not seem to help staring at
her. Behind him, Vorzheva was also staring at the newcomer, although her expression was different than the
prince's. "Of course," he repeated. "Sit down, please."

The Sitha sank to the floor in a single movement, light
as thistledown. "Are you certain this is a good time,
Prince Josua?" Her tuneful voice contained a hint of
amusement. "You do not look well."

"It has been a strange morning," the prince replied.

"So they have already ridden to Hernystir?" Josua
spoke carefully. "This is unexpected news indeed."

"You do not seem pleased," Aditu commented.

"We had hoped for Sithi aid—although we certainly
did not expect it, or even think that it was deserved." He
grimaced. "I know you have no cause to love my father,
and so no reason to love me or my people. But I am glad
to hear that the Hernystiri will hear the Sithi's horns. I
have wished I could do more for Lluth's folk."

Aditu stretched her arms high over her head, a gesture
that seemed oddly childlike, out of place with the gravity
of the discussion. "As have we. But we have long exiled
ourselves from the doings of all mortals, even the
Hernystiri. We might have remained that way, even at the
expense of honor," she said with casual frankness, "but

events forced us to admit that Hernystir's war was ours, too." She turned her luminous eyes on the prince. "As is yours, of course. And that is why, when Hernystir is free, the Zida'ya will ride to Naglimund."

"As you said." Josua looked around the circle, as though to confirm that the others had heard the same thing as he. "But you did not say why."

"Many reasons. Because it is too close to our forest, and our lands. Because the Hikeda'ya must not have any foothold south of Nakkiga. And other worries I am not at leave to explain."

"But if the rumors are true," Josua said, "the Norns are already at the Hayholt."

Aditu cocked her head on one side. "A few are there, no doubt to reinforce your brother's bargain with Ineluki. But, Prince Josua, you should understand that there is a difference between the Norns and their undead master, just as there is a difference between your castle and your brother's. Ineluki and his Red Hand *cannot* come to Asu'a—what you call the Hayholt. So it falls to the Zida'ya to make sure that they cannot make a home for themselves in Naglimund either, or anywhere else south of the Frostmarch."

"Why can't the . . . why can't he come to the Hayholt?" Simon asked.

"It is an irony, but you can thank the usurper Fingil and the other mortal kings who have held Asu'a for that," Aditu said. "When they saw what Ineluki had done in his final moments of life, they were terrified. They had not dreamed that anyone, even the Sithi, could wield such power. So prayers and spells—if there is a difference between the two—were said over each handspan of what remained of our home before the mortals made it their own. As it was rebuilt, the same was done over and over again, until Asu'a was so wrapped in protections that Ineluki can never come there until Time itself ends, when it will not matter." Her face tightened. "But he is still unimaginably strong. He can send his living minions, and they will help him rule over your brother and, through him, mankind."

"So you think that is what Ineluki plans?" Geloë asked. "Is that what Amerasu thought?"

"We will never know for certain. As Simon has no doubt told you, she died before she could share with us the fruits of her pondering. One of the Red Hand was sent into Jao é-Tinukai'i to help silence her—a feat that must have exhausted even Utuk'ku and the Unliving One below Nakkiga, so it says much of how greatly they feared First Grandmother's wisdom." She briefly crossed her hands over her breast, then touched a finger to each eye. "So the Houses of Exile came together in Jao é-Tinukai'i to consider what had happened and to make plans for war. That Ineluki plans to use your brother to rule mankind seemed to all the gathered Zida'ya the most likely possibility." Aditu leaned down to the brazier and picked up a piece of wood that smoldered at one end. She held it before her, so that its glow crimsoned her face. "Ineluki is, in a way, alive, but he can never truly exist in this world again—and in the place he covets most, he has no direct power." She looked around the gathering, sharing her golden stare with each in turn. "But he will do what he can to bring the upstart mortals under his fist. And if he can also humble his family and tribe while he does so, then I do not doubt he will." Aditu made a noise that sounded a little like a sigh and dropped the wood back into the embers. "Perhaps it is fortunate that most heroes who die for their people cannot come back to see what the people *do* with that hard-bought life and freedom."

There was a pause. Josua at last broke the silence.

"Has Simon told you that we buried our fallen here on Sesuad'ra?"

Aditu nodded. "We are not strangers to death, Prince Josua. We are immortal, but only in the sense that we do not die except by our own choice—or the choice of others. Perhaps we are all the more enmeshed with dying because of it. Just because our lives are long when held against yours does not mean we are any more eager to give them up." She allowed a slow, coolly measured smile to narrow her lips. "So we know death well. Your

640 *Tad Williams*

people fought bravely to defend themselves. There is no
shame to us in sharing this place with those who died."

"Then I would like to show you something else." Josua
stood and extended his hand toward the Sitha. Vorzheva,
watching closely, did not look pleased. Aditu rose and
followed the prince toward the door.

"We have buried my friend—my dearest friend—in the
garden behind Leavetaking House," he said. "Simon, perhaps you will accompany us? And Geloë and
Strangyeard, too, if you would like," he added hurriedly.

"I will stay and talk with Vorzheva for a while," the
wise woman said. "Aditu, I look forward to a chance to
speak with you later."

"Certainly."

"I think I will come, too," Strangyeard said, almost
apologetically. "It's very pretty there."

"*Sesu-d'asú* is a sad place now," said Aditu. "It was
beautiful once."

They stood before the broad expanse of Leavetaking
House; its weatherworn stones glinted dully in the sunlight.

"I think it is still beautiful," Strangyeard said shyly.

"So do I," Simon echoed. "Like an old woman who
used to be a lovely young girl, but you can still see it in
her face."

Aditu grinned. "My Seoman," she said, "the time you
spent with us has made you part Zida'ya. Soon you will
be composing poems and whispering them to the passing
wind."

They walked through the hall and into the ruined garden, where a cairn of stones had been built over
Deornoth's grave. Aditu stood silently for a moment, then
laid her hand atop the uppermost stone. "It is a good,
quiet place." For a moment, her gaze grew distant, as
though she beheld some other place or time. "Of all the
songs we Zida'ya sing," she murmured, "the closest to
our hearts are those which tell of things lost."

"Perhaps that is because none of us can know something's true value until it is gone," said Josua. He bowed

his head. The grass between the broken paving stones rippled in the breeze.

Strangely, of all the mortals living on Sesuad'ra, it was Vorzheva who most quickly befriended Aditu—if a mortal could truly become a friend to one of the immortals. Even Simon, who had lived among them and had rescued one of them, was not at all certain that he could count any of them as friends.

But despite her initial coolness toward the Sitha-woman, Vorzheva seemed to be drawn by something in Aditu's alien nature, perhaps the mere fact that Aditu *was* alien, the only one of her kind in that place, as Vorzheva herself had been for all the years in Naglimund. Whatever Aditu's attraction, Josua's wife made her welcome and even sought her out. The Sitha also seemed to enjoy Vorzheva's company: when she was not with Simon or Geloë, she could often be found walking with the Thrithings-woman among the tents, or sitting by her bedside on days when Vorzheva felt ill or tired. Duchess Gutrun, Vorzheva's usual companion, did her best to show good manners to the strange visitor, but something in her Aedonite heart would not let her be fully comfortable. While Vorzheva and Aditu talked and laughed, Gutrun watched Aditu as though the Sitha were a sort of dangerous animal that she had been assured was now tame.

For her part, Aditu seemed oddly fascinated by the child Vorzheva carried. Few children were born to the Zida'ya, especially in these days, she explained. The last had come over a century before, and he was now as much of an adult as the eldest of the Dawn Children. Aditu also seemed interested in Leleth, although the little girl was no more expressive with her than with anyone else. Still, she would allow Aditu to take her for walks, and even to carry her occasionally, something that almost no one else was permitted to do.

If Aditu was interested in some of the mortals, the or-

dinary citizens of New Gadrinsett were in turn both fascinated and terrified by her. Ulca's tale—the truth of which
was strange enough—had grown in the telling and retell-
ing until Aditu's arrival had come in a flash of light and
puff of smoke; the Sitha, the story continued, enraged by
the mortal girl's flirtation with her intended, had threatened to turn Ulca into stone. Ulca quickly became the
heroine of every young woman on Sesuad'ra, and Aditu,
despite the fact that she was seldom seen by most of the
hill-dwellers, became the subject of endless gossip and
superstitious mumbling.

To his chagrin, Simon also continued to be a subject of
rumor and speculation in the small community. Jeremias,
who frequently loitered in the marketplace beside
Leavetaking House, would gleefully report the latest
strange tale—the dragon from whom Simon had stolen
the sword would come back someday and Simon would
have to fight it; Simon was part Sitha and Aditu had been
sent to bring him back to the halls of the Fair Folk; and
so on. Simon, hearing the fantasies that seemed to be
woven from empty air, could only cringe. There was
nothing he could do—every attempt he made to quell the
stories merely convinced the folk of New Gadrinsett that
he was either manfully modest or slyly deceptive. Sometimes he found the fabrications amusing, but he still could
not help feeling more closely observed than was comfortable, leading him to spend his time only with people he
knew and trusted. His evasiveness, of course, only fueled
more speculation.

If this was fame, Simon decided, he would have preferred to stay a lowly and unknown scullion. Sometimes
when he walked through New Gadrinsett these days,
when people waved to him or whispered to each other as
he passed, he felt quite naked, but there was nothing to do
but walk by with a smile on his face and his shoulders
back. Scullions could hide or run away; knights could
not.

"He is outside, Josua. He swears you are expecting him."

"Ah." The prince turned to Simon. "This must be the mysterious messenger I spoke of—the one with news of Nabban. And it *has* been a fortnight—almost to the day. Stay and see." To Sludig he said: "Bring him in, please."

The Rimmersman stepped out, then returned a moment later leading a tall, lantern-jawed fellow, pale-complected and—Simon thought—a little sullen-looking. The Rimmersman stepped back beside the wall of the tent and remained there with one hand on the handle of his ax, the other toying with the hairs of his yellow beard.

The messenger dropped slowly to one knee. "Prince Josua, my master sends his greetings and bids me give you this." As he put his hand in his cloak Sludig took a step forward, even though the messenger was several paces away from the prince, but the man withdrew only a roll of parchment, beribboned and sealed in blue wax. Josua stared at it for a moment, then nodded to Simon to fetch it to him.

"The winged dolphin," Josua said as he gazed at the emblem stamped into the melted wax. "So your master is Count Streáwe of Perdruin?"

It was hard not to call the look on the messenger's face a smirk. "He is, Prince Josua."

The prince broke the seal and unrolled the parchment. He scanned it for a few long moments, then curled it up and set it on the arm of his chair. "I will not hurry through this. What is your name, man?"

The messenger nodded his head with immense satisfaction, as though he had been long expecting this crucial question. "It is . . . Lenti."

"Very well, Lenti, Sludig will take you and see that you get food and drink. He will also find you a bed because I will want some time before I send my answer—maybe several days."

The messenger looked around the prince's tent, assessing the possible quality of New Gadrinsett's accommodations. "Yes, Prince Josua."

Sludig came forward and, with a jerk of his head, summoned Lenti to follow him out.

"I didn't think much of the messenger," Simon said when they had gone.

Josua was inspecting the parchment once more. "A fool," he agreed "jumped up beyond his capabilities, even for something as simple as this. But don't confuse Streáwe with his minions—Perdruin's master is clever as a marketplace cutpurse. Still, it doesn't speak well of his ability to deliver on this promise if he can find no more impressive servitor to bear it to me."

"What promise?" Simon asked.

Josua rolled the message and slid it into his sleeve. "Count Streáwe claims he can deliver me Nabban." He stood. "The old man is lying, of course, but it leads to some interesting speculation."

"I don't understand, Josua."

The prince smiled. "Be glad. Your days of innocence about people like Streáwe are fast disappearing." He patted Simon's shoulder. "For now, young knight, I would as soon not talk about it. There will be a time and place for this at the Raed."

"You're ready to have your council?"

Josua nodded. "The time has come. For once, *we* will call the tune—then we will see if we can make my brother and his allies dance to it."

"That is a most interesting deception, clever Seoman." Aditu stared down at the game of shent she had constructed from wood and root-dyes and polished stones. "A false thrust played falsely: a seeming that is revealed as a sham, but underneath is a true thing after all. Very pretty—but what will you do if I place my Bright Stones here . . . here . . . and here?" She suited action to words.

Simon frowned. In the dim light of his tent, her hand moved almost too swiftly to be seen. For an unpleasant moment he wondered if she might be cheating him, but another instant's reflection convinced him that Aditu had no need to cheat someone to whom the subtleties of shent were still largely a mystery, any more than Simon would trip a small child with whom he was running a race. Still, it raised an interesting question.

"Can you cheat at this game?"

Aditu looked up from arranging her pieces. She was wearing one of Vorzheva's loose dresses; the combination of her unusually modest attire and her unbound hair made her look a little less dangerously wild—in fact, it made her seem disconcertingly human. Her eyes gleamed in the light of the brazier. "Cheat? Do you mean lie? A game can be as deceptive as the players wish it to be."

"That's not what I mean. Can you do something on purpose that is against the rules?" She was eerily beautiful. He stared at her, remembering the night she had kissed him. What had that meant? Anything? Or was it just another way for Aditu to toy with her one-time lap-dog?

She considered his question. "I am not sure how to answer. Could you cheat against the way you are made and fly by flapping your arms?"

Simon shook his head. "A game that has so many rules must have some way to break them. . . ."

Before Aditu could try again to answer, Jeremias burst into the tent, out of breath and agitated. "Simon!" he shouted, then drew up short, seeing that Aditu was there. "I'm sorry." Despite his embarrassment, he was having trouble containing his excitement.

"What is it?"

"People have come!"

"Who? What people?" Simon looked briefly to Aditu, but she had returned to her study of the arrangement before her.

"Duke Isgrimnur and the princess!" Jeremias waved his arms up and down. "And there are others with them, too! A strange little man, sort of like Binabik and his trolls, but almost our size. And an old man—he's taller than you, even. Simon, the whole town has gone down to see them!"

He sat for a moment in silence, his mind whirling. "The princess?" he said at last. "Princess . . . Miriamele?"

"Yes, yes," Jeremias panted. "Dressed as a monk, but she took off her hood and waved to people. Come on, Simon, everyone is going down to meet them." He turned and took a few steps toward the doorway, then pivoted to look at his friend in astonishment. "Simon? What's wrong? Don't you want to go see the princess and Duke Isgrimnur and the brown man?"

"The princess." He turned helplessly to Aditu, who gazed back at him with feline disinterest.

"It sounds like something you will enjoy, Seoman. We will play our game later."

Simon stood and followed Jeremias out of the tent and into the hilltop wind, moving as slowly and unsteadily as a sleepwalker. As if he passed through a dream, he heard people shouting all around, a rising murmur of sound that filled his ears like the roar of the ocean.

Miriamele had come back.

21

Answered Prayers

It **had grown** steadily colder as Miriamele and her companions made their way across the wide grasslands. By the time they reached the seemingly endless plain of the Meadow Thrithing, there was snow on the ground, and even in full afternoon the sky remained a dull pewter stained with streaks of black cloud. Huddled in her traveling cloak against the predatory wind, Miriamele found herself almost grateful that Aspitis Preves had found them; it would have been a long and miserable journey indeed if they had been forced to make it on foot. Cold and uncomfortable as she was, however, Miriamele was also experiencing a curious sense of freedom. The earl had haunted her, but now, although he lived, and might still conceivably seek some kind of vengeance, she no longer feared him or anything he might do. But Cadrach's flight was another thing altogether.

Since their escape together from the *Eadne Cloud,* she had begun to see the Hernystirman in a different way. He had betrayed her several times, certainly, but in his odd way he had semed to care for her as well. The monk's own self-hatred had continued to loom between them—and had apparently driven him away at last—but her own feelings had changed.

She deeply regretted the argument over Tiamak's parchment. Miriamele had thought she might slowly continue to draw him out, might somehow reach through to the man beneath—a man she liked. But, as though she had tried to tame a wild dog and had moved too quickly to pet it, Cadrach had startled and bolted. Miriamele could not rid herself of the obscure feeling that she had missed an opportunity that was more important than she could understand.

Even on horseback, it was a long journey. Her thoughts were not always good company.

They rode a full week to reach the Meadow Thrithing, traveling from first light until after the sun had vanished . . . on those days that they saw the sun at all. The weather grew steadily colder, but remained something just short of unlivable: by mid-afternoon of most days the sun struggled through like a tired but determined messenger and chased away the chill.

The meadowlands were wide and, for the most part, flat and featureless as a carpet. What slope there was to the land was almost more depressing: after a long day's ride up a gradual incline, Miriamele found it hard to rid herself of the idea that they would eventually reach a summit and that it would be *somewhere*. Instead, at some point they would cross a flat table of meadow no more interesting than the upward slope, then gradually find themselves moving down an equally uninspiring decline. Even the *idea* of having to make such a monotonous journey on foot was disheartening. Acre after empty acre, mile after trying mile, Miriamele whispered quiet prayers of gratitude for Aspitis' unwitting gift of horses.

Riding on the saddle before her, Tiamak quickly recovered his strength. After some encouragement, the Wrannaman told her—and Isgrimnur, who was happy to have someone else share the burden of storytelling—more about his childhood in the marshes and his difficult year as an aspiring scholar in Perdruin. Although his natural reticence prevented him from dwelling on his ill-treatment, Miriamele thought she could feel every slight, every little cruelty that wound through his tale.

I'm not the first person to feel lonely, to feel misunderstood and unwanted. This seemingly obvious fact now struck her with the force of revelation. *And I'm a princess, a privileged person—I've never been hungry, never been afraid that I would die unremembered, never been told that I wasn't good enough to do something that I wished to do.*

Listening to Tiamak, watching his wiry but somehow fragile form, his precise, scholarly gestures, Miriamele was dismayed by her own willful ignorance. How could she, with all her native good fortune, be so consumed with the few inconveniences that God or fate had put in her way? It was shameful.

She tried to tell Duke Isgrimnur something of her thoughts, but he would not let her slide too far into self-loathing.

"Each one of has our own sorrows, Princess," he said. "It's no shame to take them to heart. The only sin is to forget that other folk have theirs, too—or to let pity for yourself slow your hand when someone needs help."

Isgrimnur, Miriamele was reminded, was more than just a gruff old soldier.

On their third night in the Meadow Thrithing, as the four sat close to their campfire—very close, since wood was scarce on the grasslands and the fire was a small one—Miriamele finally worked up the courage to ask Tiamak about his sack and its contents.

The Wrannaman was so embarrassed he could scarcely meet her eye. "It is terrible, Lady. I remember only a little, but in my fever I was certain that Cadrach meant to steal it from me."

"Why would you think that? And what *is* it, anyway?"

After a moment's consideration, Tiamak reached into his bag, drew out the leafy bundle, and peeled away the wrappings. "It was when you spoke of the monk and Nisses' book," he explained shyly. "I can believe now that it was innocent, since Morgenes also said something about Nisses in his message to me—but in the depth of my illness, I could only think that it meant my treasure was in danger."

He handed her the parchment. As she unrolled it, Isgrimnur moved around the fire to look over her shoulder. Camaris, seemingly oblivious as always, stared out into the empty night.

"It's some kind of song," Isgrimnur said crossly, as though he had been expecting more.

"... *'The manne who though blinded canne see'* ..." Miriamele read. "What is it?"

"I am not sure myself," Tiamak replied. "But look, it is signed 'Nisses.' I think it is part of his lost book, *Du Svardenvyrd.*"

Miriamele took a sudden breath. "Oh. But that's the book Cadrach had—the one he sold off page by page." She felt something squeeze in the pit of her stomach. "The book that Pryrates wanted. Where did you get this?"

"I bought it in Kwanitupul almost a year ago. It was part of a pile of scraps. The merchant could not have known it was worth anything, or else he never inspected what he had probably bought as scrap himself."

"I don't think Cadrach actually knew what you had," said Miriamele. "But, Elysia, Mother of Mercy, how strange! Perhaps this is one of the pages that he sold!"

"He sold pages of Nisses' book?" Tiamak asked. Outrage mingled with wonder. "How could that be?"

"Cadrach told me he was poor and desperate." She weighed the idea of telling them the rest of the monk's story, then decided she should consider the matter more carefully. They might not understand his actions. Even though he had fled, she felt the urge to protect Cadrach from those who did not know him as she did. "He had a different name then," she offered, as though somehow it might absolve him. "He was called Padreic."

"Padreic!" Now Tiamak was nothing short of astounded. "But I know that name! Can he be the same man? Doctor Morgenes knew him well!"

"Yes, he knew Morgenes. He has a strange history."

Isgrimnur snorted, but now he, too, sounded a little defensive. "A strange history indeed, it seems."

Miriamele hurried to change the subject. "Perhaps Josua will understand this."

The duke shook his head. "I think Prince Josua, if we

find him, will have other things to do than look at old parchments."

"But it may be important." Tiamak looked sideways at Isgrimnur. "As I said, Doctor Morgenes wrote in a letter to me that he thought these were the times that Nisses warned about. Morgenes was a man who knew many things hidden from the rest of us."

Isgrimnur grunted and moved back to his own place in the fire-circle. "It's beyond me. Well beyond me."

Miriamele was watching Camaris, who was surveying the darkness as calmly and possessively as an owl poised to glide from a tree branch. "There are so many mysteries these days," she said. "Won't it be nice when things are simple again?"

There was a pause, then Isgrimnur laughed self-consciously. "I'd forgotten the monk was gone. I was waiting for him to say, 'Things will never be simple again,' or something like it."

Miriamele smiled despite herself. "Yes, that's just what he would have said." She held her hands closer to the fire's reassuring warmth and let out a sigh. "Just what he would have said."

Days passed as they rode north. Snow thickened on the ground; the wind became an enemy. As the last leagues of the Meadow Thrithing disappeared behind them, Miriamele and the rest grew more and more downhearted.

"It's hard to imagine Josua and the rest are having any luck in this weather." Isgrimnur was almost shouting to be heard above the wind. "Things are worse now than when I came south."

"If they are alive, that will be enough," Miriamele said. "That will be a start."

"But, Princess, we don't really know where to look for them." The duke was almost apologetic. "None of the rumors I heard said much more than that Josua was somewhere in the High Thrithing. There's more than a hundred leagues of grassland up ahead, no more settled or civilized than this." He waved his broad arm at the bleak, snowy expanses on either side. "We could hunt for months."

"We will find him," Miriamele said, and in her own heart she felt almost as certain as she sounded. Surely the things she had been through, the things she had learned, must be for *something*. "There are people who live on the Thrithings," she added. "If Josua and the others have made themselves a settlement, the Thrithings-folk will know."

Isgrimnur snorted. "The Thrithings-folk! Miriamele, I know them better than you may think. These are not town-dwellers. For one thing, they do not stay in one place, so we may not even find them. And we might be just as glad if we don't. They are barbarians, just as likely to knock our heads off as offer us news of Josua."

"I know you fought against the Thrithings-men," Miriamele replied. "But that was long ago." She shook her head. "And we have no choice that I can see, in any case. We will solve that when we come to it."

The duke stared at her with a mixture of frustration and amusement on his face, then shrugged. "You are your father's daughter."

Strangely, Miriamele was not displeased by this remark, but she frowned anyway—as much to keep the duke in his place as anything. A moment later she laughed.

"What's funny?" Isgrimnur asked suspiciously.

"Nothing, in truth. I was just thinking of all the times when I was with Binabik and Simon. Several times I had decided that within a few moments I would be dead— once when some terrible dogs almost got us, another time a giant, and men shooting arrows at us . . ." She shook her hair from her eyes, but the maddening wind immediately flung it back. She tucked the offending strands back into her hood. "But now I don't think that any more, no matter how dreadful things are. When Aspitis captured us, I never believed that he would truly manage to take me away. And if he had, I would have escaped."

She slowed her horse for a moment, trying to put her thought into words. "You see, in truth it's not funny at all.

But it seems to me now that there are things happening that are beyond our strength. Like waves on the ocean, huge waves. I can fight them—and drown—or I can let them carry me, and swim just enough to keep my head above the water. I *know* I'm going to see Uncle Josua again. I just know. And Simon and Binabik and Vorzheva—there's more to be done, that's all."

Isgrimnur looked at her warily, as though the little girl he had once knee-dandled had become a Nabbanai star-reader. "And then? When we're all together again?"

Miriamele smiled at him, but it was only the bitter-sweet tip of a great sorrow that washed through her. "The wave will crash, dear old Uncle Isgrimnur ... and some of us will go down and never come up. I don't know how it will be, of course not. But I'm not as frightened as I used to be."

They were silent then, three horses and four riders fighting their way into the wind.

Only the amount of time they had been riding told them when they had crossed over into the High Thrithing: the snow-mantled meadows and hills were no more memorable than anything they had crossed in the first week of their journey. Strangely, though, the weather did not worsen as they continued to move northward. Miriamele even began to believe that it was growing a bit warmer, the wind a little less biting.

"A hopeful sign," she said one afternoon when the sun actually appeared. "I told you, Isgrimnur. We'll get there."

"Wherever 'there' is, exactly," the duke grumbled.

Tiamak stirred in the saddle. "Perhaps we should make our way to the river. If there are people still living in this place, they are most likely to be near moving water, where there might still be fish to catch." He shook his head sadly. "I wish that what I remembered from my dream was more precise."

Isgrimnur pondered. "The Ymstrecca is just south of the great forest. But it runs most of the length of the Thrithings—a long way to go a-searching."

"Is there not another river that crosses it?" Tiamak asked. "It has been long since I looked at a map."

"There is. The Stefflod, if I remember rightly." The duke frowned. "But it is little more than a large stream."

"Still, in the places where rivers meet you often find villages," Tiamak said with surprising assuredness. "So it is in the Wran, and in all the other places that I have heard of."

Miriamele started to say something, but stopped, watching Camaris. The old man had ridden a little way off to the side and was watching the sky. She followed his stare but saw only dingy clouds.

Isgrimnur was considering the Wrannaman's idea. "P'raps you're right, Tiamak. If we continue north, we can't help but strike the Ymstrecca. But I think the Stefflod must be a little to the east." He looked around as though seeking some landmark; his eyes stopped on Camaris. "What's he looking at?"

"I don't know," Miriamele replied. "Oh. It must be those birds!"

A pair of dark shapes were swooping toward them out of the east, whirling like cinders caught in the draught of a fire.

"Ravens!" said Isgrimnur. "Gore crows!"

The birds wheeled in a circle above the travelers as if they had found what they had been seeking. Miriamele thought she could see their yellow eyes glint. The sensation of being watched, marked, was very strong. After a few more turns, the ravens dove, their feathers shining oily-black as they approached. Miriamele ducked her head and covered her eyes. The ravens flew past, shrieking; a moment later they banked upward and hurtled away. In moments, the birds were two dwindling specks vanishing into the northern sky.

Only Camaris had not lowered his head. He watched their retreating forms with an absorbed, contemplative look.

"What are they?" Tiamak asked. "Are they dangerous?"

"Birds of ill omen," the duke growled. "In my country,

we chase them with arrows. Carrion eaters." He made a face.

"I think they were looking at us," Miriamele said. "I think they wanted to know who we were."

"That's no way to talk." Isgrimnur reached over and squeezed her arm. "And what would birds care who we were, anyway?"

Miriamele shook her head. "I don't know. But that's the feeling I have: someone wanted to know who we were—and now they do."

"They were just ravens." The duke's smile was grim. "We have other things to worry about."

"That's true," she said.

A few more days' riding brought them at last to the Ymstrecca. The swiftly flowing river was almost black beneath the faint sun. Patchy snow cloaked its banks.

"The weather *is* getting warmer," Isgrimnur said, pleased. "This is scarcely colder than it should be at this time of the year. It is Novander, after all."

"Is it?" Miriamele was unsettled. "And we left Josua's keep in Yuven. Half a year. Elysia's mercy, we have been traveling a long time."

They turned and followed the river eastward, stopping at dark to make camp with the sound of the water loud in their ears. They started early the next morning beneath a gray sky.

In late afternoon they reached the edge of a shallow valley of wet grass. Before them, like the leavings from some ruinous flood, lay the weather-battered remains of a vast settlement. Hundreds of makeshift houses had stood here, and most of them seemed to have been recently inhabited, but something had drawn or driven out the residents; but for a few lonely birds poking among the abandoned dwellings, the ramshackle city seemed deserted.

Miriamele's heart sank. "Was this Josua's camp? Where have they gone?"

"It is on a great hill, Lady," Tiamak said. "At least, that was what I saw in my dream."

Isgrimnur spurred his horse down toward the empty settlement.

On inspection, much of the impression of disaster was revealed to be the nature of the settlement itself, since most of the building materials were scraps and deadwood. There did not seem to be a nail in the whole of the city; the crudely woven ropes that had held together most of the better-constructed buildings appeared to have frayed and given way in the clutch of storms that had lately battered the Thrithings—but even at the best of times, Miriamele decided, none of the dwellings could have been much more than hovels.

There was also some sign of orderly retreat. Most of the people who had lived here seemed to have had time to take their possessions with them—although, judging by the quality of the shelters, they could not have had much to start. Still, there was little left of the everyday necessities: Miriamele found a few broken pots and some rags of clothing so miserably tattered and mud-soaked that even in a cold winter they had probably not been missed.

"They left," she told Isgrimnur, "but it looks as though they chose to."

"Or were forced to," the duke pointed out. "They could have been marched out in a careful manner, if you see what I mean."

Camaris had climbed down from his horse and was rooting in a pile of sod and broken branches that had once been someone's home. He stood up with something shiny in his hand.

"What is that?" Miriamele rode over. She held out her hand, but Camaris was staring at the piece of metal. At last she reached out and gently pried it from the old knight's long, callused fingers.

Tiamak slid forward onto the horse's shoulders and turned to examine the object. "It looks like a clasp to hold a cloak," he offered.

"It is, I think." The silvery object, bent and muddy, had a rim of molded holly leaves. At the center was a pair of crossed spears and an angry reptilian face. Miriamele felt a wisp of fear rise inside her once more. "Isgrimnur, look at this."

The duke brought his mount alongside hers and took the brooch. "It's the badge of the king's Erkynguard."

"My father's soldiers," Miriamele murmured. She could not restrain the urge to look around, as though a company of knights could have been lying in wait unobserved somewhere nearby on the empty grass slope. "They have been here."

"They could have been here after the people left," Isgrimnur said. "Or there could be some other reason we can't guess." He did not sound very convinced himself. "After all, Princess, we don't even know who was living here."

"*I* know." She was angry just imagining it. "They were people who had fled my father's reign. Josua and the others were probably with them. Now they have been driven away or captured."

"Pardon, Lady Miriamele," Tiamak said cautiously, "but I think it would not be good to make our minds up so quickly. Duke Isgrimnur is right: there is much we do not know. This is not the place I saw in the dream Geloë sent me."

"So, then, what should we do?"

"Continue," said the Wrannaman. "Follow the tracks. Perhaps those who lived here have gone to join Josua."

"That looks promising over there." The duke was shading his eyes against the gray sun. He pointed toward the edge of the settlement, where a series of wide ruts wound out from the trampled acres of mud toward the north.

"Then let us follow." Miriamele handed the brooch back to Camaris. The old knight looked at it for a moment, then let it drop to the ground.

The ruts ran close enough together to make a large muddy scar through the grasslands. On either side of this makeshift road lay the marks of the people who had used it—broken wagon spokes, sodden fire ashes, numerous holes dug and filled in. Despite the look of it, the ugly scatter across an otherwise pristine land, Miriamele was heartened by how new the signs seemed: it could not have been more than a month or two at most since the road had been traveled.

Over a supper culled from their dwindling Village Grove stores, Miriamele asked Isgrimnur what he would do when they reached Josua at last. It was nice to talk about that day as something that *would* happen, not just as something that *might:* it made it seem certain, real and tangible, even though she still felt a wisp of superstitious fear at talking of good things not yet come to pass.

"I'll show him that I kept my word," the duke laughed. "Show you to him. Then I think I will catch up my wife and hug her until she squeaks."

Miriamele smiled, thinking of plump, always-capable Gutrun. "I want to see that." She looked over at Tiamak, who slept, and Camaris, who was polishing Isgrimnur's sword with the fascinated absorption he usually gave only to the movements of birds in the sky. Before the duel with Aspitis, the old knight had not wanted even to touch the blade. She felt a little sad now as she watched him. He handled the duke's sword as though it were an old but not quite trusted friend.

"You really miss her, don't you?" she said, turning back to Isgrimnur. "Your wife."

"Ah, sweet Usires, I do." He stared at the fire as though unwilling to meet her eyes. "I do."

"You love her." Miriamele was pleased and a little surprised: Isgrimnur had spoken with a heat she had not expected. It was strange to think that love could burn so strongly in the breast of someone who seemed as old and familiar as the duke—and that grandmotherly Duchess Gutrun could be the object of such powerful feelings!

"Of course I love her, I suppose," he said, frowning. "But it's more than that, my lady. She's a part of me, my Gutrun—we've grown together through the years, twined 'round each other like two old trees." He laughed and shook his head. "I always knew. From the moment I saw her first, carrying mistletoe from the ship-grave of Sotfengsel ... Ah, she was so beautiful. She had the brightest eyes I've ever seen! Like something in a story."

Miriamele sighed. "I hope someone feels that way about me someday."

"They will, my girl, they will." Isgrimnur smiled. "And when you are married, if you are lucky enough to marry the right one, you will know just what I mean. He will be a part of you, just like my Gutrun is for me. Forever until we die." He made the Tree on his breast. "None of this southlander nonsense for me—widows and widowers taking another spouse! How could anyone ever match her?" He fell silent as he considered the monumental impertinence of second marriages.

Miriamele, too, reflected in silence. Would it be her lot someday to find such a husband? She thought of Fengbald, to whom her father had once offered her, and shuddered. Horrid, swaggering oaf! That Elias, of all people, should attempt to marry her to someone she did not love, when he himself had been so crippled by the death of Miriamele's mother Hylissa that he had been like a man lost in the dark since the hour of her death. . . .

Unless he was trying to spare me from such awful loneliness, she thought. *Maybe he thought it would be a blessing not to love so, and never to feel such a loss. That was the heartbreaking thing, to see him so lonely for her. . . .*

With the suddenness and enormity of a lightning flash, Miriamele saw the thing that had been teasing her mind since Cadrach had first told her his story. It was all there before her, and it was so clear—so clear! It was as though she had groped in a blackened chamber, but now a door had abruptly opened, spilling light, and she could finally see all the strange shapes she had touched in darkness.

"Oh!" she said, gasping. "Oh! Oh, Father!"

She astonished Isgrimnur by bursting into tears. The duke tried his best to soothe her, but she could not stop crying. Neither would she tell him what had caused it, except to say that Isgrimnur's words had reminded her of her mother's death. It was a cruel half-truth, although she did not intend cruelty: when Miriamele crawled away from the fire, the duke was left perturbed but helpless, blaming himself for her misery.

Still sniffling quietly, Miriamele rolled herself in her

blanket to stare at the stars and think. There was suddenly so much to think about. Nothing important had changed, but at the same time, everything was vastly different.

Tears came to her again before she finally fell asleep.

A brief flurry of snow came up in the morning, not enough to slow the horses much, but sufficient to make Miriamele shiver most of the day. The Stefflod was sluggish and gray, like a twining stream of fluid lead, and the snow seemed thickest just above it, so that the fields on the river's far side were much murkier than the nearer bank. Miriamele had the illusion that the Stefflod drew snow like the lodestone in Ruben the Bear's smithy drew scraps of iron.

The land sloped upward, so that by late afternoon, when the light had already fled and they rode in cold twilight, they found themselves climbing into a rank of low hills. Trees were nearly as scarce as they had been in the Lake Thrithing, and the wind was sharp and raw on Miriamele's cheeks, but there was a sort of relief in the changing scenery.

They climbed high into the hills that night before making camp. When they arose in the morning, feet and fingers and noses bright pink and smarting, the company lingered over the fire longer than usual. Even Camaris got on his horse with a look of obvious reluctance.

The snow grew less, then vanished by late morning. Toward noon the sun emerged brilliantly from the clouds, sending down great arrow-flights of beams. By the time they had reached what seemed to be the summit of the hills in mid-afternoon, the clouds had returned, this time bearing a chill but delicate rain.

"Princess!" Isgrimnur shouted. "Look here!" He had ridden a short way ahead, looking for any possible hazards in their journey downslope: an easy ascent did not guarantee an equally simple descent, and the duke was taking no chances in unknown country. Half in fear, half in exhilaration, Miriamele rode forward. Tiamak leaned forward in the saddle before her, straining to see. The duke stood in a break in the sparse treeline, waving his hand toward the gap between the trunks. "Look!"

Spread below them was a wide valley, a bowl of green patched with white. Despite the soft rain, a sense of stillness hung over it, the air somehow taut as an indrawn breath. At the center, rising up from what looked like a partially frozen lake, was a great stony hill mantled in snow-flecked greenery. The slanting light played across it so that its western face seemed almost to glow, warmly inviting. From the top, pale smoke rose from a hundred different sources.

"God be praised, what is it?" Isgrimnur said in astonishment.

"I think it is the place from my dream," Tiamak murmured.

Miriamele hugged herself, awash in feeling. The great hill seemed almost too real. "I hope it is a good place. I hope Josua and the others are there."

"*Somebody* is living there," Isgrimnur said. "Look at all the fires!"

"Come!" Miriamele spurred her horse down the trail. "We can be there before nightfall."

"Don't be in such a hurry." Isgrimnur urged his own mount forward. "We don't know for certain that it's anything to do with Josua."

"I would willingly be captured by almost anyone if they'd take me to a fire and a warm bed," Miriamele called back over her shoulder.

Camaris, who had brought up the rear, paused at the gap in the trees to stare down into the valley. His long face did not change expression, but he remained where he was for a long time before following the others.

Although it was still light when they reached the lake shore, the men who came to meet them carried torches— flowers of fire that reflected yellow and scarlet in the black lake water as the boats made their way slowly through floating ice. Isgrimnur held back at first, cautious and protective, but before the first boat touched shore he recognized the yellow-bearded figure in the bow and swung down from his saddle with a shout of delight.

"Sludig! In God's name, in Aedon's name, bless you!"

His liege-man sloshed the last few steps to shore. Before he could bend his knee before the duke, Isgrimnur snatched him up and crushed him to his broad chest. "How fares the prince?" Isgrimnur cried, "and my lady wife? And my son?"

Although Sludig was himself a large man, he had to free himself from the duke's clutches and catch his breath before he could assure Isgrimnur that all were fine, although Isorn had left on a mission for the prince. Duke Isgrimnur did a clumsy, enthusiastic, bearlike dance of glee. "And I've brought the princess back!" the duke said. "And more, and more! But lead on! Ah, this is as fine as Aedonmansa!"

Sludig laughed. "We have been watching you since midday. Josua said: 'Go down and find out who they are.' He will be quite surprised, I think!" He quickly arranged for the horses to be loaded on one of the barges, then helped Miriamele onto the boat.

"Princess." His touch was firm as he helped her to one of the benches. "You are welcome to New Gadrinsett. Your uncle will be happy to see you."

The guardsmen who had accompanied Sludig examined Tiamak and Camaris with great interest as well, but the Rimmersman did not allow them to waste time. Within moments they were heading back across the ice-studded lake.

Waiting on the far side was a cart drawn by two thin and disgruntled oxen. When the passengers were loaded on board, Sludig smacked one of the beasts on the flank and the cart began to roll creakily up the stone-shod road.

"What is this?" Isgrimnur peered over the side of the cart to look at the pale stones.

"It is a Sithi road," Sludig said with more than a touch of pride. "This is a Sithi place, very ancient. They call it 'Sesuad'ra.' "

"I have heard of it," Tiamak whispered to Miriamele.

"It is famous in lore—but I had no idea it still existed, or that it was the Stone Geloë showed me!"

Miriamele shook her head. She cared little where they were being taken. With Sludig's appearance, she felt as though a vast load had been taken from her back; only now did she realize how tired she truly was.

She felt herself nodding a little with the movement of the ox cart, and tried to fight back a wave of exhaustion. Children were running down the mountainside to join them. They fell in behind the travelers, shouting and singing.

By the time they reached the top of the hill, a great crowd had gathered. Miriamele found the immense sea of people almost sickening; it had been a long time since the swarming wooden streets of Kwanitupul, and she found herself unable to look at so many hungry, expectant faces. She leaned against Isgrimnur and closed her eyes.

At the top, the faces suddenly became familiar. Sludig helped her down from the cart and into the arms of her uncle Josua, who pulled her to him and hugged her almost as firmly as Isgrimnur had embraced Sludig. After a moment he held her out at arm's length to stare at her. He was thinner than she remembered, and his garments, although colored his habitual gray, were odd and rustic. Her heart opened a little wider, letting in both pain and joy.

"The Ransomer has answered my prayers," he said. There could be no doubt, despite his lined and troubled face, that he was very happy to see her. "Welcome back, Miriamele."

Then there were more faces—Vorzheva, wearing an odd, tentlike robe, and the harper Sangfugol, and even little Binabik who bowed with mocking courtliness before taking her hand in his small, warm fingers. Another who stood silently by seemed oddly familiar. He was bearded, and a streak of white marred his red hair and capped the pale scar on his cheek. He looked at her as though he would memorize her, as though someday he might carve her in stone.

It took a long moment.

"Simon?" she said.

Astonishment turned rapidly to a kind of strange bitterness—she had been cheated of so much! While she had been busy elsewhere, the world had changed. Simon was no longer a mere boy. Her friend had disappeared, and this tall young man had taken his place. Had she been away that long?

The stranger's mouth worked, but it was a moment before she heard him speak. Simon's voice seemed deeper, too, but his words were halting. "I am glad you're safe, Princess. Very glad."

She stared at him, her eyes burning as tears began to come. The world seemed topside-round.

"Please," she said abruptly, turning to Josua. "I think . . . I need to lie down. I need to sleep." She did not see the one-time kitchen boy lower his head as though he had been spurned.

"Of course," said her uncle, full of concern. "Of course. As long as you like. Then, when you arise, we will have a feast of thanksgiving!"

Miriamele nodded, dazed, then let Vorzheva lead her away toward the rippling sea of tents. Behind her, Isgrimnur's arms were still locked about his giggling, weeping wife.

22

Whispers in Stone

The water poured out of the great crevice and splashed across the shelf of flat black basalt before surging over the edge and down into the pit. For all its fury, the waterfall was nearly invisible in the dark cavern, which was lit only by a few small, glowing stones embedded in the walls. The impossibly high-ceilinged chamber was called *Yakh Huyeru*, which meant Hall of Trembling; and although the cavern had been given that name for another reason, the walls did seem to shiver ever so slightly as *Kiga'rasku*, the Tearfall, rolled ceaselessly down into the depths. It made very little noise in its passage, whether because of some trick of the vast chamber's echo or because of the void into which it fell. Some of the mountain's residents whispered that Kiga'rasku had no bottom, that the water fell through the bottom of the earth, pouring endlessly into the black Between.

As she stood at the chasm's edge, Utuk'ku was a minute stitch of silvery white against the tapestry of dark water. Her pale robes fluttered slowly in the wind of the falls. Her masked face was lowered as though she sought Kiga'rasku's depths, but at the moment she was not seeing the mighty rush of water any more than she saw the dim sun that rolled past the mountaintop overhead, on the far side of many hundred furlongs of Stormspike stone.

Utuk'ku considered.

Odd and unsettling shifts had begun to take place in the intricate pattern of events that she had undertaken so long ago, events she had studied and delicately modified over the course of more than a thousand thousand sunless days. One of the first of those shifts had caused a small tear in her design. It was not irreparable, of course—Utuk'ku's weavings were strong, and more than a few strands would have to snap completely before her long-planned triumph would be threatened—but patching it would require care, and work, and the diamond-sharp concentration that only the Eldest could bring to bear.

The silver mask turned slowly, catching the faint light like the moon emerging from behind clouds. A trio of figures had appeared in the doorway of Yakh Huyeru. The nearest kneeled, then placed the heels of her hands over her eyes; her two companions did the same.

As Utuk'ku considered them and the task she would set for them, she felt a moment of regret for the loss of Ingen Jegger—but it was a moment only. Utuk'ku Seyt-Hamakha was the last of the Gardenborn: she had not survived all of her peers by many centuries through wasting time on useless emotions. Jegger had been eager and blindly loyal as a coursing hound, and he had possessed the particular virtues, for Utuk'ku's purposes, of his own mortal nature, but he had still been only a tool—something to be used and then discarded. He had served what had been at the time her greatest need. For other tasks, there would be other servitors.

The Norns bowing before her, two women and a man, looked up as though awakening from a dream. The desires of their mistress had been poured into them like sour milk from a pitcher, and now Utuk'ku raised her gloved hand in a brittle gesture of dismissal. They turned and were gone, smooth, swift, and silent as shadows fleeing the dawn.

After they had vanished, Utuk'ku stood for another long silent time before the falling water, listening to the ghostly echoes. Then, at last, the Norn Queen turned and made her unhurried way toward the Chamber of the Breathing Harp.

As she took her seat beside the Well, the chanting from the depths of Stormspike below her rose in pitch: the

Lightless Ones, in their unfathomable, inhuman way, were welcoming her back to her frost-mantled throne. Except for Utuk'ku herself, the Chamber of the Harp was empty, although a single thought or flick of her hand would have raised a thicket of bristling spears clutched in pale hands.

She lifted her long fingers to the temples of her mask and stared into the shifting column of steam that hung above the Well. The Harp, its outlines shiftingly imprecise, glinted crimson, yellow and violet. Ineluki's presence was muted. He had begun to withdraw into himself, drawing strength from whatever ultimate source nurtured him as air fed the flame of a candle. He was preparing for the great test that would be coming soon.

Although it was in some ways a relief to be free of his burning, angry thoughts—thoughts that often were not intelligible even to Utuk'ku except as a sort of cloud of hatred and longing—the Norn Queen's thin lips nevertheless compressed into a thin line of discontent behind her gleaming mask. The things she had seen in the dreamworld had troubled her; despite the machinations she had set underway, Utuk'ku was not altogether content. It would have been a relief of sorts to share them with the thing that was focused in the heart of the Well—but it was not to be. The greatest part of Ineluki would be absent from now until the final days when the Conqueror Star stood high.

Utuk'ku's colorless eyes suddenly narrowed. Somewhere on the fringes of the great tapestry of force and dream that wove through the Well, something else had begun to move in an unexpected way. The Norn Queen turned her gaze inward, letting her mind reach out and probe along the strands of her delicately balanced web, along the uncountable lines of intention and calculation and fate. There it was: another parting of her careful work.

A sigh, faint as the velvet wind across a bat's wing, fluted through Utuk'ku's lips. The singing of the Lightless Ones faltered for a moment at the wave of irritation that washed out from Stormspike's mistress, but a moment later their voices rose again, hollow and triumphant. It was only someone dabbling with one of the Master Witnesses—a youngling, even if of the line of Amerasu Ship-Born. She would treat the whelp harshly. This damage, too, could be repaired. It would merely require a bit more of her concentration, a bit more of her straining thought—but it would be done. She was weary, but not so weary as that.

It had been perhaps a thousand years since the Norn Queen had smiled, but if she had remembered how, she might have smiled at that moment. Even the oldest of the Hikeda'ya had known no other mistress but Utuk'ku. Some of them could be pardoned, perhaps, for thinking that she was no longer a living thing, but like the Storm King a creature made entirely of ice and sorcery and endless, vigilant malignity. Utuk'ku knew better. Although even the millennial lives of some of her descendants spanned but a small portion of her own, beneath the corpse-pale robes and shimmering mask was still a living woman. Inside her ancient flesh a heart still beat—slow and strong, like a blind thing crawling at the bottom of a deep, silent sea.

She was weary, but she was still fierce, still powerful. She had planned so long for these coming days that the very face of the land above had shifted and altered beneath Time's hand as she waited. She would live to see her revenge.

The lights of the Well flickered on the empty metal face she showed the world. Perhaps in that triumphant hour, Utuk'ku thought, she would once more remember what it was to smile.

"Ah, by the Grove," Jiriki said, "it is indeed Mezutu'a—the Silverhome." He held his torch higher. "I have not seen it before, but so many songs are sung of it that I feel I know its towers and bridges and streets as though I had grown here."

"You haven't been here? But I thought your people

built it." Eolair moved back from the stair's precipitous edge. The great city lay spread below them, a fantastic jumble of shadowed stone.

"We did—in part—but the last of the Zida'ya had left this place long before *my* birth." Jiriki's golden eyes were wide, as though he could not tear his gaze from the roofs of the cavern city. "When the Tinukeda'ya severed their fates from ours, Jenjiyana of the Nightingales declared in her wisdom that we should give this place to the Navigator's Children, in partial payment of the debt we owed them." He frowned and shook his head, hair moving loosely about his shoulders. "Year-Dancing House, at least, remembered something of honor. She also gave to them Hikehikayo in the north, and sea-collared Jhiná-T'seneí, which has long since disappeared beneath the waves."

Eolair struggled to make sense of the barrage of unfamiliar names. "Your people gave this to the Tinukeda'ya?" he asked. "The creatures that we called *domhaini?* The dwarrows?"

"Some were called that," Jiriki nodded. He turned his bright stare on the count. "But they are not 'creatures,' Count Eolair. They came from The Garden that is Lost, just as my people did. We made the mistake of thinking them less than us then. I wish to avoid it now."

"I meant no insult," said Eolair. "But I met them, as I told you. They were . . . strange. But they were kind to us, too."

"The Ocean Children were ever gentle." Jiriki began to descend the staircase. "That is why my people brought them, I fear—because they felt they would be tractable servants."

Eolair hastened to catch up to him. The Sitha moved with assured swiftness, walking far nearer to the edge than the count would have dared, and never looking down. "What did you mean, 'some of them were called that'?" Eolair asked. "Were there Tinukeda'ya who were *not* dwarrows?"

"Yes. Those who lived here—the dwarrows as you call them—were a smallish group who had split off from the main tribe. The rest of Ruyan's folk stayed close to water, since the oceans were always dear to their hearts. Many of them became what the mortals called 'sea-watchers.' "

"*Niskies?*" In his long career, during which he had traveled often in southern waters, Eolair had met many sea-watchers. "They still exist. But they look nothing like the dwarrows!"

Jiriki paused to let the count catch up, and thereafter, perhaps out of courtesy, kept his pace slower. "That was the Tinukeda'ya's blessing as well as their curse. They could change themselves, over time, to better fit the place that they lived: there is a certain mutability in their blood and bones. I think that if the world were to be destroyed by fire, the Ocean Children would be the only ones to survive. Before long, they would be able to eat smoke and swim in hot ashes."

"But that is astounding," said Eolair. "The dwarrows I met, Yis-fidri and his companions, seemed so timid. Who would ever dream they were capable of such things?"

"There are lizards in the southern marshes," Jiriki said with a smile, "that can change their color to match the leaf or trunk or stone on which they crouch. They are timid, too. It does not seem odd to me that the most frightened creatures are often the best at hiding themselves."

"But if your people gave the dwarrows—the Tinukeda'ya—this place, why are they so afraid of you? When the lady Maegwin and myself first came here and met them, they were terrified that we might be servants of yours come to drag them back."

Jiriki stopped. He seemed to be transfixed by something down below. When he turned to Eolair once more, it was with an expression so pained that even his alien features did not disguise it. "They are right to be frightened, Count Eolair. Amerasu, our wise one who has just been taken from us, called our dealings with the Tinukeda'ya our great shame. We did *not* treat them well, and we kept from them things that they deserved to know ... because we thought they would make better servants if they labored in ignorance." He made a gesture of frustration. "When Jenjiyana, Year-Dancing House's mistress, gave them this place in the distant past, she was opposed by many of the Houses of Dawn. There are those among the Zida'ya, even to this day, who feel we should have kept Ruyan Ve's children as servants. They are right to fear, your friends."

"None of these things were in our old legends of your folk," Eolair marveled. "You paint a grim, sad picture, Prince Jiriki. Why do you tell me all this?"

The Sitha started down the pitted steps once more. "Because, Count Eolair, that era will soon be gone. That does not mean I think that happier things are coming—although there is always a chance, I must suppose. But for better or worse, this age of the world is ending."

They continued downward, unspeaking.

Eolair relied on his dim memories of his previous visit to lead Jiriki through the crumbling city—although, judging by the Sitha's impatience, which seemed bridled only by his natural courtesy, Jiriki might have been just as capable of leading him. As they walked through the echoing, deserted streets, Eolair again had the impression of Mezutu'a as not so much a city as a warren for shy yet friendly beasts. This time, though, with Jiriki's words about the ocean still fresh in his mind, Eolair saw it as a sort of coral garden, its countless buildings growing one from another, shot through with empty doorways and shadowed tunnels, its towers joined together by stone walkways thin as spun glass. He wondered absently if the dwarrows had harbored some longing for the sea deep inside themselves, so that this place and its additions—even now, Jiriki was once again pointing out some feature that had been added to Mezutu'a's original buildings—had gradually become a sort of undersea grotto, shielded from the sun by mountain stone instead of blue water.

As they emerged from the long tunnel and its carvings of living stone into the vastness of the great stone arena, Jiriki, who had now taken the lead, was surrounded by a nimbus of pale, chalky light. As he stared down into the arena, the Sitha raised his slim hands to shoulder height, then made a careful gesture before striding forward, only his deerlike grace hiding the fact that he was moving very quickly.

The great crystalline Shard still stood at the center of the bowl, throbbing weakly, its surfaces full of slow-moving colors. Around it, the stone benches were empty. The arena was deserted.

"*Yis-fidri!*" Eolair shouted. "*Yis-hadra! It is Eolair, Count of Nad Mullach!*"

His voice rolled across the arena and reverberated along the cavern's distant walls. There was no reply. "*It is Eolair, Yis-fidri! I have come back!*"

When no one answered him—there was no sign of life at all, no footfalls, no gleam of the dwarrows' rose-crystal batons—Eolair walked down to join Jiriki.

"This is what I feared," said the count. "That if I brought you, they would vanish. I only hope they have not fled the city completely." He frowned. "I imagine they think me a traitor, bringing one of their former masters here."

"Perhaps." Jiriki seemed distracted, almost tense. "By my ancestors," he breathed, "to stand before the Shard of Mezutu'a! I can feel it singing!"

Eolair put his hand near the milky stone, but could feel nothing but a slight warming of the air.

Jiriki raised his palms to the Shard but paused short of touching it, bringing his hands to a stop as though he embraced an invisible something that followed the stone's outline but was nearly twice as large. The light patterns began to glow a little more colorfully, as though whatever moved in the stone had swum closer to the surface. Jiriki watched the play of colors carefully as he moved his fingers in slow orbits, never touching the Shard directly, positioning his hands around the stone as though partnering the unmoving object in some ritual dance.

A long time passed, a time in which Eolair felt his legs beginning to ache. He sat down on one of the stone benches. A cold draft was wafting down the arena and scraping at the back of his neck. He huddled a little deeper into his cloak and watched Jiriki, who still stood before the gleaming stone, locked in some silent communion.

More than a little bored, Eolair began to fidget with his long horsetail of black hair. Although it was hard to tell exactly how much time had passed since Jiriki had approached the stone, the count knew it had not been a brief interval: Eolair was famous for his patience, and even in these maddening days, it took a great deal to make him restless.

Abruptly, the Sitha flinched and took a step back from the stone. He swayed in place for a moment, then turned to Eolair. There was a light in Jiriki's eyes that seemed more than just a reflection of the Shard's inconstant glow.

"The Speakfire," Jiriki said.

Eolair was confused. "What do you mean?"

"The Speakfire in Hikehikayo. It is another witness—a Master Witness, like the Shard. It is very close, somehow—close in a way that has nothing to do with distance. I cannot shake it free and turn the Shard to other things."

"What other things do you want to turn it to?"

Jiriki shook his head. He glanced quickly at the Shard before beginning. "It is hard to explain, Count Eolair. Let me put it this way—if you were lost and surrounded by fog, but there was a tree you could climb that would allow you to move *above* the mist, would you not do it?"

Eolair nodded. "Certainly, but I still do not quite see what you mean."

"Simply this. We who are used to the Road of Dreams have been denied it of late—as surely as thick fog can make a person afraid to wander any distance from his home, even when his need is great. The Witnesses I can use are minor; without the strength and knowledge of someone like our First Grandmother Amerasu, they are of use only for small purposes. The Shard of Mezutu'a is a Master Witness—I had thought of searching for it even before we rode out of Jao é-Tinukai'i—but I have just found that its use is denied me, somehow. It is as though I had ascended that tree I spoke of, clambering up to the upper limits of the fog, only to find that someone else was above me, and that they would not let me climb high enough to see. I am balked."

"I'm afraid it is all still largely a mystery to a mortal like me, Jiriki, although I think I see a little of what you are trying to explain." Eolair considered for a moment. "Saying it another way: you wish to look out a window, but someone on the other side has covered it. Is that right?"

"Yes. Well put." Jiriki smiled, but Eolair saw weariness beneath the Sitha's alien features. "But I dare not go away without trying to look through the window again, as many times as I have the strength."

"I will wait for you, then. But we have brought little food or water—and besides, although I cannot speak for yours, I fear *my* people will have need of me before too long."

"As to food and drink," Jiriki said distractedly, "you may have mine." He turned back to the Shard once more. "When you feel it is time for you to return, tell me—but do not touch me until I say it is permitted, Count Eolair, if you will promise. I do not know exactly what I must do, and it would be safer for both of us if you leave me alone, no matter what it may seem is happening."

"I will not do anything unless you ask me to," Eolair promised.

"Good." Jiriki raised his hands and began making the slow circles once more.

The Count of Nad Mullach sighed and leaned back against the stone bench, trying to find a comfortable position.

Eolair awakened from a strange dream—he had been fleeing before a vast wheel, treetop-tall, rough and splintered as the beams of an ancient ceiling—into the abrupt realization that something was wrong. The light was brighter, pulsing now like a heartbeat, but it had turned a sickly blue-green. The air in the huge cavern was as tense and still as before a storm, a smell like the aftereffects of lightning burned Eolair's nostrils.

Jiriki still stood before the gleaming Shard, a mote in

the sea of blinding light—but where before he had been as poised as a Mircha-dancer readying a rain prayer, now his limbs were contorted, his head thrown back as though some invisible hand was squeezing the life out of him. Eolair rushed forward, desperately worried but unsure of what to do. The Sitha had told the count not to touch him, no matter what seemed to be happening, but when Eolair drew close enough to see Jiriki's face, nearly invisible in the great outwash of nauseating brilliance, he felt his heart plummet. Surely this could not be what Jiriki had planned!

The Sitha's gold-flecked eyes had rolled up, so that only a crescent of white showed beneath the lids. His lips were skinned back from his teeth in the snarl of a cornered beast, and the writhing veins in his neck and forehead seemed about to burst from his skin.

"Prince Jiriki!" Eolair shouted. "Jiriki, can you hear me!?"

The Sitha's mouth opened a little wider. His jaws worked. A loud rumble of sound spilled out and echoed across the great bowl, deep and unintelligible, but so obviously full of pain and fear that even as Eolair clapped his hands over his ears in desperation he felt his heart lurch with sympathetic horror. He reached out a tentative hand toward the Sitha and watched in amazement as the hairs on his arm lifted straight up. His skin was tingling.

Count Eolair only thought for a moment longer. Cursing himself for the fool he was, then flicking off a quick, silent prayer to Cuamh Earthdog, he took a step forward and grasped Jiriki's shoulders.

At the instant his fingers touched, Eolair felt himself suddenly overrun by a titanic force from nowhere, a rushing black river of terror and blood and empty voices that poured through him, sweeping his thoughts away like a handful of leaves in a cataract. But even in the brief moment before his real self spun out into nothingness, he could see his hands still touching Jiriki, and saw the Sitha, overbalanced by Eolair's weight, toppling forward into the Shard. Jiriki touched the stone. A great bonfire of sparks leaped up, brighter even than the blue-green radiance, a million gleaming lights like the souls of all the fireflies in the world set free at once, dancing and swooping. Then everything faded into darkness. Eolair felt himself falling, falling, cast down like a stone into an endless void. . . .

"You live."

The relief in Jiriki's voice was clear. Eolair opened his eyes to a pale blur that gradually became the Sitha's face bent close to his. Jiriki's cool hands were on his temples.

Eolair feebly waved him off. The Sitha stepped back and allowed him to sit up; Eolair was obscurely grateful to be allowed to do it himself, even though it took him no little time to steady his shaking body. His head was hammering, ringing like Rhynn's cauldron in full battle cry. He had to close his eyes for a moment to keep himself from vomiting.

"I warned you not to touch me," Jiriki said, but there was no displeasure in his voice. "I am sorry that you should have suffered so for me."

"What . . . what happened?"

Jiriki shook his head. There was a certain new stiffness in his movements, but when Eolair thought of how much longer the Sitha had endured what he himself had survived for only a moment, the count was awed. "I am not sure," Jiriki answered. "Something did not want me to reach the Dream Road, or did not want the Shard tampered with—something with far more power or knowledge than I have." He grimaced, showing his white teeth. "I was right to warn Seoman away from the Road of Dreams. I should have heeded my own advice, it seems. Likimeya my mother will be furious."

"I thought you were dying." Eolair groaned. It felt as though someone was shoeing a large plow-horse behind his forehead.

"If you had not pushed me out of the alignment in which I was trapped, worse than death would have awaited me, I think." He laughed suddenly, sharply. "I owe you the Staja Ame, Count Eolair—the White Arrow. Sadly, someone else already has mine."

Eolair rolled toward his side and struggled to stand. It took several tries, but at last, with Jiriki's help, which Eolair accepted gladly this time, he managed to drag himself upright. The Shard again seemed quiescent, flickering mutedly in the center of the empty arena, casting hesitant shadows behind the stone benches. "White Arrow?" he murmured. His head hurt, and his muscles felt as though he had been dragged behind a cart from Hernysadharc to Crannhyr.

"I will tell you some day soon," said Jiriki. "I must learn to live with these indignities."

Together they began to walk toward the tunnel that led out of the arena, Eolair limping, Jiriki steadier, but still slow. "Indignities?" Eolair asked weakly. "What do you mean?"

"Being saved by mortals. It has become a sort of habit for me, it seems."

The sound of their halting footsteps sent echoes fluttering across the vast cavern and up among the dark places.

"Here, puss, puss. Come now, Grimalkin."

Rachel was a little embarrassed. She wasn't quite sure what one said to cats—in the old days, she had expected them to do their job keeping the rat population down, but she had left the petting and pampering of them to her chambermaids. As far as she had been concerned, handing out endearments and sweetmeats was no part of her obligation to *any* of her charges, two-footed or four. But now she had a need—if admittedly a daft and soft-headed one—and so she was humbling herself.

Thank merciful Usires no human creature is around to see me.

"Puss, puss, puss." Rachel waved the bit of salt-beef. She slid forward half a cubit, trying to ignore the ache in her back and the rough stone beneath her knees. "I'm trying to *feed* you, you Rhiap-preserve-us filthy thing." She scowled and waggled the bit of meat. "Serve you right if I *did* cook you."

Even the cat, standing just a short distance out of Rachel's reach in the middle of the corridor, seemed to know that this was an idle threat. Not because of Rachel's soft heart—she needed this beast to take food from her, but otherwise would just as happily have smacked it with her broom—but because eating cat flesh was as inconceivable to Rachel as spitting upon a church altar. She could not have said why exactly cat meat was different than the flesh of rabbit or roe deer, but she did not need to. It was not done by decent folk, and that was enough to know.

Still, in the last quarter of an hour, she had more than once or twice toyed with the idea of kicking this recalcitrant creature down the steep staircase and then turning to some idea that did not require the assistance of animals. But the most irritating thing was that even the idea itself was of no practical use.

Rachel looked at her quivering arm and greasy fingers. All of this to help a monster?

You're slipping, woman. Mad as a mooncalf.

"Puss . . ."

The gray cat took a few steps closer and paused, surveying Rachel with eyes widened by suspicion as much as the bright lamplight. Rachel silently said the Elysia prayer and tried to move the beef enticingly. The cat approached warily, wrinkled its nostrils, then took a cautious lick. After a moment's mock-casual washing of whiskers, it seemed to gain courage. It reached out and pulled loose some of the meat, stepping back to swallow it, then came forward once more. Rachel brought up her other hand and let it brush the cat's back. It started, but when Rachel made no sudden move, the cat took the last piece of beef and gulped it down. She let her fingers trail lightly against its fur as the cat nosed her now-empty hand questioningly. Rachel stroked it behind the ears, gamely resisting the impulse to throttle the particular little beast. At last, when she had worked loose a purr, she clambered heavily to her feet.

"Tomorrow," she said. "More meat." She turned and stumped wearily up the corridor toward her hidden room. The cat watched her go, sniffed around on the stone floor

for any scraps it might have missed, then lay down and
began to groom itself.

Jiriki and Eolair emerged into the light blinking like
moles. The count was already regretting his decision to
choose this entrance into the underground mines, one that
was so far from Hernysadharc. If they had come in
through the caverns where the Hernystiri had sheltered, as
he and Maegwin had the first time, they could have spent
the night in one of the recently-inhabited dens of the
cave-city, saving themselves a long ride back.

"You do not look well," the Sitha commented, which
was probably no more than the truth. Eolair's head had at
last stopped ringing, but his muscles still ached mightily.

"I do not feel well." The count looked around. There
was still a little snow on the ground, but the weather had
improved greatly in the last few days. It was tempting to
consider staying right here and traveling back to the Taig
in the morning. He squinted up at the sun. Only mid-
afternoon: their time underground had seemed much
longer ... if this was still the same day. He grinned
sourly at the thought. Better a painful ride back to the
Taig, he decided, than a night in the still-cold wildlands.

The horses, Eolair's bay gelding and Jiriki's white
charger, which had feathers and bells braided into its
mane, stood cropping the meager grass, stretched to the
ends of their long tethers. It was the work of only a few
moments to make them ready, then human and Sitha
spurred away toward the southeast and Hernysadharc.

"The air seems different," Eolair called. "Can you feel
it?"

"Yes." Jiriki lifted his head like a hunting beast scent-
ing the breeze. "But I do not know what it might mean."

"It's warmer. That's enough for me."

By the time they reached the outskirts of Hernysadharc,
the sun had finally slipped down behind the Grianspog and
the base of the sky was losing its ruddiness. They

rode side by side up the Taig Road, threading through the not inconsiderable foot- and cart-traffic. Seeing his people once more out and about their business eased the pain of Eolair's aches. Things were far from ordinary, and most of the people on the road had the gaunt, staring look of the hungry, but they were traveling freely in their own country again. Many seemed to have come from the market; they clutched their acquisitions jealously, even if they held no more than a handful of onions.

"So what did you learn?" Eolair asked at last.

"From the Shard? Much and little." Jiriki saw the count's expression and laughed. "Ah, you look like my mortal friend Seoman Snowlock! It is true, we Dawn Children do not give satisfactory answers."

"Seoman. . . ?"

"Your kind call him 'Simon,' I think." Jiriki nodded his head, milk-white hair dancing in the wind. "He is a strange cub, but brave and good-natured. He is clever, too, although he hides it well."

"I met him, I think. He is with Josua Lackhand at the Stone—at Ses . . . Sesu . . ." He gestured, trying to summon the name.

"Sesuad'ra. Yes, that is him. Young, but he has been caught up by too many currents for chance alone to be the explanation. He will have a part to play in things." Jiriki stared into the east, as if looking for the mortal boy there. "Amerasu—our First Grandmother—invited him into her house. That was a great honor indeed."

Eolair shook his head. "He seemed little more than a tall and somewhat awkward young man when I met him—but I stopped putting trust in appearances long ago."

Jiriki smiled. "You are one in whom the old Hernystiri blood runs strong, then. Let me consider what I found in the Shard a while longer. Then, if you come with me to see Likimeya, I will share my thoughts with both of you."

As they made their way up Hern's Hill, Eolair saw someone walking slowly across the damp grass. He raised his hand.

"A moment, please." Eolair passed the Sitha his reins,

then swung down from his saddle and walked after the figure, which bent every few moments as though plucking flowers from among the grass-stems. A loose scatter of birds hovered behind, swooping down and then starting up again with a flurry of wings.

"Maegwin?" Eolair called. She did not stop, so he hurried his steps to catch up to her. "Maegwin," he said as he came abreast of her. "Are you well?"

Lluth's daughter turned to look at him. She was wearing a dark cloak, but beneath it was a dress of bright yellow. Her belt buckle was a sunflower of hammered gold. She looked pretty and at peace. "Count Eolair," she said calmly, and smiled, then bent at the waist and let another handful of seed corn dribble from her fist.

"What are you doing?"

"Planting flowers. The long battle with winter has withered even Heaven's blooms." She stooped and sprinkled more corn. Behind her, the birds fought noisily over the kernels.

"What do you mean, 'Heaven's blooms'?"

She looked up at him curiously. "What a strange question. But think, Eolair, of what beautiful flowers will spring from these seeds. Think of how it will look when the gardens of the gods are a-blossom once more."

Eolair stared at her helplessly for a moment. Maegwin continued to walk forward, sprinkling the corn in little piles as she went. The birds, stuffed but not yet sated, followed her. "But you are on Hern's Hill," he said. "You are in Hernysadharc, the place where you grew up!"

Maegwin paused and pulled her cloak a little tighter. "You do not look well, Eolair. That is not right. Nobody should be ill in a place like this."

Jiriki was making his way lightly across the grass leading the two horses. He stopped a short distance away, unwilling to intrude.

To Eolair's surprise, Maegwin turned to the Sitha and dropped into a curtsy. "Welcome, Lord Brynioch," she called, then rose and lifted her hand to the reddening western horizon. "What a beautiful sky you have made for us today. Thank you, O Bright One."

Jiriki said nothing, but looked to Eolair with a catlike expression of calm curiosity.

"Do you not know who this is?" the count asked Maegwin. "This is Jiriki of the Sithi. He is no god, but one of those who saved us from Skali." When she did not reply, but only smiled indulgently, his voice rose. "Maegwin, this is not Brynioch. You are not among the gods. This is Jiriki—immortal, but of flesh and blood just like you and I."

Maegwin turned her sly smile onto the Sitha. "Good my Lord, Eolair seems fevered. Did you perhaps take him too close to the sun on your journeying today?"

The Count of Nad Mullach stared. Was she truly mad or playing some unfathomable game? He had never seen anything like this. "Maegwin!" he snapped.

Jiriki touched his arm. "Come with me, Count Eolair. We will talk."

Maegwin curtsied again. "You are kind, Lord Brynioch. I will continue with my task now, if I have your leave. It is little enough to repay your kindness and hospitality."

Jiriki nodded. Maegwin turned and continued her slow walk across the hillside.

"Gods help me," Eolair said. "She is mad! It is worse than I had feared."

"Even one who is not of your kind could see that she is gravely troubled."

"What can I do?" the count mourned. "What if she does not recover her wits?"

"I have a friend—a cousin, by your terms—who is a healer," Jiriki offered. "I do not know that this young woman's problem can be helped by her, but there could be no harm in trying, I think."

He watched Eolair clamber back into his saddle, then mounted his own horse in a single, fluid movement and led the silent count up the hillside toward the Taig.

❧

When she heard the approaching footfalls, Rachel almost pushed herself farther back into the shadows before she remembered that it would make no difference. Inwardly, she cursed herself for a fool.

The steps were slow, as if the one making them was very weak or was carrying a huge burden.

"Now where are we going?" It was a harsh whisper, deep and rough, a voice that was not used very often. "Going. Where are we going? Very well, then, I'm coming." There was a thin wheeze of sound that might have been laughing or crying.

Rachel held her breath. The cat appeared first, head up, certain now after nearly a week that what was waiting was dinner rather than danger. The man followed a moment later, trudging forward out of the shadows into the lamplight. His pale, scarred face was covered in a long, gray-shot beard and the parts of him that were not covered by his ragged, filthy clothes were starvation-thin. His eyes were closed.

"Slow down," he said raspingly. "I'm weak. Can't go fast." He stopped, as though he sensed the lamplight on his face, on the lids of his ruined eyes. "Where are you, cat?" he quavered.

Rachel leaned down to pet the cat, which was butting at her ankle, then slipped it a bit of its expected salt-beef. She straightened up.

"Earl Guthwulf." Her voice seemed so loud after Guthwulf's whisper that it even shocked her. The man flinched and fell back, almost toppling over, but instead of turning to run he raised his trembling hands before him.

"Leave me alone, you damnable things!" he cried. "Haunt someone else! Leave me with my misery! Let the sword have me if it wants."

"Don't run, Guthwulf!" Rachel said hastily, but at the renewed sound of her voice, the earl turned and begin to stagger back down the corridor.

"There will be food for you here," she called after him. The tattered apparition did not answer, but vanished into the shadows beyond the lampglow. "I will leave it and

then go away. I will do that every day! You do not need
to speak to me!"

When the echoes had died, she put down a small helping of jerked meat for the cat, which began to chew hungrily. The bowl full of meat and dried fruit she placed in
a dusty alcove on the wall, above the cat's reach, but
where the living scarecrow could not fail to find it when
he worked up the nerve to return.

Still not quite sure what her own purpose was, Rachel
picked up her lamp and started back toward the stairwell
that would lead to the higher, more familiar parts of the
castle's labyrinth. Now she had done it and it was too late
to turn back. But *why* had she done it? She would have to
risk the upper castle again, since the stores she had laid in
were planned to feed one frugal person only, not two
adults and a cat with a bottomless stomach.

"Rhiap, save me from myself," she grumbled.

Perhaps it was the fact that it was the only charity she
could perform in these terrible days—although Rachel
had never been obsessed with charity, since so many mendicants were, as far as she could tell, perfectly able-
bodied and most likely merely frightened of work. But
perhaps it *was* charity after all. Times had changed, and
Rachel had changed, too.

Or perhaps she was just lonely, she reflected. She
snorted at herself and hurried up the corridor.

23

The Sounding of the Horn

Several odd things happened in the days after Princess Miriamele and her companions arrived at Sesuad'ra.

The first and least important was the change that came over Lenti, Count Streáwe's messenger. The beetle-browed Perdruinese man had spent his first days in New Gadrinsett strutting around the small marketplace, annoying the local women and picking fights with the merchants. He had shown several people his knives, with the thinly-veiled implication that he was prone to use them when the mood was upon him.

However, when Duke Isgrimnur arrived with the princess, Lenti immediately retired to the tent he had been given as his billet and did not come out for some time. It took a great deal of coaxing to get him to emerge even to receive Josua's reply to his master Streáwe, and when Lenti saw that the duke was to be present, the knife-flourishing messenger became weak in the knees and had to be allowed to sit down for Josua's instructions. Apparently—or so the story was later told in the market—he and Isgrimnur had met before, and Lenti had not found the acquaintanceship a pleasant one. Once given a reply for his master, Lenti left Sesuad'ra hurriedly. Neither he nor anyone else much regretted his departure.

The second and far more astounding event was Duke Isgrimnur's announcement that the old man he had brought to Sesuad'ra out of the south was in fact Camaris-sá-Vinitta, the greatest hero of the Johannine

Age. It was whispered throughout the settlement that when Josua was told this on the evening of the return, he fell to his knees before the old man and kissed his hand—which seemed proof enough that Isrimnur spoke truly. Oddly, however, the nominal Sir Camaris seemed almost entirely unmoved by Josua's gesture. Conflicting rumors quickly swept through the community of New Gadrinsett—the old man had been wounded in the head, he had gone mad from drink or sorcery or any number of other possible reasons, even that he had taken a vow of silence.

The third and saddest occurrence was the death of old Towser. On the same night that Miriamele and the others returned, the ancient jester died in his sleep. Most agreed that the excitement had been too much for his heart. Those who knew the terrors through which Towser had already passed with the rest of Josua's company of survivors were not so sure, but he was after all a very old man, and his passing appeared to be natural. Josua spoke kindly of him at the burial two days later, reminding the small party gathered there of Towser's long service to King John. It was noted by some, though, that despite the prince's generous eulogy, the jester was interred near the other casualties of the recent battle rather than beside Deornoth in the garden of Leavetaking House.

The harper Sangfugol made sure that the old man was buried with a lute as well as his tattered motley, in memory of how Towser had taught him his musical art. Together, Sangfugol and Simon also gathered snowflowers, which they scattered atop the dark earth after the grave was filled.

"It's sad that he should die just when Camaris had returned." Miriamele was stringing the remaining snowflowers, which Simon had given to her, into a delicate necklace. "One of the few people he knew in the old days, and they never had a chance to talk. Not that Camaris would have said anything, I suppose."

Simon shook his head. "Towser *did* speak to Camaris, Princess." He paused. Her title still felt strange, especially when she sat before him in the flesh, living, breathing. "When Towser saw him—even before Isgrimnur said who it was—Towser went pale. He stood in front of Camaris for a moment, rubbing his hands like this, then whispered, 'I did not tell anyone, Lord, I swear!' Then he went off to his tent. Nobody heard him say it but me, I think. I had no idea what it meant—I still don't."

Miriamele nodded. "I suppose we never will, now." She glanced at him, then immediately dropped her gaze back to her flowers.

Simon thought she was prettier than ever. Her golden hair, the dye now worn away, was boyishly short, but he rather liked how it emphasized the firm, sharp line of her chin and her green eyes. Even the slightly more serious expression she now wore just made her all the more appealing. He admired her, that was the word, but there was nothing he could do with his feelings. He longed to protect her from anything and everything, but at the same time he knew very well that she would never allow anyone to treat her as though she were a helpless child.

Simon sensed something else changed in Miriamele as well. She was still kind and courteous, but there was a remoteness to her that he did not remember, an air of restraint. The old balance forged between the two of them seemed to have been altered, but he did not quite understand what had replaced it. Miriamele seemed a little more distant, yet at the same time more aware of him than she had ever been before, almost as though he frightened her in some way.

He could not help staring at her, so he was grateful that for the moment her attention was fixed on the flowers in her lap. It was so strange to face the real Miriamele after all the months of remembering and imagining that he found it hard to think clearly in her presence. Now that the first week since her return had passed, a little of the awkwardness seemed to be gone, but there was still a gap between them. Even back in Naglimund, when he had first seen her as the king's daughter she was, there had not been this quality of separation.

Simon had told her—not without some pride—of his many adventures in the last half-year; to his surprise, he had then discovered that Miriamele's experiences had been almost as wildly improbable as his own.

At first he had decided that the horrors of her journey—the kilpa and ghants, the deaths of Dinivan and Lector Ranessin, her not-quite-explained confinement on the ship of some Nabbanai nobleman—were quite enough to explain the wall that he felt between them. Now he was not so sure. They had been friends, and even if they could never be more than that, the friendship had been real, hadn't it? Something had happened to make her treat him differently.

Could it be me, Simon wondered. *Could I have changed so much that she doesn't like me anymore?*

He unthinkingly stroked his beard. Miriamele looked up, caught his eye, and smiled mockingly. He felt a pleasant warmth: it was almost like seeing her in her old guise as Marya, the servant girl.

"You're certainly proud of that, aren't you?"

"What? My beard?" Simon was suddenly glad he had kept it, for he was blushing. "It just . . . sort of grew."

"Mmmm. By surprise? Overnight?"

"What's wrong with it?" he asked, stung. "I'm a knight, by the Bloody Tree! Why shouldn't I have a beard!"

"Don't swear. Not in front of ladies, and especially not in front of princesses." She gave him a look that was meant to be stern, but was spoiled in its effect somehow by her suppressed smile. "Besides, even if you are a knight, Simon—and I suppose I'll have to take your word for that until I remember to ask Uncle Josua—that doesn't mean you're old enough to grow a beard without looking silly."

"Ask Josua? You can ask anyone!" Simon was torn between pleasure at seeing her act a little more like her old self and irritation at what she had said. "Not old enough! I'm almost sixteen years! Will be in another fortnight, on

Saint Yistrin's day!" He had only just realized himself that it was near when Father Strangyeard had made a remark about the saint's upcoming holy day.

"Truly?" Miriamele's look became serious. "I had my sixteenth birthday while we were traveling to Kwanitupul. Cadrach was very nice—he stole a jam-tart and some Lakeland pinks for me—but it wasn't much of a celebration."

"That thieving villain," Simon growled. He still had not forgotten his purse and the shame he had endured over its loss, no matter how much had happened since then.

"Don't say that." Miriamele was suddenly sharp. "You don't know anything about him, Simon. He has suffered much. His life has been hard."

Simon made a noise of disgust. "*He's* suffered!? What about the people he steals from?"

Miriamele's eyes narrowed. "I don't want you to say another word about Cadrach. Not a word."

Simon opened his mouth, then shut it again. *Damn me,* he thought, *you can get in trouble with girls so quickly! It's like they're all practicing to grow up to be Rachel the Dragon!*

He took a breath. "I'm sorry your birthday wasn't very nice."

She eyed him for a moment, then relented. "Perhaps when yours comes, Simon, we can both celebrate. We can give each other gifts, like they do in Nabban."

"You already gave me one." He reached into the pocket of his cloak and removed a wisp of blue cloth. "Do you remember? When I was leaving to go north with Binabik and the others."

Miriamele stared at it for a moment. "You kept it?" she asked quietly.

"Of course. I wore it the whole time, practically. Of course I kept it."

Her eyes widened, then she turned away and rose abruptly from the stone bench. "I have to go, Simon," she said in an odd tone of voice. She would not meet his eye. "Your pardon, please." She swept up her skirts and

moved swiftly off across the black and white tiles of the
Fire Garden.

"Damn me," said Simon. Things had seemed to be going well at last. What had he done? When would he ever
learn to understand women?

Binabik, as the nearest thing to a full-fledged Scrollbearer, took the oaths of Tiamak and Father Strangyeard.
When they had sworn, he in turn spoke his oath to them.
Geloë looked on sardonically as the litanies were spoken. She had never held much with the formalities of
the League, which was one reason she had never been a
Scrollbearer, despite the immense respect in which she
was held by its members. There were other reasons as
well, but Geloë never spoke of those, and all of her old
comrades who might have been able to explain were now
gone.

Tiamak was torn between pleasure and disappointment.
He had long dreamed that this might happen someday, but
in his imagination he had received his scroll-and-pen
from Morgenes, with Jarnauga and Ookequk beaming
their approval. Instead he had brought Dinivan's pendant
up from Kwanitupul himself after Isgrimnur delivered it,
and now he sat with the largely unproved successors of
those other great souls.

Still, there was something unutterably exciting even in
such a humble realization of his dream. Perhaps this
would be a day long remembered—the coming of a new
generation to the League, a new membership which
would make the Scrollbearers as important and respected
as they had been in the days of Eahlstan Fiskerne himself. . . !

Tiamak's stomach growled. Geloë turned her yellow
eyes on him and he smiled shamefacedly. In the excitement of the morning's preparations he had forgotten to
eat. Embarrassment spread through him. There! That was
They Who Watch and Shape reminding him of how important he was. A new age, indeed—those gathered here

would have to labor mightily to be half the Scrollbearers that their predecessors had been. That would teach Tiamak, the savage from Village Grove, to allow himself to become so heady!

His stomach growled again. Tiamak avoided Geloë's eye this time and pulled his knees closer in to his body, huddling on the mat floor of Strangyeard's tent like a pottery merchant on a cold day.

"Binabik has asked me to speak," Geloë said when the oaths were done. She was brisk, like an Elder's wife explaining chores and babies to a new bride. "Since I am the only one who knew all the other Scrollbearers, I have agreed." The fierceness in her stare did not make Tiamak particularly comfortable. He had only corresponded with the forest woman before his arrival in Sesuad'ra, and had possessed no idea of the force of her presence. Now, he was frantically trying to remember the letters he had sent her and hoping that they had all been suitably courteous. She was clearly not the sort of person one wanted to upset.

"You have become Scrollbearers in what may be the most difficult age the world has yet seen, worse even than Fingil's era of conquest and pillage and destruction of knowledge. You have all heard enough now to understand that what is happening seems clearly far more than a war between princes. Elias of Erkynland has somehow enlisted the aid of Ineluki Storm King, whose undead hand has reached down out of the Nornfells at last, as Ealhstan Fiskerne feared centuries ago. That is the task set before us—to somehow prevent that evil from turning a fight between brothers into a losing struggle against utter darkness. And the first part of that task, it seems, is to solve the riddle of the blades."

The discussion of Nisses' sword-rhyme went far into the afternoon. By the time Binabik thought to find something for them all to eat, Morgenes' precious manuscript was scattered about Strangyeard's tent, virtually every page having been held up for scrutiny and argued over until the incense-scented air seemed to ring.

Tiamak saw now that Morgenes' message to him must have referred to the rhyme of the Three Swords. The Wrannaman had thought it impossible that anyone could have knowledge of his own secret treasure: it was clear that no one had. Still, if he hadn't already developed a scholar's healthy respect for coincidence, this day's revelations would have convinced him. When bread and wine had been passed around, and the sharper disagreements had been softened by full mouths and the necessity of sharing a jug, Tiamak at last spoke up.

"I have found something myself that I hope you will look at." He placed his cup down carefully and then withdrew the leaf-wrapped parchment from his sack. "I found this in the marketplace at Kwanitupul. I had hoped to take it to Dinivan in Nabban to see what he would say." He unrolled it with great caution as the other three moved forward to look. Tiamak felt the sort of worried pride a father might feel on first bringing his child before the Elders to have the Naming confirmed.

Strangyeard sighed. "Blessed Elysia, is it real?"

Tiamak shook his head. "If it is not, it is a very careful forgery. In my years in Perdruin, I saw many writings from Nisses' time. These are Rimmersgard runes as someone in that age would have written them. See the backward spirals." He pointed with a trembling finger.

Binabik squinted. "*. . . From Nuanni's Rocke Garden . . .*" he read.

"I think that it means the Southern Islands," Tiamak said. "Nuanni . . ."

"—Was the old Nabbanai god of the sea." Strangyeard was so excited that he interrupted—an amazing thing from the diffident priest. "Of course—Nuanni's rock garden—the islands! But what does the rest mean?"

As the others bent close, already arguing, Tiamak felt a glow of pride. His child had met with the Elders' approval.

"It's not enough to stand our ground." Duke Isgrimnur sat on a stool facing Josua in the prince's darkened tent. "You have won an important victory, but it means little to Elias. Another few months and no one will remember it ever happened."

Josua frowned. "I understand. That is why I will call the Raed."

Isgrimnur shook his head, beard wagging. "That's not enough, if you'll pardon my saying so. I'm being blunt."

The prince smiled faintly. "That is your task, Isgrimnur."

"So then let me say what I need to say. We need more victories, and soon. If we do not push Elias back, it won't matter whether this 'three swords' nonsense will work or not."

"Do you really think it is nonsense?"

"After all I've seen in the last year? No, I wouldn't quickly call *anything* nonsense in these times—but that misses the point. As long as we sit here like a treed cat, we have no way to get to Bright-Nail." The duke snorted. "Dror's Mallet! I am still not used to thinking that John's blade is really Minneyar. You could have knocked my head off with a goose feather when you told me that."

"We all must become used to surprises, it seems," Josua said dryly. "But what do you suggest?"

"Nabban." Isgrimnur spoke without hesitation. "I know, I should urge you to hasten to Elvritshalla to free my people there. But you're right in your fears. If what I have heard is true, half the able-bodied men in Rimmersgard were forced into Skali's army: it would mean a drawn-out struggle to beat him. Kaldskryke's a hard man, a canny fighter. I hate his treacherous innards, but I'd be the last to call him an easy match."

"But the Sithi have ridden to Hernystir," Josua pointed out. "You heard that."

"And what does that mean? I can make neither hide nor hair of the lad Simon's stories, and that white-haired Sitha witch-girl doesn't strike me as the kind of scout whose information should be used to plan an entire campaign." The duke grimaced. "In any case, if the Sithi and the Hernystiri drive Skali out, wonderful. I will cheer louder and longer than any. But those of Skali's men we would even *want* to recruit will still be scattered far and wide across the Frostmarch: even with the weather getting a little better, I would not want to have to try to round them up and convince them to attack Erkynland. And they're *my* people. It's my country, Josua . . . so you'd better listen to what I say." He worked his bushy eyebrows furiously, as if the mere thought of the prince's possible disagreement called his own good sense into question.

The prince sighed. "I always listen to you, Isgrimnur. You taught me tactics as you held me on your knee, remember."

"I'm not *that* much older than you, pup," the duke grumbled. "If you don't mind your manners, I'll take you out in the snow and give you an embarrassing lesson."

Josua grinned. "I think we will have to put that off for some other day. Ah, but it is good to have you back with me, Isgrimnur." His expression grew more sober. "So, then, you say Nabban. How?"

Isgrimnur slid his stool closer and dropped his voice. "Streáwe's message said the time is right—that Benigaris is very unpopular. Rumors of the part he played in his father's death are everywhere."

"The armies of the Kingfisher Crest will not desert because of rumors," said Josua. "There have been more than a few other patricides who ruled in Nabban, remember. It is hard to shock those people. In any case, the elite officers of the army are loyal to the Benidrivine House above all. They will fight any foreign usurper—even Elias, were he to assert his power directly. They certainly would not throw Benigaris over on my behalf. Surely you remember the old Nabbanai saying, 'Better our whoreson than your saint.' "

Isgrimnur grinned wickedly in his whiskers. "Ah, but who is talking about convincing them to throw Benigaris over for *your* sake, my prince? Merciful Aedon, they'd let Nessalanta lead the armies before they'd let *you* do it."

Josua shook his head in irritation. "Well, who, then?"

"Camaris, damn you!" Isgrimnur thumped his wide

hand down on his thigh for emphasis. "He's the legitimate heir to the ducal throne—Leobardis only became duke because Camaris disappeared and was thought dead!"

The prince stared at his old friend. "But he's mad, Isgrimnur—or at least simple-minded."

The duke sat up. "They've accepted a cowardly patricide. Why wouldn't they prefer a heroic simpleton?"

Josua shook his head again, this time in wonder. "You are astounding, Isgrimnur. Where did you get such an idea?"

Isgrimnur grinned fiercely. "I've had a lot of time to think since I found Camaris in that inn at Kwanitupul." He ran his fingers through his beard. "It's a pity that Eolair isn't here to see what a skulker and intriguer I've become in my old age."

The prince laughed. "Well, I'm not certain that it would work, but it bears thinking about at least." He rose and walked to the table. "Would you like some more wine?"

Isgrimnur raised his goblet. "Thinking is thirsty work. Fill it, would you?"

"It is *prise'a*—Ever-fresh." Aditu lifted the slender vine to show Simon the pale blue flower. "Even after it has been picked, it does not wilt, not until the season has passed. It is said that it came from the Garden on our people's boats."

"Some of the women here wear it in their hair."

"As do our folk—men and women both," the Sitha replied with an amused glance.

"Please, hello!" someone called. Simon turned to see Tiamak, Miriamele's Wrannaman friend. The small man seemed tremendously excited. "Prince Josua wishes you to come, Sir Simon, Lady Aditu." He started to sketch a bow, but was too full of nervous exhilaration to complete it. "Oh, please hurry!"

"What is it?" asked Simon. "Is something wrong!"

"We have found something important, we think." He bounced on his tiptoes, anxious to be going. "In my parchment—mine!"

Simon shook his head. "What parchment?"

"You will learn all. Come to Josua's tent! Please!" Tiamak turned and began trotting back toward the settlement.

Simon laughed. "What a strange man! You'd think he had a bee in his breeches."

Aditu set the vine carefully back into place. She lifted her fingers to her nose. "This reminds me of my house in Jao é-Tinukai'i," she said. "Every room is filled with flowers."

"I remember."

They made their way back across the hilltop. The sun seemed quite strong today, and though the northern horizon was aswim with gray clouds, the sky overhead was blue. Almost no snow remained except in the hollows of the hillside below them, the deep places where shadows lingered late into the day. Simon wondered where Miriamele was: he had gone looking for her in the morning, hoping to convince her to take a walk with him, but she had been absent, her tent empty. Duchess Gutrun had told him that the princess had gone out early.

Josua's tent was crowded. Beside Tiamak stood Geloë, Father Strangyeard, and Binabik. The prince sat on his stool, looking closely at a parchment which was spread across his lap. Vorzheva sat near the far wall, stitching at a piece of cloth. Aditu, after nodding her greetings to the others, left Simon and went to join her.

Josua glanced up briefly from the parchment. "I am glad you are here, Simon. I hope you can help us."

"How, Prince Josua?"

The prince raised his hand without looking up again. "First you must hear what we have found."

Tiamak inched forward shyly. "Please, Prince Josua, may I tell what has happened?"

Josua smiled at the Wrannaman. "When Miriamele and Isgrimnur arrive, you may."

Simon eased over next to Binabik, who was talking

with Geloë. Simon waited as patiently as he could and listened to them discuss runes and errors of translation until he was nearly bursting. At last the Duke of Elvritshalla arrived with the princess. Her short hair was wind-tousled and her cheeks had a delicate flush. Simon could not help staring at her, full of mute longing.

"I had to climb halfway down this damnable hill to find her," Isgrimnur muttered. "I hope this is worth it."

"You could have just called to me and I would have come up," Miriamele replied sweetly. "You didn't have to nearly kill yourself."

"I didn't like where you were climbing. I was afraid I'd startle you."

"And having a huge, sweating Rimmersman come crashing down the hillside *wouldn't* startle me?"

"Please." Josua's voice was a little strained. "This is not the time for teasing. It is worth it, Isgrimnur—or I hope it will be." He turned to the Wrannaman and handed him the parchment. "Explain to the newcomers, Tiamak, if you will."

The slender man, his eyes bright, quickly described how he had acquired the parchment, then showed them the ancient runes before reading it aloud.

"... *Bring from Nuanni's Rocke Garden,*
The Man who tho' Blinded canne See
Discover the Blayde that delivers The Rose
At the foote of the Rimmer's great Tree
Find the Call whose lowde Claime
Speaks the Call-bearer's name
In a Shippe on the Shallowest Sea—
—When Blayde, Call, and Man
Come to Prince's right Hande
Then the Prisoned shall once more go Free ..."

Finished, he looked around the room. "We ..." He hesitated. "We ... Scrollbearers ... have discussed this and what it might mean. If Nisses' other words are important for our purposes, it seemed likely that these might be, too."

"So what does it mean?" Isgrimnur demanded. "I looked at it before and couldn't make horns nor hind-quarter out of it."

"You were not having the advantage that some others were having," said Binabik. "Simon and myself and some others were already facing one part of this riddle for ourselves." The troll turned to Simon. "Have you seen it yet?"

Simon thought hard. "The Rimmer's Tree—the Uduntree!" He looked over to Miriamele with more than a little pride. "That's where we found Thorn!"

Binabik nodded. The tent had grown quiet. "Yes—the 'blade that delivers the Rose' was being found there," the troll said. "The sword of Camaris called Thorn."

"Ebekah, John's wife." Isgrimnur breathed. "The Rose of Hernysadharc." He pulled vigorously at his beard. "Of course!" he said to Josua. "Camaris was your mother's special protector."

"So we were seeing that the rhyme spoke in part of Thorn," Binabik agreed.

"But the rest," said Tiamak, "we think we know, but we are not sure."

Geloë leaned forward. "It seems possible that if the rhyme speaks of Thorn, it may also speak of Camaris himself. A 'man who though blinded can see' could certainly describe a man who is blind to his past, even his own name, although he sees as well as anyone here."

"Better," said Miriamele quietly.

"That seems right." Isgrimnur scowled, considering. "I don't know how such a thing could be in some old book from hundreds of years ago, but it seems right."

"So what does that leave us?" Josua asked. "This part about 'the Call' and the last lines about the prisoned going free."

A moment of silence followed his remark.

Simon cleared his throat. "Well, perhaps this is stupid," he began.

"Speak, Simon," Binabik urged him.

"If one part is about Camaris, and another is about his

sword—maybe the other parts are about other things of his and other places he's been."

Josua smiled. "That is not at all stupid, Simon. That is what we think, too. And we even think we know what the Call might be."

From her seat by the far wall, Aditu suddenly laughed, a clear, musical trill like falling water. "So you did remember to give it to them, Seoman. I was afraid you might forget. You were very tired and sad when we parted."

"Give it to them?" said Simon, confused. "What. . . ?" He stopped short. "The horn!"

"The horn," Josua said. "Amerasu's gift to us, a gift we could see no use for."

"But how does that fit with the call-bearer's name. . . ?" Simon asked.

"It was under our noses, so to speak," Tiamak said. "When Isgrimnur found Camaris at the inn in Kwanitupul, he was called 'Ceallio'—that means 'shout' or 'call' in the Perdruinese tongue. The famous horn of Camaris was named 'Cellian,' which is the same thing in the Nabbanai tongue."

Aditu rose, smoothly as a hawk taking wing. "It was called Cellian by mortals only. It has a far older name than that—its true name, its name of Making. The horn that Amerasu sent you belonged to the Sithi long before your Camaris sounded it in battle. It is called *Ti-tuno*."

"But how did it come to be in Camaris' hands?" Miriamele asked. "And if he had it, how did the Sithi get it back again?"

"I can answer the first part of your question easily," Aditu told her. "Ti-tuno was made of the dragon Hidohebhi's tooth, the black worm that Hakatri and Ineluki slew. When Prince Sinnach of the mortal Hernystiri came to our aid before the battle of Ach Samrath, Iyu'unigato of Year-Dancing House gave it to him as a token of gratitude, a gift from friend to friend."

When Aditu paused, Binabik looked for her permission to continue. When she nodded, he spoke. "Many centuries after Asu'a was falling, when John came to his power in Erkynland, he was having the chance to make the Hernystiri his vassals. He did not choose to do that thing, and in gratitude King Llythinn sent the horn Ti-tuno as part of Ebekah's bridal dower when she was sent for being Prester John's wife." He raised his small hand in a gesture of gift giving. "Camaris was guarding her on that journey, and brought her with safety to Erkynland. John was finding his Hernystiri bride so beautiful that he gave the horn to Camaris to commemorate the day of her coming to the Hayholt." He waved his hand again, a broader flourish, as though he had painted a picture he now wished the others to admire. "As for how it was returned to Amerasu and the Sithi—well, perhaps that is a story Camaris himself can be telling to us. But that is where it was brought from: the 'ship on the shallowest sea.' "

"I do not understand that part," Isgrimnur said.

Aditu smiled. "Jao é-Tinukai'i means 'Boat on the Ocean of Trees.' It is hard to imagine an ocean shallower than one with no water."

Simon was growing confused by the flood of words and the changing litany of speakers. "What do you mean when you say Camaris can tell the story, Binabik? I thought Camaris couldn't talk—that he was mute, or mad, or under a spell."

"Perhaps he is being all those things," the troll replied. "But it is also perhaps true that the last line of the poem is speaking to us about Camaris himself—that when these things are brought together, he will be then released from the prison of sorts that he is in. We hope it will be bringing back his wits."

Again the room fell silent for several heartbeats.

"Of course," Josua added at last, "there is still the problem of how that will come to be, if the second-to-last line is to be believed." He held up his arms—his left hand with Elias' manacle still clasped about the wrist, his right arm that ended in a leather-clad stump. "As you can see," he said, "the one thing this prince does *not* have is a right hand." He allowed himself a mocking grin. "But we hope that it is not meant to be taken word for word. Perhaps just bringing them into my presence will do the trick."

"I tried to show Camaris the blade Thorn once already," Isgrimnur remembered. "Thought it might jog his mind, if you see my meaning. But he wouldn't go near it. Acted like it was a poisonous snake. Pulled free and walked right out of the room." He paused. "But maybe when everything is together, the horn and all, maybe then . . ."

"Well?" said Miriamele. "Why don't we try it, then?"

"Because we can't," Josua said grimly. "We have lost the horn."

"What?" Simon looked up to see if, improbably, the prince might be joking. "How can that be?"

"It vanished sometime during the battle with Fengbald," Josua said. "It is one of the reasons I wanted you here, Simon. I thought you might have taken it back for safekeeping."

Simon shook his head. "I was glad to be rid of it, Prince Josua. I was so afraid that I had doomed us all by forgetting to give it to you. No, I haven't seen it."

No one else in the tent had either. "So," Josua said at last. "We must search for it, then—but quietly. If there is a traitor in our midst, or even just a thief, we must not let him know that it is an important thing or we may never recover it."

Aditu laughed again. This time it seemed shockingly out of place. "I am sorry," she said. "but this is something that the rest of the Zida'ya would never believe. To have lost Ti-tuno!"

"It's not funny," Simon growled. "Besides, can't you use some magic or something to locate it?"

Aditu shook her head. "Things do not work that way, Seoman. I tried to explain that to you once before. And I am sorry to laugh. I will help look for it."

She didn't look very sorry, Simon thought. But if he couldn't understand mortal women, how could he ever in a thousand years hope to understand Sithi women?

The company slowly filed out of Josua's tent, talking quietly among themselves. Simon waited for Miriamele outside. When she emerged, he fell in beside her.

"So they are going to give Camaris back his memo-

Tad Williams

ries." Miriamele looked distracted and tired, as though she had not slept much the night before.

"If we can find the horn, I suppose we'll try." Simon was secretly quite pleased that Miriamele had been present to see how involved he was in Prince Josua's counsels.

Miriamele turned to look at him, her expression accusatory. "And what if he doesn't want those memories back?" she demanded. "What if he is happy now, for the first time in his life?"

Simon was startled, but could think of no reply. They walked back across the settlement in silence until Miriamele said good-bye and went off to walk by herself. Simon was left wondering at what she had said. Did Miriamele, too, have memories that she would be just as happy to lose?

Josua was standing in the garden behind Leavetaking House when Miriamele found him. He was staring into the sky, across which the clouds were drawn in long ribbons like torn linen.

"Uncle Josua?"

He turned. "Miriamele. It is a pleasure to see you."

"You like to come here, don't you?"

"I suppose I do." He nodded slowly. "It is a place to think. I worry too much about Vorzheva—about our child and what kind of a world it will live in—to feel very comfortable most places."

"And you miss Deornoth."

Josua turned his gaze back to the cloud-strewn sky again. "I miss him, yes. But more importantly, I want to make his sacrifice worthwhile. If our defeat of Fengbald *means* something, then it will be easier for me to live with his death." The prince sighed. "He was still young, compared to me—he had not seen thirty summers."

Miriamele watched her uncle in silence for a long while before speaking. "I need to ask you a favor, Josua."

He extended his hand, indicating one of the time-worn benches. "Please. Ask me whatever you wish."

She took a deep breath. "When you . . . when we come to the Hayholt, I want to speak to my father."

Josua tilted his head, raising his eyebrows so that his high, smooth forehead creased. "What do you mean, Miriamele?"

"There will be a time before any final siege when you and he will talk," she said hurriedly, as though speaking words that had been practiced. "There has to be, no matter how bloody the fighting. He is your brother, and you will speak to him. I wish to be there."

Josua hesitated. "I am not certain that would be wise. . . ."

"And," Miriamele continued, determined to have her say, "I wish to speak to him alone."

"Alone?" The prince shook his head, taken aback. "Miriamele, such a thing cannot be! If we are able to lay siege to the Hayholt, your father will be a desperate man. How could I leave you alone with him—I would be giving you over as a hostage!"

"That's not important," she said stubbornly. "I must speak with him, Uncle Josua. I *must!*"

He bit back a sharp reply; when he spoke, it was gently. "And why must you, Miriamele?"

"I cannot tell you. But I must. It could make a difference—a very great difference!"

"Then you must tell me, my niece. For if you do not, I can only say no; I cannot allow you alone with your father."

Tears glistened in Miriamele's eyes. She angrily wiped them away. "You don't understand. It's something I can only talk to him about. And I must! Please, Josua, please!"

A weary anguish seemed to settle on his features like the work of long years. "I know you are not frivolous, Miriamele. But neither do you have the lives of hundreds, maybe thousands, weighing down your decisions. If you cannot tell me what you feel is so important—and I believe that you think it is true—then I certainly cannot let you risk your life for it, and perhaps the lives of many others as well."

She stared at him intently. The tears were gone, replaced by a cold, dispassionate mask. "Please reconsider, Josua." She gestured toward Deornoth's cairn. A few blades of grass were already growing up between the stones. "Remember your friend, Uncle Josua, and all the things you wish you had said to *him*."

He shook his head in frustration. The sunlight showed that his brown hair was thinning near the top. "By Aedon's blood, I cannot allow it, Miriamele. Be angry at me if you must, but surely you can see that I have no other choice." His own voice grew a little more chill. "When your father surrenders at last, I will do everything I can to see that he is not harmed. If it is within my power, you will have a chance to speak with him. That is the most I can promise."

"It will be too late then." She rose from the bench and walked rapidly back across the garden.

Josua watched her go; then, as motionless as if he were rooted to the ground, he watched a sparrow flutter down to alight briefly atop the cairn of stones. After a few bouncing steps and a chain of piping notes, it rose again and flew away. He let its departure lift his gaze back to the streaming clouds.

"Simon!"

He turned. Sangfugol was hurrying across the damp grass.

"Simon, may I talk to you?" The harper pulled up, breathing heavily. His hair was mussed and his clothing seemed to have been thrown on without a thought for color or style, which was very unusual; even in the days of exile, Simon had never seen the musician looking quite this unkempt.

"Certainly."

"Not here." Sangfugol looked around furtively, although there was no one in sight. "Somewhere where we won't be overheard. Your tent?"

Simon nodded, puzzled. "If you wish."

They walked through the tent city. Several of the residents waved or called greetings to them as they passed. The harper seemed almost to flinch each time, as though every person was a potential source of danger. At last they reached Simon's tent and found Binabik just preparing to go out. As the troll pulled on his fur-lined boots, he chatted amiably about the missing horn—the hunt had been afoot for three days, and was still unsuccessful—and other topics. Sangfugol was quite visibly anxious for him to leave, a fact which Binabik could not help noticing; he cut short the conversation, made his farewells, then went off to join Geloë and the rest.

When the troll was gone, Sangfugol let out a sigh of released tension and sank to the floor of the tent, unmindful of the dirt. Simon was beginning to be alarmed. Something was very wrong indeed.

"What is it?" he asked. "You seem frightened."

The harper leaned close, his voice a conspiratorial near-whisper. "Binabik says they are still searching for that horn. Josua seems to want it very much."

Simon shrugged. "No one knows if it will do any good. It's for Camaris. They hope it will bring him back to his senses somehow."

"That doesn't make sense." The harper shook his head. "How could a horn do something like that?"

"*I* don't know," Simon said impatiently. "What is so important that you needed to talk about?"

"I imagine that when they find the thief, the prince will be very angry."

"I'm sure they'll hang him on the wall of Leavetaking House," Simon said in irritation, then stopped as he saw the expression of horror on Sangfugol's face. "What's wrong? Merciful Aedon, Sangfugol, did *you* steal it?"

"No, no!" the harper said shrilly. "I didn't, I swear!"

Simon stared at him.

"But," Sangfugol said at last, his voice trembling with shame, "but I know where it is."

"What?! Where?"

"I have it in my tent." The harper said this in the doomful voice of a condemned martyr forgiving his executioners.

"How could that be? Why is it in your tent? And you didn't take it?"

"Aedon's mercy, Simon, I swear I didn't. I found it in with Towser's things after he died. I . . . I loved that old man, Simon. In my way. I know he was a drunkard, and that sometimes I talked as though I wanted to knock his head in. But he was good to me when I was young . . . and, curse it, I *miss* him."

Despite the sadness of the harper's words, Simon was losing patience again. "But why did you keep it? Why didn't you tell anybody?"

"I just wanted something of his, Simon." He was as ashamed and sorrowful as a wet cat. "I buried my second lute with him. I thought he wouldn't have minded . . . I thought the horn was his!" He reached out to grab Simon's wrist, thought better, and pulled his hand back. "Then, by the time I realized what all the fuss and searching was for, I was afraid to admit that I had it. It will seem like I stole from Towser when he was dead. I would never do that, Simon!"

Simon's moment of anger faded. The harper seemed close to tears. "You should have told," he said gently. "No one would have thought ill of you. Now we had better go speak to Josua."

"Oh, no! He'll be furious! No, Simon, why don't I just give it to you—then you can say that *you* found it. You'll be the hero."

Simon considered for a moment. "No," he said at last. "I don't think that would be a good idea. For one thing, I'd have to lie to Prince Josua about where I found it. What if I told him I found it somewhere, then it turned out they'd already looked there. It would seem like *I* stole it." He shook his head emphatically. For once, it hadn't been Simon who had made the mooncalf mistake. He was in no hurry to take this particular blame. "In any case, Sangfugol, it won't be as bad as you think. I'll come with you. Josua's not like that—you know him."

"He told me once that if I sang 'Woman from Nabban' again he'd have my head off." Sangfugol, the worst of his fear past, was dangerously close to sulking.

"And well he should have," Simon replied. "We're all tired of that song." He stood and extended a hand to the harper. "Now get up and let's go see the prince. If only you hadn't waited so long to tell, this would be easier."

Sangfugol shook his head miserably. "It just seemed easier not to say anything. I kept thinking I could take it out and leave it somewhere that it would be found, but then I got frightened that someone would catch me at it, even if I did it in the middle of the night." He took a deep breath. "I haven't slept the last two nights for worrying."

"Well, you'll feel better once you've talked to Josua. Come on, up now."

When they emerged from the tent, the harper stood for a moment in the sun, then wrinkled his thin nose. He offered a weak smile, as though he scented possible redemption in the damp morning air. "Thank you, Simon," he said. "You are a good friend."

Simon made a noise of mocking derision, then clapped the harper on the shoulder. "Let's talk to him now, when he's just eaten breakfast. *I'm* always in a better mood when I've just eaten—maybe it works for princes, too."

They all gathered at Leavetaking House after the midday meal. Josua stood solemnly before the altar of stone on which Thorn still lay. Simon could feel the prince's tension.

The others gathered in the hall talked quietly among themselves. The conversations seemed strained, but silence in the great room might have been even more daunting. The sunlight streamed through the doorway, but did not reach the room's farthest reaches. The place seemed a kind of chapel, and Simon could not help wondering if they would see a miracle. If they could bring back Camaris' wits, the senses and memories of a man forty years gone from the world, would it not be a sort of raising of the dead?

He remembered what Miriamele said and had to repress a shiver. Perhaps it was wrong, somehow. Perhaps Camaris was indeed meant to be left alone.

Josua was turning the dragon's-tooth horn over and over in his hands, looking distractedly at the inscriptions. When it had been brought to him, he had not been as angry as Sangfugol had feared, but instead openly puzzled as to why Towser might have taken the horn and hidden it away. Josua had even been so generous, once his initial flash of annoyance had passed, as to invite Sangfugol to stay and witness whatever might happen. But the harper, reprieved, wanted nothing more to do with the horn or the doings of princes; he had returned to his bed to get some much-needed rest.

Now there was a stir among the dozen or so gathered in the hall as Isgrimnur entered leading Camaris. The old man, dressed in formal shirt and hose like a child who had been readied for church, stepped inside and looked around squinting, as if trying to see the nature of the trap into which he was being led. It did seem almost as though he had been brought to answer for some criminal act: those who waited in the hall stared at his face as though memorizing it. Camaris looked more than a little frightened.

Miriamele had said that the old man had been door warden and man-of-all-work at a hostel in Kwanitupul, and not particularly well treated there, Simon remembered; perhaps he thought he was to be punished for something. Certainly, from his nervous, sidelong glances, Camaris looked as though he would rather be anywhere than this place.

"Here, Sir Camaris." Josua lifted Thorn from the altar—by the ease with which he hefted it, it must have seemed light as a twig; remembering the sword's changing character, Simon wondered what this meant. He had thought once that the sword had wishes of its own, that it cooperated only when going where and doing what it desired. Was this its goal, now almost in reach? To return to its former master?

Prince Josua presented the blade to Camaris hilt first, but the old man would not take it. "Please, Sir Camaris—it is Thorn. It was yours, and still is."

The old man's expression became even more desperate. He stepped back, half-raising his hands as though to fend off an attack. Isgrimnur took his elbow and steadied him.

"All is well," the duke rumbled. "It's yours, Camaris."

"Sludig," Josua called. "Do you have the sword belt?"

The Rimmersman stepped forward, carrying a belt from which depended a heavy sheath of black leather studded with silver. With his master Isgrimnur's help, he strapped it around Camaris' waist. The old man did not resist. In fact, Simon thought, he might as well have been turned to stone. When they were finished, Josua carefully slid Thorn into the scabbard, so that its hilt came to rest in the space between Camaris' elbow and his loose white shirt.

"Now the horn, please," said Josua. Freosel, who had been holding it while the prince carried the blade, handed him the ancient horn. Josua slipped the baldric over Camaris' head so that the horn hung beside his right hand, then stepped back. The long-bladed sword seemed made to fit its tall owner. A shaft of sunlight from the doorway glinted in the knight's white hair. There was an unquestionable *rightness* to it; everyone in the room could see it. Everyone except the old man himself.

"He's not doing anything," Sludig said quietly to Isgrimnur. Simon again had the impression of attending a religious service—but now it felt as though the sexton had neglected to put out the reliquary, or the priest had forgotten part of the mansa. Everyone was caught up in the embarrassing pause.

"Perhaps if we are reading the poem?" Binabik suggested.

"Yes." Josua nodded. "Please read it."

Binabik instead pushed Tiamak forward. The Wrannaman held up the parchment in a trembling hand and, in an equally unsteady voice, read Nisses' poem.

"... *When Blayde, Call, and Man,*"

he finished in firmer tones—he had gained courage with each line,

> "*Come to Prince's right Hande*
> *Then the Prisoned shall once more go Free ...*"

Tiamak stopped and looked up. Camaris stared back at him, offering a faintly wounded look to the companion of many weeks who was now doing this inexplicable thing to him. The old knight might have been a dog expected to perform some degrading trick for a previously kind master.

Nothing had changed. A shock of disappointment went through the room.

"We have perhaps been making some mistake," Binabik said slowly. "We shall have to be at studying it further."

"No." Josua's voice was harsh. "I don't believe that." He stepped up to Camaris and lifted the horn to the level of the old man's eyes. "Don't you recognize this? This is Cellian! Its call used to strike fear into the hearts of my father's enemies! Sound it, Camaris!" He moved it toward the old man's lips. "We need you to come back!"

With a hunted look, a look almost of terror, Camaris pushed Josua away. So unexpected was the old man's strength that the prince stumbled and nearly fell before Isgrimnur caught him. Sludig snarled and took a step toward Camaris as though he might strike the old knight.

"Leave him be, Sludig!" Josua snapped. "If anyone is at fault here, it is me. What right do I have to trouble a simple-minded old man?" Josua bunched his fist and stared at the stone tiles for a moment. "Perhaps we *should* leave him be. He fought his battles—we should fight ours and leave him to rest."

"He never turned his back on any fight, Josua," said Isgrimnur. "I knew him, remember. He always did what was right, what was ... needful. Don't give up so easily."

Josua lifted his gaze to the old man's face. "Very well.

Camaris, come with me." He gently took his elbow. "Come with me," he said again, then turned and led the unresisting knight toward the door that led to the garden behind the hall.

Outside the afternoon was growing chill. A light mist of rain had darkened the ancient walls and stone benches. The rest of the company gathered in the doorway, uncertain of what the prince meant to do.

Josua led Camaris to the pile of stones that marked Deornoth's grave. He lifted the old man's hand and placed it on the cairn, then pressed his own down atop the knight's.

"Sir Camaris," he said slowly. "Please listen to me. The land that my father tamed, the order that you and King John built, is being torn to pieces by war and sorcery. Everything you worked for in your life is threatened, and if we fail this time, I fear there will be no rebuilding.

"Beneath these stones my friend is buried. He was a knight, as you. Sir Deornoth never met you, but the songs of your life he heard as a child led him to me. 'Make me a knight, Josua,' he told me on the day I first saw him. 'I wish to serve as Camaris served. I wish to be your tool and God's, for the betterment of our people and our land.'

"That is what he said, Camaris." Josua laughed abruptly. "He was a fool—a holy fool. And he found out, of course, that sometimes the land and people do not seem worth saving. But he took a vow before God that he would do what was right and he lived all his days in an effort to measure up to that pledge."

Josua's voice rose. He had found some wellspring of feeling within himself; the words came tumbling out, strong and effortless. "He died defending this place—a single battle, a single skirmish took his life, yet without him, the chance of a greater victory would have been lost long ago. He died as he lived, trying to do what was not humanly possible, blaming himself when he failed, then getting up and trying again. He died for this land, Camaris, the same land that you fought for, the order that you struggled to create, where the weak could live their lives in peace, protected from those who would use strength to force their wishes on others." The prince leaned close to Camaris' face, catching and holding the old man's reluctant gaze. "Will his death mean nothing? For if we do not win this fight, there will be too many graves for one more to make a difference, and there will be no one left to mourn for people like Deornoth."

Josua's fingers tightened on the knight's hand. "Come back to us, Camaris. Please. Don't let his death be meaningless. Think of the battles of your time, battles I know you would prefer not to have fought, but did because the cause was just and fair. Must all that suffering become meaningless, too? *This is our last chance.* After us comes darkness."

The prince abruptly let go of the old man's hand and turned away, eyes glistening. Simon, watching from the doorway, felt his own heart catch.

Camaris still stood as if frozen, his fingers splayed atop Deornoth's cairn. At last he turned and looked down at himself, then slowly raised the horn and stared at it for a long time, as though it were something never before seen on the green earth. He closed his eyes, lifted it carefully to his lips with shaking hand, and blew.

The horn sounded. Its first thin note grew and strengthened, becoming louder and louder until it seemed to shake the very air, a shout that seemed to have the clash of steel and the thunder of hooves in it. Camaris, his eyes squeezed shut, sucked in a deep breath and blew again, louder this time. The piercing call winded out across the hillside and reverberated in the valley; the echoes chased themselves through the air. Then the noise died away.

Simon discovered he had his hands over his ears. Many others in the company had done the same.

Camaris was staring at the horn again. He lifted up his face to those who watched him. Something had changed. His eyes had become deeper somehow, sadder: there was a glint of awareness that had not been there before. His mouth worked, striving for speech, but no sound came out except a rasping hiss. Camaris looked down at the hilt of Thorn. With slow and deliberate movements, he drew it from the scabbard and held it up before him, a line of glinting black that seemed to slice right through the light of the failing afternoon. Tiny drops of misty rain gathered on the blade.

"*I . . . should have known . . . that my . . . torment was not yet finished, my guilt not forgiven.*" His voice was painfully dry and rough, his speech strangely formal. "Oh, my God, my loving and terrible God, I am humble before You. I shall serve out my punishment."

The old man fell to his knees before the astonished company. For a long time, he said nothing, but seemed to be praying. Tears ran down his cheeks, merging with the raindrops to make his face shine in the slanting sunlight. Finally, Camaris clambered to his feet and allowed Isgrimnur and Josua to lead him away.

Simon felt something tugging at his arm. He looked down. Binabik's small fingers had caught his sleeve. The troll's eyes were bright. "Do you know, Simon, it is what we had all forgotten. Sir Deornoth's men, the soldiers of Naglimund, do you know what they were calling him? 'The prince's right hand.' And even Josua did not remember, I am thinking. Luck . . . or something else, friend Simon." The little man squeezed Simon's arm again, then hurried after the prince.

Overwhelmed, Simon turned, trying to catch a last glimpse of Camaris. Miriamele was standing near the doorway. She caught Simon's eyes and gave him an angry look that seemed to say: *you are to blame for this, too.*

She turned and followed Camaris and the others back into Leavetaking House, leaving Simon alone in the rainy garden.

24

A Sky Full of Beasts

Four strong men, sweating despite the cold night breeze and panting from the exertion of heaving the covered litter up the narrow stairway, carefully lifted out the chair containing the litter's passenger and carried it to the middle of the rooftop garden. The man in the chair was so swaddled in furs and robes as to be practically unrecognizable, but the tall, elegantly dressed woman immediately rose from her own seat and came forward with a glad cry.

"Count Streáwe!" said the dowager duchess. "I'm so glad you could come. And on such a chill evening."

"Nessalanta, my dear. Only an invitation from you would bring me out in such ghastly weather." The count took her gloved hand in his own and drew it to his lips. "Forgive me for being so discourteous as to remain seated."

"Nonsense." Nessalanta snapped her fingers at the count's bearers and indicated they should bring his chair closer to hers. She seated herself again. "Although I think it is growing a little warmer. Nevertheless, you are a jewel, a splendid jewel for coming tonight."

"The pleasure of your company, dear lady." Streáwe coughed into his kerchief.

"It will be worth your while, I promise." She gestured floridly at the star-sprinkled sky as though she herself had commanded it spread before them. "Look at this! You will be so glad you came. Xannasavin is a brilliant man."

"My lady is too kind," said a voice from the stairwell.

Count Streáwe, somewhat limited in his mobility, craned his neck awkwardly to see the speaker.

The man who emerged from the entranceway onto the rooftop garden was tall and thin, with long fingers clasped as though in prayer. He wore a great curling beard of gray-shot black. His robes, too, were dark, and bespotted with Nabbanai star symbols. He moved between the rows of potted trees and shrubs with a certain storklike grace, then bent his long legs to kneel before the dowager duchess. "My lady, I received your summons with great pleasure. It is always a joy to serve you." He turned to Streáwe. "The Duchess Nessalanta would have been a splendid astrologer, had she not her greater duties to Nabban. She is a woman of great insight."

Beneath his hood, Perdruin's count smiled. "This is known to all."

Something in Streáwe's voice made the duchess hesitate for a moment before she spoke. "Xannasavin is too kind. I have studied a few rudiments only." She crossed her hands demurely before her breast.

"Ah, but could I have had you for an apprentice," Xannasavin said, "the mysteries that we might have plumbed, Duchess Nessalanta. . . ." His voice was deep and impressive. "Does my lady wish me to start?"

Nessalanta, who had been watching his lips move, shook herself as though suddenly coming awake. "Ah. No, Xannasavin, not yet. We must wait for my eldest son."

Streáwe looked at her with real interest. "I did not know that Benigaris was a follower of the mysteries of the stars."

"He is interested," Nessalanta said carefully. "He is . . ." She looked up. "Ah, he is here!"

Benigaris strode onto the rooftop. Two guards, their surcoats kingfisher-blazed, followed a few paces behind him. The reigning duke of Nabban was going a little to fat around the middle, but was still a tall, broad-shouldered man. His mustache was so luxuriant as to hide his mouth almost entirely.

"Mother," he said curtly as he reached the small gathering. He took her gloved hand and nodded, then turned to the count. "Streáwe. I missed you at dinner last night."

The count lifted his kerchief to his lips and coughed. "My apologies, good Benigaris. My health, you know. Sometimes it is just too difficult for me to leave my room, even for hospitality as famed as that of the Sancellan Mahistrevis."

Benigaris grunted. "Well, then you probably shouldn't be out here on this freezing roof." He turned to Nessalanta. "What *are* we doing here, Mother?"

The dowager duchess put on a look of girlish hurt. "Why, you know perfectly well what we are doing here. This is a very favorable night to read the stars, and Xannasavin is going to tell us what the next year will bring."

"If you so desire, Highness." Xannasavin bowed to the duke.

"I can *tell* you what the next year will bring," Benigaris growled. "Trouble and more trouble. Everywhere I turn there are problems." He looked to Streáwe. "You know how it is. They want bread, the peasants do, but if I give it to them they just want more. I tried to bring in some of those swamp men to help work the grain fields—I have had to expend a lot of soldiers in those border skirmishes with the Thrithings savages and now all the barons are screaming about having their peasants levied and their fields fallow—but the damnable little brown men won't come! What am I to do, send troops into that cursed swamp? I'm better off without them."

"How well do I know the burdens of leadership," Streáwe said sympathetically. "You have been doing a heroic job in difficult times, I am told."

Benigaris jerked his head in acknowledgment. "And then those damned, damned, thrice-damned Fire Dancers, setting themselves on fire and frightening the common folk." His expression turned dark. "I should never have trusted Pryrates. . . ."

"I'm sorry, Benigaris," said Streáwe. "I didn't hear you—my old ears, you know. Pryrates. . . ?"

The Duke of Nabban looked at the count. His eyes narrowed. "Never mind. Anyway, it's been a filthy year, and I doubt the next will be any better." A sour smile moved his mustache. "Unless I convince some of the trouble-makers here in Nabban to become Fire Dancers. There are more than a few that I think would look very good in flames."

Streáwe laughed, then broke into a fit of dry coughing. "Very good, Benigaris, very good."

"Enough of this," Nessalanta said pettishly. "I think you are wrong, Benigaris—it should be a splendid year. Besides, there is no need to speculate. Xannasavin will tell you everything you need to know."

"I am but a humble observer of the celestial patterns, Duchess," the astrologer said. "But I will do my best. . . ."

"And if you can't come up with something better than the year I've just gone through," Benigaris muttered, "I may just toss you off the roof."

"Benigaris!" Nessalanta's voice, which had so far been wheedling and childlike, turned suddenly sharp as the crack of a drover's whip. "You will not speak that way before me! You will *not* threaten Xannasavin! Do you understand!?"

Benigaris almost imperceptibly flinched. "It was only a jest. Aedon's Holy Blood, Mother, don't take on so." He walked to the half-canopied chair with the ducal crest and sat down heavily. "Go on, man," he grunted, waving at Xannasavin. "Tell us what wonders the stars hold."

The astrologer pulled a sheaf of scrolls from his volu-minous robe, brandishing them with a certain drama. "As the duchess mentioned," he began, his voice smooth and practiced, "tonight is an excellent night for divination. Not only are the stars in a particularly favorable configu-ration, but the sky itself is clear of storms and other hin-drances." He smiled at Duke Benigaris. "An auspicious sign in and of itself."

"Continue," said the duke.

Xannasavin lifted a furled scroll and pointed up at the wheel of stars. "As you can see, Yuvenis' Throne is di-rectly overhead. The Throne is, of course, much tied to the ruling of Nabban, and has been since the old heathen days. When the lesser lights are moving through its aspect, the heirs of the Imperium do well to take notice." He paused for a moment to let the import of this sink in. "Tonight you can see that the Throne is upright, and that on its topmost edge, the Serpent and Mixis the Wolf are particularly bright." He swung around and pointed to another part of the sky. "The Falcon, there, and the Winged Beetle are now visible in the southern sky. The Beetle always brings change."

"It is like one of the old Imperators' private menageries," Benigaris said impatiently. "Beasts, beasts, beasts. What does it all mean?"

"It means, my lord, that there are great times ahead for the Benidrivine House."

"I knew it," Nessalanta purred. "I knew it."

"What tells you that?" Benigaris asked, squinting at the sky.

"I could not do justice to your majesties by trying to make an explanation that was too brief," the astrologer said smoothly. "Suffice it to say that the stars, which have long spoken of hesitation, of unsureness and doubt, now proclaim that a time of change is coming. Great change."

"But that could be anything," Benigaris grumbled. "That could mean the whole city burned down."

"Ah, but that is only because you have not heard all that I have to say. There are two other factors, factors most important. One is the Kingfisher itself—there, do you see it?" Xannasavin gestured toward a point in the eastern sky. "It is far brighter than I have ever seen it— and at this time of year it is generally quite hard to see. Your family's fortunes have long risen and fallen with the waxing and waning of the Kingfisher's light, and it has not been so gloriously illuminated before in my lifetime. Something of great moment is about to happen to the Benidrivine House, my lord. Your house."

"And the other?" Benigaris appeared to be growing interested. "The other thing you mentioned?"

"Ah." The astrologer unrolled one of his scrolls and examined it. "That is something that you cannot see at this moment. There will be a reappearance soon of the Conqueror Star."

"The bearded star that we saw last year and the year before?" It was Streáwe who spoke, his voice eager. "The great red thing?"

"That is the one."

"But when it came, it frightened the common folk out of their shallow wits!" Benigaris said. "I think that is what started all this doom-saying nonsense in the first place!"

Xannasavin nodded. "The celestial signs are often misread, Duke Benigaris. The Conqueror Star will return, but it is not a precursor of disaster, merely of change. Throughout history it has come to herald a new order appearing out of conflict and chaos. It trumpeted the end of the Imperium, and shone over the final days of Khand."

"And this is good!?" Benigaris shouted. "You are saying that something which speaks of the downfall of an empire should make me happy!?" He seemed ready to leap from his chair and manhandle the astrologer.

"But my lord, remember the Kingfisher!" Xannasavin said hurriedly. "How could these changes be to your dismay when the Kingfisher is burning so brightly? No, my lord, pardon your humble servant for seeming to instruct you in any way, but can you think of no situation in which a great empire might fall, yet the fortunes of the Benidrivine House might improve?"

Benigaris sat back swiftly, as though repelled by a blow. He stared at his hands. "I will talk to you of this later," he said at last. "Leave us now for a while."

Xannasavin bowed. "As you wish, my lord." He bowed again, this time in the direction of Streáwe. "A pleasure to meet you at last, Count. I have been honored."

The count absently bobbed his head, as lost in thought as Benigaris.

Xannasavin kissed Nessalanta's hand, swept the rooftop with a low bow, then stowed his scrolls once more and walked to the stairwell. His footsteps gradually dwindled down into echoing darkness.

"Do you see?" Nessalanta asked. "Do you see why I value him so? He is a brilliant man."

Streáwe nodded. "He is most imposing. And you have found him reliable?"

"Absolutely. He predicted my poor husband's death." Her face assumed a look of profound sorrow. "But Leobardis would not listen, despite all my warnings. I told him if he set foot on Erkynlandish soil, I would never see him again. He told me it was nonsense."

Benigaris looked at his mother sharply. "Xannasavin told you Father would die?"

"He did. If only your father had listened."

Count Streáwe cleared his throat. "Well, I had hoped to save these matters for a different time, Benigaris, but hearing what your astrologer had to say—hearing of the splendid future he sees for you—I think perhaps I should share my thoughts with you now."

Benigaris turned from his dissatisfied contemplation of his mother to the count. "What are you talking about?"

"Certain things I have learned." The old man looked around. "Ah, forgive me, Benigaris, but would it be an imposition to ask your guards to step back out of hearing?" He made a crabbed gesture toward the two armored men, who had stood motionless and silent as stone throughout the proceedings. Benigaris grunted and gestured them back.

"So?"

"I have, as you know, many sources of information," the count began. "I hear many things that even others more powerful than myself are not able to discover. Recently I have heard some things that you might wish to know. About Elias and his war with Josua. About ... other things." He paused and looked to the duke expectantly.

Nessalanta, too, was sitting forward. "Go on, Streáwe. You know how much we value your counsel."

"Yes," Benigaris said, "go on. I will be very interested to discover what you have heard."

The count smiled, a vulpine grin that showed his still-bright teeth. "Ah, yes," he said. "You *will* be interested. ..."

Eolair did not recognize the Sitha who stood in the doorway of the Hall of Carvings. He was dressed conservatively, at least in Sithi terms, in shirt and breeches of a pale creamy cloth that shimmered like silk. His hair was nut-brown—the closest to a human shade the count had yet seen—and had been pulled into a knot on top of his head.

"Likimeya and Jiriki say that you must come to them." The stranger's Hernystiri was as awkward and as archaic as that of the dwarrows. "Must you wait for a moment, or is it that you can come now? It is good that you come now."

Eolair heard Craobhan take a breath as if to protest the summons, but the count laid a hand on his arm. It was only this immortal's imperfect speech that made it sound peremptory—Eolair guessed that the Sithi would wait for him for days without impatience.

"One of your people, a healer, is with the king's daughter—with Maegwin," he told the messenger. "I must talk to her. Then I will come."

The Sitha, face impassive, bobbed his head swiftly in the manner of a cormorant seizing a fish from a river. "I will tell to them." He turned and left the room, his booted feet soundless on the wooden floors.

"Are they the masters here now?" Craobhan asked irritatedly. "Should we step to their measures?"

Eolair shook his head. "That is not their way, old friend. Jiriki and his mother simply wish to speak to me, I am sure. Not all of them speak our tongue as well as those two."

"I still do not like it. We had to live with Skali's boot on our necks long enough—when are the Hernystiri going to take their rightful place in their own land again?"

"Things are changing," Eolair said mildly. "But we have always survived. Five centuries ago, Fingil's

Rimmersmen drove us into the hills and the sea-cliffs. We came back. Skali's men are on the run now, so we have outlasted them, too. The weight of the Sithi is a far easier burden, don't you think?"

The old man stared at him, eyes wrinkling in a suspicious squint. At last, he smiled. "Ah, my good count, you should have been a priest or a general. You take the long view."

"As you do, Craobhan. Else you would not be here today to complain."

Before the old man could respond, another Sitha appeared in the doorway, this one a gray-haired woman dressed in green with a cloak of cloudy silver. Despite the color of her hair, she looked no older than the just-departed messenger.

"Kira'athu," the count said, rising. His voice lost its lightness. "Can you help her?"

The Sitha stared at him for a moment, then shook her head; the gesture seemed curiously unnatural, as though she had learned it from a book. "There is nothing wrong with her body. But her spirit is somehow hidden from me, gone deep inside, like a mouse when the owl's shadow is upon the night-fields."

"What does that mean?" Eolair struggled to keep impatience out of his words.

"Frightened. She is frightened. She is like a child who has seen its parents killed."

"She has seen much death. She has buried her father and her brother."

The Sitha-woman waved her fingers slowly, a gesture that Eolair could not translate. "It is not that. *Anyone*, Zida'ya or Sudhoda'ya—Dawn Child or mortal—who has lived enough years understands death. It is horrible, but it is understandable. But a child does not understand it. And something has come to the woman Maegwin in this way—something that is beyond her understanding. It has frightened her spirit."

"Will she get better? Is there anything you can do for her?"

"I can do nothing more. Her body is sound. Where the

spirit goes, though, is another matter. I must think on this. Perhaps there is an answer I cannot see at this time."

It was difficult to read Kira'athu's high-boned, feline face, but Eolair did not think she sounded very hopeful. The count balled his fists and held them hard against his thighs. "And is there anything *I* can do?"

Something very much like pity showed in the Sitha's eyes. "If she has hidden her spirit deep enough, only the woman Maegwin can lead herself back. You cannot do it for her." She paused as though searching for words of solace. "Be kind. That is something." She turned and glided from the hall.

After a long silence, Old Craobhan spoke. "Maegwin's mad, Eolair."

The count held up his hand. "Don't."

"You can't change it by not listening. She grew worse while you were gone. I told you where we found her—up on Bradach Tor, raving and singing. She'd been sitting unprotected in the wind and snow for Mircha only knows how long. Said she'd seen the gods."

"Perhaps she did see them," Eolair said bitterly. "After all *I* have seen in this cursed twelve-month, who am I to doubt her? Perhaps it was too much for her. . . ." He stood, rubbing his wet palms on his breeches. "I will go now and meet Jiriki."

Craobhan nodded. His eyes were moist, but his mouth was set in a hard line. "Don't ruin yourself, Eolair. Don't give in. We need you even more than she does."

"When Isorn and the others come back," the count said, "tell them where I've gone. Ask them to wait up for me, if they would be so good—I don't think I will be too long with the Sithi." He looked out at the sky deepening toward twilight. "I want to talk to Isorn and Ule tonight." He patted the old man's shoulder before walking out of the Hall of Carvings.

"Eolair."

He turned in the outer doorway to find Maegwin standing in the entrance hallway behind him. "My lady. How are you feeling?"

"Well," she said lightly, but her eyes belied her. "Where are you going?"

"I am going to see . . ." He caught himself. He had almost said "the gods." Was madness contagious? "I am going to speak with Jiriki and his mother."

"I do not know them," she said. "But I would like to go with you in any case."

"Go with me?" Somehow it seemed strange.

"Yes, Count Eolair. I would like to go with you. Is that so dreadful? We are not such dire enemies, surely?" There was a hollowness to her words, like a jest made on a gibbet's top step.

"Of course you may, my lady," he said hurriedly. "Maegwin. Of course."

Although Eolair could not discern any new additions to the Sithi camp that stretched across the broad expanse of Hern's Hill, still it seemed more intricate than it had just a few days before, more connected to the land. It looked as though, instead of the product of a few days' work, it had stood here since the hill was young. There was a quality of peace and soft, natural movement: the multicolored tent houses shifted and swayed like plants in an eddying stream. The count felt a moment of irritation, an echo of Craobhan's dissatisfaction. What right did the Sithi have to make themselves so comfortable here? Whose land was this, after all?

A moment later, he caught himself. It was just the nature of the Fair Ones. Despite their great cities, mere bathaunted ruins now if Mezutu'a was any indication, they were people who were not rooted to a place. From the way Jiriki had talked about the Garden, their primordial home, it seemed clear that despite their eon-long tenancy in Osten Ard they still felt themselves to be little more than travelers in this land. They lived in their own heads, in their songs and memories. Hern's Hill was only another place.

Maegwin walked silently beside him, her features set as though she hid troubled thoughts. He remembered a time many years before when she had brought him to watch one of her beloved pigs give birth. Something had gone wrong, and near the end of the birthing the sow had begun to squeal in pain. By the time the two dead piglets had been removed, one still wrapped in the bloody umbilicus that had strangled it, the sow in her panic had rolled on one of her other newborns.

All through that blood-spattered nightmare, Maegwin had worn a look much like the one she bore now. Only when the sow had been saved and the rest of the litter were nursing had she allowed herself to break down and cry. Remembering, Eolair realized suddenly that it had been the last time she had let him hold her. Even as he had sorrowed for her, trying to understand her grief over the deaths of what to him were only animals, he had felt her in his arms, her breasts against him, and had realized that she was a woman now, for all her youth. It had been a strange feeling.

"Eolair?" There was just a hint of a tremor in Maegwin's voice. "May I ask you a question?"

"Certainly, Lady." He could not lose the memory of himself as he had held her, blood on their hands and clothes as they kneeled in the straw. He had not felt half so helpless then as he did now.

"How ... how did you die?"

At first he thought he had misheard her. "I am sorry, Maegwin. How did I what?"

"How did you die? I am ashamed I have not asked you before. Was it the sort of death you deserved, a noble one? Oh, I hope it was not painful. I don't think I could bear that." She looked at him quickly, then broke into a shaky smile. "But of course that doesn't matter, for here you are! It is all behind us."

"How did I die?" The unreality of it struck him like a blow. He pulled at her arm and stopped. They were standing in an open stretch of grass with Likimeya's enclosure only a stone's throw away before them. "Maegwin, I am not dead. Feel me!" He extended his hand and took her cool fingers. "I am alive! So are you!"

"I was struck down just as the gods came," she said dreamily. "I think it was Skali—at least his ax being raised is the last thing I remember before I woke up here." She laughed shakily. "That's funny. Can you wake up in Heaven? Sometimes, since I have been here, it feels as though I sleep for a little while."

"Maegwin." He squeezed her hand. "Listen to me. We are not dead." Eolair felt himself about to weep and shook his head angrily. "You are still in Hernystir, the place where you were born."

Maegwin looked at him with a curious gleam in her eyes. For a moment the count thought he might have finally reached her. "Do you know, Eolair," she said slowly, "when I was alive, I was always frightened. Frightened that I would lose the things I cared about. I was even frightened to talk to you, the closest friend I ever had." She shook her head. Her hair streamed in the breeze moving across the hill, exposing her long pale neck. "I could not even tell you that I loved you, Eolair— loved you until it burned inside me. I was frightened that if I told you, you would push me away and I would not even have your friendship."

Eolair's heart felt as though it would crack right through, like a flawed stone struck by a hammer. "Maegwin, I . . . I didn't know." Did he love her, too? Would it help her to tell her he did, whether it was true or not? "I was . . . I was blind," he stammered. "I didn't know."

She smiled sadly. "It is no matter now," she said with terrible certainty. "It's too late to worry about such things." She clutched his hand and led him forward once more.

He took the last few steps toward the blue and purple of Likimeya's compound like a man arrow-shot in the dark, so surprised that he walks on without realizing he has been murdered.

Jiriki and his mother were in quiet but intense conversation when Eolair and Maegwin stepped through the ring of cloth. Likimeya still wore her armor; her son was attired in softer clothing.

Jiriki looked up. "Count Eolair. We are happy you

could come. We have things to show you and tell you."
His eyes lit on Eolair's companion. "Lady Maegwin.
Welcome."

Eolair felt Maegwin tense, but she made a curtsy. "My
Lord," she said. The count could not help wondering what
she saw. If Jiriki was the sky-god Brynioch, what did she
make of his mother? What did she see when she looked
at the rippling cloth all around them, the fruit trees and
the dying afternoon light, at the alien faces of the other
Sithi?

"Please sit." It was strange how musical Likimeya's
voice was, for all its roughness. "Will you have refresh-
ment?"

"Not for me, thank you." Eolair turned to Maegwin.
She shook her head, but her eyes were distant, as though
she were somehow pulling away from what lay before
her.

"Then let us not wait," Likimeya said. "We have something to show you." She looked over to the brown-haired
messenger who had earlier visited the Taig. This one
stepped forward, lowering the sack that he held in his
hands. With a deft movement, he unlaced the drawstring
and turned it upside-down. Something dark rolled out
onto the grass.

"Tears of Rhynn!" Eolair choked.

Skali's head lay before him, mouth open, eyes wide.
The full yellow beard was now almost entirely crimson,
stained by the gore that had wicked up from his severed
neck.

"There is your enemy, Count Eolair," said Likimeya. A
cat who had killed a bird might drop it at her master's
feet with just such calm satisfaction. "He and a few dozen
of his men turned at last, in the hills east of Grianspog."

"Take it away, please." Eolair felt his gorge rising. "I
did not need to see him like this." For a moment he
looked worriedly to Maegwin, but she was not even
watching: her pale face was turned toward the darkening
sky beyond the walls of the compound.

Unlike her flame-red hair, Likimeya's eyebrows were
white, two streaks like narrow scars above her eyes. She

raised one of them in a curiously human expression of
mocking disbelief. "Your Prince Sinnach displayed his
defeated enemies this way."

"That was five hundred years past!" Eolair recovered a
little of his usual calm. "I am sorry, Mistress, but we mortals change in such a length of time. Our ancestors were
perhaps fiercer than we are." He swallowed. "I have seen
much death, but this was a surprise."

"We meant no offense." Likimeya gave Jiriki what appeared to be a significant glance. "We thought it would
gladden your heart to see what came to the one who conquered and enslaved your people."

Eolair took a breath. "I understand. And I mean no offense either. We are grateful for your help. Grateful past
telling." He could not help looking again at the blood-
matted thing on the grass.

The messenger stooped and plucked Skali's head up by
the hair and dropped it back into the sack. Eolair had to
restrain an urge to ask what had happened to the rest of
Sharp-nose. Probably left for the vultures somewhere in
those cold eastern hills.

"That is good," replied Likimeya. "Because we wish
your aid."

Eolair steadied himself. "What can we do?"

Jiriki turned to him. His face was blandly indifferent,
even more so than usual. Had he disapproved somehow of
his mother's gesture? Eolair pushed the thought aside. To
try to understand the Sithi was to invite perplexity border-
ing on madness.

"Now that Skali is dead and the last of his troops scattered across the land, our purpose here is fulfilled," Jiriki
said. "But we have only set our feet to the path. Now the
journey begins in earnest."

As he spoke his mother reached behind her and drew
out a jar, a squat but oddly graceful object glazed in dark
blue. She reached two fingers into it and then withdrew
them. The tips were stained gray-black.

"We told you that we cannot stop here," Jiriki continued. "We must go on to *Ujin e-d'a Sikhunae*—the place
you call Naglimund."

Slowly, as if performing a ritual, Likimeya began to daub her face. She began by drawing dark lines down her cheeks and around her eyes.

"And . . . and what can the Hernystiri do?" Eolair asked. He was having trouble tearing his gaze away from Jiriki's mother.

The Sitha lowered his head for a moment, then raised it and held the count's eye, compelling him to pay attention. "By the blood that our two peoples have spilled for each other, I ask you to send a troop of your countrymen to join us."

"To join you?" Eolair thought of the shining, trumpeting charge of the Sithi. "What help could we possibly be?"

Jiriki smiled. "You underestimate yourselves—and you overestimate us. It is very important that we take the castle that once belonged to Josua, but it will be a fight like no other. Who knows what surprising part mortals may play when the Gardenborn fight? And there are things you can do that we cannot. We are few now. We need your folk, Eolair. We need you."

Likimeya had drawn a mask around her eyes, on her forehead and cheeks, so that her amber gaze seemed to flame in the darkness like jewels in a rock crevice. She drew three lines down from her bottom lip to her chin.

"I cannot compel my people, Jiriki," Eolair told him. "Especially after all that has happened to them. But if I go, I think that others would join me." He considered the needs of honor and duty. Revenge against Skali had been taken from him, but it seemed the Rimmersman had only been a catspaw for Elias—and for an even more frightening enemy. Hernystir was free, but the war was by no means ended. The count also found a certain seductiveness in the idea of something as straightforward as battle. The tangle of reoccupying Hernysadharc and coping with Maegwin's madness had already begun to overwhelm him.

The sky overhead was dark blue, the color of Likimeya's pot. Some of the Sithi produced globes of light which they set on wooden stands around the enclosure; the branches of the fruit trees, lit from below, burned golden.

"I will come with you to Naglimund, Jiriki," he said at last. Craobhan could watch over the folk of Hernysadharc, he decided, and watch over Maegwin and Lluth's wife Inahwen as well. Craobhan would continue the work of rebuilding the land—it was a task that would suit the old man perfectly. "I will bring as many of my fighting men as will come."

"Thank you, Count Eolair. The world is changing, but some things are always true. The hearts of the Hernystiri are constant."

Likimeya put down her pot, wiped her fingers on her boots—they left a broad smear—and stood up. By her face-painting, she had changed herself into something even more alien, more unsettling.

"Then it is agreed," she said. "When the third morning from tonight comes, we will ride to Ujin e-d'a Sikhunae." Her eyes seemed to spark in the light of the crystal globes.

Eolair could not brave her gaze for long, but neither could he still his curiosity. "Your pardon, Mistress," he said. "I hope I am not being impolite. May I ask what you have put on your face?"

"Ashes. Mourning ashes." She made a sound in the back of her throat, a thin exhalation that could have been a sigh or a huff of exasperation. "You cannot understand, mortal men, but I will tell you anyway. We go to war on the Hikeda'ya."

After a moment's pause, while Eolair tried to puzzle out what she meant, Jiriki spoke up. His voice was gentle, mournful. "Sithi and Norns are of a single blood, Count Eolair. Now we must fight them." He lifted a hand and made a gesture like a candle flame being extinguished—a flutter, then stillness. "We must kill members of our own family."

Maegwin was silent most of the way back. It was only when the Taig's sloping roofs loomed before them that she spoke.

"I am going with you. I will go to see the gods make war."

He shook his head violently. "You are going to stay here with Craobhan and the rest."

"No. If you leave me behind, I will follow you." Her voice was calm and certain. "And in any case, Eolair, what makes you sound so fearful? I cannot die twice, can I?" She laughed a little too loudly.

Eolair argued with her in vain. At last, just as he was on the verge of losing his temper, a thought came to him. *The healer said she must find her own way back. Perhaps this is part of it?*

But the danger. Surely he could not think of letting her take such a risk. Not that he *could* stop her from following if he left her behind—mad or no, there was no one in all of Hernysadharc half as stubborn as Lluth's daughter. Gods, was he cursed? No wonder he almost longed for the brutal simplicity of battle.

"We will speak of this later," he said. "I am tired, Maegwin."

"No one should be tired in this place." There was a subtle note of triumph in her voice. "I worry about you, Eolair."

Simon had picked an open, unshaded spot near Sesuad'ra's outer wall. The sun was actually shining today, although it was windy enough that both he and Miriamele wore their cloaks. Still, it was pleasant to have his hood down and to feel the sun on his neck. "I brought some wine." Simon produced a skin bag and two cups from his sack. "Sangfugol said it's good—I think it's from Perdruin." He laughed nervously. "Why would it be better from one place than another? Grapes are grapes."

Miriamele smiled. She seemed tired: shadows lay beneath her green eyes. "I don't know. Maybe they grow them differently."

"It doesn't really matter." Simon carefully aimed a stream from the winesack into first one cup, then the other. "I'm still not sure I even like wine—Rachel would never let me drink it. 'The Devil's blood,' she called it."

"The Mistress of Chambermaids?" Miriamele made a face. "She was a nasty woman."

Simon handed her a cup. "I used to think so. She certainly had a temper. But she tried to do her best for me, I suppose. I made it hard on her." He lifted the wine to his lips, letting the sourness run over his tongue. "I wonder where she is now? Still at the Hayholt? I hope she's well. I hope she hasn't been hurt." He grinned—to think of having such feelings for the Dragon!—then looked up suddenly. "Oh, no. I've already drunk some. Shouldn't we say something—have a toast?"

Miriamele lifted her cup solemnly. "To your birth-day, Simon."

"And to yours, Princess Miriamele."

They sat and drank for a while in silence. The wind pressed the grass sideways, flattening it in changing patterns as though some great invisible beast rolled in restless sleep. "The Raed is beginning tomorrow," he said. "But I think that Josua has already decided what he wants to do."

"He will go to Nabban." There was quiet bitterness in her voice.

"What's wrong with that?" Simon motioned for her cup, which was empty. "It's a start."

"It's the wrong start." She stared at his hand as she took the cup. The scrutiny made him uneasy. "I'm sorry, Simon. I am just unhappy with things. With lots of things."

"I will listen if you want to talk. I've gotten to be a good listener, Princess."

"Don't call me *'Princess'!*" When she spoke again, her tone was softer. "Please, Simon, not you, too. We were friends once, when you didn't know who I was. I need that now."

"Certainly . . . Miriamele." He took a breath. "Aren't we friends now?"

"That's not what I meant." She sighed. "It's the same problem as I have with Josua's decision. I don't agree with him. I think we should move directly to Erkynland. This is not a war like my grandfather fought—it's much worse, much darker. I am afraid we will be too late if we try to conquer Nabban first."

"Too late for what?"

"I don't know. I have these feelings, these ideas, but I have nothing that I can use to prove they are real. That's bad enough, but because I am a princess—because I am the High King's daughter—they listen to me anyway. Then they all try to find a polite way to ignore me. It would almost be better if they just told me to be quiet!"

"What does that have to do with me?" Simon asked quietly. Miriamele had closed her eyes, as though she looked at something inside herself. The red-gold of her eyelashes, the minute fineness of them, made him feel as though he were coming apart.

"Even you, Simon, who met me as a serving-girl—no, a serving-boy!" She laughed, but her eyes remained shut. "Even you, Simon, when you look at me, you are not just looking at me. You are seeing my father's name, the castle I grew up in, the costly dresses. You are looking at a ... a *princess*." She said the word as though it meant something terrible and false.

Simon stared at her for a long time, watching her wind-shifted hair, the downy line of her cheek. He burned to tell her what he really saw, but knew he could never find the proper words; it would all come out as a mooncalf babble. "You are what you are," he said at last. "Isn't it just as false to try and be something else as it is for others to pretend they're talking to *you* when they're only talking to some ... princess?"

Her eyes opened suddenly. They were so clear, so searching! He suddenly had an idea of what it must have been like to stand before her grandfather, Prester John. It reminded him, too, of what he himself was: a servant's awkward child, a knight only by virtue of circumstance. At this moment she seemed closer than she had ever been, but at the same time the gulf between them also seemed as wide as the ocean.

Miriamele was staring at him intently. After a few moments, he looked away, abashed. "I'm sorry."

"Don't be." Her voice was brisk, but it somehow did not match the fretful expression on her face. "Don't be, Simon. And let's talk of something else." She turned to look across the swaying grass of the hilltop. The strange, fierce moment passed.

They finished the wine and shared bread and cheese. For a treat, Simon produced a leaf-wrapped package of sweetmeats that he had bought from one of the peddlers at New Gadrinsett's small market, little balls made of honey and roasted grain. The talk turned to other things, of the places and strange things they had both seen. Miriamele tried to tell Simon of the Niskie Gan Itai and her singing, of the way she had used her music to stitch sky and sea together. In his turn, Simon tried to explain something of what it had been like to be in Jiriki's house by the river, and to see the Yásira, the living tent of butterflies. He tried to describe gentle, frightening Amerasu, but faltered. There was still a great deal of pain in that memory.

"And what about that other Sitha-woman?" Miriamele asked. "The one who is here. Aditu."

"What do you mean?"

"What do you think of her?" She frowned. "I think she has no manners."

Simon snorted softly. "She has her own manners, is more like it. They're not like us, Miriamele."

"Well, then I think little of the Sithi. She dresses and acts like a tavern harlot."

He had to suppress another smile. Aditu's current style of dress was almost bogglingly reserved in comparison to the garb she had worn in Jao é-Tinukai'i. It was true that she still often exhibited more of her tawny flesh than the citizens of New Gadrinsett found comfortable, but Aditu was obviously doing her best not to outrage her mortal companions. As for her behavior . . . "I don't think she's so bad," he said.

"Well, you wouldn't." Miriamele was definitely cross. "You moon after her like a puppy."

"I do not!" he said, stung. "She is my friend."

"That's a nice word. I have heard my father's knights use that word also, to describe women who would not be allowed across the threshold of a church." Miriamele sat up straight. She was not just teasing. The anger he had sensed earlier was there, too. "I do not blame you—it is the nature of men. She is very fetching, in her strange way."

Simon's laugh was sharp. "I will never understand," he said.

"What? Understand what?"

"No matter." He shook his head. It would be good to move the conversation back to safer ground, he decided. "Ah, I almost forgot." He turned and reached for the drawstring bag which he had leaned against the weather-polished wall. "This is a celebration of our birth-days. It is time for the giving of gifts."

Miriamele looked up, stricken. "Oh, Simon! But I don't have anything to give you!"

"Just your being here is enough. To see you safe after all this time . . ." His voice broke, making an embarrassing squeak. To cover his chagrin, he cleared his throat. "But in any case, you have already given me a fine present—your scarf." He pulled his collar wide so she could see it where it nestled about his long neck. "The finest gift that anyone ever gave me, I think." He smiled and hid it again. "Now I have something to give to you." He reached into his bag and pulled out a long slender something wrapped in a cloth.

"What is it?" The care seemed to slide from her face, leaving her childlike in her attention to the mysterious bundle.

"Open it."

She did, unwinding the cloth to disclose the white Sithi arrow, a streak of ivory fire.

"I want you to have it."

Miriamele looked from the arrow to Simon. Her face went pale. "Oh, no," she breathed. "No, Simon, I can't."

"What do you mean? Of course you can. It's my gift to you. Binabik said that it was made by the Sithi fletcher

Vindaomeyo, longer ago than either of us can imagine.
It's the only thing I have to give that's worthy of a princess, Miriamele—and like it or not, that's what you are."

"No, Simon, no." She pushed the arrow and its cloth
into his hands. "No, Simon. That's the kindest thing anyone has ever done for me, but I can't take it. It's not just
a thing, it's a promise from Jiriki to you—a pledge. You
told me so. It means too much. The Sithi do not give
these things away for no reason."

"Neither do I," said Simon angrily. So even this was
not good enough, he thought. Under a thin layer of fury
he felt a great reserve of hurt. "I want *you* to have it."

"Please, Simon. I thank you—you do not understand
how kind I think you are—but it would hurt me too much
to take it from you. I cannot."

Baffled, pained, Simon closed his fingers on the arrow.
His offering had been rejected. He felt wild and full of
folly. "Then wait here," he said, and rose. He was on the
verge of shouting. "Promise me you won't leave this spot
until I come back."

She looked up at him uncertainly, shielding her eyes
from the sun. "If you want me to stay, Simon, I will stay.
Will you be gone long?"

"No." He turned toward the crumbling gateway of the
great wall. Before he had gone ten steps, he quickened his
pace to a run.

When he returned, Miriamele was still seated in the
same place. She had found the pomegranate he had hidden as a last surprise.

"I'm sorry," she said, "but I was restless. I got this
open, but I haven't eaten any yet." She showed him the
seeds lined up on the split fruit like rows of gems. "What
have you got in your hand?"

Simon drew his sword out of the tangle of his cloak. As
Miriamele watched, her apprehension far from gone, he
kneeled before her.

"Miriamele ... Princess ... I will give you the only
gift I have left to give." He extended the hilt of his sword
toward her, lowering his head and staring fixedly at the

jungle of grass around his boots. "My service. I am a knight now. I swear that you are my mistress, and that I will serve you as your protector . . . if you will have me."

Simon looked up out of the corner of his eye. Miriamele's face was awash in emotions, none of which he could identify. "Oh, Simon," she said.

"If you will not have me, or cannot for some reason I'm still too stupid to know, then just tell me. We can still be friends."

There was a long pause. Simon looked down at the ground again and felt his head spinning.

"Of course," she said at last. "Of course I will have you, dear Simon." There was an odd catch in her voice. She laughed raggedly. "But I will never forgive you for this."

He looked up, alarmed, to see if she was joking. Her mouth was curved in a trembling half-smile, but her eyes were closed again. There was a gleam like tears on her lashes. He could not tell if she was happy or sad.

"What do I do?" she asked.

"I'm not sure. Take the hilt and then touch my shoulders with the blade, I suppose, like Josua did to me. Say: 'You will be my champion.' "

She took the hilt and held it for a moment against her cheek, then lifted the sword and touched his shoulders in turn, left and right.

"You will be my champion, Simon," she whispered.

"I will."

The torches in Leavetaking House had burned low. It was long past time for the evening meal, but no one had said a word about eating.

"This is the third day of the Raed," Prince Josua said. "We are all tired. I beg your attention for just a few moments more." He drew his hand across his eyes.

Isgrimnur thought that of all those assembled in the room, it was the prince himself who most showed the strain of the long days and the acrimonious arguments. In

attempting to let everyone have his or her fair say, Josua
had been dragged along through many a side issue—and
the onetime master of Elvritshalla did not approve at all.
Prince Josua would never survive the rigors of a campaign against his brother if he did not harden himself. He
had improved some since Isgrimnur had seen him last—
the journey to this strange place seemed to have changed
everyone who made it—but the duke still did not think
Josua had grasped the trick of listening without being led.
Without that, he thought sourly, no ruler could long survive.

The disagreements were many. The Thrithings-men did
not trust the hardiness of the New Gadrinsett folk and
feared that they would become a burden on the wagon-
clans when Josua moved his camp down onto the grasslands. In turn, the settlers were not certain that they
wanted to leave their new lives to go somewhere else
since they would not even have new lands to settle until
Josua took some territory from his brother or Benigaris.

Freosel and Sludig, who had become Josua's war com-
manders after the death of Deornoth, also disagreed bitterly over where the prince should go. Sludig sided with
his liege-lord Isgrimnur in urging an attack on Nabban.
Freosel, like many others, felt an excursion into the south
missed the true point. He was an Erkynlander, and
Erkynland was not only Josua's own country, but also the
place that had been most blighted by Elias' misrule.
Freosel had made it clear that he felt they should move
westward to the outer fiefdoms of Erkynland, gathering
strength from the High King's disaffected subjects before
marching on the Hayholt itself.

Isgrimnur sighed and scratched his chin, indulging for
a moment in the pleasure of his regrown beard. He longed
to stand up and simply tell everyone what they should do
and how to do it. He even sensed that Josua would secretly welcome having the burden of leadership lifted
from his shoulders—but such a thing could not be allowed. The duke knew that as soon as the prince lost his
preeminence, the factions would dissolve and any chance
of an organized resistance to Elias would collapse.

"Sir Camaris," Josua said abruptly, turning to the old knight. "You have been mostly silent. Yet if we are to ride on Nabban, as Isgrimnur and others urge us, you will be our banner. I need to hear your thoughts."

The old man had indeed remained aloof, although Isgrimnur doubted it was from disapproval or disagreement. Rather, Camaris had listened to the arguments like a holy man on a bench in the midst of a tavern brawl, present and yet separate, his attention fixed on something that others could not see.

"I cannot tell you what is the right thing to do, Prince Josua." The old knight spoke, as he had since regaining his wits, with a sort of effortless dignity. His old-fashioned, courtly speech was so careful as to seem almost a parody; he might have been the Good Peasant from the proverbs of the Book of the Aedon. "That is beyond me, nor would I presume to interpose myself between you and God, who is the final answerer of all questions. I can only tell you what I think." He leaned forward, staring down at his long-fingered hands, which were twined on the table before him as if he prayed. "Much of what has been said is still incomprehensible to me—your brother's bargain with this Storm King, who was only a dim legend in my day; the part you say the swords are to play, my black blade Thorn among them—it is all most strange, most strange.

"But I do know that I loved well my brother, Leobardis, and from what you said, he served Nabban honorably in the years I was insensible—better than I ever could have, I think. He was a man who was made to govern other men; I am not.

"His son Benigaris I knew only as a bawling infant. It gnaws at my soul to think that someone of my father's house could be a patricide, but I cannot doubt the evidence I have heard." He shook his head slowly, a tired war-horse. "I cannot tell you to go to Nabban, or to Erkynland, or anywhere else upon the Lord's green earth. But if you decide to march on Nabban, Josua . . . then, yes, I will ride before the armies. If the people will use my name, I will not stop them, although I do not find it knightly: only our Ransomer should be exalted by the voices of men. But I cannot let such shame to the Benidrivine House go unheeded.

"So if that is the answer you seek from me, Josua, then you have it now." He raised his hand in a gesture of fealty. "Yes, I will ride to Nabban. But I wish I had not been brought back to see my friend John's kingdom in ruins and my own beloved Nabban ground beneath the heel of my murderous nephew. It is cruel." He dropped his gaze to the table once more. "This is one of the sternest tests God has given me, and I have failed Him already more times than I can count."

When he had finished speaking, the old man's words seemed to linger in the air like incense, a fog of complicated regret that filled the room. No one dared to break the stillness until Josua spoke.

"Thank you, Sir Camaris. I think I know what it will cost you to ride against your own countrymen. I am heartsick that we may have to force it upon you." He looked around the torchlit hall. "Is there anyone else who would speak before we are finished?"

Beside him, Vorzheva moved on the bench as though she might say something, but instead she stared angrily at Josua, who slipped her gaze as though he found it uncomfortable. Isgrimnur guessed what had passed between them—Josua had told him of her desire to stay until the child was born—and frowned; the prince did not need any further doubts clouding his decision.

Many cubits down the long table, Geloë stood. "I think there is one last thing, Josua. It is something that Father Strangyeard and I discovered only last night." She turned to the priest, who was sitting beside her. "Strangyeard?"

The archivist stood up, fingering a stack of parchments. He lifted a hand to straighten his eyepatch, then looked worriedly at some of the nearby faces, as though he had suddenly found himself called before a tribunal and charged with heresy.

"Yes," he said. "Oh, yes. Yes, there is something important—your pardon, something that *may* be important . . ." He riffled through the pages before him.

"Come, Strangyeard," the prince said kindly. "We are anxious to have you share your discovery with us."

"Ah, yes. We found something in Morgenes' manuscript. In his life of King John Presbyter." He held up some of the parchment sheets for the benefit of those who had not already seen Doctor Morgenes' book. "Also, from speaking to Tiamak of the Wran," he gestured with the sheaf toward the marsh man, "we found that it was something that much concerned Morgenes even after he began to see the outlines of Elias' bargain with the Storm King. It worried him, you see. Morgenes, that is."

"See what?" Isgrimnur's rear end was beginning to hurt from the hard chair, and his back had been griping him for hours. *What* worried him?"

"Oh!" Strangyeard was startled. "Apologies, many apologies. The bearded star, of course. The comet."

"There was such a star in the skies during my brother's regnal year," Josua mused. "As a matter of fact, it was the night of his coronation we first saw it. The night my father was buried."

"That's the one!" Strangyeard said excitedly. "The *Asdridan Condiquilles*—the Conqueror Star. Here, I'll read what Morgenes wrote about it." He pawed at the parchment.

> *". . . Strangely enough,"*

he began,

> *"the Conqueror Star, instead of shining above the birth or triumph of conquerors as its name might suggest, seems instead to appear as a herald of the death of empires. It trumpeted the downfall of Khand, of the old Sea Kingdoms, and even the ending of what may have been the greatest empire of all—the Sithi mastery of Osten Ard, which came to an end when their great stronghold Asu'a fell. The first records collected by scholars of the League of the Scroll tell that the Conqueror Star was bright in the night sky above*

*Asu'a when Ineluki, Iyu'unigato's son, pondered
the spell that would soon destroy the Sithi castle
and a large part of Fingil's Rimmersgard army.*

*   "It is said that the only event of pure conquest
that ever saw the Conqueror Star's light was the
triumph of the Ransomer, Usires Aedon, since it
shone in the skies above Nabban when Usires
hung on the Execution Tree. However, the argument could be made that there, too, it heralded
decline and collapse, since Aedon's death was the
beginning of the ultimate collapse of the mighty
Nabbanai Imperium. . . ."*

Strangyeard took a breath. His eyes were shining now:
Morgenes' words had driven out his discomfort at speaking to a crowd. "So you see, there is some significance to
this, we think."

"But why, exactly?" Josua asked. "It already appeared
at the beginning of my brother's regnal year. If the destruction of an empire has been forecast, what of it? No
doubt it is my brother's empire that will fall." He showed
a weak smile. There was a small rustle of laughter from
the assembly.

"But that is not the whole story, Prince Josua," Geloë
said. "Dinivan and others—Doctor Morgenes, too, before
his death—studied this matter. The Conqueror Star, you
see, is not yet gone. It will be coming back."

"What do you mean?"

Binabik rose. "Every five hundreds of years, Dinivan
was discovering," he explained, "the star is in the sky not
once, but three times. It is appearing for three years,
bright the first, then almost too dim for seeing the second,
then most bright of all for the last."

"So it is coming back this year, at the end of the winter," Geloë said. "For the third time. The last time it did
that was the year Asu'a fell."

"I still don't understand," Josua said. "I believe that
what you say may be important, but we already have
many mysteries to think about. What does the star mean
to us?"

Geloë shook her head. "Perhaps nothing. Perhaps, as in the past, it heralds the passing of a great kingdom—but whether that would be the High King's, the Storm King's, or your father's if we are defeated, none of us can say. It seems unlikely that an occurrence with such a fateful history would mean *nothing,* however."

"I am in agreement," Binabik said. "This is not the season for the dismissing of such things as coincidence."

Josua looked around in frustration, as though hoping someone else at the long table could provide an answer. "But what does it *mean?* And what are we supposed to do about it?"

"First, it could be that only when the star is in the sky will the swords be of use to us," Geloë offered. "Their value seems to be in their otherworldliness. Perhaps the heavens are showing us when they will be most useful." She shrugged her shoulders. "Or perhaps that will be a time when Ineluki will be strongest, and most able to help Elias against us, since it was five centuries ago he spoke the spell that made him what he is now. In that case, we will need to reach the Hayholt before that times comes 'round again."

Silence descended on the vast chamber, broken only by the quiet murmuring of the fireplace flames. Josua shuffled absently through a few pages of Morgenes' manuscript.

"And you have learned nothing further about the swords on which we have staked so much—nothing which would be of use to us?" he demanded.

Binabik shook his head. "We have been speaking now many times with Sir Camaris." The little man gave the old knight a respectful nod. "He has been telling us what he knows of the sword Thorn and its properties, but we have not yet learned of anything that tells us what we may do with it and the others."

"Then we can't afford to bet our lives on them," Sludig said. "Magic and fairy-tricks will turn traitor every time."

"You speak about things you do not know . . ." Geloë began grimly.

Josua sat up. "Stop. It is too late in the day to abandon

the three swords. If it was my brother alone we fought, then perhaps we might chance it. But the Storm King's hand has apparently been behind him at every step of his progress, and the swords are our only thin hope against that dark, dark scourge."

Miriamele now stood. "Then let me ask again, Uncle Josua ... *Prince* Josua, that we go directly to Erkynland. If the swords are valuable, then we need to take Sorrow back from my father and recover Bright-Nail from my grandfather's grave. From what Geloë and Binabik are saying, we seem to have little time."

Her face was solemn, but Duke Isgrimnur thought he sensed desperation behind her words. That surprised him. Important, all-important as these decisions were, why should little Miriamele sound like her own life was so absolutely dependent on going straight to Erkynland and confronting her father?

Josua's look was cool. "Thank you, Miriamele. I have listened to what you say. I value your counsel." He turned to face the rest of the assembly. "Now I must tell you my decision." The desire to be finished with all this was audible in his every word.

"Here are my choices. To remain here—to build up this place, New Gadrinsett, and hold out against my brother until his misrule turns the tide in our favor. That is one possibility." Josua ran his hand through his short hair, then held up two fingers. "The second is to go to Nabban, where with Camaris to march at the head of our army, we may quickly gain adherents, and thus eventually field an army capable of bringing down the High King." The prince raised a third finger. "The third, as Miriamele and Freosel and others have suggested, is to move directly into Erkynland, gambling that we can find enough supporters to overcome Elias' defenses. There is also a possibility that Isorn and Count Eolair of Nad Mullach may be able to join us with men recruited in the Frostmarch and Hernystir."

Young Simon rose. "I beg your pardon, Prince Josua. Don't forget the Sithi."

"Nothing is promised, Seoman," said the Sitha woman Aditu. "Nothing can be."

Isgrimnur was a little taken aback. She had sat so quietly during the debate that he had forgotten she was here. He wondered if it had been wise to talk so openly before her. What did Josua and the rest truly know about the immortals, anyway?

"And perhaps the Sithi will join with us," Josua amended, "although as Aditu has told us, she does not know what is happening in Hernystir, or what exactly her folk plan to do next." The prince closed his eyes for a long moment.

"Added to these possibilities," he said at last, "is the need to recover the other two Great Swords, and also what we have learned here today about the Conqueror Star—which is little, I must say frankly, except that it may have some bearing on things." He turned to Geloë. "Obviously, if you learn more I ask to hear it at once."

The witch woman nodded.

"I wish that we *could* stay here." Josua looked quickly at Vorzheva, but she would not meet his eyes. "I would like nothing better than to see my child born here in something like safety. I would love to see all our settlers make of this ancient place a new and living city, a refuge for all who sought one. But we cannot stay. We are nearly out of food as it is, and more outcasts and war victims are arriving every day. And if we stay longer, we invite my brother sending a more formidable army than Fengbald's. It is also my sense that the time for a defensive game is past. So, we will move on.

"Of our two alternatives, I must, after much thought, choose Nabban. We are not strong enough to confront Elias directly now, and I fear that Erkynland is so much reduced that we might find it hard to raise an army there. Also, if we failed, we would have nowhere to run but back across the empty lands to this place. I cannot guess how many would die just trying to flee a failed battle, let alone in the battle itself between Elias' troops and our ragtag army.

"So it will be Nabban. We will go far before Benigaris

can bring an army to bear, and in that time Camaris may lure many to our banner. If we are lucky enough to force Benigaris and his mother out, Camaris will also have the ships of Nabban to put at our service, making it easier for us to move against my brother."

He raised his arms, silencing the gathering as whispers began to fill the room. "But this much of the Scroll League's warnings about the Conqueror Star will I take to heart. I would rather not ride out in winter, especially since it has long seemed the tool of the Storm King, but I think that the sooner we can make our way from Nabban to Erkynland, the better. If the star is a herald of empire's fall, still it need not be *our* herald as well: we will try to reach the Hayholt before it appears. We will hope that this mildness in the weather will hold, and we will leave this place in a fortnight. That is my decision." He lowered his hand to the tabletop. "Now go, all of you, and get some sleep. There is no point in further arguing. We leave this place for Nabban."

Voices were raised as some of those gathered began to call out questions. "Enough!" Josua cried. "Go and leave me in peace!"

As he helped herd the others out, Isgrimnur looked back. Josua was slumped in his chair, rubbing his temples with his fingers. Beside him Vorzheva sat and stared straight ahead, as though her husband were a thousand miles away.

Pryrates emerged from the stairwell into the bell-chamber. The high-arching windows were open to the elements, and the winds that swirled around Green Angel Tower fluttered his red robe. He stopped, his boot heels clicking once more on the stone tiles before silence fell.

"You sent for me, Your Highness?" he asked at last.

Elias was staring out across the jumble of the Hayholt's roofs, looking toward the east. The sun had dropped below the western rim of the world and the sky was full of heavy black clouds. The entire land had fallen into shadow.

"Fengbald is dead," the king said. "He has failed. Josua has beaten him."

Pryrates was startled. "How could you know!?"

The High King whirled. "What do you mean, priest? A half-dozen Erkynguardsmen arrived this morning, the remnants of Fengbald's army. They told me many surprising tales. But you sound as though *you* knew already."

"No, Highness," the alchemist said hastily. "I was just surprised that I was not informed immediately when the guardsmen arrived. It is usually the king's counselor's task . . ."

". . . To sift through the news and decide what his master is allowed to hear," Elias finished for him. The king's eyes glittered. His smile was not pleasant. "I have many sources of information, Pryrates. Never forget that."

The priest bowed stiffly. "If I have offended you, my king, I beg your forgiveness."

Elias contemplated him for a moment, then turned back to the window. "I should have known better than to send that braggart Fengbald. I should have known he would muck it up. Blood and damnation!" He slapped his palms on the stone sill. "If only I could have sent Guthwulf."

"The Earl of Utanyeat proved himself a traitor, Highness," Pryrates observed mildly.

"Traitor or not, he was the finest soldier I have ever seen. He would have ground up my brother and his peasant army like pig meat." The king bent and picked up a loose stone, holding it before his eyes for a moment before flinging it out the window. He watched its fall in silence before speaking again. "Now Josua will move against me. I know him. He has always wanted to take the throne from me. He never forgave my being firstborn, but he was too clever to say so aloud. He is subtle, my brother. Quiet but poisonous, like an adder." The king's pale face was drawn and haggard, but he seemed nevertheless full of an awful vitality. His fingers curled and uncurled spasmodically. "He will not find me unready, will he, Pryrates?"

The alchemist allowed a smile to curl his own thin lips. "No, my lord, he will not."

"I have friends, now—powerful friends." The king's hand dropped to the double hilt of Sorrow, sheathed at his waist. "And there are things afoot that Josua could never dream of if he lived for centuries. Things he will never guess until it is too late." He drew the sword from its scabbard. The mottled gray blade seemed a living thing, something pulled against its will from beneath a rock. As Elias held it before him, the wind lifted his cloak, spreading it above him like wings; for a moment, the blotchy twilight made him a pinioned *thing,* a demon out of dark ages past. "He and all he leads will die, Pryrates," the king hissed. "They do not know who they meddle with."

Pryrates regarded him with genuine uneasiness. "Your brother does not know, my king. But you will show him."

Elias turned and brandished the sword at the eastern horizon. In the distance, a flicker of lightning played across the turbulent darkness.

"Come, then!" he shouted. "Come, all of you! There is death enough to be shared! No one will take the Dragonbone Chair from me. No one can!"

As if in answer, there came a dim rumble of thunder.

25

The Semblance of Heaven

They rode down out of the north on black horses—steeds raised in cold darkness, surefooted in deep night, unafraid of icy wind or high mountain passes. The riders were three, two women and one man, all Cloud Children, and their deaths were already being sung by the Lightless Ones, since there was little chance they would ever return to Nakkiga. They were the Talons of Utuk'ku.

As they departed Stormspike, they rode through the ruins of the old city, Nakkiga-that-was, sparing hardly a glance to the tumbled relics of an age when their people had still lived beneath the sun. By night they passed through the villages of the Black Rimmersmen. There they met no one, since the inhabitants of those settlements, like all the mortals in that ill-fated land, knew better than to stir our of doors once twilight had fallen.

Despite the speed and vigor of their mounts, the three riders were many nights crossing the Frostmarch. Except for those sleepers in remote settlements who suffered unexpectedly bad dreams, or the rare travelers who noticed an added chill to the already freezing wind, the riders went unperceived. They continued on in silence and shadow until they reached Naglimund.

They stopped there to rest their horses—even the cruel discipline of the Stormspike stables could not prevent a living animal from tiring eventually—and to confer with those of their kind who now made Josua of Erknyland's desolated castle their home. The leader of Utuk'ku's Talons—although she was only first-among-equals—paid

uncomfortable homage to the castle's shrouded master,
one of the Red Hand. He sat in his gray winding sheets
peeping ember-red at every crease, on the smoldering
wreckage of what had once been Josua's princely throne
of state. She was respectful, although she did nothing
more than that which was necessary. Even to the Norns,
hardened through the long centuries, blasted by their cold
exile, the Storm King's minions were unsettling. Like
their master, they had gone *beyond*—they had tasted
Unbeing and then returned; they were as different from
their still-living brethren as a star was from a starfish.
The Norns did not like the Red Hand, did not like the
singed emptiness of them—each one of the five was little
more than a hole in the stuff of reality, a hole filled by
hatred—but as long as their mistress made Ineluki's war
her own, they had little choice but to bow before the
Storm King's chief servants.

They also found themselves distanced from their own
brethren. Since the Talons were death-sung, the
Hikeda'ya of Naglimund treated them with reverent silence and boarded them in a cold chamber far from the
rest of the tribe. The three Talons did not stay long in the
wind-haunted castle.

From there they rode over the Stile, through the ruins
of Da'ai Chikiza, and then westward through the
Aldheorte, where the travelers made a wide circle around
the borders of Jao é-Tinukai'i. Utuk'ku and her ally had
already had their confrontation with the Dawn Children
and received its full benefit: this task was one that required secrecy. Although at times the forest seemed actively to resist them with paths that abruptly vanished and
tree limbs so close-knit they made the filtered light of the
stars seem different and confusing, still the trio rode on,
heading inexorably southeast. They were the Norn
Queen's chosen: they were not so easily put off their
quarry.

At last they reached the forest's edge. They were close
now to that which they sought. Like Ingen Jegger before
them, they had come down from the north bearing death
for Utuk'ku's enemies, but unlike the Queen's Huntsman,

who had met defeat the first time he had turned his hand against the Zida'ya, these three were immortals. There would be no hurry. There would be no mistakes.

They turned their horses toward Sesuad'ra.

"Ah, by the good God, I feel a weight lifted from my shoulders." Josua took a deep breath. "It is something fine to be moving at last."

Isgrimnur smiled. "Even if all do not agree," he said. "Yes. It's good."

Josua and the Duke of Elvritshalla were sitting their horses by the gate stones that marked the hilltop's edge, watching the citizens of New Gadrinsett decamp in a most disorderly fashion. The parade wound past them down the old Sithi road, spiraling around the bulk of the Stone of Farewell until it vanished from sight. As many sheep and cows seemed to be setting out as people, an army of unhelpful animals bleating, lowing, bumping along, causing chaos among the overloaded citizenry. Some of the settlers had built crude wagons and had piled their possessions high on them, which added to the strange air of festival.

Josua frowned. "As an army, we look more like a town fair being moved."

Hotvig, who had just ridden up with Freosel the Falshireman, laughed. "This is how our clans always look when they travel. The only difference is that most of these are your stone-dwellers. You will become accustomed."

Freosel was watching the process critically. "We need all cattle and sheep we can get, Highness. Many mouths that need feeding." He awkwardly urged his horse forward a few paces—he was still not used to riding. "Ha, there!" he shouted. "Give that wagon some room!"

Isgrimnur thought that Josua was right: it *did* look like a traveling fair, although this company showed something less than the cheerfulness that usually attended such things. There were children crying—although not all the children were displeased to be traveling, by any means—as well as a steady undercurrent of bickering and complaint from the citizens of New Gadrinsett. Few among them had wanted to leave this place of relative safety: the idea of somehow forcing Elias from his throne was remote to them, and almost all the settlers would have preferred to stay on Sesuad'ra while others dealt with the grim realities of war—but it was also clear that staying in this remote place after Josua had taken all the men-at-arms away was no real alternative. So, angry but unwilling to risk more suffering without the protection of the prince's makeshift army, the inhabitants of New Gadrinsett were following Josua toward Nabban.

"We would not fright a nest of scholars with this lot," the prince said, "let alone my brother. Yet, I do not think the less of them—of any of us—for our rags and poor weaponry." He smiled. "In truth, I think I know for the first time what my father felt. I have always treated my liege-men as well as I could, since that is what God would have me do, but I never felt the strong love that Prester John did for all his subjects." Josua stroked Vinyafod's neck meditatively. "Would that the old man could have saved some of that love for both his sons as well. Still, I think I finally know what he felt when he rode out through the Nearulagh Gate and down into Erchester. He would have given his life for those people, as I would give mine for these." The prince smiled again, shyly, as if embarrassed by what he had revealed. "I will bring this beloved rabble of mine safe through Nabban, Isgrimnur, whatever it takes. But when we get to Erkynland, we are putting the dice into the hands of God—and who knows what He will do with them?"

"Not a one of us," Isgrimnur said. "And good deeds do not buy His favor, either. At least your Father Strangyeard said that to me the other night, that he thought it might be as much a sin to try to buy God's love by good deeds as it is to do bad ones."

A mule—one of the few such on all of Sesuad'ra—was balking at the rim of the road. His owner was pushing at the cart to which the mule was tethered, trying to urge him along from behind. The beast had gone stiff and spread-legged, silent but implacable. The owner moved forward and laid a switch across the mule's back, but the creature only dropped back its ears and lifted its head, accepting the blows with mutely stubborn hostility. The owner's curses filled the morning air, echoed by the people trapped behind his stalled cart.

Josua laughed and leaned closer to Isgrimnur. "If you would see what I look like to myself, gaze on that poor beast. If it were uphill, he would pull all day and never show a moment's weariness. But now he has a long and dangerous downward track before him and a heavy cart behind him—no wonder he digs in his heels. He would wait until the Day of Weighing-Out if he could." His grin faded and he turned to fix the duke with his gray eyes. "But I have interrupted you. Say again what Strangyeard told you."

Isgrimnur stared at the mule and its drover. There was something both comic and pathetic about it, something that seemed to hint at more than it revealed. "The priest said that trying to buy God's favor with good deeds was a sin. Well, first he apologized for having any thoughts at all—you know how he is, skittery mouse of a man—but said it anyway. That God owes us nothing, and we owe Him all, that we should do right things because they are right and that is closest to God, not because we will be rewarded like children given sweetmeats for sitting quietly."

"Father Strangyeard is a mouse, yes," said Josua. "But a mouse can be brave. Small as they are, though, they learn it is wiser not to challenge the cat. So it is with Strangyeard, I think. He knows who he is and where he belongs." Josua's eyes strayed upward from the futile flogging of the mule to the western hills that walled the valley. "I will think on what he said, though. Sometimes we *do* act as God bids us out of fear or hope of reward. Yes, I will think on what he said."

Isgrimnur suddenly wished he had kept his mouth closed.

That's all Josua needs—another reason to fault himself.

*Keep him moving, old man, not thinking. He is magical
when he throws away his cares. He is a true prince, then.
That is what will give us a chance of living to talk about
such things over the fire someday.*

"What do you say we move this idiot and his mule out
of the road?" Isgrimnur suggested. "Otherwise, this place
is going to be less like a town fair and more like the Battle of Nearulagh soon."

"Yes, I think so." Josua smiled again, sunny as the
cold, bright morning. "But I don't think it's the idiot drover who will need convincing—and mules are no respect-
ers of princes."

"Yah, Nimsuk!" Binabik called. "Where is Sisqinanamook?"

The herder turned and raised his crook-spear in greeting. "She is by the boats, Singing Man. Checking for
leaks so the rams' feet don't get wet!" He laughed, displaying an uneven mouthful of yellow teeth.

"And so you don't have to swim, since you'd sink to
the bottom like a rock," Binabik grinned back. "They'd
find you in the summer when the water went away, a little
man of mud. Show some respect."

"It's too sunny," Nimsuk replied. "Look at them frisk!"
He pointed to the rams, who were indeed very lively, several of them playing at mock combat, something they
almost never did.

"Just don't let them kill each other," Binabik said. "Enjoy your rest." He bent and whispered into Qantaqa's ear.
The wolf leaped forward over the snow with the troll
clinging to her hackles.

Sisqi was indeed inspecting the flatboats. Binabik released Qantaqa, who shook herself vigorously and trotted
off to the nearby skirts of the forest. Binabik watched his
betrothed with a smile. She was examining the boats as
distrustfully as a lowlander might count the lashings on a
Qanuc chasm-bridge.

"So careful," Binabik chided her, laughing. "Most of

our people are crossed already." He waved his arm at the stippling of white rams dotted across the valley floor, the knots of troll herdsmen and huntresses enjoying the short hour of peace before the journeying began once more.

"And I will see every single one across safely." Sisqi turned and opened her arms to him. They stood face-to-face for a while, unspeaking. "This traveling-on-water is one thing when a few are fishing on Blue Mud Lake," she said eventually, "another when I must trust the lives of all my people and rams."

"They are fortunate in your care," Binabik said, serious now. "But for a moment, forget the boats."

She squeezed him hard. "I have."

Binabik lifted his head and looked out across the valley. The snow was melted in many places, with tufts of yellow-green grass showing through. "The herds will eat until they are sick," he said. "They are not used to such abundance."

"Is the snow going away?" she asked. "You said before that these lands were normally not snowbound at this time of year."

"Not always, but the winter has spread far south. Still, it does seem to be falling back again." He looked up into the sky. The few clouds did not in the least diminish the strength of the sun. "I do not know what to think. I cannot believe that he who made the winter reach down so far has given up. I do not know." He freed a hand from Sisqi's side and bumped it once against his breastbone. "I came to say that I am sorry I have seen you so little of late. There has been much to decide. Geloë and the others have been working long hours with Morgenes' book, trying to find the answers we yet seek. We have been studying Ookequk's scrolls as well, and that cannot be done without me."

Sisqi raised the hand of his she retained up to her cheek, pressing it there before letting it go. "You have no need for sorrow. I know what you do . . ." she inclined her head toward the boats bobbing at the water's edge, ". . . just as you know what I must do." She lowered her eyes. "I saw you stand at the lowlander's council and speak. I could not understand most of the words, but I saw them watching you with respect, Binbiniqegabenik." She gave his full name a ritual sound. "I was proud of you, my man. I only wish my mother and father could see you as I did. As I do."

Binabik snorted, but he was obviously pleased. "I do not think that the respect of lowlanders would count for much on your parents' tally stick. But I thank you. The lowlanders think highly of you, too—of all our people, after having seen us in battle." His round face grew serious. "And that is the other thing I wished to speak of. You told me once that you thought to go back to Yiqanuc. Will you do that soon?"

"I am still considering," she said. "I know we are needed by my mother and father, but I also think there are things we can do here. Lowlanders and trolls fighting together—perhaps that is something that will make our people safer in days ahead."

"Clever Sisqi," Binabik smiled. "But the fighting may grow too fierce for our folk. You have never seen a war for a castle—what the lowlanders call a 'siege.' There might be scant place for our people in such a battle, yet much danger. And at least one or two battles of that kind lie before Josua and his people."

She nodded her head solemnly. "I know. But there is a more important reason, Binabik. I would find it very hard to leave you again."

He looked away. "As I found it hard to leave you when Ookequk took me south—but both of us know that there are duties that make us do what we wish we did not have to." Binabik slid his arm through hers. "Come, let us walk for a while, since we will not have much time to be together in days ahead."

They turned and made their way back toward the base of the hill, avoiding the press of people waiting for boats. "I regret most that these troubles prevent us from our marriage," he said.

"The words, only. The night I came for you, to set you free, we were married. Even had we never seen each other again."

Binabik hunched his shoulders. "I know. But you should have the words. You are the daughter of the Huntress."

"We have separate tents," Sisqi smiled. "All that is honorable is observed."

"And I do not mind sharing mine with young Simon," he shot back. "But I would prefer sharing with you."

"We have our times." She squeezed his hand. "And what will you do when this is all over, my dear one?" She kept her voice steady, as if there were little question whether there would be an afterward. Qantaqa appeared from the curve of the forest and loped toward them.

"What do you mean? You and I will go back to Mintahoq—or, if you have already gone, I will come to you."

"But what about Simon?"

Binabik had slowed his pace. Now he stopped and pushed snow from a hanging branch with his stick. Here in the hill's long shadow, the raucous noise of the departing throngs was less. "I do not know. I am bound to him by promises, but the day will come when those can be discharged. After that . . ." He shrugged, a trollish gesture made with his palms held out. "I do not know what I am to him, Sisqi. Not a brother, not a father, certainly. . . ."

"A friend?" she suggested gently. Qantaqa was beside her, nosing at her hand. She scratched the wolf's muzzle, running her fingers along jaws that could swallow her arm to the elbow. The wolf growled contentedly.

"Certainly that. He is a good boy. No, he is a good man, I suppose. I have watched him growing."

"May Qinkipa of the Snows bring us all through this safely," she said gravely. "Simon to grow happily old, you and I to love each other and raise children, our kind to keep our mountains as our home. I am not frightened of lowlanders any more, Binabik, but I am happier among people I understand."

He turned and pulled her close. "May Qinkipa grant what you ask. And don't forget," he said, reaching out to lay his fingers next to hers where they touched the wolf's neck, "we must wish for the Snow Maiden to protect Qantaqa, too." He grinned. "Come, go with me a little farther. I know a quiet spot on the hillside, sheltered from the wind—the last private place we may see for day upon day upon day."

"But the boats, Singing Man," she teased. "I must look at them again."

"You have looked at each one a dozen times," he said. "Trolls could swim laughing through that water if they had to. Come."

She put her arm around him and they went, heads leaning close together. The wolf padded after them, silent as a gray shadow.

"Blast you, Simon, that hurt!" Jeremias fell back, sucking on his wounded fingers. "Just because you're a knight doesn't mean you have to break my hand."

Simon straightened up. "I'm just trying to show you something Sludig taught me. And I need the practice. Don't be a baby."

Jeremias gave him a disgusted look. "I'm not a baby, Simon. And you're not Sludig. I don't even think you're doing it right."

Simon took a few deep breaths, fighting down a cross remark. It wasn't Jeremias' fault that he was restless. He hadn't been able to speak to Miriamele for days, and despite the huge and complicated process of breaking camp on Sesuad'ra, there still seemed little of importance for Simon to do. "I'm sorry. I was stupid to say that." He lifted the practice sword, made of timbers rescued from the war barricade. "Just let me show this to you, this thing where you turn the blade . . ." He reached out and engaged Jeremias' wooden weapon. "Like . . . *so* . . ."

Jeremias sighed. "I wish you would just go and talk to the princess instead of beating on me, Simon." He raised the sword. "Oh, come on, then."

They feinted and engaged, the blades clacking loudly. Some of the sheep pasturing nearby looked up long enough to see if the rams were fighting again; when it proved instead to be a contest of two-legged younglings, they turned back to their grass.

"Why did you say that about the princess?" Simon asked, panting.

"What?" Jeremias was trying to stay out of reach of his opponent's longer arms. "Why do you think? You've been moping around after her since she got here."

"I have not."

Jeremias stepped back and let the point of his stave-sword sag to the ground. "Oh, you haven't? It must have been some other hulking, red-haired idiot."

Simon smiled, embarrassed. "That easy to tell, is it?"

"Usires Ransomer, yes! And who wouldn't? She's certainly pretty, and she seems kind."

"She's . . . more than that. But why aren't *you* moping after her, then?"

Jeremias darted him a quick, hurt look. "As if she would notice me if I fell dead at her feet." His face grew mocking. "Not that she seems to be flinging herself at *you*, either."

"That's not funny," said Simon darkly.

Jeremias took pity. "I'm sorry, Simon. I'm sure being in love is horrible. Look, go ahead and break the rest of my fingers if it will make you feel better."

"It might." Simon grinned and raised his blade once more. "Now, damn you, Jeremias, do this *right*."

"Make someone a knight," Jeremias huffed, dodging a downward blow, "and you ruin his friends' lives forever."

The noise of their conflict rose again, the irregular smack of blade on blade fierce as the hammering of a huge and drunken woodpecker.

They sat gasping on the wet grass, sharing a water skin. Simon had untied the neck of his shirt to let the wind at his heated skin. Soon he would be uncomfortably chilly, but at the moment the air felt wonderful. A shadow fell between the two of them and they looked up, startled.

"Sir Camaris!" Simon struggled to rise. Jeremias just stared, wide-eyed.

"*Hea,* sit, young man." The old man spread his fingers, gesturing Simon back down. "I was only watching the two of you at your bladework."

"We don't know much," Simon said modestly.

"That you do not."

Simon had been half-hoping that Camaris would contradict him. "Sludig tried to teach me what he could," he said, trying to keep his voice respectful. "We haven't had much time."

"Sludig. That is Isgrimnur's liege-man." He looked at Simon intently. "And you are the castle-lad, are you not? The one that Josua knighted?" For the first time, it was apparent that he had a faint accent. The slightly over-rounded roll of Nabbanai speech still clung to his stately phrases.

"Yes, Sir Camaris. Simon is my name. And this is my friend—and my squire—Jeremias."

The old man flicked his gaze to Jeremias and dipped his chin briefly before returning his pale blue eyes to Simon. "Things have changed," he said slowly. "And not for the better, I think."

Simon waited a moment for Camaris to explain. "What do you mean, sire?" he asked.

The old man sighed. "It is not your fault, young fellow. I know that a monarch must sometimes make knights upon the field, and I do not doubt that you have done noble deeds—I heard you helped find my blade Thorn—but there is more to knighthood than a touch of a sword. It is a high calling, Simon . . . a high calling."

"Sir Deornoth tried to teach me what I needed to know," Simon said. "Before I had my vigil, he taught me about the Canon of Knighthood."

Camaris sat down, astonishingly nimble for a man of his age. "But even so, lad, even so. Do you know how long I was in service to Gavenaxes of Honsa Claves, as page and squire?"

"No, sire."

"Twelve years. And every day, young Simon, every single day was a lesson. It took me two long years simply to learn how to care for Gavenaxes' horses. You have a horse, do you not?"

"Yes, sire." Simon was uncomfortable yet fascinated. The greatest knight in the history of the world was talking to him about the rules of knighthood. Any young nobleman from Rimmersgard to Nabban would have given his left arm to be in Simon's place. "She's called Homefinder."

Camaris gave him a sharp look, as though he disapproved of the name, but went on as though he did not. "Then you must learn to care for her properly. She is more than a friend, Simon, she is as much a part of you as your two legs and two arms. A knight who cannot trust his horse, who does not know his horse as well as he knows himself, who has not cleaned and repaired every piece of harness a thousand times—well, he will be of little use to himself *or* to God."

"I am trying, Sir Camaris. But there is so much to learn."

"Admittedly it is a time of war," Camaris continued. "So it is quite permissible to slight some of the less crucial arts—hunting and hawking and suchlike." But he did not look as though he was entirely comfortable with this thought. "It is even conceivable that the rules of precedence are not so important as at other times, except insofar as they impinge on military discipline; still, it is easier to fight when you know your place in God's wise plan. Little wonder the battle here with the king's men was a brawl." His look of severe concentration abruptly softened; his eyes turned mild. "But I am boring you, am I not?" His lips quirked. "I have been as one asleep for two score years, but still I am an old man, for all that. It is not my world."

"Oh, no," Simon said earnestly. "You are not boring me, Sir Camaris. Not at all." He looked at Jeremias for support, but his friend was goggle-eyed and silent. "Please, tell me anything that will help me be a better knight."

"Are you being kind?" asked the greatest knight in Aedondom. His tone was cool.

"No, sire." Simon laughed in spite of himself, and had a momentary fear that he would dissolve into terrified giggling. "No, sire. Forgive me, but to have you ask if you're boring me . . ." He could not summon words to describe the magnificent folly of such an idea. "You are a hero, Sir Camaris," he said at last, simply. "A hero."

The old man rose with the same surprising alacrity with which he had seated himself. Simon was afraid he had somehow offended him.

"Stand, lad."

Simon did as he was told.

"You, too . . . Jeremias." Simon's friend rose to the knight's beckoning finger. Camaris looked at them both critically. "Lend me your sword, please." He pointed to the wooden blade still clutched in Simon's hand. "I have left Thorn scabbarded in my tent. I am still not quite comfortable having her near me, I confess. There is a restless quality to her that I do not like. Perhaps it is only me."

"Her?" Simon asked, surprised.

The old man made a dismissive gesture. "It is the way we talk on Vinitta. Boats and swords are 'she,' storms and mountains are 'he.' Now, attend me well." He took the practice-sword and drew a circle in the wet grass. "The Canon of Knighthood tells that, as we are made in the image of our Lord, so is the world . . ." He made a smaller circle inside the first. ". . . made in the semblance of Heaven. But, woefully, without its grace." He examined the circle critically, as if he could already see it populated with sinners.

"As the angels are the minions and messengers of God the Highest," he went on, "so does the fraternity of knighthood serve its various earthly rulers. The angels bring forth God's good works, which are absolute, but the earth is flawed, and so are our rulers, even the best. Thus, there will be disagreement as to what is God's will. There will be war." He divided the inner circle with a single line. "By this test will the righteousness of our rulers be made known. It is war that most closely reflects the knife edge of God's will, since war is the hinge on which earthly empires rise or fall. If strength alone were to determine victory, strength unmitigated by honor or mercy, then there would *be* no victory, because God's will can never be revealed by the mere exercise of greater strength. Is the cat more beloved of God than the mouse?" Camaris shook his head gravely, then turned his sharp eyes on his audience. "Are you listening?"

"Yes," Simon said quickly. Jeremias only nodded, still silent as if struck dumb.

"So. All angels—excepting The One Who Fled—are obedient to God above all, because He is perfect, all-knowing and all-capable." Camaris drew a series of ticks on the outer circle—representing the angels, Simon supposed. In truth, he was a little bit confused, but he also felt that he could grasp much of what the knight was saying, so he clung to what he could and waited. "But," the old man continued, "the rulers of men are, as aforesaid, flawed. They are sinners, as are we all. Thus, although each knight is loyal to his liege, he must also be loyal to the Canon of Knighthood—all the rules of battle and comportment, the rules of honor and mercy and responsibility—which is the same for *all* knights." Camaris bisected the line through the inner circle, drawing a perpendicular. "So no matter which earthly ruler wins a struggle, if his knights are true to their canon, the battle will have been won according to God's law. It will be a just reflection of His will." He fixed Simon with his keen gaze. "Do you hear me?"

"Yes, sire." In truth, it did make a kind of sense, although Simon wanted to think about it on his own for a while.

"Good." Camaris bent and wiped the mud-daubed wooden blade as carefully as if it had been Thorn, then handed it back to Simon. "Now, just as God's priest must render His will understandable to the people, in a form that is pleasing and reverent, so, too, must His knights prosecute His wishes in a similar fashion. That is why war, however horrible, should not be a fight between animals. That is why a knight is more than simply a strong man on a horse. He is God's vicar on the battlefield. Swordplay is prayer, lads—serious and sad, yet joyful."

He doesn't look very joyful, Simon thought. *But there is something priestlike about him.*

"And that is why one does not become a knight just by the passing of a vigil and the tapping of a sword, any more than one might become a priest by carrying the Book of the Aedon from one side of a village to another. There is study, study in every part." He turned to Simon. "Stand and hold up your sword, young man."

Simon did. Camaris was a good handspan taller than he, which was interesting. Simon had become accustomed to being taller than nearly everyone.

"You are holding it like a club. Spread your hands, thus." The knight's long hands enfolded Simon's own. His fingers were dry and hard, as rough as if Camaris had spent his life working the soil or building stone walls. Abruptly, by his touch, Simon realized the enormity of the old knight's experience, understood him as far more than just a legend made flesh or an aged man full of useful lore. He could feel the countless years of hard, painstaking work, the unnumberable and largely unwanted contests of arms that this man had suffered to become the mightiest knight of his age—and all the time, Simon sensed, enjoying none of it any more than a kind-hearted priest forced to denounce an ignorant sinner.

"Now feel it as you lift," said Camaris. "Feel how the strength comes from your legs. No, you are off your balance." He pushed Simon's feet closer together. "Why does a tower not fall? Because it is centered over its foundation."

Soon he had Jeremias working, too, and working hard.

The afternoon sun seemed to move swiftly through the sky; the breeze turned icy as evening approached. As the old man put them through their rigorous paces, a certain gleam—chill, but nevertheless bright—came to his eye.

Evening had descended by the time that Camaris finally turned them loose; the bowl of the valley was filled with campfires. This day's work to bring everyone across the river would enable the prince's company to leave with the first light in the morning. Now the people of New

Gadrinsett were laying out their temporary camps, eating belated suppers, or wandering aimlessly in the deepening dark. A mood of stillness and anticipation hung over the valley, as real as the twilight. It was a little like the Between World, Simon thought—the place before Heaven.

But it's also the place before Hell, Simon thought. *We're not just traveling—we're going to war ... and maybe worse.*

He and Jeremias walked silently, flushed with exertion, the sweat on their faces rapidly growing cold. Simon had a soreness in his muscles that was pleasant now, but experience told him that it would be less pleasant tomorrow, especially after a day on horseback. He was suddenly reminded of something.

"Jeremias, did you see to Homefinder?"

The young man looked at him in irritation. "Certainly. I said I would, didn't I?"

"Well, I think I'm going to go have a look at her anyway."

"Don't you trust me?" Jeremias asked.

"Of course I do," Simon said hastily. "It's nothing to do with you, truly. What Sir Camaris said about a knight and his horse just ... just made me think about Homefinder." He was also feeling an urge to be on his own for a little while: other things Camaris had said needed to be thought about as well. "You understand, don't you?"

"I suppose so." Jeremias scowled, but didn't seem too upset. "I'm going to go and find something to eat, myself."

"Meet me at Isgrimnur's fire later. I think Sangfugol is going to sing some songs."

Jeremias continued on toward the busiest part of the camp and the tent that he, Simon, and Binabik had erected that morning. Simon peeled off, heading for the hillslope where the horses were tethered.

The evening sky was a misty violet and the stars had not yet appeared. As Simon picked his way across the slushy meadowland in growing darkness, he found himself wishing for a little moonlight. Once he slipped and

fell, cursing loudly as he wiped the mud off his hands
onto his breeches, which were muddy and damp enough
after the long hours of swording. His boots had already
become thoroughly soaked.

A figure coming toward him through murk turned out
to be Freosel, returning from seeing to his own horse as
well as to Josua's Vinyafod. In this way, if no other,
Freosel had taken Deornoth's place in the prince's life,
and he seemed to fulfill the role admirably. The
Falshireman had told Simon once that he came from a
smithing family—something that Simon, looking at the
broad-shouldered Freosel, could readily believe.

"Greetings, Sir Seoman," he said. "See you didn't
bring torch either. If you don't be too long, y'may not
need it." He squinted upward, gauging the fast-
diminishing light. "But have a care—there be a great mud
pit half a hundred steps behind me."

"I already found one of those," Simon laughed, gesturing to his mud-clotted boots.

Freosel looked at Simon's feet appraisingly. "Come by
my tent and I'll give you grease for 'em. Won't do to
have that leather crack. Or be you comin' to hear the
harper sing?"

"I think so."

"Then I'll bring it with." Freosel gave him a courtly
nod before walking on. "Mind that mud pit!" he called
back over his shoulder.

Simon kept his eyes open and managed to make his
way without incident around a patch of sucking slime that
was indeed a larger brother of the one with which he had
already made acquaintance. He could hear the gentle
whickering of the horses as he approached. They were
tethered on the hillside, a dark line against the dim sky.

Homefinder was where Jeremias had said he had left
her, staked to a longish rope not far from the twisted
black form of a spreading oak. Simon cupped the horse's
nose in his hand and felt her warm breath, then laid his
head on her neck and rubbed her shoulder. The horse
scent was thick and somehow reassuring.

"You're my horse," he said quietly. Homefinder flicked an ear. "My horse."

Jeremias had draped her with a heavy blanket—a gift to Simon from Gutrun and Vorzheva, one which had been his own cover until the horses were moved from their warm stables in Sesuad'ra's caves. Simon made sure that it had been tied in place well but not too tightly. As he turned from his inspection, he saw a pale shape flitting through the darkness before him, passing through the scatter of horses. Simon felt his heart jump within his chest.

Norns?

"Wh–who's that?" he called. He forced his voice lower and shouted again. "Who's there? Come out!" He let his hand fall to his side, realizing after a moment that he carried no weapon but his Qanuc knife, not even the wooden practice sword.

"Simon?"

"Miriamele? Princess?" He took a few steps forward. She was peering around at him from behind one of the horses, as if she had been hiding. As he moved closer, she moved out. There was nothing unusual in her dress, a pale gown and a dark cloak, but she had an oddly defiant look on her face.

"Are you well?" he asked, then cursed himself for the stupid question. He was surprised to see her out here by herself and couldn't think of anything to say. Another time, he supposed, when it would have been better to say nothing than to speak and prove himself a mooncalf.

But why did she look so guilty?

"I am, thank you." She looked past his shoulders on either side as if trying to decide whether Simon was alone. "I was out seeing to my horse." She indicated an undifferentiated mass of shadowy shapes farther down the hill. "He's one of those we took from ... from the Nabbanai nobleman I told you about."

"You startled me," Simon said, and laughed. "I thought you were a ghost or ... or one of our enemies."

"I am *not* an enemy," Miriamele said with a little of her

usual lightness. "I'm not a ghost either, so far as I can tell."

"That's good to know. Are you finished?"

"Finished ... with what?" Miriamele looked at him with a strange intensity.

"Seeing to your horse. I thought you might ..." He paused and started again. She seemed very uncomfortable. He wondered if he had done something to offend her. Offering her the White Arrow as a gift, perhaps. The whole thing seemed dreamlike now. That had been a very odd afternoon.

Simon started again. "Sangfugol and a few others are going to play and sing tonight. At Duke Isgrimnur's tent." He pointed down the hillside to the rings of glowing fires. "Are you going to come and listen?"

Miriamele appeared to hesitate. "I'll come," she said at last. "Yes, that would be nice." She smiled briefly. "As long as Isgrimnur doesn't sing."

There was something not quite right in her tone, but Simon laughed at the joke anyway, as much from nervousness as anything else. "That will depend on whether any of Fengbald's wine is left over, I'd guess."

"Fengbald." Miriamele made a noise of disgust. "And to think that my father would have married me to that ... that *pig*. . . ."

To distract her, Simon said: "He's going to sing a Jack Mundwode tune—Sangfugol is, I mean. He promised me he would. I think he's going to sing the one about the Bishop's Wagons." He took her arm almost without thinking, then had a moment of apprehension. What was he doing, grabbing her like that? Would she be insulted?

Instead, Miriamele seemed almost not to notice. "Yes, that would be very nice," she said. "It would be good to spend a night singing by the fire."

Simon was puzzled again, since something like that had been going on most nights somewhere in New Gadrinsett, and even more frequently of late, when people had been gathered for the Raed. But he said nothing, deciding just to enjoy the feeling of her slender, strong arm beneath his.

"It will be a very good time," he said, and led her down the hillside toward the beckoning campfires.

After midnight, when the mists had finally fallen away and the moon was high in the sky, bright as a silver coin, there was a stir of movement on the hilltop that the prince and his company had so recently abandoned.

A trio of shapes, dark forms almost completely invisible despite the moonlight, stood near one of the standing stones at the outermost edge of the hilltop and looked down at the valley below. Most of the fires had burned low, but still a perimeter of flickering flames lay around the encampment; a few dim figures could be seen moving in the reddish light.

The Talons of Utuk'ku watched the camp for a long, long time, still as owls. At last, and without a word spoken between them, they turned away and walked silently through the high grasses, back toward the center of the hill. The pale bulk of Sesuad'ra's ruined stone buildings lay before them like the teeth in a crone's mouth.

The Norn Queen's servants had traveled far in a short time. They could afford to wait for another night, a night that would doubtless come soon, when the great, shambling company beneath them was not quite so vigilant.

The three shadows slipped noiselessly into the building the mortals called the Observatory, and stood for a long time looking up through the cracked dome at the newly emergent stars. Then they sat together on the stones. One of them began very quietly to sing; what floated within the crumbling chamber was a tune bloodless and sharp as splintered bone.

Although the sound did not even make an echo in the Observatory, and certainly could not have been heard across the windy hilltop, some sleepers in the valley below still moaned in their sleep. Those sensitive enough to feel the song's touch—and Simon was one of them—dreamed of ice, and of things broken and lost, and of nests of twining serpents hidden in old wells.

26

A Gift for the Queen

✦

The prince's company, a slow-moving procession of carts and animals and straggling walkers, left the valley and edged out onto the plains, following the snaking course of the Stefflod south. The fray-edged army took close to a week to reach the place where the river joined with its larger cousin, the Ymstrecca.

It was a homecoming of sorts, for they made camp in the hill-sheltered valley that had once been the site of the first squatter town, Gadrinsett. Many of those who laid down their bed rolls and scavenged for firewood in the desolation of their former home wondered if they had gained anything by leaving this place to throw in their lot with Josua and his rebels. There was a little mutinous whispering—but only a little. Too many remembered the courage with which Josua and others had stood against the High King's men.

It could have been a more bitter homecoming: the weather was mild, and much of the snow that had once blanketed this part of the grasslands had again melted away. Still, the wind raced through the shallow gulleys and bent the few small trees as it flattened the long grass, and the campfires jigged and capered: the magical winter had abated somewhat, but it was still nearly Đecander on the open plains of the Thrithings.

The prince announced that the great company would rest there three nights while he and his advisers decided what route would best serve them. His subjects, if they could be called by such a name, seized eagerly at the days of rest. Even the short journey from Sesuad'ra had been difficult for the wounded and infirm, who were many, and for those with young children. Some passed rumors that Josua had reconsidered, that he would rebuild New Gadrinsett here on the site of its predecessor. Although the more serious-minded tried to point out the foolishness of leaving a protected high place for an unprotected low one, and the fact that whatever else he might be, Prince Josua was no fool, enough of the homeless army found the idea a hopeful one that the rumors proved impossible to quell.

"We can't stay here long, Josua," Isgrimnur said. "Every day we remain will add another score of folk that won't follow us when we go."

Josua was scrutinizing a tattered, sun-faded map. The ragged prize had once belonged to the late Helfgrim, New Gadrinsett's onetime Lord Mayor, who had become, along with his martyred daughters, a sort of patron saint of the squatters. "We will not stay long," the prince said. "But if we bring these folk to the grasslands, away from the river, we must be sure of finding water. The weather is changing in ways none of us can foretell. It is quite possible we will suddenly be without rain."

Isgrimnur made a noise of frustration and looked to Freosel for support, but the young Falshireman, still unreconciled to Nabban as a destination, only stared back defiantly. They could have followed the Ymstrecca all the way west to Erkynland, his expression said clearly. "Josua," the duke began, "finding water will not trouble us. The animals can get theirs from dew if need be, and we can fill a mountain of water bags from the rivers before we leave them—there are dozens of new streams just sprung up from snowmelt, for that matter. Food is more likely to be a problem."

"And that is not solved either," Josua pointed out. "But I don't see that our choice of routes will help us much with that. We *can* pick our track to bring us near the lakes—I just don't know how much I trust Helfgrim's map. . . ."

"I had never . . . never realized how hard it is to feed this many people." Strangyeard had been reading quietly from one of the translations Binabik had made of Ookequk's scrolls. "How do armies manage?"

"They either drain their king's purse dry, like sand from a sackhole," Geloë said grimly, "or they simply eat everything around them as they pass through, like marching ants." She stood up from where she had squatted by the archivist. "There are many things growing here that we can use to feed people, Josua—many herbs and flowers and even grasses that will make sustaining meals, although some who have only lived in cities might find them strange."

" 'Strange becomes homely when people are hungry,' " Isgrimnur quoted. "Don't remember who said it, but it's true, sure enough. Listen to Geloë: we'll make do. What we need is haste. The longer we stay in any place, the sooner we do what she said, eat the place up like ants. We'll do better if we keep moving."

"We have not halted just so I can think about things, Isgrimnur," the prince said a little coldly. "It is too much to expect an entire city, which is what we are, to get up and walk to Nabban in one march. The first week was a hard one. Let us give them a little time to grow used to it."

The Duke of Elvritshalla tugged at his beard. "I didn't mean . . . I know, Josua. But from now on, we need to move quickly, as I said. Let those who are slow catch up when we do finally stop. They won't be the fighters, anyway."

Josua pursed his lips. "Are they any the less God's children because they cannot wield a sword for us?"

Isgrimnur shook his head. The prince was in one of *those* moods. "That's not what I mean, Josua, and you know it. I'm just saying that this is an army, not a religious procession with the lector walking at the back. We can start whatever we have to do without waiting for every last soul who pulls up lame, or every horse that throws a shoe."

Josua turned to Camaris, who sat quietly by the small fire, staring intently at the smoke rising up to the hole in the tent roof. "What do you think, Sir Camaris? You have been on more marches than any of us, except perhaps for Isgrimnur. Is he right?"

The old man slowly turned his gaze away from the flickering fire. "I think that what Duke Isgrimnur says is just, yes. We owe it to the people as a whole to do what we have set out to do, and even more than that, we owe it to our good Lord, who has heard our promises. And we would be presumptuous to try to do God's work by holding the hand of every foot-weary traveler." He paused for a moment. "However, we also wish—nay, need—the people to join us. People do not join a hurrying, furtive band, they join a triumphant army." He looked around the tent, his eyes calm and clear. "We should go as swiftly as we can while still maintaining our company in good order. We should send riders out, not just to search what lies before us, but to be our heralds as well, to call to the people: 'The prince is coming!' " For a moment it seemed he might say more, but his expression grew distant and he fell silent.

Josua smiled. "You should have been an escritor, Sir Camaris. You are as subtle as my old teachers, the Usirean brothers. I have only one disagreement with you." He pivoted slightly to include the others in the tent. "We are going to Nabban. Our criers will shout: 'Camaris has come back! Sir Camaris has returned to lead his people!' " He laughed. " 'And Josua is with him.' "

Camaris frowned slightly, as if what the prince said made him uneasy.

Isgrimnur nodded. "Camaris is right. Haste with dignity."

"But dignity does not allow us to plunder inhabited lands," Josua said. "That is not the way to gain the people's hearts."

Isgrimnur shrugged; again, he thought the prince was cutting the point too fine. "Our people are hungry, Josua.

They have been cast out, some of them living in the wildlands for almost two years. When we reach Nabban, how
will you tell them not to take the food they see growing
from the ground, the sheep they see grazing the hills?"

The prince squinted wearily at the map. "I have no
more answers. We will all do our best, and may God bless
us."

"May God have mercy on us," Camaris corrected him
in a hollow voice. The old man was again staring at the
rising smoke.

Night had fallen. Three shapes sat in a copse of trees
overlooking the valley. The music of the river rose up to
them, muted and fragile. They had no fire, but a blue-
white stone that lay between them glowed faintly, only a
little brighter than the moon. Its azure light painted their
pale, long-boned faces as they spoke quietly in the hissing
tongue of Stormspike.

"Tonight?" asked the one named Born-Beneath-
Tzaaihta's-Stone.

Vein-of-Silverfire made a finger-gesture of negation.
She laid her hand on the blue stone for a long moment
and sat in unmoving silence. At last, she let out a long-
held breath. "Tomorrow, when Mezhumeyru hides in the
clouds. Tonight, in this new place, the mortals will be
watchful. Tomorrow night." She looked meaningfully at
Born-Beneath-Tzaaihta's-Stone. He was the youngest,
and had never before left the deep caverns below
Nakkiga. She could tell by the tautness in his long, slender fingers, the gleam in his purple eyes, that he would
bear watching. But he was brave, of that there was no
doubt. Anyone who had survived the endless apprentice-
ship in the Cavern of Rending would fear nothing except
the displeasure of their silver-masked mistress. Overea-
gerness, though, could be as harmful as cowardice.

"Look at them," said Called-by-the-Voices. She was
staring raptly at the few human figures visible in the en-

campment below. "They are like rockworms, always wriggling, always squirming."

"If your life were but a few seasons," Vein-of-Silverfire replied, "perhaps you, too, would feel that you could never pause." She stared down at the twinkling constellation of fires. "You are right, though—they are like rockworms." The line of her mouth hardened minutely. "They have dug and eaten and laid waste. Now we will help put an end to them."

"By this one thing?" Called-by-the-Voices asked.

Vein-of-Silverfire looked at her, face cold and hard as ivory. "Do you question?"

There was a moment of tight-stretched silence before Called-by-the-Voices bared her teeth. "I seek only to do as She wishes. I want only to do what will serve Her best."

Born-Beneath-Tzaaihta's-Stone made a musical sound of pleasure. The moon reflected tombstone-white in his eyes. "She wishes a death ... a *special* death," he said. "That is our gift to Her."

"Yes." Vein-of-Silverfire picked up the stone and placed it inside her raven-black shirt, next to her cool skin. "That is the gift of the Talons. And tomorrow night, we will give it to Her."

They fell silent, and did not speak again through the long night.

"You are still thinking too much of yourself, Seoman." Aditu leaned forward and pushed the polished stones into a crescent that spanned the shore of the Gray Coast. The shent-stones winked dully in the light of one of Aditu's crystalline globes, which sat on a tripod of carved wood. A little more light, this from the afternoon sun, leaked in through the flap of Simon's tent.

"What does that mean? I don't understand."

Aditu looked from the board to Simon, her eyes suggesting a deep-hidden amusement. "You are too much in yourself, that is what I mean. You are not thinking about what your partner is thinking. Shent is a game played by two."

"It's hard enough to try to remember the rules without having to think as well," Simon complained. "Besides, how am I supposed to know what you're thinking about while we're playing? I *never* know what you're thinking about!"

Aditu seemed poised to make one of her sly remarks, but instead she paused and laid her hand flat over her stones. "You are upset, Seoman. I have seen it in your play—you play well enough now that your moods carry over to the House of Shent."

She had not asked what was bothering him. Simon guessed that even if a companion showed up with a leg missing, Aditu or any other Sitha might wait while several seasons passed without asking what had happened. This evidence of what he thought of as her Sithi-ness irritated him, but he was also flattered that she thought he was becoming good at shent—although she probably only meant "good for a mortal," and since he was the only mortal he'd ever heard of who played, that was a rather lackluster compliment.

"I'm not upset." He glared down at the shent board. "Maybe I am," he said at last. "But it's nothing you could tell me anything about."

Aditu said nothing, but leaned back on her elbows and stretched her long neck in her oddly-jointed way, then shook her head. Pale hair fell loose from the pin that held it and gathered around her shoulders like fog, one thin braid coiling in front of her ear.

"I don't understand women," he said suddenly, then set his mouth in a scowl as though Aditu might contradict him. Evidently she agreed that he didn't, for she still said nothing. "I just don't understand them."

"What do you mean, Seoman? Surely you understand some things. I often say I do not understand mortals, but I know what they look like and how long they live, and I can speak a few of their languages."

Simon looked at her in irritation. Was she playing with

him again? "I suppose it's not all women," he said grudgingly. "I don't understand Miriamele. The princess."

"The thin one with the yellow hair?"

She *was* playing with him. "If you like. But I can see it's stupid to talk to you about it."

Aditu leaned forward and touched his arm. "I am sorry, Seoman. I have made you angry. Tell me what is bothering you, if you would like. Perhaps even if I know little about mortals, speaking will make you feel happier."

He shrugged, embarrassed that he had brought it up. "I don't know. She's kind to me sometimes. Then, other times, she acts as if she hardly knows me. Sometimes she looks at me like I frighten her. *Me!*" He laughed bitterly. "I saved her life! Why should she be frightened of me?"

"If you saved her life, that is one possible reason." Aditu was serious. "Ask my brother. Having your life saved by someone is a very great responsibility."

"But Jiriki doesn't act like he hates me!"

"My brother is of an old and reserved race—although among the Zida'ya, he and I are thought to be quite youthfully impulsive and dangerously unpredictable." She gifted him with a catlike smile; there might as well have been a mouse tail-tip protruding from the corner of her pretty mouth. "And no, he does not hate you—Jiriki thinks very highly of you, Seoman Snowlock. He would never have brought you to Jao é-Tinukai'i otherwise, which confirmed in the minds of many of our folk that he is not entirely trustworthy. But your Miriamele is a mortal girl, and very young. There are fish in the river outside that have lived longer than she has. Do not be surprised that she finds owing someone her life to be a difficult burden."

Simon stared at her. He had expected more teasing, but Aditu was talking sensibly about Miriamele—and she was telling him things about the Sithi he had never heard her say. He was torn between two fascinating subjects.

"That's not all. At least, I don't think it is. I . . . I don't know how to be with her," he said finally. "With Princess Miriamele. I mean, I think about her all the time. But who am I to think about a princess?"

Aditu laughed, a sparkling sound like falling water. "You are Seoman the Bold. You saw the Yásira. You met First Grandmother. What other young mortal can say that?"

He felt himself blushing. "But that's not the point. She's a princess, Aditu—the High King's daughter!"

"The daughter of your enemy? Is that why you are troubled?" She seemed honestly puzzled.

"No." He shook his head. "No, no, no." He looked around wildly, trying to think of a way to make her see. "You are the daughter of the king and queen of the Zida'ya, aren't you?"

"That is more or less how it would be said in your speech. I am of the Year-Dancing House, yes."

"Well, what if someone who was from, I don't know, an unimportant family—a bad house or something like that—wanted to marry you?"

"A . . . bad house?" Aditu looked at him carefully. "Do you ask whether I would consider another of my folk to be beneath me? We have long been too few for that, Seoman. And why must you marry her? Do your people never make love without being married?"

Simon was speechless for a moment. Make love to the king's daughter without a thought of marrying her? "I am a knight," he said stiffly. "I have to be honorable."

"Loving someone is not honorable?" She shook her head, mocking smile now returned. "And you say you do not understand *me,* Seoman!"

Simon rested his elbows on his knees and covered his face with his hands. "You mean that your people don't care who marries who? I don't believe it."

"That is what tore asunder the Zida'ya and Hikeda'ya," she said. When he looked up, her gold-flecked gaze had become hard. "We have learned from that terrible lesson."

"What do you mean?"

"It was the death of Drukhi, the son of Utuk'ku and her husband Ekimeniso Blackstaff, that drove the families apart. Drukhi loved and married Nenais'u, the Nightingale's daughter." She raised her hand and made a gesture like a book being closed. "She was killed by mortals in the years before Tumet'ai was swallowed by the ice. It was an accident. She was dancing in the forest when a mortal huntsman was drawn to the glimmer of her bright dress. Thinking he saw a bird's plumage, he loosed an arrow. When her husband Drukhi found her, he went mad." Aditu bent her head, as though it had happened only a short while before.

After she had gone some moments without speaking, Simon asked: "But how did that drive the families apart? And what does that have to do with marrying whoever you want?"

"It is a very long story, Seoman—perhaps the longest that our people tell, excepting only the flight from the Garden and our coming across the black seas to this land." She pushed at one of the shent-stones with her finger. "At that time, Utuk'ku and her husband ruled all the Gardenborn—they were the keepers of the Year-Dancing groves. When their son fell in love with Nenais'u, daughter of Jenjiyana and her mate Initri, Utuk'ku furiously opposed it. Nenais'u's parents were of our Zida'ya clan—although it had a different name in those long-ago days. They were also of the belief that the mortals, who had come to this land after the Gardenborn had arrived, should be permitted to live as they would, as long as they did not make war on our people."

She made another, more intricate arrangement of the stones on the board before her. "Utuk'ku and her clan felt that the mortals should be pushed back across the ocean, and that those who would not leave should be killed, as some mortal farmers crush the insects they find on their crops. But since the two great clans and the other smaller clans allied with one or the other were so evenly divided, even Utuk'ku's position as Mistress of Year-Dancing House did not permit her to force her will on the rest. You see, Seoman, we have never had 'kings' and 'queens' as you mortals have.

"In any case, Utuk'ku and her husband were fiercely angry that their son had married a woman of what they considered to be the traitorous, mortal-loving clan that opposed them. When Nenais'u was slain, Drukhi went

mad and swore that he would kill every mortal he could
find. The men of Nenais'u's clan restrained him, although
they were, in their own way, as bitterly angry and horrified as he. When the Yásira was called, the Gardenborn
could come to no decision, but enough feared what might
happen if Drukhi was free that they decided he must be
confined—something that had never happened this side of
the Ocean." He sighed. "It was too much for him, too
much for his madness, to be held prisoner by his own
people while those he deemed his wife's murderers went
free. Drukhi made himself die."

Simon was fascinated, although he could tell from
Aditu's expression how sad the story was to her. "Do you
mean he killed himself?"

"Not as you think of it, Seoman. No, rather Drukhi just
. . . stopped living. When he was found lying dead in the
Si'injan'dre Cave, Utuk'ku and Ekimeniso took their clan
and went north, swearing that they would never again live
with Jenjiyana's people."

"But first everyone went to Sesuad'ra," he said. "They
went to Leavetaking House and they made their pact.
What I saw during my vigil in the Observatory."

She nodded. "From what you have said, I believe you
had a true vision of the past, yes."

"And that is why Utuk'ku and the Norns hate mortals?" he asked.

"Yes. But they also went to war with some of the first
mortals in Hernystir, back long before Hern gave it the
name. In that fighting, Ekimeniso and many of the other
Hikeda'ya lost their lives. So they have other grudges to
nurse, as well."

Simon sat back, wrapping his arms about his knees. "I
didn't know. Morgenes or Binabik or someone told me
that the battle of the Knock was the first time that mortals
had killed Sithi."

"Sithi, yes—the Zida'ya. But Utuk'ku's people clashed
with mortals several times before the shipmen came from
over the western sea and changed everything." She lowered her head. "So you can see," Aditu finished, "why we
of the Dawn Children are careful not to say that someone

is above someone else. Those are words that mean tragedy to us."

He nodded. "I think I understand. But things are different with us, Aditu. There are rules about who can marry who . . . and a princess can't marry a landless knight, especially one who used to be a kitchen boy."

"You have seen these rules? Are they kept in one of your holy places?"

He made a face. "You know what I mean. You should hear Camaris if you want to find out how things work. He knows everything—who bows to who, who gets to wear which colors on what day . . ." Simon laughed ruefully. "If I ever asked him about someone like me marrying the princess, I think he'd cut my head off. But nicely. And he wouldn't enjoy doing it."

"Ah, yes, Camaris." Aditu seemed to be about to say something significant. "He is a . . . strange man. He has seen many things, I think."

Simon looked at her carefully but could not discern any particular meaning behind her words. "He has. And I think he means to teach them all to me before we reach Nabban. Still, that's nothing to complain about." He stood up. "As a matter of fact, it's going to be dark before too long, so I should go and see him. There was something he wanted to show me about using a shield . . ." Simon paused. "Thank you for talking to me, Aditu."

She nodded. "I do not think I have said anything to help you, but I hope you will not be so sad, Seoman."

He shrugged as he swept his cloak up from the floor.

"Hold," she said, rising. "I will come with you."

"To see Camaris?"

"No. I have another errand. But I will walk with you down to where our paths part."

She followed him out through the tent flap. Untouched, the crystal globe flickered and dimmed, then went dark.

"So?" asked Duchess Gutrun. Miriamele could clearly hear the fear beneath her impatient tone.

Geloë stood. She squeezed Vorzheva's hand for a moment, then set it down atop the blanket. "It is nothing too bad," the witch woman said. "A little blood, that is all, and stopped now. You have had your own children, Gutrun, and grandmothered many more. You should know better than to fret her this way."

The duchess set her chin defiantly. "I have had and raised my own children, yes, which is more than some can say." When Geloë did not even raise an eyebrow at this sally, Gutrun continued with only a little less heat. "But I never bore any of my children on horseback, and I swear that is what her husband means for her to do!" She looked to Miriamele as though for support, but her would-be ally only shrugged. There was little point in arguing now—the deed was done. The prince had chosen to go to Nabban.

"I can ride in the wagon," Vorzheva said. "By the Grass-Thunderer, Gutrun, the women of my clan ride on horses sometimes until their last moon!"

"Then the other women of your clan are fools," Geloë said dryly, "even if you are not. Yes, you can ride in a wagon. That should not be too bad on open grassland." She turned to Gutrun. "As for Josua, you know he is doing what seems best. I agree with him. It is harsh, but he cannot halt everybody for a hundred days so his wife can bear their child in peace and quiet."

"Then there should be some other way to do things. I told Isgrimnur that it was cruelty, and I meant it. I told him to tell Prince Josua as well. I don't care what the prince thinks of me, I can't bear to see Vorzheva suffer this way."

Geloë's smile was grim. "I am sure your husband listened to you carefully, Gutrun, but I doubt that Josua will ever hear it."

"What do you mean?" the duchess demanded.

Before the forest woman could reply—although Miriamele thought she looked in no hurry to do so—there was a soft noise at the door of the tent. The flap slid back, revealing for the merest instant a spatter of stars, then Ad-

itu's lithe form slipped through and the cloth fell back
into place.

"Do I intrude?" the Sitha asked. Oddly, Miriamele
thought that she sounded as though she meant it. To a
young woman raised on the false politeness of her father's court, it was strange to hear someone asking that as
though they wanted an answer. "I heard you were ill,
Vorzheva."

"I am better," said Josua's wife, smiling. "Come in,
Aditu, you are very welcome here."

The Sitha sat on the floor near Vorzheva's bed, her
golden eyes intent on the sick woman, her long, graceful
hands folded in her lap. Miriamele could not help staring.
Unlike Simon, who seemed quite accustomed to the Sithi,
she had not yet grown used to having such a foreign creature among them. Aditu seemed as strange as something
from an old story, but stranger still because she was sitting right here in the dim rushlight, as real as a stone or
a tree. It was as though the past year had turned the entire
world upside down, and all the hidden things remembered
only in legends had come tumbling out.

Aditu pulled a pouch from her gray tunic and held it
up. "I have brought something to help you sleep." She
spilled a small cluster of green leaves into her palm, then
showed them to Geloë, who nodded. "I will brew them
for you while we talk."

The Sitha appeared not to notice Gutrun's disgruntled
stare. Using a pair of sticks, Aditu levered a hot stone
from the fire, knocked off the ashes, then dropped it into
a bowl of water. When a cloud of steam hung over it, she
crumbled in the leaves. "I am told we will remain here
one more day. That will give you a chance to rest, Vorzheva."

"I do not know why everyone is so frightened for me.
It is only a child. Women bear children every day."

"Not the prince's only child," Miriamele said quietly.
"Not in the middle of a war."

Aditu was using the hot stone to further crush the
leaves, pushing it about with a stick. "You and your mate
will have a healthy child, I am sure," she said. To

Miriamele, it sounded incongruously like the kind of thing a mortal might have said—polite, cheerful. Maybe Simon was right after all.

When the stone was removed, Vorzheva sat up to take the bowl, which still steamed. She took a small sip. Miriamele watched the muscles in the Thrithings-woman's pale neck move as she swallowed.

She's so lovely, Miriamele thought.

Vorzheva's eyes were huge and dark, though heavy-lidded with fatigue; her hair was a thick black cloud about her head. Miriamele's fingers crept up to her own shorn locks and felt the ragged ends where the dyed hair had been cut off. She could not help feeling like an ugly little sister.

Be still, she told herself angrily. *You're as pretty as you need to be. What more do you want—do you need?*

But it was hard to be in the same room with boldly beautiful Vorzheva and the feline, graceful Sitha and not feel a little frowsy.

But Simon likes me. She almost smiled. *He does, I can tell.* Her mood soured. *But what does it matter? He can't do what I have to do. And he doesn't know anything about me, anyway.*

It was strange, though, to think that the Simon who had pledged her his service—it had been a strange and painful moment, but sweet, too—was the same person as the gangling boy who had accompanied her to Naglimund. Not that he had changed so much, but what *had* changed ... He was older. Not just his height, not just the fuzzy beard, but in his eyes and in the way he stood. He would be a handsome man, she now saw—something she would never have said when they stopped in Geloë's forest house. His prominent nose, his long-boned face, had gained something in the intervening months, a rightness that they hadn't had before.

What was it that one of her nurses had said once of another Hayholt child? "He has to grow into that face." Well, that was definitely true of Simon. And he was doing just that.

Little surprise, though, she supposed. He had done so

many things since leaving the Hayholt—why, he was almost a hero! He had faced a dragon! What had Sir Camaris or Tallistro ever done that was braver? And although Simon played down his meeting with the iceworm—while at the same time, Miriamele had seen, he was dying to boast a little—he had also stood at her side when a giant had charged. She had seen his bravery then. *Neither* of them had run, so she was brave, too. Simon was indeed a good companion . . . and now he was her protector.

Miriamele felt warm and strangely fluttery, as though something swift-winged moved inside of her. She tried to harden herself against it, against any such feelings. This was not the time. This was definitely not the time—and soon there might not be time for anything. . . .

Aditu's quietly musical voice pulled her back to the tent and the people who surrounded her. "If you have done all that you wished to do for Vorzheva," the Sitha was saying to Geloë, "I would like to have your company for a little while. I wish to speak to you of something."

Gutrun made a rumbling noise, which Miriamele guessed was meant to convey the duchess' impression of people who would go off and tell secrets. Geloë either ignored or did not hear her wordless comment, and said: "I think what she needs now is sleep, or at least some quiet." Now she turned at last to Gutrun. "I will look in on her later."

"As you wish," said the duchess.

The witch woman nodded to Vorzheva, then to Miriamele, before following Aditu out of the tent. The Thrithings-woman, who was lying back now, raised her hand in farewell. Her eyes were almost closed. She appeared to be falling asleep.

The tent was silent for some moments except for the tuneless humming of Gutrun as she sewed, which continued even as she held the cloth close to the fire to examine her stitchery. At last, Miriamele stood up.

"Vorzheva is tired. I will leave, too." She leaned forward and took the Thrithings-woman's hand. Her eyes opened; it took them a moment to fix on Miriamele.

"Good night. I'm sure it will be a fine baby, one that will make you and Uncle Josua very proud."

"Thank you." Vorzheva smiled and closed her long-lashed eyes again.

"Good night, Auntie Gutrun," Miriamele said. "I'm glad you were here when I came back from the south. I missed you." She kissed the duchess' warm cheek, then delicately untangled herself from Gutrun's motherly embrace and slipped out through the door.

"I haven't heard her call me that for years!" Miriamele heard Gutrun say in surprise. Vorzheva mumbled something sleepily. "The poor child seems so quiet and sad these days," Gutrun went on. "But then again, why shouldn't she. . . ?"

Miriamele, walking away through the wet grass, did not hear the rest of what the duchess had to say.

Aditu and Geloë walked beside the whispering Stefflod. The moon was covered in a net of clouds, but stars glinted higher up in the blackness. A soft breeze was blowing from the east, carrying the scent of grass and wet stones.

"It is strange, what you say, Aditu." The witch woman and the Sitha made a peculiar pair, the immortal's loose-limbed stride reined in to match Geloë's more stalwart tread. "But I do not think there is harm in it."

"I do not say that there is, only that it bears thinking about." The Sitha laughed hissingly. "To think that I have grown so embroiled in the doings of mortals! Mother's brother Khendraja'aro would grind his teeth."

"These mortal concerns *are* your family's concerns, at least in part," Geloë said matter-of-factly. "Otherwise, you would not be here."

"I know that," agreed Aditu. "But many of my people will walk a long way around to find some other reason for what we do than anything that smacks of mortals and their affairs." She leaned down and plucked a few blades of grass, then held them to her nose and sniffed. "The grass here is different than that which grows in the forest, or even on Sesuad'ra. It is ... younger. I cannot feel as much life in it, but it is sweet for all that." She let the loose blades flutter to the ground. "But I have let my words wander. Geloë, I do not see any harm in Camaris at all, except that in him which would harm himself. But it is odd that he keeps his past a secret, and odder still when there are so many things he might know that could aid his people in this struggle."

"He will not be pushed," said Geloë. "If he tells his secrets, it will be in his own time, that is clear. We have all tried." She shoved her hands into the pocket of her heavy tunic. "Still, though, I cannot help being curious. Are you sure?"

"No," Aditu said thoughtfully. "Not sure. But an odd thing Jiriki told me has been at the back of my thoughts for some time. We both, he and I, thought that Seoman was the first mortal to set foot in Jao é-Tinukai'i. Certainly that is what my father and mother thought. But Jiriki told me that when Amerasu met Seoman she said that he was *not* the first. I have long wondered about that, but First Grandmother knew the history of the Garden-born better than anyone—perhaps even better than silver-faced Utuk'ku, who has long brooded on the past, but never made its study an art, as Amerasu did."

"But I still don't know why you think the first might have been Camaris."

"In the beginning it was only a sense I had." Aditu turned and wandered down the bank toward the soft-singing river. "Something in the way he looked at me, even before he recovered his wits. I caught him staring at me several times when he did not think I was looking. Later, when his sense had returned, he continued to watch me—not slyly, but like someone who remembers something painful."

"That could have been anything—a resemblance to someone." Geloë frowned. "Or perhaps he was feeling shame over the way his friend John, the High King, hunted your people."

"John's persecution of the Zida'ya occurred almost entirely before Camaris came to the court, from what the archivist Strangyeard has told me," Aditu replied. "Don't stare!" she laughed. "I am curious about many things, and we Dawn Children have never been afraid of inquiry or scholarship, although we would not use either of those words."

"Still, there could be many reasons Camaris stared. You are not a common sight, Aditu no-Sa'onserei—at least not for mortals."

"True. But there is more. One night, before his memory was returned, I was walking by the Observatory, as you named it—and I saw him walking slowly toward me. I nodded, but he seemed absorbed in his shadow-world. I was singing a song—a very old song from Jhiná-T'seneí, a favorite of Amerasu's—and as I passed him, Geloë, I saw that his lips were moving." She stopped and squatted by the riverside, but looked up at the forest woman with eyes that even in the darkness seemed to glimmer like amber coals. "He was mouthing the words to the same song."

"Are you sure?"

"As certain as I am that the trees in the Grove are alive and will blossom again, and I feel that in my blood and heart. Amerasu's song was known to him, and although he still wore his faraway look, he was singing silently along with me. A playful song that First Grandmother used to sing. It is not the sort of tune that is sung in the cities of mortal men, or even in the oldest sacred grove in Hernystir."

"But what could it mean?" Geloë stood over Aditu, looking out across the river. The wind slowly shifted direction, blowing now from behind the encampment that lay just uphill. The normally imperturbable forest woman seemed faintly agitated. "Even if Camaris somehow knew Amerasu, what could it mean?"

"I do not know. But considering that Camaris' horn was once our enemy's, and that our enemy was also Amerasu's son—and once the greatest of my people—I feel a need to know. It is also true that the sword of this knight is very important to us." She made what was, for a Sitha, an unhappy face, a faint thinning of the lips. "If only Amerasu had lived to tell us her suspicions."

Geloë shook her head. "We have been laboring in shadows too long. Well, what can we do?"

"I have approached him. He does not wish to talk to me, although he is polite. When I try to guide him toward the subject, he pretends to misunderstand, or simply pleads some other necessity, then leaves." Aditu rose from the grass beside the river. "Perhaps Prince Josua can compel him to talk. Or Isgrimnur, who seems the nearest thing to a friend Camaris has. You know them both, Geloë. They are suspicious of me, for which I do not blame them—many mortal generations have passed since we could consider the Sudhoda'ya to be our allies. Perhaps at your urging, one of them may convince Camaris to tell us whether it is true that he was in Jao é-Tinukai'i, and what it might mean."

"I will try," promised Geloë. "I am to see the two of them later tonight. But even if they can convince Camaris, I am not sure there will be any value in what he has to say."

She ran her thick fingers through her hair. "Still, we have learned precious little else that is of use lately." She looked up. "Aditu? What is it?"

The Sitha had gone rigid, and stood with her head cocked in a most unhuman way.

"Aditu?" Geloë said again. "Are we attacked?"

"*Kei-vishaa,*" Aditu hissed. "I smell it!"

"What?"

"Kei-vishaa. It is ... there is no time to explain. It is a smell that should not be in the air here. Something bad is happening. Follow me, Geloë—I am suddenly fearful!"

Aditu sprang away up the river bank, swift as a flushed deer. Within a moment she had vanished into the darkness, heading back toward the encampment. Following her, the witch woman ran a few more paces, muttering words of worry and anger. As she passed into the shadow of a congregation of willows that grew on a hill overlooking the streambank, there was a convulsive movement; the faint starlight seemed to bend, the darkness to coalesce and then burst outward. Geloë, or at least Geloë's shape, did not reemerge from the tree-shadows, but a winged form did.

Yellow eyes wide in the moonlight, the owl flew in pursuit of swift Aditu, following the whisper-faint mark of her passage across the wet grass.

Simon had been restless all evening. Talking with Aditu had helped, but only a little. In a way, it had made him even more unsettled.

He desperately wanted to speak with Miriamele. He thought about her all the time—at night when he wanted just to fall asleep, during the day whenever he saw a girl's face or heard a woman's voice, at odd moments when he should be thinking of other things. It was strange how she had come to mean so much to him in the short time since she had returned: the smallest change in the way she treated him stayed in his mind for days.

She had seemed so strange when he had met her by the horses the night before. And yet, when she had accompanied him to Isgrimnur's fire to hear the singing, she had been kind and friendly, if a little distracted. But now she had avoided him all day today—or at least so it seemed, for everywhere he looked for her he was told that she was somewhere else, until it began to feel as though she was staying a step ahead of him on purpose.

The twilight had gone and darkness had settled in like a great black bird folding its wings. His visit with Camaris had been brief—the old man had seemed fully as preoccupied as he was, barely able to fix his attention on explaining the rank of battle and the rules of engagement. To Simon, consumed with worries more heated and more current, the knight's litany of rules had seemed dry and pointless. He had made excuses and departed early, leaving the old man sitting by the fire in his sparsely-furnished campsite. Camaris seemed just as happy to be left alone.

After a fruitless exploration of the camp, Simon had

looked in on Vorzheva and Gutrun. Miriamele had been there, the duchess said—whispering so as not to wake the prince's sleeping wife—but had left some time before. Unrewarded, Simon had returned to his search.

Now, as he stood at the outer edge of the field of tents, at the beginnings of the wide halo of fires that marked the camps of those members of Josua's company to whom a tent was, at this moment, an unimaginable luxury, Simon puzzled over where Miriamele might be. He had walked along the riverbank earlier, thinking that she might be there keeping company with her thoughts by the water, but there had been no sign of her, only a few New Gadrinsett folk with torches, night-fishing with what appeared to be little success.

Maybe she's seeing to her horse, he thought suddenly.

That was, after all, where he had found her the night before, not too much earlier in the evening than it was now. Perhaps she found it a quiet place after everyone else had gone down to supper. He turned and headed for the dark hillside.

He stopped first to say hello to Homefinder, who received his greeting with a certain aloofness before condescending to snuffle at his ear, then he headed uphill toward the spot where the princess had said her horse was picketed. There was indeed a shadowy figure moving there. Pleased with his own cleverness, he stepped forward.

"Miriamele?"

The hooded figure started, then whirled. For a moment he could see nothing but a smear of pallid face in the depths of the hood.

"S–Simon?" It was a shocked, fearful voice—but it was her voice. "What are you doing here?"

"I was looking for you." The way she spoke alarmed him. "Are you well?" This time the question seemed tremendously appropriate.

"I am . . ." She moaned. "Oh, why did you come?"

"What's wrong?" He took a few paces toward her. "Have you. . . ?" He stopped.

Even in the moonlight, he could see that the silhouette

of her horse seemed somehow wrong. Simon put out his
hand and touched the bulging saddlebags.

"You're going somewhere ..." he said wonderingly.
"You're running away."

"I am *not* running away." The earlier tone of fear gave
way to pain and fury. "I am not. Now leave me alone, Simon."

"Where are you going?" He was caught up in the
strange dreaminess of it—the dark hillside with its few
lonely trees, Miriamele's hooded face. "Is it me? Did I
make you angry?"

Her laugh was bitter. "No, Simon, it's not you." Her
voice softened. "You have done nothing wrong. You have
been a friend when I didn't deserve one. I can't tell you
where I'm going—and please wait until tomorrow to tell
Josua you've seen me. Please. I beg this of you."

"But ... but I can't!" How could he tell Josua that he
had stood by and watched as the prince's niece had ridden
away by herself? He tried to slow his excited heart and
think. "I will go with you," he said finally.

"What!?" Miriamele was astonished. "You can't!"

"I can't let you go off by yourself, either. I am your
sworn protector, Miriamele."

She seemed on the verge of crying. "But I don't want
you to go, Simon. You are my friend—I don't want you
hurt!"

"And I don't want you hurt, either." He felt calmer
now. He had a strange but powerful feeling that this was
the right decision ... although another part of him was
simultaneousy crying *mooncalf, mooncalf!* "That's why
I'm going with you."

"But Josua needs you!"

"Josua has lots of knights, and I'm the least of them.
You only have one."

"I can't let you, Simon." She shook her head violently.
"You don't understand what I'm doing, where I'm going. . . ."

"Then tell me."

She shook her head again.

"Then I'll just have to find out by going with you. Either you take me, or you stay. I'm sorry, Miriamele, but that is all."

She looked at him for a moment, staring hard, as though she would see into his very heart. She seemed to be in a kind of ecstasy of indecision, pulling distractedly at her horse's bridle until Simon feared the animal might startle and bolt. "Very well," she said at last. "Oh, Elysia save us all, very well! But we must go now, and you must ask me no more questions about where or why tonight."

"Fine," he said. The doubting part of him was still screaming for attention, but he had decided not to listen. He could not bear the idea of her riding away into the dark alone. "But I must go and get my sword and a few other things. Do you have food?"

"Enough for me . . . but you dare not try to steal more, Simon. There's too much chance someone would see you."

"Well, we'll worry about it later, then. But I must have a sword, and I must leave something to explain. Did you?"

She stared at him. "Are you mad?"

"Not to say where you're going, but just to tell them that you're gone of your own will. We have to, Miriamele," he explained firmly. "It's cruel, otherwise. They'll think we were kidnapped by the Norns, or that we've, we've . . ." he smiled as the thought came, ". . . we've run away to be married, like in the Mundwode song."

Her look turned calculating. "Very well, get your sword and leave a note."

Simon frowned. "I'm off. But remember, Miriamele, if you aren't here when I get back, I'll have Josua and every man of New Gadrinsett after you tonight."

She jutted her chin defiantly. "Go on, then. I want to ride until dawn and be well away, so hurry."

He threw her a mock-bow, then turned and ran down the hillside.

It was strange, but when Simon thought of that night later, during moments of terrible pain, he could no longer

remember how he had felt as he hastened toward the
camp—as he had prepared to steal off with the king's
daughter, Miriamele. The memory of all that came afterward crowded out what had throbbed in him as he pelted
down the hill.

On that night he felt all the world singing about him,
all the stars hanging close and attentive above. As Simon
ran, the world seemed poised on some vast fulcrum, teetering, and every possibility was both beautiful and terrible. It seemed for all the world as though the dragon
Igjarjuk's molten blood had come alive in him again,
opening him up to the vast sky, filling him with the pulse
of the earth.

He dashed through the encampment with hardly a
glance for any of the night life that surrounded him, hearing none of the voices that were raised in song or laughter
or argument, seeing nothing but the twisting track through
the tents and small camps toward his own sleeping
place.

Happily for Simon, as it seemed, Binabik was away
from the tent. He had not given a moment's thought to
what he would have done if the little man had been waiting for him—he might have been able to come up with
some practical reason for needing his sword, but could
certainly not have left a note. Fumble-fingered with hurry,
he ransacked the tent for something to write on, and at
last found one of the scrolls Binabik had brought from
Ookequk's cave in the Trollfells. With a bit of charcoal
plucked from the cold firepit, he laboriously scrawled his
message on the back of the sheep-leather.

> *"Mirimel has gon away and I hav gon after Her."*

He wrote, tongue gripped between his teeth.

> *"We will be well. Tell Prince Josua I am sory but
> I hav to go. I will bring Her bak soon as I can.
> Tell Josua I am a bad knigt but I am tring to do
> wat is the best thing. Your frend Simon."*

He thought for a moment, then added:

*"You can hav my things if I dont cum bak. I am
sory."*

He left the note on Binabik's bedroll, grabbed his sword
and scabbard and a few other necessities, then left the tent.
At the doorway he hesitated for a moment, recalling his sack
of beloved treasures, the White Arrow, Jiriki's mirror. He
turned and went to retrieve it, although every moment he
kept her waiting—she would wait; she *must* wait—felt like
an hour. He had told Binabik he could have them, but
Miriamele's earlier words returned to him. They were en-
trusted; they were promises. He could not give them away
any more than he could give away his name, and there was
not time now to sort out the things that could safely be left
behind. He dared not even take the time to think or he knew
that he would lose courage.

We will be alone together, just us two, he kept thinking
in wonderment. *I will be her protector!*

It took him what seemed an agonizingly long time to
find the sack where he had hidden it in a hole under a flap
of sod. With sack and scabbard clutched under his arm,
his worn saddle over his shoulder—he winced at the noise
the harness buckles made—he ran as quickly as he could
back through the camp to where the horses were tied, to
where Miriamele—he prayed—was waiting.

She *was* there. Seeing her impatiently pacing, he felt a
moment of giddiness. She had waited for him!

"Hurry up, Simon! The night is slipping away!" She
seemed to feel none of his pleasure, but only a sense of
frustration, a terrible need to be moving.

With Homefinder saddled and Simon's few belongings
hastily pushed into the saddlebags, they were soon leading the horses up toward the hilltop, moving silently as
spirits through the damp grass. They turned for a last look
down at the glowing quilt of campfires spread in the river
valley.

"Look!" Simon said, startled. "That's no cookfire!" He

pointed to a large, moving billow of orange-red flame near the middle of the encampment. "Someone's tent is on fire!"

"I hope no harm comes to them, but at least it will keep people busy until we are away," said Miriamele grimly. "We must ride, Simon."

Suiting action to words, she clambered deftly into the saddle—she was once more wearing the breeches and shirt of a man beneath her heavy cloak—and led him down the hill's far side.

He took one last look back at the lights, then urged Homefinder after her, into shadows that even the emergent moon could not pierce.

Appendix

PEOPLE

ERKYNLANDERS

Barnabas—Hayholt chapel sexton
Deornoth, Sir—of Hewenshire, Josua's knight
Eahlferend—Simon's fisherman father
Eahlstan Fiskerne—"Fisher King," founder of League of
  Scroll
Ebekah, also known as Efiathe of Hernysadharc—Queen
  of Erkynland, John's wife, mother of Elias and Josua
Elias—High King, John's oldest son, Josua's brother
Fengbald—Earl of Falshire, High King's Hand
Freobeorn—Freosel's father, a blacksmith of Falshire
Freosel—Falshireman, constable of New Gadrinsett
Guthwulf—Earl of Utanyeat
Heanwig—old drunkard in Stanshire
Helfgrim—Lord Mayor of Gadrinsett (former)

Inch—foundry master
Isaak—Fengbald's page
Jack Mundwode—mythical forest bandit
Jeremias—former chandler's apprentice, Simon's friend
John—King John Presbyter, High King, also known as "Prester John"
Judith—Hayholt Mistress of Kitchens
Leleth—Geloë's companion, once Miriamele's handmaid
Maefwaru—a Fire Dancer
Miriamele—Princess, Elias' daughter
Morgenes, Doctor—Scrollbearer, Simon's friend and mentor
Old Bent Legs—forge worker in Hayholt
Osgal—one of Mundwode's mythical band
Rachel—Hayholt Mistress of Chambermaids, also known as "The Dragon"
Roelstan—escaped Fire Dancer
Sangfugol—Josua's harper
Sceldwine—captain of the prisoned Erkynguardsmen
Shem Horsegroom—Hayholt groom
Simon—castle scullion (named "Seoman" at birth)
Stanhelm—forge worker
Strangyeard, Father—Scrollbearer, priest, Josua's archivist
Towser—King John's jester (original name "Cruinh")
Ulca—girl on Sesuad'ra, called "Curly Hair"
Welma—girl on Sesuad'ra, called "Thin One"
Wiclaf—former First Hammerman killed by Fire Dancers
Zebediah—a Hayholt scullion, called "Fat Zebediah"

HERNYSTIRI

Airgad Oakheart—famous Hernystiri hero
Arnoran—minstrel
Bagba—cattle god
Brynioch of the Skies—sky god
Bulychlinn—fisherman in old story who caught a demon in his nets

Cadrach-ec-Crannhyr—monk of indeterminate Order, also known as "Padreic"

Caihwye—young mother

Craobhan—called "Old," adviser to Hernystiri royal house

Croich, House—a Hernystiri clan

Cuamh Earthdog—earth god

Deanagha of the Brown Eyes—Hernystiri goddess, daughter of Rhynn

Diawen—scryer

Earb, House—a Hernystiri clan

Eoin-ec-Cluias—legendary Hernystiri harper

Eolair—Count of Nad Mullach

Feurgha—Hernystiri woman, captive of Fengbald

Frethis of Cuihmne—Hernystiri scholar

Gullaighn—escaped Fire Dancer

Gwynna—Eolair's cousin and castellaine

Gwythinn—Maegwin's brother, Lluth's son

Hern—founder of Hernystir

Inahwen—Lluth's third wife

Lach, House—a Hernystiri clan

Lluth—King, father of Maegwin and Gwythinn

Llythinn—King, Lluth's father, uncle of John's wife Ebekah

Maegwin—Princess, daughter of Lluth

Mathan—goddess of household, wife of Murhagh One-Arm

Mircha—rain goddess, wife of Brynioch

Murhagh One-Arm—war god, husband of Mathan

Penemhwye—Maegwin's mother, Lluth's first wife

Rhynn of the Cauldron—a god

Siadreth—Caihwye's infant son

Sinnach—prince of Hernystir, also known as "The Red Fox"

Tethtain—former master of the Hayholt, "Holly King"

RIMMERSMEN

Dror—storm god
Dypnir—one of Ule's band
Einskaldir—Isgrimnur's man, killed in forest
Elvrit—first Osten Ard king of Rimmersmen
Fingil Bloodfist—first human master of Hayholt, "Bloody King"
Frekke Grayhair—Isgrimnur's man, killed at Naglimund
Gutrun—Duchess, Isgrimnur's wife
Hengfisk—Hoderundian priest, Elias' cupbearer
Hjeldin—Fingil's son, "Mad King"
Ikferdig—third Hayholt ruler, "Burned King"
Isgrimnur—Duke of Elvritshalla, Gutrun's husband
Isorn—son of Isgrimnur and Gutrun
Jarnauga—Scrollbearer, killed at Naglimund
Nisse—(Nisses) author of *Du Svardenvyrd*
Skali—Thane of Kaldskryke, called "Sharp-nose"
Sludig—Isgrimnur's man
Trestolt—Jarnauga's father
Ule Frekkeson—leader of renegade band of Rimmersmen, son of Frekke

NABBANAI

Aspitis Preves—Earl of Drina and Eadne
Benigaris—Duke of Nabban, son of Leobardis and Nessalanta
Benidrivis—first duke under John, father of Camaris and Leobardis
Brindalles—Seriddan's brother
Camaris-sá-Vinitta, Sir—John's greatest knight, also known as "Camaris Benidrivis"
Dinivan—Scrollbearer, secretary to Lector Ranessin, killed in Sancellan Aedonitis
Domitis—bishop of Saint Sutrin's cathedral in Erchester
Eneppa—Metessan kitchen woman, once called "Fuiri"
Elysia—mother of Usires Aedon, called "Mother of God"

Fluiren, Sir—knight of Sulian House, member of John's Great Table

Gavanaxes—knight of Honsa Claves (Clavean House) for whom Camaris was squire

Hylissa—Miriamele's mother, Elias' wife, killed in Thrithings

Lavennin, Saint—patron saint of Spenit Island

Leobardis—Duke of Nabban, killed at Naglimund

Metessan House—Nabbanai noble house, blue crane emblem

Munshazou—Pryrates' Naraxi serving woman

Nessalanta—Dowager Duchess, mother of Benigaris

Nuanni (Nuannis)—ancient Nabbanai sea god

Pasevalles—Brindalles' young son

Pelippa, Saint—called "Pelippa of the Island"

Plesinnen Myrmenis—ancient scholar

Pryrates—priest, alchemist, wizard, Elias' counselor

Ranessin—Lector of Mother Church, killed at Sancellan Aedonitis

Rhiappa, Saint—called "Rhiap" in Erkynland

Seriddan, Baron—Lord of Metessa, also known as "Seriddan Metessis"

Sulis, Lord—Nabbanai nobleman, former master of Hayholt, "Heron King," also known as "The Apostate"

Thures—Aspitis' young page

Usires Aedon—Aedonite religion's Son of God

Varellan—youngest son of Leobardis and Nessalanta, Benigaris' brother

Velligis—Lector of Mother Church

Xannasavin—Nabbanai court astrologer

Yistrin, Saint—saint linked to Simon's birth-day

SITHI

Aditu, (no-Sa'onserei)—daughter of Likimeya and Shima'onari; Jiriki's sister

Amerasu y-Senditu no'e-Sa'onserei—mother of Ineluki, killed at Jao é-Tinukai'i, called "First Grandmother," also known as "Amerasu Ship-Born"

Benayha (of Kementari)—famed Sithi poet and warrior
Briseyu Dawnfeather—Likimeya's mother, wife of Hakatri
Cheka'iso—called "Amber-Locks," member of Sithi clan
Chiya—member of Sithi clan, once resident of Asu'a
Contemplation House—Sithi clan
Drukhi—son of Utuk'ku and Ekimeniso, husband of Nenais'u
Gathering House—Sithi clan
Hakatri—Amerasu's son, vanished into West
Ineluki—Amerasu's son, killed at Asu'a, now Storm King
Initri—husband of Jenjiyana
Jenjiyana—wife of Initri, mother of Nenais'u, called "the Nightingale"
Jiriki (i-Sa'onserei)—son of Likimeya and Shima'onari, brother of Aditu
Kendhraja'aro—uncle of Jiriki and Aditu
Kira'athu—Sitha healer
Kuroyi—called "the tall horseman," master of High Anvi'janya, leader of Sithi clan
Likimeya (y-Briseyu no'e-Sa'onserei)—mother of Jiriki and Aditu, called "Likimeya Moon-Eyes"
Mezumiiru—mistress of moon in Sithi legend
Senditu—mother of Amerasu
Shi'iki—father of Amerasu
Shima'onari—father of Aditu and Jiriki, killed at Jao é-Tinukai'i
Vindaomeyo—famed arrow-maker of Tumet'ai, called "the Fletcher"
Year-Dancing House—Sithi clan
Yizashi Grayspear—leader of Sithi clan
Zinjadu—of Kementari, called "Lore-Mistress"

QANUC

Binabik (Binbiniqegabenik)—Scrollbearer, Singing Man of Qanuc, Simon's friend
Chukku—legendary troll hero
Kikkasut—legendary king of birds

Nimsuk—Qanuc herder, one of Sisqi's troop
Nunuuika—the Huntress
Ookequk—Scrollbearer, Binabik's master
Qinkipa (of the Snows)—snow and cold goddess
Sedda—moon goddess
Sisqi (Sisqinanamook)—daughter of Herder and Huntress, Binabik's betrothed
Snenneq—herd-chief of Lower Chugik
Uammannaq—the Herder

THRITHINGS-FOLK

Fikolmij—Vorzheva's father, March-thane of Clan Mehrdon
Hotvig—High Thrithings randwarder, Josua's man
Lezhdraka—Thrithings-man, mercenary chieftain
Ozhbern—High Thrithings-man
Ulgart—a mercenary captain from the Meadow Thrithing
Vorzheva—Josua's wife, daughter of Fikolmij

PERDRUINESE

Charystra—landlady of *Pelippa's Bowl*
Lenti—Streáwe's servant, called "Avi Stetto"
Streáwe, Count—master of Perdruin
Tallistro, Sir—famous knight of John's Great Table
Xorastra—Scrollbearer, first owner of *Pelippa's Bowl*

WRANNAMEN

Buayeg—owner of "the spirit-hut" (Wrannaman fable)
He Who Always Steps on Sand—god
He Who Bends the Trees—wind god
Inihe Red-Flower—woman in Tiamak's song
Nuobdig—Husband of the Fire Sister in Wrannaman legend
Rimihe—Tiamak's sister

She Who Birthed Mankind—goddess
She Who Waits to Take All Back—death goddess
Shoaneg Swift-Rowing—man in Tiamak's song
They Who Breathe Darkness—gods
They Who Watch and Shape—gods
Tiamak—Scrollbearer, herbalist
Tugumak—Tiamak's father
Twiyah—Tiamak's sister
Younger Mogahib—man of Tiamak's village

NORNS

Akhenabi—spokesman at Naglimund
"Born-Beneath-Tzaaihta's-Stone"—one of Utuk'ku's Talons
"Called-by-the-Voices"—one of Utuk'ku's Talons
Ekimeniso Blackstaff—husband of Utuk'ku, father of Drukhi
Mezhumeyru—Norn version of "Mezumiiru"
Utuk'ku Seyt-Hamakha—Norn Queen, Mistress of Nakkiga
"Vein-of-Silverfire"—one of Utuk'ku's Talons

OTHERS

Derra—a half-Thrithings child
Deornoth—a half-Thrithings child
Gan Itai—Niskie of *Eadne Cloud*
Geloë—a wise woman, called "Valada Geloë"
Imai-an—a dwarrow
Ingen Jegger—Black Rimmersman, huntsman of Utuk'ku, killed at Jao éTinukai'i
Injar—Niskie clan living on Risa Island
Nin Reisu—Niskie of *Emettin's Jewel*
Ruyan Vé—patriarch of Tinukeda'ya, called "The Navigator"
Sho-vennae—a dwarrow

Veng'a Sutekh—called "Duke of the Black Wind," one of the Red Hand

Yis-fidri—a dwarrow, Yis-hadra's husband, master of the Pattern Hall

Yis-hadra—a dwarrow, Yis-fidri's wife, mistress of the Pattern Hall

PLACES

Anvi'janya—place of Kuroyi's dwelling, also known as "Hidden" or "High" Anvi'janya

Ballacym—walled town on outskirts of Hernysadharc territory

Bradach Tor—high peak in Grianspog Mountains

Bregshame—small town on River Road between Stanshire and Falshire

Cathyn Dair, by Silversea—Hernystiri town from Miriamele's song

Cavern of Rending—where Talons of Utuk'ku are trained

Chamul Lagoon—a place in Kwanitupul

Chasu Yarinna—town built around keep, just northeast of Onestrine Pass in Nabban

Elvritshalla—Isgrimnur's ducal seat in Rimmersgard

Falshire—wool-harvesting city in Erkynland, devastated by Fengbald

Fiadhcoille—forest southeast of Nad Mullach, also known as "Stagwood"

Fire Garden—tiled open space on Sesuad'ra

Frasilis Valley—valley east of Onestrine Pass (other side of pass from Commeis Valley)

Garwynswold—small town on River Road between Stanshire and Falshire

Gratuvask—Rimmersgard river, runs past Elvritshalla

Grenamman—island in Bay of Firannos

Hall of Five Staircases—chamber in Asu'a where Briseyu died

Harcha—island in Bay of Firannos

Hasu Vale—valley in Erkynland

Hekhasór—former Sithi territory, called "Hekhasór of the Black Earth"

House of Waters—Sithi building on Sesuad'ra

Khandia—a lost and fabled land

Kiga'rasku—waterfall beneath Stormspike, called "the Tearfall"

Leavetaking House—Sithi building on Sesuad'ra, later center of Josua's exile court (Sithi name: "Sesu-d'asu")

M'yin Azoshai—Sithi name for Hern's Hill, location of Hernysadharc

Maa'sha—hilly former territory of Sithi

Mezutu'a—the Silverhome, abandoned Sithi and dwarrow city beneath Grianspog

Mount Den Haloi—mountain from Book of the Aedon where God created world

Naraxi—island in Bay of Firannos

Observatory, The—domed Sithi building on Sesuad'ra

Onestrine Pass—pass between two Nabbanai valleys, site of many battles

Peat Barge Quay—dock in Kwanitupul

Peja'ura—former forested home of Sithi, called "cedar-mantled"

Pulley Road—road in Stanshire

Risa—island in Bay of Firannos

Shisae'ron—broad meadow valley, once Sithi territory

Si'injan'dre Cave—place of Drukhi's confinement after Nenais'u's death

Soakwood Road—a major thoroughfare of Stanshire

Spenit—island in Bay of Firranos

Taig Road—road leading through Hernysadharc, also known as "Tethtain's Way"

Venyha Do'sae—original home of Sithi, Norns, Tinukeda'ya, called "The Garden"

Vinitta—Island in Bay of Firannos

Wealdhelm—range of hills in Erkynland

Ya Mologi—("Cradle Hill") highest point in Wran, legendary creation spot

Yakh Huyeru—("Hall of Trembling") cavern beneath Stormspike

Yasirá—Sithi sacred meeting place

CREATURES

Bukken—Rimmersgard name for diggers, also called "Boghanik" by trolls

Cat—a gray (in this case) and undistinguished quadruped

Diggers—small, manlike subterranean creatures

Ghants—chitinous Wran-dwelling creatures

Giants—large, shaggy, manlike creatures

Drochnathair—Hernystiri name for dragon Hidohebhi, slain by Ineluki and Hakatri

Homefinder—Simon's mare

Hunën—Rimmersgard name for giants

Igjarjuk—ice-dragon of Urmsheim

Kilpa—manlike marine creatures

Niku'a—Ingen Jegger's chief hound, bred in kennels of Stormspike

Oruks—fabulous water monsters

Qantaqa—Binabik's wolf companion, mount, and friend

Shurakai—fire-drake slain beneath Hayholt whose bones make up the Dragonbone Chair

Vildalix—Deornoth's horse

Vinyafod—Josua's horse

Water-wights—fabulous water monsters

THINGS

A-Genay'asu—("Houses of Traveling Beyond") places of mystical power and significance

Aedontide—holy time celebrating birth of Usires Aedon

"Badulf and the Straying Heifer"—a song Simon tries to sing to Miriamele

Battle of Clodu Lake—battle John fought against Thrithings-men, also known as "Battle of the Lakelands"

"Bishop's Wagon, The"—a Jack Mundwode song

Boar and Spears—emblem of Guthwulf of Utanyeat

Breathing Harp, The—Master Witness in Stormspike

Bright-Nail—sword of Prester John, formerly called "Minneyar," containing nail from the Holy Tree and finger-bone of Saint Eahlstan

"By Greenwade's Shore"—song sung at Bonfire Night on Sesuad'ra

Cellian—Camaris' horn, made from dragon Hidohebhi's tooth. (Original name: "Ti-tuno")

Citril—root for chewing, grown in south

Cockindrill—Northern word for "crocodile"

Conqueror Star—a comet, ominous star

Day of Weighing-Out—Aedonite day of final judgment

Door of the Ransomer—seal of confession

Du Svardenvyrd—near-mythical prophetic book by Nisses

Falcon, The—Nabbanai constellation

Fifty Families—Nabbanai noble houses

Floating Castle, The—famous monument on Warinsten

Frayja's Fire—Erkynlandish winter flower

Gardenborn, The—all who came from Venyha Do'sae

Good Peasant—character from the proverbs of the Book of Aedon

Gray Coast—part of the shent board

Gray-cap—mushroom

Great Swords—Bright-Nail, Sorrow, and Thorn

Great Table—John's assembly of knights and heroes

Green Column, The—Master Witness in Jhiná T'seneí

Hare, The—Erkynlandish constellation name

Harrow's Eve—Octander 30, day before "Soul's Day"

Hesitancy, a—Norn spell

High King's Ward—protection of High King over countries of Osten Ard

Hunt-wine—Qanuc liquor

Indreju—Jiriki's witchwood sword

Juya'ha—Sithi art: pictures made of woven cords

Kei-vishaa—Substance used by Gardenborn to make enemies drowsy and weak

Kingfisher, The—Nabbanai constellation

Kvalnir—Isgrimnur's sword

Lobster, The—Nabbanai constellation

Mansa Nictalis—Night ceremony of Mother Church

Market Hall—a domed building in central Kwanitupul

Mist Lamp—a Witness, brought out of Tumet'ai by Amerasu

Mixis the Wolf—Nabbanai constellation

Mockfoil—a flowering herb

Muster of Anitulles—Imperatorial battle-muster from Golden Age of Nabban

Navigator's Trust—Niskie pledge to protect their ships at all cost

Night Heart—Sitha star-name

Ocean Indefinite and Eternal—Niskie term for ocean crossed by Gardenborn

Oldest Tree—Witchwood tree growing in Asu'a

One Who Fled, The—Aedonite euphemism for the Devil

Pact of Sesuad'ra—agreement of Sithi and Norn to part

Pool of Three Depths, The—Master Witness in Asu'a

Prise'a—"Ever-fresh," a favorite flower of Sithi

Quickweed—Wran herb

Rabbit-nose—mushroom

Red knifebill—Wran bird

Rhao iye-Sama'an—the Master Witness at Sesuad'ra, called the "Earth-Drake's Eye"

Rhynn's Cauldron—Hernystiri battle-summoner

Rite of Quickening—Qanuc Spring ceremony

Saint Granis' Day—a holy day

Saint Rhiappa's—a cathedral in Kwanitupul

Sand Beetle, The—Wran name for constellation

Serpent, The—Nabbanai constellation

Shadow-mastery—Norn magics

Shard, The—Master Witness in Mezutu'a

Shent—a Sithi game of socializing and strategy

Snatch-the-feather—Wran gambling game

Sorrow—Elias' sword, a gift from Ineluki the Storm King

Speakfire, The—Master Witness in Hikehikayo

Spinning Wheel—Erkynlandish name for constellation

Sugar-bulb—Wran tree

Tarbox, The—inn at Falshire

Tethtain's Axe—sunk in the heart of a beech tree in famous Hernystiri tale

Thorn—black star-sword of Camaris

Ti-tuno—Camaris' horn, made from dragon's tooth, also known as "Cellian"
Tree, The—(or "Holy Tree," or "Execution Tree") symbol of Usires Aedon's execution
Twistgrass—Wran plant
Uncharted, The—subject of Niskie oath
Wailing Stone—dolmen above Hasu Vale
Wedge and Beetle, The—Stanshire inn
Wind Festival—Wrannaman celebration
Winged Beetle, The—Nabbanai constellation
Winged dolphin—emblem of Streáwe of Perdruin
Wintercap—Erkynlandish winter flower
"Woman from Nabban"—one of Sangfugol's songs
"Wormglass"—Hernystiri name for certain old mirrors
Yellow Tinker—Wran plant
Yrmansol—tree of Erkynlandish Maia-day celebration
Yuvenis' Throne—Nabbanai constellation

Knuckle Bones—Binabik's auguring tools.
  Patterns include:
  Wingless Bird
  Fish-Spear
  The Shadowed Path
  Torch at the Cave-Mouth
  Balking Ram
  Clouds in the Pass
  The Black Crevice
  Unwrapped Dart
  Circle of Stones
  Mountains Dancing

WORDS AND PHRASES

QANUC

Henimaatuq! Ea kup!—"Beloved friend! You're here!"

Inij koku na siqqasa min taq—"When we meet again, that will be a good day."

Iq ta randayhet suk biqahuc—"Winter is not being the time for naked swimming."

Mindunob inik yat—"My home will be your tomb."

Nenit, henimaatuya—"Come on, friends."

Nihut—"Attack"

Shummuk—"Wait"

Ummu Bok—"Well done!" (roughly)

SITHI

A y'ei g'eisu! Yas'a pripurna jo-shoi!—"You cowardly ones! The waves would not carry you!"

A-Genay'asu—"Houses of Traveling Beyond"

Hikeda'ya—"Cloud Children": Norns

Hikka Staja—"Arrow Bearer"

Hikkà Ti-tuno—"Bearer of Ti-tuno"

M'yon rashí—(Sithi) "Breakers of Things"

Sinya'a du-n'sha é-d'treyesa inro—"May you find the light that shines above the bow"

Sudhoda'ya—"Sunset Children": Mortals

Sumy'asu—"Fifth House"

Tinukeda'ya—"Ocean Children": Niskies and dwarrows

Venyha s'ahn!—"By the Garden!"

Zida'ya—"Dawn Children": Sithi

NABBANAI

á prenteiz—"Take him!" or "At him!"

Duos preterate!—"God preserve"

Duos Simpetis—"Merciful God"

Em Wulstes Duos—"By God's will"
Matra sá Duos—"Mother of God"
Otillenaes—"Tools"
Soria—"Sister"
Ulimor Camaris? Veveis?—"Lord Camaris? You live?"

HERNYSTIRI

Goirach cilagh!—"Foolish (or mad) girl!"
Moiheneg—"between" or "empty place" (a neutral
   ground)
Smearech fleann—"dangerous book"

RIMMERSPAKK

Vad es ... Uf nammen Hott, vad es ... ?—"What? In the
   name of God, what?"

OTHER

Azha she'she t'chakó, urun she'she bhabekró ... Mudhul
   samat'ai. Jabbak s'era memekeza sanayha-z'á ...
   Ninyek she'she, hamut 'tke agrazh'a s'era yé ..."—
   (Norn song) means Something Very Unpleasant
Shu'do-tkzayha!—(Norn) "mortals" (var. of Sithi
   "Sudhoda'ya")
S'h'rosa—(Dwarrow) Vein of stone

A GUIDE TO PRONUNCIATION

ERKYNLANDISH

Erkynlandish names are divided into two types, Old
Erkynlandish (O.E.) and Warinstenner. Those names
which are based on types from Prester John's native is-

land of Warinsten (mostly the names of castle servants or John's immediate family) have been represented as variants on Biblical names (Elias—Elijah, Ebekah—Rebecca, etc.) Old Erkynlandish names should be pronounced like modern English, except as follows:

a—always *ah,* as in "father"
ae—*ay* of "say"
c—k as in "keen"
e—*ai* as in "air," except at the end of names, when it is also sounded, but with an *eh* or *uh* sound, i.e., Hruse—"Rooz-uh"
ea—sounds as *a* in "mark," except at beginning of word or name, where it has the same value as *ae*
g—always hard *g,* as in "glad"
h—hard *h* of "help"
i—short *i* of "in"
j—hard *j* of "jaw"
o—long but soft *o,* as in "orb"
u—*oo* sound of "wood," never *yoo* as in "music"

HERNYSTIRI

The Hernystiri names and words can be pronounced in largely the same way as the O.E., with a few exceptions:
th—always the *th* in "other," never as in "thing"
ch—a guttural, as in Scottish "loch"
y—pronounce *yr* like "beer," *ye* like "spy"
h—unvoiced except at beginning of word or after *t* or *c*
e—*ay* as in "ray"
ll—same as single *l:* Lluth—Luth

RIMMERSPAKK

Names and words in Rimmerspakk differ from O.E. pronunciation in the following:

j—pronounced *y:* Jarnauga—Yarnauga; Hjeldin—Hyeldin *(H* nearly silent here)

   ei—long *i* as in "crime"

   ë—*ee*, as in "sweet"

   ö—*oo*, as in "coop"

   au—*ow,* as in "cow"

NABBANAI

The Nabbanai language holds basically to the rules of a romance language, i.e., the vowels are pronounced "ah-eh-ih-oh-ooh," the consonants are all sounded, etc. There are some exceptions.

   i—most names take emphasis on second to last syllable: Ben-i-GAR-is. When this syllable has an *i*, it is sounded long (Ardrivis: Ar-DRY-vis) unless it comes before a double consonant (Antippa: An-TIHP-pa)

   es—at end of name, *es* is sounded long: Gelles—Gel-leez

   y—is pronounced as a long *i*, as in "mild"

QANUC

Troll-language is considerably different than the other human languages. There are three hard "k" sounds, signified by: *c, q,* and *k.* The only difference intelligible to most non-Qanuc is a slight clucking sound on the *q,* but it is not to be encouraged in beginners. For our purposes, all three will sound with the *k* of "keep." Also, the Qanuc *u* is pronounced *uh,* as in "bug." Other interpretations are up to the reader, but he or she will not go far wrong pronouncing phonetically.

SITHI

Even more than the language of Yiqanuc, the language of the Zida'ya is virtually unpronounceable by untrained tongues, and so is easiest rendered phonetically, since the chance of any of us being judged by experts is slight (but not nonexistent, as Binabik learned). These rules may be applied, however.

i—when the first vowel, pronounced *ih*, as in "clip." When later in word, especially at end, pronounced *ee*, as in "fleet": Jiriki—Jih-REE-kee

ai—pronounced like long *i*, as in "time"

' (apostrophe)—represents a clicking sound, and should not be voiced by mortal readers.

EXCEPTIONAL NAMES

Geloë—Her origins are unknown, and so is the source of her name. It is pronounced "Juh-LO-ee" or "Juh-LOY." Both are correct.

Ingen Jegger—He is a Black Rimmersman, and the "J" in Jegger is sounded, just as in "jump."

Miriamele—Although born in the Erkynlandish court, hers is a Nabbanai name that developed a strange pronunciation—perhaps due to some family influence or confusion of her dual heritage—and sounds as "Mih-ree-uh-MEL."

Vorzheva—A Thrithings-woman, her name is pronounced "Vor-SHAY-va," with the *zh* sounding harshly, like the Hungarian *zs*.

Orbit titles available by post:

☐	The Dragonbone Chair	Tad Williams	£6.99
☐	Stone of Farewell	Tad Williams	£6.99
☐	To Green Angel Tower: Storm	Tad Williams	£7.99
☐	Otherland: City of Golden Shadow	Tad Williams	£6.99
☐	Otherland: River of Blue Fire	Tad Williams	£6.99
☐	Otherland: Mountain of Black Glass	Tad Williams	£7.99
☐	Caliban's Hour	Tad Williams	£4.99
☐	Tailchaster's Song	Tad Williams	£5.99

The prices shown above are correct at time of going to press. However, the publishers reserve the right to increase prices on covers from those previously advertised, without further notice.

ORBIT BOOKS
Cash Sales Department, P.O. Box 11, Falmouth, Cornwall, TR10 9EN
Tel: +44 (0) 1326 569777, Fax: +44 (0) 1326 569555
Email: books@barni.avel.co.uk

POST AND PACKING:
Payments can be made as follows: cheque, postal order (payable to Orbit Books) or by credit cards. Do not send cash or currency.

U.K. Orders under £10	£1.50
U.K. Orders over £10	**FREE OF CHARGE**
E.C. & Overseas	25% of order value

Name (Block letters) . . . .

Address . . . .

. . . .

Post/zip code: . . . .

☐ Please keep me in touch with future Orbit publications

☐ I enclose my remittance £ .

☐ I wish to pay by Visa/Access/Mastercard/Eurocard

Card Expiry Date